by Abraham Rothberg

Novels

THE THOUSAND DOORS

THE HEIRS OF CAIN

THE SONG OF DAVID FREED

Children's Books

THE BOY AND THE DOLPHIN

ABRAHAM

Nonfiction

EYEWITNESS HISTORY OF WORLD WAR II

The Other

Man's Shoes

by ABRAHAM
ROTHBERG

SIMON AND SCHUSTER · NEW YORK

Grateful acknowledgment for permission to quote several lyrics is made to the following:

For the song *J'Attendrai*, to the Southern Music Publishing Company, Inc. Copyright 1938, P. Leonardi, Milan. Copyright renewed 1965, Southern Music Publishing Co., Inc. All rights for the Western Hemisphere controlled by Southern Music Publishing Co., Inc. Used by permission.

For the song *Over There*, by George M. Cohan. Copyright 1917 (renewed), to Leo Feist, Inc., New York, New York. Used by permission.

For the song *Keep Your Head Down "Fritzie Boy."* Words and Music by Lieut. Gitz Rice. Copyright 1918 (renewed), Leo Feist, Inc., New York, New York.

For the poem "Ode in Memory of the American Volunteers Fallen for France," to Charles Scribner's Sons. From the volume *Poems*, by Alan Seeger, 1916.

FOR *Fay*
Midge
Jean
—all sisters, all loved

Life can only be understood backward, but must be lived forward.

—Soren Kierkegaard

One

The more a thing knows its own mind, the more living it becomes.

—SAMUEL BUTLER

THE first step was to talk to Elizabeth Marshall Christiansen. It took him only minutes to find her number in the phone book and then he felt like a fool because he was sure the number was in the address book, was bound to be. Though he let the phone ring half a dozen times there was no reply and only after he had set the receiver down did he realize his stupidity. What would he say to her over a telephone and what could he learn in a few minutes of metallic conversation? I knew your husband in the Far East. We were in the war and we ate together, slept together, fought together, talked about life; and one day on a Saigon sidewalk he died for me. Can you explain why he'd want to do such a thing? Courteous and cruel—and utterly inept. Stupid! Stupid! Why should she tell him anything? Name, rank and serial number—that's all you told the enemy. No, he had to proceed more slowly, carefully, use the intuitive subtlety and skill for which he was known as a journalist, the indirection and concern (or was it only the illusion of concern?) that had made him so successful with minister and milkmaid alike. The enemy—he caught himself: am I really the enemy? Her enemy? His? My own? Then he recalled that never once had Christiansen talked about his wife, or mentioned her name. There had been more than one nerve leaping in that twitch, more than one hesitation and knot in that tic.

In talking to Tessier he had felt his own intuition was sound, and he would follow it. He'd asked for three months' leave and it would take at least that long for him to establish sufficient intimacy with Elizabeth Marshall Christiansen to make any kind of estimate of George. Intimacy? The word alarmed him because he knew what was required. The most haphazard reconstruction of a rudimentary event was immensely difficult—often, usually, impossible; possible only when intimacy with the people involved, the history of what had preceded, the setting were all there and one steeped oneself in them; and even then one arrived only at the most tentative version of what had taken place, only a kind of pencil sketch of what was, in reality, an immensely complicated nuanced colored landscape. Journalism being a cruel and difficult taskmaster for those few who retained a sense of craft and truly used it—and he prided himself on being one of those—even the simplest facts were difficult to root out or verify; but the fluttering changing-colored butterfly of intent was the most elusive thing to pin down, or almost the most elusive, for if intent was slippery to seize and hold, then how much more fugitive was motive in the deeper sense of what was buried in the larva and pupa's cocoon before the full-fledged adult took wing? Memory must speak and record, and reason and intuition disentangle that silken skein of protestation and protection, of egotism and evasion, before the blurred outline of what might pass for truth emerged.

❈　❈　❈

The drive from San Francisco down to Palo Alto runs for a short but somber time along the barren salt flats which rim the great Bay. Before that were the signs of power—power lines on pylons, factory after new factory, planes in a continual circle and spiral over the airport—and Sanders was again reminded of how strong were the sinews of his native land. His momentary elation of return home was intensified by the tastes of American foods he had not had for a long time—milk and butter, coffee and ice cream—and by the swiftness of the services—the telephones worked, establishing bank credit was easy and renting an automobile so simple that he had a sudden rush of affection and admiration for the land and the people. But on the freeway the speeding cars reminded him of the

German death-urge driving on the autobahns; the eyesore billboards and gasoline stations, the rusting pyramids of used-car chas-
sis, the cairns and funeral pyres of the civilization, made him long
for the potholes and poplars of French roads; and the grim grainy
salt flats depressed him. The evening, settling now, was also grainy
and monotonous, like poorly developed film, and he could taste it in
his mouth, feel it like a twist in his wounds. Well, what had he expected? More, much more. This was the country of his growing up;
no, he corrected himself, of his youth, but not of his growing up.
His youth had been the time when his life looked as if it were going
to run straight and smooth as a freeway, before he saw how quickly
a human life could disintegrate, not at the edges but at its very center, the tree rotting from the cambium core of the trunk, not inward
from the outer bark and branches.

A ranch-style house of dark-red brick and redwood shingle, it
stood in a quiet section of Palo Alto, blending with the green rise
which set it off from its neighbors. In the new dark only a finger-
print of light on the door shone, the bell, the eye of a watching,
waiting animal. The bell clanged to his touch somewhere in the recesses of the house and when there was no response Sanders moved
to press it again but the door was abruptly opened and a voice
asked, "Yes?"

"I'm Elliott Sanders," he said.

Silent, she stood there without acknowledging him or giving him
her name, almost completely hidden in the shadows, a white blur in
the darkness.

"I wrote you that I was coming—"

"Come in," she interrupted, then even more brusquely, "follow
me." He followed her through the house, out past full-length glass-
and-screen doors into a small garden made private by the walls of
the house on three sides and screened in the back by a windbreak
of evergreens and a high woven redwood fence. She motioned him
to a wicker chair and sat in another. What, following her, had
seemed like a white dress Sanders now saw was a nurse's uniform,
which surprised him, reminded him of Cathy Sullivan, but this
woman was older, tall and thin. In the brief flare of her match as
she lit a cigarette he saw an angular very pale face framed in short

[13]

black hair, a striking face. Again in the same angry voice, she asked, "Yes?"

"I'm Elliott Sanders," he began.

Again she cut him off. "You said that."

"Perhaps I should come another time," he offered. "Perhaps you're tired or this is an inconvenient evening."

"Now is as good a time as it will ever be."

"You *were* expecting me?"

"Yes. I got your note."

Sanders sensed the hostility, the barbed wire in the voice, and couldn't understand it. It was difficult enough to begin but this volatile anger was something he had not anticipated at all. "Your garden is beautiful," he said. "I like this way of building houses to shelter a garden or a court. Makes it private."

She took the cue, but not easily. "Part of our Spanish heritage."

"That's right. I've been away for so long I forget my American history. San Francisco, El Camino Real, Palo Alto, Spanish names. This was once all Spanish and Mexican, wasn't it?"

"It's only a little more than a hundred years since we—they—took it away from Mexico," she said. Swaying slightly in the beginning night breeze beyond her was an old-fashioned hammock, slung between two medium-sized live oaks whose trunks bore the rope marks. Was she Spanish? Mexican? The pale skin, high cheekbones and dark hair revealed in the match flare could have come from varied antecedents; but the speech and manner were contemporary American. As she smoked, the end of her cigarette glowed and faded and Sanders felt her hatred like another presence in the garden, heavy and heady as the leftover heat of the day, the musk of the flowers and the damp of the dew.

"What do you want from me?" she asked.

"Want *from* you? Why, nothing." He spoke the lie smoothly but was aware of it. "I came to tell you about George. I thought you'd want to know."

"I don't," she replied shortly.

Sanders pushed his chair back, a grating sound on the flagstones, and stood. "I'm sorry," he said stiffly. "I didn't mean to intrude." He walked the three steps to her chair, swiftly, and with both hands, as if bestowing on her something infinitely precious, he laid in her lap the box he'd brought. "George bought this chess set in Hong Kong. I thought you might want it." Gingerly, her face half averted, she ran her fingers down the polished wooden surface several times before she opened the box. When she did she picked one of the sallow, intricately carved ivory pieces from the green baize, the king, held it in front of her, turning it first one way then another as if searching in the Chinese inscrutability for an angle which would give its features some special meaning. As its elongated shadow fell crookedly across her legs she brushed her skirt with one hand as if to sweep it away; then in a fury, with the other she flung the king with all her strength toward the trees, overturning the box and sending the rest of the pieces clattering onto the flagstones. "Get lost!" she yelled. "Get lost!" In the half-darkness Sanders could not see her face clearly but her mouth was working, her teeth bared; and although he was not sure she was shouting at him, he turned to leave. He picked his way among the chessmen with the odd notion that they were the dead and wounded of a battlefield and that he, too fastidiously, was threading his way among corpses, until he was out of the house and back in the car. He sat there for twenty minutes trying to compose himself, but no light shone in the house and no sound or movement was apparent there. Even before he had returned to the hotel, he knew he had miscalculated; what he'd set out to do was going to be far more difficult than he imagined.

❖   ❖   ❖

Sanders had met Elaine Huntington for the first time at one of the many parties he went to in those days. Parties were where he could meet pretty and compliant women, where at the least he could drink and dance away the frequent nights he couldn't sleep, where the music might drown out the static of mourning and despair that sparked in his skull. The woman who brought him there, Thérèse Guilmant, was a junior editor on the magazine who did women's stories on fashion, child rearing, society gossip. A twenty-eight-year-old jet-haired daughter of an Algerian *colon* father, who was now in bitter exile from his native sun under the lowering skies of France, she had for months been using her marvelous Carthaginian profile

[15]

to provoke him into asking her for a date. Put off by her façade of cool sophistication that seemed adopted from a Françoise Sagan heroine, he'd been remote, but that evening she had caught him still at his desk and he had agreed, because he had no other arrangements, to make her party rounds with her. He was already bored with her fashionable chitchat and psychoanalytic and anthropological jargon, her clinical dissertation on the decline of the *nuclear* family (the *double-entendre* of the prophetic and barbarous term was lost on her and horrified him)—so she explained her unfeelingness for the tragedy which had overtaken her family, though she did permit herself, as who did not, to loathe the General—and the rise of the *kinship* family—into which she intimated she would initiate him later that night after this last party which she had to attend.

A literary party given by a Paris publisher to launch a new female novelist whose book was sure to win the Fémina or the Goncourt, the party was indistinguishable from the three others they had attended earlier that evening, but the pain of this one was less, Sanders reflected, as they walked through the seven- or eight-room apartment which ran the length of an old building on the Rue du Bac, although it was only because he recognized that he was already three sheets in the wind. Thérèse moved against him with the promise of better things to come, soon, if only he was patient, and told him someone special at the party wanted to meet him. Thérèse had said the same thing at the earlier parties but none of the people she introduced him to had the remotest interest in him—nor should they have—but this time, it turned out, was different.

"Look at her," Thérèse grated and pointed out a woman at the far end of the room standing with her back to the wall, hemmed in by four men, two in evening dress, "surrounded as usual by male admirers. The pack. She, that one, was asking about you." Thérèse was jotting furiously in a small morocco notebook with a slender gold pencil she'd taken from her purse. "Imagine," she muttered as she wrote, "who else would dare to wear a black velvet evening skirt with a sheer white chiffon blouse and a flounce of jabot! The picture of an innocent virgin! Her! And with an eyelet camisole beneath and ruffled cuffs on her sleeves!"

[16]

Only then did Sanders' not quite steady eyes search out the woman and, as if she had felt his glance like a touch, Elaine Huntington looked up, their eyes met, clashed and held. At that moment the music began, she handed her glass to one of the four men and stepped into the arms of another to dance, her eyes holding Sanders' until her partner whirled her around, when Sanders saw that she had stepped out of her shoes to dance, left her two high-heeled black pumps at the center of the circle of her three remaining admirers.

Thérèse, next to him, sensed his interest. "Her name's Elaine Huntington. American. You like her?"

Sanders, cruelly, because he heard the unspoken "better than me?" in Thérèse's voice, said yes nonetheless and nodded to emphasize it.

"She's evil," Thérèse spat out suddenly. "With all that careful, calculated, innocent getup, all flounces and frills and furbelows, all so white and untouched, that woman is evil like"—Thérèse was at a loss for words—"like Scarlett O'Hara."

"Evil?" Sanders asked, piqued, his voice unbelieving, certain she was being melodramatic, journalistic, jealous, Grand Guignol: evil was a big word. He didn't wait for her to go on; instead, he threaded his way unerringly through a dozen dancing couples to cut in, and when he held Elaine Huntington in his arms, a cloud of lily-of-the-valley perfume warmed by a body, he said in French, "I am called—"

"—I know," she interrupted in English.

"Are you sure?" Sanders asked.

"I'm sure," she said, and he noticed how they'd switched languages, he to hers, she to his.

In the half-dozen foxtrot turns they took she told him how much and how long she'd looked forward to meeting him, how she'd enjoyed his writing and his photographs in the magazine, how she'd learned from them, which was more than she could say for most of the journalism she read; and all the while she talked a quaver of recognition, a premonition of disaster, passed silently, secretly between them before another of her four swains cut in and danced her away, and when he did Sanders felt a startled internal pain as if a placenta as yet imperfectly placed and connected had been abruptly torn loose.

[17]

Sanders watched her for a while until Thérèse, once again at his side, suggested that she had enough for her story now, they could leave and go to her place. Sanders shook his head; he didn't want to take his eyes off Elaine Huntington. "She's a whore," Thérèse said, after watching her with him for some time; the word she used was argot, *conasse*, a woman who has a profession but whores only incidentally.

"So much the better," Sanders commented.

The music stopped as Thérèse added, in a voice so loud in the silence that it carried all over the room. "And you are a *zob*." That too was argot, an Arabism for prick.

Elaine and the man in the tuxedo had stopped dancing only a few feet from them and she, as indeed everyone around them, had heard Thérèse's expletive. Walking toward them, she smiled and in a clear, lilting voice remarked, "Ah, M. Sanders, so you really are a *zob*, an *aobi*. You see, you have an enviable reputation and you're living up to it." She made him a mocking bow.

Enraged, Sanders replied, "And yours, Mlle. Huntington, as well. A *zob* is recognized by a *conasse* only." He took a handful of franc notes from his pocket and deliberately tossed them on the floor in front of her stockinged feet. The intake of a dozen breaths was like an audible wind.

Elaine took two steps forward, eyes blazing, and slapped him hard across the face.

If he had not been drunk he would probably not have done it; but he *was* drunk and without an instant's hesitation, with a great open-palmed smack across the jaw, Sanders knocked her down. Sprawled like an odalisque, she lay there, a sudden tear up the seam of her black skirt like a cheongsam slit. Her escort leaped forward but she clutched his trouser leg and, as if she were restraining a hound, held him back. "No, Claude," she commanded, "don't touch him. Just help me up." Claude whirled and helped her to her feet.

Elaine walked up to him and said, in English, "I thought everything here was phony, all con. The whole world's con, Mr. Sanders, but that was real, wasn't it?" She fingered her cheek gingerly.

"Yes," he answered, also in English, suddenly sobered, "pain is always real."

[18]

"The *only* reality." A statement, her questing eyes pleaded for him to say there was more.

He said it. There were many other realities he recognized, far more than he cared to, but he knew the one she wanted acknowledged, that he himself wanted affirmed, that already stirred him. "No, not the only reality," he asserted caressingly, not caring a damn for all the staring faces, "there's love."

She broke free from Claude's arm and, ignoring Thérèse altogether, asked him to take her home.

"It will be my pleasure," Sanders agreed.

Elaine walked to where her shoes still stood, fitted her feet carefully into them and then, taller, more stately, returned to him. After she had found her cape, a black velvet drama lined with scarlet silk whose stiff Chinese collar opposed its flowing softness but made the new cheongsam slit in her skirt more appropriate, they left the party arm in arm before the outraged eyes and pursed mouths of all, including Claude and Thérèse, who stood there, her mouth gaping, holding the handful of his francs she had swept from the floor.

From the beginning theirs was a Paris romance, but with dark things unspoken and implied. In that first meeting Sanders knew he had encountered someone from whom he could not easily disengage, a bruising, jarring love, but one which wholly involved him and made him feel that he had, somehow, come home, made home. The possibility of the normal life he coveted, wife and children, an end to his sense of nomadism and rootlessness that others sometimes envied by calling it freedom and being footloose, seemed only a little beyond his grasp.

On the surface all was spring Paris sunshine and candlelit chestnut trees. No amount of self-mockery about Paris in the spring, tra-la, tra-la, no poking fun at their having the traditional, even cliché Paris love affair, perhaps a little belatedly for both of them, could stop the lyrical joy he felt. They did everything young lovers in Paris had done for ages: They danced at the *boîtes;* they walked through the spring rains into the white mornings and went to Les Halles for soup; they drank on the *terrasses* of the cafés and watched people stroll by on the boulevards; they dined at the Eiffel Tower and over their wineglasses looked gloatingly and happily down on Paris as if

[19]

they owned it from the splashing fountains brightly lit before the white portico of the Chaillot to the whited sepulcher of the Sacré-Coeur.

And they talked. He was able to talk to her about his mother and Lovett Carpenter Sanders, about how he had searched for family and home, had found it only in wars and on the magazine. But Elaine always spoke about her parents with scalding contempt, when she could be persuaded to talk about them at all. That she hated the Huntingtons was not in itself a surprise to him, it was common enough; that she was so intractable in her hatred, so unforgiving and unrelenting, alarmed him. Like himself an only child, she seemed to have found her childhood a hell without a single redeemed day, from which she had sought to escape by the swiftest growth into womanhood and out of the household. For all he remembered of Lovett Carpenter Sanders, for all the accumulated bitterness of the years, his family and his childhood had been two of the touchstones of his life that had given him strength and solace, affection and hope; and talk of marriage, or having children, or of the future, Elaine sheered away from abruptly—and left him uneasy and apprehensive. For all Elaine's talk of being conned, snowed, fooled, which she surely meant, and for all his own sense of being cheated, deceived, manipulated, which he too meant though perhaps less passionately, Sanders knew that their choice of words revealed a chasm between the way they saw themselves and their lives.

And they never made love. If Sanders never asked Elaine to go to bed with him, it was because he wanted her to give herself to him freely. What he craved was more than a mere gesture; he wanted the spontaneous offering from her depths which asking for or demanding destroyed, but she made no such move. She was gay, charming, funny, she was a wonderful companion whether they were dancing at the Embassy ball or driving into the country for picnics of bread and cheese and wine, while she chaffed him about "a Jug of Wine, a Loaf of Bread—and Thou beside me singing in the Wilderness." It was as if sex was too serious, too heavy and cumbersome to undertake or even mention because it would overwhelm and spoil their relaxed ease and pleasure in one another. Yet Sanders felt the smoldering of her flesh when they kissed and embraced; even that they did but sparingly, usually only when they met and parted, and he could for hours thereafter feel the impress of her flesh and bones in his. Not to make love was for him indeed to die a little, more than a little. At first it seemed unbelievable to him that he could sustain any relationship with a woman without going to bed with her—he never had before. The longer they went without lovemaking, however, the longer they did not discuss it—that too was new to him —the more it seemed that they were reserving something special for each other, some sacramental champagne which could not simply or capriciously be quaffed; however much he was convinced that lovemaking was the daily domestic *vin ordinaire* to be drunk from the glass and not the holy-day wine from the chalice, the abstinence sharpened the edge of his thirst. What perturbed him greatly was that Elaine seemed not to feel deprived or aware of the strain until at last, one night as he was kissing her goodbye outside of the Avenue Foch apartment, she thrust her body against his as if wanting to wedge herself into his marrow. "Take me, Elliott," she said, biting hard on his shoulder. "Marry me." The two were not the same commands and her tone was so ambiguous he did not know how to respond; but he did note that, order or plea, it was the gesture, the act, he'd hoped for and, kissing her throat, exploring her breasts for the first time with a tentative tenderness that made him feel juvenile and painfully vulnerable, he said he would. When she broke away, her features in disarray, her hands begging, waving him off, warning him that he didn't know what he was getting into, that she was an albatross, a jinx, would make an impossible wife, he stopped her mouth with his kisses.

❉ ❉ ❉

The next morning Sanders drove up to see Christiansen's father. A two-hour drive from San Francisco, the veterans' hospital was set away from the eyes of men among the ridges and arroyos south of Livermore. As he made inquiries and saw some of the patients, he remembered going with his father to a small hospital in Clichy to see the *mutilés* of World War I, men who had lost parts of their faces and who could not be repaired by the process doctors quaintly called plastic surgery. One particular patient stood out in his mind,

[21]

an immense blond Norman who wore a mask and would not remove it though Lovett Carpenter Sanders had had the gall to ask him to. The nurse who finally knew who Joseph Farnum Christiansen actually was looked askance, a bitter knowing mouth pursed as only the mouth of an unattractive woman can be who knows how unattractive she is. "Nobody ever comes to see him," she said, doing those small useless things to her hair with her hands that such women do. When she saw the expression on his face, she relented: "Well, almost nobody comes nowadays," she amended. She rose from behind her desk without alacrity, a big-boned, awkward woman, and led him down a long bare corridor painted a nauseating pale green, her rubber heels making small complaining sounds just out of step with his own clacking leather soles.

"Did they once?" he asked.

She nodded, more emphatically than was required, and Sanders saw how lonely she was, hungry for even the smallest change of conversation. "His son used to come visit, regular, and then, for a while, his daughter-in-law, but no more, not lately."

"His son is dead," Sanders told her.

She caught her breath, her eyes lovely with compassion, her thin-lipped mouth mean with revenge. "Oh, I didn't . . . does the old sonofabitch know?" she asked.

"The government notifies parents," he said.

"Yeh," she said, after a pause, "that's the way it works. They send the kid a letter first, then the folks get the telegram." She glanced at him over her shoulder, her hand an organ apart and unknowing still fussing with the tight roll of her chignon. "Sometimes," she mused aloud, "I'm glad I never had no kids," but she didn't look very glad.

The doors at the end of the corridor opened onto a large screened and louvered porch filled with the early-morning sunlight. In the far corner, his back to them, a man in a maroon corduroy bathrobe sat erect, a chessboard on the table in front of him. He was playing chess against himself, so absorbed that he didn't hear them, and the nurse had to tap him on the shoulder and say he had a visitor before he turned. His face looked as if it had been carved of ice: Snowy hair, sparse and regularly waved, was parted precisely in the center, the direct white line perfectly bisecting his head; beneath the rimless eyeglasses with their gold bridge and earpieces, the carefully barbered face was clean-shaven and powdered; the long, beautifully cut features were the same as his son's except for the mouth, but so cold that even in the warm morning sunlight Sanders was chilled by them. "What do you want?" the man asked, his rimless lenses glinting so that the cold eyes burned. His voice, cool and remote, gave no quarter and asked none, yet it too had a vague disconcerting resemblance to his son's.

"I'm Elliott Sanders," he introduced himself, "a friend of your son, George."

The frosty blue eyes appraised him, slowly, clinically, without embarrassment, taking their time. "So you're the one *she* called about." The emphasis on the *she* was so patent it couldn't be ignored, but even before Sanders could ask who *she* was, Joseph Farnum Christiansen, eyes even icier, turned on the nurse. "G'wan, Miss Macon, beat it!" In his mouth the Miss became an epithet, the order an insult.

"You're such a nice man, Mr. Christiansen," she said, hurt in spite of herself.

"Ugly old sow!"

Miss Macon turned and flounced away, her seeking hand reaching for her chignon once again, the questing fingers already shaped to receive.

"I hate ugly women," Christiansen said, not raising his voice an iota but obviously knowing that the nurse could still hear him, "always have." His speech had an even more pronounced Southern rise and fall than his son's, with a glassy hardness all its own. "Little Miss Muffet warned me you might come a-calling," Christiansen continued, "but I didn't think you'd be so soon."

"George's wife?" Sanders asked stupidly, knowing it could be no one else yet feeling betrayed; still, how could she betray him when he hadn't told her he was planning to see George's father?

"Not much of a wife, I expect, but then my George wasn't much of a man for her either." Something lascivious slithered across his lips, turning them into pink snakes. "Comes of marrying an older woman, I guess."

[23]

"She older than George?" Sanders asked, trying to regain his composure.

"George never say? You couldn't have been much friendly then, because he was always telling everybody about that. You a Yankee?" the old man asked suddenly.

Sanders nodded. "From Connecticut."

"Your granddaddy fight agin us?"

Sanders wondered if the whole Confederate pitch and Southern accent were being shrewdly used to mock, but he couldn't be sure. "Both grandfathers," he said. "One was killed at Chickamauga. My father's father was with Sherman."

"Quite a record—for Yankees. Your daddy a fightin' man too?"

My father a fighter? It was the question he dreaded, but he knew what the old man wanted and replied shortly. "He was killed in the Second World War."

"That's a right good record your people have there, boy."

"We have a lot of dead to show," Sanders said, unable this time to contain the irony.

"Well, now, don't look so sad. A man's gotta die sometime. A little sooner, a little later don't make so much difference as people think." The old man gave him a shrewd look and quit. He turned to his chess game again, pondering his next move a long while before he asked, "You play chess?"

"A little. George and I used to play out there."

"Was he good?"

Sanders couldn't tell whether the old man was talking about fighting and dying or chess so he took the easier way. "He beat me often enough."

For the first time Christiansen smiled, a dazzling sun-on-ice display of teeth. "I taught him to play, taught him good, but—" proudly now—"he couldn't hardly ever beat his old man."

Looking at the cheap black-and-white plastic pieces, Sanders regretted giving those beautifully carved ivory ones to Elizabeth Christiansen. "I gave that chess set of his, the one he bought in Hong Kong," Sanders murmured, "to his wife." By now he almost believed that the chess set had been Christiansen's, not his own.

"Better to have given it to me. Beth don't play no chess. Hates it.

[24]

Hated it when George played—because I taught him, I guess. Poor Beth."

Sanders sat in silence, wondering by what labyrinthine schizophrenia Christiansen contrived not to let his right hand know what his left was doing as he plotted against himself, carefully considering each move, and Sanders admired the way the old man took equal time and trouble over both sides.

The squealing shoes told of Miss Macon's arrival even before she reached them and announced, "It's time, Mr. Christiansen."

"Don't I know it? Don't you think I can tell time, you fool?" he replied irascibly. He stood and Sanders stood with him, noting now that the old man was half a head taller than he and broader, a once powerfully built man with a gauntness that seemed to have come from flesh recently lost. "Go on!" he roared at the nurse, dismissing her. "I'll be right there."

"You know where?" Macon persisted.

"I been there often enough, ain't I?"

She stalked off and Christiansen turned, the *US Army* embroidered on the bathrobe for the first time visible on his left breast, stark as a military decoration. "Keep foolin around. Can't let a man die any more. Know so much nowadays they keep you goin forever almost, like a blasted used car, patchin you up all the time, givin you blood transfusions—most likely nigger blood at that—givin you all those goddam rays make you wear on and on. Don't know when to pull the cork and let a man go peaceably down the drain." He stretched and yawned a cavernous yawn. Sanders saw perfect white teeth, not a filling, and wondered if they were plates. The old man shook himself, then asked, "The boy leave me any money?"

Unable to reply, Sanders nodded.

"Half?"

Sanders found his voice. "No, a quarter."

"Half the insurance to that bitch, Beth? And me splittin with that crazy nigger friend, what's his name, Pete King?"

Sanders nodded again.

"I figured. Just like George. A snotty bastard to the end."

"Don't you want to know how he died?" Sanders asked softly.

Christiansen shrugged. "What for? He's dead, ain't he?" The sun focused on the old man's glasses made his eyes burn like molten ball bearings. "You wanna tell me. Is that it?"

"No," Sanders replied, holding his anger in check. "You're right. He's dead and it doesn't matter."

The old man, shuffling in felt house slippers, took him to the porch doors. "Come see me, boy. Any time. We'll play some chess." He shook hands, a hard handclasp, then went his way.

Passing her desk, Sanders said goodbye to Miss Macon and in a small deliberate gesture lit two cigarettes for them from a single match and handed her one. Greedily she drank in the first puff and the attention, then cupped the cigarette in her hand, hiding it, smiled and said, "No smoking on duty."

"That's tough," Sanders sympathized.

"For a two-pack-a-day type like me, it really is," she agreed.

"What's wrong with the old man?" he asked, though he had already surmised.

"Leukemia," Miss Macon answered.

"Got much time?"

"Hard to say. Some go in six months, some in six years. All depends."

"Even at his age?"

"Even at his age. He's a mean sonofabitch and they live the longest."

❁   ❁   ❁

Their apartment was on the Right Bank on the Quai de Passy just before it becomes the Avenue de New York. High up for Paris, on the sixth *étage*, which really meant the seventh floor, it overlooked the Seine and faced toward the Eiffel Towel and the Invalides. From the windows and balcony the view was spectacular; on a clear day you could see downriver as far as St. Cloud and upriver to where the Seine gracefully flowed through the heart of the city. They'd taken the apartment together, though at Elaine's insistence, touted and guided by a fairy real-estate agent whose bleached blond pompadour, purple shirt and pink tie and red velvet waistcoat were a sight to behold. While showing them the bedroom, its windows also looking out on the Tower, M. Jacques—that was the way he liked people to address him; having only a single name, he thought, gave

[26]

him a kind of éclat—nakedly ogled him so that Sanders felt Elaine's fingers tighten on his arm, smirked as he drew the portieres open to reveal the dark-brown squalid thrust of the skeleton frame into the gray sky. And then, because even if they did speak French, they were after all only Americans, M. Jacques pointed to it and, never taking his eyes off Sanders' fly, said, since they would surely know the one joke almost all Americans knew and therefore certainly appreciate the *double-entendre,* "*C'est beau,* eh?" Without moving a muscle, the two of them had deadpanned together, "*C'est beau? Mais, c'est magnifique!*" not smiling, not showing they had understood, enjoying his raging homosexual pique that he had, so to speak, not been able to make his point.

They'd taken it for a good omen, that they'd responded together like that, instinctively, without premeditation or coaching, but now Sanders wondered what those portents really meant. M. Jacques had looked so downcast at first, so disappointed, that they thought he would burst into tears or that they would lose themselves to laughter, but his disappointed face was soon covered with contempt—*these* Americans didn't even know *that* joke—only to be replaced by greed when they'd gotten down to the hard bargaining about francs and the lease. When at last they had reached an agreement, it had not kept M. Jacques from a *sotto voce* parting to Sanders which implored and invited him "to make a change."

A fortnight later, when he and Elaine moved in together, with only the flea-market furniture from his old apartment, the difficulties began. Elaine had no furniture of her own in Paris, having lived in the lap of luxury on the Avenue Foch in the de Besancourts' flat—the de Besancourts were among the friends, the many friends, the Huntingtons had everywhere, Paris, Cannes, Madrid, Málaga, Rio, wherever the rich and footloose stayed—which had been lent to her, an apartment magnificently furnished in Louis XVI and Directoire antiques. Her refusal to share his big old double bed, insisting instead on the guestroom cot, opened the battle. She gave all kinds of reasons, some in earnest, some in jest, but all equally strenuously insisted on so that he was never sure which she really believed. "I won't sleep in that bed where I know you've had other women, your cheap Boulevard Haussmann harlots." "I'm uncomfortable in a

[27]

double bed; I'm used to twin beds." "We *nice* girls make love but don't sleep over." "Well, really, Elliott, we aren't married yet, are we?" And so on, one contradictory, perverse, funny, frustrating excuse and pretext after another. How was he to know which, if any, made sense? How was he to understand what the omens really were?

"You can't sleep on that cot," he protested, "unless you're dead drunk. It's too damned uncomfortable."

"I'm used to being uncomfortable," she replied. "You forget I was a campfire girl and learned to be uncomfortable and smile. Besides, I can get dead drunk every night. Wonderful excuse."

"What is it? For God's sake, Elaine, what's it all about?"

"I know what you want," she breathed, in her best little-girl manner, all saucy and saucer-eyed, a manner which could and did still charm in those days. "All you want is to . . . to"—abruptly her blue eyes were those of a Gare de l'Est whore in a hurry—"to fuck me." The word, brutal and unexpected, stood between them, impenetrable.

"That's what you want, isn't it?" she growled, her mouth frightened and furious, meek and mocking together. "That's what all you men want, isn't it?" She pushed him into the leather armchair and crawled into his lap like a little girl. "Isn't it?" she repeated, beginning to undo his clothes in a way that was anything but a little girl's way, but when he was ready and they lay together on the old Persian carpet she stalled him off, fought him off and finally brought him off against her thighs with an expertness and toughness that relieved his flesh but assaulted his spirit.

* * *

He took the wrong turn, then found his way back over the San Mateo Bridge, driving straight into the setting sun. As the car moved out onto the causeway over the dark choppy waters, clouds on the far shore piled one on the other were high and golden, the sunset spectacular, as if once again the other side of the Bay, the river, the hill, promised perfection. The question framed in his mind then was "Am I going to absorb his life into mine or let mine be absorbed into his?" The drive back had seemed longer than the drive up as he thought over the talks with George's wife and father. He saw that

he had miscalculated on at least two counts: Not only had he underestimated the difficulty of inquiring into a man's life, but he had not
calculated the intensity which drove him, to find out what it was
that had driven George. He should have, when he had the chance,
gotten on a plane to Europe, or perhaps even earlier have heeded
Fillmore's advice and simply sent those damned letters, the diary
and the address book by mail and forgotten the whole business.
Tessier's rational skepticism had also been warranted; three months
was not going to be enough: He was going to have to settle in, find
a flat and, at least temporarily, a job. Sanders squinted into the sun
over the Bay and abruptly the whole Saigon café sprang out of the
clouds, sight, sound and smell: He saw George Christiansen's face
again, the twitch of the eye and cheek now unremitting, as if an
electric current had the flesh in thrall and would never leave it free;
and he began uncontrollably to hiccup. Only when the freeway rose
over the ridges and the city came into view, its houses stacked in
diagonal lines on the hillsides, pastel and shadow and white geometric shapes, did the hiccuping leave him, sides sore and head
muddled, because those lines of houses became the hillside houses
in that mining town in Wales Tessier had sent him to for a picture
story. Among those funereal Welsh houses the very air itself was
coal-colored and there he had reported and photographed the accidental death of the town's schoolchildren, buried with their school
under a shifting slide of a mountain of slag. "The mines giveth and
the mines taketh away," one dour old miner, searching for his two
sons, had intoned bitterly, the only white on the grime of his face
the tracks of tears, "nothing is mine."

In the hotel bar Sanders bolted three brandies before the dry lump
in his throat and the aching in his sides gave signs of going away
and before he knew he wanted a girl. "America," he thought, "I
bring you back my problems and my seed, relieve me of both." He
laughed aloud, a quick constrained laugh he cut off as soon as he
saw the bartender's head look up in his direction.

San Francisco's Chinatown was not Cholon or Kowloon and Grant
Avenue was not Nathan Road or Singapore's Cathay Street, still,
being there comforted him. Why he was always comfortable among
the Chinese—was that now treasonous?—he didn't understand. Per-

haps because their color, their swarming family life, their desire to live and breed and flourish, their gambling and greed gave him confidence that mankind could survive even under the most adverse circumstances. No wonder they were called the Jews of Asia; they had the same persistence, the same lust for life, the same commercial and intellectual skills, the same close family ties, only the Chinese were a greater and more populous people. He'd argued that point often with Levi Migdal, a Polish Jew once *Hadoar's* Paris correspondent and once his best man—how Elaine and the Huntingtons had balked at that!—who insisted that this was only a refined form of Anglo-Saxon anti-Semitism. No amount of persuasion, no carefully reasoned arguments (shades of Lovett Carpenter Sanders!) that the Jews had only a great literature while the Chinese had that and almost everything else: great art and architecture, sculpture, music, science, and even one of the world's great cuisines, had sufficed. Levi reluctantly admitted the grandeur of Chinese achievements but without conceding Chinese superiority, for with only ethics and literature—and Levi emphasized the former not the latter —Hebraism's priestly toughness and prophetic loftiness had changed the whole moral temper of mankind, and what had the Chinese done? And Israel had done all that with never more than two percent of that four or six or eight hundred million Chinese horde. The Sinaitic revelation, he maintained, was more majestic than any Sinology, the Decalogue more worthy than any American Sinologue could appreciate.

What the Chinese had been able to do with an ordinary American street was remarkable. Grant Avenue seemed narrower, more crowded, instinct with life; there were people everywhere, old men and women, young children, infants at the breast, the whole panoply of human life from beginning to end. To the façades of undistinguished buildings they had added their Chinese cupolas, whose looping lines lifted the heart, and the marvelous complication and artistry of their ideographic signs, which intrigued the eye; and over and through it percolated the odors of Chinese food and cooking and the high-pitched sounds of Chinese speech and laughter. The shops were filled with all kinds of goods, the spirit of commerce rampant: food—

live fish, dried fish, shellfish, sausage, suckling pigs; roast ducks with their long necks and heads still attached hung browned from hooks; cool green and white Chinese lettuce and celery and snow peas; decks of spices—and the whole procession of expensive silks and porcelains, teaks and jades, on down to the simple bamboo ornaments, the brass wind chimes, and the cheap bare-wood back scratchers, as well as the whole range of gimcracks made in Japan. The carved ivory chess sets were there too, more expensive than they'd been in Hong Kong, with the same fine humanity, sad and downcast, carved into them, so different from the bellicose inhumanity of European knights and rooks and horses. For a long time he stood in front of one shopwindow where a particular set took his fancy trying to decide whether to buy it for old man Christiansen, but the recollection of that brusque man prevented him from doing it.

This was a more sedate bourgeois American Chinatown, less teeming, cleaner, more modern and prosperous, than the medieval Chinese colonies he'd seen in Asia. From the church on St. Mary's Square a Chinese wedding party burst out onto the street, the bride in conventional white gown and veil, her flat-cheeked face exotic and strange in such clothing, the groom in black tie; and six young bridesmaids, all in identical sunny yellow gowns with ruffled hems, held bouquets of yellow daisies. They clustered around the bride and groom, kissing and being kissed, hugging and making a fuss over a small Chinese ring boy who suffered himself to be picked up and petted. The wedding guests, all in Occidental clothes, the women wearing not cheongsams but white gloves and pillbox hats with little veils and fur stoles, milled around speaking English in polite and modulated voices.

"It doesn't seem right, does it?" someone next to him asked.

"No, I don't suppose it does," he said, unthinkingly, "but then what would be here and in our time?"

"A bacchanal! A genuine Soochow saturnalia! A fine old Chinese whoop-de-do!"

Sanders turned. The voice belonged to a girl in tight-fitting blue jeans and a loose buckskin fringed vest worn over a man's white button-down shirt with a frayed collar. A cascade of tawny hair

[31]

flowed down her back and her eyes had the same tawny lioness color and quality. "Americans aren't built for bacchanals," Sanders demurred.

"*I* am."

He gave her a second look before he realized that she was walking barefoot beside him and carrying a pair of Greek-style leather-thonged sandals in her hand. "You're a lucky girl," he said.

"And you're a lucky man."

"I am? Why?"

"Because I like you and I'm going to let you take me to dinner," she replied, firmly taking his arm.

"Is that a request or a command, a privilege granted—or is it that you're hungry?" Sanders asked.

"Hey," she said, letting go of his arm, "you're hip."

"Hip?"

"You know—with it, cool."

Pointing to her bare feet, he remarked that she was looking pretty cool herself. Her laugh was wide-mouthed, showing even white teeth. This country and all its beautiful teeth; milk, meat, orange juice and green vegetables their wonders do perform; not to speak of orthodontia. "Man," she continued, "I take it back, you *are* square."

"Careful, madam, you are referring to the only figger I have," he said, parodying an English ducal style, "and I don't think that's square."

In an upper-floor Chinese restaurant overlooking a small green park that had been manufactured over a subterranean garage, Sanders ordered for both of them but mostly listened, drank and watched her eat. Her name was Laura Martin and she came from "near Davenport," Iowa. Her father, a middling-well-off farmer and also a skillful carpenter and stonemason, had made a killing in contracting local construction during the Second World War. With his four sons exempt from the draft because farming was "essential" industry, her father had not only managed to keep the farm growing, buying additional parcels when he could, but was able to build a profitable construction business. Laura was their only daughter,

[32]

the last child, and eighteen years younger than her closest brother, almost an afterthought of passion by her fifty-year-old father and forty-two-year-old mother on a hot Iowa summer afternoon in 1943. "You know," Laura said, between healthy bites of duck in apricot sauce, "he used to screw her once a week, regular as clockwork—"

"*Clock*work?"

"Say," she said, "that's cool, real cool. You're right, of course, regular as *cock*work. Never thought of it." She pointed a greasy forefinger across the table at him. "My old man was just like that too. Every Sunday afternoon after lunch. Church in the morning, big Sunday lunch and then a little afternoon . . . nap. That's how little old me was conceived."

"Sin on the Sabbath. Desire under the elms. The same old American story of transgression."

Midway into a duck's wing she stopped. "It wasn't funny, really. He was a mean, dirty-minded, miserly old bastard."

"That why you came to California?"

"I cut out. Couldn't stand it. Always riding my back and humping my mother ragged."

"Only on Sundays?"

"No," she grinned, "*never* on Sundays. Do you know that song?" She began to hum it, then, apologetically, "Always sounds better on those goddam Greek tools, zithers and bouzoukis, or whatever you call them. . . . D'you see the movie? That dame sure had the right idea. Never, but never, on Sundays."

"Today Sunday?" Sanders asked.

She stopped eating and reappraised him. "You *are* cool."

"*And* square?"

"*And* square," she reaffirmed.

"A crazy mixed-up kid," he added, realizing how different his idiom was from hers—and how dated.

Puzzled, she asked, "You turned on? Like on grass or acid or speed?"

"*You* turn me on," Sanders said, sardonically grimacing inside at the perversities of the language of gallantry and at the absolute consistency of their intent. It was good he'd come back to the States

[33]

for that alone; the language was threatening to grow away from him and evidently not only the language but what it stood for in the way of manners and morals.

Laura said she wanted air and a walk after such a good dinner, so they strolled through the small park behind the restaurant. A line of poplars screened the border separating it from the buildings of the street and reminded him of France; in the park itself shrubs, cactus, grass and white birches were strategically placed as were the benches. The park paths converged on a concrete base from which a stainless-steel statue reared upward. Sleek, powerful and unblemished, it had the face of a Buddha but where the classical Buddha was imperturbable, this countenance was implacable; what was once serenity was here turned into a steely purpose, and the simple uniform in which Sun was encased was, logically, both the Jesuit's cassock and medieval armor breastplate. Opposite the statue was a bronze plaque at which Sun stared, announcing, WE SALUTE THOSE AMERICANS OF CHINESE ANCESTRY WHO GAVE THEIR LIVES FOR AMERICA IN WORLD WARS I AND II. Beneath a list of Chinese names was appended. As Sanders read them in the uncertain light, the damp night wind whose moving sounds in the poplars had induced his nostalgia for France now chilled him to the bone. He shivered and Laura moved closer to him. "You need a drink," she said. "Come on, we'll go up to my pad." Leaving the park, he noticed under the church clock the simple but imperative admonition of all the fathers: SON, OBSERVE THE TIME AND FLY FROM EVIL. It's too late for me, he thought, too late for everybody; but he was not quite sure what he meant for the world or for himself.

Laura lived in North Beach near Telegraph Hill, high up enough so that the Bay below, occasionally revealed through rifts in the low-lying mist, looking like a distant surface of smoked glass. As they passed the Memorial Tower, half hidden in the clouds on the bluff, Laura pointed and said, "We got two big hard-ons like that in this area—besides yours, baby," and she touched him lightly but surely, "that there Coit-us Tower there and old Herbie Hoover's erection down at Stanford. Ooo!" she exclaimed. "You should see that one in Palo Alto, like outta this world. Not that you're so bad yourself." She brushed him again and he was back on the Quai de Passy, the

Eiffel Tower rising into the night, the Seine noiseless and flowing below, and Elaine beside him making jokes about whether M. Jacques' fairy friends called him, admiringly, the Tour St.-Jacques.

Sanders had seen apartments like Laura's in half a dozen countries; with only minor variations the flat could have been set down in Soho or Montparnasse or Greenwich Village. The high-ceilinged room with long narrow windows and a skylight, the small stove with electric burners encrusted, the refrigerator of ancient vintage with cauliflower-head cooling unit, and furniture to match: threadbare pieces of old maroon carpet; a large divan with a bedspread of colorful Mexican serapes sewn together; old-fashioned nineties-style furniture scavenged from the Salvation Army and who knows where else—American versions of the Flea Market—repainted black and gold or scraped down to bare wood. But another sort of decor was unique for him and told him that he was being introduced to a new generation. The walls were plastered with signs, tintypes, etchings, and of the many posters and pictures he could recognize only a few of the less hairy. One was of Jean-Paul Belmondo, cigarette dripping from the side of his mouth as in À Bout de Souffle. A six-foot photograph of James Dean, the vaguely rebellious and wistfully forlorn face so enlarged that the pores were like craters on the moon, was stuck to the ceiling directly over the bed. A Diego Rivera-type portrait of Joan Baez, strong India-ink lineaments and hair contrasted with warm sepia skin, decorated a large announcement of one of her concerts and was attached to the tassel of the rolled-up window shade, thereby covering most of the length and breadth of the window. Nearby was a poster with an old World War I biplane as its main illustration: LSD: TAKE A TRIP AND FLY! Two stickers pasted on the lintels above the windows read, GET OUT OF VIETNAM! and MAKE LOVE NOT WAR.

Laura went to the cupboard, brought out a half-full bottle of vodka and two champagne glasses. "I love champagne glasses and brandy snifters," she explained. "Drink anything from them," she giggled, "even water. How do you take it, straight or with . . . I think I've got some tonic water." When he made no reply she turned, gave him a dry look and said, "Ah-ha, you're ready, aren't you? And you've had enough to drink. I don't want you to drink too much.

[35]

Like you drink a lot, huh? You were, that is, back there in that Chinese restaurant. You oughtta try grass. Easier on the head. And like great for the sex, doesn't put you out." She put the vodka bottle down, turned to him fully and unself-consciously began to undress. There was no flirtatiousness, no embarrassment, only the simple awkward act of taking her clothes off that she somehow made graceful, and Sanders watching her remembered how different it had been with Elaine, how every snap undone, every silken sheath removed, was a brush of flame deliberately applied to his flesh. Laura stepped out of her panties, the small lace-edged triangle of silk so inadequate for such a powerful girl, a woman really who might have been molded on those generous lines copied by Rodin or Gaston Lachaise or Henry Moore, and tossed them back over a cane-bottomed chair straight out of some pre-World War I Iowa ice-cream emporium. Naked, she walked to him naturally, pulled him down on the divan and began to help him off with his clothes. "How do you make the scene?" she inquired, then seeing his incomprehension, explained, "You know, how do you get your kicks?" and finally, exasperated, "What kind of hangups do you have?"

It's been a long time, Sanders thought, longer than the weeks and months he could count, somewhere years back on a plateau in time before that village in the Delta and Christiansen had happened. When he asked Laura if she wanted the lights out, she shook her head and only after the long caresses, when he was inside her, her arms and legs binding him to her, his fingers tangled in her hair, did he cry out in gratitude and anguish for her open welcome and did she breathe in his ear, her lips pale and parted, her eyes closed. "Be gentle," she murmured, "please be gentle with me." And he was; in spite of Elaine, he was.

When he came back Laura had turned all the lights down except the bed lamp and sat, lotus position on the divan, with a champagne glass of vodka in each hand. "Here," she offered, "I want to drink to you."

Sanders took the glass. *She* wanted to drink to *him*. He couldn't even summon up a smile.

"You may be square," she toasted, a mischievous grin on her face,

[36]

"but you're straight." She was enjoying his embarrassment. "Real groovy."

His head bowed, seeing himself naked, with a champagne glass in his hand, ridiculous, unable to speak, Sanders was moved almost to tears. *She* wanted to toast *him!*

"You know," she continued, serious now, "I almost forgot it could be done that way. It's been so long"—she flushed—"since I saw someone face to face."

* * *

For the moment he had almost persuaded himself that he was back in Paris. The sky over the river was blue, the Dauphines and the Deux Chevaux scuttled past like swift crabs, the outdoor café gave him the same kind of vantage point from which he could watch people go by as his own café in the disreputable Fourteenth gave; even the black coffee and brandy in front of him had the same taste and odor. Only the suffocating heat that pasted his khakis to his damp flesh and his sense of smell dispelled that comforting illusion: He was not in Europe but in the Orient, and the momentary sense of safety and security that four *noirs* and four *fines* together, the streets and the sidewalks, and the bustle of the city had brought to him sluiced away like the coffee his trembling hand sloshed over the side of the table. That he should think of Paris as home was ironic, he knew, even a bitter irony, yet as he listened to George Christiansen's soft-voiced California drawl, almost but not quite Southern, Sanders realized that he hadn't thought of the States as home for a long time and perhaps, just because of that, it was time to go back.

"I don't think it's a matter of generations either," Christiansen was saying. "You're what, ten, twelve years older than I am, Elliott? That's not all that much, is it?"

A dozen years didn't seem much yet it really was critical. From the eminence of thirty-seven, twenty-four seemed boyish and innocent, a whole lifetime away though he remembered how old he had seemed to himself at twenty-four, even at fourteen. No, he corrected himself, not yet at fourteen; he'd been sixteen before he'd really been kissed. Most of all, he knew that even beyond the generations and the ages that separated them it was because George was a soldier and he was a civilian; the boy had to be there and he had chosen to come. Chosen? Well, perhaps that was not the word; impelled might be more accurate, but not, certainly not, compelled.

"You haven't taken a word I've said seriously," Christiansen protested, his face showing his disappointment, but only a little and under good control. George had poise. The way Levi Migdal had had. "And it *is* serious."

"At twenty-four everything seems serious," Sanders said, feeling his ennui a posture but his world-weariness real, and thinking that perhaps at twenty-four everything seemed so serious because it really was: youth is the seed time. He couldn't have replied to what Christiansen had been saying because he'd been listening to his own inner voices, but now he listened.

"None of it, none of it, makes much sense, and you know it doesn't. Men are out there in the boondocks dying, and women and children too, and for what? For nothing. Why can't you make people see that? Why don't your words and your pictures do anything?" The outrage was a healthy flush on George's tanned skin, and the rays of the setting sun caught his close-cropped blond hair, illuminating his skull and making him look like a painted Byzantine martyr with a fourteen-karat-gold dish coming out of his skull. For an instant the play of light seemed to catch a muscle leaping or a nerve twitching in the boy's cheek, then it was gone, the face calm and classic.

"There are men, women and children dying all the time, everywhere, and mostly for no reason, George." Sanders paused, tired before he'd really begun. "Monkeys and rats and sacred cows eat the crops, the rains don't come or they come too much and too often, sickness infects the people, the princes or generals or plantation owners decide to have a war or stumble into a depression. . . . And people are likely to go right on dying, mostly for nothing, the way most of them go on living, the way most *of us* go right on living for nothing."

Christiansen's face was very stern. A fogginess pervaded his voice like the prelude to a storm. "It doesn't *have* to be."

"Nothing *has* to be, I suppose," Sanders said flatly, hearing the accents and intonations of arguments *ad nauseam* with Levi Migdal long past, and feeling nausea once again. *What is is best in this best of all possible worlds.* How far he was from believing that he knew, but how far he was from Christiansen and from believing that much could be done about it he also knew. There was where he differed from Lovett Carpenter Sanders and from Elaine; they were duped not by others, not even by life, but by themselves, by that burning necessity to assert that somehow something could be done about it all even at the expense of . . . their lives. Voltaire had been right; the only answer was to till your own garden. If they let you. . . . And why was it that when he tried to till his own garden he felt like a clod?

"You can still talk like that after—the village?" Christiansen's voice was hoarse now, as if he'd caught cold; his blue eyes were hard and remote and his boyishness had disappeared: He looked like a man, and a determined one.

The last warmth of the coffee and brandy seemed to dissipate with the last long light of the pyrotechnic sunset, chilling him. He shivered, drank the rest of the coffee, the dregs, and the few remaining drops of brandy, not enough there even to bite his tongue. On the fluorescent film of his brain the tanks hosed the village down with flamethrowers, burning, burning, and the bulldozers flattened the scorched remains of thatched-roofed houses, sowing splinters into the ash-strewn earth until nothing was left but garbage heap— nothing, that is, but the charred baby they unearthed from beneath the floor of one of the huts, a great roasted lamb with sizzling sockets where once its eyes had been. The villagers had seen. Loaded on trucks, looking back, back, as the trucks pulled away, they were abject; and Sanders wondered that they did not on the instant, on the spot, soldiers and farmers alike, turn into pillars of salt or stone. Some of the peasants in the copters being taken back to headquarters for interrogation looked wildly down, eyes spinning as crazily in their sockets as the rotor blades; dark growing things torn out of their element, their homes and their earth, they hung their heads, shamed, let their hands dangle, impotent with rage.

Home. Sanders tried not to remember, groping instead for the recollection of his Paris house, the narrow building in the Fourteenth Arrondissement which, like some skinny interloper, had shouldered

[39]

its three stories up between two old squat ten-story apartment houses on either side; but the fourteenth kept dissolving into a column of remembered fire and the hoarse cloud of George Christiansen's voice behind him. "You're drunk," Sanders told himself, "you should have something to eat." Four *fines* on an empty stomach. *Ma foie!* The Frenchman's permanent plaint—at least in that he was acculturated—the cirrhotic principal paid on the alcoholic's interest; but he knew that even eating wouldn't help now, no distraction or ruse would work. "It's getting dark," he said slowly, the consonants sticking suddenly to his teeth and the roof of his mouth because the words slowed and broke as he spoke them. The sudden gray melancholy of evening, the sun and the light about to be lost. *I hate to see that evenin' sun go down. . . .*

Christiansen's profile was abruptly thin-lipped, patrician. "What happened to the good men?" he asked, so softly that Sanders strained to hear him. "Where are all the honorable men? Where did they go?" The nerve and muscle together leaped in his face, momentaneously, then was gone.

Looking past that now adamantine profile, thinking how his friend so young yet echoed his father's sentiments so old, the hoarse complaint hanging unanswerable in the stifling air, Sanders saw the man coming down the street on the trishaw, pedaling slowly next to the curbstone as if he had with his last and failing energies only just managed to survive the ravages of the day. Washboard ribs showed through the shirt plastered against them, and his narrow chest was heaving with great effort. He pedaled past an old lady in black pajamas so bent by age and the burdens of life that her body seemed to be inexorably bowed toward the earth and her final resting place. Holding her hand, a beautiful young girl no more than twelve years old, slim and pale as bamboo, swayed along next to her in a spotless white *ao dai* looking as though her youth would, if anything could, straighten the old woman's bones until once again she might hold her spine and her head erect, and regain the posture of her prime. The trishaw man gave them only a glance as he pushed past. His conical coolie hat was back on his head; sweat poured over his hooded eyes and protruding cheekbones; his mouth, filled with misshapen yellow teeth, was gasping; and in the hollow of his

[40]

right cheek a long smudge was engraved like a scorched knife scar. As he came abreast of the café, slowly, as if the air were thick or his muscles hamstrung, he put his hand into the crotch of his trousers as if to scratch himself. The hand came out a bunched fist and from it something rolled gently along the sidewalk and, spinning foolishly, stopped in front of the café three scant feet from their table. The trishaw man was abruptly peddling furiously off, the balloon sweat stains on the shoulder blades of his shirt like the X-rays of distended and diseased lungs. Only then did it register: a grenade. And an American one.

It seemed like hours before he could cry out, to George, to the old lady and the girl, to the other people drinking on the café terrace, before he rolled off the chair and knocked the table down in front of him, the crockery going smash before the explosion. Muffled, it sounded as if something inside the earth had erupted and Sanders felt the concussion and the pain together, the tearing of his flesh by flying glass and metal and wood. The brutal silence was like being suddenly deaf until, gradually, movement in the café behind him began, voices cried out, and finally, as if he'd returned from a great distance, an impossible journey, he opened his eyes and knew that miraculously he was still alive. Hurt but alive. He pulled himself shakily to his feet, unable at first to focus his vision. And then, when he could, he saw. On the sidewalk beyond, where Christiansen had thrown himself on the grenade, his body was almost blown in half, the legs akimbo, the arms hugging the ground, the profile now that of an old and wizened man, the sunny flesh itself ashen, burined on the gray concrete. A little way away the old lady in the black pajamas, blood bubbling from her toothless mouth, keened over the young girl who like a cut-down bamboo lay slender and silent, her long hair spread out like a great black fan, her white *ao dai* blooming with changing bloody flowers.

"Why?" Sanders croaked. "Why did he do it?"

An ARVN major, automatic drawn, came cautiously out of the café to look up and down the street but the trishaw man had long since disappeared. Staring the major down, Sanders saw the bland face outraged and frightened by the deaths before him and, likely, by the ones he feared awaited him still. Sanders stumbled toward

[41]

the old lady and the girl to see if he could help, but as she saw him the old lady threw up her hands as if to ward off an attack or an accusation—or was it to make one?—and then, as he drew near her, with a windy "Aa . . . iee . . . ee!" she collapsed across the dead girl's body.

"Why did he do it?" Sanders continued to repeat stupidly, looking down at them, then up at the major who now stood next to him. The major, unwittingly pointing the automatic at him, looked at him as if he were insane, and then, laughing, Sanders keeled over.

❊   ❊   ❊

Later, he awoke with a start and Laura was asleep, arms and legs akimbo, a lioness who had just run down its prey, eaten and was now content to slumber. So that he wouldn't wake her he took his clothes into the bathroom to dress and there, washing his face, he could not muffle his laughter when he saw the balloon-glass brandy snifter sitting next to Laura's toothbrush and toothpaste. Walking downhill to his hotel through the deserted streets, aware of the Coit Tower on Telegraph Hill behind him and what Laura had imputed to it, Sanders remembered together that graceful brandy glass, its fine edge rimmed with the scum of that morning's mouth rinse and Laura's pained confession about making love face to face, and felt sad and empty and full of remorse for not having stayed the night and had breakfast with her in the morning.

At the hotel desk the night clerk gave him his room key and three telephone messages, all from Mrs. Elizabeth Christiansen, the last one marked shortly after midnight. The lobby clock read 4:37, not quite the right time to return her call, but Sanders wondered what could have been so urgent to Beth Christiansen to have made her call him three times and that late at night.

In his room he took off his clothes, had a hot shower and went to bed; but he couldn't fall asleep. His wounds began to ache and from the past he knew that when sex, liquor and a hot shower didn't work nothing short of Nembutal would. " 'Take what you want and pay for it,' " he thought, the phrase coming unbidden to his mind. "There I have it, the whole American tradition of guilt from the beginning, in Emerson's words and from Lovett Carpenter Sanders' mouth." Well, to give credit where it was due, his father had lived and died by those words: He'd taken and he'd paid but what he'd forgotten, or deliberately ignored, was that other people paid too. *His* tariff. Or had he ever realized that?

And then he was walking in the Place des États-Unis. In all the years he'd lived in Paris, he had come there only three times, once by chance with his father, once after the war, and that last time after Elaine and the Avenue Foch. The first time, so distant now, his father had walked him through the gardens to the statue commemorating the dead of World War I. Only a boy, he'd stood there, awed, looking up at the doughboy and the poilu cast in stone, hands joined, before the winged victory of peace behind them which encompassed them both in her embrace. He could still hear his father's voice, that eloquent unguent, which, broadcast and magnified, so many had come to know wherever news—which in his lifetime meant war—was made: "This is Lovett Carpenter Sanders reporting from"—the Rhineland, Addis Ababa, Nanking, Madrid, Vienna, speaking the words of Alan Seeger's poem engraved on the base of that statue:

> *Hail, brothers, and farewell; you are twice blest, brave hearts.*
> *Double your glory is who perished thus,*
> *For you have died for France and vindicated us.*

While he was led around to the other side of the statue to see where the other lines were carved, his father's voice had not missed a word or a beat:

> *Yet sought they neither recompense nor praise,*
> *Nor to be mentioned in another breath*
> *Than their blue-coated comrades whose great days*
> *It was their pride to share—ay, share even to the death!*

Standing there, truly moved, his father had said, "Elliott, these are the two countries I've loved best. Paris is my second home as France is my second native land. I hope that someday it will be that way for you." It was one of those rare occasions Sanders could remember

[43]

that voice and presence descending from the regal and omniscient *we* to the personal and mundane *I,* one of the few times his father had spoken to him father to son, man to man, and he cherished it. He was ten years old. Cherished it and profited from it, for if there was one heritage he had gotten—taken?—from Lovett Carpenter Sanders, it was that Paris was his second home and France his second native land. Or had it grown beyond that; was America his second native land and New Canaan his second home? If there was an explanation for his father's death, or forgiveness for it, Sanders thought, even if he could not accept or understand it, he got it in that park in front of that statue in tribute to those French and Americans whose bodies fertilized the wheat fields and vineyards of France, not at Clichy where the reporter, another man, a man he would have disowned as his father, could ask that wretched man to remove the mask from his shattered face.

The last time he had come there was in springtime, after the second Great War, a lifetime, several lifetimes, later. Alone, blind with pain and anger after the scene he'd witnessed at de Besancourt's Avenue Foch apartment, the scene with Elaine he could never wipe from his mind, he had wandered along the Avenue d'Iéna unable to forget what he'd just seen and unable to come to terms with it as he was unable to forget or come to terms with his father's life and death. He'd found the small park then, after having left the cab blindly, simply stopping it at a street corner, coming on the park as something altogether new, an enclave of bright and dark greens, with workmen in blue coats quietly talking, gesticulating and smoking, a couple of old khaki-colored barrels for removing leaves neatly overturned in the paths. He'd walked past old ladies in big, old-fashioned hats designed to shade their faces from the sun and from close scrutiny, and the young girls, bareheaded and barefaced, past the statue of Washington and Lafayette, huge and mediocre, wondering at the faint ripple of anticipation and recollection that distracted him from that great anguish he had just fled. Only the faintest spring sunshine filtered through the dark-green umbrella of the trees overhead that made a pale green and yellow light beneath, remote and healing, bathing lilacs and rhododendrons, andromedas and azaleas alike. Birds sang, literally sang, not chirped, and for one

[44]

rancorous pungent moment Sanders felt that the whole world, human and natural, was unnatural and inhuman, unhinged; and was baiting him, biting him, egging him on over the brink.

Then, once more, he came to the poilu and the doughboy, the statue now somehow more touching because it had been broken—by the Germans?—and because there was a kind of ludicrousness in its having been broken across the poilu's belly and the doughboy's buttocks and clumsily repaired—by the French?—in the same places. Above was another statue he could not recall at all, a metal statue of a doughboy, slightly bandylegged, his rifle slung over his shoulder, his hand holding his doughboy hat high in triumph, all of him covered with verdigris and black stain. Although the verse as spoken by his father's sonorous voice still rang in his ears, he was saddened most of all to see that even in stone the words of the poem were dimmed, in some places almost effaced. He sat on a nearby bench staring at the base where once those words had been so sharp and clear; now they were more sharply engraved on his so fragile brain, and his lips repeated, "It was their pride to share—ay, share even to the death," but this time for himself and for Elaine, for what he had witnessed and suffered at the de Besancourts' apartment—and before. Where did he go now, after the Avenue Foch? As he sat there in that park so ironically named, he was puzzled by the fact that he had only twice in twenty years found it though it was almost in the center of the city, and as he repeated that single line of poetry, he knew he was speaking the obsequies over his marriage: He had endured the funeral rites on the Avenue Foch but here were the final burial ceremonies, the interment beyond resurrection. "Till death us do part," the marriage ceremony said, but what partings death in life called for it did not specify.

❋   ❋   ❋

From the moment in San Francisco that Sanders heard James Needham's voice on the telephone the old specter of having altogether disappeared, of having become the invisible man, haunted him; again he was no more than his father's son, an extension of his father's reputation—less. He listened to Needham's sentimental reminiscences about his father, what a great newspaperman he'd been,

[45]

how sad that he should be cut off in his prime, the detailed rehashing of some of Lovett Carpenter Sanders' great scoops, and felt sure that his shaking hand which held the telephone would in a moment fade and disappear. Only after Needham asked what he could do for him did his voice grow more cautious, now the voice of a newspaper executive, not that of the old roving foreign correspondent. Sanders told him and instantly Needham began to hedge. "I thought you were already located, working for that French news-picture magazine—what's the name? Goddam, I can never remember French names—in Paris and reporting from the Far East."

Sanders told him the magazine's name and admitted that he was still on the staff, then added that he had just come back from Saigon. He heard the skepticism in Needham's voice, the professional journalist's perennial suspicion of people's motives, the probing for greed, failure, hypocrisy, the "What's in it for him?" and the "What's he covering up?" What great gaffe had been charged against Elliott Sanders so that he was sent home and looking for a job? Which of the arcane gods had he offended? Yet Needham's way was his own way, had been his father's way, was probably the most fruitful attitude for a reporter to adopt most of the time with most people; but the adoption became before long the permanent possession, the attitude the reality. Only the really good reporters learned when it was not appropriate, when to suspend disbelief, however rarely: Sanders doubted that Needham had been one of them. Needham would have to be played back in the same terms: greed, ambition, curiosity, the unvaried lust for a scoop. Deliberately Sanders let the pause be prolonged so that when he did finally tell him not only would Needham's curiosity be piqued, his relish for the newsbeat and his hankering for the exclusive provoked, but Needham's guilt would be intensified, his embarrassment heightened, his sentimentality called into play. Slowly, carefully, Sanders explained that he'd been wounded by the VC, that he'd come back to the States for rest and rehabilitation, and wanted, after such a long absence from home, to get reacquainted with life in the United States. Needham interrupted, his sentences replete with hasty and apologetic repetitions of "I see," "I didn't realize," "Is that the way it was?" until they got down to cases. "We're only a small-town paper, Elliott, not a big metropolitan daily. We can't pay a hotshot correspondent like you the kind of money you're used to. We don't even cover your kind of story. We take most of the foreign news off the wire-service tickers. Mostly we deal with local stories." His voice now turned artificially hearty and self-deprecating. "You know the kind of stuff, fires, weddings, divorces, auto crackups, hippies, the Rotary and the Legion. . . ."

Sanders let him run on until he'd run down, then in the most understated fashion, because he knew that would be the most effective, opened the gambit. "Well, Mr. Needham, since I covered the war out there for the last half year, my second trip out there, I thought a good story would be to cover the other half of it back here, the antiwar movement in the States the way I'd covered the war out there." *The lure.*

"Say, that's a good idea!"

"I remembered reading that you'd bought a paper down on the Peninsula and thought I'd talk to you first—"

"The Vietcong and the Vietniks, what a story!"

"And some other people were interested, but I thought a big paper would cramp my style." *Another lure.*

"Make a great series—"

"They'd want all rights and I wouldn't give them anything but American. Exclusive, of course, but all the rest would be mine. Still exclusive for the whole country." *The bait.* "I'm still on the magazine's payroll so I feel obliged to give them the French rights. The salary's not so important since I'm getting half pay from them anyway, so I could take the Guild scale or slightly above." *The hook.*

"Look, Elliott, why don't you come in and let's talk it over. Maybe we *could* arrange something."

"Well, I wouldn't want to put you out." *The hurt withdrawal.* "And there were a couple of other people I was going to talk to." *The hint of others interested. The club.* "If it's not your kind of story, if it's too big for you . . ." *The subtle imputation of being small-time, having limited horizons, being blind to opportunity.*

"No, Elliott, of course it's our kind of story. It's anybody's kind of story. You free for lunch today?"

"I'm sorry, Mr. Needham—"

"Jim, boy, Jim."

"Today's really rough." *Important things cooking.*

Needham was disappointed. "A drink later on, dinner, maybe this evening?"

"No," Sanders replied. "I'm really booked solid for all day." *Lots of people to see.*

"You won't take it to someone else?" Needham's anxiety and eagerness were now open, keen.

"No, I promised you first crack at it." *Emollient.*

"You wouldn't fool me, now, would you, Elliott?" The edge of fear in his voice was mixed with suspicion.

"I wouldn't fool *you*, Jim. I give you my word." *Confidence. The old Paris Lovett Carpenter Sanders tie.*

They agreed on an appointment for the next day after lunch.

When Sanders put the receiver back into the cradle, his hand was still trembling, yet for an instant he couldn't see it, was sure it was invisible. Then the hot sense of triumph was like the taste of berries in his mouth, sweet and sharp at once. He'd landed his fish. And the series *was* a good series, it *was* a good idea. If he could do it, even Tessier would be satisfied, more than satisfied. But the elation drained swiftly away because he knew he had worked, performed, operated, in exactly the way he remembered his father had, the way he'd been told since by a hundred people his father had worked. *Tel père, tel fils;* he really was an invisible man. *Take what you want and pay for it,* the voice of New England and America had spoken through his father; but his father had been able to afford it.

*   *   *

It was as if no time and months had passed when he awoke in the darkened ward. He remembered being fitfully conscious when they brought him into the base hospital, recognizing the building because he'd been there several times to do features on the wounded and on the staff. They set him down with the really war-wounded— or was he himself really now war-wounded?—and his newspaperman memory repeated blurred snatches of events and talk he wanted to clarify, but it was like staring through a fogged window; every time he tried to wipe it clear, it clouded once again and he knew and did

[48]

not know he was heavily drugged. The bandages around his middle told him he'd already been to surgery as did the pain deep inside that was a violation, and he remembered reaching down and finding himself whole as the only moment of gladness and relief. The single question burned like napalm in his brain. Why? Why? *Greater love hath no man.* . . . They'd known each other for such a short time, been on operations together, shared being shot at. They'd come down to Saigon on the same plane, George for a weekend leave, himself to recover from that village and the stink of killing—and the fear. They'd talked, too much perhaps, with the timorous intimacy that comes of being near death together too often, and now Sanders found himself carrying those conversations on, extending, amplifying them, going off on tangents in his mind, but returning always to the same final question.

For days, fitfully awake, he knew he was aware mainly because with returning consciousness the question came back to him like a neon-lighted sign flickering in front of a storefront Pentecostal church. Once, and he remembered it in the remote, drug-frayed way he was remembering all the nights and days, a long time before, in a small Midwestern town, he had taken a billboard down from in front of just such a storefront—JESUS SAVES!—and carried it to the front of the town's main bank, carefully positioning the sign under the façade of the false Corinthian columns right next to the night depository; and then only just managed to escape the local gendarmes who saw and chased him.

In one of his more lucid moments Sanders called for his musette bag. Only after asking three or four times and receiving the same if increasingly sharply spoken rejoinder did he realize that it was gone, misplaced or stolen, and he felt utterly bereft, naked as the day he was born. If he couldn't find it, something irrevocable was lost, though just what he couldn't remember, and so he tried to get out of bed to search for it himself and twice crawled several yards on the floor before they found him, put him back into bed and angrily shot him full of morphine while muttering threats that they would tie him into the bed with sheets. He would have tried again except that he was finally convinced that the musette bag was irretrievably lost.

[49]

On the first morning he could see the outlines of beds and doors and windows with precision, the first morning his pain had diminished to where he could manage it and the loss of the musette bag no longer seemed catastrophic, he was displeased to see a chaplain standing at the foot of his bed, a tall spare man whose ruff of hair had been shaved so close to his skull that he looked altogether bald. "I thought I had no religious markings on my dogtags," Sanders growled, realizing how much he sounded like his father at his most bearish, "because they wouldn't put A for *atheist* on them."

"So they told me," the chaplain said softly, fingering the gold cross on his collar not nervously but with a sure patience that irritated Sanders still further. "Which is why I came."

"To reclaim me . . . from my fate?" He began to stutter. "I mean to reclaim me for the faith?"

"What faith should I reclaim you for?"

Sanders shrugged and the motion sent waves of pain through him.

"I came to visit," the chaplain said mildly, "because a couple of your newspaper cronies told me you were a chess player."

"I play a little," Sanders admitted grudgingly.

"Good. Need a partner?"

"No. Just an opponent."

"Okay, an opponent then. So be it." He put his hand out and reluctantly Sanders took it. "My name's Murray Fillmore," he said, "but some of the more sacrilegious call me Filly."

"I've got a good portable chess set but it's in my musette bag. Bought it in Hong Kong, folding board and small, lovely ivory pieces. Could you find that bag for me?" Sanders asked, innocently, yet feeling cunning and covert.

"I think so. Let me have a try anyway."

"Sure." Sanders shrugged and, hurting again, inhibited the movement. "What have I got to lose?"

"Yep, that's what Pascal always said."

In what seemed to him the first and only certifiable miracle he'd ever witnessed—until almost simultaneously he remembered Christiansen broken on the grenade and knew he'd seen another before, far more marvelous—Sanders saw Fillmore return after two days with his musette bag. The bald black stenciling of his name on the

[50]

pouch startled and relieved him and he had a sudden rush of feeling out of his maimed surgical numbness, an upsurge of such sharp and bitter love that had Fillmore not been standing there dangling its dirty, blood-spattered weight by its shoulder strap, he would have crushed the musette bag to him and embraced it. But even as he held himself back, restrained his feelings, his shaking hand reached out for it because he could not altogether contain himself.

"You really want that bag," Fillmore remarked, handing it over.

"I would have gone through hell for it," Sanders replied, knowing that he was speaking literally, knowing that he'd gone through hell, was still in it.

"Well," Fillmore said, not at all shocked, "perhaps that won't be necessary." His warm smile was shy, the even white teeth making his long, twitching nose and its almost invisible gill-like slits seem more human and less fishlike, so that Sanders was moved even more.

"The whole . . . world goes away," Sanders tried awkwardly to explain. "You're nothing . . . you're left with nothing."

Fillmore nodded. " 'Naked I came into the world . . .' "

Sanders shied away from his sacerdotal tone and, propping the bag up against his hip, held it so that the open flap hid the contents from the chaplain. As he looked inside, searching for the chess set, he saw and remembered Christiansen's packet of letters, his leather diary and black morocco address book. He took the chess set out, small, beautifully made wooden board opening to show the carved Chinese chessmen relaxed on the baize. They set the board up on the bed, Sanders propped against a couple of pillows, Fillmore sitting on a small antiseptic white medical stool next to the bed. Sanders played absent-mindedly but not unaware of Fillmore's querulous glances when he missed an obvious gambit or made a stupid mistake; but the chaplain said nothing. Christiansen had given him those things to keep in the musette bag on the flight down to Saigon. He'd carried only a small canvas kit for toilet articles and always kept a valise with spare clothing at a friend's in town, he said, and now, suddenly, Sanders wondered why. What friend did an American soldier have in town with whom he kept a wardrobe? The question distracted him and although he was sure he would normally

[51]

have beaten Fillmore soundly, the best he could manage was a draw.

Inert and innocent-looking but deceptive as grenades, those three items in his musette bag were Christiansen's explosive heritage to him, for him, and however unwittingly they had been put in his trust—if unwitting was it really accidental?—Sanders knew they were a burden and an opportunity, one to be shouldered, the other explored; or perhaps only opportunities had to be shouldered and only burdens explored. Suddenly he felt as if he had taken at last the first but long-considered slippery step past the edge of a precipice over which he had before only gingerly thrust his nose, a first step which sent him stumbling down, scattering stones and debris, trying to keep his feet, but falling to his knees, bruised, his clothes tearing, rolling over and over, slowly at first, but knowing that soon the ominous momentum would grow swifter, clutching at shrubs and stunted trees for handholds, anything to hang on to, to arrest his descent, to save himself from that plunge. Those pale-blue airmail envelopes with their discreet red-and-blue *fourragère* borders, that leather diary, frayed as a breviary too often pressed against a *prie-dieu,* the prim pebbly morocco address book with its dignified gold-and-black alphabetical epaulets, were all keys to another life, perhaps even to another man's death, keys to doors Sanders was afraid he would have to open, yes, afraid, yet doors he was eager to vault through to discover what was beyond, to see what had made Christiansen do what he had done. And that twitch, that strange evanescent tic, why?

"You look like you just saw a ghost," Fillmore said, standing over him.

"I have."

"A holy one, I hope," Fillmore joked, slipping easily into the humor but not seeming at all profane.

"I don't know."

"Are you feeling all right?" Fillmore asked. "Here, let me take that musette bag." He reached for it, and Sanders lurched back as if he'd been pushed.

"No," he said, more sharply than he'd intended. "Just leave it alone."

[52]

"I'm sorry. I didn't mean—"

"Yes, I know, I'm sorry too."

So the chess game ended in a huff and a flurry of tight-lipped apologies, with Fillmore stalking off down the ward, stiff-backed, his fingers irately kneading his collar cross.

After he had gone Sanders tied the musette bag around a post at the head of the bed where he could keep an eye on it, where it was within easy reach, but after the first time, when he returned the chess set to it, each time thereafter when he tried to open it to examine the contents he grew drowsy and dozed.

❋   ❋   ❋

Sanders had gone to the telephone to call her, reached out for the receiver when the telephone jangled against his palm. He let it ring three times, certain that it was she, prepared now to deal with her on his terms. "Hello," she said, her voice remote, breath short, "this is Beth Christiansen."

"Yes, Mrs. Christiansen," he replied, "I recognized your voice. Good morning. I got your message last night and was going to call you but I didn't have a chance. Is anything wrong?"

Silence. Then, "No, not exactly wrong, Mr. Sanders . . . just that I'd like to apologize for the other night."

"No apologies are necessary."

"I was terribly rude."

"You were overwrought."

Silence again before "I know I hurt your feelings the other night. I even meant to, but I can explain—"

"No explanations are necessary either." He was not going to make it easier for her. He waited the silence out.

"Look," she began abruptly, "could I see you?"

"Well . . ." His hesitation was calculated.

"Please, I'd like to talk to you. I could drive in and meet you at your hotel."

"Today?" He gave the word all the unwillingness he could muster, all the illusion that it was a terrible imposition.

"Yes," she said hesitantly, "it's my day off."

Sanders let the silence continue for a long time before he acquiesced, cheerlessly, and arranged to meet her in the lobby of his hotel.

Dressed in a fitted black suit with a white ruffle at the throat, Beth Christiansen looked like a different woman, not quite so thin, taller and much younger. The angular face seemed softer, probably because she wore her hair differently, and her smooth skin skillfully made up hid her pallor, but it was the green and hazel-flecked eyes hidden beneath stiffly mascaraed heavy black eyelashes and the slender high-bridged nose that were most arresting; it was the face of a stranger, with the familiar yet vague outlines of a single encounter vividly remembered. When he took her elbow to lead her to the elevators, he felt her stiffen and, relenting, assured her that he'd made a reservation for lunch at the hotel's rooftop restaurant. Glassed in on four sides, it gave a magnificent almost unobstructed view of the city, the harbor and the bridges and she seemed entranced by the panorama, so much so that when the waiter arrived she didn't even hear his request for drink orders until it had been repeated. "Will you join me?" she asked, demure, even diffident.

He nodded and gratefully she told him to order for her. He did, a daiquiri for her, white wine and soda for him, aware that the image of an abstemious Elliott Sanders he was creating was another part of a lie. She said nothing until the drinks arrived, simply staring at the scene spread below, and then, holding up her glass, she whispered, "To your homecoming."

They clinked glasses and drank and as the glasses rang he remembered the warmth and welcome of Laura Martin's toast and beyond that a dinner at the Tour d'Argent with Elaine. They'd sat at the window too, overlooking the river and Notre Dame, after a large number of francs to the *maître* had assured the table for them. It had been a *son-et-lumière* evening, the rose windows glowing in the medieval gray stone of the cathedral like a beating heart, the illuminated spires and gargoyles casting great satanic shadows; in the azure twilight that was a cloak of romance it was Paris at its loveliest. "It's the way it is with us, Elliott," Elaine said. He could see her wide eyes unblinking over the wine. "You know it's not going to improve . . . but it's not going to get worse."

"Could it?"

She nodded. "It could. Easily."

[54]

The Seine, silent, sinuous, slithered past beneath them like a snake, and Sanders felt that same serpentine quality in Elaine, a serpentine constriction around his heart.

"You know I love you"—the wicked, glittering smile—"after my fashion."

"You don't know what the word means."

"Fashion?" The smile was even more provoking.

"And if I can't bear it?"

"Can't?" Her proud, petulant mouth looked as if she would spit. "You mean won't."

"That too."

For an instant anger and fear sparkled in her eyes like diamonds, then she shrugged, a gesture defiant and indifferent together, and raised her glass once again. "To your patience, my darling, and the marriage bond: *Till death us do part. . . .*"

Sanders heard her voice from a great distance and was surprised to feel her hand on his forearm, gently shaking him, to hear her asking if he was all right. "Yes, fine, Mrs. Christiansen, fine. I'm sorry," he apologized. "I was in another country."

"And besides the wench is *not* dead?" Beth Christiansen asked. When her face swam into focus he was surprised to see the shrewish and shrewd appraisal of those extraordinary wide-irised eyes.

"Something like that," he admitted, "but she *is* dead, at least as far as I'm concerned."

"But the ghost will not be laid?" In the momentary pause, recognizing the *double-entendre,* she was embarrassed and a slow flush rising from her throat reddened her cheeks and forehead.

Sanders, seeing his advantage, took it. "The lady, if one can call her that, was once my wife. We were divorced a few years ago."

She had recovered herself. "That makes it easier for me," she said.

"My being married or divorced?"

"Both." She paused, sipped her daiquiri, and went on. "I don't know how much . . . George"—she labored to produce the name—"told you about me, about us." She waited for some reaction, some reply, but Sanders gave her none. "I don't know how well you knew him."

"I knew him. How well you know a person is always hard to say."

[55]

"Well, that at least is honest." She smiled bitterly. "And it does sound like George. I was married to him for more than three years and that's about the way I felt, about the way I still feel. I'm telling you this only because otherwise my behavior the other night would make no sense and would be unforgivable."

"Do you need forgiveness?" he asked.

"Don't you?"

"Yes," he answered too casually, "I suppose we all do."

She let that pass. "George and I were not on . . . very good terms when he left for Vietnam. In fact, I'd asked him for a divorce but he insisted that I wait until he got back, said that the time would serve as a trial separation and that we could make a final decision then."

"You agreed?"

She nodded. "I didn't feel I could insist."

"Why not? Another man?"

She looked shocked. "No, nothing like that. It was just between me and George. It just hadn't worked out. And then, when I got the telegram, I was shattered."

"Because you felt guilty?"

"That and"—she looked straight into his eyes—"because by then there *was* another man."

Jealousy and desire raked his flesh although until that moment Beth Christiansen had not even seemed attractive to him. "Now?" he asked.

"Now," she repeated, her eyes masked, gazing at the panorama of the city behind him. "I got a note from his commanding officer saying that George had been very brave, had been killed in action and was likely to receive a decoration which, of course, they would send to me. I didn't want it. I don't deserve it. I felt like one of those soldier-heroes' horses in the moving pictures on whose saddles they pin the posthumous medals and who from then on are expected to be put out to pasture, to go riderless forever after."

"Guilt," Sanders commented, not calling her attention to the figure of speech she'd used so revealingly.

"I suppose so," she confessed. "Then, weeks later, the chaplain's letter arrived—"

"Fillmore's?" Sanders interrupted.

Leaning back in her chair, she moved away from him and the table. "Yes, Fillmore. Here, I have the letter in my purse." She began to rummage in her bag for it and Sanders signaled the waiter for more drinks. When she found it, she handed the airmail envelope across the table to him with only a momentary hesitation before she said, "Please read it. It concerns you . . . too."

The letter was postmarked the day after he'd flown out of Saigon. That goddam skypilot, that nosy old woman, Sanders thought, couldn't keep his cottonpicking hands out of other people's business. But that particular epithet also applied to him, he realized. The letter was handwritten on two sheets of paper that bore the embossed letterhead of the base hospital and in the upper right-hand corner Chaplain Murray Fillmore's name. It said:

DEAR MRS. CHRISTIANSEN:

By now your husband's commanding officer will have written to you about your husband's death. I want you to know that I was able to see that he had Christian burial. If you make proper application to the Graves Registration Service his remains will be sent for burial to any designation you specify.

Most of your husband's effects are being forwarded to you by his commanding officer, but some were in the possession of a friend of his, a foreign correspondent for a French news-magazine, though an American by birth, who was with your husband when he died and whose life your husband saved. Though this man survived, he was severely wounded in the action and I believe that the combination of his wounds, his sense of guilt about having survived while a friend and younger man died, and his stay at the hospital here have worsened an already disturbed mental state induced by a long term of service in this area and frequent reporting from other zones of great danger and combat. He has the fixed idea that your husband died in his place and that consequently he must in some way make up for that death, perform some atonement, though just what atonement is not clear to him. Though this is a common enough obsession in men badly wounded in combat, especially where saved by a close friend, it is usually overcome in time by the simple, healthy and necessary gratitude at being alive. And so it should be. Nothing is to be gained by shouldering unbearable burdens or undertaking unpayable debts.

Because this obsession has not left Elliott Sanders I am writing to you. He has with him your husband's diary, address book, and some letters, most of which I assume are yours, and when you see him—Sanders plans to get in touch with you as soon as he returns to the United States—I think you should ask him for them. They are yours by right and they are also the tangible symbols of Sanders' obsession, the sooner delivered to their rightful owner the better for him as well.

Do not misunderstand me: Elliott Sanders is not unhinged, not a madman, though he is, I believe, seriously troubled. Our base psychiatrist agrees with me in this but we had no way in the case of a civilian of doing much about it. And, to be altogether candid, I doubt we could have done much more even if he'd been a member of the armed forces.

I am sorry to impose this added burden on your present grief, but I felt I had to forewarn you of Sanders' impending arrival and of his possession of your husband's effects. Sanders will, I believe, try to visit other people connected with your husband—certainly his father and a Mr. King, both of whom are listed with you as Sergeant Christiansen's beneficiaries, and whose names and addresses Sanders knows—and I would appreciate your informing them of the contents of this letter.

Please accept my deepest condolences for your loss.

> Yours in Christ,
> MURRAY FILLMORE,
> CAPTAIN, U.S. ARMY

"You do have those things, the diary and the letters, don't you?" Beth Christiansen asked, her face working.

"You believe him?"

"Absolutely."

"That I'm deranged?"

"Well, perhaps not that," she replied, and he saw that only politeness spoke.

"Only perhaps?"

"I'm a nurse. I see people do unbelievable things almost every single day."

"Like throw chess pieces around?"

She ignored that. "Fillmore's letter has the ring of truth. Besides what has the chaplain got to gain by writing such a letter to me?"

"And what do I have to gain by coming to see you?"

She closed her eyes and drank the daiquiri all in a single abrupt gulp, then very carefully set the glass down and took a deep breath before she spoke. "I don't know what you have to gain or why you came here, Mr. Sanders. I don't know why you went to see Mr. Christiansen at the hospital. I don't know what you want from me, so why don't you tell me?" Her eyes were out of focus, her voice raised, her speech thicker and less controlled, and she looked as if she was going to be sick. On two drinks? Sanders thought. Impossible. "Are you feeling sick?" he asked.

"I'm all right," she replied, blinking her eyes as if it were a terrible effort for her to keep them open. She leaned her elbows on the table and propped her head up with both hands. "I'm fine." Her eyes closed and her head drooped.

Sanders signaled the waiter for the check and paid it. "Come on, Mrs. Christiansen," he said, "I think you'd better lie down." He steadied her when she stood, picked up the white gloves she dropped, retrieved her purse and led her to the elevator. "Lie down," she muttered, her eyes shut tight, "lie down." She leaned against him, her breast soft against his arm, her flank shaking against his thigh, and he fought down the flush of painful feeling that welled up in him. With the fastidious distaste of the sober for the drunk, the other passengers on the elevator stared and looked away as she continued to murmur, "Lie down, lie down," but Sanders ignored them until his floor came and then, bracing her, he half carried, half walked her to his room. When she sat on the bed, he pushed her back, picked up her legs and swiveled her around so that she was lying full length. "Down," she said, a slow, pleased, foolish smile lighting her face, "lie down." He took off her shoes, unsnapped the white ruff at her throat and unbuttoned her jacket. He would also have tried to loosen her brassiere, but he didn't trust himself.

* * *

They wheeled the new man in from surgery and put him into the empty bed on Sanders' right, a big white tent over his body. When the orderlies had gone a nurse remained behind, standing between their beds filling out the man's chart until she dropped her pen. "Shit!" she exclaimed softly. Crouching to recover it, she pulled her skirt up, exposing white strong thighs and kneecaps flushed with blood, like wounds beneath the medically white stockings. She was young, with a close-cropped dark curly head and a pale neck that showed a strong line of vertebrae. Sanders stared at her, at the freckled Irish face, the small breasts, the powerful thighs and was surprised to feel no desire. When she found the pen she stood up and held it to the light. "Damn, it's broken," she said, biting her lip.

"I can fix it," he told her quietly. She was startled. "Let me have it," he asked, and reached out his hand.

"I thought you were asleep and you should be," she admonished.

"I can fix it, I tell you," he insisted.

"Sure, sure," she said placatingly and handed the pen over but her skeptical blue eyes spoke louder than her hesitation in doing so. Carefully, Sanders bent the point back straight, pushed the tube and socket into place and trickled a bubble of ink out to make sure it was working properly before he handed the pen back to her. "You're old-fashioned," he remarked, "still using a fountain pen."

"I never did like ball-points," she said, then heard the echo of her words and flushed. Her quick squiggles on the back of the chart pleased her. "You *did* fix it," she said, pleased, surprised.

"I said I would."

"Lots of people say they can do things they can't."

"I know a lot of those, but not me."

"I know plenty of them too."

"It figures."

Her black brows rose and arched. "Why?"

[60]

"Nurses always know such things."

"Oh," she murmured, no longer offended.

"What's wrong with him?" Sanders gestured toward the new patient and as he did noticed the sleeping man's aquiline nose, the jutting cheekbones beneath the tight bronze skin and the crow-black hair. A warrior's face if ever he'd seen one.

"This is a chest and belly ward," the nurse replied. "Mortar wound. He's got a colostomy, poor thing."

"Is that what's under the Conestoga wagon?"

She chuckled and nodded.

"That funny?"

"It does look kind of like a Conestoga wagon, you know, and in this case I suppose it is funny. He's an Indian, Cherokee I think." She put the chart back, then turned to his. "Oh, you're that reporter—"

"Foreign correspondent." He tried to grin. Something in her tone and expression had upset him. "More glamorous. Even have a regulation trench coat but too hot for this climate."

She was quick on the uptake. "You'll be all right," she assured him, replacing the chart.

"You're sure?" he asked somberly. "You guarantee it yourself?"

For the first time she looked into his face. "Mr. Sanders, you have my word you're going to be just fine."

"I don't really think so."

"You're going to be up and out of here in a couple of weeks at the very most."

"I know that."

"Then what's eating you?" she asked.

"How about Chief Cherokee?"

Her face fell. "He'll make it," she replied.

"With the colostomy?"

She nodded and was all business then. "Now, enough of this talk," she began.

"Lie down!" he caroled, remembering the joke.

She ignored that and continued, "Let me plump your pillow."

She leaned over him and said, "Here, put your arms around my neck and hold on to me." He did and was overcome by her softness

[61]

and cleanness, the softness of her breasts, her arms, even the tiny soft hairs of her forearms that tickled him, the fine smell of her soap and fragrance. How filthy it had been out there, dirty clothes, muddy ground, hard ground, dirty killing, hard killing. Now, soft white clean linen. Soft. Nurse. "What's your name?" he breathed into her ear. "Cathy Sullivan," she whispered back. She lifted him, and her breasts against him were the softest most healing flesh he could remember. He let his pillow be plumped and held her until carefully, tenderly, she lowered him back to the bed and to sleep.

In the morning he was in pain, and fever raged through him in such waves, burning crests and chilling troughs, that the world around him blurred and tilted, and he had a vertigo like seasickness. He kept seeing Christiansen's face, that medallion profile burned first into the concrete and then turned full-face transposed onto the shoulders of the old lady in the black pajamas while her wizened head in turn was attached to the beautiful little-girl body in the *ao dai*. Their faces and bodies trembled with a wild dancing frenzy like St. Vitus' dance or epileptic fits, so they leaped and jerked like puppets whose strings were being pulled, *petit mal, grand mal,* until staring woodenly through the circle of those people in spasms he came face to face with the solid-mahogany Cherokee countenance in the next bed.

He awoke in the middle-of-the-night darkness, the only light a single dim yellow bulb in the outside corridor, feeling his bedclothes soaked with sweat, his own body foreign, an enemy and a betrayer. The restless sounds of the ward, moans and groans, turnings and tossings, afflicted him and then he heard the rustling of sheets and the Conestoga wagon on the Cherokee's bed rocked and quaked as if in a prairie storm that wailed "Ah . . . ee . . . eee!" the same cry the black-pajamaed grandmother had keened on the street. The sheets went black with blood just as the *ao dai* had stained scarlet and in the darkness the white moon scythe of the Indian's teeth reaped the air.

Sanders called for help, hearing his voice weak, little, forcing it bit by bit bigger, shouting as loud as his faintness and weakness would permit, hoping that this time he would be quicker, more effective, in a faraway recess of his brain convinced that it was already too late. They heard. Running swiftly on their squeaking shoes, orderlies, nurses, doctors came and raced the Cherokee up to the surgery, but for Sanders the conclusion was foregone and even before he was able to ask Cathy Sullivan he knew what had happened. "He tore out his colostomy," she told him, her voice choking, unshed tears in her eyes.

"You said he'd make it," Sanders accused.

"He would have, but—"

"But he didn't want to?"

She nodded. "You've got to want to live."

"Why?"

"Just because."

"No, why did he do it?"

She shrugged off the question irritably.

"When a man dies deliberately, you've got to know why," he told her, and found himself choosing every word too carefully.

"The only thing he said"—she hesitated—"was that he was the son of a chief. Does that make any sense?"

"The son of a chief." It did make sense, its own insane sense, its own courageous sense.

Later he took it up with Fillmore. "We are all sons of chiefs," Fillmore replied.

"We're all sons of bitches!" Sanders exploded.

"I don't think so. Neither," he added, looking significantly at the musette bag, "do you."

"These local types are a lot smarter than us Christians."

"Us?" Fillmore's tone was insinuating.

"At least they know how to make their people burn!"

"We keep a little hellfire in reserve too, you know." He smiled, then was serious. "I never thought that was a Christian idea." Bitterly, outraged, he went on, "Those Buddhist leaders promised those martyr monks pills that would keep them from feeling the flames—but the pills are only aspirin!"

"Psychiatry and placebos everywhere. Or only Pavlov? What a way to make saints and martyrs."

"Their willingness to die *is* impressive," Fillmore admitted with obvious reluctance, "if willingness to die is a criterion of belief, of faith, of love."

"Is there another?"

Fillmore's fingers sought the collar cross once again. "Yes, willingness to live."

"And ability?"

"And ability," Fillmore confirmed.

"What gives someone that ability?"

"I don't know. I don't even know if all men have it. My father, he thought he knew." Fillmore paused, the personal difficult for him to speak. "He wasn't a religious man, you see. That was something for women, for my mother and sister, but for him, for me, for us men, a fairy tale." He waved his hand as if he had a wand in it. "But my father loved the earth and sky and the things that grew and walked the earth, the way only a prosperous dirt farmer can, one with two hundred and fifty acres of river-bottom Iowa land." A mixture of respect and envy, anger and affection deepened his voice. "I suppose you could give it a fancy label, say he had a reverence for life, and that would be true, but it was more than that, and less too. It was a lust for living and living things. I've seen him taste the cornstalks for their greenness, or touch the tassels for their silkiness, or stroke a heifer's flank for the simple joy of the feel. I've seen him roll in the stubble of a sheared wheat field, or plunge his head into a barrel of cold rainwater and come up roaring with delight. That, he insisted, was what made a man what he was and what made a man want to live."

"The flesh? The skin? The song of oneself?"

"Only that. Simple sensuous pleasure. Everything flowed from that."

"But man?"

"He thought man was a pestilence come to destroy the earth, all four horsemen of the Apocalypse together."

"I would have liked your old man," Sanders said.

"I suppose you would have." Fillmore shook his head sadly.

"You sound as if you liked him too," Sanders went on, suppressing the "almost" he sensed was true, pushing the recollection of Lovett Carpenter Sanders from his mind.

[64]

"I did. I do."

"Your father's still alive?"

"In a manner of speaking. He had a bad stroke."

"How bad?"

"He hears but he can't see or speak."

"A vegetable?"

"No. That might be easier. I think he's all there."

"What a punishment for a man like that!"

"Perhaps it fits the crime," Fillmore said, trying to be gentle but not succeeding.

Fillmore began the silent tedious ritual of lighting his pipe, and Sanders, amazed and annoyed that anyone could endure all those details for such a minor vice, observed. For other more intensely passionate vices he understood all too well the endurance and the enduring; Elaine had given him unnumbered lessons. "What happened to the chief?" he asked, aware that he was weak because he was remembering; fatigue and depression were always his undoing, cracks in the wall through which recollection at first seeped, then poured. "He tore his guts out, didn't he?" The cruelty of the language was more to inure himself than to outrage Fillmore.

"He went into shock and—"

"Good old Sanders, always in the nick of time."

"It wasn't your fault and you mustn't blame yourself."

"Why? Or why not?"

"Do you always ask that question?" Fillmore's irritation showed.

Sanders laughed. "I guess I do. You know what they try to teach you in journalism school? Who? What? When? Where? The unholy four W's of the reporter's creed. The bedrocks of good reporting on which so many have stumbled. But I've made my own reputation, such as it is, as a 'different'-style reporter, a fancier foreign correspondent, because I also ask *How?* and *Why?*" That was true as far as it went, he knew, but there was more, much more, to be explained.

"Why?" Fillmore responded, smiling to take the sting out of what was intended as a riposte.

"Mostly because I couldn't keep a job the usual way. I was a loner, an out, and I kept making the newspaper and magazine editors who employed me angry. I needed an equalizer to keep myself in the running, to make a living. Maybe even to prove myself. The *How?* and the *Why?* were my equalizers." It was too pat an answer, too clear, and rubbed smooth with use; he knew that he had other virtues, and other vices, that applied.

"Is that all?"

"No," Sanders said, "not quite. My father taught me to ask those questions all the time, of everyone, of myself, and I've never been able to kick the habit." He tried to say it calmly but it didn't sound that way.

"Your *father* taught you that?" Fillmore seemed surprised.

"I may seem like a bastard to you but that's only metaphorically. I *did* have a father and I *was* born on the proper side of the blanket."

"I wasn't questioning that. Did your father teach you to ask why of him too?"

"I'm sorry to say he did."

"And did he answer when you asked?"

"As long as he lived, he did."

"He's dead, then. I'm sorry."

"He was killed in the war."

Fillmore struck a match and with an audible breath lit the pipe. Words and smoke came oracularly out of his mouth together. "You ought to give me that boy's stuff, you know."

Sanders sat upright and cunningly looked puzzled. "What stuff?"

Fillmore pointed at the musette bag with his pipestem, and hypnotically Sanders watched the smoke snake from the mouthpiece. "I looked in there before I brought it to you."

"Pretty unethical, and sneaky too, wouldn't you say?"

"I'm not an inquisitive man, Sanders, but sometimes when effects are sorted out, mistakes are made. I was only checking."

"Mistakes are mankind's métier," Sanders replied, "but not in this case. Christiansen gave me those things to hold for him."

"To keep?"

Sanders shook his head.

"Why not give those things to me and let me send them home?"

[66]

"I'm going to return them myself, *in person*," Sanders said stubbornly, realizing as he said it that that was exactly what he intended to do.

"Now it's my turn to ask *why?*"

"I don't know, Fillmore. I haven't even looked at what George left, not yet, but I want to take the stuff back to the States to deliver them to his—" His what? Wife? Parents? Family? He didn't even know whether George was married or not, whether he had a family, or where he lived. California, that he knew, but just where? He'd have to find out, not just that but a lot of other things as well.

"Next of kin," Fillmore supplied.

"Foul phrase."

"Have you thought this through?"

"What's there to think through?"

"Why you should want to take Christiansen's things home personally, why you won't let these things be sent home officially, through channels." Fillmore exhaled divided streams of smoke from his pinched nostrils. "The rest of his effects go home via the military."

The rest? What else was there? What had Christiansen kept in town and with whom? "Do you think I want to steal something from a dead man? from a dead friend?"

"Well, don't you?"

"There's only a packet of letters, a diary and an address book, as you know, if you looked. Total value maybe five bucks."

"Total monetary value, perhaps, but not total worth."

Whatever he said to Fillmore, he sensed something morbid in his desire to return those things to Christiansen's hearth himself and in his oblique way Fillmore was warning him not to. "What is it you're trying to tell me?" he finally asked the chaplain.

"You're treading a dangerous road, invading privacies you have no right to invade."

"By returning the property of a friend who saved my life?"

"That could be done as easily by mail as in person, perhaps better."

"Yes, I suppose it could."

"You will want to, you will have to, tell them how Christiansen died," Fillmore said flatly, "and then you'll want to find out why he was willing to die, what made him the kind of man he was."

"What's wrong with that?"

"Is that a newspaperman's proper curiosity?"

"No, a human being's proper curiosity."

"Not journalistic voyeurism and desire to manipulate men and events, *make* news rather than report it?" He switched his tack.

"I don't have to tell them *exactly* how it was, do I?" he asked, knowing how that obsession had been with him all his life, knowing how it had first bound him to words and the struggle with making them a precise description of what he learned about and saw in an occurrence, and was increasingly less satisfactory so that he had found himself more and more relying on the camera rather than the typewriter to make them see, to make them feel. He had always had to tell them exactly how it was and to do so to find out exactly how it was, if and when he could.

"You're trifling with a human life, with a human soul, Sanders. And in cold blood. There's no greater sin." Though his voice was soft, its timbre was heated and his face white.

"You're imagining things, Fillmore."

"Am I, Sanders, am I really? Or are you imagining things, imagining that you can find your own self by discovering someone else's self?"

"I know my own self, all too well."

"Then why do you persist in doing this?"

"Because Christiansen saved my worthless hide; he gave me a lease on life, a new life, another life."

" 'Greater love hath no man than this, that a man lay down his life for his friends,' eh?"

"Exactly." The word kept repeating itself.

"Let me return those things to Christiansen's family, Sanders, I beg you."

"I can't."

Not until three days later did Fillmore return for their usual chess game and he was no longer the same man. "Have you read the diary or those letters?" he asked.

"Have you?" Sanders countered.

Fillmore looked affronted.

"You feel perfectly justified in asking me such a question but if I return the compliment, you're insulted, aren't you? Do you think that cross on your collar gives you an automatic halo over your head?"

"If I thought that, I'd never have taken that cross on," Fillmore responded angrily. Then, apologetic, he continued, "But you have as much right to ask me such a question as I have to ask you."

"More, because George left those things *in my care*."

"Would he have, if he had known he was going to die?"

"How do I know?"

"The executor of the estate," Fillmore commented sarcastically.

"The executor of his will," Sanders said.

"Have you read those private papers?" Fillmore repeated.

"I can't even bring myself to touch them."

"But you *intend* to read them?" Fillmore was persistent, insistent.

"Go away," Sanders suddenly shouted. "You hear me, Pastor Captain Fillmore, just get the hell out of here and leave me alone." With that he turned his back and closed his eyes.

*　*　*

The telephone call came in the middle of the night and the moment Sanders heard John Ballinger's ponderous legal voice he knew she was dead. He was at journalism school in the Midwest then, but he'd been expecting that call every day and night for five years, since his father's death. As he sat at the desk, bleary-eyed, having fallen asleep there only a few hours before while studying for a history exam, the desk calendar reminded him that it was the fifth anniversary of his father's death. His mother had needed no reminder. Ballinger said it was an accident, soft shoulder, road markings obscured. She'd taken the turn on Taylor Hill going more than seventy, skidded off the road, hit a tree and then smashed into the stone wall of the Adams estate; her neck was broken; she died instantly. A police car found her at dawn and called Ballinger—she carried a little card in her wallet instructing anyone to call Ballinger in case of emergency, giving his home and office numbers, some-

[69]

thing Sanders had not forgiven her for—and Ballinger had telephoned him immediately after identifying the body.

"Was she drunk?" Sanders asked.

"Your mother was a lady, Elliott, she didn't drink to excess." The same old Ballinger bull. He was a gentleman; she was a lady; his father had been anything but a gentleman, in spite of his family, nothing but a nobody journalist upstart.

Ballinger told him what the funeral arrangements were—it was all in his mother's will which Ballinger had drawn—and that he was expected back as soon as he could get a plane. Three hours later Sanders was on a plane for Chicago; by evening he was in Connecticut. Ballinger had, indeed, taken care of everything as if he himself were the only bereaved; and, of course, in a sense he was. Sanders had known about Ballinger and his mother for years, though the proprieties were kept. All during the war, after they got home from France, while his father was in Europe covering the "big one" he'd waited all his life for, Ballinger had come to dinner three times a week, deviating from that routine that first and last and only time Lovett Carpenter Sanders had come home before the invasion, that single week of the three weeks' leave he had, when Ballinger had not come to visit at all. "One in Washington, one in New York, one in Connecticut, one week each for the politicians, the news editors and the family," Lovett Carpenter Sanders had written and as usual he was as good as his word; he took what he wanted and was prepared to pay the price; and as always he was also prepared for them to pay his price as well.

Ballinger had, surely, taken care of everything. There were banks of his mother's favorite rust-colored chrysanthemums; the services at St. Thomas' Episcopal were simple and tasteful, and the private burial, attended by a few old friends and relatives, was in the family plot, the raw red earth where Stuarts had been buried for a hundred and fifty years scarred with another grave carefully disguised by a mat of artificial green grass. There was no unseemly display of grief, though Ballinger wept quietly into a monogrammed handkerchief as they lowered the coffin into the grave; but he kept his place, as he had in the church, one step back here, one row back there. Yet no one saw fit to mention that his mother was not quite forty years old, her birthday still two months off, and because Ballinger had also seen to it that the coffin remained sealed because she'd been badly battered in the "accident," Sanders never had a chance to have a last look at her, to see her face once more, one last time, before the earth claimed her.

The double tombstone, narrow, white and prim as the New England faces around it, was there, already prepared: his mother's work, with Ballinger's help. On the right Lovett Carpenter Sanders, born 1904, died 1944; on the left Marian Stuart Sanders, born 1909 and only the blank façade of stone to fill in with the date of death. Even here there was sham and mystery, hypocrisy and hope, for there was neither body nor coffin beneath his father's stone, only a ritual urn, because no one had found his father's body or knew what had happened to it. *Somewhere in France. The Unknown Correspondent.* His father would have enjoyed that hugely; it would have appealed to his sense of cosmic comic farce.

Lovett Carpenter Sanders had come home that last time, thinner, browner, more tightly drawn than Sanders ever remembered him. When he'd run down the path to embrace him, his father had held him off at arm's length, looking him over, shaking him first by the shoulders, then by the hand. "You're almost a man," his father had said admiringly. "Look at you! I'll bet you've grown a foot and a half since I last saw you." As always he was the observant reporter and Sanders knew because there was a place in the cellar of the house where his mother had marked his growth half-year by half-year during those five years since they'd left his father in Paris. Sanders had been ten years old then and four feet eight inches tall; he was fifteen and six feet one inch tall now, two inches taller than his father, an inch taller than his father's quick estimate. Playfully, Lovett Carpenter Sanders had punched his biceps and said, "Here, watch this hand," raising his right arm high as if to strike him, and then, swiftly, with his left and using the weight of his body, had thrown Sanders to the ground. As he lay there sprawled headlong on the grass, his father, standing over him, chortled, "You've got to keep your eyes peeled. Don't watch what they tell you to, what they want you to watch; that's camouflage. Watch what they don't tell you, what they don't want you to see; that's where the truth is that they're hiding. Don't listen to what they say; watch what they do." It was good advice to a man, he realized later, better counsel still to a reporter; but to a son who had not seen his father for five years it was torment.

The next day Ballinger saw him at his office to talk about the estate. The will, Ballinger explained, would leave Elliott an independently wealthy young man. "You can do almost anything you want to now"—Ballinger smiled his tight smile—"within reason." Sitting in a red leather armchair behind a magnificent mahogany desk so highly polished that Sanders could see both their faces and trunks clearly reflected in it, Ballinger seemed almost proud, boastful.

"Like buy a Bugatti and go to Paris to chase Follies girls?" Sanders asked tartly.

Ballinger was put out. "That wasn't exactly what your mother had in mind," he said primly. Ballinger was thinking that he was just like his father; that that was exactly the sort of thing Lovett Carpenter Sanders would have done, and done again.

"Look, Mr. Ballinger," Sanders said, "let's level, you and me. I don't particularly like you and you never really cared much for me either. I knew about you and Mother"—Ballinger began to protest, to bluster, but Sanders cut him off with a wave of his hand—"and it was okay with me if it made things easier, happier, for her. Lord knows my father made it neither." At that last Ballinger subsided but his thick neck and features were red, stark contrast to the clipped fringe of white hair. In that instant he looked vulnerable, even helpless, not at all like the haughty practical lawyer he was and had the reputation for being. Sanders, sorry for him, decided not to go on to mention Ballinger's wife who had for years, as far back as he could remember, been confined to a mental institution.

Ballinger took a cigar out of a humidor on his desk and, head down, gave it all his attention for a time, cutting and piercing the end, lighting up with a lovely veined green onyx lighter, drawing and puffing a few tentative streams of redolent cigar smoke. When he looked up again his features had resumed their staid pallor, his mouth was judiciously drawn and he said quietly, "Your mother asked me to be the executor of the estate, *and* your guardian."

"My guardian!"

"You're still a minor, Elliott, legally."

"I'll be twenty-one next spring," he replied defensively.

"Your mother's will calls for me to administer the estate until you're thirty. You're to have the income from the principal to live on during those years and to use at your discretion. The principal, however, is not available to you until your thirtieth birthday."

"Until I'm thirty," he protested.

"That looks like a long way off, but it isn't."

"Ten years is half my life!"

"It'll only be a third of your life then," Ballinger said, a smile narrowing his eyes and touching the corners of his mouth. For that instant he was a human being with a sense of humor, not the family lawyer and his mother's lover.

"How much was there?" Sanders asked finally.

"The will's got to go through probate, you understand, and there are some expenses to pay—"

"You get paid as executor, don't you?"

Again Ballinger colored. "Yes," he answered.

"Did she leave you anything in the will?" Sanders persisted.

"I believe she left me a small bequest."

"What's a *small* bequest?" Sanders asked sarcastically.

Ballinger shifted uncomfortably in his chair. "The estate after taxes should be a little under two hundred and fifty thousand dollars. She left me a ten-thousand-dollar bequest. Attorney's fees will be about five thousand."

"The laborer is worthy of his hire, huh?"

Ballinger's face froze and his teeth bit almost through the cigar. "There's the house, of course, and it's worth another sixty thousand or so—"

"Get rid of it. I don't want it."

"I thought you might want to keep it."

Their sentences were virtually simultaneous and they were then left speechless, looking at each other across the mirrorlike desktop until Ballinger rose, a portly lawyer in a neat pin-striped suit, dignified and looking very tired now. He walked to the window and turned his back. Slowly, distinctly, he spoke. "I loved your mother.

[73]

I wish I could have married her, though very likely she deserved better than me, or your father. But my wife, my wife—" He couldn't finish the sentence. "You're a boy, a bright boy but only a boy, and you don't understand any of these things. Yet. You think you do but you don't. You just haven't lived long enough to know how complicated life is."

Then he was walking across the room, had him out of the chair and led him by the shoulder to the door. "Go back and finish school, Elliott. I'll keep you informed. If you want anything, just let me know." His secretary had appeared out of nowhere and Ballinger, in a voice full of authority now, said, "Will you show Mr. Elliott out, please, Mrs. Tanner," and Sanders found himself in the corridor facing the glazed door pane and the gold letters: J. C. BALLINGER, ATTORNEY-AT-LAW.

Sanders had gone back to Iowa the next morning but not without having first paid a visit the night before to the freshly dug grave to take his own personal and private parting from his mother. A few nights later, in Iowa City, having for the first time in his life failed a school examination and having gotten drunk for the first time in his life as well, he had picked up that JESUS SAVES sign from that storefront Pentacostal church and carried it down the main street to the bank. Ballinger had discharged his duties as executor impeccably, though they conducted their necessary relations by mail or over the telephone; and he had never imposed himself as a guardian. But Ballinger had kept the house for him and that was truly to prove a boon. It was only years later when he was already living in France that Sanders learned that the lawyer had used both the bequest and his legal fees, and a considerable sum of his own money, to set up a scholarship fund at Amherst in the name of Marian Stuart Sanders, not in journalism, of course, but in religion; also, Ballinger had paid for the entire cost of his mother's funeral out of his own pocket. By then, however, it was too late to say he'd been wrong or to admit that he was sorry, much less that he was grateful, because John C. Ballinger had died three months before of prostatic cancer.

*   *   *

Shortly before Sanders was due to be discharged from the hospital Fillmore dropped into the ward one evening, an unusual time for him to be there and in an unusual mood. "Remember," he asked without preliminaries, "you told me that Christiansen was keeping his clothes somewhere in town?"

"You found out where?"

"Yes."

"I told you, Fillmore, you'd make a good reporter. Did you find the dolly too?"

Fillmore laughed sourly. "It took some doing, especially for a man of—the cloth. Some people don't like to tell us things because they're afraid to shock us. Well, we're not so very easily shocked. We hear and see and understand a great deal more than some people give us credit for."

"It's because they think of you as out of this world." Sanders was deliberately snide.

"We may be otherworldly and some of us are unworldly, but you know, Sanders, we see a lot of human pain. We're there when people marry and give birth and get into trouble and are sick and die. The prisons and the hospital wards and the cemeteries are part of our natural habitat and you learn a lot there. And many people do talk to us about themselves, maybe because they have no one else to talk to these days, maybe because no one else comes there, maybe because to us confidences are privileged, maybe just because we're cheaper and more available than psychoanalysts."

"What did you find?" Sanders impatiently brought him back to the point.

"I talked to a few people, some who knew Christiansen, and I finally tracked his place down. Near the river, just past one of the smaller Buddhist temples. It wasn't much of a place, but I found it." A curious note of triumph rang through his voice.

"Did you find any of his stuff?"

"Wasn't much there. A Japanese transistor radio, a French electric hot plate, some American food and clothing. International enough, but nothing he'd have wanted to send home."

"What did you do with it?"

"I gave it to the children."

"Children!" Sanders sat bolt upright, feeling the twinges in his belly. "You mean he had children! I didn't think he was here long enough for that."

Fillmore looked at him with an austere wiliness.

"And the dolly?" Sanders went on. "Who was the girl? What little Annamese dancer did he corral? A bar girl? Or was it a Chinese girl? Some Americans seem to prefer them."

"He *adopted* two children whose parents were killed."

"By us," Sanders said, certain even before he spoke the words.

"By us," Fillmore confirmed, "one of those regrettable accidents."

"That stupid, saintly sonofabitch!" Sanders swore. "And there was no dolly?"

"No dolly, no bar girl, no dancer, no whore," Fillmore said, as if he had won something, "only an old amah to take care of the boy and girl."

The time came for him to leave the hospital. His wounds had healed and except for the scar across his belly the doctors said he was fine; and he was happy to be leaving the hospital and the country, though not quite so sure he was fine. Fillmore and Cathy Sullivan were even more skeptical about his departure and both tried to persuade him to stay a while longer. Fillmore was very helpful even after Sanders overruled him. He shopped for the Hermès scarf and the *muguet* perfume that Sanders wanted to give Cathy Sullivan, those old favorites of Elaine, Parisian wiles, as goodbye gifts; and he spoke bitterly only about the corruption of a country where such French luxuries—he used the word French with the usual Anglo-Saxon sense of France as a place of brothels and cancan girls—were available, and any others you wanted, for a price after more than twenty-five years of war.

Fillmore brought his flight bag from the hotel, already packed, and even had a jeep for the drive to the airfield. While Sanders was putting his few remaining possessions into the musette bag, his eye as usual flicked over the letters, diary and address book, and he promised himself again that he would make himself read them, but he saw his fingers avoid touching them as he put things into the bag. The time will come soon, he assured himself, on the plane, when I land, but soon. Then he saw Fillmore watching him, closed the bag, and buckled it down.

Outside Cathy Sullivan waited to say goodbye, looking less antiseptic in khakis than in the whites she usually wore, and he felt her sexuality, her womanliness, like an impact at the base of his spine. I must be getting better, he thought, or worse, and regretted that aside from some few sly caresses there had been nothing between them. No, he reminded himself, not nothing; just no sex. She embraced him and as she closed her eyes and lifted her face to him, he leaned down and kissed her French-style on both cheeks; "For gallantry beyond the call of duty," he said. But she didn't laugh or even smile. Her lips, still pursed, seemed frozen. In the bright uncompromising sunshine outside the hospital flecks of gray and green and hazel burned in those startled and startling blue eyes. She looked powerful and determined and impressive—and as if he had somehow disappointed her. "Are you sure you're okay?" she asked, her chaste speech clashing with the giving posture of her body.

"Fine."

"Then go back to Paris!" she ordered shortly.

"I will. After I see the States again. Time I went home for a little while. You don't want me to become one of those St.-Germain-des-Prés beatniks with a beard, do you? A permanent Left Bank expatriate? Where's your red-blooded American patriotism, your love of country?" he asked, but his anger drove through the humor roughshod.

"Listen," she said, clearly picking her words, "I'm not a very bright girl, I never was. And I'm not very pretty. Which is why I became a nurse. But I have an instinct about people, about some things, that makes me a good nurse, so just try listening to me for a change."

Sanders smiled and brushed her cheek with two fingers. "Yes, nurse."

"Something's wrong with you. You're still sick. That wound isn't healed up here"—she tapped his head—"even if it is down there." She poked his belly with a stern forefinger.

"You've been talking to the old skypilot again."

[77]

She half shook her head. "Yes and no. I knew something was wrong first, then I talked to Captain Fillmore and *I* asked *him*, so he said you were going to the States and he told me why."

"He doesn't know why."

"Don't do it."

"Do what?"

"Don't try to jam yourself into George Christiansen's shoes."

"Why? The size too big?"

"If the shoe pinches—" She essayed a smile, but couldn't complete it. "You can't put yourself into another man's shoes. Especially when he's dead."

"Why not? I thought that's what civilization was all about, and the skypilot's Christianity, being able to put yourself into another man's shoes so you could understand him, tolerate him, even endure him. Even Victor Charley. Maybe even learn then not to spend all your time killing him, the way we're doing here."

"You can't put yourself into anyone else's position. You can't even put yourself into another woman's bed," she said, her face desolate for the first time he'd ever seen it.

He put his arms around her and drew her close. "Is that how it is with you?" he asked her softly and she nodded her head, pounding it against his chest so he felt it like an outside heart beating in concert with his own.

"It can't be done," she said softly, "and it's better not to try."

Sanders pressed the scarf and perfume into her hands then, sadly instead of joyously, kissed her briefly again and got into the jeep next to Fillmore.

"Where will you be, Elliott?" she called, the first time she'd called him by his Christian name.

"Somewhere around San Francisco. I'll send you a picture postcard with the Golden Gate Bridge on it," he promised.

"You're haywire," she said, "you just won't listen."

Fillmore gunned the motor and they drove off, but as they turned into the road, Sanders saw her still standing there, her head bowed, the bottle in one fist like a grenade, the scarf hanging like a forlorn banner from the other.

Fillmore got him through the red tape with dispatch and efficiency, then sat next to him on the bench in the waiting room, not speaking for a long time. "You've made up your mind and you won't change it," he said finally, "and you haven't been able to read the letters or the diary either. Do the decent thing, the sensible thing. Give them to me. This is your last chance to turn back. You know that, don't you?" But none of the statements were really questions.

Suddenly Sanders felt a light-headed weakness, a burning nausea he had to bite back so that he couldn't speak a word.

"I want to give you something," Fillmore said, with such a painful wrench it seemed physical. From out of his tunic he took a thick red manila envelope and handed it over. "In there is some information you'll find useful. Most of it is official but I'm giving it to you unofficially. Read it. Sleep on it a couple of days before you get in touch with Christiansen's family."

"You're helping me?" Sanders asked unbelievingly.

"I thought I was helping you all along."

"Don't be the professional parson."

"But that's what I am."

"Then don't be deliberately ambiguous."

"How can I help it, with a deliberately ambiguous man?"

"*Touché!*" Sanders said, drawing his own finger across his throat.

Fillmore stood up and for a moment Sanders was certain that he was going to make the sign of the cross over him and give him a benediction, but Fillmore did neither. Instead he looked long and hard until his eyes seemed about to start from his head, then he walked away. After a few steps he returned and put his hand on Sanders' shoulder. "Walk gently," he admonished, "very gently. And, bless your heart." Without looking back once, then, he strode out of the air terminal.

❄   ❄   ❄

The telephone ringing prodded him out of his depths and Sanders heard his own voice, faraway and husky, speak "Yes?" into the mouthpiece and simultaneously saw Beth Christiansen stir on his bed and moan softly. Without thinking, Sanders covered the phone and heard the voice at the other end grow louder and sharper. "Hullo! Hullo! Mr. Sanders?" She rolled over on her stomach, her

[79]

face burrowing into the pillow, half hidden now, her hair disheveled, her skirt hiked over her thighs so that the darker tops of her stockings and a band of white flesh were rings that he wanted to adjust, blend, touch; the outstretched legs were fine, long and shapely. Lying there like that, looking bereft, her face and body turned away, those legs ever so slightly, reluctantly parted, she might have been Elaine, and again he felt the treacherous current run through him and threaten to sweep him away. "You're a passionate man," Levi Migdal had once told him, "and in love as in politics you should remember Talleyrand's advice: 'Not too much zeal!'" Well, he'd learned that in politics, learned it long before Levi had advised it; would that he'd been able to learn it in love. Passion was bad enough, he knew, but pity was more pernicious, the trap door to the dungeons of another soul from which there was no exit unscarred. "Are you there, Mr. Sanders?" the metallic voice insisted. "Are you all right?"

Clearing his throat, Sanders said that he had just swallowed the wrong way and was having a little trouble catching his breath. He wheezed once or twice for the effect, yawned, and then found himself having to do both again of necessity.

"This is Steven Prescott, Dr. Steven Prescott here."

"Dr. Prescott? Are you sure you have the right Sanders?"

"I'm Beth Marshall's—Beth Christiansen's—fiancé. I thought she might have mentioned my name to you." He sounded disappointed that she hadn't. "I'd like to speak to her if she's there."

The sight of those legs made his mind up. "She's already left," he said.

"But she was supposed to meet me here at four. I was going to drive her back."

"Perhaps she was delayed."

"That's not like her."

"A woman who comes on time? That's hard to believe." As he began to laugh he recognized the double meaning and stopped.

Prescott was sharp. "Beth isn't like that," he snapped. "She's not ordinary. Anything but. Besides she hasn't got her car and she knew I was scheduled for surgery at five-thirty so she wouldn't

[80]

delay deliberately. She knows I've got to be back on time. How long ago did she leave?"

Offended by the proprietary tone and curtness, Sanders said he didn't remember.

"You don't remember!"

"No, I don't live with my eye on the clock. Besides, Dr. Prescott, I don't know that I'd tell you even if I did remember. How do I know what you tell me over the phone is true? How do I know that Mrs. Christiansen knows you or wants you to know where she is and when she went there?"

"Dammit, Sanders, don't you play games with me!" The man's concern was genuine but so was his *amour propre* at being denied.

"To me, Dr. Prescott, you're just a voice on the phone. As a newspaperman I've learned to distrust voices on the telephone." And, he thought, after living in France all these years.

The doctor's effort to control himself was almost palpable and when he resumed, his voice was quiet, if baleful. "I suppose you have a point there. If Mrs. Christiansen calls you, please tell her I had to go back to the hospital. Ask her to call me there or to leave a message with my service to say she's okay and how and when she's getting back."

"I'll be glad to do that," Sanders said, "if she should call. I'll even volunteer to drive her home if she'd like that."

"That won't," Prescott began, but drew back from the "be necessary" just in time and said instead, "that would be kind of you."

The phone came down hard and Sanders had the eerie feeling that he had just made an implacable enemy.

Beth Christiansen did awaken shortly before dinnertime, with a start, and the first thing she did, perhaps following his eyes, was to pull down her skirt. It was a move he could have predicted. She sat at the edge of the bed, her legs too long to be dangling or they would have been, her hands limp in her lap, her thighs squeezed tightly together. Still loose with sleep, her face was having difficulty in recomposing itself, and she did not look at him. "Mrs. Christiansen," he began softly, but she cut him off with a shake of her head that said *no* much more definitively than words. For a quarter of an hour her only movements were flickers of feeling in her face that ran through her entire body. They were not twitches like her husband's, fitful, spasmodic, painful; hers were undulant tremors which swept her whole body like long rhythmic waves until one wave finally lifted her from the bed to her feet. She found her purse, took out her cigarettes, but her hands were shaking so badly that Sanders finally had to light one for her.

"Such politeness," she remarked, drinking in the smoke, "and without even having made love to the lady." Eyebrow cocked, her eyes searched his. "Or have you?"

Stung, Sanders replied angrily, "I don't make love to drunken females."

"I forgot your European gallantry," she retorted sardonically. "In America, a drunken lady, a hotel room and a man are an unholy trinity: they mean only one thing." She looked at him melodramatically and hissed, "*Seduction!*" The cigarette dangled from the corner of her mouth, and she closed one eye against the rising smoke while with the other she looked down at herself, rearranged her skirt and blouse, expertly smoothed the stockings taut on her legs, then found her shoes and stepped into them. It was such a performance that he had to laugh and that raised her ire.

"I'm sorry," he apologized. "You look so—how can I say it politely? —professional. So knowing, tough, hard, having just turned another trick—"

"You know about such things," she accused.

He nodded. "I confess that I do."

"Your wife, your ex-wife I mean, must have liked that." She gauged the sentence and delivered it like a blow, and he felt it. The Rue Daunou came back, Monique and her big brass bed, his return home to Elaine—but he closed the door on it as on a scene he refused to witness again, got up and opened the hotel window as if he could thereby air out the stale, bad smell of his nightmares.

She thanked him for opening the window, remarked how stuffy it was and then, awkwardly, asked if she might use the facilities. Sanders pointed her to the door, watched her go in and with a pang heard the too careful turning of the door lock. Memories of Monique and Elaine, of the old musty hotel on the Rue Daunou, the apart-

[82]

ment on the Avenue Mozart, their own bedroom on the Quai de Passy began seeping in under the door of his resolve like malodorous gas. The de Besancourt apartment on the Avenue Foch. To save himself he walked to the open window, breathing the outside colder air deeply into his lungs, but instead of San Francisco's bay and bridges he saw only the oily green Seine and the frothing Paris fountains. Why, he rebuked himself, do you remember only your personal horrors with such detailed intensity? Why not the personal joys? And the same applied, as Tessier had told him, and he knew himself, to his political recollections. Why that British policeman's throat in the Wanchai district in Hong Kong, the longshoreman's hook still imbedded in his neck, the slant eyes already white with death, the great carotid artery pumping a cataract of blood over his khaki uniform? Why the *flics* closing in on that Algérie-Française "patriot" after his *plastique* killed the waiter, a passerby, two Swedish tourists, but didn't even knock the *vin rouge* out of the hand of the pro-FLN journalist he was after? The bulky baldheaded man ran swiftly and lightly, as big men sometimes do, his head down, but the *flics* surrounded him and when he tried to butt his way out of their circle they beat him with their clubs and leaded capes until, vomiting and bleeding, he went down on the cobbles like a broken bull. Or that Hungarian boy torn by a land mine on the Austrian border, jackknifed on the barbed wire, his long flaxen hair like corn tassels, his arms and legs flailing the wind like a scarecrow's. He'd seen the vultures in green uniforms come anyway, as he himself sat comfortably on the Arlberg Express drinking Pilsener beer, the scene flashing by so quickly he sometimes tried to persuade himself he'd only imagined it.

Why, he thought, must I recall the horrors, personal or professional, not the happy times? Even the calm and pastoral times. Had his life been such unrelieved darkness? He knew that wasn't true, and teetering on the verge of an insight he felt he was groping desperately for, he heard her cough and realized that she'd been standing beside him for a while, silent, observant, waiting. He turned and motioned her to a chair and she sat, her silken knees so primly together, her glistening hair still wet at the temples and shining from the brush, the white frilly ruff at her throat now buttoned and in place, and her suit as neat as under the circumstances it could be; she had courageously tried to repair the ravages of the day. "I seem to be apologizing again," she spoke up apprehensively. "I'm sorry about lunch"—she pointed to the bed—"and conking out like that."

"Again, no apologies are called for."

"George's death knocked the framework of my life apart," she rushed on, as if afraid that if she stopped she'd be unable to continue. "I suppose it was jerry-built anyway but I didn't realize that until the telegram. Then Chaplain Fillmore's letter came and I had to talk to Mr. Christiansen. And finally you arrived and I was so upset I couldn't cope any more. Steven—Dr. Prescott—gave me some tranquilizers but, as you saw, they don't mix well with alcohol. After those daiquiris I felt as if someone had hit me with a mallet. Here." She touched the base of her skull. "Otherwise"—there was pride and pique in her voice—"two drinks wouldn't quite knock me out that way ordinarily."

"Then it's my turn to apologize. I thought you were drunk." Sanders told her about Prescott's call and saw dismay, then consternation, spread over her face. Anxiously she looked at her watch and said to no one, "It's six o'clock," then leaped to her feet as if she were going to run off. "You shouldn't have done that," she said, "you should have awakened me.'

"I hate waking people. I never have liked waking anyone since childhood. Besides"—he grinned—"I'm not sure I could have waked you even if I'd tried."

"Steven will be furious," she said, more to herself than to him.

"Do you care?" he asked, and then, seeing her face, blurted, "He's *the* man."

She made a mute helpless gesture with her hands.

"If I'd known," he averred, but he knew he'd have been even more adamant had he known. "He didn't strike me as the kind of man I could tell you were drunk and sleeping on a hotel-room bed in a strange man's room."

She looked scared, then laughed out loud. "No, he certainly is not." She blinked at him shrewdly. "You knew that just from talking on the phone; you're very perceptive."

[84]

"Journalist's instinct"—he passed it off—"saves you from making a lot of useless trips to check out stories."

Beth Christiansen accepted his offer to drive her home and agreed to phone Prescott first to say that she was all right, but he could see her reluctance to call in his presence so he went into the bathroom to wash up. When he came out, she was saying, "Yes, Steven, I'm fine. No, it was okay. I'll see you tomorrow," and she hung up.

Hunched over the phone like that, she looked so forlorn that he was impelled to say he was sorry he'd caused her any trouble, but he wasn't sorry and when she swiveled to face him he could see that she knew that too. If he was not a troublemaker, her expression said, he was a trouble-bringer, which was just as bad—or even worse. Her face was so disconsolate that intuitively he made the decision and took up their conversation of hours before as if it had never been interrupted. "You asked me what I wanted and I want to tell you, but first—" He strode to the chest, took the letters, diary and address book from the top drawer, turned back, and put all of them into her hands. "These are the things George asked me to hold for him and that Fillmore wrote to you about."

She took them without relish, her whole demeanor an unspoken question.

"You want to know why?" He shrugged. "I'm not sure."

"Is it because of George?"

"Yes. No. Because of him. Because of me. Because of you."

"Me?" Her astonishment was overdone, the hand turned in against her breast a shade too considered.

"I want to have as few lies between us as possible. I almost said no lies, but I tried that once and it's cruel and doesn't work."

"Your wife?"

"Yes. I'm not sure anyone's capable of telling no lies and living. I'm not even sure that's a good way to live. Lies have their importance in life, in human relations."

"Please." She held up her hand like a traffic cop. "Don't say any more now."

They drove along the freeway in silence while she smoked one cigarette after another, her purse and George's effects between them on the seat, the silence heavy until he turned on the car radio.

Booming out of it came the electric thrumming of rock-and-roll music, then an automobile salesman with a hard-sell pitch—they were, if you hurried, *giving* away new cars—and finally a whining baritone, brassy and sentimental, sang of leaving his heart on a hill in San Francisco and how eventually he'd come home to the city and to his love. He saw she was crying and reached out to turn the radio off but she stopped his hand, held it tightly until the song was ended, then switched it off herself. "A stupid song," he commented vehemently.

She went on crying, so Sanders pulled the car off the highway, put his arm around her and held her while she shook with sobs. When he tried to draw her closer, to sweep to the floor her purse and George's things which lay between them, she drew away and said, "Please, Elliott, take me home," and because she had stopped weeping and used his Christian name he felt he had won a victory.

This time when she led him into the house she put the lights on as they went, before leaving him by himself in the living room. It was a soothing place of jade greens and bright yellows, and its decor was, surprisingly, Chinese. On the wall above the deep-green couch hung three classical Chinese scroll drawings lit from below by two sunshine-yellow porcelain lamps squatting on polished teak tables. The facing wall was glass entirely and opened out on the garden in which they had so briefly talked the other night. Another wall was all bookshelves and held books, record player, records and two speakers as well as several pieces of elaborately carved ivory figures of people, sampans, animals, pagodas, rickshaws, the whole caravan of Chinese life on a simple arch of tusk and a black wooden base. The last wall was almost all a wide white-brick fireplace which rose like a column from the black-and-white mosaic-tiled floor to the white wood-beamed ceiling.

Sanders sat back on the couch and let the quiet and color of the room wash over him. His wounds ached, he was very tired, but he felt unburdened, felt he had taken another sure step in making a new life and in understanding the old, though not in discovering what that twitch had meant, or that unholy sacrifice, both of which he was certain could tell him so much. Why, he asked himself, did you give her George's things without having read them first? The

[86]

clues to what had made Christiansen die for him he was convinced were in those letters and diary, or at least the first leads that might ultimately take him to insight. You're well rid of them, another internal voice said; they weren't yours and couldn't be. Fillmore was right. No man is known by such tokens anyway; a man is known by his life, by what he did and by those who were a genuine part of his life.

The clacking of the dial and her voice were faint but unmistakable. "Steven? Yes, darling, it's me. I'm home. Mr. Sanders drove me. No, it's too late and I'm very tired. I just wanted you to know that I was here and fine. I do. I can't say it. No, no one's here. Yes, you know that I do," but Sanders didn't want to hear any more and walked out into the garden and the eucalyptus-smelling night. The night wind blew cool and shook the hammock. Enfolded by it, Sanders was suddenly transported, rocked in his childhood and the recollection of his mother's reedy soprano singing, "Rockabye baby on the tree top" and its last plunging line, "Down will come baby, cradle and all," which had terrified him then and whose astringent cruelty he had only comprehended much later.

"Elliott?" Her voice interrupted his train of recollection. "Are you out there?"

"In the hammock," he called back, knowing how muffled it would sound, knowing too that she would come out and pry the hammock folds apart to see if he was there. She did and her face above him, still tearful, was another moon. She'd changed her clothes and was wearing a fitted pair of blue slacks and a matching blouse which displayed her shapely body.

"What are you doing in there?" she asked.

"Reliving my childhood." He swung himself out and on his feet. "I love hammocks and did even before I had a couple of South American assignments and learned to sleep in them. We had four of them at my mother's house in Connecticut. Is this one a single or married one? What do they call it now, *matrimonio?*"

"A married one. George bought it, before . . ." She changed the subject. "Come on in. I've spoiled your lunch and dinner so I'll make you some supper."

They ate together in the kitchen, cold steak sandwiches, salad and milk, and he felt altogether American. No wine, no coffee, no brandy. When they were done he asked if any of the letters were hers.

"Most of them, I think. I looked at only one." Her eyes began to fill again. "Let me read it to you, just the kind of letter a loving wife should send to a soldier at war." She was back with it in a moment, and as she began to read, began once more to weep:

> The wars are distressing and yesterday I felt suicidal because of my own private, seemingly hopeless wars, but I fought my own over-powering negation. I'd sprained my ankle and went to the clinic but the sights there, after what I'd seen in my own radioactive clinic during the day, was too much and I went home, having taped my own ankle, trying to be my own doctor, to my body as well as my spirit.
>
> I feel I'm growing old. One of the nurses who'd had a year up at Mendocino now writes me gaily from Cannes. I tried to help her when she was down but now she has her divorce and a comfortable alimony, and has ended up better than I. At least for now. She came to visit before she left for France and when I tried to air my own distress to her (which was damn foolish anyway), she said I was a natural-born victim, then added hastily that she really meant I was empathetic, but I knew it was the first she really meant.
> And, afterwards, for days, I was paralyzed by despair, fear, anxiety, self-hatred, all standing between me and action. Partly, I guess, it's exhaustion, partly it's me too, but not completely. It's a mad world of which I'm a part (and you are too) and I've never lost my vulnerability. I ache for myself, and for others too. And I'm alone, lonely, though I see people. . . .

She broke off and began to sob uncontrollably, the letter shaking in her hand like a leaf in the wind. With her face in her hands, the nakedness of her grief and guilt and anguish so moved him that Sanders stood behind her and, guiltily, massaged her neck and shoulders with the techniques he had learned from Monique and which had brought him some respite. The house of joy had been for him a *poule de luxe,* though he knew that that was both inaccurate and unfair, the too clear-cut New England rubric of what passed for conscience. Monique had given him more than Elaine when he needed it; the prostitute had been richer and more giving than the wife, and perhaps it was because she had more to give so that it might have meant altogether less. That was the kind of casuistry, he reminded himself, that his mother must have indulged in every time his father came home smelling of someone else's body or perfume, a thousand times over the long years. He needed the unceasing, acid reproof he knew Lovett Carpenter Sanders would surely have given him had he lived: A woman did not give like a cow with a teat full of milk which had to be relieved of its burden; a woman gave only where she wanted to. And when she wanted to. And when she could and did give a great deal, that was love.

Sanders left her in the kitchen and in the garden watched the scythe of moon harvesting the night. How is it that these are the women I am drawn to, the convoluted, the distraught, the lost? Why not the simpler ones, the Moniques, the Laura Martins, the Cathy Sullivans? Because—he could almost hear his father's voice berating his mother—they are the people who live where you live, in the house of pain. I know that can be remedied, I know it can be changed, but I couldn't do it with Elaine so why should I imagine I can do it now? You're older, wiser, tougher, he said to himself, but he was not reassured. When he came back from the dark windbreak of trees and shrubbery that masked the back fence, Beth was sitting in one of the wicker chairs, silhouetted by the light in the house behind her so that he couldn't see her face. "We have gotten off on the wrong foot in every way we could have, haven't we?" she said. He sensed that she was not trying to placate him or to apologize but was groping for some common ground on which they could stand and perhaps—or was he merely deluding himself?—even build a relationship on. "You said you were going to tell me what you wanted," she continued. "Don't pace, then. Sit down and tell me."

It was only one more small but inexpiable step to tell her just how George had died and he would be unburdened. He would already have given her her husband's effects; he would already have told her how he had died; he would have performed the time-honored rituals of the survivor. But he refused his own weakness; to tell her when she was already so riddled with guilt would only persuade her that she had caused George's death, forced him to it, that her depressed and depressing letters, their estrangement, her affair with Prescott, had made George Christiansen commit what was, in effect, suicide. Though he was averse to believing that, he knew it could be true, knew it was quite possible. Maybe that was all the answer he needed, all the answer there was, to explain Christiansen's falling on that grenade; but he was not convinced. That might be enough to explain the twitch but not the death; Christiansen's had not been an act of despair but of affirmation, not a negative withdrawal from the value of human life but a positive assertion of it. Of that, if only of that, Sanders was certain.

He sat. "You said before that the framework of your life had been shattered by George's death. Well, so was the framework of mine. My life was probably no less jerry-built than yours; if anything, more so. I had two dead parents to show, two university degrees, one ex-wife and a traumatic divorce, and a large number of newspaper articles and photographs, even some pretty good ones, that were forgotten by readers almost as soon as they were looked at."

"Was that really all? No good times?"

"I know that there were good times, there must have been, yet, mostly, when I look back, what I seem to remember is pain, unhappiness, despair, all those things you wrote to George in your letter."

"That *is* the way it's been with me," she said dolorously, "but I can't believe life is like that, only me . . . only us."

"Maybe. Anyway George's death and his heroism, no matter how old-fashioned that word, saved my life. I was wounded, yes, and almost glad of it. I don't think I could have borne his death—two others were killed also—if I'd gotten away unscathed. There, in the hospital, the more I thought about it, the more I felt I had a debt to pay."

"To George?"

"Yes, but not just to him. To the people he knew and loved. Perhaps, if that doesn't sound too grandiose, to his life, to life itself." Although he didn't say it, he knew that he meant to his mother and father, to John C. Ballinger, to Levi Migdal, to Monique. Perhaps even to Elaine, perhaps even to her.

Beth nodded. "I understand that. The same thing happened to me. Not when George died, but before." She chose not to elucidate further. "And so, you decided to come back here?"

"I decided to come back to the States for a while to see—"

[90]

"If you could make a new life here?" Her laughter was strident. "What damn fools we all are."

"For wanting to make new lives? For looking for some meaning in them?"

"For wanting *to start new lives, to be reborn,* instead of trying to reshape our old lives, what we have and what we are, and that's stupid, Elliott, believe me, that's stupid because it can't be done." The words were so woefully heartfelt that he wished he could see the expression on her face. "And?"

"And that's it," Sanders said. "I came back. I saw you. I saw George's father. I want to see his friend."

"Peter King?"

"Yes, him, and others if I can find them. That was one of the reasons I kept those things, to get the addresses from the letters and the address book."

"That was all? Then you'd leave?" Outlined in the light, her face still in darkness, not moving, almost not breathing, at last she whispered, "What you really wanted was more, to find out what made George Christiansen the kind of man he was, the man you knew, who saved your life. Wasn't that it?"

The naked explanation—it was an accusation too—took him back. "I don't know," he said. "I'm not sure."

"Isn't that the new life you're looking for? His life? You want to pick up his life for him, live it, become part of our lives in his place? Isn't that it?" Her voice was harsh.

"I don't know," he repeated, hearing the agony in his voice. "I'm just not sure."

"You'd better be sure. This isn't some kind of game in which you can begin and then simply quit when you feel like it. Such actions have real consequences and they're far-reaching."

"That I do know."

"I don't think so. That chaplain understands that. I doubt you do. I've seen the difference in the hospital a hundred, a thousand, times over. Everybody knows he's going to die but then a man finds out he has cancer and he knows in another way, not in some vague and distant future, but in a week, a month, six months. His time has run out. What looked like an unending road that might end eventually

[91]

somewhere over the horizon now has a definite stop sign on it that he can see: the end of the road. He knows he's driven himself, or been driven, into a real dead end. And when he knows, Elliott, he changes. His face, his hands, his posture change—and you can see it. Like stigmata, it shows. Then he *really* knows. Only then. It's the same with this. You're only guessing, you don't really know."

"If I don't stay," he asked stubbornly, "how can I ever find out?"

"There's a terrible price for discoveries."

"My father always told me: 'Take what you want and pay for it.'"

Beth frowned. "George's father always said that too, only more vulgarly: 'You pays your money, you takes your choice.'" She mimicked the old man's speech with such fidelity that Sanders was there in that hospital ward again. "Did your father pay his money and take his choice?" she asked.

"He did, but I think what he said and meant was different. My father would have said, 'You pays your money and takes your *chance*.' Or maybe he'd have preferred, 'You take your road and pay your toll.'"

"Your father paid but others paid with him too, for him, didn't they? You? Your mother? You're willing to pay here but others may have to pay even more heavily and they may *not* be willing."

"Are *you* willing?"

She struck a match to light a cigarette and he saw her face again, remote, sibylline. Smoke poured from her nostrils as from some ancient goddess's stone mask whose thunder foretold the future, and when she spoke her voice was so stony it scarcely seemed her own. "Go away, Elliott," she said. "Go away and leave us all alone. Save yourself."

The cold night wind seemed snared in his spine, and a chill wave percolated up to his brain. To save himself, he was convinced, he had to stay, not leave. "Do you want me to leave?"

"Yes—and no. But that doesn't matter. You should go away. Part of the reason for my advice that you should go is that I might want you to stay and that's precisely what should persuade you to go."

Sanders laughed, but the laugh was forced and frightened and he heard it that way himself. "You sound like a tearoom gypsy reading the leaves or the cards," he joked, "breathing auguries of disaster from her nostrils with every puff of cigarette smoke," but the joke was labored.

Beth stood up and when they were both indoors, even before she told him, he saw from her eyes that she had taken more of the tranquilizers. When he mentioned his appointment with Needham, she seemed obscurely pleased and said that all he needed now was a place to live. "A place to live," she repeated as if that were a prayer and a warding off of evil, smiling sleepily, her eyes already out of focus. "Just a minute," she said, and returned with the chess set. "Here, give this to old Christiansen. He's a chess player and I don't play games any more." There was just the hint of coquetry in the last line, but when he asked her if she'd go with him to visit Christiansen, she seemed confused, shook her head, nodded, shrugged. He took the chess set and said good night, but when he leaned over to kiss her, her mouth escaped because she'd already turned away and he only nuzzled her hair. "Save yourself," she advised again. He'd been taught "Know thyself"; could he do both?

*   *   *

Needham's paper was housed in a two-story, L-shaped sandstone building roofed with red Spanish tiles and in pseudo-Romanesque style. Set in the middle of a grove of thick-trunked date palms and flourishing pines, its building and parking lot coolly shaded from the blazing sun, it was an inviting sight. Sanders had expected a big, fat, florid cigar-smoking man; what he found was a short bronzed muscular man, smartly dressed in a dark-green tweed jacket and light-green slacks, his white sport shirt open at the throat. Though Sanders knew Needham had to be at least sixty, if not more, he appeared more like forty-five, brisk and athletic.

"You look just like him," Needham said, as if he'd seen a ghost, not taking his eyes off him. "Just like him. Real chip off the old block. My God," he exclaimed, "time flies! It must be more than twenty years and you must be just about his age now . . . I mean the age he was then. Lemme see, he was killed in '44. Lov musta been no more than—"

"My father was thirty-nine when he died, only a few days before his fortieth birthday," Sanders told him precisely. He hated to hear his father referred to by his nickname, though almost everyone, even those who had met him only once, called him that. *Lov.* "I'm thirty-seven."

"Just about, just about." Needham shook his head wonderingly. Eyeing him carefully, clearly looking at him now not as the son, the image of his father, but as himself, Needham commented, "Must be tough to be a reporter and Lov Sanders' boy."

"It's not too bad. Got some advantages, some disadvantages, plenty of both. Gets me through doors I wouldn't get through otherwise. A lot of his old cronies remember him and are nicer to me. Like you."

"Yeh, I suppose it does have that," Needham agreed. "Still I'm glad that my old man was just a dumb boatwright. Came out here before the first big one, in 1907, and settled in Alameda, a dumb sailor off a boat. Went to work in a shipyard in Oakland and stayed there for fifty years! Can you imagine anyone staying in one place, doing one job, for fifty years nowadays? Didn't care a damn for anything except making and sailing boats. Used to sail Alameda Creek, San Leandro Bay, the big bays, knew the waterways like the back of his hand, and when he wasn't sailing or working, always hanging around the waterfront yakking it up with the old salts.

"When I told him I wanted to go to college to study journalism he thought I was nuts but he put up the money, enough to get me started anyway. Aw hell." He broke off. "You don't want to hear the story of my life. Another self-made American. No news in that, is there, now?"

Needham seemed embarrassed though why Sanders couldn't tell. To turn the conversation he commented about the building and the setup, saying how much he liked it, how well planned it was.

"Not a bad setup, eh?" Needham laughed. "Designed the whole thing myself. Printing plant in one wing, editorial in another. Works like a charm. Even got a swimming pool out back when anyone wants to jump in. Keep a cool head that way. Or try. And it does all right so long as the advertising money keeps up. I was lucky when I came back from the war to get me a small radio station and now I got the local TV too. That's where the real money is, Elliott, television. Goddam, your old man would have been a great TV commentator, that wonderful voice and those good looks and that big Eastern Ivy-League-school air of authority. And he'd've been in on the ground floor too, believe you me. Newspaper business in this country's about finished and Lov would've known it before anyone else." Sanders listened patiently as Needham talked on about how newspapers were dying left and right, how people didn't even read any more, only looked at the "boob tube" instead, and as he talked, Sanders tried to dredge up something he knew he'd heard about Jim Needham from his father but what it was he couldn't quite recall.

"All right," Needham said finally, "let's get down to cases. You gave me an idea over the phone that I liked. Tell me a little more and you've got yourself a job. At least," he amended cautiously, "a temporary assignment."

"I don't want anything more than a temporary assignment, Mr. Needham—"

"Jim."

"Okay, Jim, maybe three, maybe six, months. I haven't been back in the States for almost a decade. It makes a difference."

"Believe it!"

"And there have been a lot of changes, some problems are filed, some have gotten out of hand, some are first priorities and you've got them all around here, in the Bay Area, a real harvest."

"You can say that again, boy!"

As Sanders talked, Needham nodded his agreement enthusiastically. He thought they could do business, and before long they had a deal worked out. Sanders would be a special correspondent on a staff by-line basis, with a regular reporter's status at a regular Guild salary. Needham would get an exclusive on any Vietnik story he did, and the press-service exclusive too; on TV and radio in America, they'd share fifty-fifty. The rest of the rights Sanders retained for himself, especially the rights on his own pictures. Needham called his secretary in and twenty minutes later their agreement was typed out and signed, Sanders was on the payroll and had his press card, and they shook hands on the deal. "You do business like your old man did. No fooling around, straight down the pike. I wish I had a newspaperman like you for a son to take all this over." He waved his arms at the office appointments. Regret and loss were in his voice and Sanders knew he'd been paid a great compliment.

"Do you have children, Jim?"

"No, Sheila and I never had any. Couldn't."

"No chance to adopt?" Sanders asked, very gingerly.

"At first we thought we'd have our own and then"—Needham spread his hands in the first uncertain, helpless gesture he'd displayed—"I guess it was my fault, I just couldn't buy it. I wanted my own flesh and blood and by the time I realized that didn't matter so much it was too late."

"That's tough," Sanders sympathized.

Needham inclined his head. "Wasn't so hard on me as on Sheila. She took it hard. I got used to it, she never has."

* * *

Instead of driving back into the city and the hotel, Sanders called in and, as he hoped, Beth had left a message for him: He was to call her at the hospital if he returned before four, at home if after six. When he telephoned to the hospital they could not at first locate her and she had to be paged before she spoke breathlessly into the phone: "Elliott?"

"Beth? How do you feel?"

"Better. No, good. Thank you for yesterday. You were very considerate. And you?"

"Needham gave me the assignment."

"Congratulations! All you need is a place to live," she said, but it did not carry the freight or fright of meaning it had the night before.

"Not all I need, Beth," he said cautiously, "but the first step."

"Don't quibble. I think I've found you a place, if you want it. One of the doctors at the hospital is off for a year on a Rockefeller. He's got a lovely apartment at Los Pueblos, a big modern high-rise, all furnished and air-conditioned too. You could move right in. It's only a few minutes from Needham's paper too."

"How far from you?"

"By foot or by car?" she asked, her laughter young and gay.

"As the crow flies," he said.

"Don't crow," she laughed.

"No, I'm flying," he replied, but he felt like crowing too, and felt that little jar that told him, reminded him, that he always ate crow soon after that.

Beth gave him the address and promised to meet him there in half an hour. Sanders stopped for coffee at a drive-in and, as he sipped it, hot and black, missing a *fine* with it, he wondered at the elation he felt. A new job, a new flat, new friends and colleagues. A new life? There were, there could be, incursions into the house of joy without the *filles de joie*.

Los Pueblos was an eight-story-high apartment house, a long slim rectangle of glass and concrete in the modern style surrounded by closely shaved greensward, meticulously clipped shrubs and a stand of thin-leaved ash trees planted with almost orchardlike regularity. He parked the car in the parking lot and as he walked down the crushed-stone paths toward the entrance he flushed a flight of swallows which rose from the trees like bounding spume and took his heart soaring with them. I'm happy, he thought, I'm happy. Happy? his other voice questioned. Well, content, quiet, he defended himself against himself. That's enough. For now, the black part echoed, for the moment, but for how long?

Beth was waiting in front of the glassed-in reception hall. When she saw him she waved and ran up the path, her blue, red-lined cape a swirl behind her like a *flic's*, but a few steps before they met she slowed and sedately put out her hand. Sanders took it and this time, though not yet unself-consciously, raised it to his lips. A glitter of laughter shone on her mouth and she curtsied, graceful though constrained by the tightly fitted nurse's uniform. "Sir," she said.

"Madam," he rejoined. "My arm. Shall we go in?"

"We shall," she agreed, "as soon as Steven arrives."

"Your Steven, Dr. Prescott?" He let go of her arm and stepped back a pace.

"Yes," she said, "he has the key to the apartment," and explained that Jason Howe, the surgeon whose apartment it was, was one of Prescott's colleagues and had given him the key with the under-

[97]

standing that if anyone reliable showed up and wanted to rent it Prescott was free to make the arrangements. "Don't be like that," she said, impulsively touching his arm.

"Like what?" he said, shuddering and turning away. "Should I be joyous to have your lover find apartments for me?"

"What's that got to do with anything?" she inquired weakly. "It's an apartment. *I'm* getting it for you. Steven simply has the key."

"You know what it's got to do with everything, Beth, you're not a fool."

"I haven't been to bed with Steven since I got the telegram about George," she said, her face stern.

"Very chaste," he remarked bitterly, "but you will again, soon, won't you?"

"And what did you want me to do, become a nun?" she flared angrily. "What business is it of yours, anyway? Are you my guardian? Meddling in my life, telling me what to do and what not to do . . ."

A wave of melancholy and nausea swept over him and he walked away from her. There was a bench nearby and he went up the stone path to it, sank down there and rested his head in his hands.

The steps he heard were distant but audible, strong and determined on the stone and mixed with the flutter of leaves and the fluting of birds. Beth was pleading at his elbow. "Please, Elliott, no scenes. If you don't want the apartment, all right. Just look at it, first, and then find some fault with it. Steven won't care."

Sanders stood up and they walked together, not touching or speaking, to the entranceway. As they reached it Prescott rounded a turn in the path from the other direction, a tall, well-set man wearing a navy-blue suit and a woven brown coconut straw hat with matching navy band. Tremulously, Beth introduced them and Sanders found the handshake noncommittal and very powerful. "Glad to meet you, Sanders," Prescott said in a beautifully modulated bass voice that shimmered with bedside manner. "I'm sorry I was rude to you on the phone yesterday, but Beth gave me a scare." Again the proprietary tone irritated him and then Prescott leaned over and kissed her in what was clearly a practiced gesture, but also now quite calculated. Heavily lined, thin and mercurial, Prescott's face was older than Sanders had anticipated, that of a man almost his own age; in all it was a face given to command and expecting obedience without question although some uncertainty was trapped in the glossy sensual pink lips that were snapped together between the strong Indian jut of nose and the heavy black mustache.

Jason Howe's apartment was on the top floor of Los Pueblos and the moment Prescott let them through the door Sanders knew he was going to agree to rent the apartment. Interrupted by only a few beams, one whole wall was glass and through it in the distance mountains loomed in the mist and a burning ball of sun about to set behind them. "The Santa Cruz," Beth murmured. "Beyond is the Pacific."

The place's appointments brought back their flat on the Quai de Passy and persuaded him. Scandinavian furniture with its naked uncluttered honesty was comfortably placed around the rooms; it was furniture that, he had to admit, lacked subtlety, perhaps even warmth, but its simplicity was appealing. That was another thing Elaine had held against him, censured him for. "This is furniture without a history, furniture without complexity, and you fly to it from the complexities of your life and the histories of the people you're involved with. Your little simplified modern oasis in the complicated desert of one of the oldest cities in Europe." He could still hear the scorn dripping from her words, still feel its acid drip on his vulnerabilities. Perhaps she'd been right at that, though what should he have said about the intricacy of the furniture of the de Besancourt flat on the Avenue Foch, and what it meant to her? But that Quai de Passy flat had given him a remarkable ease and peace of mind, or at least the furnishings had. Here, Howe had varied the Scandinavian pieces with dark African masks and shields covered with zebra skins, primitive African sculpture on shelves and tables, and, beneath an impala skin tacked to the wall over the couch, three different long spears and a crude stringed instrument that looked like the remotest forebear of the violin hung together, contradictory diagonals of the arts of peace and war, instruments which gave men their opportunity to play their different, differing songs. Jason Howe was clearly a man torn between the primitive and the civilized, between violence and peace, between blood and brain.

[99]

"Dr. Howe's a Negro, single, from a poor family and educated by scholarships, isn't he?" Sanders asked, showing off.

Prescott froze as he was showing how the glass windows and full-length screens opened onto the small railed balcony outside. "Do you know Jason?" he asked suspiciously.

"Never met the man or heard of him until today, but you can tell a great deal from the way his flat is furnished."

Beth studied him admiringly. "You're describing Jason to a T. Except that he may not be all Negro. I think he might have had a white father or grandfather."

"Why not a white mother or grandmother?" Prescott asked cuttingly.

"It's possible, Steven, but less likely," she replied reasonably. "Do you know which it was?"

"His grandfather was white," Prescott said, but he was surly.

"Like Peter King?" she asked.

"That miserable pansy," Prescott burst out, slamming the door with a shudder of glass, "that troublemaking black faggot. God only knows where he comes from!"

Sanders tried to catch Beth's eye but she looked away. Was George Christiansen's best friend homosexual? And what did that mean? Did that have something to do with Beth's dissatisfactions with their marriage? How were Prescott and Howe involved? Before he could think further Prescott had turned on him and asked nastily, "Why, does Jason's being a Negro or having been poor offend your sensibilities, Mr. Sanders? Make the place uninhabitable for a proper middle-class white man?"

"Steven!" Beth protested.

"If you're asking whether I'm a bigot or a racist or a snob, Dr. Prescott, I think the answer is no."

"Only think?"

"Think. That's the best I can do."

"Then why make such an unnecessary comment?" Prescott asked.

"I'm sorry. I was just showing off, demonstrating what an acute and sensitive observer I am," Sanders confessed. "In fact, I find the apartment quite congenial, Dr. Howe's taste excellent, and I'd like to rent it."

Sanders saw that Prescott was on the verge of saying no, that he realized who the showing off was intended for and didn't like it, any more than he liked Beth's pleading look. "The rent is two hundred and fifty dollars a month plus the utilities," Prescott said. "That doesn't include a maid who comes in once a week on Thursdays to clean. You pay her separately."

"I think I can manage that," Sanders said mildly. "Who do I pay, you?"

"You make the checks out to Jason Howe and mail them to me. I deposit them in his account," Prescott replied, but he didn't like the explanation.

Downstairs Prescott offered to drive Beth home but she had her own car and would, she promised, meet him later on. He strode off without a goodbye and she stayed for moments only because she seemed to know that Prescott would stop and wait for her up the path, as he shortly did. She whispered, "Why do you have to antagonize him?"

"I don't *have* to," Sanders replied.

"You mean you *want* to?"

"Something like that."

Beth stepped back, disconcerted. "In some ways," she said, "you're just like him, crazy."

"Who, Prescott?"

"No. George! Your precious George!" she growled, her teeth bared, her eyes blazing; then she turned and fled up the path to the sanity of Steven Prescott.

❖ ❖ ❖

Two telephone messages and a letter awaited him at the hotel desk. The letter was from Tessier and he read it going up in the elevator and walking to his door. It was formal confirmation of his three months' leave in America *at half pay*. The French greed. Even over a continent and an ocean Philip Tessier's voice had carried command. Was he drunk? What the hell was he doing in San Francisco? Three months' leave? With pay? Who did he think he was, Jean-Jacques Schreiber? The silence over the transatlantic telephone was filled with sounds of birds shrieking until Sanders replied that

he was in San Francisco because his wounds were not healed, metaphorically true, that he needed treatment and rest, absolutely true,
and that he wanted to see what the States was like now, partially
true.

"*Merde!*" Tessier exploded. While he was there diddling himself
and getting drunk there was a good hot war for him to cover in the
Middle East.

"Three months is a short time."

"A quarter of a year. Three issues." Leave it to Tessier, always the
editor, to put a bad face on things he didn't like approving.

"I'll bring a couple of good articles on California back to Paris
with me," Sanders promised.

"That will be marvelous on the Côte d'Azur," Tessier rasped.

Sanders let the cacophonous telephone gulls squawk for him until
Tessier barked that the call was costing more than the whole affair
was worth, had given him permission for three months, but warned
that he'd better come back with some first-class articles and pictures.

"I will, don't worry."

"If there are two injunctions I hate, that no intelligent man can
abide and that you Americans are addicted to, it's 'Don't worry' and
'Relax.' If anyone could do either, he would, without your advice,"
Tessier grated and hung up. He was, as ever, a master at having the
last word.

Sanders decided to write to Tessier immediately, explain the
Needham deal before he could put any misconstructions on it, and
give Tessier his new address. Tessier could have the new articles he
was going to do but only on a full-pay basis and the understanding
that these assignments were *not* leave, but regular on-the-job assignments. As conditions changed, you had to change plans. Tessier
would know that such articles, if they were good, would be *sensass*
in France, and even if they were mediocre, French audiences would
be interested. Tessier was a realist; he would understand and approve.

A postscript to the letter was in Tessier's own pointed calligraphy:
"If you have any ideas of repeating your stupidities with and about
American women, *don't!* Life allows most men one major accident

[102]

of that type," he cautioned further, "but more than that one is character, and character, as even an American must know, is fate. Don't tempt fate."

Tessier's notes were always to be considered carefully. He had met Elaine only a handful of times and cordially detested her, a feeling Elaine reciprocated with equal intensity if less cordiality. Would Tessier react to Beth in the same way? Probably. Tessier's relations with women were half medieval-French troubadour, half Byzantine tyrant, a combination by no means unattractive to many; but Elaine, after meeting him the first time, had commented frigidly that Tessier treated women as if they were either concubines or guardians of children and property, things, not people—a comment so abruptly feminist that he was amused, until she went on scornfully to poke fun at the Legion of Honor rosette he wore in his buttonhole, his *haut-école* snobbery, his *haut-bourgeois* arrogance and bad manners, and Sanders realized that she was attracted to Tessier and that Tessier knew it. What was unlike Tessier, however, was to give such personal advice to anyone, least of all to him. Even now, after ten years of working on the magazine together, they never called each other *tu* and with the exception of one Bourse reporter, with whom Tessier had gone to *lycée*, he was on *tu-toi* terms with no one. If Tessier had taken time to write that postscript in his own hand, he was worried.

In his room Sanders dropped the letter on the night table and left the two telephone messages unread beneath. Swiftly he began to pack his clothes as if he had a plane to make for which he was already late. He knew it would be easier and more sensible to do it all in the morning and not have to drive back over the Peninsula still a third time in one day, but he was eager to be out of the hotel and into the apartment—eager, he recognized, because the move would connote the end of his transiency and the beginning of this new life. The bags were at the door when the phone rang and he let it ring three times before answering, loath to pick it up and delay his departure, but when he did the voice that vibrated over it was like few he had ever heard. A deep musical bass with precise almost finicky English pronunciation, it sounded like an actor's voice, a singer's, or perhaps a professional preacher's, orotund and oracular.

Clear and forceful, it almost sang in ordinary speech, and at the same time, below the surface of the melodious words, ran a counter-current, a ground bass of violence and hatred so strong that Sanders was momentarily fearful. "Mr. Sanders?" the voice inquired. "Mr. Elliott Sanders?"

"This is he," Sanders replied, more careful with his grammar than ordinarily he might be. "Who is this?"

"I understand you're looking for me. My name is Peter King." A dramatic introduction, it had the moving-picture Hollywood quality which, Sanders was certain, had been deliberately contrived. The speech gave no indication that the man who spoke was Negro; the surging virility of the voice betrayed not the slightest trace of effeminacy.

"You're George Christiansen's friend."

"I was his *best* friend," King interjected, "maybe his only friend." There was pride and a genuine sense of loss in the voice which dropped down so low in register that it sounded like a rumble and was scarcely understandable. "Were you with him when he died?"

"I was," Sanders replied, feeling himself for the first time in the presence of an unqualified grief, a true mourner for George Christiansen in a way in which neither his wife nor his father was a mourner. "I was going to get in touch with you next week," Sanders explained. "I got your address from the insurance."

"So that miserable bastard who calls himself George's father told me," King snorted. "He wrote me a sniveling, bellycrawling note saying George had left me a quarter of his insurance but that he knew it was a mistake of some kind, that in my heart I knew it too. I was young and strong and he was old and sick so I didn't need the bread and he was hard up for it so wouldn't I please just hand it over to him? After all it wasn't as if I was George's flesh and blood the way the old prick is. He can freak out before he sees a single buffalo from me, man. I wouldn't piss on him if his guts were on fire." The deep voice, the precise speech and the slang and obscenity were a singularly effective if unexpected combination.

"You don't like him," Sanders said, laughing.

"Man, you dig, you really dig."

"He's not an easy man to like."

"Few folks are, Mr. Sanders." The tone implied that neither of them was either.

"Except me and thee, eh?"

"Absolutely . . . and I'm not sure of thee." King's laughter was hearty.

"That's the general consensus," Sanders told him. "When can we meet?"

"Any time you say. I left you a message to call me for just that reason."

"I didn't get any message. Wait, hold it." He picked up the two telephone slips: One was from King, the other from Laura Martin, who had called four times that afternoon. He was to call both of them back. "Okay, it's here. How about tomorrow?"

"Tomorrow's okay with me. I'm up here in Oakland. That's only a short drive from where you are."

Sanders told him he'd be down on the Peninsula and that might take a bit longer, but they agreed to meet in Jack London Square in front of the statue. After he hung up, Sanders felt that Peter King was going to be not only able but willing to tell him a great deal more about George Christiansen than either Beth or old man Christiansen was willing to impart.

Laura Martin picked up the phone on the very first ring as if she'd been waiting for his call, and she recognized his voice before he said who he was. "Where have you been?" she asked. "I've been trying to reach you all day." Sanders told her he'd just gotten her message and was about to move out of the hotel to a new apartment down on the Peninsula, would she like to drive down with him? He had to drive back up tomorrow and would take her back to the city then. Sure, she said. She didn't ask where he was moving, or why, but offered to come help him pack, and when he told her he'd just finished packing she sounded distressed as if he had deprived her of some way of being useful that she coveted. Nonetheless she promised to be ready and waiting outside her building in twenty minutes.

Just talking to her lowered the tension, lessened the aching spasms of gut that Needham and Prescott and Beth, especially Beth, had provoked in him during the day. No coquetry, no complex jealousy,

[105]

no ambivalence, no subtle knifing or probing, just simple warmth and good spirits. She'd come along just for the ride, in both senses. The consolations of philosophy were doubtless real and profound for the age of reflection, but for the age of passion he'd take the consolations of screwing every time.

As she'd promised, Laura was waiting, in washed-out khaki trousers that fit her like a glove and a dark-blue corduroy bush jacket, carrying a big square paper bag under her arm which she tossed into the back seat as she got in front next to him. "This buggy's strictly from Dullsville, Elliott," she commented. "You need a little turned-on color, say flame-orange nostrils up front and some emerald hair streamers on the sides. Then you'd have a groovy bus for real. I could paint them on for you, if you want."

"I don't think the people I rent the car from would like that very much."

"We try harder or we give till it Hertz?"

"Huh?"

"Just being clever," she said, and explained. He laughed and she was pleased and squirmed against his shoulder, rubbing her back against him like a cat. "We're going to make a cat out of you yet, you old deadneck. And besides, that goes to show you that I'm not just a dumb little hick from Iowa."

"I'm too old a cat to teach new tricks," he said.

"Always puttin people down, you're a put-down man." Then with a chuckle, "Put me down, man, put me down."

"Later, Laura, it will be my pleasure."

"How old are you?" she asked. Because he saw she was interested Sanders almost decided not to tell her, then relented. "Thirty-seven," he replied, "old enough to be your father."

"Not unless you started a lot younger than most."

"Than you?"

"Well," she said mysteriously, "girls are different," telling him nothing.

As he drove along the freeway he couldn't help but make comparisons between Beth and Laura, the earlier trip that day with Beth and the present one with Laura. He was enjoying Laura's company more, yet thereby feeling called on to defend Beth in his mind from invidious comparisons. Laura didn't talk much either but when he told her he was a newspaperman, she frowned and the frown grew deeper and deeper as he told her about the new job until, instinctively, he brought himself up short of defining what assignments he proposed to work on. When he mentioned the name of the paper, she whistled and exclaimed, "Kee-rist!"

"You don't like the paper?"

She shook her head glumly.

"Or newspapermen?"

She was even more emphatic.

"Why?" he asked.

"They write glop. They're so square and on the make you could die. They think they're something special, like teachers or the fuzz or librarians, and they lie like hell."

"A good description of most of the members of my profession," he admitted freely.

"Then why do *you* do it?" she responded, her expression very serious.

He was tempted to say that he liked to eat or that he liked feeling special but that wouldn't have done justice to the earnestness of her concern. She'd phrased the question not as a gibe or an attack but as a serious question of integrity. She was not just showing her disapproval; she really wanted to know why he had picked "that bag."

"I said most, and most isn't all."

"No, but most is most," she insisted. "You know, I've been to some places and seen some things that got into the papers. Nothing important," she added cryptically, "but when I saw what they put in the papers, what they printed, it made me sick. They wouldn't know the truth if they fell over it. And a couple of times, when I know the guy reporting really did dig, really dug the whole scene, he couldn't write it up, or if he did, they changed it or they wouldn't print it altogether." She put both her hands to the sides of her head. "Like man, they're all crooks and liars. It's cover-up, all cover-up," Laura objected, "and who's got his hand in the till, who's on top and who's on bottom."

Her comment about hangups in bed and not having seen a lover *vis-à-vis* echoed in that, and he said, "There really are men, and

[107]

some on top, in the very highest places, who want to do things better, make them better," but he could hear the halfheartedness of the apologist in his tone. There Lovett Carpenter Sanders and Levi Migdal had the better of him: There were some ideals they could and did passionately espouse while for him there was no true cause; the Galahad in search of the Holy Grail had been left out of his makeup. All he wanted was an end to the killing and the chaos— and that, he was convinced, was beyond the power of mankind because mankind was out of its own control, had always been and would always be.

Their conversation died away, leaving her unconvinced, leaving him distraught; and her usually smiling mouth, turned down at the corners, though it tried to smile did not succeed. To divert her he asked what she'd brought in the big paper bag. She clapped her hands, her cheer restored. "A surprise! And I'm not going to tell you what it is, or show it to you, until we get to your new pad. No, no, don't ask me."

Against the night sky, only a few windows lit in its dark bulk, Los Pueblos looked more like a cliffside of real Indian pueblos than a modern apartment house. "Man," Laura exclaimed, "this really is Fat City."

"That good?"

She shook her head, the tip of her tongue just visible between her teeth. "You must have plenty bread."

"Enough," he confessed, getting his flight bag and suitcases out of the car trunk. "That bad too?"

Her laughter pealed through the parking lot. "I'm no bread baker, better not ask me." She hoisted the flight bag easily to her shoulder as if it were a sack of meal, swinging her long hair out of its way with a pitch of her head.

When he switched the first light on in Jason Howe's apartment, Sanders heard her sharp intake of breath. "Who owns this pad?" she murmured, her eyes admiring. Sanders gave her a brief if edited version of how he had come to rent it, making known Prescott's good offices and Jason Howe's name, but omitting mention of Beth altogether. Laura was curious about how much it cost and though he was tempted to evade, or lie outright, partly because of the old pang of guilt that he was living more expensively, if not better, than other people, he told her exactly. "Fat, Fat City!" she expostulated. "You *do* have bread."

To please her Sanders acceded to her insistence that he let her unpack and put his clothes away. She was so surprisingly neat and efficient, so housewifely, that he teased her about having escaped from Iowa without ending up the wife of a good Iowa farmer. Her feelings were hurt and she showed it. "You think maybe I couldn't have? You think I'm a hippie because I can't make that square scene? Well, you're wrong, because I can. I cut out because I saw how it made my mother. Like a dray horse. That cooking-cleaning-housework scene, I like it, see? It could get to be like a habit with me, like it was with her. It possessed her, became an obsession. I do it fine, I enjoy it, but I keep myself away from it because it's bad for me. Same way you oughta keep yourself off the booze."

"I'm sorry, Laura."

"Don't apologize. All you straight types think we're—what's the word?—incompetent. But like we're not. We just don't want to make your scene—even for this." Enviously she waved her hands at the room and the furnishings.

"So it's we and them, eh? And I'm one of them?" he asked, his feelings hurt now but not so hurt that he couldn't recognize that there was some truth to her including him with them.

She looked as if she were poised to throw herself at him and then she laughed. "You made me lose my cool." She went to him, put her arms around his waist, insinuated her pelvis against him, and said softly, "It's true though, isn't it?"

"All the more reason for not saying it, if it is. But it isn't. Maybe you and me, you against me, and that's bad enough; but no we and they."

"Come on," she cajoled, "cheer up. Let's forget it. Like you said this pad had a balcony. Show it to me."

From the balcony the buildings around Los Pueblos looked small and squat. On the distant mountains a few lights gleamed and were gone, and above the low moon was thin and very white; the stars were almost effaced. "It's cool, real cool," Laura breathed and Sanders, offering her his coat, abruptly realized what she meant and they both laughed together. They stood there quietly, his arm over her shoulder, hers about his waist, until they began truly to feel the chill night air. Inside again she pushed him down on the couch, told him to close his eyes and keep them closed until she said ready, and promised him his surprise. Sanders heard her moving around across from him in the living room, then in another room he couldn't place, and finally rummaging around in the large bedroom before she returned and whispered in his ear that he could open his eyes. When he did he did not believe what he saw. On the wall facing him hung a Paris street sign and, incredibly, the white letters on the blue background read clearly: PLACE DES ÉTATS-UNIS. Laura led him by the hand into the bathroom where, above the head, stood another sign, RUE DE RIVOLI, and then, though he held back because now he was certain what was coming, he let himself be dragged into the bedroom. Over the bed, the white letters shimmering like distorted moons on the square sky-blue background, was the last sign: QUAI DE PASSY. "Aren't they like great?" Laura enthused. "I saw them in a bookshop the other night and bought them for you. I would've bought a couple more but I didn't have enough bread. You talked so much about Paris I knew you'd think they were neat, especially this one," she pointed and in stumbling pronunciation said, "Kay de Pussy." He felt he was cowering, only barely restraining his impulse to run screaming out of the door, out of the apartment. "What's the matter?" she asked. "Are you sick?"

Sanders nodded, shook his head, made empty gestures with his hands, but couldn't speak a word. Fate could not reach six thousand miles across the world so casually to strike him a blow! Yet it had. There on the walls, his history, his pain, yes, his failures, were encapsulated and announced on Paris street signs. It was too apt, too devastating, to be intentional; it could therefore only be accident, coincidence, or was that itself a form of fate and foreordination? No one, not even Elaine or Levi Migdal, had known how important the Place des États-Unis had been to him, and only Elaine could know what the Quai de Passy meant.

"You're white as a sheet," Laura said. "You look like you've seen a ghost, or someone walked across your grave."

He essayed a not very successful laugh. "Both. I have. Several."

"Was it the street signs?" She was baffled.

"Yes," he blurted. He saw her dismay and was instantly sorry. He tried to salvage what he could. "Not exactly. Really just the shock of being reminded of Paris." *Noli me tangere,* he thought, and then, wryly, at least not that way.

"Lie down," she commanded him, putting her fingers against his chest and urging him toward the bed. "I'll get you a drink. Now, where did you put those whisky bottles you had in the suitcase?" she asked, but without waiting for his answer she went to the kitchen.

Sanders sat on the edge of the bed, eyes riveted on that street sign, and twice, half raising himself, tried to touch it but couldn't. Kay de pussy, Laura had pronounced it; well, perhaps key de pussy would have been more to the point.

Only the night-light was on, the tiny hooded green light that bulged from the baseboard socket like a cobra. Elaine had to have it lit or she couldn't sleep. Like so many other things between them it had at first been a joke. The first night she lit it—she'd brought one with her from the Avenue Foch apartment, confiding that she never traveled without such a gadget—she maintained she just needed a green light so she could see her way to the john at night and he teased her by demanding that they buy a red bulb instead, since it was, after all, a bedroom and needed the proper boudoirlike atmosphere. Later, when he realized she was afraid to sleep in the dark, to wake in the dark, he wanted to comfort her, to make up for all those nights when her parents had left her as a frightened child to sleep in the dark with only a nanny down the hall and three servants in the house—that last he knew as irony. Still later the eerie green and red lights took on those perverse symbolic meanings which seemed to sum up so much of their life together: They were the lights of social traffic, the stop's and go's of urban civilization: The red light was the literal and figurative symbol of the brothels he had frequented and continued to frequent; and the green light never failed to remind him of García Lorca's poem, *Verde que te quiero verde,* with such a wretchedness that he wanted to splinter the bulb with his bare toe.

Her body was angular and still under the sheets, though he knew

[111]

from her posture that she was still awake. "You're back," Elaine called from the bed. "Which *poule* was it tonight? Which little Left Bank *copain?* Which cheap St. Denis whore?" When he said nothing, her voice rose. "You might at least have enough decency, tact, to wash the smell of your nastiness off before you come home. Or did that poor little *souris* not even own a bidet?" In the green dark her voice ran the gamut from rasp to whine to coo and back again. He said nothing, but got into the double bed next to her, careful not to touch her.

Elaine sniffed loudly. "Cheap and vulgar scent!"

Since she was awake, Sanders knew how it would culminate, knew because he loved her in spite of it and knew he would permit it, no, not permit it, abet it, and then she touched him and it began.

"Do you want me to take the signs down?" Laura asked as she returned from the kitchen, clinking the ice cubes in the glass she offered to him, and gesturing at the QUAI DE PASSY sign. She had discarded her bush jacket and beneath wore a horizontally striped blue-and-white skivvy shirt that showed off her unencumbered breasts.

Sanders forced himself to politeness and the present. "No, don't take it, them, down. They're perfect . . . housewarming gifts." The outward signs of my inward journey. He drank half the liquor down in a gulp. "And thanks for this too, I needed it."

"Like I wasn't thinking of a new pad, you know, just something to cheer up that gloomy hotel room."

"How did you know it was gloomy?"

"All hotel rooms are gloomy." Laura had a cigarette in her mouth and began to fish for matches in her khakis. "You mind if I turn on?" she asked, the flame a hairsbreadth from the end of her cigarette.

"Why not?" he asked, not quite certain what she meant until, after a few sibilant puffs, the burned sickly sweet smell of marijuana floated up. "You wanna drag?" She proferred the cigarette. "You look like you can use it."

"Thanks. I'll stick to my poison."

Laura sat down on the bed, then lay back, blowing the smoke past him, one hand burrowing under his coat and shirt to play

[112]

along his backbone. "Lie down," she invited lazily in a while, "relax."

"In a minute," he promised, but drank his drink slowly to rid himself of the taste of that other room on the Quai de Passy in which he had lived, to bring himself back to the room where only a Paris street sign bought in a bookshop reigned over the bed. As he put the glass on the night table, Laura sat up, breathing a final sigh of smoke from deep in her lungs. "Ah," she crooned, "that was groovy."

Sanders took his jacket off, tossed it over a chair and lay back with her. She put her head on his chest, threw one powerful leg across his thighs, then opened his shirt and put her mouth against his breastbone as if she wanted to speak directly to his heart. Her voice was so muted he could not hear what she said, but it vibrated in his flesh. He drew her face up to him to kiss her. "I don't know what you were saying but it felt good."

"This," she responded, and pressed close to him.

Under her skivvy shirt she wore nothing, neither slip nor brassiere, and her breasts, big, globed as fruit, were a solace to his touch. When he began to undo her trousers, she held his hand and shook her head.

"Why?"

The reply cost her an effort and her downcast face was shy. "The curse," she murmured.

Amused by her diffidence, he said that was no hindrance, he didn't mind if she didn't, and her puzzlement said plainly that she couldn't tell if he was teasing her; but when he persevered she still pushed his hands away. Her head sank to his chest, went to his belly, her hands exploring before. "Let me do you," she said, lifting her head to look up at him, "anyway. This will be my party."

The QUAI DE PASSY sign burned blue-and-white at the edge of his vision and turned into the Avenue Foch. "No!" he barked and sat bolt upright. "No," he repeated into her silent, questioning, undecided eyes.

They sat on the edge of the bed until she said sadly, "I thought you had no hangups," and if it was an indictment, and it was, she spoke it with such tenderness and concern that Sanders was stirred.

[113]

The blue Parisian street sign still burned on the periphery of his vision and he shifted slightly to make it disappear, to shut it out of his sight, but as he moved he felt her recoil and realized that she thought he was turning away from her and forced himself back to face her and the Quai de Passy sign above her head full on. "It's not what you think," he said, considering every word carefully. "I'm not puritanical, square"—his attempt at a smile he knew was at best a grimace—"about that kind of thing."

"But?" she asked, her face expectant and full of dread, and she pulled the skivvy shirt down to cover her breasts, as if she no longer wanted those red eyes focused on him, those soft breasts offering their comfort, her person available to him.

He wanted to tell her, he wanted a great deal to tell her and to tell her a great deal, but he couldn't. He breathed deeply, trying to catch the right words in his mouth, but he couldn't even pronounce Elaine's name. Laura put her arms around him, her cheek against his. "If it's that hard, don't try, Elliott," she whispered, "just let it be."

His mouth was dry, his throat constricted, and his stomach, like a wild animal, surged against the walls of his chest. She held him close, crooning an unrecognizable tune in his ear until he no longer shook so badly and then when she let him go, held him at arm's length to see if he was better, the bell clanged. It was one of those semi-Oriental chimes that sound a series of bamboolike notes, and they echoed and reechoed through the rooms. Their eyes met and Laura's, puzzled, asked without words who could be calling him at midnight and Sanders replied aloud, "I don't know." The bell echoed again and he left her on the bed and walked quickly through the living and dining rooms into the hall. As he reached the small entrance foyer, a key turned in the lock, the door was pushed open and Steven Prescott walked in. "Oh, it's you," Prescott said, his face severe and disapproving. Abruptly Sanders was conscious of his dishevelment, aware that his hair was mussed, his shirttails out, his belt open, his fly half unzipped, but the satisfaction he saw on Prescott's face as it took in those details angered him and he made not the slightest effort to repair his disarray.

[114]

"Who did you expect?" Sanders asked, feeling his anger begin to build.

Casually Prescott ignored the question, his aplomb unruffled. Instead he reported, "Beth and I were driving home—" he waited a moment for some reaction before continuing, but Sanders denied him the satisfaction of a response—"and Beth saw the light on in Jason's apartment. I thought that maybe I'd left the light on when we were here earlier this evening so I came upstairs to put things right."

"Very considerate," Sanders said, barely restraining his temper.

"Yes, wasn't it? Jason Howe is a very good friend of mine."

"Elliott, what is it?" Laura called from behind him, and before he could answer she joined them in the foyer. Prescott's eyebrows rose, a smirk slithered across his mouth as he took in Laura's clothes, her long and now tangled hair, her once-white tennis shoes. That she felt the insult of the scrutiny Sanders felt as she clutched his arm and pressed close to him. "This is Laura Martin," Sanders announced. "A very good friend. Steven Prescott." He omitted the title by design.

"Good evening." Prescott's small bow from the waist was the condescending gallantry of a toff to a tart.

Sanders felt Laura flinch but she replied coolly enough. "Oh, you're the man who rented the apartment to Elliott, aren't you? and Sanders' heart rejoiced. She had struck precisely the right tone of indifferent curiosity: What was this rental agent doing there so late at night? Prescott froze. She had hit him truly, gone through the professional manner and the personal rudeness to where he lived. His head came up sharply, then, pointing like a hound's, sniffed the air. "You cooking something?" he asked her, the question far too casual. He had smelled the marijuana.

"Why, yes," Laura said, "how did you know? We missed dinner while we were moving and I was making us something to eat."

"Funny aroma," Prescott commented. "What is it?"

"Fried chicken," she bluffed him. "Would you like some? It's almost ready if you care to join us." But it was not a friendly invitation and Prescott was left no doubt that it was.

"No, no, thank you," he replied, put out. "I'll say good night, then."

"Oh, Prescott." Sanders stopped him as he was going out the door. Impatiently Prescott turned. "Yes?"

Sanders put out his palm. "I'll take that key."

Facing each other like two Arctic snowmen, immobile and rigid, they remained frozen in that tableau until it became clear that neither would relent and then Prescott said, "The key? Ah yes, I almost forgot." With a mocking glance at Laura, a glance meant to shame and demean her, to invade their privacy, he added, "You will need two keys now, won't you?" He handed the second key over and was gone.

As soon as the door closed behind him, Laura began to cry, great rolling tears that wet her cheeks. "That mean bastard, that hateful square sonofabitch!" and nothing Sanders could do would soothe her.

❋ ❋ ❋

In the daytime the Rue Daunou is a narrow, commonplace, even ugly street near the Opéra which runs its course between buildings so nondescript that they pass notice and are set so that even on the very brightest Paris days only a little sunshine filters down into it. With its bars, cafés, bistros, its *pâtisseries* and *boulangeries,* and the usual complement of other small businesses, it is an eminently forgettable street. At dusk, however, with the lighting of the yellow streetlamps, the Rue Daunou becomes shadowy and romantic, its corners and doorways replete with lounging, smoking women, its sidewalks with girls strolling very slowly always by themselves and with no apparent destination. These are Parisian *filles de joie* now driven into this and other such side streets by an uncharacteristic onset of governmental puritanism. The Rue Daunou is a good street for these women because they know that it debouches almost into the rich tourists' laps as they sit at the Café de la Paix watching and being watched, enduring and enjoying the stares of all, the swift if mercifully brief iguanalike incursions of dirty-picture peddlers, and often awaiting the lure of the prostitutes who beckon them down the dusky Daunou to small flats and hotels which serve their purposes and those of their companions.

It was on the Rue Daunou that Sanders met Monique and there it had begun. He had had a long and futile talk with Georges Ron-

[116]

valet, a minor Quai d'Orsay official, about France and European union but what he had elicited was even less informative than the written handouts of the Ministry of Information. After almost a bottle of Calvados between them, Ronvalet had unsteadily excused himself, called for a taxi and explained, as he pointedly ignored the check, that he had to be home for dinner. If he was a little late—he looked abashed; his wife went into a fury about his having a *cinq-à-sept* and made life thoroughly unpleasant. Sanders couldn't tell whether that was to explain Ronvalet's departure or his taking a cab instead of the Métro, but the conspiratorial wink, the sly shrug, and the comment "Even we French . . ." left salaciously unfinished, only thrust Sanders back into the shambles of his last weeks with Elaine. Not that he was ever far removed from it, for even as he had probed Ronvalet's ignorance and provinciality, his chauvinism and reluctance—Ronvalet was a disciplined Gaullist—Sanders had drunk the Calvados to numb the other pain, his life with Elaine which lay just beneath the surface of their talk always threatening to emerge unawares, like an interior wound bleeding into great bruises beneath the unbroken skin, visible and purpling. Ronvalet stumbled out to his taxi and Sanders poured the remainder of his Calvados into the glass, watching the last drops drip slowly from the rim of the bottle one at a time like some Chinese water torture: E . . . laine, E . . . laine.

Dusk had settled, the streetlights were lit, the terrace was emptying as people left for dinner, and he knew he ought to leave too, walk down to Fauchon's, buy Elaine the tin of Strasbourg pâté and the *fraises des bois* he knew would please her, placate her, and then bring them home to dinner; but he had no desire to return to the Quai de Passy. He didn't want to see Elaine's lovely cruel face; he didn't want once more to begin that serpentine stifling argument that repeated itself over and over again, the twists and turns and sometimes even the very words the same, as they tried to talk about why she would not have a child. Whatever she said and however she said it, the situation always came down to the same ludicrous fact: You couldn't have children without intromission and that she would not, said she could not, allow. He remembered the incomparable Louis singing and playing the trumpet in an old-style cabaret, bringing the French *le jazz hot,* the trumpet improvising, the band singing, "A *fifteen-minute intermission, boss, you hear me wishin, intermission,*" and his own mocking version, "A fifteen-min-ute *intro*mission, boss, you hear me wishin, *intro*mission," but it al-ways failed to make him laugh. "You don't understand what it's like," she continued to cry out, her face and voice hysterical, her body tensed like a beast at bay, her eyes seeking escape, "it's like being stabbed, pried apart, impaled—"

"Pricked? Is that the word you're looking for?" he'd cruelly in-terjected, and Elaine had thrown her treasured Sèvres shepherdess —always the souvenirs of the Avenue Foch—at him, missed and smashed it into bits against the wall. Sanders had left her there on her knees, crying, sweeping up the shards, to go out to meet Ron-valet, left her without a word or gesture of conciliation or compas-sion: Things between them had gone too far for either of those.

A last coffee and Calvados coursed more warmly through his blood and he could feel the heat in his face while he paid the check and waited for his change. The café's terrace had still fewer people now, but when Monique walked past the more discerning males imme-diately cocked their heads, young and old alike, French and for-eigner, and turned to watch her. Like Calvados she appealed to and warmed the blood. Though she was quietly and tastefully dressed in a nubby tweed suit with a jacket that ended just above and called attention to her superb behind, her stride was so languorously sexual that it instantly proclaimed her a *poule;* no "respectable" woman would have permitted or called attention to those contrasts of her body: the upper half puritanically straight, the head held high and erect, the posture austere; the lower half uncurbed and voluptuous, a swaying invitation to unbridled lust. Even the waiter, counting out his francs, stopped and stammered, "*Mon Dieu!*" his mouth open. Sanders pocketed his change without counting it, a thing he rarely did in tourists' places, and followed her down into the Rue Daunou where she permitted him to catch up to her and then, turning, ac-costed him. Her approach, age-old and simple, was to hold up a cigarette and ask, in English, for a light.

Sanders gave her one and, in French, brutally asked what she charged and whether she was worth it. One thin penciled eyebrow

[118]

rose and cold eyes examined him. "You speak French like a true Parisian," she said, "but you behave like a Tatar." She made as if to walk away, but Sanders knew she wouldn't and pitilessly stood his ground, glowering and leering by turn, inflamed by that walk and the Calvados, sure that with *cinq-à-sept* over and dinner under way she could not afford to leave, she would have to turn a trick. She went only four paces before she pivoted, head down, and walked back, dropping her glowing cigarette at his feet and grinding it out with the pointed toe of her shoe. "You are cruel and crude, Monsieur," she rebuked him. "It is not necessary to do such things, we are human beings too." Even through the haze of his anger and alcohol, Sanders was ashamed; he had tried to humiliate this woman, this stranger, for no better reason than that Elaine had humiliated him—and he was mortified.

Monique lived on the top floor of a nearby apartment house in what had obviously been in the past a maid's room, with a tiny kitchen, and a lavatory with a bidet but no bath. Naked about its purpose, the room was almost entirely filled by a great, old-fashioned brass bed with coarse sheets, neatly turned down. Tersely, she motioned him to it and went herself to the bidet. Only when she had returned did Sanders really see her clearly, her blond Norman grace, heavy and quiet, her small pink-tipped breasts and tiny girlish waist so disciplined and ascetic a contrast to the copious hips and buttocks, the slow somnolent movements as she came to bed. That she was expert there was no doubt but that she was not intent on demonstrating her expertise was also clear. Sensing his haste, his need, his selfishness, she took him into her quickly, without preliminaries, without even a kiss, her legs wide, the blond bush parted, the generous hiding place for a small animal, the nest for the bird, slowing him only with pleasure, giving not taking, enhancing his rhythm without insisting on her own until he burst upon her like a freshet, shuddering.

Together they sat on the edge of her bed and drank the heavily sugared black coffee she had made, peering over the rims of the cups at one another with undisguised curiosity. She asked if he lived in Paris or was just visiting, and where and how he had learned his French; and then shyly what he was called. He told her, without caution or hesitation, and was flattered when she recognized his name, her head tilted, tossing her mane of yellow hair, her gray eyes widening. "Ah-ha, the journalist." With only the sparest glance at his wedding ring she wondered aloud why he was so unhappy, so distraught—she did not say *seemed,* she said *was*—and without waiting for his reply asked if it was his wife. How did she know? The proverbial sixth sense of whores? He didn't believe in that any more than he believed in the tarot pack or the tea leaves or the lines of one's palm. What better guess, he supposed, than one's wife. Or was his unhappiness so obvious? Yet she did not seem merely to be guessing, or even inquisitive, only sad. When he asked her how she knew, his tone more skeptical than his feeling, she couldn't tell him, or wouldn't; she said she didn't know how she knew but she knew. And then, almost gratuitously, added that going to bed with many men gave her some kinds of insight that other women didn't have, it was one of the few benefits of the "trade"; then, as if to demean it, she said she thought that perhaps it was no more than she had to develop to protect herself. "I am called Monique Bardieu," she introduced herself with a diffident formality that made him think she did not often give her full name, or any name—the many uses of the ubiquitous *chérie*—to her patrons.

With equal formality, unsmiling, he stood up and kissed her hand, spoke his *"Enchanté"* as he felt it, as more than mere formality.

After she took the cups and saucers away, she lay back once more, her face screened by sheaves of hair, and spread herself for him like a cavern of earth in which he could mine the vein of joy and sample the ore of his manhood once more, conquer and forget Elaine and himself; for those plunging moments he moved and was moved and had the first faint dawning that perhaps he had also moved Monique Bardieu.

✱ ✱ ✱

Out on the balcony in the morning the air was cool and sweet with the smell of apricots, the mountains were shrouded in haze, and down below he saw for the first time the regular pattern of a fruit-tree orchard in blossom. Apricots, he thought, trusting his nose, but he could not be sure at that height. Though there was no fresh milk in Jason Howe's kitchen, there were coffee, canned milk, tomato juice and a tinned date-nut bread. Not brioches or croissants, he thought, meeting the recollection of mornings after when Elaine, contrite, hollows under her eyes dark as if bedaubed for a masquerade, would bring him *petit-déjeuner* in bed, eyes downcast, and would share it with him, the most attentive of wives, the most compliant of handmaidens. Laura was sleeping when he brought the breakfast tray into the bedroom and set it on the night table. In his pajamas she lay outstretched, her face still streaked with last night's tears, but now placidly sleeping. Opening the portières, he let the light slant across her face and when her eyes opened, focused, she smiled at him, stretched, yawned and sat up. She saw the breakfast tray and covered her face with her hands, and wept once more. Confounded, Sanders asked what was wrong, what had happened, and when her sobs resounded again, he apologized exaggeratedly for the juice, the coffee, his improvised baked date-nut bread, and told her that if she went on crying she would leave him permanently scarred about his culinary talents and hospitality, until her sobs became gasps of laughter, her face came out from behind her hands and she averred half laughing, half crying, that he would make some girl a properly domesticated husband.

"Tried it once," he joked, "didn't like it." He handed her the brandy snifter of tomato juice and when she saw the glass she almost wept again, but then restrained herself, raised her glass to him, and said, "No one ever brought me breakfast in bed before and no one ever remembered that I like everything in champagne or brandy glasses until now. Skoal!" She drank a healthy draught of the tomato juice and was hilarious.

"If that's what smoking pot does for you, maybe you ought to switch to whisky. We get bigger and better laughing jags," he said, but she, choking a little, went right on laughing.

* * *

In Oakland no one was at the statue when Sanders arrived though there were clumps of tourists seeing the sights, talking of huskies and sourdoughs, of London's adventurous life and its tragedies: the drunkenness, the blighted marriages, the talent and then the life destroyed, the bleak burned-out ruins of the Wolf House—also a

[121]

tourist's sight; but there was no sign of Peter King. As Sanders turned to walk away someone tapped him on the shoulder, startling him, for he had heard no one and seen no one coming, and when he did see he was even more startled because the blue-black Negro in front of him was at least six feet four inches tall and some two hundred and fifty pounds, a great panther of a man moving on the balls of his feet. Thick, bow-shaped lips parted to show the swiftest glimpse of white teeth before the big bass voice inquired, "Elliott Sanders?" Sanders nodded and put out his hand only to have it engulfed in a fist consciously demonstrating its strength and in so doing emphasizing the strange and irregular ridging of his palm that Sanders felt but couldn't see. "I'm Peter King," the man said.

Sanders managed to say good morning, controlling but not quite concealing his wince under the impact of that handshake. King's broad nostrils flared, sniffed the air, and his head turned to take in the plaza, the surrounding buildings and the sky. "Fog still not burned off and chilly, but any morning you make it is a good morning, eh?" Gesticulating at the London statue, he said, "Not many statues to anything but killing and killers in this country. Nice to have something different here."

"Not many in any country," Sanders replied, putting aside his own thoughts about the killer in Jack London, his boyhood hero, foisted on him by Lovett Carpenter Sanders, whose boyhood hero he was also—wasn't he the gay blade, the peripatetic journalist, the espouser and defender of unpopular causes?—and said, "First priority for generals, second for their horses."

King's peevish look faded into a smile. "That's right, isn't it? People dig those equestrian statues. You know, man on a horse, spear in one hand, flag in the other, that kind of shit." The perfect, too precise speech and diction and the obscenity again brought Sanders up short, as did King's dress, chinos worn white by too much wear and washing, an open Eisenhower battle jacket showing still the lighter space on the sleeves where once a sergeant's stripes had been sewn, a gray sport shirt beneath and a thick belt with a heavy brass buckle and high-laced yellow boots with gum soles of the kind that laborers or dockhands wear. King's demeanor seemed abruptly and

[122]

unaccountably friendlier. "Too early for you to drink, Mr. Sanders?" he asked.

"Elliott. Never too early to drink, Mr. King."

"Peter," King returned, but the hesitation in giving his first name was mastered with a wrench. King took his elbow and conducted him across the plaza to a nearby bar. There was no mistaking the fact that he was being led either: King's fingers encircled his biceps like a band and his own biceps felt as if they would spring out of his flesh like the useless inner tube of a ruptured tire. The bar was almost empty but Sanders sensed a small stir as they entered and took a table. Was it that they were a peculiar-looking pair or was it King's imposing bulk? The habitués of the bar seemed to move closer together, their heads tucked into their chests, their eyes too self-consciously elsewhere. "What'll you have?" Sanders asked.

"Same as you," King replied, looking down at his hands, the thumbs hidden beneath the table, the other fingers fanned out like the spokes of two broken wheels without either hubs or rims.

No one came to take their order and though Sanders waved at the bartender a couple of times the man didn't seem to notice, so he walked up to the bar and ordered two cognacs. The bartender didn't seem to have heard and Sanders repeated the order, but this time the barkeep looked straight at him, then deliberately turned his back. Sanders raised his voice. "What's the matter with you anyway, you out of business or hard of hearing?" he called angrily, noticing the sly nudging gestures of the half-dozen regulars at the bar all of whose eyes studiously avoided his though he could see that they were drinking in every detail of the scene and enjoying it. His fleshy face set, his pale eyes cold blue, the barkeep turned and said, "No cognac."

"All right, two bourbons, then," Sanders began and then, seeing the brandy, pointed to where the cognac bottles multiplied themselves in the bar mirror. "You've got six or eight bottles of cognac right there."

"Why, so we have, don't we?" the bartender replied, his voice and face absolutely without surprise, and he made no move toward the bottles.

"You don't understand, Mr. Sanders." King's voice was right behind him, so close he felt the breath on his neck and was again rattled by the swift, silent way in which King moved. "If I leave, this man will be delighted to serve you cognac, Scotch or anything else in the house you can pay for. That right, Whitey?"

"That right, Blackie." The barkeep's speech turned vaudeville Southern. "We don't want your business."

"There's a law—" Sanders began.

"Stick that law up your ass, mister. This is my place and I don't want niggers drinking in it. You take your—business some other place."

"You crummy honky," King said, moving warily toward him, but the barkeep immediately had the small boy's baseball bat in his hand which had appeared from under the bar and the habitués had moved around behind them, hemming them in. Two of them held longshoreman's hooks. Sanders remembered how that British policeman had looked in Wanchai with the hook in his throat.

"All right, Peter," Sanders said, estimating the odds. "Let's get out of here."

"All right, Peter," one of the longshoreman types mimicked, giving the name its slang meaning. "Let's get out of here." He made the shoulder-shaking, hip-swiveling motions of a nance, but with that hook in his hand looking more ludicrous and lethal.

"Blow!" one of the others said.

"Yeh, blow!" a couple of others chorused, bending their wrists effeminately, joining together in the raucous ridiculing double-edged laughter.

One thing was clear; it was not only that Peter King was black, it was also that he was homosexual; these men knew him or knew about him.

The shabby Negro bar King took him to was down a side street and not much friendlier, though here when King ordered their whiskies the waiter no more than looked his hostility at Sanders before he brought the glasses and sloshed them down on the table. He stood waiting until Sanders paid and tipped him before he shuffled off without acknowledging or thanking him for either. Though Sanders did not feel personally responsible—I'm home, he thought, and not at home with this—he apologized but like a horse

[124]

flicking gnats off his mane Peter King shook his head, snorted, then bolted his whisky in a single swallow. "Don't talk about it," he counseled, his big hands raised between them so that Sanders saw the raised white ridges across his pink palms. "It doesn't do any good. Words don't matter and a drink doesn't matter and not being served in a bar doesn't matter. By law we've been allowed to drink in your bars and eat at your lunch counters for almost fifteen years now, Mr. Sanders, but the drinks are piss-warm now and the hamburgs cold and greasy. It's too late for all that and Mister Charley better know it. We want more—and we're gonna get more."

Sanders caught the *your* and the *Mister* and he didn't let them pass. "Not *my* bars and lunch counters and my name is still Elliott," he said, signaling for the lounging waiter to bring two more whiskies. For a fleeting instant he was tempted to say that he was an expatriate, that he'd lived abroad almost continuously for most of his adult life, and for much of his childhood too, but he wasn't sure whether that absolved him of responsibility or simply convicted him more profoundly.

"It's impossible, Mr.—Elliott—don't try," King said.

"What's impossible?"

"White men and black men living together like human beings. We're not ready. You're not ready. The whole goddam country's not ready."

Sanders didn't argue the point; he wasn't sure he could, but he did say, "You and George Christiansen were friends and he was white, wasn't he?"

King's eyes glittered. "How did he die?"

"He died well," Sanders answered, knowing that with King, unlike the others, he wouldn't be able to get away with that, but hoping King would let it go by.

King didn't. "What the hell does that mean? Who dies well? Where did he buy it? What was he doing?" King's questions were imperious. "George didn't cop out, did he? I can't believe he'd do that, he had too much guts."

"He had guts," Sanders affirmed and then, in detail, but without embellishment, reliving that afternoon in his guts so that his wounds ached again, Christiansen buried and disinterred in his brain, he

[125]

told Peter King how George had thrown himself on that grenade, how the whole thing had happened on that sidewalk in Saigon. King's head swayed from side to side like a pendulum measuring time, saying, "No, no, no. It couldn't have happened that way, it didn't." But it had. "Why?" King finally asked despairingly, after a quarter of an hour of silence. "Why did he do it?"

"I don't know," Sanders admitted. "I'd like to find out and not only because he saved my life."

King was instantly alert. "So that's why you went to see his old man, and his wife."

"And you."

"And me."

"I thought they'd, you'd, help me find out why."

"Why should they help? They hated George. They must be glad he's dead. Besides, how could they know? They didn't even know him here, he was a stranger to them."

"I think you're wrong, at least about his wife," Sanders countered, realizing as he did so that once again he had leaped too obviously to Beth's defense only this time not in the privacy of his mind.

King eyed him sardonically. "You believe all that hand-wringing and wailing routine? Shit, man, Beth sent him a Dear John letter after he was in Vietnam only a couple of months. And she's been jouncing that doctor, what's his name?"

"Prescott?"

"Yeh, that Bircher sonofabitch. If you're a believing man, Elliott, you believe a lot but you learn nothing."

A believing man. How he wished he were. "If you don't believe," Sanders said, "you don't learn anything worth much."

"From broads?" King looked his contempt. "They're from nothing. Dirt. Holes you put your peg in. Or don't."

"I like women," Sanders said mildly, knowing how hyperbolic that was, wondering how much of King's impassioned hatred was the spillover from the pent-up anger and the insults of those white longshoremen at the bar.

"You really like them, like to be with them, talk to them, go places with them, or you just like humping them, getting your wick wet?" King asked savagely.

"I enjoy their company. They're different from us and I like the difference. They pique me and I'm curious about them," Sanders retorted, as blandly as he could manage, but he knew he enjoyed women's company only sometimes, only liked and understood some of the differences and loathed and feared others; but this was the time and the place for neither a blanket indictment of the sex, nor hedging and careful qualification.

"You're a lucky man," King said, and Sanders couldn't tell if King was intending sarcasm, was envious or both.

"My relations with women are a history of catastrophe," Sanders confessed, trying to cool down King's heated tone, unwilling to travel under false colors but not yet ready for candor either. Elaine. E . . . laine.

"Maybe you ought to try men," King proposed, the invitation bold, the eyes trying to stare him down.

"It's not my kick," Sanders said, holding King's gaze, the grin he managed pasted to his lips, painfully reminded by his language, Laura's language, of Laura's anxious desirous "How do you get your kicks?" Your hangups and your hangdowns.

"How do you know until you've tried it?" King pressed.

Sanders shrugged. "I don't have to eat oysters to know I don't like them. I can tell just by looking."

"Even oysters Rockefeller?"

"Even the best. But," he added, as kindly as he could, "I'm not one of those who mind other people eating oysters or liking them, even at the same table. See?" It was a lie, or at best a half-truth, but he could see no other way to cope with King's aggressiveness and sensitivity.

"I see," King mocked him, "you're one of the *tolerant* ones." He spat the word out, an affront.

"Peter, the world's full of strange creatures and they don't have to be like me for me to like them."

"You mean they can even be black and queer." King's sneer was uncertain.

"I mean they can be the way they are. It's no skin off my nose. Besides, they haven't got too much choice anyway." But enough, Sanders amended to himself, more than enough.

[127]

"Did George tell you about me?" King seemed to mean about his homosexuality, so Sanders replied that George hadn't talked much about people back home.

King laughed harshly. "Discreet to the last. Issues. Problems. Institutions. Right?"

"Yes, and no. He thought people made the institutions, not the other way round. But he said that good men, brave men, could always change things, improve matters." Shamefaced, Sanders recalled the thin-lipped patrician face calling, crying out, for the good men, the honorable men; it was a cry that hung over Lovett Carpenter Sanders' entire life, a barbaric yawp heard over and behind the cynical appraisal of human, political and national motive.

"Did he tell you about himself?" King asked, his eyes hard, his mouth set. Without waiting for an answer he hurried on. "People don't tell you about themselves, do they? They tell you only what they want you to know. George wasn't much of a teller even that way. But he told me because I was his friend and he trusted me. Maybe he told me because like me he had no one else to talk to, no one else who gave a damn."

"Not even his wife, or his father?"

"Especially not them."

"Why?"

"Because he didn't belong to them. He belonged to me. He was my friend, my brother, my father."

Your lover? Sanders wondered, but he didn't ask. "Even if he was white?" he asked instead.

"*Because* he was white and I was black."

"Then there's a chance some of us can live together, as friends and brothers?"

King considered that in sullen silence for two whiskies before he spoke again. "Maybe. But George was not just another Mister Charley. He was an extraordinary man."

Sanders had no quarrel with that; men who deliberately fell on hand grenades were, by definition, extraordinary.

"We were brothers where it counted," King maintained, "*under the skin*. I didn't even have to tell George what it was like, what I was feeling; he knew."

Sanders had his own irrational confidence in rapport and intuition but he knew that more was needed—words, gestures and actions —or else communication if it occurred at all was incomplete and unsatisfactory. Not that he knew what words or gestures or behavior would be appropriate and when, any more than King apparently did. Or probably than George Christiansen had. Or had he? What more seemly act or proper gesture than Christiansen's commitment to death for another's life? It was an act beyond compare, but sometimes you need a word too, to explain, to mitigate, to relieve guilt; and he said so.

King stared gloomily into his whisky glass, the signs of alcohol now plain in his speech which had grown slower and even more precise. "History repeats itself in curious ways that don't make sense," he reflected. "George was one of the leaders of the peace movement in this area. Did you know that? He hated the war, he hated the idea of killing anyone. Not like me." He laughed harshly. "I loved that idea. I wanted them to give me a chance to kill. Even yellow men, but Whiteys would have been better. Much better. But they wouldn't let me. I freaked out on them. I was a psycho. Me a nut. How do you like them persimmons?" he asked, in mock-Southern farmers' speech, but Sanders didn't know if he was mocking the individual or the type, or himself. "Even the Army didn't want me, even they rejected me. What a laugh! 'Stones by the builder rejected.' I wasn't even equal enough for killing. Man, some guys pray to stay out, some guys break a leg or take castor oil until they shit their guts on the floor, and some just play being 'conshie'—not like George, he was for real—and let the cops cart them away. But me, Peter Simon King, I *wanted* to go. I wanted to kill anybody, if they'd give me a gun, and they wouldn't let me."

The waiter, lounging not too far off, a cigarette pasted to his lip, was uneasy and began to fidget when King, raising his voice, made himself heard. "I'm a killer. George, he was a saint. They should have left him here and taken me. Besides, I had nothing to lose." His shrug shook him like a tic. "Maybe you'd be dead if they had. What makes a cat drop on a grenade?"

"What kind of psychiatric difficulty did they say you had?" Sanders asked softly, wondering what would have happened had it been Peter King instead of George Christiansen he'd been sitting with that day in Saigon.

"Difficul*ties*, Mr. Sanders, *ties*. I'm black. I *am* black. That's the big one." Pushing up the sleeve of his combat jacket to expose a mighty forearm, he plucked the black skin with his fingers angrily. "That's it, the skin, the hide—ain't no hidin place down there." His arm shot out, hinged over Sanders' forearm. "Don't feel sorry for me, you smug honky prick!" He began to squeeze. Sanders sat, countering the pressure as best he could by flexing his muscles, resisting, but the pain was intense. With a sharp, flailing movement, he managed to free his arm. He stood up. "That way you get nowhere and nothing."

"Niggers get nowhere and nothing regardless," King said, clenching and unclenching his fist. Then, forcefully, he slammed his fist down on the table. "Goddam, I'm sorry he's dead. I'd rather *you* were dead. He . . . my only friend, my soul brother, and he had to kill himself."

"Had to?" Sanders sat down again, awed by the nakedness of King's grief. He had known grief firsthand himself; if he feared it, and he did, he respected it too.

"Had to," King repeated. "You know why? Because George was really a killer like me, only he didn't know he was, couldn't admit he was. He said I was full of hatred and he was full of love, but"— he grinned crookedly—"he was only full of shit. He was an outsider like me, black like me, only his black was inside."

"Is that why he went to Vietnam?"

King waved for another round and the waiter went to get it. "I don't know why he went. What George told me didn't make any sense. He said that honor and love of fellow man had changed his mind. Honor, mind you! Christ! Love of fellow man! D'you dig that? When I asked him how that racked up with the burning and the killing, he told me that he belonged on the front line, that that was the only place honor and love of one's fellow men could be defended and protected, the only place where peace could be saved. I thought he'd flipped."

"Had he?"

"You mean he was sick up here?" King tapped his forehead knowingly. "Nah. George was one of the sanest types I ever knew. Black inside, but not screwy. He had good reasons to freak out here, plenty of them, no matter what he said. And Vietnam was far away, plenty far away, from Beth, from his old man, from—"

"From his whole life?" So, Sanders thought, Christiansen too had looked for a new life, perhaps tried to give up his old life, but he'd taken himself along, and he was doing the same thing exactly. For the moment Sanders was distracted from what King was saying.

"That's too big for me. I don't know. But he had had it up to here." King drew a finger across his throat. "He was up at Berkeley then, in graduate school, with a juicy student deferment. There wasn't a thing to keep him from sitting it out, but he volunteered for Vietnam."

"But why?"

The waiter returned then and, ignoring Sanders as he set the drinks down, said to King, "Whyn't you cool it, Peter? Man, you got too much lip. Why you shootin your mouth off to the Man? You gonna git your ass in a jam."

"I need instruction from you, Dever, I ask you," King replied, arrogantly copying the common lilt of the waiter's speech and pushing his chest so hard with his finger that the waiter staggered back a step or two.

"You a helluva soul brother," the waiter said.

"Believe it!" King retorted.

The waiter turned and slunk away.

"You see how it is," King said, pointing after him, "not much brotherly love for Whitey here. Not much for niggers"—the word gritted from his teeth—"down there, so how you gonna make it work? Black and white worlds don't talk to each other and even when they talk they don't speak the same language. We live on this same land but in different countries."

"Yet you and George spoke the same language, lived in the same country—with different-colored skins."

King knocked back his whisky, again in a single gulp. Increasingly he was showing the effects. "I told you," he said unsteadily. "George was black like me. Inside. He was outside, way outside, so he belonged with us."

"Even with white skin?"

"You get out far enough, you freak out of your skin. You got no color at all. Just your insides show. And all human insides are black —and bloody."

Sanders remembered George Christiansen's easy, laughing camaraderie with colored troops in the field, the hard, precise careful support on operations, and he also remembered that George was one of the few who fraternized with Negro troops in the rec areas. And those two Vietnamese kids Fillmore had reported that Christiansen had adopted. Did the color line disappear for him because he'd been Peter King's friend or because he was really what King said, black inside? And what did being black inside mean and how did an ordinary middle-class American boy like George Christiansen get to be black inside? No, Sanders corrected himself, not ordinary, not middle-class, not a boy; but an American truly.

"You don't get it, do you?" King asked, pitying and condescending. "It doesn't make a goddam bit of sense to you, does it? Well, let me throw a little more light on it for you, because you look like you really want to know."

"I do."

"Why?"

"He died for me. He saved my life."

"Don't be a horse's ass! Nobody dies for nobody else. George died for himself. Your life getting saved was an accident."

"It was no accident."

"You're sure?"

"I'm absolutely certain."

King looked at him and then, unexpectedly, impulsively placed his hands on the table, palms up, fingers rigidly outstretched. "See those!" he commanded, and Sanders stared down and with a shudder noted the white welts like pale serpents across King's palms. "Knife scars. Each one from my mother. She used to cut me across the palms to punish me. First, because she was a nut, a real psycho, and said she couldn't *do nuthin with me.* And then because I was too big and strong for her to punish any other way. *'You sassed the teach.'* Slash! *'You copped them gloves offa tha Jew.'* Slash! *'You ben playin hooky an they come an see me.'* Slash! *'Ah catch yuh runnin*

[132]

fa tha numbers, ah cut yo arm off.' Slash!" Abruptly the palms disappeared into clenched fists and King's voice, steely, said, "White boys don't get cut up like that, do they? And not by their mothers."

Speechless, Sanders couldn't take his eyes off those fists, already unable to believe the stigmata of those palms he had just a moment ago seen; but not even his horror contradicted what he knew, that there were nonetheless other welts and scars which cut across the soul and seared the spirit as deeply and ineradicably as a knife, and if they were neither so visible nor so melodramatic, they were incredibly painful. Sanders had his own and knew they were neither his property solely, nor King's, neither black nor white, neither Jew nor Greek; they were the irredeemable heritage of the human family at large, the undeniable heirlooms handed down from father to son, from mother to daughter. *The sins of the fathers are visited on the children unto the third and fourth generation.* . . . That kind of ineluctable fatality, that inherent foreordination, had driven his father from the church and religion and left his mother to the dubious comforts of both. Yet, now, after all these years, Sanders understood that "You take what you want and then you pay for it" was as much a way of life that involved inevitable retribution as the other.

"George Christiansen was just like these"—again the gashed palms appeared and were gone—"only inside, where his father had cut him. You see white boys' fathers, they cut them up different, inside, where the neighbors can't see the scars. Niggers they don't give a shit what the neighbors think. Why should they? They all alike, beatin up on each other, shittin all over each other. Every man gotta have somebody to shit on. That's why people git married, ain't it?" He giggled. "Old Joe give it to George even worse after George's mother died, his wife, and couldn't stand between them any more." King spoke as if he'd eavesdropped on Sanders' thoughts.

"What was she like?" Sanders asked, relieved by the diversion.

"Kind. Even to black boys," King said dreamily. "Thin, dark hair, pretty. Like a cameo I once saw in a pawnshop, too rarefied for where it was, too precious. And sickly. The old man used to whale the shit out of her too. I never saw her once when old Joe was around that she didn't have a bruise, a cut, a shiner, something to

[133]

show he'd paid her court, really loved her. But she stuck it out, she stayed, she didn't cop out, didn't take a powder, because she loved George. God, how she loved that boy! I think that burned the old bastard most of all. Every time he came home with a snootful— and that was often enough—he shared things equally with both of them, a fist in the gut for George, a slap in the kisser for her; fair is fair and you can't say old Joseph Farnum Christiansen wasn't a fair man."

"But why? Why?" Sanders heard but couldn't control the entreaty in his voice and knew that King heard it too.

"You're one of those *why* men. A Y-man. Y is a crooked letter! It's the way it is, the way it was," King shouted angrily, responding to that entreaty and giving the waiter such a start that he dropped his cigarette butt, glared at them, then kicked it out. "Old Joe was a shit. So what if you know he was a hero in the First World War, a real gung-ho Marine with a drawerful of decorations and a bellyful of honor, courage, and love of country. Belleau Wood, Château-Thierry, the Meuse, you name the battle and that twenty-one-year-old craphead was there. And he had the medals to prove it too. The sonofabitch told me once he was never even scared and you know something, Sanders, I believe him. That bastard wasn't afraid of the devil himself."

"George comes of brave stock."

"Now isn't that the most smart-assed bullshit you ever heard! 'George comes of brave stock.' You been seeing all that Hollywood turd about Marines charging up Iwo Jima or Guadalcanal, 'Semper Fi' and 'From the Halls of Montezuma,' and beating the balls off the Japs, those cute little banzai yellowbirds. No wonder you can be a reporter, you really believe all that crap." As King dressed him down, cutting and contemptuous, Sanders was surprised how much what he said sounded like Lovett Carpenter Sanders. His father had handed down his heritage and sins too: It was no accident that his father had taken him to the Place des États-Unis that day; it had been part and parcel of the sense of his life, and only now, belatedly, did he believe that his father had done it purposely, deliberately, to pass on to him and to memorialize some hard-earned wisdom of his own. He knew now that that was a truth; however Hollywoodian

[134]

it sounded, however absurd, it was an essential part of human life and its survival: the courage to stand, to fight, even to kill. Brave stock. Had he only been a graft on that stock, not really a Sanders at all, but a Stuart? Yet he knew the Stuarts went back to wild skirling Highlanders whose reckless bravery was legendary. No, he couldn't blame it on his forebears, only on himself. He remembered his father singing one night, having come home late from one of his "assignments," singing albeit drunkenly those oh so simple words:

> *Over there, over there.*
> *Send the word, send the word*
> *Over there . . .*
> *We'll be over,*
> *We're coming over,*
> *And we won't come back*
> *Till it's over over there.*

How green and trusting and gullible, how inexperienced and innocent, it sounded now. How little it had to do with his world, however much it might have been appropriate to Lovett Carpenter Sanders'. Two world wars had made that song pitiful, an object of ridicule, yet not ridiculous. Only in this new world, this present world, it was never going to be over over there and so the Yanks wouldn't be getting back for a long, long time. It had been a shorter way to Tipperary; it would be a much longer way back from Saigon, and from all the other Saigons thereafter.

"Old Joe was always mainlining that horseshit too." King's voice and manner became Christiansen's father's now and had Sanders closed his eyes he would have been certain that he was back in the Veterans' Hospital ward with Joseph Christiansen. "We come from old pioneer stock. We tamed the West and settled California and killed the Indians and took it from the Mexicans and came over the Sierras eating bear and our buckskins and sometimes, like the Donner party, each other. My great-grandfather came from Massachusetts to California in 1835. My grandfather was nine years old then, only a boy, but he could fight and shoot like a man. And by God he did. By the time he was twenty he was fighting with Frémont in the

Mexican War. . . ." King's own voice and manner, irascibly alcoholic, returned. "What a drag! Who gives a damn?"

"He must have," Sanders replied. "My own father did. Lots of people do, and did, and I'm not sure they're all wrong."

King was having increasing trouble focusing his eyes. "You mean because my people, the soul folk, were slaves for three hundred years, Sanders," he asked belligerently, "I can't be brave and all niggers gotta be cowards?"

"Come on, Peter, that's not what I said or what I meant," Sanders protested. "George was a brave man and so was his father, apparently, but I didn't say and I don't say that all white men or all Englishmen are brave or all black men or Italians cowards." For that matter, my black friend, how many white fathers like mine would think their white sons black sheep with white feathers?

King placed both his elbows emphatically on the table. "We come from thousands of years of warriors, Zulus and Ashantis, Masai and Sudanese, chiefs and warriors, the sons of chiefs and warriors." The Indian in the hospital, the Cherokee tearing his colostomy out, came back with the smell of blood and bile and disinfectant fogging his brain. King's elbows slipped and slowly, with exertion, he brought them back up on the table. "It takes goddam brave men to grow up a nigger in America," he said confidentially, "it takes heroes just to stay alive and not cut his own throat. D'you hear?" His confusion of singular and plural made what he said more poignant.

"I hear," Sanders said and he knew it for the truth as he knew that King was describing another kind of bravery.

King's head lowered gradually onto his forearms, resting there, his face turned up, his eyelids so heavy that his eyes were only slits. "D'you understand?"

Placatingly Sanders said he did understand and then with a childlike smile King closed his eyes and slept. Sanders sat silently and sadly, smoked two cigarettes, and watched that magnificent blue-black face and the hands, now relaxed, palms open, the scars pleading. God, he thought, how did they survive, how did they endure the bleakness and the blackness of their life in America?

Since the drinks had been paid for round by round there was no check, so that when Sanders finally stood up to find the waiter at his elbow, he said softly, "I'm going to get my car and drive him home. Keep an eye on him until I get back, will you?" The waiter's bloodshot eyes looked through him and the man said nothing.

When Sanders returned the table had been cleared and wiped dry, the ashtrays were empty, and there was no sign of King. The same waiter slouched against the wall in the same place, another butt pasted to his lips, but he gave no sign of recognition. Sanders asked him where Peter had gone, but got no reply. The waiter took a long drag instead and sent streams of smoke out of his broad nostrils and into Sanders' face. Controlling his temper, Sanders repeated the inquiry, and slowly, lazily, the waiter said, "Who?"

"You know who, Peter King."

"Nevah heard of no Peter King."

"The man I was just drinking with," Sanders pointed to the booth. "Right over there. Not fifteen minutes ago. You knew him. You called him by name."

"You makin some kinda mistake, man. I don even member seein you. You sure you got de right bar? This a *colored* bar."

"Now, listen," Sanders began angrily, knowing he was being made sport of.

Pale with rage, the veins of his neck standing out blue and corded, the waiter spat, "No, you listen, you motherfuckin ofay! I don know you. I don know no Peter King. An if'n I did, I wouldn say nohow. We soul brothers ain't got nuthin to do with you Charleys, so git lost, beat it, fuck off, Charley."

It was then that Sanders remembered that American soldiers in Vietnam, white and black alike, called the VC Charley too, and his rage sluiced away. Maybe, he thought, you called the enemy by the same disparaging names always, depending on where you were fighting and which war. "Okay," he said reasonably, "but you're making a big mistake."

"Naw, Whitey, you makin tha mistake."

"Not all of us are your enemies," Sanders said evenly, intent on salvaging something he could not define but felt strongly, some sense of fairness, some dim illusion of brotherhood, "except if you make

[137]

us your enemies." And then he walked out of the bar, his ears ringing with "Ofay! Motherfuckin ofay!"

*　*　*

It was the kind of party his parents gave often in that flat, the last they had lived in in Paris and his favorite by far, and that party he remembered best, or was it really remembering the worst? On the Left Bank, high on the eighth floor of an old ivory-colored building near La Motte-Picquet, not far from the Invalides, it was a splendid flat of eight high-ceilinged sprawling rooms most of which, in spring and summer, looked out into the lit candles and green leaves of great old chestnut trees over whose tops one could see the crown of the Eiffel Tower. The party had begun late, after he was in bed and supposed to be fast asleep, and it had gone on all the night well into the early morning hours. Even if he had wanted to sleep, and he had tried, playing the game of dropping the curtains on all sides of the four-poster bed so that there would be less light and so he could make believe he was really in his own little private hut, they would have awakened him with their noise. There was too much loud music and singing, talking and arguing, there was too frequent smashing of glass and crockery, and people kept stumbling drunkenly into his room looking for the *pissoir*. Sometimes one of them would pick up the bed curtains to see who was sleeping inside and he always pretended he was asleep, keeping his eyes tightly shut until they'd gone away because he didn't want to talk to them, didn't want to be led out to be shown to the company and to see his mother and father, as had happened too often before; he even tried hard not to breathe because he hated the smells of wine and brandy, cigars and cigarettes they brought into his bed with them.

The sky outside was beginning to gray when it was all over and the final flurry of drunken voices had been cut off by the slammed door, and Elliott heard only his father's voice, loud and jocose with drink, contending with his mother's, penetrating and peevish with fatigue. They made no effort to keep their voices down, and someone, the last stumbling drunk who had opened his bedroom door and, not bothering to flick on the light, had considerately urinated

[138]

on the rug and then departed, leaving the door ajar so that Elliott could hear them all the more clearly in the salon.

"Lovett," his mother said crossly, "the war is only months, maybe even weeks, away. We've got to leave. We've got to take Elliott home." By the tight meticulous way she talked, Elliott knew that she had been waiting all through the party, all night, to talk to him.

"Home?" He heard the clinking of glass against decanter that meant his father was having still another nightcap. "Where's that, the ancestral acres in Connecticut?"

"Anywhere in the United States will do. It doesn't have to be Connecticut, if you don't like it there. New York, Boston, Washington would do. Anywhere you say, but in America."

"I'd like to stay in Europe."

"There's going to be a war." His mother's voice rose shrilly.

"I know, my dear. I've been predicting it. Probably in the fall, after the harvest."

"Then you know the risks."

"I want to see it. I missed the last one and I want to see this one. I believe in this war. Hitler is a pestilence they should have stopped long ago and now they're going to have to stop him, they've got to be brave in spite of themselves, and I want to see how and if they can. I want to be a part of it."

"Don't read me one of your editorials, Lovett!"

"Please don't pace like that, Marian. It makes me nervous. Sit down and have a drink."

"You want to deprave me, Lovett, you really do. Make me into a drunkard . . ."

"Only a connoisseur of fine wine, let us say." Elliott heard the labored humor in his father's voice.

In the silence, he got out of bed, put his slippers on and went silently to the door, feeling the squish of the wet rug beneath his soles and smelling the ammonialike stink. He saw his mother, her face livid and drawn, but his father was hidden by the chair he was sitting in, hidden except for the long crossed legs and the top of his head.

"Why, Lovett, why?"

"I'd like to see you enjoy something, Marian, anything. Wine, sex, food, anything, not watch the corners of your mouth turning downward more and more every day, your face perpetually disappointed and disapproving. Is that depraving you?"

"You'd like me to do as you do, live as you do."

"Why not, don't you get bored this way?"

His mother nodded. "Yes, I get bored and lonely and wrought up and resentful, but I'm not like you, not like that."

"If you know that"—his father's voice was not jocose now—"then why can't you let me be? Accept that I'm not like you either, that I'm this way and need to be."

"Why did you marry me, Lovett? You knew what I was like."

"I thought you'd change, that I'd be able to change you. Besides I didn't really know what I was like myself then. I thought you'd be different and therefore that I'd be different, it would be different after we were married."

"But it wasn't?"

"You know it wasn't, Marian, you're not disposed that way, not interested."

"Not passionate, not sexual enough? Is that it again? Is that always it?"

"Do you think it goes away? That's an everyday matter and time doesn't improve such things, it makes them worse."

"Isn't there anything else that counts with you? A home? Companionship? Children?"

"That wasn't what I was looking for," his father replied stubbornly. "I'm a newspaperman. I wanted change and travel and excitement, yes, excitement."

"Victims and vicious rumors and underhanded political deals! Assassinations and briberies and embezzlements and smuggling! Strange hotels and drinking and cheap whores! Is that what excitement is for you?"

"Yes, those too. They're part of my business, part of my life. I should have let you marry John Ballinger, good, staid, responsible John C. Ballinger, Attorney-at-Law, and left you in that nice comfortable dull, dull, dull big house in Connecticut."

"That would have been kinder."

"Kinder! Goddam it, Marian, I'm not kind, people are not kind, the world isn't kind. Kinder! When we met, I loved you, passionately, yes, sexually, the only way I knew how to love anybody, and I wanted you. I didn't want to be kind to you."

"Yes, you wanted me as you've wanted every skirt that ever walked by. Wanted! To you that word means only one thing: to fuck!"

"Marian!"

"What's the matter, Lovett, are you shocked that I know the word? Do you think I don't know all those words because I don't toss them around casually the way your companions do? Do you think I learned nothing in Connecticut before you, or that you've taught me nothing yourself after a dozen years of marriage? Or don't you like such words on your own wife's chaste lips?"

His father's voice was weary. "Let's go to bed, Marian. We're both overtired and saying things we don't mean, that we'll regret in the morning."

"Let's go to bed, let's have a drink, let's make love, your solutions to everything. It's because we're tired that we're saying the things we mean. At least I am and maybe you should be too."

"Five o'clock in the morning is not a sensible time to make important discussions the order of the day."

"You're going to decide now, Lovett. You don't have much choice, in fact. *Force majeure* is what it is, that phrase you love so much I can almost identify your dispatches or your broadcasts by it. I've booked passage for the three of us on the *Île de France*. It leaves in ten days. If you want to come, fine; if not, we're going without you." It was an ultimatum.

His father stood up and Elliott saw how stern and forbidding he was. "You've really done it this time, Marian, you've really gone and done it."

His mother rose out of her chair to defy him. "I'm taking that boy home. I want him out of this war, out of this dreadful, corrupt, wicked country. I want him to grow up in his own land, speaking his own language, going to school with his own people."

"And if I refuse to let you go, stop you from taking Elliott?"

"You won't, Lovett, you won't. I know you too well for that. You're

[141]

too damn selfish to keep him yourself. He'd get in the way of your precious prostitutes and parties and political conventions. Besides you never wanted him anyway. Right from the beginning you wanted to be the only child in this family, all by yourself, petted and catered to, and my wanting to have a child, this one and others, dethroned you. You never forgave me for that. You never forgave Elliott. That's what it was, wasn't it?" Her words lashed him and he shrank back before he recovered himself.

"No, I *didn't* want him. I didn't want children altogether. I wanted another kind of life—not kitchen, kirk and kids. And I didn't want that kind of life for myself alone either, I wanted it for you too—"

"Yes, Lovett, I know, you wanted to lead me out of New Canaan to old Canaan, Moses leading his willing flock to the promised land, out of the Goshen suburbs into the greater worlds and greener fields of Paris and London and Berlin."

"But that doesn't mean that I don't love Elliott *now*. It doesn't mean that I don't want him with me *now*."

His mother's voice was iron, gray. "Then, if you want him, if you want me, come home with us. *Now*."

"I can't do that, Marian, and you know I can't."

"Can't?"

"This is where I belong. I'm thirty-five years old and that's getting on for a newspaperman in the field. The big boys afterwards will be the ones who see this war through and cover it. And I know it better than most, the issues, the problems, the people. I've watched it grow up all the way from Manchuria and the Reichstag fire. I want to see it finished."

"You're not staying to advance your career, Lovett, I know you better than that. You're staying for the same reason you chase chippies. You want to see what's going to happen."

"And you don't?"

"I *know* what's going to happen. Death and destruction, murder and pillage and conquest. And I want my son out of it."

"You can't take him out of the world."

"No, but I can take him out of France, away from Europe."

"Even at the price of leaving your husband behind, of breaking up your marriage?" He reached out for her, but she slipped away, backed off.

"You know your own treasured Emersonian motto, the one you repeat so proudly at every opportunity?"

"Take what you want and pay for it!"

"Right. You've always used and touted that New England apothegm, Lovett, but you're one of those who know the price of everything but the value of nothing. You've taken what you wanted, now you start paying for it. *Force majeure.*"

They stood there like duelists, the drinks in their hands, until his father in a blind fury smashed his glass against the wall, splintering and splashing everything. His mother's hand went up to her cheek and when she took it away a small trickle of blood flowed down the side of her face. Their son's gasp must have startled them for they turned wide-eyed together to stare at him. He met their eyes, one set at a time, and then quietly, weeping inside but giving them no sign of it, he turned his back on them, closed the bedroom door behind him and walked across the damp carpet to his bed.

❊ ❊ ❊

In the weeks that followed the meeting with Peter King, Sanders' days took on a routine both lonely and difficult. Usually he spent the mornings at the office going through the morgue, reading, looking at photos, making notes, reviewing his own notebooks and dispatches from Vietnam. In the afternoons he got into the car and drove all over the city and the Bay Area, talking to anyone who would talk to him, except officials and newspapermen. He talked to businessmen at lunch in posh restaurants on Nob Hill, to suburban housewives and office workers shopping at Gump's and I. Magnin's, to Tenderloin panhandlers and Sixth Street hookers, hippies in the Haight-Ashbury and ex-beatniks in North Beach, to fishermen down at the Marina and to longshoremen on the Oakland and Alameda docks, to barbers and shoeshine boys and taxi drivers, to soldiers at the Presidio and to sailors and fliers from Alameda and Moffett naval air bases, to grocers and tailors and small pawnbrokers living off the heartbreak and desolation of the poor, to the Chinese on

Grant Avenue, to Japanese and Mexicans, to Negroes in the Fillmore, out on Hunter's Point, and in Oakland, slums all. The more he heard and saw, read and thought, the more he was driven to the libraries to remedy his ignorance, about the Oriental Exclusion Act, about the American missionaries' role in China, Hay's "Open Door" and Teddy Roosevelt's maneuvering for a Far Eastern balance of power that did not exclude the United States when he negotiated the Treaty of Portsmouth ending the Russo-Japanese War and sowed the seeds of Japanese resentment to bloom at Pearl Harbor. He had to learn about the civil-rights movement and went back to Marcus Garvey, Nat Turner, W.E.B. DuBois, Malcolm X. He was forced to try to work out some solution to the problem of America's ethnic variety, its lamp beside the golden door to the melting pot which did not melt, its brutal treatment of Indians, Mexicans, Orientals, Irish, Italians, Jews—but most of all Negroes—and could not. He found himself in a technological-economic maze of the new industrial revolution: automation and atomic power and the problems of cities for which no adequate plan, no adequate housing, education, policing, transport and tranquility had yet been devised. He saw the American naïveté and commitment to the pursuit of moral ends in politics and the American *realpolitik* of the pursuit of power and purchase and how both the politicians and the press had confused the minds of the people on which was which and, ultimately, also confused themselves. He saw the intricate network of personal ambition and greed continually cloaked in high-minded morality, and everywhere the corruption, the fix, the kickback, the payoff. He saw the confusion of ends and means, of private interest and public weal, and he understood why such things as Manifest Destiny and the Monroe Doctrine and the rollback of Communism appealed and were both sincere and hypocritical.

In short, he shook hands with his country once more, in older and more mature ways, and found he loved and hated it, for over everything hung the specter of war, the sparks of stars that flared in such dark places as Vietnam that might suddenly burst into a conflagration that would turn all the heavens into flame. And he found its violence and pacificism, its isolationism and one-worldism were also his heritage. What continued to amaze him was not only how much

America had changed in the years that he'd been away, but how little he now knew of his own country and his own people—and yet how much. That he could approach his own native land as if he were a stranger did not surprise him, seeing it through another vision, probably astigmatic, but surely different. It was an advantage he had exploited in other countries too, to the fullest in France as an American, but in Algeria as a Frenchman and as an American, in England as a Frenchman and as an American, for examples, but more often than he liked to admit he found himself in a strange land without the empathic eyes or the sympathetic heart, without either the sensitive ear that heard the popular feeling beneath the words or the sensitive finger that felt the popular pulse as in Japan or in Bulgaria where the faces, the hearts, the language were closed to him. But if he loved America and France, as he did, and England too, for that matter, he was, he knew, and his reacquaintance with his native hearth more than ever convinced him, a man without a country, a man of the world, rootless perhaps but no longer parochial. Neither his father nor his mother had given him what they had hoped; he'd taken what they would have considered the worst of both their worlds, yet he could console himself that it had given him some of the distinguishing marks he had as a journalist, distinguishing him not only from others in the clan but from Lovett Carpenter Sanders.

When Sanders remained in the office he took his lunch at his desk though he knew it was resented. He had overheard the comments being made, deliberately within earshot, about big-time correspondents being too stuck-up to talk or lunch or drink with the local working press. That disturbed him, but not too much, because his position there was as anomalous as his position in France on the magazine; he was not and couldn't really be one of the boys in either place. More important, he knew that one of the downfalls of newspapermen was journalistic incest, seeing, listening, talking to other newspapermen until you had the official view, the professional sunglasses that sometimes, often, made you miss the sun for the glare. Most important, he knew it was a reflection of the chief anomaly of his professional life, that his parents had inoculated him, unwillingly but effectively, against the two most powerful forces he saw in the life around him, personal greed and nationalist fervor, his father by forcing him to leave home and live abroad and learn languages and different ways of life, his mother by leaving him enough money to cover his foreseeable needs and the ethical residue of her stern religiosity.

Late one evening as he sat at the typewriter trying to make sense of what he'd seen and heard that afternoon, and to put it down simply and accurately—a blue-chalked graffito on the wall, TODAY IS GOD DAY: CELEBRATE! and another Telegraph Avenue one, WAR IS GOOD BUSINESS; INVEST YOUR SONS! had disturbed him deeply—Needham spoke to him. He'd come in without Sanders' noticing him, and leaning his muscular body against the doorframe, his suntan deeper than before, he looked more like a tough circus acrobat than a newspaper publisher but his shrewd light eyes were inquisitive. "Hello, Elliott," he said, "you've been burning a lot of midnight oil, they tell me. And doing the overtime bit. And not even asking for extra cash. What do you want to do, bring the Guild down on my neck?"

Sanders leaned back in his chair, stretching and barely stifling a yawn. "Trying to get things to make some sense to me," he finally said.

"They don't often these days, do they?"

"Not much. Not yet."

"Gave me a start, you sitting there like that, just like your old man in Paris. Only usually come now he'd be through with news-hawking and phone calls and ready for the evening's serious business: drinking and dames." Needham paused. "You making any headway?" he asked. It was clearly courteous curiosity; Needham was not hurrying him or jogging his hand.

"A little, I think," Sanders replied hesitantly.

"When you get a little more, cue me in, will you?"

"You're the boss," Sanders said but it didn't sound the way he'd meant it to and the disappointment flickered across Needham's face. Needham asked if he'd had dinner and offered to take him home for potluck with Sheila and, sensing Sanders' reluctance, added, "That is, if you haven't got a date or a girl."

"No date, no girl."

"No girl?" Needham looked skeptical. "You've been here long

enough, haven't you?" He smiled. Sanders thought of Beth and
Laura and, for a single instant, Elaine, then simply shook them out
of his mind.

Needham's fire-engine-red Corvette roared out of the parking lot
like a jet and Sanders was hard put to keep up with him. He followed in his own car at a respectful distance and went faster than
he liked to keep Needham in sight. A twenty-minute drive from the
paper, their route rose gradually from bay land and marsh up
through rolling yellowing grassland and chaparral into the foothills
until Needham soared up through a canyon on a narrow road that
wound through stands of oak and laurel, tall and austere, to where
a modern redwood house with a flat white crushed-stone roof and
expanses of glass window jutted from a ridge. Against the orange sky
left by a sun that had just dropped beyond the mountains into the
Pacific, the house was strikingly silhouetted. Sheaves of salvia, glad-
iolus and roses, all in bloom, were planted along the path, and beyond them in the doorway of the house Sheila Needham waited. A
strawberry blonde gone sandy gray, she would have looked washed-
out but for bright makeup and a colorful Hawaiian muumuu. After
greeting Needham with a perfunctory kiss and hug, she turned and
gripped his shoulders and appraised him in the failing light. "So,
you're Lov Sanders' boy," she said. "You look like him, in a way,
profile, but full-face more like your mother, I think." Catching his
surprise, she went on, "You didn't know I knew your parents but I
did. In the old days, in Paris. Didn't Jim tell you?" She looked scathingly at Needham as she led them into the house and Sanders wondered now even more why Needham had hired him, what obscure
or not so obscure impulse had impelled him. A comfortable, conventionally furnished living room with two walls of glass overlooked
the flatlands, and below, the first evening lights, like distant dande-
lions in a meadow, shone yellow and small.

"What a marvelous view," Sanders exclaimed, watching those
lights glimmer, feeling lonely and melancholy, wondering if Beth
was in bed with Prescott.

Sheila Needham hadn't heard him because she was standing at
a fully stocked bar stirring a pitcherful of ice-cold martinis with a
long glass rod. "Marti?" she asked. "I make the best in the county."

Needham sank into a wing chair, shaking his head to her invitation, suddenly subdued and saddened. "It is a good view, isn't it?" he asked, as if he needed to be reassured that it was. "I planned it for a long time before we bought this piece of land and had the house built."

"But you'll have one, won't you, Elliott?" Sheila Needham asked. "To keep me company? I hate drinking alone and Jim is such a spoilsport. I think he'd like to have me in the WCTU. 'Lips that touch liquor shall never touch mine.' It didn't used to be like that, did it, darling?" She was too eager and coquettish so that her anger showed beneath and Needham shrank back into the wing chair, looking pained and smaller.

Sanders agreed to have a "marti" and was rewarded with a smile so dazzling that for a flashing instant he saw how beautiful Sheila Needham must have been when young.

"Good! Chip off the old block," she applauded. "I never saw your father turn down a drink or a good time. Always full of jokes, making people laugh and enjoy themselves. A great guy, wasn't he, Jim?"

"Yep. A great drinker and carouser, full of piss and vinegar," Needham confirmed, but the tone belied his concurrence.

Cold and wet, the glass Sheila gave him chilled and burned his fingertips while he remembered his father, drunk, making funny faces and sounds, cavorting and leaping to get him to smile, calling him all the while "old sobersides."

Sheila raised her glass and toasted Paris and Sanders drank to that willingly. Though San Francisco thought of itself as the Paris of the Pacific, Sheila said she missed the original, the one and only City of Light. Or perhaps she was only fooling herself, she added sadly, and what she missed simply was her youth. She began to reminisce about the parties, the drinking, the lovemaking, and her face aglow seemed once more that of the young beautiful girl she had obviously been. She'd been a newspaperwoman herself, she told him, on the old Paris *Herald*, and a damn good one too. That last she directed belligerently at Needham who grew increasingly uncomfortable. And that's where she'd met old Lov Sanders and what a love he'd been. Needham interrupted her several times to ask when dinner would be ready and again to admonish her about her third "marti," but she blithely ignored him until, excusing himself, he said he'd see how dinner was faring.

Sheila watched him walk out of the room, her face a confusion of contempt and affection, and when he'd gone, she said softly, "He's always looking over my shoulder, always telling me not to do this or not to do that, as if he were my father. Goddam, that was why I left home in the first place, because I didn't like that. And he's as jealous and horny as a June bug."

"Are June bugs jealous?" Sanders asked, his face hot, reaching for the second martini she was offering him.

Sheila giggled and took a fourth for herself. "Dunno. Jim Needham sure is. You should have seen him in Paris, with Lov and the gang. Jim and I were sort of going together, not bedding down yet, mind you, but we had what used to be called an "understanding.' God, he used to try to chaperone me like a housemother with a randy sorority girl. Your father and mother had been married for years by then and you were three years old and cute as a button." She gargled her martini and swallowed most of it. "I wanted to see you, see what you looked like, but Lov would never bring me to your flat. We had a little thing going, in spite of old Jim's bed check, and Jim suspected it, maybe even Marian did, though she'd never try to find out the way Jim did. He couldn't find out either, never prove anything. Jim doesn't know to this day and don't you go and tell him either!" She waved her empty glass commandingly at him before pouring herself another martini. "So I surprised Lov one afternoon when he was walking you in the pram in the Luxembourg Gardens and he was furious at first, but only at first, then he kissed me and let me hold you."

So Sheila Needham had been his father's mistress. It was an odd feeling sitting there looking at this middle-aged, faded woman, her body thick, her face slack with drink, the tiny sequin sparkles of some curious eye shadow glittering on her lids, trying to remember that she had once been quick and passionate to his father's touch, young and beautiful. Half a dozen women had been pointed out to him before who were reputed to have been his father's bedmates— even Elaine had taken a perverse joy in pointing one out one day

[149]

when they were meeting some friends at the George V bar—and he had actually met two or three others personally, but, except for Nathalie Blanchot, Sheila Needham was the first to tell him to his face, so that he was really sure. Or was he?

"Lov was the most exciting man I ever knew, the most—so full of life." Her eyes filled with tears and for a few seconds her moving lips made no sounds. "It's hard to believe he's dead."

"He's dead all right," Sanders said flatly, putting his martini down quickly because his hand was trembling.

"Yes," she said, stifling a sob, "he *is* dead."

When Needham returned to announce that dinner was ready, she had already regained her composure; her eyes were red, she had finished her martini, and had still another in hand which she took with her to the dinner table. Linens, china and silver shone in the candlelight, the wine bottles glowed red and gold, and next to each of their plates was a single blood-red rose, a Don Juan, Sheila informed him mischievously. The meal, served by an elderly Mexican woman, was superb: crêpes enclosing small Bay shrimps, tournedos Rossini, tiny pommes de terre soufflées, green salad full of sliced calavos, chilled Spanish melon and *fraises des bois* in kirsch. It was like eating again in Paris and the taste of it made him long to be there once again. When, finally, Needham brought out cigars and a crusted bottle of Napoleon brandy, Sanders said, "That's the best meal I've had in the States, as good as, better than, the view."

"Sheila's a marvelous cook, isn't she?" Needham inquired, his face flushed with wine and pleasure.

"Jim married me for two reasons only, Elliott: I'm a good cook and I'm good in bed," Sheila proclaimed.

"Sheila!" Needham delivered the reprimand primly.

"Sheila!" she echoed. "It's true, isn't it, Jim?" But her face pleaded for him to say that there was more to it, that he loved her, needed her, and his silence brought the frustration and pain plainly to her eyes. Sardonically, then, Sheila said she was leaving them to their brandy and cigars while she went to the kitchen to direct Alicia with the cleaning up. Sanders was more comfortable alone with Needham, the tension in the room relaxed, and they sat back in their respective wing chairs, silently smoking and sipping cognac.

[150]

As he held the brandy snifter up, watching the play of light in the fluid, Sanders was reminded of Laura's toothpaste-rimmed balloon glass and the sparkle of Sheila Needham's silver-sequined eyelids and was made melancholy by both.

"I'm pleased you came to dinner," Needham said, breaking the silence. "We don't see enough people. At least Sheila doesn't. And that's bad for her."

"The 'martis'?"

"The 'martis,'" Needham affirmed.

Another silence settled, filled with the aromas of brandy and cigar smoke, before Needham said, "You look so like your father, Elliott, it's disconcerting. You talk like him and sometimes you make a gesture and I'm back there in Paris with him, sitting in an office or a bar, or a cathouse, or waiting in the Quai d'Orsay for an announcement. But I've just finished reading your last six months' dispatches from Vietnam and they don't read like Lovett Sanders at all, not at all."

"Our styles are different."

"You know that's not what I mean. You can read your hatred of war, your horror and disgust with it, in every line of every article. Patriotism, honor, *esprit de corps* don't exist there. No human sacrifice, no personal courage, no ideals, however small or personal, no aspect of policy makes up for the destruction, for the wanton use of power, for the *machtpolitik*"—he pronounced it so that it sounded like *make politics*—"nothing changes things or, if I can use such an old-fashioned term, ennobles them. Lov didn't see things quite like that."

"Did you read the French, Jim?" Sanders asked, knowing he was deliberately being evasive.

Needham shook his head. "My French is rustier than a San Joaquin irrigation pipe in spring, but I got some Xeroxes and Sheila did the translating for me. Kept her busy for a little bit and she had fun doing it. *She* liked your stuff. She's got a flair for languages, like she has for cooking and . . ." He left the sentence unfinished. He was silent, as if waiting for a rebuttal, before he spoke up again. "It wasn't that I didn't have confidence in you, Elliott. I wanted to see what you had to say about that goddam war." There was no apology in his tone. "I gave you the job only half because you were Lov Sanders' son. The other half was because you had a good idea, and the right experience, and I thought it was about time somebody did it. But I don't want to see the guys out there dying made into devils and the guys carrying picket signs made into saints."

"Did I make them devils?"

"Kee-rist! Montagnards carrying VC heads and cutting off ears so they get paid by the piece. ARVNs torturing prisoners with bamboo splints under the nails and the water treatment. Aussies beating the hell out of pajamaed peasants to get information. Marines gunning down prisoners and soldiers burning villages and fliers burning and bombing innocent farmers with napalm."

"That's the way it is, Jim. It's a dirty war."

"All wars are dirty."

"You get no quarrel with me about that." He gulped the brandy and was grateful for its burn. "But this war's different, Jim, the wrong war, the wrong place, the wrong time, the wrong enemy, the wrong ally, the wrong tactics and strategy. . . . Wrong. All wrong."

"Okay," Needham replied, "it's a dumb war and we shouldn't be there, never should have gone in in the first place. Leave the goddam French to dummy up their own railroads and banks and rubber plantations. But isn't there anything in it, any human virtue at all, bravery, sacrifice, intelligence, love of buddies, love of one's own soil, religion, defense of family, anything that redeems even a small fraction of it? In your father's reporting, no matter where he was, he'd have caught some of that, felt some of it all the time."

Où sont les guerres d'antan? The Place des États-Unis once more. The stainless-steel Sun Yat-sen and the bronze plaque to the Chinese-American dead in that postage-stamp Chinatown park. And George Christiansen on a Saigon sidewalk. How did you say that either man would be obsolete or war had to be made obsolete? How did you say an era was over and no new era would even begin unless the slaughter stopped? Not better red than dead; but better men than cinders.

"Your father was my friend," Needham continued after a time, "and a good friend too. When I didn't have too many friends. We had disagreements, lots of them, but I admired him and I respected him. Envied him too, that gifted sonofabitch. He had an ear for languages, he knew history and economics, and he understood what made people and politicians—and they're a different breed of skunk, believe me—tick. And because of those things after a while he had the right connections too. A hell of a good newspaperman. Guts, brains, ingenuity, style, what we used to call in those days *class*. And integrity: he called them the way he saw them. A tough man too; if you got in his way, absolutely ruthless, didn't give any quarter and didn't give a damn."

"I know."

Needham was brought up short. "How?" he asked.

"I got in his way."

Needham thought about that for a while, then nodded. "You know what his motto was? 'Take what you want and then pay for it!' He'd make it sound better by telling you it was a quotation from Ralph Waldo Emerson—that snooty bastard!—but he meant it all the same. Try to beat him to a story or out of a girl and—pow! he was after you like a tiger. He wanted them all, or almost all, so he made a raft of enemies. He must have boarded more broads by himself than all the rest of the Paris press corps together. And he got more exclusives than the rest of them combined too."

"I'm not like Lovett Carpenter Sanders in those things either," Sanders said curtly.

"The dames? You mean you don't like 'em?"

"No, I'm not a fag," Sanders replied grimly. "I've had my share, like anyone else, I suppose, and one wife, but I don't play it like a game, with a scorecard, or like a war, with skirts painted on my fuselage for every one I've shot down."

"Neither did your father!" Sheila interrupted from the doorway. She strode into the room as if she were charging the net at tennis. "He wasn't like that, not at all. And Jim knows that too. Lov *liked* every woman he ever went to bed with and he was kind to them, good to them and for them. And every one of them stayed his friend, even after the affair was over."

"Quite an achievement," Sanders said sarcastically.

"It is quite an achievement and you're just too young to know it," she shot back.

[153]

Needham's mouth opened like a gaffed fish gasping for air, then his lips closed into a thin severe line. Looking down at his burning stub of cigar and rotating the brandy in his snifter, he said huskily, " 'Take what you want and pay for it.' "

"He paid," she said.

"Others paid too," Sanders said, pitying himself, his mother.

"Others always do," Needham added.

"But *he* paid with his life," Sheila insisted passionately.

With his wife, Sanders thought silently.

"No, with his death, Sheila," Needham said. "Other people pay with their lives." He held her gaze for a long time before she turned away.

✽ ✽ ✽

The message read that Mrs. Christiansen asked him to dinner at seven but that if he couldn't make it to call, otherwise to come right ahead. Sanders' first impulse was to tear up the little blue slip and drop it into the wastepaper basket, then to sit down at the typewriter and try to get down what he'd seen in the East Oakland slums that day where he'd gone to search out Peter King. But the nausea was already in his mouth and throat and he knew that reliving what he'd seen and heard that day, which was what he'd have to do to put it down right on paper, would make him throw up.

And he still didn't know where King was. The boy who came to the door of the apartment and held it slightly ajar was naked except for a pair of white Lastex bathing trunks that bulged and his pale yellow skin and girlish Caucasian features were streaming sweat: He couldn't have been more than seventeen and was a queen. "You lookin fer somebody?" he asked, his voice so high-pitched that automatically Sanders pitched his own voice even deeper.

"Peter King. This is where he lives, isn't it?"

"Sometimes," the boy lisped, "but he's not heah now. You wanna come in an wait fo him?" He threw the door open with a grand effeminate gesture to reveal the jumble of heaving bodies on the floor, four or five of them, shades of black and brown, yellow and tan, naked and pulsing. "We ballin'," he remarked too casually. "You wanna jine us?" His voice even higher, he had remarked on the hesitation. "Whattsamatta, man, you chickenshit?" Then, laughing wildly, he slammed the door in Sanders' face.

Although she wore dark glasses, Sanders knew immediately from the huskiness of her voice that she'd been crying and for quite a long time. In the backyard, in the late-afternoon sunshine, ashen clouds like schools of flat gray fish swam high in the heavens, but Sanders could not clear his mind of what he'd seen in the Negro slums that afternoon, of what he'd met in Peter King's flat, and how little her tears, or his own, or any tears, meant in the light of that. Beth took off her glasses so he could see her red eyelids, her lashes wet and pasted together, her whole face tear-streaked and drawn, yet he could muster no sympathy. All he could think of was what did she want, yet he was sure she would shortly tell him just that and he didn't really want to know. Elaine, he realized, had made him permanently wary and cynical about tears. Beth dabbed at her eyes with a small handkerchief before saying, hoarsely, "George's body is here."

"Where?" he said, leaping from the chair.

Hysterically she laughed. "Not here in the house, but in the city. They called last night and then I phoned Mr. Christiansen this morning."

"I thought you two weren't talking."

"We're not. We weren't. We talked all right. Had to."

"What about?"

"The burial."

"That should be easy to arrange."

"It isn't. That's why I called you. I thought you'd talk to him, persuade him."

"Of what?" Christiansen was not a man easily persuaded, of anything. "Besides, Beth, I've got a job and Livermore's half a day's driving to and from."

"He's not there any more, he's been transferred to the veterans' hospital here in town."

"Isn't that unusual?"

"No, it just usually means the case is terminal."

"You mean he's going to die."

"That's what I said," she replied irascibly.

"Then why not ask Prescott to talk to him?"

"Steven's away."

"So you called me. Second-fiddle Elliott. Where is the good doctor?"

"At a surgical conference in Texas."

"I see."

She jammed the dark glasses back on her face. "No," she said, "you don't see. You don't see anything—except your news stories and your hippie girls."

The wicker chair creaked as he stood up and walked toward the house.

"Don't go," she called after him, her voice breaking. "Please. I'm sorry. I didn't mean that."

Sanders turned. "You meant it, Beth, just as Dr. Fat Mouth meant it when he—accidentally, I'm sure—turned up at the flat that night and—accidentally, too—mentioned Laura to you."

"Laura?"

"My hippie," he replied, the phrase ludicrous and painful.

But Beth had other things on her mind. "Please, Elliott, I need your help. I want to bury George in our family vault. My people have a private burial ground," she added apologetically. "That's where he belongs. He's my husband. But his father says no, he wants George buried in an Army cemetery, the way he's going to be buried, the way so many Christiansens have been buried. He'd like Arlington, I guess, but he'll settle for the Presidio."

"Is that so unreasonable?"

"I don't give a damn whether it is or not," she shouted. "I hate their goddam war! Do you understand? I hate it. They killed George and I don't want them to have his body."

"Does it really matter to you where he's buried? George is dead. Or do you just want to get back at the old man?"

"I'd rather see him dead."

"The old man's going to be dead soon, very soon. He's dying of leukemia. You know that."

"The quicker the better."

"Beth!"

"I mean it. I hope he dies. I hope he dies tonight, now. If not for him, George would still be alive. What did he care about George anyway? He didn't even like him. Or want him. Or acknowledge him

[156]

as a son. And he never treated him like a son. He only cares now because it fits his crazy notion about his family tradition. Fighting. Killing. Bravery. Medals. 'We tamed the country. We protected the people. We crossed the mountains and hunted the buffalo and killed the Indians and defeated the Spaniards and took this country with our bare hands.' " Her voice glided between a rhetorical boom and a dramatic whisper. "That great soldier was never home. He almost never saw George until George was grown up, never helped him, never gained his confidence. And after George's mother died and the legal authorities made him responsible for George, made him make a household for George, he put a roof over his head, that's all, never made it a home, just sent him to school, that's all. When they made him do those things the old man wouldn't even talk to George. The perfect father. When George was going to high school, once a week, regularly, the old man would leave him a single dollar bill in the refrigerator. *In the refrigerator!* That miserable, coldhearted, tightfisted man. One dollar for lunch he never even handed to a teen-aged son. Is that the kind of father whose wishes should concern me? Why should I give a damn, one single damn, what Joseph Farnum Christiansen wants? The Army didn't call him, they called me. George's wife. I can do what I want. What *I* want." She was shaking so badly Sanders thought she would faint.

He asked if she had any tranquilizers and if he could get her one, but she said that she had none left and Steven Prescott wouldn't give her a prescription for more, though she could have, if she had really wanted, gotten some at the hospital. Sanders resented and was grateful to Prescott simultaneously; at least neither the man nor the doctor was altogether a fool. Yet, wanting to calm her, not knowing how, and shuddering himself again with the recollection of George's broken body, trying to stop himself from visualizing it in a crate on some indifferent San Francisco pier, he knew he had to get into the open air to breathe. "Let's go for a drive," he said desperately. "I know another kind of tranquilizer that will do us both good," and as he said it he knew it for a sensible suggestion.

It was only a short drive into the foothills, then up the turning roads into the mountains. He parked on a vista point and when he had turned the engine off the silence was tangible, accentuated by the sounds of small birds, the occasional rustle in the underbrush of fox and squirrel and badger, an uncertain wind in the redwoods and the Douglas firs. Below, the valley was spread out all the way to the Bay and the bare bleak hills beyond, the grid-patterned streets and neatly laid-out groups of houses, the great looping cloverleafs of the freeways, the rigid geometric progression of fruit trees in the orchards, all so safe, secure, serene-looking that his leaping nerves seemed to quiet and no calamity seemed possible anywhere. Not even in Saigon. He stood on the bluff until Beth came up behind him and her pointing arm drew his eye to the middle distance where a great metal webbed saucer tilted upward. "The university radio telescope," she said. "It tracks space satellites." She then turned him a little to show him the university linear accelerator nearby, a huge concrete bar like an enormously elongated coffin rammed into the hillside, and his precariously regained sense of quiet evaporated, the cold vision of George returned and with it the macabre thoughts of what was left of him to put into a coffin; he was thankful that at least the coffin would be sealed.

He would have stood there longer, uneasy in the presence of those artifacts of man, especially fascinated, and remembering the article he had written for Tessier about the space efforts of all countries. There he had taken the view that the political leaders of countries encouraging and financing space travel were doing so in order to feel that some men would escape the final nuclear holocaust somewhere on the moon or another planet, once more to take up the lugubrious and magnificent history of man when the mushroom cloud settled. Tessier had, wisely, decided not to publish the article though it had unsettled him and the other staff members who'd read it. Beth took his hand and drew him past the car, away from those thoughts, and into the trees. From the way she led him it was clear that she was familiar with the terrain and knew where she was going, so Sanders tried once more to put all that darkness from his mind. He followed her up the hillside, then down an arroyo, through the still warm and fragrant shade of pine and eucalyptus, oak and acacia, until they came to the edge of a small boulder-strewn clearing. There, the smell of balsam brightening his brain, he saw the mountain stream that ran sparkling with sunlight, steely and white, and felt it cleanse his spirit. Beth let go his hand and ran ahead with a free skip, stripping off her sandals and stepping into the cold

[158]

water with an ecstatic and painful cry, splashing ahead, holding her skirts thigh-high and laughing, and for an instant young and carefree, having apparently forgotten George and the impending burial. In midstream where two great rocks divided the waters, she lay back on one of them and waited for him, her face still lit by a smile and the leafy sunshine of the glade, inviting, challenging him to follow. Slowly he drew off his shoes, tucked his socks neatly into them, and dropped them next to her sandals on the bank. He rolled up his trousers and plunged into the stream, the icy water jarring him to the base of his skull. He skittered along over rocks and gravel and sand in the stream bed and by the time he reached her and pulled himself up onto the warm stone opposite, his teeth were chattering and his feet tingling cold. "You look blue," she said. Reaching across the narrow swift rivulet that separated their rocks, she began to rub his feet with her hands, blowing her warm breath on them, then chafing each foot between her warm palms in a gesture so artless and spontaneous that he was at first embarrassed, then moved and finally aroused. He lifted her chin to kiss her, their mouths engaged and with passion he felt her warm lips and sharp teeth together. His hands groping for her found her breasts and stayed but she flinched and drew back, her parted mouth gasping, "Not here, not now." Disconsolately he let his hands fall to his sides; then, angry, he plunged them into the stream, soaking his sleeves.

"Don't be angry," she pleaded after the silence had become insupportable. "It's me, not you. When we were students, I used to come up here with Steven. I'm so mixed up now. With Steven. With George. I don't want things mixed up any more."

The water rippled through and over his fingers like leaping glacial fish. "With Steven?" he murmured, perplexed, the chill a spasm through his hands and arms.

She nodded.

"Did you know him at school?"

"We knew each other, all of us, George and Steven and me."

"And Peter King too?"

"That was later, though George knew him earlier when the Christiansens were living up in Oakland."

"What did you do up here?" he asked harshly, looking hopefully at first then despairingly into her eyes. Her mouth trembled and she seemed to be trying but unable to speak. "What did you do up here," he repeated, "fuck?"

Something convulsed in her face and she didn't seem to hear him. She was staring down at his hands and then unceremoniously, with a lunge, she seized his sleeves and tried to yank his arms out of the stream. His fingers were stiff, his wrists numb, but he resisted her, holding them underwater to spite her, to spite himself, enduring the cold pain so that it would distract him from the hot. Again and again she tried, tearing at his arms, and he held firm against her until, finally, eyes full of tears, she implored, "Please, Elliott, take your hands out."

Reluctantly then he withdrew them, strange blue-and-white appendages that ached and burned, and held them in front of him the way a surgeon who has just scrubbed awaits his sterile gloves. She made him stand and expertly slipped his jacket from his arms, carefully folding it on the rock. She squeezed the water out of his shirt cuffs, rolled his sleeves up onto his biceps so that he could no longer feel the damp, then dried his hands on her skirt, the movements skillful and practiced—a nurse. But still he couldn't stop shaking. She took both his hands in hers and huddling over them, as she'd done before with his feet, warmed them with her breath as if she might somehow breathe life and warmth back into them. Then she stepped across the small rivulet to his rock, stood against him and took both his hands and tucked them under her separate armpits. Sanders felt her first shudder as the shock of the cold tightened the hold her arms had on his hands, pressing them against her body; gradually, lingeringly, the woolen warmth of her sweater and body began to suffuse his fingers, the soft curve of her breasts where they met her chest brought his palms achingly alive once again and the beating of her blood under her armpits became a painful pulse in his own fingers.

When his hands were agonizingly prickling they made their way back downstream, through the trees and up the canyon, Beth carrying their shoes, the jacket thrown over his shoulders not warming him. Sitting on a rock near the car, shaken, drying his feet with a sodden handkerchief and putting his shoes and socks on with stiff, awkward fingers, he watched Beth slip on first one sandal and then the other, her face remote, her movements automatic, yet, standing one-legged, she was graceful and lovely as a bird, as elusive as one about to take flight. In the valley where the lights were now throbbing yellow below, the evening was falling like dark dew and all seemed serene, but still the telescope skein unseeing scanned the skies and the linear accelerator burrowed blindly into the land.

Though she offered to drive back he wouldn't permit it and he was glad because the driving warmed and steadied him, occupied him and kept him from asking the questions she had left unanswered. Under the carport the smell of the climber roses in the portico was heavy and heady and he savored them, their sweetness suddenly so poignant it brought tears to his eyes. "Come inside and have a drink," she said, eyes pleading. "You need one." Her hand was outstretched to lead him once again. Her pale face was paler, altogether without makeup now, her lips almost white, her hazel-green eyes the color of murky seawater. "Please, Elliott." He went with her but did not take her hand, nor walk with her, but he followed where she led, into the warm chinoiserie of the living room. While she went to the bar to get drinks, taking balloon glasses, an unprepared-for irony, and the brandy bottle, Sanders abandoned the living room for the green garden and the new evening dusk rife with bustling shadows. It was as if he were walking into the past from the present—escaping?—and as he sat and rocked on the edge of the hammock, his heels grazing the ground, the childish song echoed again through his memory, his mother's dim soprano singing:

When the wind blows, the cradle will rock,
When the bough breaks, the cradle will fall,
Down will come baby, cradle and all.

You tried, you risked, you got out on a limb and then—the bough broke. Inevitably, the bough broke. Was that what was happening to mankind, the boughs the radio telescope, the nuclear acclerator, the space capsule? Was that what his father had learned early and known so well and therefore grasped so greedily of his life? I've known it forever, it seems, all my life, yet other people don't, and because they don't seem happier for it.

And what had the knowledge done for him? It had been part of what had, at the very least, made him a good journalist. At most it had made him cautious and kept him a live journalist. Cautious. *I am cautious, you are timid, he is an arrant coward.* The conjugation, he knew, reflected the way he saw himself, the way his mother had seen him, and the way most scathingly his father and Elaine had seen him: an arrant coward.

In Paris and in Connecticut on that last visit his father had lamented, his own tireless lament, that there would be other wars, wars in which Elliott might fight, but in which he, Lovett Carpenter Sanders, would be too old to participate, the disappointment jagged in his voice. Then he added, spitefully, that very likely Elliott wouldn't care to fight in any wars, would pass them up anyway; his tone was snide, certain, insulting, yet it contained a genuine wistfulness, an uncertainty about himself and his life, the desire to test and define it, that only now, more than two decades and two lives removed, Sanders understood. "No, Lovett," his mother had countered, "you think that everyone who isn't always aching for extremes, longing for battle and hardship and conflict, is cowardly. You're like a small boy chasing ambulances or fire trucks. Elliott is cautious, perhaps even still a little timid—after all he's a boy and not a man—but he's no coward. Scarcely. In some ways . . . in fact, mark my words, he'll be a braver man by far than you have ever been or will be." But his mother's confident and prophetic voice had spoken before his father had gone to his death in the liberation of Paris, and he had since been in how many wars, though he had fought in none, always forcing himself to the point scout positions, always unarmed in the fighting, always blooding his editors and readers to expect words and pictures from where the fighting was hottest.

"Elliott?" Beth's voice startled him. She handed him a brandy snifter, put her fingers over his mouth and filled his nostrils with the clean astringence of eau de cologne. "Please don't talk. Just drink and get warm and listen to me. There's a coverlet in the hammock. If you're still cold, wrap yourself in it. It's very hard for me to say what I want to say, especially hard to say it to you." She paused while Sanders savored that *especially*, tormented by it, knowing it for the straw that the emotionally drowning proverbially seize. She sat down, leaning back in the wicker lounge chair, her long slender legs outstretched, the brandy bottle at her feet, and began to tell him.

The three of them had met as students at the university, though Beth and George were undergraduates when Prescott was already well along in medical school. George had achieved a brilliant high school record, although she couldn't imagine how, for he and his mother had lived like gypsies, moving all over the Bay Area in those years—San Francisco, Alameda, Oakland, San Jose, Los Altos, Berkeley—when for one reason or another the Marine allotment did not arrive in time, when George's mother had to find a new job, when George's father did not send money. They had lived from hand to mouth but it had not kept George, even with part-time jobs he worked at to help out, from being advanced several years in school, from being valedictorian of his high school class, though he borrowed a schoolmate's suit to deliver the oration, and from winning half a dozen scholarships, and from entering Stanford on one of them the second or third youngest member of the class. In that last year in high school his mother had died, swiftly and mysteriously, so that George was never sure she had not committed suicide although the doctors said it wasn't that at all and tried to explain to him what had happened. "I suspect now that it was an aortic aneurism, from what he described, but I never saw the death certificate so I don't really know, and what's important, I suppose, is that George never really believed what they told him: He was convinced that she was a suicide.

"You should have seen him then, Elliott, the first time I did, when he walked into the Commons. In the doorway with the sun behind him, its very rays emanating from his head, his body, he looked like a god. That fine profile—he'd turned his head to look for someone—that golden head of hair scintillating, his face and bare arms brown as wood because he'd worked the summer down in the valley picking melons with the Mexicans, all caught in my throat. I couldn't breathe. A line sprang into my mind that my aunt had occasionally quoted from French poetry, the kind of line I thought she'd learned at Mills forty years before from some other maiden lady teaching proper girls French verse, the kind of line I would never have thought such a repressed, warped and militant virgin would have known, and which I had never understood before, though I knew the words by heart. Suddenly, then and there, I knew what the words meant for the first time, with wonder, but with surprise that

my aunt should even have glimpsed their meaning and still continued to cherish them:

Je veux m'anéantir dans ta gorge profonde,
Et trouver sur ton sein la fraîcheur des tombeaux!

Baudelaire, Sanders thought; of all things, Baudelaire whose
flowers of evil Elaine had always thought to pluck and strew. If he
did not know what Beth had felt like, he did know what George
must have looked like, not very different from the way he had looked
when he died in Saigon, except perhaps for the crew cut and the
new, fine, but deeply etched lines of war drawn about his mouth
and eyes.

"*La fraîcheur des tombeaux,*" Beth repeated. "How prophetic!
How could I have known then that one day in the not too distant
future I would find the freshness of the tomb on his breast and so
annul my being?" She shrugged. "I didn't. I was too excited, too
upset. Instead I thought of it then as a kind of approval from the
grave—I sat there in a tizzy, anxious for him to look at me, worried
that he might find the person he was looking for, sit down with him,
or—catastrophe!—her, with anyone else but me, and wondering how
I could meet him then and there without seeming brazen.

"It sounds insane, I know, a schoolgirl crush, a Hollywood fantasy
of love at first sight, a hysterical hallucination a young girl only just
released from the prison of girls' schools and a puritanical guardian
might indulge herself in. Probably it was all those things, but it was
more. I knew even then that it wasn't love; and I didn't think it was
passion, or at least what I knew then about passion. A part of me
responded to him here"—she put her palm over her breasts—"as if he
were my brother, flesh of my flesh, blood of my blood. I knew that
if only he would lay his hands on me, I'd be healed of everything
that ailed me, as if he had some miraculous gift, some unique Queen
Anne's touch that cured the halt and the lame—of which, believe
me, I knew I was one. But if he knew me, held me, I'd be transformed, everything would change, the world would be improved,
and so would I.

"The way I describe it now is not really how I felt it then. How
can you describe such a feeling in words? As if a god had just come

[164]

into your life who would revolutionize your whole being. It's like trying to put words to a tune you dimly remember, but powerfully, from your sleep, or to a child's song your first kindergarten friend hummed in your ear, a secret from the teacher and the others. You're aware that the words don't really match or describe the tune, but you're also aware that you want to sing it to your own child or describe it to your husband"—she realized the implications of the words as she spoke them, started, but made no apology—"so that he, they, can get the feeling of it."

"I know what you mean," Sanders said, wanting to help her, and he was sure he did for how could he describe the Place des États-Unis to anyone, or the statue there and its meaning?

"Maybe," she replied, "but with a man it's different."

"Isn't it always?"

"Always," she admitted somberly and there was acceptance in her voice but no affirmation. She seemed suddenly sunk in torpor but roused herself. "And then, as by a miracle, George came and asked if the chair at my table was taken. There were other seats vacant, although the Commons was pretty crowded, but my table was at the window, almost out of his line of sight, *but he came to my table.*" A strange elation rang in her voice. "I was delighted. I knew he would talk to me and that everything would turn out fine."

"Didn't you ever ask afterwards how he came to take that seat?"

She shook her head. "I never had the courage. It was a miracle and I didn't want to know what brought him to me."

"Even though it turned out as it did?"

"Especially because it went sour. Especially. Because that was only the beginning, our beginning, and"—her face was stark in the shadows, a confusion of broken ashen gray planes—"now, soon, it's almost the end."

"The end?"

"The end is when George is buried, the bitter end, the final end."

"Not as long as you can think of him, talk about him, the way you just have," Sanders said. That was how he had kept Lovett Carpenter Sanders alive, and his mother, and John C. Ballinger, and even George Christiansen, because they peopled his mind, alive, jostling out of the recesses of his brain for his attention, and getting it. It was never *loin des yeux, loin du coeur,* for him, not even with the living: Elaine he kept alive, wherever she was, by letting her live, in his memory.

"Do you really believe that, Elliott?"

"He lives in you and his father, and—"

"And you?"

"Yes," Sanders admitted reluctantly, "and me."

Night had fallen, the moon was up and the first faint green stars stirred. In the blue-green darkness of the garden, her voice was halting, the elation altogether gone out of it. "How ironic that I imagined George's touch would perform the miracle I craved. Ironic and perhaps what I deserved. My just deserts, Aunt Katharine would have said, my desire bringing my undoing. But when George touched me, my flesh crawled and rebelled. I couldn't control it though God knows I tried and tried and tried again, but I came to dread his touch, yet I wanted to have him near me all the time."

She looked down at her outstretched legs, the planes of her face being rearranged by the play of light and shadow. "The touch, the passion, came from Steven. Yet he wasn't at all my type."

"Your type?"

"Yes, Elliott, that sounds schoolgirlish but people do have types. There are chemical mysteries, sexual mysteries, we don't understand, so we deny that anything exists of that kind. There are sexual types just the way there are blood types. If I'd only realized that then I'd have saved myself so much grief, and perhaps saved George even more. Steven appealed to me in a way George never did and probably never could. I didn't even particularly like him but when he touched me I was like a river in spring thaw."

"Am I your type?" he asked, at last, caustic and defensive.

Her eyes and mouth were hidden in shadow so he couldn't see her expression and she held the brandy glass with both hands as if it were a chalice; it was poised at her lips but not tilted so she could drink. Because she spoke half into the brandy snifter her voice was distorted in pitch and timbre. "It's because you do appeal to me, *that way,* that I'm saying these things, because your being here has made things so difficult for me."

"Difficult," he remarked. "Imagine that. Didn't Steven's arrival on the scene make things difficult too with George already there?"

Beth shifted uncomfortably in her chair, tilted the brandy glass

[166]

and sipped, then continued: "One of my favorite songs in those days was 'Night and Day.' Remember it? The two of them were like that, night and day. I met George in the Commons in bright sunshine and Steven at night in the hospital emergency room. I'd been in an automobile smashup. I drove a lot too fast in those days and so did all the kids I ran with, and they took me there. Steven was on duty. I had only one really bad cut, across my palm, of all places, but it took sixteen stitches to sew it up and Steven sewed me up." She reached her left hand across to him, palm up, and peering closely he was able to see a scar that had healed so well that now it looked like one of the natural lines of her palm except that it ran against the grain and direction of the others. "That's how it began. He sewed me up."

"He had you sewed up."

"No, Elliott, you're wrong. It was George who had me sewn up in that way."

"But you slept with both of them."

"Yes, yes. It got so I couldn't even stand the smell of George's skin. And I loved him, I really loved him. I think he must have known it after a while because he used to raise gardenias and jasmine in our garden." She was crying now, again. "He'd wait until the house was quiet and the lights were out, then he'd go out into the yard and pick a gardenia or a clump of jasmine and bring it back to bed with him. We made love in a cloud of jasmine, an aura of gardenias, the way they describe lovemaking in romantic novels, and I hated every moment, every touch, of it."

Sanders sniffed. "No jasmine or gardenia here."

"That was in another house," she sobbed, "one I sold after George went overseas, but before I sold it I tore up every one of those goddam gardenias and jasmine plants by the roots. Every single one. And I threw away every bottle of cologne or perfume that had the faintest trace of jasmine or gardenia, every cake of soap. I never want to smell those odors again."

"It must have been pretty bad," he said, trying as much to suppress his sympathies for George, his loyalties, as to express his feeling for her.

Beth laughed at him. "You don't know how bad. You don't know what it's like to spread your legs, yes, spread your legs, open yourself wide to someone whose touch nauseates you. You men and that little penis you're so goddam proud of. It's outside of you, an appendage, a tool you dig with the way some blind mole burrows into the ground, so you don't care where you put it, just so you can bury it somewhere, just so you're relieved. But you put it *into* us, into the very depths of where we live, and you leave your casual spurt *inside us* to nourish and bring to birth. . . . 'It must have been pretty bad!'

"His touch was like filthy spider webs on me and set my flesh crawling. I lay there under him gripping the sheets, choking with the musk of his body, his sweat, his hair, trying not to breathe, and drenched in his odor and the odor of jasmine or gardenias. Each time he moved into me, I went stiff. I knew he felt it and that filled me with more panic, because I didn't want to hurt him, because I loved him. So I learned to lie and cheat and feign things. I ground my teeth in a facsimile of passion to fool him and to assuage him and I bit back my vomit, and my hands tore those thick-leaved gardenias to shreds and crushed the jasmine he had brought to bed with him as I would have torn him to shreds, crushed him, if I could have."

"Then," Beth continued, her voice skirting a yowl, "came that twitch, leaping across his face like some sick thing trapped beneath his skin, some underground animal, some groundhog fighting to come up to the surface for signs of spring. I knew it was my fault, I knew it just as I knew he knew it, though he told me he'd had it before, many times, when he was a boy and his father used to beat his mother and he couldn't stop it, and then afterwards, after his mother died and his father wouldn't talk to him, after a while the twitch would go away. But this time it didn't and I hated myself, and I hated him, and when I saw that twitch I wanted to tear it out of his bones with my nails."

So the tic had come from where it had to come from, way back in the womb of George's pain. He felt an intense sticking pain through the scars of his wounds and drew his breath in sharply through his teeth.

She misconstrued that. "So now you understand a little more and it doesn't seem so simple after all." She tilted the brandy glass and drank, then ran her tongue over her lips as if she could not keep her lips moist. "If he'd been my first lover, I might have thought *it* was like that, that *it should* be like that, that Aunt Katharine was right and that *it* was all men wanted from you but that *it* was ugly and disgusting, degrading and demeaning, and you weren't supposed to enjoy *it*, only endure *it* to have children and please your husband. But George *wasn't* my first—"

"Who was?" he interrupted, the jealousy naked in his voice.

"You want it all, Father, the I-have-sinned, the confession from the beginning?"

"I'm not your father confessor," he said.

The silence between them was charged and in the shadows her eyes were those of a jungle cat about to spring. "What difference does it make?" she asked finally, not speaking to him but to the moon and stars. "A friend of my father's, Bill Daulton, William really, but no one dared call him Bill except me, when I wanted to tease him or make him angry."

"Was he a man your father's age?"

"Nothing so Oedipally simple. He was a younger friend of my father's, a banker too, very shrewd. He had a green thumb for money; everything he touched turned into money, every investment grew. My father had asked him once to look after me and my mother if anything happened to him, and Bill tried. He took that kind of promise seriously. Though I was Aunt Katharine's ward, he looked after the money, advised her on investments, and me, and very well."

"For a return?"

Her eyes narrowed. "If you think *he* seduced *me,* you're wrong. He was married and I was just about the age of his eldest daughter, so he tried to carry out his obligations as he saw them. Upright, responsible, sober, avuncular. It was *I* who seduced him. Nastily too. If what a seventeen-year-old virgin can manage can be truly called a seduction. The chemistry was right, though I didn't know it for chemistry in those days; and I was curious, hungry for experience and passion and affection. I toyed with him, teased him and, as he would put it, 'overcame his scruples.' "

"What a fine Victorian phrase."

"He was a fine Victorian gentleman; the phrase was therefore apt. A man of the old school."

"Yes, a very good old school," Sanders snapped peevishly.

"At first it was fun. It was illicit and new and he did teach me things." Her eyes sparkled. "But it turned sour because he was dull and stodgy and wanted to divorce his wife and leave his children and marry me. 'Do right by me,' he called it, that idiot! He couldn't keep his hands off and he was always coming up from Santa Barbara where he lived, hanging around on the off-chance we'd get an hour or two in bed together in some motel. But Aunt Katharine got suspicious and that was when she sent me east to boarding school. It wasn't any fun any more.

"At school I used to dream of him, my first lover, though not my first love—George was that—and occasionally he would turn up there, a sad man now, changed and older and somehow pitiful, wanting desperately to go to bed with me, kiss me, touch me, do anything for me, and spoiling the romantic memory I had of him. I hated him for that, yet I liked him too. Sometimes I let him make love to me when he came up to the school to visit and sometimes I met him in New York where he kept a *pied-à-terre*, but only after he begged and insisted. He gave me a key and when I knew he wasn't there I went there with other boys, with other men, to spite him and to please myself. Yet I dreamed about him often, I had no one else to dream about, and in dreams he was cruel to me and I kind to him; when we actually met it was the reverse: I was cruel to him and he was kind to me, so I knew it was all over, over and done with."

It wasn't any fun any more. The thrill is gone. It's all over. It was just one of those things. The cliché phrases of popular love songs, yet all true and sad, sad, sad, unarguable as their moon, June and spoon, neither tawdry nor grand, romantic nor passionate, only full of a withered bloom and a desperate hopelessness, a yearning full of tears.

"Had enough?" Beth laughed, a crippled chortle. "There's more, lot's more."

Sanders stood, his hands raised in a gesture of surrender meant to be humorous. *"Kamerad,"* he pleaded, but it wasn't funny and then he drew her up from her chair, held her, embraced her, eased her back into the hammock with him, kissing her tear-salty mouth until his lips were briny, his tongue bitter, his teeth on edge, feeling as if he had drunk the sea. The length of her body against his, the heave of her breasts and thighs, made his wounds ache, caught his scars and twisted them, but his flesh rose and yearned for her even through the still-luxuriant smell of jasmine and gardenias that pervaded his skull like a thick cloud and left, with the salt of her tears, the taste of flowers on his tongue.

It was she who finally lifted him from the hammock and in a prolonged embrace that was also a dance led him out of the garden through the house to the bedroom on the far side of it, where he had never been, leaving behind them a trail marked with discarded pieces of their clothing. And when, on the green-velvet-covered bed, she lay back and took him to her, the nipples of her breasts rose to greet him and her thighs to embrace him like old friends, and the short fall downward seemed from a great height and dizzying, and their cries locked them together as if they were caught in an avalanche that had swept them down a mountainside to death. Later, much later, when she was asleep in his arms and he lay wakeful but warmed, what she had cried out on the peak came back to him, a brutal clamor out of the mountain ravines into which they had tumbled, a screech in the eyries of his mind: "I love you," she had cried out, "I love you, George."

* * *

The dream he woke from was of Elaine and Beth and Prescott, full of the sound of *Et trouver sur ton sein la fraîcheur des tombeaux,* the smell of jasmine and gardenias, and the nightmare fury concerning his last letter to Elaine which he had mailed to their old Quai de Passy flat because he thought she had returned, not abandoned it, because he did not see her or any of the people they had known together. The letter had come back undelivered with the poetic and poignant French postmark brusquely red-inked on the heavy white linen stationery she had bought and he still had and used: *Parti sans laisser d'adresse, n'habite pas à l'adresse indiquée.* Where had she gone and why had she left no forwarding address? Though she hadn't needed the money, he'd wanted to leave her what he had if anything happened to him in Vietnam, but there'd been no way, no time to find her, then; and he had to rest content

[171]

with the fact that he had left her with everything they'd owned in that apartment, their joint checking account, and even their Peugeot.

The film of stale brandy on his teeth and tongue was bitter, his swollen mouth tasted like wet sawdust, and his wounds burned. *I love you, George:* Beth. It could as easily have been Elaine, had been in fact, though the words had been different, more scalding, and the feeling virtually identical. The intent too. His fate. Character *is* destiny, and his had shaped his fate as truly as it had shaped his father's, as it had shaped George Christiansen's.

Strange shadows moved on the walls, the glass wall glistened beyond the bed. With the portières undrawn, he could see jagged starfish shapes of andromedas, the thick-fingered blots of rhododendrons, the bell-tinkling droop of fuchsias in the garden silhouetted by the moonlight, the movement of the night wind in their leaves. Beth slept, her body in a ballet pirouette, a sleeping beauty in a fairy tale, all passion spent, and husbanded, waiting for the prince to leap the thicket and thorns, to kiss her back to life and feeling. Her long legs, slender hips, the belly scooped out flat so that the pelvic bones were stark and uncushioned, the unseeing eye of the navel stern, all seemed ready to spring out of bed into the night garden in a baleful and luminous *Spectre de la Rose.* The specter. Monique. The schoolboy phrase he had learned: *Voulez-vous faire la rose avec moi,* the resonance of boyhood romance before he had learned the harsher, realer names for it. Even then, still, no *tu-toi.* As he drew himself gently away from Beth so that he wouldn't wake her, Sanders noticed the horizontal ridged lines between the deep eye of her belly and the darkness below. Stretch marks! The stigmata of childbearing. Beth had given birth to a child, or at least been pregnant almost to term, but when and whose? *Parti sans laisser d'adresse? N'habite pas à l'adresse indiquée!* The matronly revealing lines in that otherwise youthful flesh were disturbing, moving, disappointing, yet he knew that no other explanation for them was possible: Those corrugations were the relaxed issue of skin stretched to its farthest limits to accommodate the expanding flesh of new life within.

Two

A new heart also will I give you,
And a new spirit I will put within you:
And I will take the heart of stone out of your flesh,
And I will give you a heart of flesh.

—Ezekiel

The veterans' hospital was only a quarter hour's drive from Los Pueblos, a dozen immense, low-slung buildings of modern design in sand-colored brick and white stone set in the foothills among prosperous industrial neighbors, drug, electronics and dietetic food firms in their own modern glass, brick and reinforced concrete cubes, and here and there an occasional stretch of interspersed ranch or orchard which they had not yet bought up for bulldozing and building. The hospital itself blended into the landscape, looking like any other building in the vicinity, and had it not been plainly marked, Sanders would surely have passed it by. As he was about to turn into the drive marked for visitors' parking, his eye was caught by four horses and two colts cantering up the side of a yellow hill beyond the highway, two roans, a palomino and a jet-black mare, the two colts, both bays too, gamboling around the horses as they worked their way up out of the blazing afternoon sun into the cool shade of the live oaks. Sanders stopped the car and watched them, the sweat pouring down his sides, his clothing already soaked, though he had gone back to the apartment from the paper to shower and change clothes and get the chess set, and felt his legs itching with desire to run free with those horses. Then, reminding himself that visiting hours were limited, he put the car in gear and drove into the parking lot.

The hospital was so big that it took him longer to find Christiansen's room than it had taken to drive to the hospital from his flat. Christiansen was in a room that had only two beds, both neatly made up as if no one had ever slept in them, hospital corners tucked in, blankets taut, pillows plumped. Christiansen was there alone, erect in a chair in front of the windows that looked out on the yellow hills and the drug company buildings beyond and the horses Sanders had seen before now quietly grazing beneath the trees. Seen in profile, his eyes closed, his mouth slightly ajar, Christiansen seemed to be asleep, but when Sanders made a slight sound, his head turned and the same frigid blue eyes opened, unfocused but even more intense and frosty now, their color perhaps reinforced by the blue pajamas and navy-blue robe he wore. His hands appeared out of his lap with the rimless glasses and gold earpieces and he fitted them onto his face with measured unhurried movements. "Sanders," he said, his eyes now focused, "I was expecting you."

"Were you?" Sanders asked, smiling and walking forward with his hand outstretched. "Why?"

Christiansen ignored the hand and spoke up at him, sharply. "Because I know her, that bitch Beth, I know my fine daughter-in-law very well."

To cover embarrassment and resentment, Sanders put the chess set forward. "Here," he said, grateful that he could do something with that outstretched hand, "that was George's chess set. I brought it because Beth wanted you to have it."

The turn of Christiansen's face made his blue eyes black. "Beth told you she wanted me to have that?" The gesture was deprecating. "I don't believe it." The voice, the manner, the man still gave no quarter and asked none, though it was clear that he had declined physically. He was thinner, paler, his face drawn and more heavily lined; even his voice was weaker, scratchy and occasionally out of his control.

"Beth said she knew you liked to play chess and since she doesn't play any more herself, she wanted you to have this last memento from George. When I saw you up at Livermore, you were using those miserable plastic pieces so I thought you'd enjoy these."

Reluctantly, Christiansen's liver-spotted hands, the veins blue and elevated in them, undid the cord and wrapping and he opened the teak box, grumbling, "I don't need any mementos from George. He left me part of his insurance, didn't he? Why don't she give me the part of the money he left her?" For a time he simply stared at the carved ivory pieces, then picked one up and held it in the sunlight. "Beautiful," he murmured softly, "beautiful to look at"—he caressed the piece, a castle—"beautiful to touch." The aesthetic response followed the greed so swiftly that Sanders wondered if he had been put off by the hardness and, confused, missed some depth in the old man.

"*She* wants *you* to persuade *me* to let *her* bury George in *their* family plot, doesn't she?" Christiansen asked. He emphasized each pronoun by shaking the black castle in his fingers. "And these are part of the bait, the bribe, aren't they?"

"She said you wanted George buried at the Presidio."

Christiansen nodded.

"Why?" Sanders inquired.

"Because I don't want him buried among them Marshalls."

"Proud?"

"Yeh, proud. Is that bad?" the old man asked, his head rigid, his neck craning, the glassy hardness not even scratched.

"I never said it was."

"Then don't, boy, don't." He pointed to another chair, facing him and facing away from the window. Sanders took a last, lingering look at the horses still peacefully cropping grass under the live oaks and sat.

"My people fought and died for this country. We came from the Atlantic to the Pacific, from the East Coast to the West, pioneers, yes, pioneers. This is the end of the line, California. I want George buried looking out to the Pacific. I'm dying and I want to be buried there too, next to him if it can be managed, near to him if it can't. George is the end of the line too, for me, for us Christiansens, and all because of that spoiled little richbitch Miss Elizabeth Marshall." He spoke in a flat hard voice without even a trace of Southern accent or adornment to soften it, without a trace of self-pity to hollow it out.

"You hate her quite a bit, don't you?" Sanders said.

"Hate her? I suppose so. Despise her more. I despise her and her kind for what they made of the country. We fought for it and died for it and they put up the billboards and live off the fat of the land. The high and mighty. We made it and they took it away. And I hate her for what she done to George." He put up a warning finger. "Don't you look at me like I'm a foolish old man, boy. I don't like it. I still got all my marbles and a little bit of *cojones* left too, if they had a decent-looking enough nurse here to make it with. I know what I'm saying, I know the way it happened, and you don't."

"The way what happened?"

"*It.* It happened. The whole thing. . . . We been in this country for a long time. My grandfather, John Christiansen, he came out here in 1835. 1835, mind you, more than a hundred and thirty years ago. No smog, no automobiles, no Hollywood trash, only clean air and mountains, trees and water, fishing and hunting and people full of piss and vinegar. He fought with Frémont in the Mexican War and again in the Civil War, and at the Red River in 1864 he left my gramma a widow. They buried him there, in Arkansas, but my daddy got him dug up and brought out here to California and buried him once again in the Presidio.

"My daddy—that was James Frémont Christiansen, named after General Frémont—fought with Dewey in the Philippines during the Spanish-American War and left his right arm up to the elbow buried there, and two or three toes off'n his left foot, but he come back and died in bed, like a proper gentleman. And he's buried up to the Presidio too.

"Then there's me. My father named me Joseph Farnum after his captain, company commander, who saved his life on Luzon. I was in the First World War, and then in China and Mexico, Nicaragua and Haiti. And in the Second World War all over them islands, 'Canal and Peleliu, and Saipan. That 'from the Halls of Montezuma to the shores of Tripoli' crap is for real. So they're gonna bury me up there on the Presidio too.

"Now, that's a long line, three generations and more, and five big goddam wars and a couple of little bitty ones, and who the hell knows what they fought back in Massachusetts and in England before that. Grandpa John got the family Bible burned up in his Conestoga wagon when the Indians tried to ambush them coming west, just before they made it to California, so I don't know much about them before him."

The Conestoga wagon brought back the Indian chief and that tent of sheets in the hospital ward, and Sanders felt the first twinge of sympathy for Christiansen, saw that the old man, like the chief, was tearing out his own guts, yanking out his own colostomies.

"So that's why I want George buried up there," he said very slowly, "because it's the end of the line, because he's the end of the line for us Christiansens, the last male." For a fleeting instant there was strong emotion in the glasslike hardness of the face but it was rapidly erased. "After I go, nobody's left. Should've had a couple more kids, but I made a few mistakes too. Didn't care for 'em. Didn't even want him. Should've listened to the old lady. Probably the only time in her whole life she was right about something." He put the black castle carefully back into its slot.

"You like a pretty face," he said after a while, "a nice ass and a good pair of tits. Well, so do I. But don't let them addle your brains, boy. Beth Marshall's a good-lookin woman. I give her that. I don't know she's much in bed but I expect George was no great shakes in the sack either. Like his mother, not like me. But Beth'll do you in—count on it, boy—just the way she done him in."

"Women don't do men in," Sanders said, only half believing it, only half wanting to believe it, and conscious that he was talking about himself. "Men choose women to do themselves in so they don't have to take the responsibility themselves."

Christiansen nodded, once, tersely. "Same thing. Was that way with George—and her."

"What did she do to him that was so bad?" Sanders asked.

"Married him. Couldn't do nothing worse. Under false pretenses. She was knocked up—"

"Pregnant?" Sanders asked, remembering the corrugations in her flesh, feeling them in his fingertips, hearing them confirmed.

"That's what 'knocked up' means, boy. And not by George either. Oh, not that he wasn't getting into her pants too. He was. But there was some other sonofabitch she was humping too, some sawbones—"

"Steven Prescott?"

"Yep. That's the man. You know him?"

[179]

"I met him a couple of weeks ago."

"So he's still sniffin around."

"He's still around."

"He was in school then, studyin to be a doctor. Didn't have a pot. And he was on the make, you know, one of them Tennessee crackers from the hill country wanting something terrible to be respectable and re-e-fined. Wouldn't marry little missy Beth. Guess he didn't know how much cash she had then so he passed her by."

"You sure the child was Prescott's?"

"Sure? You don't even get sure of those things if you're layin under the bed, or on it."

"But surely George knew," Sanders protested.

"A born sucker, George was," Christiansen said. "Didn't care, he said, one time I asked, didn't care a damn. Said it didn't matter who put the spurt in, it was who took care of a kid that made a man a real father, lookin at me real red-eyed, like I committed some sin for askin. Never saw him so mad, never. Said I was crazy—crazy, mind you—with family name and blood line and history. Said we Christiansens were no different from any other goddam carpetbaggers— so help me, *goddam carpetbaggers* were his exact words, who come out west to get rich quick and cheap, pan a little gold outta the streams or stick a toothpick in the ground to get some oil to spout. Said we weren't much more than a bunch of jailbirds and refugees— *refugees!*—anyway, just managed to get outta debtors' jails in England to come to America to escape the law."

"What happened to the child?" Sanders asked.

"It was a boy child. We Christiansens always make sons," the old man said proudly. "What happened to it? I never saw it. George and I weren't on speaking terms those days. When he told me he was gonna marry Beth Marshall, I told him you married you a rich woman, you were her servant and bein a servant to any female was death to any man."

"What happened to the boy?" Sanders persisted. "Did they put him out for adoption?"

Christiansen's face set in melancholy, his eyes pools of blood in the sinking sun. "I told you George is dead now and I'm last of the line. Last of the line." He seemed distracted, remote. "They buried it," he said finally, "the two of them. Never even saw the boy. Died. Didn't even ask me to the funeral. Last of the line. My only grandson. Don't even know where they buried him."

"Why'd they do that?"

"I told you, we weren't talkin.'"

"Not much of a reason."

"Enough for them. Didn't need any more. George and I didn't never see exactly eye to eye."

"Never saw a father and son who did," Sanders rejoined, speaking for himself, for Lovett Carpenter Sanders, for life. Was it I to I that made eye to eye impossible? he wondered, and set the question aside.

Christiansen's cocked right eye rolled warily behind the shelter of its lens. "You speak from experience, I take it?"

His long unresolved war with Lovett Carpenter Sanders, he knew, qualified him to speak. "Bitter experience."

"Had any other kind of experience except bitter?"

"Some," Sanders said, "not much."

"Had *any* other, you're lucky."

"I suppose."

With the fading light their conversation seemed to have run down. They sat in the lengthening shadows until Sanders stood and went to the window. In the dusk, although things seemed to move under the live oaks, he couldn't tell if it was the evening breeze in the leaves muddying the shadows or the horses still galloping, grazing, gamboling. "You won't change your mind?" he said to Christiansen while his eyes burned with trying to discern the outlines of horses and colts.

"About what, Sanders, dying?" A macabre smile flitted across his defiant mouth.

"About letting Beth bury him in the family plot."

"Her family's or mine? Mine's the Presidio. George doesn't belong with her family—or her kind."

"The decision, then, I take it, is no."

Christiansen's set face and pale hands crossed on the teakwood chess case were answer enough. In the dying light the bridge of Christiansen's nose and one eye were still visible but the rest of his

[181]

face was eaten away by darkness; yet the nose was firm, as patrician as his son's, his single eye determined. Someone, somewhere, pulled a switch, the corridor lights went on, and then a squawk box announced that the day's visiting hours were over. Sanders asked if there was anything Christiansen wanted, feeling stupid asking the question, for what else could he want but his life. Christiansen said he wanted nothing, but he was grateful for the chess set, it would be useful. His pale hands patted the dark wood and for the moment Sanders was touched by that somber, baleful pride, then enraged by the mulishness that went with it. "So that's the way it's going to be," he said.

"That's the way. It's arranged for the Presidio day after tomorrow," Christiansen said, just a touch of apprehension under the gloating. "Tell my daughter-in-law."

"They asked her, you know. She was his wife."

"I know, but he's a Christiansen."

"I'll tell her," Sanders replied ironically, but the irony was lost on the old man.

"See you at the funeral," Christiansen said, pointing a finger. Neither a question nor a request, it was only a command and Sanders had to fight down his almost automatic "The hell you will."

Walking out to the car, he peered into the trees again until his eyeballs ached, hoping to catch even a glimpse of those horses running free but now the darkness was still, without an eddy; although he was sure he heard one high tremulous whinny in the distance, it might have been a railroad train or a ship in the Bay. "I'll see you at the funeral all right," he said softly, and only after he had got into the car, turned on the engine, and put the car into gear, did he realize that not once had the old man called George "my son."

❊   ❊   ❊

Sanders found Peter King in the simplest but most time-consuming way: He stationed himself across the street from his house at six the next morning and stayed there without eating or drinking or going to the john, enduring the suspicion and hostility of neighbors and passersby who muttered "fuzz" and "nark," "Whitey" and "the Man." While he waited, his mind in that curious floating state he so often felt when he was on a story and waiting for an interview, a result, combat, he thought of how Beth had cried the night before when he called to say that the old man wouldn't permit George to be buried in the Marshall family plot. When, after the first rebellious hysteria of "He won't permit, who the hell is he? I'm the one they called and told, the body is consigned to me!" and the weeping, Sanders tried to persuade her that perhaps it was best to indulge Joseph Farnum Christiansen, to acquiesce as graciously as possible because the old man was dying, and if worse came to worst, once he was dead, which Sanders thought could not now be far off, Beth could then have George's coffin disinterred and reburied in her family's ground.

"Laid to rest," she said, wearily sardonic, conscious, he thought, of only one of the meanings.

"You're not fighting me."

"You're on his side," she accused.

"I'm not. He's a thoroughly unlikable man, but I understand what the Presidio stands for with him and it's not all mean-spirited jingoism." Could he have explained by telling her about the Place des États-Unis and Lovett Carpenter Sanders? He didn't think it would matter, but he could no more tell her than he could have told Elaine.

"It's phony."

"Some of it, maybe, not all."

"You're so compassionate," she said caustically, "so understanding."

He ignored that. "It's fixed for day after tomorrow."

"Day after tomorrow," she repeated.

"At the Presidio."

"At the Presidio."

"Do you want me to drive you up to the city?" he asked.

"Steven will be back late tomorrow," she replied. "He'll want to be there and he'll take me."

"Steven," he blurted.

Her embarrassed silence told him that she too was remembering the previous night. "Stay with me tonight," she invited. "I'm lonely and depressed." There was no attempt to lure or attract him, though he knew she wanted him to make love to her. He saw her body fitted for the arrow like a bent bow, but he felt the corrugations of her

[183]

belly in his fingertips, tasted the gardenias and jasmine in his mouth, and the entreaty he heard in her voice made his temper flare.

"Do I fill in only in Steven's absences?" he asked. "Or am I at least scheduled for alternate nights?"

Her gasp was naked and unprepared, then the phone had clicked off.

It was not only his bulk that dwarfed the people around him and even reduced the size of the street, not even the leonine grace and brilliant ebony color, but the powerful aggressive thrust of his walk, high on the balls of his feet, like a boxer or a runner, his shoulders pushed forward as if he were about to plunge through a line or dive off a board, which summoned all to him and simultaneously announced that everyone had better get the hell out of his way. As Sanders tried to grasp just what quality it was that made Peter King look like the prow of some great black ship whose hull easily pried the waves of people apart so that he might pass unhindered, he knew it for a quality that Lovett Carpenter Sanders had had, that Needham still had, that old man Christiansen had too, a quality he admired and loathed, knew in the innermost confines of his skull intimately yet could not define.

"I hear you've been looking for me," King said.

"I have."

"Something important?"

"I thought so."

"You trying to find some more answers about George?" The white smile was insolent.

"No, I came to invite you to George's funeral."

"Aw, sh-i-i-i-t, man, George is already dead and buried."

"Dead but not buried."

King was brought up short. "Not buried?" he asked nervously. "They cremate him and put him into one of those little urns?"

"No, a lead-lined sealed coffin. He's going to be buried tomorrow up at the Presidio. I've been trying to get you because I thought you'd want to come to the funeral. I also sent you a couple of telegrams, tried calling, but I couldn't reach you, so—"

With a lift of his head King invited him to follow and Sanders crossed the street behind him and went into the building, up the

[184]

narrow stairs which smelled of urine, bacon fat, cheap wine and disinfectant, the stains of all on the walls and staircase. No one was in
the room now, but for a flash, when the door swung open, the furor
of those grappling bodies, the bulging Lastex swimming trunks, the
lilting lisp of that pansy queen's "We ballin . . . you wanna jine
us?" shot crazily before his eyes like moving picture films run backward. The room was almost bare, saved from looking altogether un-
tenanted by a black metal cot with a gray mattress and striped-
ticking pillow that looked more like a prison paillasse than a bed.
What once must have been grocer's shelves were filled with paper-
back books here and there interrupted by the rigid spines of case-
bound volumes.

"Come into the library," King invited, his irony heavy but
good-humored, "and have a seat." He pointed to a couple of heavy
wood-and-metal beer cases. "You eat anything today while you were
staking me out?" King inquired.

Sanders shook his head.

"The fuzz has advantages. Those motherfuckers do it in relays
so one of them can go take a piss or have a coffee and sandwich
while the other one keeps his eyes peeled. The facilities are that
way." He pointed. "I'll get us both a sandwich and a beer."

They ate the thick ham-and-cheese sandwiches from paper plates
and drank beer from glass jars that had held other things—peanut
butter and chocolate syrup—while King sprawled on the cot and
Sanders, sitting on one beer box, used the other for a table. "Tastes
good," he said, conscious of how hungry and thirsty he'd been.

"My international sandwich," King announced. "Polish ham, Dutch
cheese and French mustard. Dijon mustard. Brings out the flavor."

"A touch of home."

"Like the black bread, my touch of home. You live in France?"

"Paris is home."

"I'd really like to see that town."

"Come and visit. Any time. I'll put you up. I've got an old house
in the Fourteenth Arrondissement, plenty of spare rooms."

"You're joking."

"No, I mean it."

"Be serious, man. Where would a dropout nigger get the bread

[185]

to make the miles? Ain't nobody walked on water since the late J.C. and I ain't likely to be the next miracle."

Sanders maintained that it wasn't that expensive, explained about excursion and off-season rates, until the naked chagrin on King's face stopped him. "You don't know how much bread it takes just to stay alive here," King said, and so Sanders let it drop.

When they'd finished eating, King wrapped the debris in old newspapers and took the bundle out to the kitchen. He brought back another quart bottle of beer and refilled the glass jars. "They all coming to the funeral?" he asked.

Sanders told him briefly about the quarrel between Beth and Joseph Farnum Christiansen, about the Marshall family plot and the Presidio military cemetery, and explained that there wasn't going to be much of a funeral, perhaps a half-dozen people all together, those two, the two of them, and a guy named Steven Prescott.

King snorted. "A guy named Steven Prescott. The *good* doctor. He's still with it, still with her."

"You know him?"

"I sure do. Man, how can you figure life? Every time you get knocked on your ass and finally get up off the floor, thinking maybe your luck's changed and there's no more coming, watch out! The shit is sure to hit the fan! That sonofabitch haunted George, made his life miserable, almost drove him out of his gourd."

"His *bête noire?*" Sanders asked unthinkingly.

"What does that mean?"

Embarrassed, Sanders translated and was ashamed because King's face worked.

"You Whiteys got it made. You don't miss a trick. You even got it built into the language. *Bête noire,*" he repeated, his French accent flawless. "It's a *black* day. *Black* market. *Blacken* his good name and reputation. Whatever's bad is black and unlucky; whatever's good is always white and shining."

" 'Black is the color of my true love's hair,' " Sanders sang softly.

"Black but not kinky. And not her skin, Sanders, not her skin."

" 'I am black but comely.' "

"Don't you hear how loud that *but* comes on?" King asked softly.

"Moses and Solomon, sure they had a taste for poontang, and so I hear did George Washington and Jefferson catch their deaths of cold down in the quarters, but they made sure you hear that *but*."

Or butt. Pursuing it would only make matters worse, so Sanders turned the talk back to Prescott. "When did you meet him?" he asked.

"A long time ago, when George was going to Stanford. You see, I knew George from way back when we were kids, when he and his mother were living in Oakland and Alameda and Berkeley, up this way, before they moved down on the Peninsula. His mother used to invite me down then because she knew what a freakout my old lady was, she knew about these." He opened those great balled fists to show the white fibrous scars. "Lord knows she cleaned and band-aged enough of them. Even took me to the hospital clinic to get one of the deep ones stitched, and another, infected one, treated. Had enough penicillin for that—my hand blew up like a balloon—to cure a case of the clap. And after Mrs. Christiansen died, George'd invite me down to that bungalow they rented down there, old and dilapidated enough for nigger fruit pickers to live in.

"My mother was back up in the hatch then, up at Napa, for the sixth or seventh time, and I was working the Alameda docks, shaping up with the boys. George was a sophomore and headed for another scholarship. He was one of those whiz kids who went all the way through on scholarships. Had to. That cheap old sonofabitch wouldn't give him a dime to get through college, unless maybe it was West Point or Annapolis. Old Joe was down in Tijuana then, with some old Marine buddies on a bat, when George asked me down. We went fishing up in King's Canyon and caught a mess of trout, camping out, freezing our asses off in the cold water up there, and then came back on down to his bungalow. Must've been June or early July, I guess, because George was on vacation between semesters. He was always in such a Christ of a hurry. Gotta make time, gotta hurry. Those accelerated programs ran right on through the summer.

"We went to the University Commons the first day we got back from the Sierras, for a Coke, I thought, and I saw Beth sitting there with some joker. I wanted to go over and say hello, or wave, but

[187]

George held my arm like iron—he was one strong sonofabitch when he wanted to exert himself—and dragged me over to another table. He sat down with his back to them as if he didn't know they were there, didn't want to see them, and looked right through me, talking gibberish. Then I began to get the picture. I'd met Beth a couple of times before and I knew she and George were making it together. She'd even stayed at the bungalow overnight some times when I was there.

"I didn't really catch on at first and dumbbell that I am, I pointed and said, 'Hey, George, Beth is over there.' I thought maybe he hadn't seen her.

"But he had. 'Don't point!' he said, his face so furious I thought he was going to slug me. 'Haven't you got any manners?' " King took a long sip of the beer and wiped his mouth on the back of his hand. "That made me so mad I said no I didn't have any manners and what was the matter with him, didn't he have any manners, not saying hello to girls he was bedding down with.

" 'Not when they're with another man they're bedding down with,' he said, his face pale under the tan he'd gotten up at King's Canyon, and that shut my mouth quick. He sat there hunched over his Coke, the slab of lemon in his teeth, and I thought he was going to vomit all over the table. He looked sick, real green.

"What I didn't know until later was that that was the first time George had seen Prescott, the first time he met him, that he knew they were going to be in the Commons because little bitch Beth had warned him to stay away."

"She met George in the Commons too," Sanders interjected.

King sat up on the cot, his legs drawn up under his chin, his back against the wall. "I didn't find out about that until much later either."

"Why did he go there if he knew?"

"Why did he go? How to hell do I know why he went? I don't even know if *he* knew. Because he was a man. Because he liked snatch. Because cunt kills by taking you in, squeezing you dry, then cutting you off and spitting you out. Because he had to see what he was up against, maybe. Or who. Or maybe just because Beth told him she'd be there and not to come, to show he could come and go as he pleased."

Peter King might have been looking into his own heart to dissect and question what Sanders had felt that day he'd come back to Paris from Vienna, without warning, the articles on the Austrian elections all wound up, to find Elaine gone. She was not in the Quai de Passy flat and hadn't been, he could tell, for some nights. He counseled himself well, warned himself to stay there, shower, shave, go to sleep, cajoled himself to wait for her to come back and not to search and not to ask any questions. But he hadn't been able to because he knew, in his flesh and bones, that she was at the Avenue Foch apartment and a part of his desolated spirit already surmised what she was doing there. So he had gone and he would be forever sorry and forever delivered because he had.

"Man, Beth had moxie though," King said. "She could've walked right by us, made believe she didn't even know we were there, but she didn't. She brought Prescott right up to our table and introduced us all around. Good manners. Very well-bred. All that shit. You should've seen George and Prescott like two hound dogs around a bitch in heat, circling, bristling, gauging each other. If it hadn't been so mean, it would've been funny."

"Hah!" Sanders croaked lugubriously, not quite having completed the trip from the Avenue Foch.

"That's where you straight cocks don't see it right. All that biting and baying and howling at the moon, for what? For a roll in the hay and five minutes in the greased pocket."

"Was that all it was?"

"What else?"

Sanders shrugged. If King didn't know, no explaining would make it clear to him. As much try to explain the delights of lovemaking to a eunuch—harder: A eunuch might at least remember what it had been like once.

"Besides, you could see Beth enjoying it, two cocks fighting over a chick, her eyes shiny and her lips wet like she was creaming in her jeans right then and there." King chuckled, a throaty humorless rasp. "She had to tell them about each other, show them to one another, put them against each other—*and may the best man win!* Man, what horseshit!"

"Maybe that was her way of trying to be honest with them, and with herself," Sanders suggested.

"What broad is honest with a john? What chick is straight with herself? Everyone's a hooker and crooked as a Y."

"Human beings aren't very honest with themselves," Sanders admitted, broadening the base of the indictment.

King winked, pointing his finger happily. "Sanders, you got something there. At least with us, with men, there's not so much of all that love shit. You got a bone, you want to lay it into somebody, you want to get your ashes hauled, not so much come-on to come off. You ought to try it."

"That what you advised George?"

"Matter of fact, I did. And more than one time too. Especially when Beth got herself knocked up and he told me he was gonna marry her. That doesn't happen with us," he said.

"No," Sanders replied sadly, "it doesn't, does it? Automatic population control."

King missed it or passed it by. "Marry her! Shit, man, he didn't even know whose jocko it was, his, or that motherfucker Prescott's."

"He knew."

"You mean tests and all that crap? Don't mean a cottonpickin thing. She told him it was the good doctor's but she might not know herself."

"She knew too."

King eyed him strangely. "You got a lot of confidence, ain't you?"

"Not much. Newspapermen are short on confidence and long on suspicion. But I don't think Beth lied to him about that. About other things, maybe, but not about that."

"George looked at it like that, way back then. He believed her too when she said it was Prescott's and when she told him the way the good doctor took it, he was almost out of his skull. Prescott laughed and told her he'd arrange for an abortion if she *really* had a bun in the oven. Besides, how did he know it wasn't George's? Wouldn't do the job, the scrape thing, himself because that might get out and ruin the pretty little career he'd worked so hard for. Wouldn't even recommend the a.b. man himself. Got someone to telephone Beth with the info, someone she didn't know, never saw, wouldn't even give his name."

"Didn't she go?"

"Told him and Prescott to bugger off. Wouldn't have any part of an abortion, said she'd have the kid no matter what. And it sure was no matter what. For true."

"You mean the baby was stillborn?"

"No. Something went haywire all right but the kid came out a monster, no arms, no legs, a basket case. Big, strong boy. Couldn't tell what it looked like, or who, but more like the good doctor than like George."

A birth defect, a child without arms or legs and they had let it come out of the delivery room alive. Barbarians. No wonder Joseph Farnum Christiansen hadn't mentioned that to him. Family name. Bloodlines. How could the old man live with that if the child had really been George's? He had to make it Prescott's, no matter what.

"George married her in the fourth or fifth month, right after Beth got out of nursing school, so the kid was his. All legitimate, so no one could call it a little bastard. It was touch and go there, because if they found out she was preggers, no graduation, so Beth and George kept it all pretty dark—you see what the language will do for you?—and later named it John King Christiansen."

"After you?"

"Me and his grand-, no, his great-granddaddy, I think. I was his godfather, me a blackass nigger godfather to a white child." His face turned stormy and he stretched his fingers as if reaching for something to crush, the ridged palms protruding scarred as a tiger's hide. "I jinxed it. Put the hex on it. Maybe old Granddaddy John too. Old Joe told me he was pretty young when Granddaddy John bought his on the Red River. Real proud of it too, old Joe was." Suddenly King began to sing in a rich, melodious deep bass voice:

> *I'm comin, I'm comin, for my head is bendin low.*
> *I hear those gentle voices callin*
> *Ole black Joe . . .*

"Jinxed it, sure as hell. A black bastid godfather for a po white bastid godchild."

"You don't believe that, do you?"

"Sometimes I do, Sanders, sometimes I do."

"You can't believe such superstitions."

"I know I can't, but I do."

"You'll come to the funeral though?"

"Can't jinx George any more now, man, he's dead; but there's none of them going to be happy to see me there."

"You give a damn?"

"Shit, no. Don't like it, they can lump it. I'll be there."

King sat with his hands resting on his knees, palms upward, looking down at them as if he saw some reading of his past and future in their scars, lines of fate, life lines. "You ever had a man, Sanders, even once?" he asked, without looking up.

"No," Sanders answered, "never."

"Not even some of them old white-boy locker-room college jim-jam, that shower-room drop-the-soap game? Not even the boy-scout, YMCA-kid-stuff hand jobs?"

Trying to smile, Sanders said, "I guess I was deprived." How ironic, he thought, that King's invitation to homosexual heaven had just the same vocal and sexual resonance as his college classmates' invitations to accompany them down to the Negro district in Boston or in Cedar Rapids to "change their luck."

"I guess you were," King agreed humorlessly. "Ever watch men have sex?"

"Not even that. Never curious enough, I guess." Actually there had been more than one opportunity to observe such displays among the Arabs in Algeria, the international faggots in Paris and in Greece, the Viennese *lustknaben,* but he'd avoided such voyeurism and when he had seen things, he'd turned away.

"George was more curious." King's voice was an insinuation, his eyes faraway and reminiscent. "I took him to show him."

If King had had to show George, then George couldn't have been a homo, although that perhaps had been the first step, the initiation. Why couldn't he bring himself to ask King straight out if George had or had not been? King might conceivably tell him and yet Sanders knew that he wouldn't be sure no matter what King avowed. "And?" Sanders asked.

"And? You still want to know whether he was gay, don't you, or working both sides of the street? I think that's what Beth always

[192]

thought, that he was a closet queen, that George was queer for me."

Was that what explained the distaste Beth had felt, the jasmine and the gardenias? Had George Christiansen been a homosexual trying to live a straight life with a wife and child? Did that account for why the marriage had gone bust? Sanders tried to recall any effeminacy of movement, the odd flicker of hands, the pansy lisp, anything that might have borne out such a conclusion, but he could remember nothing of that kind. Or, he speculated further, had the dissatisfactions with Beth eventually driven George into the alternative Peter King offered?

"Come on," King invited, popping off the bed like a jack-in-the-box, "I'll take you cruising, give you a guided tour."

Sanders tried to lie his way out gracefully, saying that he had things to do before the funeral and a date in San Francisco besides.

"It'll only take an hour or so," King said, looking at his wristwatch. "The night is young. What are you, Sanders, chicken? Afraid you'll get *con*verted or *per*verted?" He laughed uproariously. It was the oldest gambit in the world, the meaningless gibe he should have been able to resist easily and rarely could. Half a lifetime of trying to prove to Lovett Carpenter Sanders that he wasn't a coward and the other half to prove to his mother that he was properly cautious fought inside him and, as usual, the former won.

"Where's your journalist curiosity?" King teased.

"Okay," Sanders agreed finally, "but I'll have to make a call first."

King nodded at the telephone which sat on the floor in the corner of the room at the foot of the bookshelves where Sanders had not noticed it before. As he dialed Laura Martin's number King went out to the kitchen with that self-conscious gait that announced he was giving Sanders whatever privacy to speak he required. When after a dozen rings Laura didn't answer, Sanders called Beth's number too but there was no response. For an instant he had a crazy disorganized impulse to call Elaine and his finger automatically began to trace the number of their Quai de Passy telephone when between his eyes and the phone the envelope of his last letter to her fluttered like a spectral leaf hacked off a pale linen tree marked by a red scrawled ". . . *n'habite pas à l'adresse indiquée.*"

"Ready?" King stood in the kitchen doorway, his head bowed

[193]

slightly to accommodate the lintel, and Sanders, the dial tone a wail in his ear spoke a brusque goodbye into the mouthpiece as though he were finishing a conversation and hung up. "Let's go," he said.

"You can't go like that. You'll stick out like a sore thumb." He pointed scornfully at Sanders' tweed jacket and whipcord trousers. "I'll have to lend you something so you—blend into the landscape." He laughed. "Maybe even a little burnt cork."

"Your clothes won't fit me," Sanders said shortly.

Gauging his size, King replied, "I get a lot of traffic through here, visitors, you might say. You saw some of them—" he paused, his eyebrow raised questioningly "—and sometimes they leave clothes behind, boys' and girls' clothing." He came back with a pair of khaki trousers whitened by many washings, an ironed green sport shirt and badly creased light tan poplin jacket. "Here, try these." Sanders held them against him and saw that they'd fit well enough not to make him conspicuous. Sanders changed quickly, while King watched him with a detached candor and a contemptuous smile on his face when Sanders, about to take his pants off, turned his back.

"They'll fit," he said.

"Those drag parties come in handy sometimes," King said without irony. He nodded approvingly at the clothes, but gestured contemptuously at Sanders' heavy English brogues. "Those shoes are out, but I can't help you there, unless you'd like to wear a couple of pointy-toe styles with high heels or some Greek sandals—in gold."

"I've got some tennis shoes in the car."

"Dirty?"

"They'll never be white again."

"Good! They'll do on a black man's party."

They drove toward the docks and Sanders did not see a single white man. It was like being lost in the Casbah or in Wanchai where no familiar white face broke the strangeness. King was explaining how he'd learned to speak proper English from the nuns and how one of them, Sister Agatha, had taken him under her wing, treated him like a son, more like a son than his mother ever had, for sure, though that wasn't saying much. A tall, blue-eyed Irish nun, Sister Agatha had never even seemed to notice that he was black.

That had been helpful in many ways but each time he left school and the plays that Sister Agatha directed and produced, and in which he was soon taking leading roles—the only time he ever felt really at home in the world, King confessed, was on the stage, playing someone else's life, and like as not, someone else's color—it was like being knocked down a flight of stairs because white people on the outside not only noticed that he was a black man but treated him that way. And so did his mother and his black friends. The only other white person who had also not seemed to notice his black skin was George Christiansen.

"You *are* black," Sanders said irascibly, his irritation at having permitted himself to be compromised into the foolish expedition finding voice in this. "It should not only be noticed but approved of as something different, a Roman nose, or flaxen hair, or a Scottish brogue."

"Separate but equal?"

"No, different but equal."

"Now there's a great political slogan. *Equal but different rights!* A great political shit-eating program." King's sarcasm was savage.

"Goddam it," Sanders said angrily, "you're going to eat shit just so long as you're set on having the white folks love you, so long as you're full of self-pity and self-righteousness and self-hatred when they don't. *They're not going to love you.* They're not even going to like you. They don't love each other or themselves, so why should they love you? They can barely tolerate each other and maybe that's all you can ask of human beings right now, to stay off each other's backs and out of each other's hair as much as they can." Ashamed of his outburst, halfway through he heard himself moderating what he would otherwise have bitten out.

" 'Thou shalt love thy neighbor as thyself,' the Bible says. That's the stuff you white folks sold us black folks."

The quarrels between his parents about religion began to recapitulate themselves in his skull: his father's acid estimates of human nature and its limitations, his mother's refusal to accept the bounds his father's experience of men—and women—had taught him, refusing to admit that the reporter's view of life was anything but a distortion, refusing to accept politics as anything but the warping of

[195]

man's natural goodness, not, as his father saw it, the expression in all its violence and ugliness of man's nature. Their arguments equally reasonable, equally rooted in human life, had never convinced him because he saw how they used the arguments to refuse the meaning each assigned to his own and the other's life. The discord had the same reverberations as George's terrible plaint "Where are all the honorable men?" and the same impossibility of producing a clear-cut sensible answer.

King was telling him how only two women had ever treated him decently, Sister Agatha and George Christiansen's mother, and Sanders could barely restrain the sardonic "But both of them were white." Both had given him the only disinterested and consistent love of his childhood and youth, and both had taught him. Sister Agatha had taught him to act and to sing, training his voice, his diction, his movements, his "presence." Mrs. Christiansen had instructed him in smaller but no less necessary things—table manners, routine courtesies—and imbued him with some confidence that something could be done with his life even if he was a Negro. "Sister Agatha forgot I was black but Mrs. Christiansen, she never forgot. Sister Agatha lived as if it didn't make any difference and never even reminded me; Mrs. Christiansen always reminded me, said it did make a difference, a great difference, and that I had to live as if it made a difference.

"Then, in my last year in high school, I was the lead in *Othello*. Playing the Moor, of course. Paul Robeson had shown that one nigger could do it so it was safe for me. Sister Agatha invited the Oakland and San Francisco critics to come down to see the premiere because she said she'd never seen a better Othello than me, not even Robeson, and I was ready to begin my professional career. She was sure I'd get some notices, though she didn't think any but the second-string reviewers would come, but even on the strength of their notices she was certain I'd get a scholarship to one of the big universities—in drama. It looked so perfect, my motherfucking, all-American big shiny white chance, onward and upward into that Whitey world where people would treat me like me, Peter King, as if my sinful black skin was pure as the driven white snow.

"Goddam, I was set up. Man, I knew my soul was white even if the color of my skin wasn't. I knew because Sister Agatha treated me that way, because she'd taught me to read Blake with solace aforethought:

My mother bore me in the southern wild,
And I am black, but O! my soul is white;

and I was ready to prove it to her and everyone else too. Me, Peter King, actor. I saw myself on Broadway, my name in lights, with all the Whiteys applauding and waiting for me at the stage door; I saw myself in Hollywood, on the wide screen, *in color,* with all the young blond starlets coming to my dressing room for a fast boff before we went on the set; I saw myself in a big white Cadillac driving home to show Sister Agatha and my mother, my mother especially, what I'd *made of myself.* A man. Not white or black, but a man. What a laugh. I'd forgotten the rest of that Blake quatrain:

White as an angel is the English child,
But I am black, as if bereav'd of light.

Though I remembered it plainly enough later; they made me remember it, to my sorrow.

"Sister Agatha had us give a couple of previews first, with students, neighborhood people, parents, some of the nuns, because she wanted us to get the feel of performing in front of a live audience, and it was then I blew it, the whole thing, the dream and the McCoy together. You know the play?"

Sanders nodded, not taking his eyes off the road and the traffic, listening to King's interspersed traffic directions, his voice calm and ordinary, turn right there, second red light, turn left, before it rose intense and passionate again. "Remember in the last act where Othello kills Desdemona? The stage is dark and Othello comes in with a candle to wake Desdemona in her bed. I *was* the Moor by then, the jealousy and love incendiary inside me, in my flesh and bones, yet at the same time I knew I'd played it better than I ever had before. Then, in the dark, as I was about to speak my first lines in that scene, someone said in a hoarse whisper—from the wings or from the audience or maybe from backstage—'Look at the spade!

Black bastard, I hate to see that buck nigger put his spunky hands on her even in a play.'

"I almost dropped the candle and went off crazy to look for whoever spoke the words, but Sister Agatha's discipline and the audience kept me in the part. It was dark and I couldn't see who'd said the words, I didn't even really know where the voice came from, or I doubt I could've gone on. If the lights were up things might have been different. But after that every word I spoke was a poison in my blood, a fever in my brain that turned me half crazy. What kept running through my mind was that even there, on the stage, I couldn't escape." His voice suddenly became Othello the Moor's, a hoarse resounding *sotto voce:*

> . . . *Yet I'll not shed her blood,*
> *Nor scar that whiter skin of hers than snow,*
> *And smooth as monumental alabaster.*
> *Yet she must die, else she'll betray more men.*
> *Put out the light, and then put out the light.* . . .

When I came to kill Desdemona, a beautiful seventeen-year-old French girl, dark-eyed and brunette, a good friend and a girl I liked, who'd always been decent to me, I really began to choke her. Her throat became the whole world's throat I was choking, keeping it from ever speaking those words again, those hateful words— *spook! jigaboo! boogie! spade! nigger! nigger! nigger!* She screamed and fainted, but I kept right on until the house lights came up and I realized what was happening. And then I remembered myself, and forgot myself, and ran off the stage and left her lying there. I never went back. I never even said goodbye to Sister Agatha, or apologized to the girl, I just ran."

"What happened to the girl?" Sanders asked, flickering a glance at those immense powerful hands that now lay in King's lap.

"I hitched up north, past Redding, expecting the cops to come looking for me any day, sure I'd killed her. I got a job in a lumber mill and worked my tail off up there, working like a dog all day and then drinking myself into a stupor every night. And then one day, maybe six months later, I ran into another Oakland nigger I knew who was hitching up to Portland looking for a job and he told me the girl was all right. She'd had bruise marks on her throat and was hoarse for a couple of weeks, but she was alive and well."

"Did you go back then?"

"I went back. And my old lady said, 'I told you so. You mis'able nigger. You gonna end in tha gas chamber.' But she was afraid of me now and didn't cut my hands any more because she was afraid, so that something good came out of the whole thing."

"It's an ill wind," Sanders commented. "But why didn't you go back to see Sister Agatha and finish school, and try for the drama scholarship then?"

"You think like the Man, Sanders—can't help yourself. A black boy choking a white girl, for real, even in a make-believe play? That gets around. Think anyone would trust him again, ever? Even the sympathetic ones would say he was a nut, psycho like his mother, especially with mine in and out of the hatch—Napa, Mendocino, Agnews, maybe eight, maybe nine times. I was afraid they'd ship me off to one of those nut houses too. And you can imagine what the *un*sympathetic ones would say: Buck nigger gits his hands on a white gal's flesh and is so hot in the pants he wants to jump her, goes off his head and tries to choke the life outta her. No, going back made no sense."

"Did you talk to Sister Agatha about it?"

"Too ashamed. I'd put her on the spot too. They canceled the play out after that and they didn't let her produce any more. Finish to her dramatic program." He paused. "No, I never called her or talked to her again. I'd jinxed her enough."

When King finally motioned to park and said they'd walk from there, Sanders pulled over, stowed his shoes and clothes in the trunk and sat on the front seat putting his sneakers on while King impatiently paced the sidewalk. When he turned off the car lights the street was suddenly quite dark. A moonless night without stars above seemed to grow even darker and thicker around them as they walked toward the waterfront, the yellow streetlamps grew fewer and farther between, the buildings bulking larger and without any lights, and the faint smell of fish on the night breeze growing stronger and sharper. Only the necklace lights of the Bay Bridge off on the right lifted quivering and obscured by darkness into the skies. At his side King was like a great cat on the prowl, tense, alert, sniffing the air as if searching for the spoor of his prey. "Down here, just do what I do. Follow me. Don't say anything if you can help it. Nod. Grunt, Keep it to yes and no, which is *yeh* and *naw* down here. Understand?"

"Yeh." Sanders imitated him to relieve the tension but King didn't laugh and his own apprehensions mounted.

"We'll get a drink first," King suggested nervously. "There's a leather place down a block from here. Come on, give you your first look at the denizens of the dark."

"A leather place?"

"You live too cautious and confined a life for a foreign correspondent," King taunted. "I'm going to see that you expose yourself to a little far-out adventure."

It was the kind of sentence Lovett Carpenter Sanders himself might have spoken. Pursuing far-out adventures got you killed, more often than not.

Outside the bar a small fisherman's lantern, yellow and flickering, illuminated a weatherbeaten sign on which was painted a white whale with a tower of spume geysering out of his blowhole, and over it, an arc of Victorian italics, the legend read: THE SPERM WHALE. The windows were wild with color, gyrating loops and serpentine swirls, and in the heart of each of them the same snowy whales with columns of water jetting out of their heads. Inside, the bar was dimly lit with hurricane lamps and pervaded by the smell of beer and kerosene and fish. Sawdust on the floors, models of old sailing vessels behind the bar and everywhere else posters, pictures and photographs of motorcycle types in black leather jackets, leather caps, visors, goggles, masks and scarves. Almost all wore boots. Some, like those of Marlon Brando and James Dean, Sanders recognized, as well as one or two of the less well-known moving-picture actors, "heavies," whose names he couldn't remember. Around the tables and at the bars, instead of chairs there were bollards, though what boats were to be moored to those uprights seemed more likely to be motorcycles. The few people there looked exactly like the posters, young men with long and unkempt hair, mustachioed and bearded, some of them with jutting brutal faces and lowering brows. There were only a very few women. As they ordered whiskies at the bar, King said out of the side of his mouth, "Nothing here tonight. These aren't the real leather, just some auntyish faggots and a couple of queens in drag." Only then did Sanders realize that what he'd taken for women were really men. A large picture of George Washington was hung over the bar, a print completely out of place, the traditional Gilbert Stuart portrait of the Father of his Country. Unbelievingly Sanders saw that someone had with superb and malicious humor skillfully superimposed a leather motorcycle jacket over the hero of Valley Forge's shoulders.

King impatiently tugged his elbow, said there'd be no excitement there and they'd look elsewhere.

They finally came down to the wharves and the water, to a particular dock that jutted out over the oily bay where great trailer trucks without their cabs were parked parallel to each other, so close together that it seemed impossible for a man to squeeze through the narrow spaces between the trucks' sides. King murmured something about Oakland's inner harbor, Alameda beyond and poplars that Sanders didn't understand, and began to lead him through the dark between the great trailer trucks. The aisle was so narrow they couldn't walk normally but had to sidestep in a shuffling Stepin Fetchit jig, King's right hand holding his left, and Sanders, conscious of the fluting of scars on King's palms, felt the panic mounting into his throat. Where was he being led and what for? It was so dark he couldn't see more than three feet ahead and even that dimly, and the looming trucks on either side hemmed him in like gray elephants and gave him claustrophobia. After they had gone what almost seemed the interminable length of a single truck, Sanders unable to swallow the lump of fear that was now stuck in his throat, they came on a small freer and lighter darkness, six or eight feet of open space between the back of the first truck and the great greased disc protruding from the second which was used to hook the trailer to the cab that pulled it. When they had passed the third such in the line and were coming to the gray intermission between it and the next one, King stopped and whispered, "Now, come on real casual," and then he drew him out into the lighter area. There, lounging in a casual semicircle, were five men: a sailor in blues, two leather-jacketed types, a truck driver, and another dressed like a stevedore, smoking, passing around two pints of sneaky pete, and watching a Negro sailor in whites, his bell-bottom trousers around his ankles, leaning into the rear of a hairy white-buttocked wriggling queen.

With a nod of recognition one of the leather types gave King one of the wine bottles and he drew on it, two long swallows, then passed it to Sanders. Sanders feigned a gulp, then passed it on to the sailor in blues next to him, shamelessly eavesdropping on King's "Not much action tonight, is there?" to the leather jacket while not taking his eyes off the coupling pederasts.

"Cops raided night before last," the leather jacket replied slowly. "But the night's still young."

"Anything doing back there?" King nodded toward the end of the dock.

"Could be," the leather boy said noncommittally.

They watched the thrusting buttocks grow swifter and heard the short grunts from the black sailor and the soughing sighs of the white queen whose stiffened body, like a bracket at right angle to the pier, braced by his pleading arms against the truck, held fast. Grunts and sighs blended into a long "Ooooh!"—the sound of a distant foghorn on the waters of the bay—and the two bodies, black and white, their color now murky and blended in the shadows, went limp and clinging. The white boy turned, repeating the muted foghorn call, fell on his knees and embraced the sailor, clutching his buttocks, pressing his face into the wavering Negro's groin. Entangled in their half-discarded clothes, they looked like a disorderly Pietà.

Lazily, the leather jacket asked, "You wanna rock now?" and Sanders heard King's "Nah" simultaneous with his own.

Following King's shadow, once more pressed between two expanses of truck, the darkness even more menacing, Sanders struggled to wipe the scene from his mind and the excitement from his loins, guilt and distaste, no, more than distaste, aversion, struggling to understand each other inside him. Not one of those men had been obviously effeminate except the white queen; if anything, they'd

[202]

looked like more conventionally masculine men than most; all were young, in their twenties and thirties, the queen perhaps in his teens, and almost aggressively male. Was this what George Christiansen had come to see and felt? Had the same revulsion and agitation moved him toward instead of away? Still not adjusted to the darkness Sanders' eyes could make out only the vague shapes ahead and those took on the fantastic silhouettes of the de Besancourt apartment, the two blending and melding and coalescing with the broken body of George Christiansen on that Saigon sidewalk, but all always just out of focus, blurred apparitions and all abhorrent. In front of him he heard King mutter something unintelligible and felt the corrugated palm release his hand. As he strained to see, King's amorphous bulk seemed to blend into the shadows, and Sanders, afraid to be left behind, hurried after him, took a step forward, then another, and felt himself walking in space, then plunging downward. About ten feet below he hit the water with a shock and went under. "I don't believe it," he said aloud. "This isn't happening to me." It had been like flying, stepping out and unexpectedly finding nothing underfoot, and the whole thing began to seem like a nightmare from which he would soon have to awaken, or a comic movie he'd soon grow bored with and leave behind in the darkened theater. But the words he'd spoken aloud had filled his mouth with water and, choking, he began to stroke to the surface. When he got there King's voice floated down, a grating whisper, "Don't yell, or anything, you'll bring the fuzz. I'll fish you out."

The alarm and responsibility in King's voice was amusing, and Sanders, treading water, replied in his normal voice, "You'd better and quick. This goddam water is cold enough to freeze your tail off."

"Yours, buddy"—he saw King's white grin and relief—"not mine." With King leaning over the edge of the pier, Sanders was able to see what had happened. The trucks, using the wharf as a depot, were parked back to front right up to the very lip of the pier, and when King had stepped around the end of the last truck, gingerly working his way around the edge of the truck and the wharf to go back down another aisle of trucks, he had instead gone straight ahead—and into the drink.

"Swim around to the side of the pier. Grab hold of one of the pil-ings," King called. Sanders followed instructions and King's moving shadow above him and swam slowly through the viscid water to the corner of the pier where one of the pilings rose. He tried to clasp it and haul himself up but it was so covered with slime that he couldn't get enough leverage to lift himself far enough out of the water for King, leaning way down over the wharf edge now, to reach down to him.

"Don't panic, don't panic," King cautioned when he saw that their hands wouldn't engage, sounding far more frightened than Sanders felt, "we'll figure a way."

Sanders was a strong swimmer and he felt less anxious than oddly apathetic, almost as if the whole experience was happening to some-one else, as if he were simply a bemused spectator. But the cold struck his muscles like fists and he began to feel the first knottiness that might soon become cramps. He sidestroked beneath the pier to see if there was any other way up and found the crossbeams which supported both deck and pilings, a framework of two-by-fours which was halfway between the surface of the water and the level of the wharf and ran around the entire rim of the pier. It was a narrow scaffolding but one on which a man could, if he got up there, even stand. If he could hold the slippery piling long enough to haul himself a few feet out of the water, he might be able to grab the framing and hoist himself out of the water up onto the scaffolding by himself. From there he should be high enough to reach King's hand. Three times he shinnied up the piling only to fall splashing back into the water, but on the fourth attempt, slowly, determinedly, bracing his feet against the wood, his wet sneakers squeaking and sliding, he managed to get enough purchase to work himself up to within clutching distance of the beams; then, as he began to slip back, he leaped, a frantic reaching for the boards, grabbed them, and in spite of the tearing strain in his armpits, the splinters in his fingers, held on. "Here, over here," he called stri-dently. "Give me a hand."

King's shoes clattered above him and then, just as the black arm descended to him, the board broke and he was pitched back into the water. "That's the right idea," King encouraged, "try it again

[204]

at the next piling, the wood's rotten here. And don't make so much noise."

Recovering himself, Sanders swam to the next piling and again tried until, this time on the fifth attempt—he could feel himself growing weaker, cramped with cold, tireder—his frenzied grasp caught the supports and he managed to heave himself up onto the network of beams. Breathing heavily, precariously balanced on the two-by-four on slimy canvas soles, he held on to the piling with one arm and with the other reached up and felt King's corrugated palm slide over his hand and close around his wrist. "Grab my wrist and when I say go, push off with as much spring as you can manage," King called and then in a slow count of three called for go. A moment later King had pulled him up onto the wharf, wet, covered with slime and kelp, shivering in the warm air and laughing.

Suspiciously King peered into his face. "You okay? Not hysterical?"

"Nah, the whole thing was funny. At least the swim part of it was."

"Wanna go on from here? There's usually a good daisy chain in the middle truck in the third row but inside the van so you can take off your clothes and get dry. They've got some candles too so you can see what's going on."

Sanders wrung the water out of his jacket. "No, thanks. I'm chilled to the bone. I've had enough."

"Yeh, I guess you have," King agreed, reluctant and disdainful. "Better get you back to the car and get you a drink."

"If you want to stay, I can find my way back myself," Sanders said.

"You sure?" A vibrato of suppressed excitement glittered in his voice.

Swiftly, unerringly, King led him by the hand down the narrow aisle between trucks past two other sporting groups in this aisle back out onto the paved street. There, hands on hips, he waited awkwardly, almost as if he expected to be rebuked, then finally he spoke up. "I'm sorry it didn't turn out," he said. Just what he meant by that equivocal statement was unclear and at that juncture Sanders didn't even care.

"What the hell do you need this kind of thing for," Sanders asked irately, "with the"—at a loss for words, he made a sweeping gesture with his arm, taking in the whole nighttime landscape, the pachydermous trucks, the stinking piers, the scummy waters of the Bay— "this whole goddam mess, the chance the cops will break in and pick you up—"

"The danger turns me on," King replied urbanely. "The risks make it more exciting, set me up." But the urgency fought the urbanity in him, the braked lust to return to the trucks and the daisy chain barely contained.

Not for me, Sanders thought, not for me, but he didn't say it. When they shook hands and said good night, he felt again the ridged palm and knew the scars for only the superficial marks a mother had handed on to her son, only the skin-deep welts; the profounder wounds to the spirit, the burned and crusted sores of the soul, though not declared on the skin, were just as prominent in every word and movement. He knew he should feel that there but for the grace of God went he, but he didn't: Whatever Lovett Carpenter Sanders and Marian Stuart Sanders had done to him, they had not burdened him with that, they had not left his hands with that mess of corrugated scars.

He found his car without any trouble and, grateful for the dark privacy of the lonely street, stripped off the wet slimy shirt, trousers and underwear and left them in an untidy pile on the curbstone. Standing there naked, the night wind drying and chilling him, he rummaged in the trunk of the car, found an old piece of toweling he kept there and rubbed himself as clean and dry as he could. When he was dressed, he sat in the front seat next to the curb, the door open and the dim dashboard light illuminating his kelp-covered tennis shoes and socks, and something Levi Migdal had once said to him came back. They were drinking brandy on a beautiful autumn Saturday outside of Fouquet's some months after he and Elaine were separated and Levi was trying to cheer him out of his depression. "When I was learning English," Levi remarked, "there were two words I kept using interchangeably when I talked, but which I didn't know were spelled differently and meant different things. A *queen*, which meant a female monarch, and a *quean*, which meant a slut. Elaine, my friend, was both." Sanders dried his feet with the toweling and uncomfortably got into his shoes without socks, wondering if the two words had a single root, and recognizing how well they might. As he was tying his shoes and remembering the complete democracy of color in the leather bar and in the interstices between those trucks, he heard movements and stood up to find himself facing two black men. They looked like Halloween figures, silk stockings over their heads and faces, the smaller holding a bayonet in his fist, the taller with a cut-down baseball bat. "Don't talk loud, mistuh," the shorter warned softly.

"An don move," the taller added.

"Git up yo cash," the smaller one ordered.

As Sanders reached for his wallet the baseball-bat man raised the bat overhead, ready to crush his skull. "Come on out mighty slow, mistuh," he cautioned. Sanders took the wallet out and handed it over.

Efficiently the smaller one emptied it, then tossed the wallet on the pavement. "Turn out tha pockets too."

Sanders turned them out.

Some loose change and his car keys clattered to the pavement. The smaller one swept them up so swiftly and agilely Sanders barely followed his movements. Quickly pocketing the bills and change, he then put the point of his bayonet against Sanders' chest and almost in a whine said, "Git in yo car an drive out. Skedaddle. Goddam quick. You ain't seen no one, you ain't lost nuthin, an don talk to no fuzz."

"My car keys and driver's license are there." Sanders pointed to the wallet and his key case.

"Smart-ass, huh?" the bigger man said menacingly.

"Leave offa him," the shorter one commanded. "Pick em up," he said to Sanders.

The taller one shoved him toward the car and stumbled over the pile of wet clothes. "Whut that stuff?" he asked, probing them with the toe of his shoe.

"Clothes," Sanders said.

"I kin see that. Yourn?"

"Yes."

The smaller one reached down and touched them. "They wet," he exclaimed. "You ben swimming?"

"No. Fell off the dock."

"How cum?"

"Accident," Sanders said. He stooped and retrieved both his wallet and key case. As he stooped to get into the car the bigger man stopped him with the baseball bat across his chest. "You mis'able Whitey faggot," he said. "We know what you down heah fo." Deliberately he spat in Sanders face, then shoved him into the car. "Move out, you honky cocksucker, fo we make you eat shit too."

Sanders put the key in the ignition and when the motor roared into life, reached over but the door was kicked closed in his face before he could pull it to. Furiously he wiped his sleeve across his face, put the car in gear and turned it in the street, keeping the two black men in sight in his rear and side mirrors. They were running down the street and he drove the car after them, racing it up onto the sidewalk after them, so blind with rage that he knew if he could catch them he would run them down, grind them under the wheels of the car with joy, with a sense of justice and without an iota of remorse or regret. They outwitted him at almost the last moment by dodging into an alley though not before the big one had thrown the baseball bat at him and left a clanging dent in the car fender. Then the two of them disappeared into the darkness.

* * *

Established to protect the port and bar enemy entrance into the harbor, the Presidio is a military reservation which preempts the strategic northwest shore and heights of San Francisco. Though it has played a role in every major American war since the Marines replaced the Mexican garrison there in 1846, the Presidio has achieved its martial glory by combat once-removed, and at some distance, serving as a shipping, marshaling and communications center rather than as a battleground. Headquarters of the Sixth Army, it is today a city within a city with its own garrison, housing, clubs, hospital and even its own airstrip, and continues to play its role in the wars of the Far East.

High on the Presidio's rocky headlands, as they curve away from the Golden Gate Bridge toward Land's End, where gray-green San Francisco Bay churningly debouches into the gray-green Pacific, is the National Military Cemetery where, partially hidden in groves of laurel and cypress, fir and eucalyptus, and masked by many flowering shrubs, lie more than fifteen thousand American military dead enjoying the final tribute of a grateful nation.

There, though it was close to noon, the sun had not yet burned off the shrouds of sea mist which rolled in from the Pacific through a ghostly gray-green eucalyptus windbreak to hover over the gravestones. Walking past row after row of the neat chalk-white tombstones, identical and anonymous in spite of their neatly engraved names and dates, Sanders felt sick, the nausea of the night before having tightened into a fist in his throat which made swallowing difficult and painful. Everywhere he'd ever been, from Normandy and Flanders, Ypres and Verdun to the rolling country of Connecticut, Massachusetts and Washington, he'd been witness to the burying grounds of the young who had died in battle, the continuing cairns of civilization, the unanimous and anonymous graveyards in out-of-the-way places to commemorate great and generally forgotten battles, to be kept from the sight of the live and the quick except for those whose fathers and sons lay buried there and who, sometimes, infrequently, came and remembered.

At the grave six soldiers in dress uniforms, their rifles held in white-gloved hands, lounged around a parked olive-drab weapons carrier, smoking, looking absurdly youthful and self-conscious, and so beautifully alive; a young second lieutenant smoked by himself near another grave decorated with a withered autumnal brown wreath; and separate from all of them, an older, grizzled sergeant, his face smocked with the broken capillaries of the heavy drinker, fingered a highly polished bugle and made strange faces to exercise his lips. All ignored his arrival, looking away from him as if by recognizing his presence they might embarrass him. Only a military chaplain, a first lieutenant who at first watched him warily for a full five minutes, took note of him and then approached and asked if he was Elliott Sanders. When Sanders confessed that was his name, the chaplain, uneasy and furtive, turned his back to hide his movements from the second lieutenant, brought a sealed khaki envelope from his tunic, and handed it over with the advice that he read it later at his leisure in some "more appropriate" place. Then he backed off and stood at the foot of the open grave chafing his Bible in his palms as if trying to warm it.

Walking arm in arm up the hill toward them, Prescott and Beth were next, Beth in black, her head and face veiled by a black lace mantilla, Prescott in a dark blue suit, bareheaded and suntanned, looking every inch the prosperous, dignified surgeon. With a pang Sanders recognized in them that similarity of posture and expression that comes of intimacy, the look of dancing partners, lovers, of husbands and wives. The soldiers, seeing them coming, doused their cigarettes and stood at attention, rifles at present arms, until Beth stood at the head of the grave next to the chaplain. A few moments later Peter King emerged from the mist, richly if oddly dressed in gray flannel trousers and a blue double-breasted blazer with brass buttons and an emblem on the pocket over his heart, looking as if he had just stepped ashore from a yachting trip or was about to embark on one. Lastly, old man Christiansen came, helped by a uniformed attendant, leaning on a knob-headed cane, so thin and pale now that he looked as if he were compounded of the very mist around them and might almost without effort turn and melt into it without leaving a trace. None of them spoke to anyone else or gave more than the faintest nod of recognition that was acknowledgment of the others' presence. Together they formed a small semicircle at the head of the grave, each of them a pace or two away from the others.

The funeral service was mercifully brief and with its ancient ritual dignity seemed to Sanders to have as much relevance to the way George had died as a wedding celebration has to a marriage: The ceremonial grandeur masked and mitigated the mundane and often horrible reality. When the honor guard brought the casket out of the weapons carrier, it was covered with the flag and pinned on it were two medals. The bugler took them off and handed them to the second lieutenant who, in turn, marched over to Beth and pinned them one next to the other over her left breast. "What are they?" Christiansen asked aloud, his voice clear and carrying, military, and the lieutenant told him they were the Bronze Star and the Purple Heart. Having stripped the flag from the casket, the bugler deftly folded it and when he was done a bulky triangle of material remained, revealing only the white stars on the blue background. The bugler took the flag to Beth, marching right past the old man who had extended his free hand for it and then, when he saw it was not intended for him, withdrawn it, standing taller and straighter thereafter, digging his stick deeper into the sod.

After tentative glances at their dour faces and squinting into the mist as if he expected a numerous train of mourners to materialize suddenly, the chaplain, head down, began to read the service so swiftly and in such a reedy voice that his words were carried off on the dank breeze that blew in over them from the sea. Sanders couldn't make out the words the chaplain spoke although once he thought he heard something that resembled "I am the Resurrection and the Life" and "Earth to earth, ashes to ashes, dust to dust . . ." In the overcast above, the sun burned like a bleeding wound swathed in gray gauze, the great red breasts of the bridge now and again jocularly revealed in the rolling fog, and twice the naked brown flanks of the Marin hills appeared, but mostly everywhere, everything seemed monotonously gray and funereal, as if they were all at a burial at sea watching some fisherman being lowered into the waves from a boat off the Grand Banks or in the North Sea.

The chaplain's "Amen" was abrupt and muddled, more like "Ah men!" sighed in regret, and in the silence the lumbering sounds of the coffin being lowered into the grave were like the poundings of his heart, irregular and painful. Sanders felt a part of himself, a literal, physical part of himself, being lowered into the earth, as if one of his limbs had been cut off, and he tried to recall George's face but couldn't, tried again and again, in panic, but all he could see in his mind's eye was the sprawled and broken body and a featureless void of countenance. He tried to remember his father's face, his mother's face, any of his beloved dead, but he couldn't, and the panic grew. The honor squad raised its rifles; the bolts, metallic and certain, shot home, and at command they fired a volley toward the sky, a final ragged period to George Christiansen's life, a firecracker sound muffled by the mist. The bugler blew a high and mournful taps, faltering on the highest notes, the thin brassy lament distorted by the wind into a cacophonous animal roar, a wild cry that hung on the clumps of fog like streamers of human keening, the only relevance to the death he'd seen and George had endured. Slowly the bugle notes faded and tore at his throat, at the swollen Adam's apple where there was buried a broken siren whose wail would not be clamped off. Only then did he recognize that he was crying, the sound torn out of his unwilling throat past that steel ball bearing which was his Adam's apple. Abruptly he felt weighted down, heavier, for the words that shaped themselves soundlessly in his head were intolerably oppressive: "Now I bear the burden of his life." Sacerdotal and self-pitying together, they were words he tried uneasily to shrug off, but their weight pressed him down.

As if someone had given a signal they all turned from the grave and the sight of the blood-colored clods and swinging shovels. His vision blurred by tears, his throat containing a swollen Adam's apple of nausea, his wounds aching—and all of it heightened by his panic, his terror that he could not remember George's face, or his father's and mother's—Sanders only just made out the chaplain's approach but the man's voice was uncomfortably close and jarring. "You won't mention that I gave you that letter," the chaplain asked fearfully, "if anyone asks? You know how it is."

Here, in the presence of death, and still afraid. Well, however petty the fear, what better place to be fearful, to be made afraid? "Sure," Sanders said, "I know how it is."

Then the chaplain, soldiers and weapons carrier were gone, the other mourners dispersed, and Sanders found himself alone, staring at the red scar in the green sod, the narrow hummock beaten into shape with spades. "Thanks for my life, George," he said desperately, to the grave and the mist and the chill. "Maybe I can live for both of us with it." But even as he added that, he knew it was sentimental cant, that however successful he might be with his old life or this new one, he might perhaps have two, or at least more than one, but George would have none, no more.

*   *   *

It was fall in Connecticut, a bright, brisk day in which the earth was carpeted with red, gold and yellow leaves and the sky faultless; an auburn month in a dying year, November seemed to augur spring instead of winter. The Colonel arrived at the door unannounced, having marvelously for that time of gasoline rationing driven up to their front door in a dark-red convertible with the top down. A big rawboned man who looked as if he had not slept for a month got out; his eyes, bloodshot and staring, did not really seem to take them in and his skin was so tightly drawn over his bones that Sanders saw the blood beating in the protuberant blue veins at his gray temples. They knew he was a colonel only because he told them he was, formally announcing himself as Colonel Michael Robinson from Washington, but he was in mufti, swaddled in an old-style camel's-hair overcoat that had once fitted him well and wearing a broad-brimmed, mud-brown fedora with a sweat-stained band.

His mother already surmised disaster but she had to some extent been prepared by the long silence from his father and the evasiveness of his New York and Washington offices when she'd called them to find out what had happened. They had not heard from Lovett Carpenter Sanders for almost four months, since midsummer, which would not in itself have been disturbing, for he was not much of a letter writer; but what alarmed them more was that they saw none of his dispatches in the papers and heard no more of that familiar and resplendent voice on the radio. At first Sanders wondered at his mother's concern, but after Paris fell and they had still not had a letter or card, or seen his column printed or heard his voice on the air, he became frightened himself. Not that he could believe anything would happen to his father: Lovett Carpenter Sanders was invincible; but he was also convinced that his father could never, would never willingly, have passed up the opportunity to record the liberation of Paris. His father had, he knew, lived for that day with a stoic patience, a roweling impatience, eager to see his beloved second home—and perhaps if he had been altogether honest, he would have confessed that it was his first and preferred home. In his mind Sanders could see the words of the column and in his head he could hear their echo as he knew Lovett Carpenter Sanders would have recorded them: "This is Lovett Carpenter Sanders speaking to you from Paris once more. A little more than four years ago on June 14, 1940, I saw Nazi flying columns enter and occupy Paris and as their jackboots echoed down the Champs-Élysées and through the Arch of Triumph those who loved the city and France wept. Today, August 25, 1944, after six days of fighting, I saw the City of Light liberated, returned to its citizens and to France. Allied forces led by an American and Free French division, and aided by the French Forces of the Interior, the FFI, once again cleared the city of the hated Boches."

Though he saw that his mother was upset, Sanders was sure that Colonel Robinson would never have known it. She asked the Colonel to take off his coat, seated him in his father's big wing chair, brought him a drink of their now almost never used Scotch, and had Sanders lay a fire in the living room to take the November chill off the air. When she had finished making the Colonel as comfortable as she could with her small talk about his trip and gasoline rationing and would he like a bite to eat, she grew silent, her beautiful hands lying folded in her lap, apprehensively waiting. Robinson drank the three fingers of whisky silently in two spasmodic gulps and held out his glass for more. While Sanders brought the decanter and poured him a second, setting it next to him on the table and within easy reach, the Colonel looked from one of them to the other before he said, "The Greeks used to kill bearers of ill tidings and I now see why. They deserve it."

"You have bad news about Lovett," his mother said.

"I have," he said outright. "We think he's dead."

"You *think* he's dead?" his mother said, her emphasis on the word so critical that the Colonel leaned back in his chair as if he'd been slapped.

"He's missing," Robinson said.

"In action?" Sanders asked. "He'll get back. He knows France like a book, he speaks fluent French, he—"

"It's not like that, son," Robinson interrupted. His head wobbled as if the effort to keep it erect on his neck was almost too much for him.

"How is it, then?" Sanders asked.

"A long complicated story," Robinson replied, sipping the Scotch slowly with catlike pleasure.

"Isn't that what you came here for, to tell us?" Sanders persisted.

"Elliott," his mother interposed, "please let Colonel Robinson tell us what he wants to in his own way and in his own good time. Whatever it is, it cannot be easy for him."

Robinson looked his gratitude. "What I have to say is more difficult because we don't exactly know what happened. Not nearly. But I'll tell you what we do know."

"Yes, do," his mother said dryly, but Sanders saw her agitation in her hands.

"Where shall I begin?" the Colonel said rhetorically.

"At the beginning," his mother advised.

"Sorry," Robinson apologized. "I've only just gotten back from there, from France I mean, and I'm not myself. Washington for a week and not much sleep there, briefings and all, and—" he smiled —"I guess the old classroom manner sticks. Not even the military can brush off the academic manner."

"You came here directly from Washington, without going home?" his mother asked. "Thank you."

"It was on my way," Robinson explained. "I live in Cambridge, and they gave me coupons so that I could drive up." He waited for her to say more but she didn't.

"There's an American intelligence service," he began again with a sigh, "called the OSS, the Office of Strategic Services. You may have heard of it. We've had to recruit many and not-quite-orthodox persons into the service, overage, broken-down professors like me, journalists like your husband, scientists, others."

"One volunteers for that?" his mother inquired.

"Yes, it's voluntary."

"Then Lovett volunteered?"

"Well, yes and no. We asked him to work with us because he knew things that so few of our people do. We sent him into France and brought him out, several times. In fact, before the invasion he performed admirably—"

"But we saw his columns and heard him on the radio regularly," Sanders protested.

"Yes, yes, I know," Robinson agreed. "Recordings. Columns. Even letters. All made up in advance. We took care of that. Simple. All carefully thought out and planned."

"Not carefully enough, apparently," his mother commented.

Robinson's head hung lower. "No, I suppose not." He poured himself another dollop of Scotch. "When we were close to the invasion, we needed someone to go into France a good while before us on an assignment of some delicacy. It required a man who knew Paris, France, the French intimately—and who could be trusted. Lovett Sanders was just the man and when we told him what we needed, he volunteered."

"He would," his mother said and Sanders couldn't tell if she was proud or sarcastic or both. "What did you have him do?"

"I'd rather not tell you, if you don't mind."

She stood up, her fingers toying with the single strand of pearls at her throat. "Good afternoon, Colonel, I'm sorry you had to drive so far out of your way."

"You're not angry, I hope," the Colonel said, still seated.

"I'm not angry, I'm furious. As soon as you leave, I am going to put in a person-to-person call to Washington to our Senator who happens to be an old family friend. I'm going to tell him precisely what you've told me." Though her voice was agitated, her manner remained composed.

"I hope you won't do that," the Colonel said uneasily.

Her fury broke through her composure. She turned on her heel, deliberately showing him her back, and walked to the windows. "You come here and tell me you think—you *think!*—my husband is dead. You inform me that he volunteered for a mission behind the German lines about which you will tell me nothing. You declare that he was working for an organization I never heard him mention. And you expect me to nod, complacently, accept it without further information or proof, and say thank you? What kind of idiot do you take me for?"

"Mrs. Sanders, it's your patriotic duty—" Robinson began.

She turned on him like a cat, teeth bared, eyes blazing, spitting the words out. "Don't you dare lecture me about patriotism! You have the effrontery to sit there and tell *me* what *my* duty is! Let me tell you *your* duty. If my husband died, I want to know how, when and where, and what for. Do you understand that? And if you have nothing more to say, then, Colonel, you just get yourself up out of that chair and out that door. I'll find out what happened in my own way."

Sanders had never seen her so angry in his life, nor so fierce; not even in her worst fights with his father could he remember her being so savage. Suddenly, with a hot rush of embarrassed feeling, with a new and uncomfortable sensation of adult complexity, he realized that his mother loved his father, separation or not, fancy women or not, John C. Ballinger or not, and would continue to love him as long as she lived.

"There's a war on, Mrs. Sanders," Robinson unnecessarily and sententiously reminded her, "and there are other lives in danger. I'm under orders to tell you only that we are pretty certain that your husband is dead."

"Good afternoon, Colonel Robinson," his mother said. "Elliott, show the Colonel out, please." She strode out of the room without giving the Colonel another glance and Sanders heard her heels sharp on the staircase.

For a long time Robinson sat looking into the melting ice of his drink, then he stood up. "Your father was a very brave man," he said. "Your mother should leave it at that, leave well enough alone."

"Would you?" Elliott asked him.

Robinson hesitated, then reluctantly shook his head. "No, I suppose not. But it won't do you any good. You can't bring your father back."

"Eventually we'll find out," Sanders said and he knew he was making a threat and a vow, to the Colonel, but also to himself.

"You may—"

"We will. *I* will."

Robinson surveyed him again, reappraising him. "You're a lot like your father," he said. "You know, I have a son about your age and I wish I could believe he'd feel the way you do if someone came and told him what I've just told your mother and you." Robinson finished the drink, set the glass on the table, turned and made his way out. Elliott followed and, from the vestibule, through the multicolored leaded windows on either side of the door, watched him. The Colonel sat stiffly in the seat, then folded his arms on the steering wheel and collapsed his head on his arms as if he were overwhelmed with the need to sleep. He rested there for what seemed an age until, abruptly, his car horn sounded and he jerked erect. He cast a quick eye to see if anyone had been alarmed, then started the car and drove out of the driveway. It was the end and the beginning.

Sanders called to his mother several times before the silence frightened him and he went up the stairs two at a time to her bedroom. No one answered his knocking and when he went inside he heard the shower in her adjoining bathroom going full blast, felt a momentary relief, then knocked and shouted at the bathroom door until she answered, her voice, even through the clamor of the shower, filled with tears. "I'm quite all right, Elliott," she called, the effort to reassure him plain. "I'll be down to dinner in a little while." He stood listening to her sobs sounding over the noise of the shower, expecting, hoping, that the sobs might bring on his own tears, but all he felt was rage and a fanatic urge to know what had happened to his father that he could free only by a wild screaming that congealed in his throat like an icy snowball. The sobbing in the bathroom was steady as the rain of the shower and when he could bear it no longer and was ready to leave, he noticed the small slip of paper that lay on her dressing table and with uncertain fingers picked it up. It read, a combination of bold black type and slender graceful italics:

A MESSAGE TO YOU

Be not deceived; God is not mocked: for whatsoever a man soweth, that shall he also reap.

For he that soweth to his flesh shall of the flesh reap corruption; but he that soweth to the Spirit shall of the Spirit reap life everlasting.
JESUS CHRIST: Take Him and Live; Neglect Him and Die!

TAKE HIM TODAY

Sanders let the paper slip from his fingers, and like an autumn leaf it floated back down onto her dressing table.

❉   ❉   ❉

It had taken him more than ten years to find out most, but not by any means all, of what had happened with a reasonable degree of certainty and it had changed his entire life. By then his mother was long dead, although it was she, true to her word, who had begun the investigation by going to Washington to see their Senator who had in earlier times been a law partner and friend of her father's. There, his mother had discovered that the American OSS and the British SOE, Special Operations Executive, had parachuted his father into France in January 1944, five months before the invasion. The Senator told her that, as far as he could find out, Lovett Carpenter Sanders had volunteered for what on the surface seemed like a fairly simple assignment, the delivery of a newly invented radio transmitter to the French Resistance, a transmitter that was supposed to make contact with London swifter, easier and less dangerous. Later, at the Senator's insistence, an intelligence report had been made available to his mother stating that his father had successfully completed his mission but subsequently been apprehended in Paris and executed by the Germans. Just when, it said, they were not sure but they believed it to be shortly before or shortly after the June 6 Allied landings. If that was the case, his mother inquired, how then had they continued to receive mail from him up through August, seen his dispatches late into spring and even heard his voice on the air from time to time? The Senator didn't know and the intelligence people wouldn't say. A few months after the war was over the Senator had informed her that her husband had been awarded the highest decoration conferred on civilians for war service, but what he had done to earn the award was not specified, nor was any formal citation or decoration then forthcoming.

Obsessed, Sanders had gone on to put the story together piece by piece, learning more in doing so of how to be a good newspaperman than journalism school or any subsequent assignment had taught him, comprehending more through it about power and politics in their starkest forms than the study of either history or political science had given him the slightest inkling of. All of it, the long road through five foreign countries and the United States, through chancelleries and several secret-service "front" offices, into police records and beyond to the individuals who had worked in and for all those agencies, had more than prepared him for what he eventually saw and reported in Algeria, in South America, in Eastern Europe, in Southeast Asia. Finally, he was able to make some sense of what had happened, a broken mosaic to be sure, with parts missing, but a mosaic that made a picture nonetheless, though it was the archeologist's reconstruction more than the live reality; and when he had finished he wasn't sure that he wouldn't have been wiser in one sense to follow Colonel Robinson's advice to let well enough alone. His confidence in the whole technique of journalism had been permanently undermined and warped and he was less sure than ever that he had made the right choice in following in his father's footsteps—in both senses—by becoming a journalist, the only way he felt he could competently carry out his vow and the search instead of becoming a lawyer, as his mother had wished, or a historian, as he had himself hoped.

In 1951, in London, he had gotten his first real break. After a fortnight of being shunted from office to office, from one shabby pipe-smoking civil servant and ex-Army officer to another, he'd been casually approached in his hotel lobby by a small dark Englishman with fair hair slicked down and a nasty thin-lipped mouth. The man had worn only a brown Harris tweed suit and a red plaid scarf flung jauntily around his throat though it was a bitterly cold winter day. His mean gray eyes had taken his measure like a psychological tailor, and behind the eyes a cash register that rang up the total said more plainly than speech that Elliott Sanders was a man one didn't have to worry about too much. "You're Lov Sanders' boy?" the man had asked and when Sanders admitted that he was, the man had led him to a nearby pub where, over double whiskies, he'd told him coldly that his father had been betrayed to the Gestapo by a double agent in the French Resistance. "You know," he remarked morosely, "the Germans had the French underground completely infiltrated; it was as full of holes as termite-ridden wood."

"We were told," Sanders countered, "that the Wehrmacht took my father."

"You speak German?" the man asked, a light flickering in his face.

"Yes, why?"

"French?"

"I grew up in France."

"Yes, I know."

"Did you know my father?"

"In a manner of speaking."

"What does that mean?"

"Interesting. You ever do the kind of job your father did for us? No, of course not, you're much too young. Ever want to?"

"Definitely not. I'm only interested in finding out what happened to my father."

The Englishman's face closed. "I've told you what I know."

Sanders stood up. "Thanks for the whiskies," he said, but the man held his forearm and wouldn't let him pass.

"Leave it be, why don't you?" he asked.

Sanders glowered at the man's hand on his forearm until it was removed. "I can't," he said then.

"Well"—the Englishman shrugged—"if you can't, you can't." He fingered the tiny scrub of stiff blond hairs protruding from his nostrils. "Why don't you have a talk with Albert Guitton. He was a good friend of your father's."

"Where do I find him?"

"Paris, I suppose. Lived somewhere out near St. Cloud last I heard."

"No address?"

The man shrugged again.

"Thanks."

"Don't mention it," he said blithely and turned back to his whisky and cigarettes.

*　*　*

Buck Kiely was press attaché at the London Embassy then—his card read PATRICK KIELY, SECOND SECRETARY—a tall, thin Irishman with a pale face pitted and scarred by adolescent acne. At fifty he was balding and gray with heavy black eyebrows that made him look incongruously youthful, like a Studs Lonigan crony left over from the Chicago South Side where, in fact, Kiely'd been born and raised. "How can you tell with those Limey bastards?" Kiely was saying as they walked along the border of Hyde Park away from Marble Arch, Kiely kicking at the powdery snow like a kid testing it for sledding. "They're cold fish, every goddam one of 'em."

"But if he gave me the name, why not the address?" Sanders persisted.

"Albert Guitton. Now, where the hell do you find him? Paris isn't New Canaan, Connecticut, y'know."

[221]

"Why give me the name?" Sanders repeated.

"Blames it on the French, of course. Puts the Limeys in the clear, takes them off the hook, gets you out of their hair."

"They don't know me."

"Don't kid yourself; they know *who* you are. Some of it I can't explain, some I can, not much, but some. We worked out of the same office in those days, your father and I, for the same paper but not the same network. I mean the broadcasting network. Our cloak-and-dagger boys asked me to come in with them about the same time Lov did, but the Limeys didn't trust a Chicago Irishman any more than I trusted any of those snooty bastards, so I didn't get the whole scoop. Damn near no one did, except the top boys. You know, *Eyes Only*, and all that crap. The postcards and letters our boys mailed home to your mother and you. The dozen broadcasts or so, in those first months of '44, were prerecorded and I know because I helped Lov write and research 'em so they wouldn't go stale. The columns I wrote myself. I was a good imitator and could mimic his style like it was my own, so it went by. Besides I expect the boys in the home office must've been in on it and went along.

"But I didn't like the sound of it from the beginning. Too risky. Too long. Lov'd been in twice before, but only for a couple of weeks. This time was for keeps until we came and got him—which, though those cagey creeps didn't say it right out, they implied would be pretty soon."

"It was only six months or less before the landings."

"*Only!* Jesus H. Christ! Do you know what six months' underground is like?"

Sanders shook his head dumbly.

"But that new radio transmitter *was* important. I knew that, and so did your old man. Which is, I guess, why he agreed to take it in. The Resistance boys working with those old-style keys, tapping their stuff out in Morse, were getting picked off like flies—the Nazi radio-detection units were damn good—and we were losing a lot of information. And boy, we were hungry for information then, everybody had the jitters about the invasion being a blood bath. The technical boys said this new gadget would give the Frogs voice communication with London so they could transmit fast and get the hell out of where they were before the German radio-intelligence outfits triangulated them and came busting in. The 'old firm' —the SOE—said those transmitters would be tough to monitor altogether."

"And?"

"I don't know too much more. Lov got in and made contact. That much I know personally. He delivered the goods. The rest I only heard. The Limeys had three very short broadcasts from that network, all of them interrupted—by the Germans, they assumed—and then . . . nothing."

"When was that?"

"I'm not sure. He went in in January. Must've been early spring then, April I'd say."

"Isn't there a file on that operation somewhere?" Sanders asked.

"There *was*."

"If there was, there must still be."

Kiely scooped up a handful of the light wet snow and began to pack it into a snowball which he threw in a high long arch into the park. "The SOE files were burned after the war. Orders from on high."

"So there's only Albert Guitton."

"Or some of the guys who were controls for the 'old firm.'" Kiely snapped his fingers. "Wait a minute. There's more than that. Your father—I'm sorry, Elliott, you know he was a great swordsman—had two special dames in France, both of them in the Resistance, Nathalie Blanchot and Claudia . . . Morrisette. He used to joke that he had to parachute into France to get a good meal and a good piece of ass."

"Have you got their addresses?"

"No, not personally, but I might be able to get them for you. I'll call you at your hotel tonight."

That evening when Sanders returned to his room after dinner a sealed envelope awaited him. It had been slipped under his door and contained a single sheet of paper without either note or letterhead, but with the typewritten addresses of both women.

❖   ❖   ❖

[223]

Sanders had lived and worked in France for two years before he found Nathalie Blanchot and then only after he had spent fourteen months tracking Claudia Morrisette through four flats—only one of them in her own name—five different men and three arrondissements and finally traced her to a grim and grimy brick hospital near the Flea Market where she had died a few months earlier. The doctor remembered her well, a frail large-eyed brunette who had the whole range of alcoholic ailments—pancreatitis, ileitis, cirrhosis—a very unusual and interesting "case." The doctor continued talking about how unusual "the case" was, you didn't often get women who drank that much, but Sanders stopped listening to him.

Of Nathalie Blanchot there was not a trace until, purely by accident, he located her in an item in the papers announcing that a painter with that name was giving a show. Sanders didn't go to the show, but by then, having established himself as a journalist and photographer for both French and American papers, it was not hard to get her address from the gallery simply by dangling the hope of an interview and a picture spread.

Nathalie Blanchot lived high up on Montmartre in one of the small streets from which, if one craned one's neck, one could see the whited sepulcher of the Sacré-Coeur, and which, with only two brandies inside you, might seem like a typical Utrillo scene. She lived on the top floor in a studio that had a skylight and little black scrollwork balconies chipped and rusting around the windows just wide enough to hold potted and blooming geraniums. When Sanders knocked she looked at him through the judas first and he could see her mouth become an *O* of consternation. The door opened slowly, as if by itself, and a tall, once-beautiful woman in her late thirties, wearing a paint-smeared blue artist's smock, gazed at him with great green eyes fixed like a sleepwalker's. "Lovett," she said, staring, pronouncing his father's name like *love eet*, "it cannot be you."

"Nathalie Blanchot?" Sanders asked, though he knew the question was superfluous.

She nodded, like one drugged.

[224]

"I'm *Elliott* Sanders," he introduced himself, emphasizing his first name so that she would understand.

"Elliott?" she repeated, perplexed. "Ah yes, the son, the boy. You're Lovett's son." She seemed released from a spell, smiling to show two prominent gold teeth, and asked him into an impeccably neat but sparsely furnished flat with only one part of it, separated from the rest by two shoji screens which showed faceless Japanese peasants drawing an aristocrat's cart with a bullock between the shafts, used for a studio. Equally orderly, the studio was bathed in the early-morning light and all the canvases, stacked against the walls with their frames toward the room, looked skeletal, naked, except the canvas on the easel which was face-out but empty. Without taking her eyes from his face, she motioned him to a chair. "You speak French?" she asked in heavily accented English and then, with an impatient gesture, answered herself. "But certainly, you speak French. You are a *vrai petit de Paris*. You grew up here." Before he could speak, she held her hand up and said, "Elliott—I may say *tu* to you? I feel I know you very well—I think you are here to find out about Lovett, about your father, no?"

Sanders nodded, not trusting himself to words.

She brought a carafe of red wine from the breakfast table where there was a *café filtre* percolator and demitasse cups and filled two water-spotted glasses. She gave him one, held hers up in a toast. "To Lovett Sanders, one of the finest men I have ever known."

Uncomfortably Sanders drank to that and when she had asked how he had searched her out, Sanders told her about the Englishman, about Kiely, about Claudia Morrisette, and then the accident of seeing her show announced. "Ah, Claudia I knew. She was in our network during the underground days. It was difficult for her after the war, she couldn't find herself and so she lost herself." She lifted her glass again, not without pity, and sipped the wine for Claudia now dead. Her eyes grew pensive. "Claudia was also your father's lover, as I was. Perhaps I should not say that to you, you Americans are so much puritan, but I am relying on your young days in France so you will not tell your mother."

"My mother is dead," Sanders said, with effort.

"I am sorry," Nathalie Blanchot said and she seemed genuinely saddened. Her sadness increased through two or three more glasses of wine before she began to talk.

"I met your father in 1939, just before you and your mother went back to the United States. I was twenty-two years old, working at the old Havas Agency—you are a newspaperman, no?" And when he nodded, she continued, "Of course, what else could Lovett Sanders' son be?—and he took me out for an aperitif. He was handsome and gallant and really interested in me, and I was lonely—my family always at me to come back to Lyon and marry and settle down—and we had an affair. Then the war came and Lovett went, had to go, to England, and I remained behind in Paris, and I found I was in love with him. You are not embarrassed that I talk like this?" she asked.

Sanders felt his cheeks hot but feigned the necessary sophistication, and said no.

"Good! It was a bad time, an ugly time, for France. You could trust no one and every day people were betrayed to the Boches, not only Jews but Frenchmen, and all those poor refugees who had run from Hitler elsewhere, Austrians and Czechs and Dutch and even some Germans. Then, one day, Albert Guitton came to visit me."

"Albert Guitton!"

"You know him?"

"No, but I want to know him."

"It is simple. He is with the Sûreté."

"A policeman?"

"Probably with the Deuxième."

"Go on," Sanders urged her, struggling to control his impatience, his curiosity.

Nathalie Blanchot sipped her wine meditatively. "Guitton told me he was in the Resistance, that he had been to London and been sent back to organize a . . . network. He had seen Lovett in London and Lovett had sent him to me, told him that I could be relied on absolutely. *Relied on absolutely*. How flattering that was to a girl of my age, young and so naïve then, and if you will pardon me, so full of passion for your father. When the Germans came I quit Havas—I had a small income left to me from my grandmother's inheritance—and I went to the École des Beaux Arts to study painting. I wanted no part of politics then—though I thought of myself with pride as a *political*—but I hated the Boches and Vichy, so though I said the hell with them all, I knew I could not stay out for long. But the Communists made me sick to my stomach, and the others—well, the others did not seem like much. Guitton was my opportunity—I took it. I joined the Resistance.

"At first I didn't have much to do and there was little danger. I worked as a courier for the underground. Because I was a student and could take my easel and go almost anywhere to paint, it was easy for me to travel so I was useful to Guitton. But later I had to do other things I did not like and which were more dangerous and I was frightened and sickened. That was how I met Claudia Morrisette and learned"—she laughed, a humorless grimace that showed her wine-stained tongue and teeth—"that Lovett had also told Guitton that Claudia too could be 'relied on absolutely' and that Claudia had also been his 'little friend.' I was hurt and jealous and angry, but they talked to me about duty, about France, about the Boches, and how such things were greater than individuals. Bah!

"Claudia's work was more dangerous than mine and I was grateful and envious. She was a singer, in a small boîte near Pigalle—you know, one of those skinny, big-eyed, big-breasted chanteuses who usually make half their living as prostitutes. But not Claudia. She really thought she could be Piaf, without tears, without suffering, without all the dying; she was not very well educated or very intelligent, she had no politics at all; she was in all things an innocent.

"Until Guitton arrived. Guitton sensed what she could do—he was that kind of man, he had something feminine in him; like a wolf, he could sniff out your weaknesses and your dreams and use them against you and for the underground; it made him what he was, a hero—and a scoundrel—and he used Claudia. German officers came to the club where Claudia worked. They came to drink and sing and carouse and to find girls who would 'play' with them for money or for excitement or just for a man; those were the girls we so kindly and so bravely shaved the heads of afterwards—when everyone was suddenly brave, when everyone said he had been in the Resistance, when there was no more risk and no more danger. Guitton wanted information from the Germans. At first Claudia was only to drink with them, really only make-believe drinking, because the bartender would see that she got colored water or ginger ale. Then, later, when the officers were of higher rank, Herr Majors and Herr Obersts, and one even a young Herr General, it went further. Claudia was ordered to become their *copain*.

"Three years is a long time, longer in the life of a young girl than any man can know. It is different for men. We have different calendars, rhythms. Men have a longer time to fulfill their destiny and so they are less aware of how time passes for us who come to flower and to fruit sooner and whose urgencies are so intense, so imperative. You know, we French say, woman has only two passions: cupidity and mother love; but it is not true: We women have only one passion, men, through which we realize the other two and through which we are ourselves realized.

"And so it was with Claudia. She began to drink in earnest herself because she was afraid, because she was at heart an innocent and hated what she had to do, because she thought she could drown out the schoolgirl conscience she had learned from the nuns. Somehow, perhaps one of them was kind to her, or perhaps she was lonely, or perhaps because she fell in love with someone on the rebound from Lovett, the Boches 'doubled' her. She began to give our information to them as well as theirs to us. Perhaps they had even known about her being part of our 'net' and deliberately set out to penetrate it; perhaps it was 'accidental.' I don't know. I told you, Claudia had no politics, so it could not have been for that. Perhaps, too, it was the fear and the darkness of those times when it seemed that the Germans would be with us forever, always, for the rest of our lives and our children's lives. Claudia even passed along to the Boches the signal for the invasion, those beautiful Verlaine lines that the BBC was to broadcast to let us know, to alert us, so that we would be prepared:

> *Les sanglots longs*
> *Des violons*
> *De l'automne*
>
> *Blessent mon coeur*
> *D'une langueur*
> *Monotone.*

There were tears in her eyes as she recited the lines, and Sanders could see that the recollections of those autumns gone by were still wounding her heart.

"Then, in the winter of 1944, Guitton came and told me that Lov was in France on a mission, that he had brought with him a new radio transmitter that those wonderful English had invented for us, a voice transmitter, so that we could save our comrades from being taken by the Boches while broadcasting, as so many had been taken, but that the transmitter only had a short range. It could reach London from within a radius of about one hundred and fifty miles, so we had to find some place in the Pas de Calais from which we could safely transmit. We had to find someone who would broadcast and I would bring the materials to be broadcasted from Paris.

"Lov was already in Paris and would go with me to find the right place. Then he was to come back to Paris to hide here until the invasion and the liberation. Guitton had located three places where we had friends he thought we might use to broadcast from in the Pas de Calais: one at Boulogne-sur-Mer, the most dangerous because the Boches had it heavily garrisoned, a second at St. Omer, and the last at Montreuil. All were in range of London with the new transmitter and we decided to try all three."

"But why the Pas de Calais where the Germans would have had the most people, and since it was the shortest distance from England and the most logical place for the invasion, where they'd have the best security?" Sanders asked.

"Yes," Nathalie Blanchot replied, "why? That was the question." She gulped some more of the wine. "I wanted Lovett all to myself," she continued, a dreaminess taking possession of her face. "I hadn't seen him for five years and I'd carried the picture of him in my head, exaggerated by time and distance and romance; but I was no longer the girl of twenty-two, I was a woman of twenty-seven, and those five years made a difference, a very great difference. How great I knew but Lovett didn't. He thought we could be together as we'd been before the war and have a carefree, passionate, illicit affair without responsibilities, but that was no longer enough for me. I wanted more, much more, but I knew he wasn't willing to give it, perhaps couldn't give it. He was still married to your mother and

[229]

in his own strange way he loved her. I don't think he could admit that to himself but he wouldn't talk of divorce. And of course he would never have considered giving up his son." She pointed a long finger, nail rimmed with paint, at him. "You."

"I'm sorry," Sanders murmured awkwardly, not sure what he was apologizing for, his own existence as his father's hostage to fortune, or his father's failures of commitment to Nathalie Blanchot. He hid his awkwardness behind his wineglass, emptied it, remembering that when you took what you wanted others paid for it too.

"Yet having him there again in Paris was wonderful. He was, as he had always been, cheerful, charming, gallant, brave, and I wondered why I couldn't have been lucky like your mother to have such a man to myself. Until I realized, of course, that she didn't have him to herself either and it was not, if you will pardon me, altogether a matter of what he said about her coldness in bed. I knew Lovett wasn't and probably never would be for one woman, but I wanted his child anyway. Right there, right then, in the middle of the war, in the intrigue and danger of the underground, I didn't care about anything so much as having Lovett's child. And mine. I was twenty-seven and I was ready, and I had the man I loved with me, a man I might never have again.

"But I didn't tell Lovett. I knew better than that. He would have joked and teased and laughed me out of it, told me very seriously that there was a war to be won, that it wasn't the right time for personal and private fulfillments, all the commonsense things I didn't care a damn about. If I couldn't have him, I wanted his child at least; and so I took no precautions. I hated them anyway and I prayed for a pregnancy though I had no idea how I could manage things if I became pregnant, or what I would tell Lovett. Or Guitton.

"I didn't want to tell Claudia that Lovett was back, at first, because I knew about them from Guitton, but soon it became necessary. We needed several 'safe houses' to keep him hidden so he wouldn't be seen and become familiar in any one place; and because we all had some kinds of social obligations to fulfill where his presence would have been awkward to explain, we had to use Claudia's flat from time to time. She was still singing in that cabaret but now she had only one of them for a lover, a Major Friedrich Olbracht—

her Freddie—the adjutant to Lieutenant General Boineburg-Lengs-feld, the commandant of Paris. Freddie was perfect for what we wanted; we could get information from him we couldn't get any-where else because he was in a perfect place. As adjutant all kinds of information came across his desk—troop movements, transporta-tion plans, political and economic decisions—so Guitton, of course, encouraged it and was delighted when Olbracht made Claudia his 'regular.' Claudia was not drinking so much and didn't seem so un-happy and she was singing much better; all of that should have given me a clue but it didn't. She was in love with Freddie, and eventually, when he found out about her, we think he 'doubled' her. When Lovett came back and she saw him it must have been a ter-rible shock for her. In her own way Claudia loved him and she loved Freddie too. She was caught and she tried in her own fumbling way —as I told you, she was not very intelligent—to be loyal to both.

"All the while Guitton was busy trying to set up the transmitter in the Pas de Calais. Late in February he and Lovett tried to broad-cast from Boulogne, but it was a fiasco. The Boche radio-detection units almost caught them. They tried again early in March from St. Omer and again barely escaped with their skins. Guitton had much important information for London, so something had to be done quickly—the Germans were strengthening the West Wall, new di-visions were arriving in Normandy, Brittany and the Pas de Calais—and Guitton decided to try transmitting once more, from Montreuil, the first week in April, but he was very disturbed because he couldn't understand why the Germans were picking them up even more swiftly than when they'd been sending by Morse. Something was wrong and the only thing Guitton could think of was that we had a 'leak' in our net. That was when he began to check on Claudia and her Freddie and how we found out, later, finally, that she was giving our information to Olbracht. But there were two ironies. She was not only giving us the information Olbracht 'manufactured' for us; she was giving us other information she wasn't supposed to. And the final irony was that it wasn't Claudia who had told the Boches about the new transmitter or about Boulogne or St. Omer: We did that ourselves."

"Why, in God's name?" Sanders blurted.

"Yes, why? But not in God's name. Certainly not in His name." She laughed harshly and poured herself some more wine and when he covered his glass, she raised a quizzical eyebrow. "Ah, not like father, like son? Would you like a *noir* instead?" Without waiting for his reply she got up and began to make *café filtre*.

"Please go on," he urged.

"There isn't too much more," she said from the sink, her back to him rigid. "Guitton had an old friend who owned a small farm outside of Montreuil and they set the transmitter up in the barn, but before they'd been on the air a quarter of an hour, the barn was surrounded, the Germans barged in and they were taken. They didn't even have time to put up a fight or smash the transmitter.

"And that's when they found out what fools we'd been, what dupes. The Boche captain who interrogated them laughed in their faces and asked how they could be so stupid as to broadcast on the same wavelength used by *German* tanks! Then they knew they'd been set up as sacrificial goats by the English because they knew that the English monitored German tank radio traffic so that they must have known the wavelength."

"Couldn't it have been a mistake, an error, one branch not checking with another?"

"No, my dear boy." She shook her head with absolute certainty. "It would have been criminal even if it had been a mistake. You don't make mistakes like that in underground work without having all your people killed. But it was no accident." She turned and faced him. "By a miracle we managed to rescue them. Guitton's friend had several of the local Maquis nearby and when the Germans tried to take Lovett and Guitton back to Montreuil, they were ambushed. Guitton and Lovett escaped and came back to Paris. Lovett stayed at my flat because by then we knew that Claudia was doubling and we couldn't risk his being with her. But because Claudia would be suspicious if Lovett stopped seeing her altogether, we told him nothing and let him continue to go there so that he slept with her three nights a week, the nights Olbracht was on duty, and the other four nights—he made love to me. So, you see, I was, at least, one ahead." She laughed bitterly.

She motioned him to the table, set out clean cups and saucers,

[232]

some *pain de campagne,* butter and strawberry preserves, and sat down across from him. The sound of the coffee as it dripped from the top of the percolator to the bottom was like the sound of rain, and the sipping sounds Nathalie Blanchot made smoking her cigarette were like an asthmatic's breathing while they waited for the coffee. She poured it for him when it was done but continued herself only to smoke and drink the red wine.

"Why didn't you tell my father she was a double?" Sanders asked.

Nathalie Blanchot shook her blond head; the lines around her eyes were deep and patterned crow's-feet as she squinted into her own cigarette smoke, making her seem much older than she was. "Guitton said not to. He didn't think your father could be her lover and know about her." She smiled. "Guitton said, 'A Frenchman, maybe, but an American, never.' You see, we all have these nationalist—chauvinist—illusions. Only four of us knew—Guitton, Jean Hoche and Bernard Magny, two of the men who had done the 'investigation,' and myself. Our plan was to use her to feed back false information through Olbracht to the Germans. It is a nightmare world, that underground work, where you double and triple and quadruple until, I am sure, some of them no longer truly know which side they are on. You need strong loyalties and a strong stomach for such work.

"But it was a mistake not to tell Lovett; if we had, if I had, he might still be alive." She swallowed the rest of the wine in her glass, made a face, and poured herself some coffee. "If . . . agh! All that spring the trees budded and leafed and blossomed, the candles on the chestnuts burned white as if they were all great candelabra lit up to celebrate the coming invasion. We knew the invasion must come soon, you could almost smell it. Even the Boches felt it and they were nervous and even more cruel. Networks were broken, hostages taken, people rounded up and deported to the Reich, suspects tortured and shot. But the spring was beautiful, yellow and green and fertile. . . .

"And then the BBC broadcast the *Chanson d'Automne* and we knew, at last, it was here. The waiting was over. For the first few days after the landings Lovett was quiet, depressed, worried that it might be a fiasco, a bloodbath, and that the Boches might throw

[233]

them all back into the sea, and then he turned ecstatic. 'I told you we'd come back,' he exulted. 'I told you we'd drive them out.' He hated the Boches as if he were himself not an American but French. Lovett wanted to join the Allied forces but orders came through Guitton that Lovett was to remain in Paris, that we were to keep Claudia 'alive,' and to use her Freddie to see if we could prevent Paris from becoming a battleground.

"And a week after the invasion began, I knew I was pregnant—and I told your father."

"He must have been furious," Sanders hazarded.

Sluggishly she immersed the burning end of her cigarette in the coffee which had sloshed over into her saucer, watching each glowing spark darken. "That was what I expected too, but Lovett surprised me. He was happy!" She looked up at him, her face obdurate, daring him to challenge the truth of what she'd gone through. "He *was* happy. He said he had one American son who'd lived in France long enough to be considered half French; now he'd have a French son who was half American."

"It never occurred to him that the odds were fifty-fifty that it might be a daughter, did it?" Sanders remarked.

"No, never. But it was, it was." Her face convulsed with tears that were never shed. "It was I who made the great, the fatal, mistake. I was so happy, happy because Lovett wanted the child and seemed to want me. Even if he had said nothing about divorcing your mother and marrying me, even if he was often morose because there was no way for him to communicate with you or to know how you were living, even if he was restless because the Allies were fighting and he was doing nothing, even if he continued to go to bed with Claudia three times a week, I thought he loved me. In his own way, to be sure, in his own, strange way."

"Maybe Lovett Carpenter Sanders could just love more than one woman. Maybe—he was big enough." Sanders intended the comment primarily to allay her doubts, to comfort her, but he was also conscious that he had finally accepted a conclusion he had previously always fought, that the weakness was a strength of his father's, the strength a weakness. On that, for the first time, he felt undeceived.

"It was a mistake nonetheless," Nathalie Blanchot continued. "But

[234]

I couldn't keep it to myself. I couldn't tell Guitton because I knew then that he'd drop me from the net, split me from Lovett. Oh, Guitton knew we were sleeping together but he knew Lovett was also making love to Claudia—"

"Which made it okay?"

"That Guitton could understand and countenance. But having a baby was different, serious. It posed many problems and difficulties, so instead of telling him, I told Claudia. Looking back on it, it was insane. I knew about Freddie—I lay awake tossing and turning every one of those three nights Lovett spent with her, blind with anger and jealousy—yet it was to Claudia that I turned, to Claudia that I said I was pregnant with Lovett's child." She struck the heel of her hand against her forehead. "How could I have done anything so stupid!"

"And so human." For that Sanders did not have to force his compassion.

"Human, yes, which is the same thing, isn't it?" She lit another of her Gitanes, swallowed hard and choked a little on the smoke before she spoke again. "It never occurred to me," she went on, in a voice so diminished it sounded like another, younger voice, a girl's voice, gentler, higher-pitched, naïve, a voice she might once have owned, "that Claudia would be jealous. I didn't let myself see or remember that in spite of Freddie Olbracht, Claudia also loved Lovett, that she might be jealous, that her anger and envy might be kindled into flame. Perhaps I never let myself believe that altogether because I wanted to think that what was between them was only an affair of the flesh, nothing more.

"Then and there, when I told, she went berserk, wild with anger, smashed a hand mirror she was holding, threw it to the floor and ground it under her heel. What right did I have to be pregnant when men were being killed every day, when the country was in the throes of such anguish? I thought *she* was innocent. It was *I* who was the naïve one. I asked what better time, the Allies were going to liberate Paris soon and we'd all be free to live as we wished. I didn't think that maybe she too wanted a child, with Lovett, or with Freddie, or that perhaps she was frightened by the Allied liberation, terrified that someone would find out her double role. I didn't imagine she was lonely or desperate or crying out with need for a child; I thought only of myself."

"Not quite," Sanders reassured her, but she ignored him.

"Then, suddenly, she quieted down. She petted me and stroked my belly—there was no real sign of the baby yet—and told me how happy she was for me. She promised she'd be able to get me some baby things, a bassinet, clothes, blankets, things that were hard to find in those days, and she seemed transformed, genuinely pleased that I was going to have a baby. She told me how much she wanted a baby herself, wanted to stop singing and playing these Resistance games, wanted to settle down to being a woman, a wife and a mother.

"Whether it was a ruse or she really felt it didn't make any difference. She must have made up her mind then that she was going to get rid of me—of us? I can't tell which. Afterwards, Claudia made so many explanations, I couldn't tell what was the truth, what was simply craziness."

"She told Freddie, of course."

"Of course. She told him when I'd be coming to visit her next. It was the day after Bastille Day. I remember it so well because it was the first Bastille Day in a long time that I felt like singing and dancing in the streets and I couldn't. I was nauseated. I had morning sickness, afternoon and evening sickness and I had to stay in bed. Lovett teased me that he would go dancing in the streets with Claudia and I almost believed him. When he stayed with me that night, that last night, I cried.

"The next morning because I still felt so rotten, he went with me to Claudia's though he wasn't scheduled to go. Claudia'd asked me to come by for some new information on keeping Paris an open city. Fieldmarshal von Klüge had already declared Paris an open city but we had heard rumors that Hitler wanted the city burned to the ground when the Germans retreated and the FFI wanted to prevent that.

"That was how Claudia fingered me for them and Lovett too. It was a small street she lived on in those days, looking like a cul-de-sac with only a single way out, the same way you came in, but there was a narrow alley between Claudia's building and the one next to it, so narrow you didn't notice it if you looked casually and one person could barely get through it, no more. I'd never noticed it myself though I'd been to Claudia's at least two dozen times, but Lovett had. He'd seen it and checked it out. As we came up the street toward her house, we saw a man in a raincoat lounging in front of the *boulangerie* smoking a cigarette. He had *flic* written all over him. Lovett's hand tightened on my arm, he whispered 'Gestapo,' and said to go on talking as if we hadn't seen him. I was panicky and wanted to run, but Lovett put his arm around my shoulder and carried me along a little way, half skipping like a child, half holding me up— we looked like young lovers gamboling—before he leaned me against a building and stopped my mouth with kisses. Nuzzling my throat, he told me to see if anyone was at the head of the street, behind us, and there was another raincoat there, walking toward us, hands in his pockets.

" 'All right,' Lovett said, 'stay here against me. They'll come for us. When they do, if it looks bad, I'll make a diversion. You run. Don't talk, don't look back, just run. See the little alley next to Claudia's building? Remember it?' He nudged my head around by kissing my neck. 'Go through there. Beyond is a public market that's open every day except Sunday, a good place to lose anybody chasing you. Lose them, get out of this arrondissement, and let Guitton know what happened.'

"What about you?" I whispered into his ear, biting his earlobe.

" 'They're coming now,' he said and pulled me closer.

"The raincoats approached from the two different directions and tapped our shoulders. They were Gestapo. They asked for our papers and as Lovett was taking his out, I looked up and there was Claudia standing in her window, looking down at us. At that moment I knew with absolute certainty that she had betrayed us and I vowed that I would revenge myself on her if it took me the rest of my life."

"But you didn't, did you?" Sanders asked, alarmed by and hoping for some mercy in that implacable face behind the coffee cup.

"You sentimental, forgiving Americans. I *finished* her," Nathalie Blanchot grated, "with Guitton's help. I paid her off."

"The doctor at Clichy told me she died only a few months ago, of acute alcoholism."

"I know. I was with her when she died."

"Then how? Why?"

"You are puzzled, Elliott? You think there's only one way to deal with the Claudias of the world, eh? Shoot them? Poison them? Kill them? No, that would have been too easy, too quick, too good for my Claudia. I didn't want her to die easily; I wanted her to suffer, as I had suffered, as Lovett must have suffered. For a long time." Her cup clattered as she set it down in the saucer.

"You couldn't just let her go?"

She looked at him as if she thought he was insane. "Do you understand? It was Claudia who was responsible for your father's death. Would you have just let her go?"

He shrugged.

She looked forbidding. "We did not let her go. First we finished her Herr Major Freddie. *Sale Boche!* The Germans were abandoning Paris, the Allies had not yet come and the FFI decided to hurry them along, both of them. It was on August 20 and Freddie went to Claudia's flat to say goodbye, to promise her, she told me later, that he would come back for her when the war was finished—by then even Herr Olbracht knew that the Boches were done for—and marry her. For that moment, it must have seemed to Claudia that it had all paid off, the doubling, the cheating, the lying, the betraying, the fear, the risk, everything.

"It was that same cul-de-sac and Guitton and Bernard Magny were there. While Freddie was upstairs with Claudia they strapped two sticks of dynamite to his car and waited. The Herr Major came down and got into the car, waved to her as she stood up there in her window, blowing a farewell kiss to him, and then he started the car—and blew himself to pieces. While she watched. While Claudia watched, the kiss still on her fingers and her lips. And she knew it was us, she knew her time had come because she saw Guitton and Magny afterwards, just for a moment, as we wanted her to see them, to know who had given Olbracht his reward, and who would give her hers."

"Why didn't she run?"

Nathalie Blanchot showed her teeth, the gold ones gleaming iridescently in the lustrous morning light. "To where? There was nowhere for her to run. In a few days Leclerc and the Americans were

[238]

here and Paris was free. Free. For us it was all over but not for her. For her it was only beginning. Guitton would have killed her—simple, swift justice—but I said no. Perhaps I persuaded him that death was a gift we should not bestow on Claudia Morrisette; perhaps it was that I was berserk and he did not wish to oppose me.

"It was almost November before we were certain about Lovett. We had been almost sure before, but now we knew there was no real possibility that he was still alive. No possibility at all. And then I had the miscarriage, a girl, a tiny, perfectly formed little female, quite dead. I fell. I suppose that's what caused it, but even before I fell—a flight of stairs, steep, and I was dizzy when Guitton called and told me there was no more hope—I knew that what lay beneath my breast and my beating heart was not life but death.

"The first thing was to shave her head. Claudia was proud of her hair, long, lustrous, silky dark-brown hair that hung almost to her waist and that she sometimes wore, regally, like a crown of braids on her head, or piled high like a bouffant flower, that she brushed religiously morning and night. I cut her hair myself. I shaved her head myself. With my own two hands. She didn't even struggle, she only sat with her head bowed and wept. I took her hair and threw it into a sewer. We kept her hair cut for some time—Guitton was already with the police and helped me—so that everyone would know her for what she was. We made it impossible for her to do anything, except . . .

"Except be a whore. That was the only course we permitted. No job as a chanteuse, a mannequin, a salesgirl, nothing but a common *poule*. Because she was a whore, we made her life a whoredom. We kept her what she'd been. A whore. A drunkard. I watched her, I never let her out of my sight for too long. I saw her, irregularly, surprising her, but about every two weeks. I watched her, I never . . . I always knew where she was. I watched her as she went downhill, year after year, bed after bed, bottle after bottle, brothel after brothel, cheap hotel after cheap hotel, until she was the lowest of the low, hustling for a quick trick at the stations—Gare de l'Est, du Nord and St. Lazare—until she lost her looks, her health. And while I watched her die, slowly, month by month, I enjoyed it, I gloated over her degradation. The fires of vengeance warmed my empty womb, the womb that would never again, because of her, have any fruit."

Nathalie Blanchot left the table for the easel, stood blinking at the empty canvas, circling it several times, shifting the palette from one hand to another but not touching brush to canvas. "I was glad when Claudia died because I couldn't bear her suffering any more, because I hated my enjoyment of it, but I was never sorry for what I had done. I'm not sorry now. She betrayed us; she betrayed Lovett to his death; she killed our unborn daughter.

"To this day I can see her face up there in the window when the Gestapo took us, looking down with that hateful exultant expression. The moment they saw his papers the two raincoats exchanged glances, and I knew they were going to take him in, take us in, and so did Lovett. While they asked me for my papers, he struck them both, together, and knocked them to the ground. I ran. Right into that narrow alley. I didn't look back, except once, and they were still rolling on the ground, the three of them struggling, and one of the raincoats was trying to get a pistol out of his pocket. I ran through the alley, bruising my shoulders against the walls, scraping my knees, until I was out and into the public market. Like a frightened fool I kept right on running until a woman deliberately stood in my way, to stop me, and I crashed into her, knocked her shopping bag down and spilled her *baguette* and some potatoes onto the ground. 'Don't run,' she warned me in a low voice as she kneeled to pick up her groceries. 'Whatever it is, whoever's chasing you, walk! walk! *Flics* up ahead.' I can't even remember her face, only her hands picking up those potatoes, red, raw, calloused hands like a man's, like a farm maid's. But her voice brought me back to my senses and I began to walk. There were crowds of people shopping and it was easy to get lost among them and to pass by the *flics*. I took out my string bag, bought a cabbage and some carrots, so I'd look as if I'd been shopping, kept an eye out to see if anyone was following, pursuing—no one was—and strolled right past the police to the Métro."

"So that was how they took him?" Sanders asked somberly. A fitting end for Lovett Carpenter Sanders, the women and the gallantry to the end. And the courage. He had to admit the courage.

"Then and there."

"A few days more and the Allies would have saved him," Sanders mused aloud.

"It is the way things go. Two wars and five years in the underground, yet Bernard Magny and Jean Hoche were both killed by the Boches in the fighting two days before Leclerc arrived," Nathalie Blanchot rebuked him, but the words didn't seem to be her own; they seemed the rehearsed nostrum someone had given her to use to cope with what she otherwise found insupportable.

"The Germans executed my father right away, then?"

She hesitated. "I don't know. We couldn't find out. We tried everything to find out where the Gestapo had taken him, what they did with him, but we couldn't. Guitton even put together a group to rescue him, as they'd been rescued by the Maquis at Montreuil, but Lovett had disappeared without a trace."

"Without a trace?"

"Guitton couldn't even find out for sure that he was dead until November when the Allied Intelligence informed him that they had a German prisoner who had seen Lovett killed."

"Where do I find Guitton?" Sanders inquired.

"I shall give you his number. We haven't seen much of each other these past years, so I don't have any address. We talk on the telephone now and then, but not even much of that."

"Too many memories?" Sanders asked and heard with regret the nasty edge of the question.

She ignored it. "I called him last not too long ago to tell him about Claudia but he already knew she was dead. He'd been informed. Guitton kept track of her to the end." She put the palette down and went to a bureau. From a small red-leather address book she read out Guitton's number in a hollow voice.

"That's it?"

"That's all. No body. No grave. No tombstone." She stood motionless in the middle of the floor. "*Fin*. The end. Nothing. Not even a plot of earth, a place to go to weep, to mourn."

"Do you need a stone, a patch of ground, some broken bones to help you cry?" he asked bitterly.

Nathalie Blanchot glared at him out of tear-filled eyes. "I said you Americans were sentimental. I take that back. You are unfeeling. Cold. Harsh."

[241]

"Remember, I'm really half French, as my father said."

"So you are. *Le vrai petit de Paris* but grown older, more callous."

"One must live." It just missed irony.

"Yes," she echoed, "one must live, but why?" Her voice, low and melancholy, rose into a chant:

> *Tout suffoquant*
> *Et blême, quand*
>   *Sonne l'heure,*
> *Je me souviens*
> *Des jours anciens*
>   *Et je pleure.*

"Then, cry, goddam it, cry," he growled in English and strode to the door, repeating in his head Guitton's telephone number so that he wouldn't forget it.

Quickly she ran after him, pulling him around, embracing him, her soft blond head against his heart. "You will come back, Elliott, to visit me?" she sobbed. "I would like . . . I would like . . ." but she couldn't finish the sentence.

"I will," he replied, extricating himself from her embrace. "Of course I'll come visit," he promised as he eased himself out of the door and out of her life; but he never went back.

* * *

It took another two years before he managed to find Guitton; it was after he came back from reporting and photographing the French invasion of Port Said. Though he had kept trying during those years and though he'd tried hard, they never seemed to be able to arrange something mutually convenient. Either Guitton was out of the country, or he was, but when they did finally meet it was in true French—and Deuxième—fashion, at an outside café near St. Cloud, and Albert Guitton looked not at all like what he had imagined. A squat, powerful man, with a thick smudge of mustache, Guitton had the face of one of the Keystone Cops but it was informed by a heavy persistence and a pinched severity that made it anything but comic. It was a face Sanders might have imagined for a Javert—dark skin, heavy jowls, hooded eyes, and a heavy briar pipe to match—a face that was a sealed room, with eyes not windows to the soul but dark-brown shades hiding the mind, and the features decorated by an expression both unfathomable and menacing at the same time. After he had introduced himself and ordered a *fine* and a *noir,* Sanders sat back in the wicker chair and waited while Guitton sipped his beer and talked easily about a pelota game he had just seen, measuring him, judging, but what conclusions Guitton arrived at before he gave up the small talk of pelota and *futbol,* before he quit the darting glances around them, Sanders couldn't tell. Guitton asked him how much he knew, his voice curiously mellifluous for a man's, his accent an odd Flemish one that seemed out of place in Paris, and Sanders as succinctly as he could recounted what the others had told him. At various points in the narrative, Guitton nodded, his lips pursed around the stem of his pipe as if he were tasting what had been told him, and at the same time making tangential wet circles on the tabletop with the base of his beer glass.

"Your father," he said finally, "was a man truly brave. Not impetuous. Not without caution. Not without intelligence. He loved France. Better than many Frenchmen—and more courageously. Like all of us, however, *the* weakness betrayed him. Women. With one woman a man is on the brink, staring over the edge; with two, or more, it is always disaster. One goes over the brim eventually. With two such as Nathalie Blanchot and Claudia Morrisette, it was destined."

"Was it really they who destroyed him?" Sanders was skeptical. "Wasn't it the English and that transmitter that really did it?"

"Why that?"

"Why the Pas de Calais?"

"Ah, I see you comprehended. Good. Nathalie Blanchot never really understood."

"What, I did understand, but not why."

"Simple. Diversion. Good planning. Like politics, intelligence is cruel. What is it but politics bareknuckled, action without consensus, secret warfare without uniforms, flags, glory? The British may box with Marquis of Queensbury rules; they do not fight wars with them.

Sensibly. They are eminently practical people. The invasion was scheduled. For Normandy. But the Boches didn't know where it would come, or when. Neither did we in France. The Boches had their own intelligence reports. Many. But in this business no one can rely on such reports completely.

"London saw the whole picture, we only a sliver. London knew Berlin thought the Pas de Calais would be the place. It was logical. German logical. Not, therefore, Anglo-Saxon logical. The easiest place. The shortest distance across the Channel. So London catered to the Teutonic logic. The shortest distance between two points is always a straight line. Except in our non-Euclidean universe.

"London knew we'd be taken. They planned it that way. That's what they wanted. The transmitter was deliberately keyed to the German tanks' wavelength. They planned that too. If we were captured, as they hoped, planned, it would be another piece for the *Abwehr* to fit into the puzzle of intent that pointed away from Normandy, where they really intended to land, to the Pas de Calais."

"They never told you, or my father, of course."

"That would have negated the entire effort. They knew that if we were taken, we would be tortured. They assumed we would resist, but they were sure, too, that eventually even the most courageous talk. Everyone talks. Or dies. Either way, if we didn't know, we would not be able to tell the Boches. If we talked, or died, our presence there, the transmitter, our intelligence for London on German troop dispositions and reinforcements, would speak for the Pas de Calais. You understand?"

"In London Kiely told me that they gave my father a cyanide tablet to use if he was captured," Sanders said, but it was a question.

"That's what they told him. It was aspirin."

"Oh my God!" Sanders cried out.

Guitton's pipe came out of his mouth; his beer glass stopped describing those blurred watery circles on the table. "That way," he said indistinctly, "London could be sure the Boches would find out. And be misled. At least confused."

"They didn't know Lovett Carpenter Sanders," Sanders rejoined, the pain and perverse pride in his voice distinct and contradictory. "He would have died first."

[244]

Ponderously Guitton nodded agreement. "He did. Without talking. London knew men. It was a good plan. They did not know *that* man."

The sudden inconsolable understanding was an affliction. Grindingly Sanders asked, "How did you find out the cyanide was fake?"

"The Gestapo tried to make him talk. About us. Names, addresses, plans. He didn't know very much. We were very careful. But he knew enough to cause much trouble, many deaths. He knew names —mine, Magny, Hoche, Claudia, Nathalie, others. He knew addresses, places—safe houses, mailboxes, cutouts. And he knew about the plan for a rising in Paris. He told them nothing."

"So they killed him?"

Guitton cast a quick shrewd one-eyed glance at him. "The Gestapo tortured him. He wouldn't talk. They worked him over some more. He took the cyanide."

"The aspirin. And he didn't die. It probably didn't even help his aspiring," Sanders said, laughing hysterically at the macabre humor. Gallows humor. Guitton shifted uncomfortably in his seat.

"No, he didn't die," Guitton said.

"How did you find out?"

"It took time. Months."

"Do you know where he's buried?"

"We never found that out. Never even discovered what they did with—the body."

"Tell me, please."

"Are you sure you want to hear more now? Perhaps another time? It has been over for a long while. A decade and more. It can do you no good." The kindness from Guitton was harder to bear than the cruelty. Guitton paused for some time, sucking noisily on his pipe, giving him some time to recover himself. "They should have put up the glass panes," Guitton said finally, shivering a little in the cold November night. "They should put up the glass panes and start the stoves. It's winter. When you get older you feel the cold more. Your bones ache. They long for the south, for Nice and Cannes." He warmed his fingertips on the pipe bowl, blowing the tobacco inside alive and glowing.

"It can do *me* some good," Sanders insisted stubbornly.

[245]

"Nathalie called me within a half hour after your father was taken," Guitton began slowly, after a half-dozen breaths of smoke. "Within an hour, I had eight of us. Two cars. Submachine guns. Grenades. That may not seem like a great accomplishment now. In Paris, in 1945, it was a miracle. I alerted our best people. We had a net of observers. Informers. Telephone communications. I even authorized use of emergency radio communications. But we couldn't find him. He wasn't at any of the usual places the Gestapo took people for interrogation—or torture.

"When the fighting for Paris began there was no time for such luxuries, no time for anything but the fighting. But after it was over I kept looking. The Allied Intelligence Services looked too. We all cooperated. The first thing some of our people found was a Gestapo flimsy to Berlin HQ. Just a teletype carbon saying that an American journalist, and they named him, traveling with false papers, had been executed after a thorough investigation which had elicited no useful information."

"Who signed the teletype? Can I have the flimsy?"

"It was signed by an assistant bureau chief of the Paris Gestapo, a Gunther Mecklund. We found the flimsy in late September. By then he'd been killed in action."

"The copy?"

"I don't know who took it. OSS probably. Maybe the British. Probably destroyed by now," Guitton said cautiously. "One doesn't keep that kind of thing around. Then, in November—it was just this time of year, a dozen years ago—my God, the time flies! Lovett has been dead for a long time. It seems like yesterday, yet in another life far far past."

"You were on *tu-toi* terms with him?" Sanders asked.

Guitton nodded. "The Resistance was not a place for formality, grammatical or otherwise. In November, a Feldwebel was captured by your army in a skirmish. Military Intelligence interrogated him and 'passed him along.' He'd worked with the Gestapo. Saw them bring your father in. Saw them take him out. Overheard one of the Gestapo say to the other, 'Just think of those English bastards giving him aspirin and telling him it was cyanide.' The other one said, 'Perfidious Albion! It didn't make things any easier for us.' 'Or for him,' the first one said. Then they said something about having to get rid of him and they dragged a heavy tarpaulin out with them that the Feldwebel assumed was the body. That was all. We believed that he was dead then, for sure."

"That was when they told us," Sanders said, remembering Colonel Michael Robinson giving them the news in that Connecticut November, hearing his mother's sobs in the shower still, seeing that crudely printed sheet of religious exhortation on her dressing table.

"Under ordinary circumstances they would have kept him longer. That was what I was counting on when I tried to put that rescue team together," Guitton said, his cold detached voice suddenly genuine and regretful. "Maybe even send him to HQ, even to Berlin. He was a well-known newspaperman and they knew him there. I didn't think they'd kill him."

"Maybe that was why they killed him so quickly."

"Perhaps. He was *persona non grata* with the Nazis. But I do not think that is the reason. When they saw they had to abandon Paris almost immediately, they must have decided to finish him. Panic. Haste. Carelessness."

"Without a record of interrogation? of burial? Where was all the traditional German *Ordnung?*"

"By then their organization here had broken down. The fastidious dossier keepers had already fled with the most important files. And they burned many other records before evacuating. Maybe they did bury him. An unmarked grave. Somewhere. They were in a hurry. And those 'butcher-boy' types were not fastidious." Guitton looked down at the wet circles he'd made with his beer glass, most of them now evaporated so that little more than the stains of their presence remained. "We think they might simply have dropped that tarpaulin in the Seine. Some river barge people think they saw such a thing happen. Near the Gare d'Austerlitz. It was very late when we heard that, January in the new year. But I had the river dragged there. And up and down stream too."

"Nothing?"

Guitton smiled for the first time, showing slightly uneven buck teeth. "No, not nothing. A number of bodies. More than you'd imagine. More than a few murdered. And not just by the Germans. And other things. But not Lovett Sanders' body."

The Seine. The immemorial artery of Paris through which for

centuries the city's lifeblood had flowed. Well, perhaps the Germans had done better by him than they intended; perhaps the Gestapo had, after all, buried him where he really belonged. "*Point final.* The end of the line. The end of my father. The end of the story."

"Perhaps not," Guitton spoke up.

"No? What else?" Sanders asked.

"I'm a Catholic," Guitton replied. "Perhaps there's more."

"My God, isn't this enough?" Sanders retorted, trying to hold back the suppressed shriek in his voice. "More than enough?"

"It's not God's world, it's man's." Guitton's expression was a reproof but he didn't scold. "It is a heavy burden to be his son—and a privilege." For seconds Sanders didn't know if Guitton meant a son of God, a son of Christ, or simply the son of Lovett Carpenter Sanders. Perhaps all three. Whichever or all, it *was* a burden but the privilege seemed hidden from him, a mirage of an oasis where every man sat under his own vine and fig tree, where swords would be beaten into plowshares and spears into pruning hooks, where men lived pleasantly and in peace and loved their neighbors as themselves: It was a mirage in the desert which only lured men on to their deaths.

* * *

In the car, under the eucalyptus trees outside the cemetery where he'd parked, Sanders gaped down at the Presidio's old brick buildings and the bilious green-board barracks faded by the sun. Dazed as he was, it seemed to him more like a university or boy's school, which, he supposed, was what it was, only a boy's school of destruction, a university of death. The wizened grief on Peter King's great black face swam up before his inner eye, a rebuke, and he realized that in his reverie and regret he had not even offered him a ride back to the city. Then the image of the old man's stick, stubbornly burrowing into the upturned earth of his son's grave, poked his brain, and finally the picture of Beth, her face swathed in black lace, seductively mourning, throttled him. He'd been unable to speak a word of condolence to any of them. Guilty. Yet no one there had seemed to feel like talking to anyone else, so why should he feel most responsible for not having behaved humanely, correctly, suavely? Was he the host at the funeral, the *maître* of mourning, that he should feel so remiss?

Dully he drove along the seafront, catching occasional glimpses of the ocean frothing at the mouth and gnashing its teeth on the rocks and concrete seawalls below and knew he was seeing the lordly Pacific that way because it was exactly the way he felt. Sharply the road turned inland and abruptly he found himself back in Paris, for there before him a newer, whiter, less shabby Commanderie sat back on a rise of greensward, its feet swathed in shrubbery, HONNEUR ET PATRIE inscribed on its frieze.

Paris once more. Everywhere he went, it seemed, was Paris. Saigon, the Paris of the East; Algiers, the Paris of North Africa; even Budapest had been the Paris of the Danube; and here San Francisco, that frontier Yankee city, not only thought of itself as the Paris of the Pacific, but took such imitation so much to heart that all over the city, in spite of the hilly non-Parisian topography, there were little fragments of Paris, a view, a building, a street, French bread or a French newspaper. It was not merely his nostalgia, the regurgitation of the disasters of his past life rising into his throat like stale and undigested food, or Laura Martin's Paris street signs affixed on the walls of Jason Howe's apartment, his apartment now, signs that he had already become skillful at not seeing, to remind him of the paths he had walked, the paths he still walked; it was the city itself. And now this cream-colored stucco replica of what in Paris he knew was the hewn Caen stone of the Palais de la Légion d'Honneur erected in Pacific fog and chill. Guitton had even taken care of that, posthumously of course, and he had been informed that Lovett Carpenter Sanders had been made chevalier of the Legion of Honor for his "wartime services" to France.

Above him was a triumphal arch whose entablature was decorated with trumpet-blowing angels announcing what victory—the end of the world? the Day of Judgment? the Days of Wrath?—and he heard the Connecticut carols of his youth ringing in the Christmas echoes of his mind: "Hark, the herald angels sing!" Dreamily he walked up the path between great expanses of dandelion-studded lawn where military equestrian statues of El Cid and Joan of Arc, both in armor, sword and spear raised for the charge, rode their horses champing at the bit, wide-nostriled for war. *Honneur et Patrie?*

The court beyond, peaceful beyond belief, was stamped suddenly with golden sunshine, gilding the colonnade of simple Ionic columns that supported the roof, and there, seated in the center of the court, as if he were baffled by the silence and the serenity, was a Rodin bronze of *The Thinker,* bent over, bowed, chin jutting against the protuberant knuckles of a powerful green fist. *Honneur et Patrie?*

Gingerly Sanders went around that tribute to hamstrung thought only to be stopped at the portico by a plaque whose broken single branch of gold-leafed laurel, stark and lovely, grew out of mausoleum-cold marble in which was engraved the legend: HOMMAGE DE LA FRANCE AUX HÉROS CALIFORNIENS—MORTS POUR LA DÉFENSE DU DROIT ET DE LA LIBERTÉ. Once more *Honneur et Patrie?* And could one have both honor and country, right and freedom? Could these things really be held for very long? Mankind, as even Jefferson must have known, was incapable of eternal vigilance. Still blinking from the abrupt and brilliant onset of the sunlight, Sanders entered the rotunda to meet, when his eyes had adjusted to the gloom, only a single sculpture, apelike and menacing, the statue of a Neanderthal scratching his head, a stone adze clutched bellicosely in his other hand. *Honneur et Patrie! Droit et Liberté!* The farther he walked through the California Palace of the Legion of Honor, echoing its European counterpart, the more he felt he had intruded into a history that was all anachronism, strolling backward through a nightmare landscape where everything was palpable and real—and so, absolutely immutable. Seventeenth-century Louis XIV *antechambres* and eighteenth-century Louis XVI *salons* and *boiseries,* full of gilded cornices and gold-wreathed ceilings, vitrines, ormolu-mounted porcelains, floors of alternating white and purple marble squares, French rooms, rooms that had once contained and delighted living, hurting, hurtful men and women aware that they ruled a great nation and were the scourge of Europe and its cynosure, rooms and furnishings and art that were a legacy so rich as to seem obscene—like the magnificent and degrading Sedan chair that sat in the center of one gallery, its summation and vilification. Was it any wonder that the Jacobins had come? And the Terror? And their heirs the Bolsheviks? And their terror? *Honneur et Patrie.*

As Sanders turned out of the last of the antique French rooms, the lump in his throat more painful now, as if he had been struck in the throat with a fist, his knees weak, he felt he had walked with the tumbrils to the guillotine. And walked alongside with the sans-culottes and cursed and spat on—himself. He found himself in a long gallery in which yellow slatted folding chairs had been set up for an audience far larger than the few individuals who were seated there. Beyond was an organ console at which a man had just now begun to play. In an unexpected crashing thunder the great chords of organ music pounded down on him, the heavy cool rain of Bach, and Sanders, sitting on one of the uncomfortable and ugly yellow chairs, closed his eyes and let that music wash his memory clean of the filth of history, his own and that of his countries: Elaine and his father, Beth and Prescott, even old man Christiansen and George, or especially them: *Honneur et Patrie; Droit et Liberté; les sanglots longs* which wounded the heart, the cyanide and the aspirin. To hell with them all; what they led to, everywhere and always, was a wooden box and that coppery dirt scar in the cemetery, or the muck of a riverbed, or a ditch at the side of the road.

How long he sat there with his eyes closed through what thunder-claps and cloudbursts of music Sanders didn't know until the haven offered by "Sheep May Safely Graze" shimmered in his ears like water rippling over rocks and he opened his eyes without warning, certain he would find some sunlit refuge within his grasp, only to discover Beth sitting on the chair next to his, her eyes scrutinizing his face as if she'd never seen it before and might never see it again, the black mantilla now a lacy halo around her head, accenting her pale face and the great pale irises brimming with tears. "Did I wake you?" she whispered tenderly.

"No," he replied faintly. "I wasn't asleep, only coming out of a dream."

"A bad dream?" she asked, touching his hand.

Sepulchral and stubborn, he replied, "All dreams are bad, all dreams are nightmares."

"All?"

"Without exception. As dreams they begin and as nightmares they end."

"You're talking about marriages?"

"No, not only about marriages. About politics. About journalism. About life."

[251]

"Is that why you were crying back there, your dreams shattered and turned to nightmares?" Beth asked. "I didn't think George was your young dream or that he mattered so much to you."

"Was I crying?" he asked.

"They could hear you and Peter King down at the Presidio." She attempted a smile. "You'd think both of you had lost your best friend."

"I always cry at funerals," Sanders said, aware that she was needling him, hoping to give his words just the right cutting edge in return.

"Peter King's always melodramatic. He's an actor and a fairy so I expect it from him," she said. "He's always playing 'lift that barge' and 'tote that bale.' But you're supposed to be a tough foreign correspondent, through all the massacres and revolutions and wars. I thought you'd seen enough killing and burying so it wouldn't bother you any more."

To a muffled scattering of applause the organist had risen and departed and two attendants began to double up the folding chairs and stack them like yellow sheaves. The concert was over. The aura of Bach and "Sheep May Safely Graze" was dissipated in Beth's viciousness.

Her arm in the crook of his, Beth led him downstairs into the coffee shop. He sat numbly at one of the tables thinking about what she'd said, wondering if he had grown callous or ever would to even the single death much less to the moving obligatory anguish of row on row of tombstones, crosses and stars of David, the young statistically buried beneath, the most beautiful bloody fertilizer the world had ever known. He sat there until Beth went and brought back two steaming cups of coffee. "I didn't expect to find you here," she said. "Looking for another little piece of Paris?" The double meaning was evident in the turn of her lips and the deliberate baby-doll open eyes. "Or paying your further respects to our august California dead, heroes of right and freedom?" The coffee scalded his throat but swallowing remained difficult as if the fluid had to trickle through grinding millstones. He massaged his throat with his hand and practiced swallowing, but the lump remained.

"What is it?" Beth asked. "Can't swallow it all any more?"

"Something like that," Sanders replied. "My Adam's apple has turned to stone in my throat and is blocking the passage."

"Come down to the clinic for an X-ray," she said, her concern evident even through the sarcasm. "I'll do it myself. No charge. And I'm a first-class technician. Even Steven will tell you I'm better than most of the radiologists. But then, I should be. Besides, I'd like to look inside you."

"Will that really tell you anything?"

"An X-ray is but the shadow of a shadow," she said, "but then, what is man?" Her fingers, warmed by the coffee cup, explored his larynx and windpipe, felt under his ears and jaw. "Ever had a barium swallow?"

"No."

"It's like eating chalk or crow."

"I've done that," he said, "more often than I care to remember."

"Good for the psychological digestion."

"We all need a dose of spiritual salts from time to time, is that it?"

"Why wouldn't you stay with me the other night?" she asked uncertainly, the raised coffee cup half masking her face.

"I'm not a sexual dose of salts or a sleeping pill either," Sanders said. "You can't just ask me to *stand in*"—meanly he stressed those two words—"for Steven Prescott."

"Didn't it matter that I needed comfort? Or that I was lonely? Or even, if that were the case, if I needed a sexual seconal, shouldn't that be enough?" She was angry.

"I'm not that kind of man."

"You're just like him," she observed.

"Like Prescott?"

"No, like George."

Sanders shook his head, held up his hands, palms out. "See, no jasmine, no gardenias." He felt he'd committed treason to George.

"And no manners either." She stood up, almost overturning her coffee, ready to stalk off.

Sanders made no move to stop her. Glowering, she stood over him, hands on her hips, until, like an umbrella folding, she sat back down. She drank some coffee before, in a quite different tone and manner,

[253]

she said belligerently, "Well, you wanted to fit into his shoes, you wanted to take up his life and make it your own, didn't you? Well, this is the way his life was. This is his wife"—she stabbed her index finger between her breasts—"the way she was and is, and this is the way it was with him and me and Steven."

"I'm not George." And, he thought, I don't know how he could bear it.

"Are you sure?"

Sanders remembered the suffocating sense he had had at the burial of being buried himself, alive and dead, a part of him essential to him forever gone.

"You cried for yourself back there," she persisted furiously. "The only time people cry like that is when they cry for themselves."

"I cried for myself, all right," Sanders said, "but for George too, for all those others there buried under those blank-faced gravestones. Some of them only boys. Once," he added grimly, "I covered an industrial fair in Slovakia, the big stupid kind of thing Communist countries love, full of new machine tools and charts of industrial growth and boring, boring, boring. One afternoon a Russian newspaperman who was covering the fair too, an older man, invited me for a walk around the outskirts of the city with him. He was bored with all that crud about the new Slovak steel mill, a mill that after millions of dollars and a dozen years had not produced a single sheet or ingot.

"The two of us walked up the hillside overlooking Bratislava, where the trade fair was, and it turned out that the Russian had been there before during the Second World War. He'd been with the Red Army when they took the city from the Germans—a bloody battle—and now he wanted to visit the graves of friends who had died there. He took me to the Russian military cemetery, row on row, acre on acre, miles of Russian graves covering that whole goddam hillside. Next to every one of those graves, the local people, who had no special love for the Russians, had planted a rose bush so that as far as the eye could see there was a forest of blooming red roses, as if the whole earth had risen in rebellion at those deaths and bled those roses out of its heart all over its breast.

"I saw all those Russian names and ranks and dates, the tombstones of boys, many of them sixteen- and seventeen- and eighteen-year-olds, and I burst into tears. My Russian companion looked at me just the way you did a minute ago and said he didn't know I cared that much, that I was sentimental, that I was an imperialist hypocrite, that I was crying for myself, not for them. He explained, in suitable bombastic terms, how they had liberated the Soviet Motherland and the People's Democracies, and swept the Fascist vermin before them, exterminating them, and I went on crying. Stupid, stuffy ass. Looking at that forest of roses and gravestones, blood-red and bone-white, I felt diminished, I felt the whole world smaller and poorer, uglier and crueler. I felt all those unlived young lives as a personal loss, as if they were members of my own family.

"To my Russian compatriot, I suppose, it was just one more example of bourgeois class failure, false sentimentality inbred by a corrupt system, just as for some sophisticated Westerner it would doubtlessly have been some unresolved psychoanalytic problem, some Oedipal tic invoked by my father's having been killed in the war and by our never having found his grave. Maybe so, for both explanations, but I doubt such simplistic and complex keys.

"Haven't you ever cried for someone's death and not for yourself, but only for that person's unlived life?" He knew he hoped she would, could, say that she had cried that way for George's unlived life, if not at the grave then at least when she had first been informed of his death; but he knew she wouldn't say so even if she had and if she did he wouldn't have believed her.

"Once," Beth said, "only once."

"But not today," Sanders said, touching the mantilla that clung to her shoulders. "Not even that would have hidden it."

"No," she confessed, "not today, not for George."

Not ever for George. "For whom, then?"

Beth's face fell, her eyes closed, and behind the mascaraed lashes and shadowed eyelids her eyes seemed to be racing toward some secret hiding place. "For a child, for our child, for *my* child," she said at last, her voice growing stronger and more assertive with each repetition of the noun.

"The one who died?" he asked.

"They told you. I thought they would. Old man Christiansen and Peter King."

"They told me but I didn't believe them."

"It was true. I had the child," she declared, rueful, proud.

"That wasn't what I doubted. I didn't believe their story of how it happened."

"The skeptical reporter," she gibed.

"It didn't make sense—with the people involved."

"Do you know them well enough—for it to make sense?"

"It's hard to be sure what someone would do but usually not so hard to know what he *wouldn't* do." He was, he knew, still immersed in that recollection of his long trek to Guitton to discover how his father had met his fate; he was still thinking of Lovett Carpenter Sanders.

"Sometimes, Elliott," Beth said, "you can't even tell what they wouldn't do. Five years ago if someone had told me that George would volunteer for Vietnam and die a hero, I'd have thought him stupid or clinically insane."

"Why? You knew George was no coward."

"I don't even know how to explain it without explaining so many other things. And if I explain those I'm not sure I can make anything sensible of it all."

"Try."

Beth sipped her coffee, surreptitiously eyeing him as if she might find an index to his trustworthiness on his face, but she couldn't seem to make up her mind.

"You cried once," Sanders prompted her, "for someone else, for someone else's life."

"Not like you, Elliott, for another life, but for another's life."

"I understand the difference but sometimes mourning for another's life, deeply and sincerely enough, may lead you to try to *make* another life."

"But not take it?"

"Take it on, try to enrich one and make it more than one, perhaps not quite two, but more than one. And no, not take it. Not that."

She made a gesture of despair. "All those words and plays on words, those intricate and complicated double and triple meanings, until I never really know what anyone is saying, much less what anyone really means. *Language is supposed to help people communicate.*"

"And to help them obfuscate, hide, deceive."

"But why?"

"Because the words themselves are cheats and disappointments. They never get exactly what you're feeling or seeing or trying to say because the words are made to communicate, they're common denominators, common currency, rounded off for passing from hand to hand, while the thought, the feeling you have, the perception, is only your own, private, unique, individual, really impossible to communicate exactly to anyone else. It's what makes journalism even more corrupt than it need be, an even more frustrating scrambling up the cliff with your fingernails. Sometimes you can't even shape what you see into words for yourself, so how can you do it for anyone else? That's the real rub. As the thought is made flesh and the flesh made thought, it tries, it struggles to communicate—and it flounders. The moment you put the perception, the feeling, into words you have a lie. The word is never quite the right container for the thought or the feeling, the shape of the shoe distorts and cripples the foot; your wine always needs some other vessel, a goblet, a beaker, a wassail bowl, a chalice, or"—Laura Martin's face blotted out Beth's before his eyes—"a champagne glass."

"Then what's the good of it?"

"You get rough equivalents, Beth," Sanders said.

She laughed. "Rough equivalents. You do get those, all right, don't you? Mighty rough and not even very equivalent. The glass shoe never does fit Cinderella, does it?"

"That's the best anyone can do." Rough equivalents. *Honneur et Patrie*, once more, *Droit et Liberté*. Small wonder he had more and more been impelled to rely on the camera, and even that, perhaps especially that, was no more than rough equivalent. Even "Sheep May Safely Graze," even that music that was the joy of man's desiring, of man's aspiring, was only a rough equivalent.

"It's not enough, not half enough." Back stiff, jaw jutting, she was obdurate, childish and magnificent, and Sanders wanted to laugh at her, kiss her, comfort her all together.

"No," he admitted, "it's not enough."

She looked puzzled. "I don't understand you."

"Why should you?"

"I thought you were like him, like George."

"In some ways I am."

"But you're not him."

"No, I'm not him."

"Then, what—"

"Because George saved my life," Sanders said cautiously, more prudent with her than he was being with himself, "I wanted to take up his life where he had laid it down. I didn't want it just to be left—left there." He pointed in the direction of the cemetery, of Saigon, of the past. "I didn't want that to be the end."

"*You* wanted. Did you ask what any of us wanted, me, his wife, his father, his friends?"

Feeling hemmed in, unable to swallow his gorge, restlessly unwilling to confess that he hadn't even thought of what any of them wanted, Sanders stood up. "This place is stifling. Let's get out of here."

Head bent, morose, she remained seated. "I can't."

"Why?" Sanders sat down next to her again. "Are you feeling sick?"

Listlessly stirring the dregs of her coffee, not looking at him, she said, "Steven is coming here to pick me up."

"I see."

"You don't see anything," she flared.

" 'Those who have eyes and see not,' " he said, but the swagger didn't work.

"Goddam your eyes!"

"He already has," Sanders lamented sincerely. He stood up, put a half dollar on the table and thanked her for the coffee. With a swift slap of her hand she sent the coin clanging to the floor and people at other tables looked up sharply. Sanders watched the coin run its course, then walked slowly to it, excused himself to a young hippie in slovenly jeans, stooped and picked up the half dollar from next to his unwashed bare foot in its Greek-style leather sandal, and went out. Halfway up the stairs, he heard her at his elbow.

"You are just like him, you are. You make me boil with fury just the way he did. Calm, reasonable, logical, judicious—and completely without any understanding for human emotions." Her fierce voice was shrill and heads rose from among the books, placards and postcards as she followed him out into the sunshine of the peaceful court. She yanked him around to face her. "I need Steven. I needed him then, I need him now."

"Okay, you've got him."

"I need you too," she said, her eyes narrowed to slits, the irises almost black. "I need you both."

"Just like George."

She nodded vigorously. "Exactly."

"I'm sorry. I'm not made that way."

"If the game isn't according to your rules, you just don't play? You were just telling me that you had to make do, with words, with language, with communication, but not with love?"

"That's not the way I see it."

"All right, how do you see it?"

"I lived through that with my father and mother, with my wife, my ex-wife. That isn't the way I want to live."

"And you have a choice?"

"Yes, I have a choice."

"Well, I don't."

He shrugged.

"I don't because I *am* like that."

They were sullying the quiet of that court, its measured pace of colonnade, its immaculate Ionic grove, its meditative Rodin, their strident quarrel echoing discordantly there, and he tried to pull away from her but she held tenaciously to his sleeves. "You can't walk away from me, or from it, like that. It's not that easy."

"Why not? You need Steven. You have Steven. That's that."

"That's that. That's all. Just like that." She was mocking him. "You wanted to pick up George's life, you said. Well, I'm the central part of that life, and Steven is one of the important parts of mine. We're all plunged into this, even old man Christiansen, up to here." She raised her chin, showing the fine profile of her throat and head, then drew a finger across her throat as if slashing it.

Sanders knew he would have to concede. If history alone didn't justify or sanctify or even explain for Lovett Sanders, or Claudia Morrisette, or for Elaine and himself, it did at least command con-

[259]

sideration, weighing, waiting. He felt her relief as he let her walk him out under the triumphal arch, between the victorious hard-riding warriors, across the plaza and past the flurry of fountains, around another verdigrised Rodin—*The Three Shades,* as depressed and defeated-looking as he felt himself—to the quiet beyond where in the shadow of the sculpture two nuns sat, their heads together, their cowls and wimples giving them the appearance of ancient, keening women, while with young and moving lips they read a guidebook of the city.

Beyond the balustrade where they stopped and leaned, the golf course stretched away green and rustic and the people playing seemed figures of fun in a pointless diversion, an American intrusion into a French ambience. How could this, his native land, seem so outlandish to him, so strangely lacking in the sense of home and hearth? Was he the unknown and unknowing intruder, a stranger forever in both countries? Was that why *Honneur et Patrie* meant such different things to him and to his father, who was at home in both countries? Was he simply deficient in both qualities, not blessed with either country, having neither as his home nor their honors as his heritage? Was that too why he couldn't comfortably keep his feet in more than one household or have other shoes beneath the bed in which he slept? Narrowness, he told himself, was a virtue: He ran not broadly but deeply; but perhaps it was only that his spirit and passions were starved in scope, undernourished in richness.

"The history may be more than you can bear," Beth warned. He was amazed to find that she was still there beside him, astonished to realize that for minutes he had been oblivious to her presence. "When Aunt Katharine brought me back home from the East it was on condition that I never see Bill Daulton again and that I do well in school. She'd permit me to enter Stanford, even permit me to be a premed, though she didn't think medicine was a ladylike profession, provided that I behaved with the 'proper prudence.' She was, as I said, very old-school."

"How old-school could she have been if she knew and remembered Baudelaire's *aperçu* that he could find the freshness of the tomb on a lover's breast?" Sanders asked, staring at her breasts until,

[260]

self-consciously, Beth folded her arms protectively over them.

"You have a good memory," she said, touched but shamefaced for having told him something about her aunt that seemed indiscreet.

"Man's curse and blessing. The real art is to know when to do which: remember or forget."

"If you can control either." Beth resumed her train of thought with effort, almost with a physical wrench made more plaintive by her arms still hugging herself and camouflaging her bosom. "By then I couldn't have cared less about Bill Daulton and I did really want to be a doctor, so I agreed. I had leverage with Aunt Katharine because I'd gotten top grades and honors in boarding school and she was enough of a bluestocking to respect that—she'd done honors herself in French literature at Wellesley, but that was properly lady-like for her day—and to admit that I might, just might, make a useful life as a physician."

"She doubted you could do it?"

"She never said as much, good manners forbade, but I had the feeling that her reservations were profound. She really thought I lacked the brains, the stick-to-it-iveness. I don't mean that I couldn't endure the minor unpleasantnesses, pithing frogs and fetal pigs and cutting up cadavers and that sort of thing. She knew I could do that, and gladly, and she should have. She'd seen me do enough cruel things to her dogs and cats and one of her pet canaries when I was a child."

"You were one of those."

Beth nodded. "I still am." She grinned crookedly. "George thought so and I expect you do too."

The smell of jasmine and gardenia floated through his memory and recalled the smell of roses in his youth and the incident with it. It was the fall of the year that Lovett Carpenter Sanders had chosen to come home to Connecticut for the last time. The fascia on one of the house eaves had warped and split open, showering a snow of white lead-paint fragments over his mother's roses beneath, the last yellow, white and red blossoms of that year. Because it was war-time and there were almost no carpenters or handymen available, he did all the house repairs and his mother asked him to replace the fascia and soffit boards and repaint them before the rains and the snows of winter arrived. There, under the slant roof, he had stood on the ladder and carefully broken off the twisted boards, torn out the rusted nails. He couldn't see anything in the dark space he opened up in the eave, and he had brought no flashlight. Gingerly he had felt his way inside, plucked out two dry, gray, beautifully detailed wasp honeycombs and as he drew them out accidentally spilled two recently hatched sparrow chicks and their bed of straw out onto the ground below. By the time he had jumped from the ladder the chicks were already dead, their necks and backs broken and askew, their tender short-haired pink-gray bodies smeared with blood. Still quivering, their yellow beaks turned up, their ducklike faces in death agony, they looked like tiny blond-bearded children, the children of elves. Unable to touch them, to pick them up and throw them into the garden trash pails full of dead autumn leaves he had earlier raked together, he had finally dug them a narrow grave, two spades in length, one in width, picked the two tiny corpses up on the flat of a shovel and interred them in his mother's rose garden. Back up the ladder he had laid in the carefully measured boards, and with swift angry blows of his hammer driven in the galvanized nails until everything was fitted and flush and the dangers of wasps and squirrels, termites and carpenter ants, water and snow seepage, had been warded off. The next day he had painted over the naked boards with a coat of primer, and later in the day, when that had dried, with a coat of paint, noting as he came down the ladder with brushes and paint can that the narrow hummock beneath which the sparrows had been buried had already been leveled and trodden down.

A few days later his mother remarked that she'd heard odd sounds in the rafters and that perhaps he'd been too late with the repairs, that perhaps a squirrel or two had already taken advantage of the warped boards he'd replaced. She took him out to the rose garden where she had that morning begun the autumn pruning of the thorny canes and the winter hilling up of soil and straw over the crowns, pointing with her shears to where she'd heard the chittering in the eaves. Silently, they stood listening until he heard it himself, the faint chirruping whose meaning he instantly discerned. Like a madman he had run for the ladder, set it up, and begun to tear at the newly placed and painted boards with a crowbar while his mother looked on astonished. It was only moments before he had freed the second nest and the three tiny dying sparrows he had unwittingly imprisoned in the eaves, cutting them off from light and air and their feeding mother who had before been able to bring their food in through the gaps in the warped boards. Crowbar in one hand, the warm nest and its dying birds in the other, he had stood on the ladder sobbing, knowing he couldn't save those birds—though later he tried and failed—wanting to throw himself down with those birds until his mother's clear cutting voice had torn sharply through his crying and brought him back down to earth. His fingers could remember the pubic-hair texture of the nest; his nostrils were filled with the smell of his mother's roses. Now, as he recalled it, he told Beth what had happened, knowing it was a lesson he meant her to learn that she could not heed and a lesson to him that he had not altogether absorbed, but reminding Beth that his mother had finally helped him to bury those birds and the memory. Until now, when Beth had unearthed it for him.

"You *are* like George. That's the way he would have felt—and behaved. Not me. And Aunt Katharine knew me." Her lips thinned. "She knew me all right, better than I thought. She disapproved of my character. At bottom she thought me incapable of sustained and disciplined effort; basically, as she would have said it, I was not *sérieuse.*"

"But she was wrong."

"On the contrary. She was right. I couldn't finish medical school. In fact, I never even entered; I ended up in nursing school, and only a nurse." Regret, self-hatred and self-pity underlined every word.

"Only?"

"Only I couldn't behave like an adult. I didn't have—the character. Aunt Katharine would have called it that, just that, however old-fashioned it sounds nowadays, and she'd have been right."

"Excuses, excuses," he joked, trying to erase the deep lines of dissatisfaction her frowning cut around her eyes and mouth.

"No, Elliott, reasons, real reasons, not excuses. Aunt Katharine was a very shrewd old lady and old-fashioned enough to want, in her words, to 'save me from myself.' She tried, Lord knows, but she didn't succeed."

"Did she approve of George and Prescott?"

[263]

"She met them both and heartily disapproved of both. She said George wanted to be a saint and she didn't like saints because 'they slept in a hairshirt scourge and whipped themselves bloody during the nights instead of having a sensible night's rest.'" Beth laughed, but ruefully. "Steven she despised. Said he was Southern 'white trash' on the make, wanting to marry money and live in the big house."

"Aunt Katharine sounds as if she might have been right on both counts."

"That was Aunt Katharine's trouble, there was no might-have-been with her. She was right so often she thought she was right all the time, and once she'd made up her mind, she wouldn't change it. She called that character and perseverance, but lots of time it was just plain pigheadedness. She wouldn't see either of them when she could avoid it, wouldn't get to know them better. She said she didn't have to. She didn't like them and she was too old and had too little time left to spend it with people she didn't like. As it turned out, she was right. She didn't have much time left, poor dear."

"Sounds like my grandfather, my mother's father. A man of oak and hickory my mother used to call him. I think I'd have liked your Aunt Katharine."

"Probably. And she you. You were more her style, but—"

"But not approved of me?"

"No. That would have been asking too much."

"Was her approval so important to you?"

"She was my father and mother wrapped up in one. They died when I was eight, right after the war, a little while after my father came back from the Navy. My parents went to Mexico on vacation with some friends in a private plane—it was supposed to be a second honeymoon after the long separation of the war; my father was in the Pacific for almost four years before he came home. The plane crashed and everyone was killed. I can't even remember him very clearly. He went away when I was an infant. He came back, a big man in a Navy officer's uniform full of gold braid on the sleeves and on his cap, smelling of whisky and tobacco and shaving lotion when he kissed and hugged me. Oh, I've got pictures of him in the family albums, but they're not of the father I knew. My mother I remember better, though not too well either. She looked like me, a frivolous, pretty, vain woman who wasn't interested in much beyond horses, bridge and partygoing. My aunt was always sure and terrified that I'd turn out just like my mother."

"Aunt Katharine was from your father's side of the family, I take it?"

"How did you know?" Beth chuckled, her face clearing. "She certainly was. That was the side with brains. She was my father's older sister, which is why he left her my guardian and the executor of their estate. And sober, decent, interfering, stubborn fool that Aunt Katharine was, she took her responsibilities seriously. She could have fobbed me off to some school and seen me on holidays but instead she took me to live with her. It couldn't have been easy for an old-fashioned maiden lady already set in her ways."

"There must have been some rewards for her."

"I wonder. When I began to run around at school, first with George and then with Steven, she did everything she could to stop me. She warned me that unless I buckled down to work I wouldn't get into medical school, but I didn't believe her. The dean of the med school was an old friend of hers and I thought Aunt Katharine would just put in a call to him and fix things up. But I underestimated her. She refused. She would absolutely not make such a call, or any other. She would pull no strings and use no influence. She even made sure that Bill Daulton wouldn't."

"Couldn't you get accepted anywhere?"

"Somewhere, maybe. Switzerland, Holland, but George and Steven were here, so here was where I wanted to be. The best I could manage after being rejected by all the local medical schools was the nursing school, so that was where I went."

"That was more ladylike. Maybe she was pleased."

"Not Aunt Katharine. I'd vowed to do something and failed. She was disappointed. Not, mind you, that she hadn't expected it."

"It wasn't that bad."

"It was awful. I felt as if I'd fallen off a cliff and broken all my bones. I made up my mind to buckle down and work, but I didn't. Instead, I drank more and drove faster and ran around more. Oh, I worked enough to make a passable record, but that was pretty easy for me. I was smart enough, too smart, but my mind wasn't on the work; it was on Steven and George.

"And then with only a few months to graduation, I found out that I was pregnant."

"By whom?" he asked, unable to conceal the asperity in his voice.

"By Steven. George was up at Berkeley by then and though I still saw him from time to time, mostly on weekends, and we talked a lot on the telephone, we hadn't been going to bed together for a couple of months."

"So you could be sure it was Prescott."

"Yes, I was sure and I told him. He laughed in my face and asked me how many other men I was sleeping with and which of them I'd accused of being the father. I slapped him. He slapped me back. I told him I'd slept with no one else and he smiled, completely unbelieving, and offered to find me a good abortionist."

"Why didn't he just marry you? I thought you said he loved you."

"He did. He does. But he had no money. He'd done the whole route by himself, all the way on scholarships and part-time work at night, and he didn't want to lose it all. He was terrified. He was a third-year resident then and if the pregnancy came out he'd be booted and I wouldn't be allowed to graduate. But he wouldn't marry me and that was that. He wanted money, he said, position, comfort, security, and he was going to have them; he wasn't going to let me spoil it all for him."

"But you had money."

Watching a trio of golfers standing around the sand trap while a fourth struggled to work out of it, she shook her head. "I only had an allowance my aunt gave me. Legally, I was her ward and all the money was hers. I wasn't due to get a dime of it until I was twenty-eight, but Steven didn't know that."

"Did he know that your aunt was rich, that you'd be rich?"

"I doubt it. I had a car and a small furnished flat, but that didn't look like money, especially not out here, where plenty of the 'nice' girls from 'good' families had the same."

"Besides, you didn't tell him about the money either. You didn't trust him enough."

Beth looked ashamed. "No, I didn't want Steven to know I was— well-off."

"Because he might have married you for the cash?"

"George knew," she said defensively.

"You trusted him. And you were sure he wouldn't tell Prescott."

"You really have stepped into George's shoes," Beth said, out of nowhere. "You've really begun to think his part as well as take it."

Sanders drew himself up and sat on the balustrade, his back to the golf course, and just then the two young nuns rose from behind the statue of the shades, smiled sweetly in their direction and walked away into the bright sprays of sunlit spume that masked the Palace of the Legion of Honor. Only they were happy, Sanders thought; only they could be, having given up the flesh and its wantonnesses; but he knew that that too was an illusion, that the nuns' flesh like his own and Beth's was racked with as many lusts, and as urgent, and that they had not, could not, put off the flesh. Everyone walked in the Emperor's new clothes even if no one saw and no one remarked on it. "George's shoes are uncomfortable."

Beth leaned against him. "They don't fit. They're not yours."

"The child wasn't George's either, yet he married you."

"Yes"—her voice acidly parodied her words—"he married me, he rescued my good name, he gave the child his good name—"

"That's no small thing," Sanders brought her up shortly.

"And he killed it."

"Your good name?"

"He killed the child," she said dully, "he killed it. You asked before, didn't you? Well, that was the first and only time I ever cried for anyone else, the one and only and I hope the last time."

"It won't be the last time, you can be sure of that."

"Not when my parents died. Not when Aunt Katharine died. Not even when George died."

Sanders was sure that what she said wasn't true but he didn't contest it. She rubbed her head against his sleeve like an alley cat begging to be fed and comforted, petted and approved, and he put his arm around her and felt that small shiver run through her frame that was either passion or remorse. "Steven wouldn't do the abortion himself, quietly, as I asked him to. He was afraid we might have a falling out and that I'd eventually tell someone, that someone would find out, that things might not go right and he'd have to take me to a hospital. If they found out, he'd be thrown out of medicine.

So he got someone else to do the dirty work, to call me to arrange the a.b. and that was the last straw, that stranger's cold voice on the telephone giving me those cold, cold instructions. If Steven had even offered to go with me, to take care of me afterwards—but that would have made him an accessory, he said, and he'd endanger his license. He didn't want any traceable connection between him and that abortion. But that way was too brutal and uncaring for me. I called it off. I told him I'd have the child and I'd see him in hell before I married him or took his lousy money."

"In other words, you took him off the hook."

Beth drew back and gazed up at him, her lips a cynical grimace. "No, Elliott, that was just what I didn't do. He couldn't pay me off like a whore, like his other whores, and clear his conscience. He was left on the hook, he remained guilty, and he could never get off."

"You never let him expiate."

"I could have predicted that you'd say that because that's just what George said. *Expiate,* that was his exact word, and I told him, and I tell you, that there is no such thing in life as expiation without restitution, and how could Steven make restitution to me? An eye for an eye is inadequate. If you lose the eye, what good does it do to take someone else's eye out unless your eye is replaced?"

"And I thought it was Prescott who was making you pay," Sanders marveled.

"We both paid and we both pay," she retorted. "That's human commerce. Where everybody pays, nobody goes free and everybody pays more than it's worth."

Her face was so vengeful and vicious that he had to turn away. He looked at his watch and asked casually when Prescott would be back for her. Now more than ever he didn't want to see Prescott, didn't want to be there with Beth when he arrived for her.

Beth must have heard his thoughts. "Don't go. Don't leave me here alone," she pleaded. "Stay with me. You won't have to talk to him. His car will come up from that way and park in front of the arch. I'll see it and go quickly by myself."

Sanders knew it would likely *not* be that way, knew it would be demoralizing to watch her walk away from him to meet Prescott, but he acquiesced, stroking her hair, caressing her head which lay against his ribs just under his heart. Adam's rib, he thought. Not pride goeth before the fall, but fear and hatred, he told himself: apprehension, the terrors of yesterday and the day after tomorrow. As he listened with a shudder of his flesh Beth spoke into his ribs, as if her voice and its echoes might meet and persuade the rhythms of his heart and the marrow of his bones. "I called George and told him what had happened, without any folderol or curlecues, exactly what had happened, and when I was through all I could hear at the other end of the phone was a sigh, a deep intake of breath that sounded just like the humming of the telephone wires. When he spoke up at last, he spoke very slowly, not at all like himself, as if someone was at his elbow, listening. 'Marry me, Beth,' he said. 'I'll marry you.'"

"Just like that?"

"Just like that. I didn't know what to say, or do. I wasn't even sure exactly why I'd called him but when he asked me to marry him I began to cry. I said I couldn't do that to him, that that wasn't why I'd called him, but I knew that wasn't true and so did he. He cut me off. 'I want you,' he said, 'and I want the child. I want you both.' But there was something about the way he said it that sounded like a judge pronouncing sentence, inexorable and irreversible. I was frightened and told him that the child wasn't his, that it was Steven's, and he asked me only if I was sure. When I told him I was sure, there was the only note of regret I detected in his voice. That made him sorry, he said, but it didn't change matters; a child's father was the man who took the responsibility for raising it, not merely siring it; he would take that responsibility."

Gladly? Willingly? Sanders wondered. From the balustrade, looking down on her, he saw that the planes of Beth's face were different, older, stoic, almost Indian, with reserves of stamina and strength you did not see straightforwardly. "I couldn't have done that," he confessed.

"No," she said, scanning his face for something he would have given her if he knew what she was seeking, "you wouldn't." There was only the faintest stress on the verb and only the faintest shutter-like click of the irises that showed her disappointment.

Unable to bear her scrutiny, resenting her quest for what she

[269]

sought and hadn't found, because he knew it revealed a flaw in his own character that was profound and permanent, a flaw that Lovett Carpenter Sanders had not had, either with his mother or with Nathalie Blanchot, or probably with any woman he was involved with, Sanders tried to turn her disappointment aside with a question. "So you married him?" he asked.

"*He* married me," she replied, her correction soft but insistent, "and he came down the Peninsula from Berkeley that very night so I wouldn't be alone." That, too, Sanders knew, was rebuke, invidious comparison.

"I was already in my third month. There wasn't much time left before I'd be showing so we had to be quick. There were only a few months to graduation too so that if I carried small and dressed cleverly I'd just make it under the wire and no one would be wiser. It was dead of winter then, cold and rainy, bleak and cheerless, just the way I felt inside. Graduation was at the end of May and then I'd be an RN. My due date was last week in August or the first in September, so the whole schedule was pretty tight."

"What did your Aunt Katharine say?"

"When?"

"You didn't tell her?"

"How could I?"

"How could you *not* tell her?"

"She didn't like either Steven or George, she wasn't exactly sympathetic to premarital sexual relations, certainly not promiscuous sexual relations, maybe not sympathetic to sexual relations at all, regardless of the proprieties, except for having children—"

"On that score, at least, you weren't too far out of bounds for her."

"You never miss an opportunity, do you?"

"Sorry," he apologized, genuinely abashed.

She extricated herself from his embrace. "You talk about expiation."

"There's never any expiation," he said angrily, "only sin after sin after sin. Each to the other, against the other, each to himself. What there is, when there's anything, is feeling—and forgiveness."

"You're talking to yourself, about yourself," she accused.

"That's true, but not *only* about myself." Their eyes locked, and

[270]

hers, first to look away, stared past him to the golf course, wide and unseeing, her lower lip caught by her teeth. "I told her as soon as I thought I could—respectably." She laughed harshly at that last word. "We drove out to Nevada to get married, George and I, and luckily George had already passed his twenty-first birthday or we'd have needed his old man's permission. To Reno! It was the right city, prophetic, the capital of divorce. What a place to marry! A justice of the peace, beery and with his fly half unzipped and his flabby mouth half open in a leer. Ugh!" She shuddered. "We were eloping and under the gun, so what could we expect? But I could see the knife twist in George there, and for the first time I understood what that fine phrase, *to solemnize a marriage,* really meant. Our ceremony was not even frivolous; it was obscene; it was like going to a motel without luggage and signing yourself Mr. and Mrs. with the wiseacre face of the night clerk watching, knowing that you know he knows you're a fraud."

"And then you told your aunt?"

"Aunt Katharine was a lady to the very end. She congratulated George and kissed me, all very proper, and I'd swear her eye lingered on my stomach for just the fraction of a second more than it should have. Not that anything showed yet, but I think she knew, and I felt as fraudulent with her, more, as I'd felt in front of that justice of the peace in Reno. She didn't ask why we were so hasty, she didn't inquire why we hadn't shown her the elementary courtesy of consulting or informing her, and she didn't berate us for a failure of real affection in not doing a proper wedding her way so that all the years she'd taken care of me should have a decent capstone. She was so decent and so courteous I hated her."

"No expiation."

Beth's head hung. "No," she lamented, "no expiation at all. Here she'd taken an eight-year-old brat into her household to raise, and a troublesome adolescent and young woman had come out of it in spite of her best efforts. She hadn't complained, she hadn't quit, she'd gone right on behaving like a responsible parent and this was her reward: We came back from Reno, George moved into my flat, and then a few days later we drove over to see Aunt Katharine to break the news."

"Fait accompli." Fête accomplie.

"Right. If only she'd exploded, shown me the door, dressed me down, done anything nasty so I could have felt aggrieved and justified, but she didn't. She sat us both down and told us that marriage was a very serious matter, so serious and responsible that she had never felt up to it herself—"

"What a marvelous old lady!" Sanders exclaimed.

"And that she wished us the very best of luck. She knew that we would now have some additional expenses and since we were both going to school and she didn't think either of us would want to drop out now, she'd raise my allowance so that things wouldn't be too tight financially."

"Decent, diplomatic, smart."

"Aunt Katharine was all those things. When George mentioned that he thought he ought to quit school, that he wasn't learning much, and wasn't sure he wanted the Ph.D. anyway—he didn't say that he also thought he should support a wife, though I knew he had that old-style notion—she gave him some good advice, advice he should have followed. Aunt Katharine told him that at least it kept him out of the Army where he wouldn't learn anything, and that the Ph.D. would be useful no matter what he did want to do eventually; certainly it would be no handicap. Besides, he was very young—she said that oh so kindly although I knew that was one of her major objections to George, that he was only twenty-one and too immature for a twenty-four-year-old woman like me—and he would have the Ph.D. by the time most men his age were graduating from college, especially if he didn't have to take time off to work. She knew he did all sorts of odd jobs to keep himself going even with his fellowship.

"She asked me if I needed anything, or if there was any way she could help me and I said no, she'd already helped more than enough, and I thought I saw tears start into her eyes. That wasn't like her, that wasn't like her at all, and I was surprised and upset by it. Then, while we were leaving, she embraced me and kissed me goodbye, on the cheek of course, but she hadn't done that for a very long time and I knew something was wrong."

"Maybe she was just pleased and hopeful for the two of you. Maybe she was even a little envious. You're forgetting that that maiden lady knew that Baudelaire quotation and used it."

Beth's face was contorted in vehement negation. "It wasn't like that. I wish it had been. She was sick, dying, and she knew when we came to her with our news. She'd known for a couple of days and we surprised her, but she didn't say anything then. One didn't, of course, spoil anyone else's good news with such grim tidings. Then, after a whole month, when I hadn't seen her even once, she telephoned me one afternoon when she knew George would be up at Berkeley and asked me to have tea with her. I wasn't eager. I was feeling even guiltier because she'd sent me a $2,500 check—made out in my name, of course, not George's—as a little 'emergency nest egg,' as she put it, and she'd raised my allowance from $300 to $700 a month. And the guiltier I felt, the more I hated her for making me feel guilty."

"*Making* you feel guilty! By being decent to you, and generous." Though he stood against her, was rebuking her, he knew what she meant.

"The money was mine," Beth contended.

"Not then, not until—"

"Until she died. The irony of ironies, because not only did I come into my own money but she left me all of hers too. And what she had me to tea for was to tell me that she was dying and that I'd now have to handle my own money—and my own life. She said it so regretfully, so sorrowfully, as if she'd failed to fulfill some important obligation *to me*. She had, she said, thought of setting up an executor, probably Bill Daulton, or a board of trustees for the estate, but she'd reconsidered. She didn't think it would do much good. I wasn't going to learn by having other people do things for me, take care of me; I was going to have to do things for myself, so she was leaving the whole kit and kaboodle to me. Bill Daulton would help with investments, and one or two other friends of hers had promised to be available if I needed financial or legal advice, but the decision and responsibility were to be solely mine. I was to remember that she expected me to handle the money, both my parents' estate and hers, with prudence, because it would be for our children and our grandchildren and she hated to think that what it had taken four generations to accumulate would be dissipated in one.

"For our children and grandchildren!" Beth snorted. "If she'd died earlier and left me all that money, I could've married Steven and things would have looked different."

"You couldn't and you wouldn't."

"No, I suppose you're right. I'd have been too proud to tell Steven that I was rich, that he could afford to marry me, that my parents' money and my aunt's converted me from a liability to an asset. No, I wasn't sure enough to be that candid with him. I really didn't think that, all by myself, he wanted me."

"But you wanted to be persuaded."

"What woman doesn't? If only Aunt Katharine had died before—"

"People are rambunctious that way, they never do die on schedule, when it's convenient for others"—Sanders was snide—"sometimes they don't even die when it's convenient for themselves." Before she could take him to task, he apologized once more for having an aspish tongue.

"Aunt Katharine's tongue was like yours, waspish and cutting, but never out of control. How she managed it I don't know but she did."

"My mother called that breeding."

"My God, she was a redoubtable woman. Strong and conscientious, and perfectly adjusted to the role she had to play. A maiden lady of good family. Not like her niece. When the doctors informed her that she had cancer of the bowel, that it was metastasized to the liver and one of the lungs, she simply asked how long she had left. Perhaps six weeks, perhaps six months, if they left it as it was, but if they operated, perhaps several years. Without qualms she vetoed the operation and there was no surgery. She was not a woman to live with a colostomy. That afternoon she told me she felt she'd lived long enough, that except for me there was no special person she was responsible for and now that I was married I had George and besides I was old enough to look after myself. If there was just a shade of caustic in her comments I didn't notice it at the time, but I did notice the disdain she had for the world, a fastidiousness about it which made her want to hold it off at least at arm's length, farther if she could, and she didn't seem to regret leaving it.

"She didn't ask for my pity—and she didn't get it. She told me simply and matter-of-factly that she was going to die and I accepted it just as simply and matter-of-factly—and quite callously. I thought it was a terribly inconvenient time but when she told me that I'd be in control of my own money and would get hers as well, that almost seemed to make up for the inconvenience. It was quite all right with me for a sixty-two-year-old woman to get cancer and die without complaint, without rebellion, even without regret. And, clearly, without my love or sense of loss. It was a long time afterward before I knew that I loved her, a long time before I knew what she meant to me, what I meant to her."

The colostomy. Cherokee chiefs and maiden aunts. Did anyone really leave life that simply and matter-of-factly, so without regret and with so much disdain? He remembered the Indian's Conestoga wagon of sheets careening and the sheets black with blood. The sons—and daughters—of chiefs. "You conferred motherhood on her without birth. It was her own form of immaculate conception and it gave her a child, someone to love and someone who helped give meaning and shape to her life. She understood those words by Baudelaire, Beth. You've just underestimated her."

"I haven't come to terms with Aunt Katharine yet. I'm still not sure what she felt about me or I about her. I only know the sense of loss, her absence. Luckily, she wasn't in much pain. She just got weaker and weaker, thinner and thinner, until she couldn't get out of bed any more, so that at the end she was helpless and dependent, which she hated. But she was dead ten days before I graduated from nursing school in an absolutely flamboyant spring that seemed to be celebrating the kicking I felt in my womb, not the gradual fading from life of my Aunt Katharine; the jubilance was of birth unmarked by the sorrow of her passing."

"Did you tell her you were going to have a child?"

"No, she was even denied that. I never told her, though George and I quarreled bitterly about that—he went to visit her more faithfully than I, brought her flowers, found her special foods he knew she liked, and I'm sure she thought it was because of the money. But it wasn't. George wasn't like that. He admired her, he liked her, and he was hurt when she showed him no affection, only an exquisite courtesy which wounded him all the more."

What did Beth expect of a woman who, to all intents and purposes, had been her mother for twice as long as her natural mother, who had devoted herself to raising a child and who yet found the child she'd loved and raised callous and indifferent to her, without genuine concern for her impending death? Had Aunt Katharine come by that understanding of Baudelaire only by reading French literature at Wellesley? Sanders doubted it. Whatever romantic disappointment she'd known, and she must have known one or more, had come to be summarized in the wisdom and feeling of those poetic lines; but by an accident of fate, a mischance, she'd been given Beth as a reward. And a punishment. Though at the very last she'd found the freshness of the tomb, it had been on the indifferent breast of her niece. Aunt Katharine was like his mother, though Marian Stuart Sanders had been luckier—and unluckier—to have his father and John C. Ballinger, romantic disappointments both perhaps, but warm human relations. His mother wouldn't indulge herself or ask for what, if it was to have any force and meaning, had to be given freely; Aunt Katharine had very likely known that too, had not asked, and had not received.

"I was such a bitch," Beth was saying. "It never occurred to me that I owed my life to her, that she'd loved me better and raised me more sensibly than my own mother would have. I wasn't even grateful for the money because I thought that it was mine by right anyway, I thought I had it coming. And I was so completely involved with myself and my problems I didn't even have time for her, or feeling; all I could think about was that child squirming in my womb, trying to get myself through nursing school, trying to cope with George and Steven."

"Still Steven? Hadn't you had your fill of him by then?"

"I still wanted him. And George too. In the beginning George wouldn't make love to me any more, didn't seem to want me, as if a kind of fastidiousness kept him from intruding into a womb another man had filled. I wanted him to make love to me, not only to make me feel wanted but to make him committed to the child, to make him feel as close to fathering it as could be, not just a Sir Galahad on a white horse rescuing a damsel in distress. At first I made jokes about superfetation but he ignored them in a way that made me feel I'd committed an indecency. Then I tried to seduce him, you know, getting dressed or undressed when he was there watching me, showering while he was in the bathroom, moving against him in bed, and when after nights of tossing and turning in that big bed, when he was beginning to look thin and green as the new leaves on the trees, he finally woke me, fierce and insistent, inconsiderate and uncaring for my pleasure as he'd never been before —it was the best lovemaking we ever had together. For two weeks then I was happy, full of sunspots in my blood, warming me inside and out. I thought things were going to turn out fine.

"Then Steven called and I told him George and I were married and that I was going to have the baby and he didn't have to worry about a thing. He went berserk, howling on the telephone like an animal, threatening to kill me, to kill George, to kill the child, until I hung up on him. But the next day on the wards he was waiting for me. I was on pediatrics that week and there, among all the new-born infants, he came for me. He looked like a madman, unshaven, his mustache scraggly, his eyes wild and bloodshot. He came up behind me while I was feeding one of the babies and grunted that I'd better put the baby down that minute and go with him. When I caught the look on his face, I laid the poor child down, though it was only half fed and started to cry, and followed him. He took me to the linen closet on the second floor, locked us inside and then, without a word, put his hand under my skirt and felt my belly. 'Whore! Slut! You really have it!' he bawled. 'You really do have it.'

"I tried to push his hand away. I threatened to scream. I cursed him. I told him he'd had his chance and let it go by. Now the child was going to be George's and mine. I didn't want to see him, I didn't want to talk to him, I wanted him out of my life. His face came closer to mine, and he rasped, 'You'll see me, you'll see me all right.' I felt his hand grab me as if he were going to tear the child right out of my womb, his nails cutting my flesh, and then he bit me and his hand changed, touching me, caressing me, and there, on that pile of dirty linen on the floor he made love to me."

The lump in his throat grew until Sanders was sure he was going to puke, but when he turned away, gagging, she tore at his sleeve and cried out, "Don't turn away from me like that, that was the way George did, just that way, and it never was the same between us again. Never."

"No," Sanders croaked, his voice barely negotiating the passage in his throat, "after that it was all jasmine and gardenias, wasn't it?" After the Avenue Foch what is there?

"Elliott"—Beth's eyes widened with alarm—"what is it?"

Dumbly he pointed to the paroxysm he felt in his throat and she put her hands on it, gently, her fingers working his windpipe, massaging his flesh, but he felt she was choking him and tore her hands away and held them at her sides while he swallowed hard over and over again until his mouth was dry as sand and his throat a continuing painful spasm.

"What a touching scene," Prescott exclaimed. "A tableau in the shade of *The Three Shades*. How arty! But couldn't you have found a more private place?" He'd come up behind them unobserved, impeccable as always, blue suit perfectly tailored and pressed, maroon foulard dimpled just beneath the knot, mustache trim, the very antithesis of what Beth had just finished describing.

When Beth explained that he was sick, Prescott's manner turned professional. He ran his fingers down the sides of Sanders' throat, under his ears and jaws, before opening the shirt collar and several buttons to probe painfully into the hollows of the collarbones and under the armpits. "Come in and have Beth do a barium swallow on you," Prescott advised coolly, giving him a diagnostic look that somehow was a dismissal. "I don't think it's anything serious but let's check it out just in case." An exchange of understanding glances between Prescott and Beth, part professional, part personal, left him excluded and Sanders resented it. They were awkward until Prescott brusquely proclaimed that he had to be back at the hospital, took Beth firmly by the arm and marched her off toward his car. She turned and yelled back for him to call. Prescott waved his one arm, not looking back or letting go of Beth's elbow with the other, and said something to Beth of which Sanders caught only two words—*boule hystérique*—badly pronounced, before they were out of earshot.

Sanders refused to watch them leave together, the only protest he felt he could make, so he turned his back, leaned his elbows on the cold stone balustrade and thought of what *boule hystérique* might mean. Hysterical ball or ball of hysteria. Is that what Prescott thought the lump in his throat was, a hysterical hallucination? Running his fingers down his neck, he found nothing, but when, experimentally, he tried to swallow, the constriction and pain were real and evident.

Sitting with his back to the sad Rodin sculpture, holding his throat with one warm palm, Sanders remembered the letter the chaplain had handed him at George's grave. Groping in his pockets, he found the letter, slit the blank khaki envelope with his fingernail only to find another smaller sealed khaki envelope within bearing only his name. That envelope contained a single sheet of the same kind of paper Beth Christiansen had shown him with the base hospital letterhead embossed on it and, in the upper right-hand corner, Chaplain Murray Fillmore's name. The letter, in Fillmore's even, small but intense calligraphy, all of the *i*'s, *l*'s and *t*'s drawn with heavy sword strokes of the pen, said:

DEAR SANDERS:

Since I knew that if you were in the States you would be at Sergeant Christiansen's funeral, I took this somewhat unorthodox method of getting in touch with you. Much has happened to me since your departure and, in part, as a result of our talks together.

I have left the Army but not the cloth; or should I say that I have left the Army and resumed the cloth? I would like very much to see and talk to you again if you would care to see me. I don't yet have a telephone but my address is, temporarily, 739 Hillside Road in Berkeley.

Yours in Christ,
MURRAY FILLMORE

The letter was undated but if Fillmore had known about the funeral, then presumably it was recent enough to be applicable still. So Fillmore was back and out of the Army. Had he simply been due, his overseas tour of duty up, or had his separation been more painful, as that second paragraph of his letter seemed to imply? The tone of the note was such an odd mixture of diffidence and assertiveness that Sanders smiled in spite of himself. Well, he would see Chaplain Fillmore if only to get his t.s. slip punched.

* * *

The door was open as if she was expecting someone but Sanders couldn't see anyone inside nor did anyone respond to his two knocks at the door. Only a single lamp seemed to be lit and in the oncoming darkness the room was filled with hewn blocks of shadow so that the room seemed a stony medieval torture chamber. "Laura," Sanders called softly, but there was no answer. "Laura!" he spoke out more sharply, walking into the middle of the room before he noticed the screen, an improvised shoji triptych of posters, buttons and a simple long sheet, a diploma or papyrus proclamation on each of the three sections, all three combining to block off another part of the room where another lamp reflected a gold oval on the ceiling above. "Laura," he repeated, moving toward the light, and the wave of sobbing from behind the screen rose to meet him. Behind the shoji Laura sat, naked from the waist up, looking at herself in an old-fashioned dressing-table three-panel mirror which showed three different weeping faces and convulsed bodies. Her red swollen eyes saw him, acknowledged him, even made him welcome, but her crying continued. Approaching her, his arms outstretched, he was hurt to see her shrink back from him. "What is it?" he asked. "What is it?"

"Look at me," she cried, pointing to the mirrors and her triple reflection, flicking a demeaning hand from her throat across her bare breasts and navel into her lap. "Look at me. Who would want me? Who could want—this?" The genuine torment touched him to the quick. She'd flaunted herself, touched herself, spoken of herself with loathing as she were a side of moldy beef hung for display. Abruptly, then, her crying stopped. The smell of marijuana drifted up to his nostrils, the butt still smoking in the ashtray. Laura nodded dreamily. "Like I'm turned on, man," she said. "Been turned on for three days, on high, and uptight because the high's gone, like I'm gummy, sticky, down, down, down." She reached for the butt, couldn't get her fingers on it and picked it up with tweezers, the chrome scorched, lit the butt again and breathed in the smoke with a sigh. "You want a hit on the roach?" she asked, offering him the stub. "No, I guess not," she said when he made no move. "Like square, square, square." She began to cry again.

"What happened, Laura?" he asked.

"Nothing. That's it exactly, like nothing happened. Just got full of hangups, hung up, hangdog, hung down." Her face was a wet papier-mâché mask that had run, her eyes lacquered over, her lips pouted and full as from love. "So I had me a tea party." She raised the tweezers and butt delicately, the faint light glinting off the discolored chrome, her pinky outstretched as if she held the daintiest Spode teacup, and then she drew on the butt, drank in the smoke as if she were sipping politely the most fragrant Darjeeling, but her hand shook so badly that she had trouble steadying the cigarette.

Restraining himself from slapping the butt from her hand, Sanders asked if that was all she'd been on.

"Laura's like a good little girl. Iowa- and Ivory-pure. Ninety-nine and forty-four one-hundredths percent pure. Only high with jive. Hung high on hemp. Pulling my pod, podner. Groovy on grass. Smoking it up with Maryjane. Gutting with gauge. No acidhead, only teahead. Speed kills. Meths are freaks and freaks are meths. Good girl. Good little Laura." She made a dizzy small girl's grin to show how smart she was—and how miserable. The burned-down butt scorched her lip and she cried out and dropped the tweezers. A shower of sparks, then the glowing coal, fell on her thigh. She couldn't seem to find it and Sanders swiftly brushed it from her thigh while she yelped and sat heavy-lidded watching it burn the carpet until Sanders smeared it out with his shoe. He took a dab from an open cold-cream jar and smeared it on the reddened skin.

"When did you last eat?" he asked, keeping his voice neutral, the lump in his throat stonier because he wanted to roar and rage at her.

"*Who* did I eat last?" she asked, her face all animal cunning, lazy laughter bubbling from her lips, shrilly, rising, then cascading down while she admonished him with a finger. "Like you should not ask me questions like that. Everybody does his thing. Like you do yours, I do mine, everybody. . . ." She spread her arms helplessly, bowed her head and suddenly her laughter switched tracks, screamed over the switch and was on another line of intense sobbing, full cry, as if that was what she'd intended all along. "Look at me," she resumed, sorrowfully, bitterly, contemplating her navel. "Who wants this—this thing? Nobody ever wanted me. Nobody. Never."

I do. The lie leaped easily to his lips, the lie that would likely stop her weeping, that would, for the moment, assuage and console; but it was a lie he couldn't speak though he knew that when she came out of the hemp fog she would have forgotten his words.

A once-white terry-cloth robe hung from the back of her chair and Sanders put it over her shoulders. "Come on," he said, "get up and I'll make you some hot coffee." He lifted her to her feet, drew the robe closed, his fingers grazing, then avoiding, her breasts, and tied the sash tight around her waist as she swayed then stumbled into his arms and shivering let him rock her quiet. Slowly, painstakingly, he drew her tangled tresses out of the neck of the robe and while holding her with one hand with the other he straightened, loosened, caressed her long hair.

In the next half hour he managed to get her to eat a scrambled egg and a piece of toast, and to drink three cups of hot black coffee before he put her into a steaming-hot shower and kept her there for almost twenty minutes. When she came out Sanders toweled her dry, permitting his flesh to rise to the occasion but not exploiting it, and enjoying the way she brushed her long hair straight and stiff, vigorously brushed her teeth and rinsed her mouth from the clouded champagne glass. When at last she was in bed, the blanket up to her chin, exhaustion plain on a face that should have been girlish and glowing, she whispered, "Stay with me, Elliott," and when he hesitated, "at least for a little while." He nodded and she brought her hand out from under the blankets and uncertainly reached for his. He sat on the edge of the bed, her fingers gripping his tightly until as her breathing grew regular and shallow they relaxed and left his hand free.

Sanders reheated the coffee, poured a cup and as he drank it wandered restlessly around the room, depressed by that implacable mirror triptych, its dressing table littered with combs and brushes, powder boxes and puffs, makeup kits, pots of eye makeup and mascara, but none of it proof against the sense of worthlessness. Who would want me? This thing. And the drugs too, only one of the parts of what Laura called the scene that he hated because it was the worst of America, always boom and bust, agonies and ecstasies, typical American immoderation, to be provoked and prolonged by

drugs, yoga, diet, laxatives, aphrodisiacs, alcohol, surgery, whatever
came readily to hand or was the fad of the moment. In front of the
improvised shoji he stopped to admire how skillfully it had been
put together of painted black wood frames and green baize-covered
plywood, American bulletin boards made Japanese. Tacked to one
section was a mass of buttons filled with mottoes: MAKE LOVE NOT
WAR; KISS DON'T KILL; WE SHALL OVERKILL; and HAPPINESS IS A YELLOW
BANANA; LEGALIZE BROWN RICE; KAFKA IS A KVETCH; and WOMAN
SHOULD BE OBSCENE NOT HEARD; LXIX; IT IS BETTER BY FAR TO COME
TOGETHER THAN TO GO TOGETHER. Tacked to another were posters of
the kind he'd seen all over the city but mostly in the Haight, the
largest of them of Allen Ginsberg as Uncle Sam, in starred top hat
and red-and-white-striped pants; but the last panel was the most
interesting, because it contained only a single long scroll printed
in seventeenth-century-style type, the f's and s's serpentine and confusing. The scroll was titled simply *Desiderata:*

*Go placidly among the noise & haste, & remember what peace
there may be in silence. As far as possible without surrender be on
good terms with all persons. Speak your truth quietly & clearly; and
listen to others, even the dull & ignorant; they too have their story.
Avoid loud & aggressive persons, they are vexations to the spirit. If
you compare yourself with others, you may become vain & bitter;
for always there will be greater & lesser persons than yourself. Enjoy your achievements as well as your plans. Keep interested in
your career, however humble; it is a real possession in the changing
fortunes of time. Exercise caution in your business affairs; for the
world is full of trickery. But let this not blind you to what virtue
there is; many persons strive for high ideals; and everywhere life is
full of heroism. Be yourself. Especially, do not feign affection.
Neither be cynical about love; for in the face of all aridity & disenchantment it is perennial as the grass. Take kindly the counsel of
the years, gracefully surrendering the things of youth. Nurture
strength of spirit to shield you in sudden misfortune. But do not
distress yourself with imaginings. Many fears are born of fatigue &
loneliness. Beyond a wholesome discipline, be gentle with yourself.
You are a child of the universe, no less than the trees & the stars;
you have a right to be here. And whether or not it is clear to you, no*

doubt the universe is unfolding as it should. Therefore be at peace with God, whatever you conceive Him to be, and whatever your labors & aspirations, in the noisy confusion of life keep peace with your soul. With all its sham, drudgery & broken dreams, it is still a beautiful world. Be careful. Strive to be happy.

Beneath with becoming modesty was the attribution: "Found in Old Saint Paul's Church, Baltimore: dated 1692." *Plus ça change.* More than two hundred and fifty years ago some unnamed man, secular or cleric, had anonymously inscribed the essentials for wisely meeting and supporting life. Two thousand years before, Micah had called for every man under his fig tree and Isaiah for turning the swords of life into plowshares and the spears into pruning hooks, but over the generations so few, so pitifully few, had paid any attention and those inconstantly. To this day. The lights such men lit, often consuming themselves in the incandescence, seemed only to scorch the maculae of men's minds' eyes, blinding them, yet the wisdom of man—like the stupidity, the sanity and the madness, the hatred and the love—went back a long way and was everywhere manifest, persisted still, and here in San Francisco, two thousand years after Christ, was tacked on the baize of a green girl's decorative screen the right way, so clearly described, so tangibly, you thought you could reach out and pluck it like a fruit: the joy of man's desiring, but forever unattainable. I have had enough of killing, Sanders thought, as if that was both logical and coherent, I have had more than enough of killing.

The insistent question which had lumpishly caught in his mind and been trapped in his throat like his gorge was suddenly loosed: Beth had told him that George had killed the child. The wildness of her grief speaking, the desire for revenge and self-justification, the hatred of the castoff, mother, wife, and mistress scorned? Why would George have killed the child anyway; only because of Prescott's paternity? *Only?* Men killed for a great deal less than that, he knew, but not men like George Christiansen: That didn't seem to be the man he knew. Yet who was the man he knew? The George in Vietnam seemed very different from the man in whose shoes he found himself; no, he corrected himself, the man whose footprints he was following. Sanders could have understood killing Beth but that was perhaps because he had walked through his own raging fire, burned on his own bed of coals that afternoon on the Avenue Foch. He'd have to find out more about what had happened to the child because if George *had* murdered the child, that might force him to give credence to the idea that George Christiansen had simply committed suicide, immolated himself on that sidewalk in Saigon, found himself in the situation that permitted himself to punish himself for some crime or sin—and what sin more primal than the killing of a son by his father, real or surrogate, except perhaps the killing of a father by his son? " 'Let this not blind you to what virtue there is,' " he reminded himself; "many persons strive for high ideals; and everywhere life is full of heroism.' "

His mother would have talked and behaved in that fashion without even the conscious awareness that such was her commitment. His father would never have admitted that, much less talked of it in such simple yet grand terms. No, Lovett Carpenter Sanders would have wanted to see himself and convey the picture of himself as a necessitarian, a cold, tough, practical man, not romantic, idealistic or quixotic. If his mother might not have been able to understand that "Strive to be happy" admonition, then his father was evidently incapable of absorbing the wisdom of "Be careful"; their heritages to him had torn him asunder, left him riding horses in different directions. Courage and cowardice. Love and sex. Prudence and pettiness. Or was the chasm he saw himself suspended over merely a chimera that required no bridge except the clear perception that there was no chasm at all?

Sanders got himself another cup of coffee and while he waited for it to cool he went past Laura's bed. As she, turning, uncovered herself, he drew the blankets up chastely over her breasts without a tremor of his hand or his flesh. The sudden pounding on the door was startling and he opened it to find two small muscular young men, dark glasses like blind eyes turned on him, their whole stance a silent belligerence, an unasked questioning of who this interloper was. The one closest to the door, in a dirty sheepskin-lined black leather jacket and denims, was so closely backed up by the man behind him, who wore a leather band Indian-style across his forehead, that they seemed both one person, some hirsute shaggy Siamese twins attached back to front and so when they spoke together, their voices harshly harmonizing, Sanders was not surprised that their words were identical. "This Laura's pad?" they asked in chorus. When they saw her in bed, asleep, the two heads looked at each other, then at him. "She freaked out? Bad trip?" the first one asked, carelessly fingering a Maltese cross suspended from a silver chain around his neck so that it hung on his breastbone like an award, a talisman. "She uptight?" the second asked.

"I'm sorry," Sanders said, spilling a little of his coffee. "I don't know what that means."

They exchanged glances of silent contempt. They shoved through the door past him and into the room, and Sanders, coffee cup in hand, feeling foolish and domestic-looking, asked if they were Laura's friends and were expected. They ignored him and the question, but from the way they walked around the room examining things as if they were at an auction he was reasonably sure that they'd never been in the flat before. After their tour they ended up standing in front of the panel of buttons, reading them aloud in the careful way people do who do not often read aloud, nudging each other's ribs and guffawing. "Ha, getta load of this. PULL OUT, LBJ— LIKE YOUR FATHER SHOULD HAVE. DON'T FLY AIR LINGUS; FLY WITH CUNNILINGUS. Say, what does that mean?" The Indian headband asked his friend.

Sanders set his coffee cup down. "I think you'd better go now, gentlemen. Laura's not been feeling well and she needs sleep. You're going to wake her."

They turned together, a *pas de deux,* and hands on hips, heads cocked hostilely, nostrils contemptuous, surveyed him. Sanders felt the anger and fear billow up together from his stomach and end simmering beneath the lump in his throat. He opened the door wide. "Now," he said.

"Like you gonna make us?" the Indian headband asked.

"I might try," Sanders replied.

"We friends of Laura's, man," the other one said, oily and menacingly reasonable. "We come pay her a visit. We like real sorry to hear she's uptight like that. Maybe *we* stay and take care of her and *you* take off."

Sanders shook his head. "Sorry," he said, "I think you'd better go."

"Sorry," the Indian headband mimicked, "*we* think *you'd* better blow."

The first one, fingering his Maltese cross, asked, "You a sawbones? Like a doctor?"

"No."

"Family?"

"No, just a friend."

"A good friend," the Indian headband leered.

"Get out," Sanders raged, his temper rising swift and ungovernable. "Beat it!"

"Like whyn't you try an make us?" The Indian headband challenged.

"Now whaddyu wanna yell like that for?" the Maltese cross asked with a hurt, exaggerated politeness. "We only trying to be like helpful. Y'know, we old friends of Laura's too."

"I'll bet."

"Not very friendly. Not hospitable like Laura be if she was with it," the Maltese cross said, the smirk in his voice all ugly innuendo. "We just come like to pay a visit."

"Okay, you paid it. Come back when Laura's feeling better—and when you're invited."

The churlish faces looked offended but whether it was feigned or real Sanders couldn't tell. "But the chick did invite us," the Maltese cross insisted amicably. "How'd you think we like find this pad anyway?"

Laura stirred restlessly and again, in turning, exposed her breasts. The two faces suddenly tightened except for their mouths which went slack as those of slavering dogs. The Maltese cross took off his dark glasses to reveal fixed pale stony eyes which never for a moment moved from the sight of those bared breasts. "Man," he said to no one, "like great, hah?"

Sanders strode across the room, irascibly yanked the blanket up to cover her, and with a violent movement of his arm waved them out the door.

"You makin it with little Laura? Like you wanna git your little wick wet in her nookie while she's out cold?" the Indian headband asked. "Like a real gennuman. That why you in such a hurry for us to cut out?"

"Get out," Sanders roared as he saw their fixed stares, their fingers twitching at their sides as if clutching were only barely under control, realizing that what the Indian headband had accused him of was what they intended, hoped for, wanted him to be gone for, "before I throw you the hell out."

"Thatta way to talk to friends of tha family?" the Maltese cross asked softly.

Sanders moved across the room toward them, his hands balled into fists, the lump in his throat choking him with bile. A click he thought was in his head until he saw the knife blade, alive and shining, leap out of the Indian headband's closed fist, didn't stop him. "Like don't get your balls in an uproar, Mac. You do, you lose em," he said, and Sanders knew that was not bluster.

A great bellow came echoing up from downstairs and through the door. "You don't cut those goddam noises out up there, I'm gonna call tha cops."

The leather jackets looked at the open door. "Neighbor," the Maltese cross noted, "downstairs."

"Think he'll ring in the fuzz?" the headband asked.

"If he doesn't, I will," Sanders assured them.

"You gonna throw us out," the headband gibed, brandishing his knife, "you like need help."

Sanders picked up one of the cane-bottomed chairs, held it with legs extended, and moved on them. "Out!" he ordered. "Right now."

"We going right now," the unruffled Maltese cross agreed. "Put the sticker away," he advised his ally, and then contemptuously turned his back on the chair. Dragging their feet, they slouched slowly to the door together as Sanders, already feeling stupid and vulgar and mock-heroic, the barroom brawler, the phony tough matador fighting the Miuras with a wooden muleta, hurried, harried them. Alert, the Indian headband watched him, half turned, the knife ready in his hand. "Like don't get your piss hot," he growled. "We on our way."

When they were at last out in the corridor, Sanders slammed the door closed with the chair legs and then threw the bolt, the Maltese cross's, "We be back, we see yah soon" echoing in his ears. Breathing hard, his hands clammy and shaking, Sanders stood the chair on the floor and sat down weakly on it. Hero, he castigated himself, bloody fool! What did you hope to accomplish with that? But he knew that he had felt he had no other choice, that no matter what had happened, no matter what violence was provoked or had to be used, he would not, could not, have left those thugs alone in the apartment with Laura even if what they wanted him to believe were true, that she had invited them and given them her address. That much, if no more, of his father remained in him.

Outside, close by, there was the muffled almost machine-gun quality of motorcycle engines being gunned, then booming away with a roar that shook the windowpanes. They'd gone, he thought, relieved; at least they'd gone. After a time Sanders put things in order, washed the dishes, refilled the percolator with water and fresh coffee and left it on the stove for Laura's breakfast. Lying there in bed, she looked so very lovely, so very young and defenseless, Sanders felt suddenly irretrievably the burden of his years. I'm middle-aged, he thought, the awareness coming with the shock and force of a cold shower; closer to forty than to thirty. As he watched her nuzzle the pillow, Sanders wondered what would have happened had he not been there; if she had invited them, it could only have been while she was high, he hoped, and he knew it was not jealousy he felt but fear that they would harm her, violate her so irrevocably that she would have no road back and none forward. He turned out the lamp and left only the little light glowing on the dressing table behind the shoji screen, the dressing table whose mirrors had shown Laura triple and fragmented, hysterically weeping her worthlessness, lamenting her youth.

The dark blue night outdoors was mottled by clumps of flannel-gray clouds; the air was cool, damp and rich with sea odors. Behind him the Coit Tower loomed darkly on Telegraph Hill, a rocket, blunt-nosed and ready to be launched, while before him the ribbon of light that was the outside elevator of the Fairmont Hotel leaped up into the night like a thermometer reading of the city's temperature. After carefully scrutinizing the street and seeing no leather jackets or motorcycles, parked or waiting, Sanders breathed easier and permitted himself the luxury of taking in the sea smells and the night sounds while he walked to where he'd left the car. He started it up quickly, headed for the freeway, keeping a dim background of musical-comedy tunes on the radio to prevent him from recalling the anger and anguish of the day. *Carpe diem,* the wise old Roman advised; but this was a day not to be seized but to be dropped from the fingers of consciousness like a hot potato.

When they picked him up or how they followed him Sanders couldn't figure out, but he didn't notice them until he was just outside the city limits, between the flat black waters of the Bay and the grim rock piles of the San Bruno Mountains, and he cursed himself for the fatigue and carelessness that had kept him from being warier. They were there quite suddenly, two speeding motorcycles, one blood-red and the other black—*le rouge et le noir,* he thought stupidly—sparkling with polished chrome and flashing mirrors and scintillating wheel spokes, roaring up behind him, cutting in front of the car, compelling him to twist and turn as they zoomed in and out, in front of and behind him, their double exhausts belching flame and smoke, and though the riders' faces were masked by goggles and their heads by crash helmets, Sanders knew they were the Maltese cross and the Indian headband. The two of them began to play "chicken" with him, one on either side, hemming his car in so closely that he was sure one or the other would hit him and he held onto the steering wheel with all his strength, exercising all his driving skill, to keep from veering even the slightest bit for fear he would kill one or both of them. And even as he did so he wished he could twist the wheel freely and kill them both because he wanted to. Abruptly they were both on his right, so close that he had to give ground, and they drove him that way across two lanes of the broad highway into the third lane until he was almost smack up against the barrier separating him from oncoming traffic and he knew he would have to either turn the car and kill them both or smash himself into that embankment and either go over it into an oncoming automobile or go ricocheting out of control and be hit by the cars coming up behind him. In either case he would almost certainly be killed. The wheel rings screeched and scraped crazily against the concrete barrier, he felt the car buck and quiver as he

[290]

fought to hold his course and then, as his nerves and strength were about to give out and he knew he would turn the wheel and slam into those two madmen, they veered their bikes away from him, their black-gloved left fists raised high, their middle fingers stuck out obscenely, their faces split by wild sadistic laughter, and then he was alone and driving past the airport, his heart still pounding in the lump in his throat, his hands so palsied on the wheel that he stayed in the slow lane, driving at thirty-five miles an hour until he got back to Los Pueblos.

* * *

In the morning, depressed, unable to rouse himself from the torpor into which he'd awakened after a nightmare-tossed sleep, Sanders sat on the balcony with his toast and coffee watching the steaming mountains in the early light, the gray clouds from the ocean scudding over their crests. It was a dismal day, even more depressing than the recollection of yesterday. Though he had already managed to get three cups of hot coffee and a slice of toast down, the lump in his throat had not appreciably diminished nor did the coffee clear his brain or make his mood more sprightly. A shower, he thought, might cheer and invigorate him, and as he rose and turned to go inside, the telephone rang. He heard Beth's voice and was aware of his disappointment that it was not Laura calling to say that she felt better, reassuring him that she was all right and that those maniacal cyclists had not returned. Though he'd taken great care to see that the door's spring lock closed after him, Laura's door was flimsy, and he'd been unable to throw the inner bolt and unwilling to wake Laura to do it. He was mumbling so incoherently that Beth had to ask him to repeat what he'd said, and before he could apologize she asked how his throat was. When he told her there'd been no change, she asked him to come down to the hospital for an X-ray.

"Now? It's Sunday," he protested.

"Hospital's open seven days a week. Sickness has no union hours."

"Funny."

"I didn't mean to be comic."

[291]

"You on duty?"

"No, but I'll be there in an hour and do the tests myself. Okay?"

He agreed to meet her there then, and she gave him brisk instructions and hung up.

The hospital was a blond brick-and-fieldstone complex of modern structures pierced by glass, stainless steel and chrome set among clumps of thick-trunked date palms, its grounds carefully landscaped with cactus, fuchsia and hibiscus. The Radiology Department was adjacent to the Department of Nuclear Medicine, at the far end of the building, buried in a subbasement in an area that gave the feeling of a bomb shelter. When he got there eight or ten patients were already seated on orange and yellow molded-plastic chairs, reading magazines, fidgeting, staring into space. Most of them were older people, but some were very young, two were children, and all waited apprehensively, funereally, except the two children, a little girl who talked quietly to her rag doll and a small boy who played with red and white plastic blocks. The waiting room had been made as cheerful as possible with lamps which had brightly colored shades, potted green plants and sunny landscape paintings on the wall. Floor-to-ceiling Mondrian block-print drapes were hung over sections of the whitewashed cinder-block walls to give the illusion that they masked real windows. Sanders could smell the air conditioning and there was an underground clamminess in the air, a catacombs quality, and he felt a sense of both Potemkin façade and *huis clos* overwhelm and oppress him. He would have turned and left if Beth had not at that moment come out of one of the highly polished wooden doors marked starkly with black letters x-ray and motioned him inside.

Everything in that room seemed from a different and ominous world, sterile and potent together. The whitewashed cinder-block walls were made more stark by various pieces of black equipment; everything was black and white, life-and-death contrasts that were terrifying. Even Beth, who was not in regular nurse's uniform but wore a long white laboratory coat over a black dress and black sheer stockings with high-heeled black shoes—an unexpectedly sexual contrast—seemed menacing. Two machines dominated the room: a great black cocoon of an X-ray machine poised over a black metal table that looked like an undraped catafalue; and a bright white fluoroscope which resembled an oversized food freezer and television set combined. "Strip to your waist and stand there," Beth commanded curtly, shaking her head at the fluoroscope.

On the ground floor the coffee shop was back in the normal world, most of one glass wall looking out on the cactuses and palmettos of the parking lot. Though many of the people inside wore medical whites and surgical greens, the rest were normally dressed and all looked committed to life not death, their expressions irate or sullen but not lugubrious. Prescott was at a table by himself, as usual smartly dressed in a gray hound's-tooth sport jacket and dark gray flannels, his white teeth nipping at the ends of his mustache, his hand absently stirring the spoon in the coffee cup before him. His face looked older, more careworn, than Sanders had noticed it before, even the Indian nose less bold, the sensual lips paler and thinned out. Prescott saw him, his face changed and resumed its sardonic self-possession. "Sit down," he said, after waving him over, but not offering his hand. He put up two fingers and a waitress swiftly brought two steaming cups. Sanders drank his black, a little at a time, from a teaspoon, the coffee scalding his throat, burning the lump he felt there.

"Throat better?" Prescott asked, not unsolicitously.

Sanders shook his head.

"Beth see anything on the scope?"

Again he shook his head. "She even let me see it in the mirror, but there wasn't anything to see."

"Probably nothing there, you know. People get shook up and then something back here"—he tapped the base of the skull—"goes click and something gives. Imaginary but real."

"*Boule hystérique.* Wasn't that what you called it?"

"*Bolus hystericus,*" Prescott said, as if using the French might be giving Sanders an advantage. "A sense or feeling of having the throat blocked though there's nothing there organically. The plates would show anything organic for sure."

"What's it from?" Sanders asked cautiously, hating to be indebted to Prescott for anything, information, a cup of coffee, even courtesy.

"From being fed up," Prescott answered shortly. "Up to here." He

[293]

held his finger over his mustache, just under his nose. "Or up to here," he moved the finger down to his Adam's apple.

Am I that fed up? Sanders asked himself silently. Am I so fed up that I'm choking myself? Certainly he'd known tension before, certainly felt as if he had hands at his throat throttling him, usually when he'd had to bottle up his anger or his fear, when he'd been in combat and wanted to run and couldn't, when he wanted to kill Elaine or Monique, but never quite like this. Always before a few brandies and a couple of nights' sleep, a long walk in the countryside, a bicycle trip in the Bois de Boulogne or Vincennes, left him relaxed and prepared to go on. Was he what the motorcycle boys had said Laura was, uptight? A good expression.

Prescott gauged him, tried to stare him down, then said, "We don't like each other much, do we?"

"Speak for yourself, Dr. Prescott."

"I always do. I don't like you because you're one of George's kind, and I hated his guts." Prescott was heated. "A bleeding heart. A do-gooder who always managed to screw things up worse than they were before he came on the scene with his compassion."

"He pulled your chestnuts out of the fire once or twice, didn't he?"

"I see Beth's given you her version of how the marriage went. But did she tell you why she married him?"

"Because you wouldn't marry her."

"I wanted her to get it aborted," he whispered, leaning across the table, looking furtively around to see if anyone was listening, "but she wouldn't."

"Makes sense. She loved you, wanted to marry you and have your child. You should've been flattered." Sanders was surprised to hear his voice calm, controlled.

"So he married her! The bleeding heart. Sir George Galahad Christiansen on his white horse. Did she tell you about the child too?" he asked, his voice low and fierce.

"It died."

"A blessing. A basket case, Sanders, without arms or legs. A hereditary freak. *And she said it was mine!*"

"Wasn't it?"

[294]

"I don't know, I don't know." It was clear that he was still in pain over it. "Beth screwed everyone and his brother."

"You mean it wasn't yours?"

"How could I be sure?"

"You might have taken her word."

"Would *you* have believed her?"

Sanders thought about how he could never believe Elaine again, no matter what protestation she might have made; after that afternoon at the Avenue Foch apartment nothing Elaine might say would wipe the scene or the suspicion from his mind. "I'm not sure," he admitted. "It's hard to tell what you'd do in someone else's shoes." Even as he spoke he knew that was what he was struggling with, the trying to do in George's shoes what George would have, might have, could have, done; and yet each time he did anything he felt that he was doing only what he would have done himself, not what George would have wanted. If that was the case, what point was there, what repayment for George, in all this involvement with George's people? Whose life was he extending, his own or George's? Surely not George's. Was that what he was fed up with, was that why the *boule hystérique* had risen to choke him?

"Beth was a very immature girl. She should have been a woman by then—she was in years—but she wasn't. She was foolish, flighty, promiscuous. I didn't even know whether to believe her when she told me she was pregnant. She wouldn't even let me see the test report, thought I should take her word. I didn't know if it was her imagination or another of her melodramatic games to rope me in."

"Were you such an attractive stallion to rope in?" Sanders asked.

"Don't be smart-alecky, Sanders. You're goddam right I was. I was on the verge of being a real surgeon and making some money, at last. I'd fought for that all my life, sacrificed all kinds of things— girls, pleasures, leisure, sleep, whisky—and I wasn't going to throw it overboard because some cock-crazy girl said I'd knocked her up." The veneer had cracked slightly, the accent and slang lapsed into another time, another class. "You middle-class bastards don't know what it's like. You get it easy and you think you got it coming, because you got the cash and your parents make it cushy for you, college and professional schools, and money for your flats and cars and charge accounts if you run short. And later more money for offices—"

"George Christiansen was no middle-class boy, and you know it," Sanders said. "He had as tough a time as you did."

"Bah!" Prescott exclaimed. "Sure he was poor but a mama's boy, an only child, pampered."

"I was an only child myself," Sanders said defensively.

"It shows. You and Beth and George Christiansen. You only children. Do you know what it's like to be one of fourteen kids? Not the first or the last either, but smack in the middle of a whole army? Do you know what it's like to fight for your food at the table with thirteen others, or a place to study or sleep, or to get into the can?"

"Being an only child's pretty lonely, you know."

"By God, I'd have given my right eye for some loneliness when I was a boy, some quiet, a place I could hide and be myself by myself. I used to get up in the middle of the night and sit in the can with the light on so I could read, until one day one of my older brothers got the same bright idea and then I had to fight him for it every night until my father caught us both and walloped us both for wasting electricity and that was the end of that."

"George didn't have an easy life. Besides, how can you hate him like that now that he's dead and you've got Beth?"

"Got Beth. You think anybody's got Beth Marshall? She's like trying to hold quicksilver in your hand. I had her more while George was here and alive. Now she's full of guilt, remembering how he married her when she needed him, how good, how chivalrous, how sensitive good old George was. Sensitive! He was the kind of man who when he used toilet paper automatically thought of chopping down redwoods and despoiling forests so he couldn't even wipe his ass!" Prescott's face was flushed, sweating, and he wiped his forehead with the back of his hand.

"George was sensitive enough to know Beth was telling the truth about being pregnant, brave enough to marry her when you copped out and wouldn't," Sanders said, enjoying the pain he saw on Prescott's face, feeling that he was paying a debt for George.

"Brave, huh?" Prescott sneered. "He couldn't get Beth, couldn't keep her any other way either, because he was no good in the kip.

So he married her. That was *his* way. And then couldn't even keep her. All my life I've seen these gallant knights in shining armor, these idealist bleeding-heart liberals, always, with all their malarkey, going after something they really wanted for themselves."

"At least he really wanted her, which was more than you did."

"You want her too, don't you?" Prescott asked.

"Not the way George did, not the way you do."

"You mean you just want to jump her. That's easy. Lady Round-heels. She'll go down on her back faster than a television wrestler and grunt and groan just as hard." Sanders saw how he was hurting himself with the words, remembering his own similar dialogues and monologues after the Avenue Foch, but he didn't stop him. "Just ask, just say please," Prescott added.

"I don't think Beth's that easy or that simple," Sanders said, fighting his impulse to agree, to agree about Beth and so agree about Elaine, about all women. "And it's not what I meant."

"What do you mean?"

"My women have to be one-man women," Sanders said, hearing himself too fervent, "just for me, not for anyone else. Not even once."

Prescott burst into raucous laughter he toned down the moment heads turned and eyes stared in the coffee shop. "You poor stupid romantic bastard," he whispered, "you think they still make them like that. I know. I know, your mother was like that." In a low, satiric growl, he sang off key, " 'I want a girl just like the girl that married dear old Dad.' "

How little Prescott understood, Sanders thought wearily, how very little.

"My mother," Prescott said, almost proudly, "was a slattern. My father was a raunchy, cornlikkering hillbilly, like old man Christiansen but once-removed, mean and tough and hot-tempered. And a billy goat to boot. He came up to Michigan from Tennessee in 1930 because of the Depression and I was born there, in Flint, two years later. He got a job at General Motors, as a paint sprayer, and he didn't give a shit for nothing nohow." Prescott's speech was abruptly full of twang and hill country. "A redneck. White trash. Kept my old lady knocked up all the time. Barefoot and pregnant was his motto, but he really meant it. Fed us and bought us shoes

[297]

some of the time. Whupped us. Got hisself likkered up whenever he could. 'Book learnin,' he used to say, 'that's *sheet*. Fer uppity niggers an Jews.' He was proud of the fact that he couldn't read and could barely sign his name. I couldn't wait to get out from under. I hated him. Goddam, if I met him on the street right now, I'd either walk to the other side to avoid him or knock him ass over teakettle for all those beatings he gave me when he came home drunk and the old lady was too pregnant or too petered out to accommodate him or he found me 'with my nose in a book.'

"I hated him so bad that once I got out of that house, that miserable, moldy, piss-smelling house, I never went back. Not even once. I won a scholarship and went down to Ann Arbor, only an hour away, but I never went back to see him, or my mother, or any of my brothers and sisters. I don't know if they're dead or alive. And I don't care. I had enough of all of them in my first eighteen years to last me a lifetime."

"They might have been proud of you if you had gone back," Sanders said in the face of that fierce onslaught.

"Proud of me? When I told my old man that I had that scholarship, that I'd won it, the first out of more than two thousand candidates, he beat me black-and-blue. That's what I got for keeping my nose in books. Wanted me to be a union apprentice, then to go to work for GM like him. Work on the line all week, get likkered up on Saturday nights, the whole thing. Who did I think I was and what did I think I was, better than him? Books! College! Medical school! He was trash and proud of it. His granddaddy had died at Shiloh, that was enough glory for one family."

"No charity for him, for them?" Sanders asked, hearing Prescott's vindictiveness echo in his heart but wanting to reject it.

"Charity's one luxury I could never afford."

"A necessity you can't afford to give up," Sanders said, speaking to his own secret self more than to Prescott.

"You talk the same mush George did. Charity. Forgiveness. Pity. Compassion. Love. I don't even know what those words mean. I can't attach them to any feelings I ever felt or anybody ever seemed to feel for me."

"Anybody?"

"Anybody." Prescott was definite, magisterial, looking down on him from below.

"Not even Beth?"

"Beth was like George, only shrewder, saying, 'Thy need is greater than mine,' but always making damn sure *her* needs were served, not yours. The original gimme girl. George wasn't in Vietnam for more than a few weeks before we were back at it again, the way we'd been before they were married."

"And the child?"

"The child was dead. Didn't she tell you that?"

"That was quick," Sanders said, avoiding an answer.

"Should've been quicker. The child should never have come out of the delivery room."

"Maybe some doctor there didn't want to take the risk either. Maybe he'd worked a long time to get to where he was and to make some money and he didn't want to throw it all away."

"You're a vengeful bastard, Sanders, maybe you're not a bleeding heart after all. And you might be right. I'm not sure I blame him, yet what's the sense of letting a child like that live?"

"What happened to it?" Sanders persisted.

"Pneumonia. Fast. Three days and out."

"That *was* fast."

"It lived eight months first, until Beth was so tied to it, so fond of it . . . She nursed it, insisted she had to nurse even though she didn't have enough to breast-feed at first, until when the boy died, she was so . . . involved with it that she had a breakdown. Postpartum psychosis, officially. Took months for her to recover."

"George saw her through that too, didn't he?" Sanders heard the edge of his voice sharpen.

"The goddam fool was on the verge of finishing his degree, but he gave it up altogether, and stayed with her. For months. He brought her through almost single-handed, better than any psychiatrist."

"Maybe bleeding hearts make good psychiatrists."

"No maybes, that's all they are."

"And then when it was done, he went to war."

"George went to war. Volunteered. Ran away and left Beth to me. He'd had enough—the marriage, the baby, the death, the break-

[299]

down, more than enough, up to here." He put his finger up to his Adam's apple.

"But without *boule hystérique?*" Sanders said, watching the man and physician struggle in Prescott's face.

"Nothing to be ashamed of," Prescott managed to say at last, the voice the physician's to the patient. "We all get those things."

"Not you."

Prescott hesitated. "No one is immune."

They sat silent and somber for a long time before Sanders could ask, "If you didn't want to marry her, why did you go on with it?"

The words were almost torn out of him. "I couldn't let her go," he said.

"You love her?"

"I don't know words like that, I don't understand them. Linear measurements, calibrated beakers, X-ray plates, temperature charts —tangible things—I understand. I know what they measure, what they describe. But not love, not feeling."

"No acts of faith?"

"No acts of faith."

"But you couldn't let her go."

"We couldn't let each other go," he said very carefully. "We tried and we couldn't." He raised his hand for more coffee, the gesture sudden and imperious, and when the coffee arrived and the stained cups and saucers were removed, he spoke with a dry despair. "I wanted to marry her, I really wanted to, not for her needs but for mine. I felt I could afford it, manage it, now, and that was why I let myself in for the whole thing again when George went overseas. Get a divorce, I told her, and we'll get married. But no, she couldn't do that to George. She couldn't write a soldier overseas fighting for his country a 'Dear John' letter, so there we were, back in the old posture, serving her needs, not mine."

He put his hands in front of his face, long, beautifully tapering fingers, with perfect manicured nails. "We went through it piece by piece, over and over again, like a daytime soap-opera serial, until I couldn't stand it but I couldn't turn it off either. 'I can't do that to George. I just can't. After all he's done for me, all he's seen me through.' It was enough to turn your stomach." He'd been talking

[300]

through his fingers, but now he bared his face once again. "Then, after she heard he was dead, she was wild with grief and guilt, saying she'd treated him so badly he'd gone to war deliberately to get killed, that she'd driven him to suicide, that his death was all her fault, that she'd crippled his will to live, cut his balls off so he didn't care any more. I tried to tell her that all that no longer mattered, that what was done was done, that we had to go ahead now and make what we could of our lives. After a decent interval, of course."

After a decent interval, Sanders thought, of course. What was decent in such intervals? Could anything be decent? Yet what else was there to do?

"But now she'd have none of it. She wouldn't marry me, she said, she couldn't do that to George. And then you arrived—"

"I arrived?"

"Yes, you arrived and Beth had some crazy idea that you were George's emissary, his substitute, a living reminder, his surrogate. First I thought it was just that she had the hots for you and that made me boiling mad. Then I saw that it was more serious than that and I thought maybe George's death and your coming here would push her, had pushed her, over the brink again, and that she was going to have to be institutionalized. She couldn't marry me, she shouldn't, she insisted, and I didn't want to buck her, didn't want to upset her more. I gave her some tranquilizers, I tried to treat her as I would a patient, objectively, medically—but I couldn't. It was long past where I was able to do that."

"You had no reservations then, you were committed?"

Prescott's laughter was nails on glass. "Committed. That's the proper word all right. I should've been committed, to a mental institution. We were hellish for each other, an explosive mixture that should be kept from flame. We should have walked away, never spoken to each other again. Every man has his *bolus hystericus;* I had mine too. I'd lie awake at night in a sweat unable to sleep thinking of that basket case, how even our genes were wrong for each other, remembering how she'd gone off her flue, terrified, paralyzed. What if every conception of ours turned out like that basket case? What if that sent Beth permanently over the border? It made

[301]

no sense, we made no sense, but we went on and on and on and we're still going on and on."

That was the way life went, on and on, until suddenly it was cut off, ended, over. His mother, Elaine, Monique. George Christiansen. Lovett Carpenter Sanders. The scarred ground. The few ritual phrases. The stone. The absence, the absence.

Beth was standing there smiling and Prescott, half rising, had shoved a chair out for her. She'd removed the lab coat and in the black dress set off only by a single strand of pale pearls she looked formal and funereal at once, and Sanders felt the tugging at his flesh as she sat and crossed the sheer-black-stockinged legs. "The plates are not quite dry yet, but I don't think there's a thing," she reported briskly.

"*Bolus hystericus*," Sanders said.

"Right. You're fed up." She made a face.

"Who isn't?" Prescott asked rhetorically.

"Well, aren't you glad it's nothing?" Beth asked.

"It isn't nothing," Sanders replied.

"It will go away," Prescott assured him. "You'll wake up one morning and the whole thing will be gone, like a bad dream."

"By *it*, you mean my life?"

"What have you been guzzling," Beth asked, "hemlock?" She leaned over the table and peered into his coffee cup.

Looking not at her but at Prescott, Sanders spoke truthfully. "Yes, hemlock. How did you know?" He felt the mutual recognition that was not conciliation between him and Prescott, knowing it bypassed and eluded her.

"My dear Socrates," Beth said blithely, stroking his cheek with her fingertips, "how can we ever teach you that suicide is no solution?"

"It may not be a solution," Prescott interposed, "but it *is* an ending."

Yes, Sanders whispered silently to himself, we all owe our cocks to Aesculapius.

"Would you look at the plates, Steven, just to make sure?" Beth requested. "They'll be dry soon."

Prescott rose, stood at rigid attention, saluted and barked, "*Dis-*

missed!" Then he made a smart about-face and marched out of the coffee shop without looking back or paying attention to the inquiring eyes and turned heads.

"What's eating him?" Beth asked, nonplussed.

"You are," Sanders reported, staring at her mouth and watching the slow flush mount to her embarrassed cheeks. "He wants to marry you."

"Then, now or later?" she asked sardonically. "Steven's a puller-away from intimacy, always was. I don't believe him." She was curt.

"Are you a pusher-toward?" he asked.

"You two comparing notes, locker-room style?" Her intention was to be cutting but she was only dismal.

"No comparisons. You're nonpareil. 'Age cannot wither, nor custom stale—' "

"My gallant enemy!"

"Are we truly enemies, Beth?"

"Not true, not truly, falsely, his enemy and mine."

"Neither. Why should I be?"

She was sullen, hesitant. "Because of George."

"George, always George. Steven thinks you imagine I'm George's surrogate, his alter ego, the reminder of his living presence, the fly in your ointment. His too."

"Isn't that just what you intended? To take up George's life? His space? The fly in the ointment, the open fly?" she added nastily. "To see if another man's shoes fit? Well, do they, Elliott, do they?"

The smell of antiseptics and anesthetics, blood, mud, sweat and the stink of pissed-on and shit-in pants filled his head and lingered as tastes in his mouth. Lying there naked on the table in Saigon, he had heard someone say as if from a great distance that he was in the chest and belly ward. A nurse? Cathy Sullivan? A batch of badly wounded had just been coptered in from the Delta, the returns on a search-and-destroy, and they were being operated on at three tables simultaneously. Everyone was busy because there'd been so many casualties and more were expected any moment. "Please take off my shoes," Sanders heard himself call. No one seemed to pay any attention and he repeated the request, his voice louder, wailing, pleading. "My shoes," he cried out, "someone take

[303]

off my shoes," wondering why it was that he didn't want to die with his boots on, what difference it made.

An orderly stopped and said, "Your shoes *are* off, soldier," but he didn't believe it, heard himself bellowing again in a voice so distorted with pain and persistence that he could barely recognize it as his own. "I tell you your shoes are off," the misty face said, a crew cut bobbing vaguely.

"Pick up my legs and show me," Sanders, still unbelieving, insisted. Instead, the medic eased him gently up, propping his back and shoulders so that he could see his bare feet jutting, his toes pale and unmoving, nails rimmed black and muddy rings like shackles around his ankles. "They're there," he gasped, "thanks," and fainted again.

"What was it like out there?" Beth asked.

"Like nothing. Like death," he replied, still inhaling that Saigon operating theater, unable to exhale, expel it. "Like all the stupid wars, rebellions, risings I've ever covered, ever been in. Killing. Maiming. Burning. Taking a few thousand yards or a hill, or a couple of miles of road or beach." Remembering the orderly, he added, "They were awfully good to you, tender and good, in a funny detached way, but the further you came back from the fighting the worse it became. The compassion diminished, the feeling for one another tapered off in proportion to the distance from where the combat was. As the immediate need became less urgent, less apparent, the direct contact, the good feeling, the intimate communication between men and men disappeared, the rules took over— and the chickenshit."

"Like the hospital, in a way. As you get away from the emergency ward and the surgery and the intensive-care unit, and the threat of swift death, the treatment grows indifferent," Beth corroborated.

"Out there, though," he said, "the medics seemed to know who would live and who would die. Everyone was pretty beat up, but they knew, the medics. Somehow. A hundred times I heard them say, 'Hasn't got enough left in him,' and that was that. *A death sentence.* They knew and didn't waste any time on those. Doped them up and just left them alone to die." He told her about the chief, the Indian who had torn his own guts out under the white sheet of his

Conestoga wagon and bled to death. "Sometimes I wondered what the hell it was that kept anybody alive there anyway. You were past caring. I know I didn't care a damn by then. But the ones from the minorities, like the chief, seemed to own something special, some pride they'd learned the hard way and held onto for dear life. The micks and the spiks, the jigs and the sheenies, the guineas and the greasers—as the slang had it—the ones who hadn't folded in the fighting, fought for their lives with all their might, with a fierce dignity—and they usually made it." He wondered if he was trying to say something good, tell her something important about Prescott, in fairness, precisely because he disliked the man so much.

"Strange, your wanting to get your shoes off."

"In the field you never even wanted to take them off because you were afraid you might never get them back on, you might get some crud on your feet, you might need them quickly—"

"No other man's shoes would do out there, eh?"

"Sometimes not even your own."

"Why do you need anyone else's shoes—George's or Steven's or Peter King's—to fill, or even mine parked under your bed?" Beth asked, her eyes reduced to pupil points boring into him.

The sudden recollection of the hospital ward, its stink of death and rack of pain, brought a ready answer to his lips, *the* ready answer that George had died for him on a Saigon sidewalk; but however swift and justifiable that response, it was too automatic, it begged the question and so lost much of its force. The months since his return to America had made clear that George's motives for throwing himself on that grenade, that George's unlived life, were not the reasons for his obsession to fill another man's shoes. His own motives for sacrificing himself, if it was that and not an aggrandizement of self, had to be accounted for: his battle with his father's ghost and his mother's presence, his choice of country and profession, his bravery and cowardice, his feelings for Beth and Laura—his own unlived life. There were, he knew, at least two kinds of buried life. In probing George's past and in trying to understand the intricate network of action and intention that George had supported and that supported him—and which apparently he had finally found insupportable—Sanders was being forced inexorably to reconsider

[305]

the threads, ropes and wires which composed the jumbled skein of his own past life. Like Odysseus he had come home from the wars only to find himself his own Penelope and Telemachus, father, mother and son, unraveling what he had knit up in the past to see if he could discern the leitmotifs of his life. In trying to look forward he'd been forced to look backward, and though he had seen Hades and Sodom and Gomorrah, he had been neither doomed to the shades nor yet turned to a pillar of salt. That's not my Lot, he thought, hearing the pun in his ear like Laura's "That's not my bag." The only way you know where you're going is to know where you've been, he reassured himself, where you've come from, the road you've traversed.

A sense of *déjà vu* surged through him, so abrupt and powerful that he felt the vivid Paris sunshine coming through the open shutters and once again squinted his eyes narrow to accommodate its brilliance; beneath his flanks he felt the old soft Oriental rug that had been spread in his parents' salon in that ivory-colored building near La Motte-Picquet and he smelled the greening chestnut trees outside. His parents were quarreling, his mother in high dudgeon, which meant that her voice was lower, tighter, more penetrating, asking the question she knew the answer to anyway but couldn't accept: "What kind of man are you anyway?" And his father's soft, turneth-away-wrath answer, jocular, reasonable, yet caustic, employing the deliberate kind of profanity he knew she despised and was enraged by: "Remember what the bull dike says: 'I know what I am because my little dog knows me. But who am I when my little dog dies?' "

"Am I your little dog, Lovett?"

Venomously: "No, just my little bitch."

And his mother walking haughtily out of the room.

"I'm not sure . . . any more," Sanders admitted falteringly.

"Shouldn't you be?" Beth was unexpectedly tender to him, reaching across the table and covering his hand with hers. "You can't fit anyone else's shoes. Most people can't even fit into their own. The best they can do, maybe, is to find out their size and width and try to grow into them. And maybe if they're lucky or work hard enough they can even learn which style suits them best."

More than that, Sanders thought, the real skill, the great virtue, the immense marvel, was simply to learn to walk in the shoes altogether, as comfortably as you could, taking out the bits of stone, the thorns and the burrs, the shards of glass, so you can do what you have to do, walk the road you have to walk, without cutting your soles completely to ribbons.

* * *

When he returned to the apartment there was a telegram under his door from Needham asking him to call immediately. He did. Sheila Needham answered the telephone after only a single ring, as if she'd been waiting next to it. "Elliott," she cried after he'd identified himself, "why don't we see anything of you? It's been weeks and weeks since you came to dinner and not even a phone call. Aren't you ashamed?" He was and confessed that he'd been remiss, explaining how busy Jim Needham had kept him. "Too busy for old friends and a couple of my special martis?" she asked, and then Sanders realized that she was a couple of sheets to the wind. Before he could reply Needham was on the wire, having obviously seized the phone from her. "Elliott"—his voice was crisp and no-nonsense-like—"glad you called. We had a tip about a big antiwar demonstration tomorrow morning in Oakland. Want to cover it?"

Unhesitatingly Sanders said he did and Needham gave him what information they had, which was little enough. "You want to phone the story in?"

"You want to make the wire services?" Sanders asked.

"If we can."

"Okay, I'll try, but I'd rather write it myself."

"Do both."

"Good idea."

"Why don't you drop by for a drink or dinner one of these evenings?" Sanders could see Sheila gesticulating silently to Needham, urgently. "Sheila'd like that and so would I. Some time soon, eh, boy?"

"I will, Jim, I meant to."

"Sure. See you."

Three

. . . the individual *dies of his internal conflicts but the* species *dies of its unsuccessful struggle against the external world, when the latter undergoes changes of a kind that cannot be dealt with by adaptations which the species has acquired.*

—FREUD

Mists were rising from the city like a slow curtain gingerly lifted when Sanders got to Oakland, long before either the induction center was scheduled to open or the demonstration to begin. In a nearby coffee shop, primed by the irony of having just driven on streets bearing the august though not exactly pacific Presidential names of Jefferson, Washington and Jackson, Sanders strategically placed himself at the counter so that he could have breakfast and not miss any of the slow gathering of forces of what at first he thought would be a routine and boring business. He had two swallows of the hot bitter coffee which reminded him that, whatever the X-rays said, hysterical or no, the lump in his throat was still there and quite uncomfortable. Moments later he watched more than two hundred uniformed police, on foot and mounted, their blue helmets glinting in the early light, mustered into the moving-van warehouse garage directly across from the induction center. Again his old instinct and usual practice had paid off: arriving earlier than anyone expected on what was to be the scene of an encounter to get the before feeling so that he could know what changes occurred during and after the event for proper contrast. Arriving at dawn had been worth it. He was pleased too that he'd brought his cameras and, using the telescopic lens on the Leica, got a dozen good shots of the police entering the garage, setting up barricades at both ends of the street,

[311]

stationing prowl cars and planning their strategy while his breakfast grew cold and the counterman's friendly face turned sour. At first the street was empty in a chill gray dawn and then it was a crush. Hundreds of people jammed the street and sidewalks, filling every doorway and alley, carefully blocking the main entrance into the induction center. Here and there, above the throng, signs and posters undulated: STOP THE DRAFT! LIFE IN AMERICA, NOT DEATH IN VIETNAM; LET THE PEOPLE VOTE ON WAR; KEEP OUT OF THE DRAFT, IT'S BAD FOR YOUR HEALTH; PATRIOTISM MEANS WAR; BURN YOUR DRAFT CARD, THE LIFE YOU SAVE MAY BE YOUR OWN; GIRLS SAY YES TO MEN WHO SAY NO; BRING THE BOYS HOME NOW. No vehicles could move through that crowd but Sanders saw police cordons at the ends of the street make room for television trucks, and then the cameramen with their portable cameras and microphones began to sift through the crowd.

With different placards it might easily have been a football game or a homecoming alumni rally. Most of the protesters were college-age boys and girls with a few groups of matronly mothers, one bunch of them carrying a WE DON'T WANT TO BE GOLD-STAR MOTHERS sign over their heads like an umbrella. There was only a sprinkling of grown men, a few of them white-haired, but most seemed to be clergy, priests, ministers and rabbis. Sanders took photographs of one of the priests in his cassock, and then of a rabbi in a skullcap before he turned his telescopic lens on one of the ministers and Murray Fillmore's face swam up in his focus. The chaplain was bareheaded, in clerical collar and attire, and his face looked older and more somber. Sanders took several photographs of him and then, uneasily drawing the attention of some of the police, waved and called out to him, "Fillmore! Fillmore!" but the minister didn't hear him in the noisy throng.

The demonstration had a picnic quality. People drank coffee from thermos bottles and paper cups, munched toast and doughnuts, ate sandwiches and candy bars, and one girl, whose picture he snapped, was eating a jellied apple. A nearby couple were gnawing at opposite ends of a long hero sandwich, alternating with swigs from a Chianti bottle they passed back and forth. Conversation was so lively that human voices filled the street like a river in flood. Crowding made movement difficult and people stayed where they were so that Sanders, shouldering his way toward Fillmore and the entrance to the building where the minister stood, made slow progress and so, too, he noted with vicious satisfaction, did the TV men with their microphones and sneaky-peekies, but the cameraman on top of the TV truck roof at the end of the street was grinding away, getting it all.

Sanders approached Fillmore from the side, the only way he could manage. Fillmore's head was turned away from him when he said, "Hello, Filly," and Fillmore froze, his profile animal, frightened and belligerent, until wheeling slowly he saw who it was. "Sanders," he said, "Elliott," his expression unbelieving, then relieved, "what are you doing out here?"

"Murray, what are you doing in there?" Sanders rejoined.

Fillmore laughed, his face relieved, younger. "You're out here on a story, Waldo, not in here with us; but I'm not going to pay my poll tax anyway, or"—his demeanor sobered—"approve this war, or the draft that supplies it with cannon fodder. . . . I'm glad to see you."

"Me too," Sanders replied, surprised by how glad he was. "I got your little note," he added, "and, in fact, I was going to look you up today until my boss called me about this shindig."

"Believe me, Elliott, it's no shindig."

"What made you do it?" Sanders asked.

"Send the note? I wanted to see you."

"No, this." Sanders gestured at the assembled multitude.

"I couldn't stand the killing any more so I got out."

"You mean they let you out, just like that?"

"Well, not just like that." Fillmore grimaced. "That's a long story and this isn't the place to tell it." He looked uncomfortably at all the people pressing in around them, but no one seemed to be paying them any attention. "I didn't even know if you'd ever get that note. Old Harvey wasn't eager to deliver it."

"You knew I'd be at Christiansen's funeral."

Fillmore nodded. "That's why I sent it there, but I couldn't be sure he'd give it to you."

"He did give it to me, but pretty surreptitiously."

"Afraid," Fillmore commented sadly.

[313]

"Sure, but he *did* do it," Sanders reminded him.

"Men of the cloth." Fillmore's disappointment was plain.

"Don't expect too much from changes in uniform," Sanders cautioned, looking at Fillmore's plain black suit. "The man remains pretty much the same underneath the clothing and the collar."

"Yes, hot under the collar."

"In both senses," Sanders agreed and had the satisfaction of seeing Fillmore flush. "How's Cathy Sullivan?" he asked, not quite irrelevantly.

Fillmore looked puzzled. "Ho, your nurse," he remembered. "Still doing one of the few things you can do out there without violating your conscience, tending the sick and wounded. Also in mortal sin because she's a professing Catholic and lives with an Air Force major who's already got a Stateside wife and children."

"Too bad."

"That she's with the major?"

"No, that she thinks of it as mortal sin. She's a healer, she takes nothing from anyone and gives something important to someone— and to herself." Before Fillmore could contest that, as clearly he was going to do, Sanders asked about Fillmore's father.

"You remember my talking about him." Fillmore was pleased. "I was home to see him before I came back out here. Terminal leave— in more ways than one. He was better, my father was, worse too. His eyesight came back gradually after the stroke and so did some of his speech, but now his mind's affected."

"Didn't he recognize you?"

"He recognized me all right." Fillmore was pained. "My mother couldn't take care of him any more so my brother and sisters put him into a nursing home. He didn't want to go, of course, and they told me he'd fought and cursed them when they'd taken him. I went there to see him the day after I got home, and when I came into his room he was dozing. They were feeding him intravenously, glucose, I guess, the bottle hanging from that metal rack with a tube joined to the needle and the needle taped into a thick blue vein that stood out in his forearm.

"I'm a minister, Elliott, and as you know, I was a military chaplain, so I've seen lots of death and dying. But this was my own father and it wasn't the same. I remembered how powerful a man he'd been. Once, when we were children, one of the neighbor's kids came running over to our place for help. Hansen, that was their name, Swedes. The axletree on their hayrack had broken in two and one of the wheels had spun off and pinned the father under it. We drove over there with the Hansen boy—my father, my brother and I. My father got under the hayrack, calmed Hansen down—he was groaning and yelling, should've been too, because he had four ribs broken and part of his breastbone crushed and God knows what else—gave him a big drink of whisky, then gradually braced his back and slowly lifted the hayrack enough off the ground so my brother and I and Mrs. Hansen, who was there too, could slide Hansen free. A *loaded* hayrack. I remembered him, straining, naked from the waist up, the sweat running off his body in that Iowa summer heat, all his muscles standing out as if they were about to burst from his skin, his dirty blue work shirt a pad between his scapula and the hayrack. Later, at school, when I learned about Atlas holding up the world, I'd think of my father holding up that hayrack. I guess I still do.

"Now he's skin and bone, his flesh and muscle melted away; like a used-up candle, there's nothing left except the ropy wick. I stood there unwilling to wake him, unable to leave, when his eyes opened. They were the same bright blue but with a thick white ring around the iris that made them seem vacant. Then he saw me. His lips moved but I couldn't hear what he was saying. I thought he spoke my name and wanted me to come closer so I walked toward the bed. With a heave he hoisted himself up in the bed, tore the needle out of his vein, plucked the bottle from the rack and threw it at me. It missed me, smashed into the wall and shattered all over the floor. "Murderer!" he called. "Murderer!"

"Is that why you left?" Sanders asked.

Fillmore shook his head. "I'd made up my mind before I left Saigon. I'd had the killing up to here." He held the cutting edge of his palm at his throat and Sanders felt again the lump of Adam's apple blocking his throat, remembered Beth's gesture and Prescott's. "He only confirmed what I already knew."

The sudden cessation of sound stopped their talk. Every face had turned toward the head of the street where two khaki-colored buses had drawn up surrounded by police. Someone in the crowd hallooed, "They're here," and voice after voice took up the call until the street resounded with "Don't let them into the building! Stop them!" The bus engines turned over and slowly the two buses nosed forward into the crowd which made way, eddying around them, until, altogether surrounded by bodies, the buses could go neither farther nor back without running over human flesh: they were stranded.

Then the police took a hand. At the end of the street, beyond the police barriers, where the television truck with the cameraman on its roof was parked, a police lieutenant with a bullhorn stood up on the roof of a prowl car. Surrounded by a circle of police with shotguns, its roof light whirling like a glaring red eye gone berserk, the police car looked like an outlandish Pleistocene animal, its voice roaring out of its tiny head, warning the crowd that it was breaking the law by obstructing entrance to a Federal building and that if by the time it counted twenty the way wasn't clear, force would have to be used to make a path to the doors. The growl of the bullhorn was met by the low rumble of the crowd: It crouched, readied itself, recoiled, then moved forward, a Neanderthal animal threatened. The numbers, methodical and spaced, bellowed forth in sequence and hung metallically over the spectators like a sentence pronounced, echoing like individual thunderclaps. After the last number there was silence; then a sibilant hiss as if from a pit of serpents rose, then a great sigh as a V-shaped wedge of mounted police flew into the crowd. Screams of pain mixed with roars of rage broke from the crowd as heads were bloodied and bodies went down beneath horses' hoofs, but no sooner had a small space been cleared than once again the crowd flowed into it and stopped the buses from moving forward. So many people were hemmed into that street that it was impossible to keep any space cleared for very long.

The police lieutenant on the prowl car saw that too and gave new instructions; the V of mounted police turned into a square, cutting off sections of demonstrators and forcing them back toward the police vans, the barriers now removed, but as foot patrolmen tried to get the protesters into the vans, they lay down on the street and the police had to carry each one bodily into the vans. As the limp bodies were carted into the Black Marias, the mounted police held

[316]

the other protesters off, a space was cleared and the buses began slowly to move forward until once again they were halted by the wall of human flesh. Again, the mounted police cordoned off another section of demonstrators, pressing them back toward the vans, but this time the demonstrators outside the Kitchener square threw themselves like Zulus against the police, the horses reared, heads were clubbed, and the police square broke. Because there were still two thousand or more people in that street it was clear that the police would have to adopt new tactics or it would take them all day to clear the street.

"Now," Fillmore whispered, aloud but to himself, "comes trouble."

A faint cheer of triumph, a single uncertain ragged note, rose from the crowd. Someone started to sing "We shall overcome" and then stopped, but while most eyes were fixed on the prowl car with the lieutenant on its roof, only a few of those at the middle of the street next to the moving-van warehouse heard the corrugated iron doors of the garage roll up and saw the mounted police come charging out into their midst. More than two hundred men and horses struck the crowd headlong, splitting into four columns and at the same time splitting the crowd into four segments. The horses plunged head on; the police, each with his head encased in a gas mask looking like another head of the horse he rode, swung their clubs tellingly as they assaulted each separate segment. Through and over those who stood in their way they cut a swath as if they were scythes and the crowd wheat. Like sheaves the demonstrators fell away from them, over each other, screaming, some bleeding, some shaking their fists in thwarted anger. Someone yelled, "Run!" Someone ran. And then the panic was on. Ducking, diving, dropping, swooping, dodging, falling, people began to run until, in what seemed like moments, the street was half cleared. To Sanders, on the steps below Fillmore, taking snapshot after snapshot of police and demonstrators, the swiftness and sureness of the police assault was stunning and beautifully organized. Some demonstrators stood and tried to fight the foot police who now advanced from both ends of the street in a loose line which permitted many protesters to plunge through with only a blow to hurry them along, but most of the protesters fled. The others, grappling with the prehistoric police

[317]

in gas masks, were clubbed and, weeping and sobbing, clubbed police back, using their fists and their signs as weapons, one even using his shoe.

Next to him Fillmore gasped, "My God, they'll be killed," and ran toward a small melee where police were beating two boys and two girls, their legs and bodies tangled, who had fallen to the ground. Taking picture after picture, Sanders ran after Fillmore until the minister had thrust himself between the police and the kids being clubbed. Two of the police turned swiftly, charged Fillmore and buffeted him to the street while the other pair went on clubbing the quartet of youngsters on the ground. As those two were about to slam into Fillmore, Sanders roared, "Hold it! He's a priest!" They stopped, clubs poised, looking uncertainly from Fillmore's clerical collar to Sanders' cameras. "Sorry, Father," one of them apologized, and helped Fillmore to his feet. Undaunted and dirty, Fillmore said firmly, "You're not to club those children." Seeing a sergeant run past, Fillmore yelled to him that he had to stop his men from using their clubs, but the sergeant brushed him aside and hotfooted it down the street. The two patrolmen who had knocked him down looked at him contemptuously and followed in the wake of the sergeant. The other pair of cops had allowed the girls to get up but continued to beat the two boys whose arms were trying to protect their heads and faces. One of the girls, her face dazed, her long loose blond hair matted with blood, took one more look and then ran screaming away from them, a wild gazelle fleeing the lions; the other, like a tigress, leaped on the back of one of the cops and bore him to the ground. As his partner turned to help him, the two boys on the ground rolled away and Fillmore helped to yank them erect. They didn't say thanks or stay to look; they ran. Calmly Sanders took pictures of the entire struggle. The policeman standing, when he saw it was a girl who had knocked his partner over, helped the girl to her feet, dragging her off the cop's back and pulling her nails away from his face; but his partner, enraged and bleeding, furiously booted her in the buttocks and sent her sprawling on her face. "There," he cried, "get your goddam ass home where it belongs," and then the two police raced off after the scattering demonstrators, Painfully, the girl stood up, wiped her hair back from her face and gaped at him as he continued to take pictures. Then, convulsed with nausea, she spat into his face and missed, the spittle striking and hanging from his Leica. "Fink!" she cried. "Shithead!" She spun around and, dignified even in her tight faded blue jeans and fringed Indian shirt, walked waveringly away. Feeling dirtied and criminal, Sanders wiped the camera clean with a paper tissue and, looking around for a trash barrel and not finding one, stuffed the tissue into his pocket.

Except for small groups being hustled and herded by foot and mounted police down to both ends of the street, most of the area was soon cleared. But a small bulwark of bodies was still clotted on the steps and in the entryway to the draft-induction building. Fillmore strode back to them to join the other clergymen there, and Sanders, guiltily, followed. He sidestepped a splintered pair of two-by-fours, their cloth streamers puddled on the ground, their mottoes unfurled and trodden on: SUPPORT DRAFT RESISTERS: REFUSE! REFUSE! REFUSE! The police now sealed off both ends of the street except for one way past the barricade through which they now brought in the first two khaki buses, a Black Maria, then five more khaki buses and a police radio-communications truck that Sanders hadn't seen before. Police manned the barriers, holding back those of the demonstrators who had returned to see the final act. The remainder of the police, reporters and photographers bunched behind them, converged on the entrance to the building in a tight semicircle, a small cleared patch of concrete separating them from the few dozen protesters who still held the fort. The prowl car came down with them, its red walleye whirling, and the police lieutenant slowly, painfully, got out of it, bullhorn in hand, and walked into the cleared space between police and demonstrators. The lieutenant, an old man, white-haired and obviously in his middle or even late sixties, had one of those leathery, seamed locomotive-engineer faces, blue-eyed and peering into the distance as though he could see beyond them, through them, into time. His voice without the bullhorn, which he now saw he didn't need, was disarmingly gentle. "All right, gentlemen," he said, "you've made your protest. Now why not be reasonable and let us bring these people in to do their work and these young men to be inducted?" He looked at each of them in turn as if he expected

[319]

someone to answer him just as reasonably, but no one answered. Instead, those on the steps and in the entryway massed together, perhaps huddled together, more closely. "Look," the lieutenant continued, "we've already arrested more of you than we want to. And more than thirty people have been hurt, a few seriously. We don't want to hurt any more of you. Or any of you. You've made your point. Now why don't you go home?"

A middle-aged priest, his high-colored Irish face flaming above his collar and cassock, spoke up. "We want to stop the drafting of boys for a cruel and immoral war, Lieutenant," he said, emphatic, with no note of apology in his tone.

Fillmore stepped forward. "Your men were clubbing people left and right with their nightsticks. Boys and girls alike. I saw them with my own eyes, Lieutenant. Is that what you meant when you said you didn't want to hurt anyone?"

"Pastor," the lieutenant replied, "you are breaking the law. When you break the law, there are risks and punishments. Getting clubbed is one of those risks."

"We are still breaking the law then," Fillmore said softly, "man's law not God's," and there was no mistaking the challenge in his voice.

"You want us to go through you? You want us to put you in jail?" the lieutenant asked, his voice weary with surprise, looking from one face to another as if hoping for someone to meet his reasonableness with theirs, but he found no answering response.

Fillmore stepped back into the ranks; the lieutenant shrugged, then turned and whispered some orders. The center workers and inductees began to pile out of the buses and were organized into neat ranks. The demonstrators stood staunch or huddled in the doorway, sprawled on the steps, or sat in what resembled the Buddhist lotus position, but no one moved out of the way or made a path. "Aw, why don't we walk them right in over the bastards?" a policeman called hoarsely, but the lieutenant shook his head. A phalanx of police came forward and brusquely began to pick up the protesters one at a time, lugging them to the paddy wagon and tossing them into it like sides of beef. Two in the doorway, one a Negro minister, the other a bespectacled school teacherish old man who stiffened with fear at the approach of three police, were hammerlocked and rushed dancing painfully across the concrete into the police van. When Fillmore's turn came, four police picked him up by the ankles and wrists, letting his back drag and bump along the ground as they carted him toward the van. Fillmore's face turned back, white and frightened but determined, seeking in Sanders something Sanders understood perfectly well without a word's being spoken, but when two other burly police turned their attention to him, Sanders flashed his press card, showed his cameras and explained that he worked for Needham's paper, and the police passed him by. He watched them load Fillmore into the van with a heaving thump and felt like Judas Iscariot.

When the last demonstrator was locked into the van it began slowly to move toward the wooden barriers. The lieutenant nodded and workers and inductees, some glaring but more looking down at their feet, began to file into the building. From the police van through the barred rear windows came a call that Sanders would have sworn was Fillmore's, magnificent and distorted: "You don't have to do it, boys. You don't have to go. Burn your draft cards. Don't kill. Don't burn innocent farmers. Don't dirty yourself in this dirty war." Other voices in the van took up a chorus, "You don't have to go! You don't have to go!" and then the low snarl of the police siren rose and blotted them out.

Setting aside the welter of his feelings, the recollection of the kids being clubbed and kicked, himself being spat on, the sight of Fillmore's pleading, rebuking face turned to him as the police carried him away, Sanders called the story in from a phone booth in a nearby bar, having first reinforced himself with a stiff straight bourbon. He heard his own crisp, detailed and yet objective description of the demonstration as he dictated it to the deskman. He heard it as if it were a recording someone else had made, a detached observer who neither took risks or sides nor played favorites, and knew it was good professional reporting of a high order, that rewrite would have almost nothing to do on it before sending it down to be set. That was what was always the most terrifying part of the work: his words, the frail exhalations of his breath and brain cast in metal. In metal: irretrievable, irrevocable, fixed. When he was done he asked that the front page be held for pictures and the final number of arrests and injuries which he'd bring in with him and was surprised to hear Needham cut in on the line to say, "Great job, Elliott. First-class. A real page-one. Should make the wire services on this one. More if the pix are right. Hurry back." And then, before ringing off, he added, "You're a chip off the old block." In the phone booth he gathered up the remainder of his change, the large quantity of it he had husbanded in anticipation of the call, leaving himself just two dimes—no, not thirty pieces of silver, he reminded himself, not that—for the phone calls he then had to make, one to police headquarters for the total number of arrests and the second to the hospital for the number of injured, jotting them down though he knew he'd remember them without that. At the bar, drinking an Irish coffee for the road, he wondered how Lovett Carpenter Sanders would have handled the demonstration. Would he, being so deeply committed to courage and love of country, yes, and war, have joined the police as most of the other photographers and reporters had? Or if he'd been convinced that the war was a lunacy and a fiasco, fumbling plus bad judgment mated with obstinacy, would he have stood off with the demonstrators, gone into the paddy wagon and jail, and reported from there? Especially if Fillmore was his friend?

Walking to the car, the cameras on his neck suddenly burdensome, Sanders almost bumped into Peter King who popped out of a doorway and, scarred palm outstretched, panhandled him. "Spare a quarter, mister?"

"Peter," Sanders said, "it's you."

"No, Elliott, it's your dark *doppelgänger*, your black-assed buddy, your fuliginous foe, your Othello of the Ghetto, your King Blear of the pavements." The smell of alcohol and something else—marijuana? —was heavy around him; and he was high as a kite. King fell into step and walked with him, talking all along. "You're a pretty hotshot newspaperman. I saw you back there, you know, right in with them all—"

"Were you watching the demonstration?"

"Watching? Man, I was one of the demonstrators, the leader of one of our *colored*"—he gave the word a nasty, demeaning stress—"contingents." He laughed. "You didn't know that was my kind of kick, huh? I've got lots of kicks and lots in the kick you don't know about, white boy. You don't swing with the gang, do you? You stay way out—on the outskirts of town, at funerals, at demonstrations. You a fringe man? You cutting out, like old George? You cutting out and leaving us, all of us, to our *dee*-vices? You newspaper boys, you just along for the ride. You don't belong with the rest of the black gang down here in the engine room. You something special, even among the honkies. I saw you cop out on your round-collar buddy back there and you wasn't even ashamed. Man, you got the whole bag licked, the whole goddam scene."

"I've got to take some pictures back to the paper to file with the story," Sanders said defensively. "You want to come with me? I'll drop you off somewhere until I finish up and then buy you some lunch later."

"Man, I'm not sure I want to ride with you. You want me to wait outside that rag you write for, outside the door with my hat in my hand waiting for you to buy me a bite"—his teeth were bared—"to eat? *She-ee-t!* Old Judas, he sold the old Man out for thirty pesos of silver, and you sell one of his preachers out for thirty lines of copy. Goddam Gresham's law everywhere nowadays. And then you ashamed to take me *into* your lousy yellow-journalism office, you leave me off, and pick me up later."

"Be serious, Peter."

"You think I'm fooling? I kid you not, Mr. Man. You better believe it because it's the rock-bottom, the real acey-deucey. I don't break no bread with you."

"You're high," Sanders said. "What are you on?"

"'One pill makes you large, and one pill makes you small, and the ones that Mother gives you don't do anything at all,'" King sang. "This trip is into the high country where the grass grows tall and Maryjane and I rode horses through the golden snow and rain." He made the announcement as if it were a travelogue with Lowell Thomas, bearing down hard on the words that had double drug meanings. Then he switched to a blues-song rasping plaint, "'Gonna mo-ove to the outskirts of to-own, ah don wan no white man to-oo-oo-oo always hang around.'"

"If you give me a chance—"

"Who gives me a chance?" King snapped.

"I'll try to explain. Not that I owe you an explanation."

"Nobody owes nobody explanations, Man. If George didn't give me any, why should you? Right?" His manner and voice turned starchy and professorial. "Now, Mr. King, things are not always the way they seem. They are much more complex, you might even say reticulated, with underlying causes and overlying motives." Then dirt-farmer Negro. "Hell, no. Nevah ah, ah theh? Mo comple-ee-cated, Massa, ain't theh? Too comple-ee-cated fo this po niggah tuh unnerstan."

"Cut it out, Peter," Sanders said, putting his hand on King's sleeve.

"You speakin tuh me, mistuh?" King said coldly, eyes slitty. "If'n you are, take yo han offa me."

Sanders released his sleeve. "If that's the way it is—"

"That *is* the way it is," King said menacingly.

"I'm your friend," Sanders reminded him, "George's friend, too."

Now minstrel-show Negro. "Man got friens lak you don need no enemies, boss. My daddy just lak that, wantta be ma frien too. Didn wantta be ma daddy-o, nohow, only ma frien. But he cum out neither." Then normally. "You really are like him. Thought of himself as above the battle, way above. A niggah aristocrat, suh, one of A. Philip Randolph's Knights of the Pullman Diner. After all he was a pullman porter of one of those fancy big transcontinental trains." Then confused, mixed speech, gutter language and high-flown in unpredictable pattern. "A real big man. Flashing plenty of the long green. Like ah say, that cat, he got bread when no one else got collard greens. But even the big man gets lonely, now and again. Travelin all tha time ain't good nohow for a man's spirit—or his dong. He has hisself one family in Noo Yawk, he gits hisself couple more 'long tha road, one in Chi, where the big trains stop over, and one out here in Oakland, tha end of tha line. Man, you can say that again, the real end of the line: He gets my mother. She come out to the Coast with her kooky family in '36 with all them white-trash Okies and Arkies from the dust bowl, comin out heah to fine tha Promised Lan, flowin with milk and money. She only sixteen an kooky herself and don know what tha hell it all about anyway, don

[324]

know which end is up. No, mebbe she do. She know how to tilt up her ass an take it inta tha right place. He finds her, my daddy-o, and he lak that. He come visit her regularly, that misable fucker, and why not? He have hisself a juicy little setup with a dicey seventeen-year-old fresh piece of ass right outta tha rhubarb, fresh as country butter, tasty as country ham. Don hurt him a bit. An every time his train in town, he got a place to soak his meat. What could be better than that? He got the bread so he sets her up in a little flat, cheap enough at half the price. Always there when he wants it and comfortable as home. Much better'n Miss Sadie's cathouse. And she so hongry to git outta where she beddin down with 'leven other little niggers on the floor those goddam Okies got in the slums, she grateful. Mind you, she grateful! She look up an admire him. A big man. He payin the bills. Washington Dancer King. He come on strong, Man, mighty strong. And so he knocks her up 'cause she don know beans about such things, nuthin attall; she know where to find it, she know where it feel good, she know how to tuck it in, to wriggle when it feel good an to milk it dry. She nuthin but a Okie country girl afta all, and Dancer King, he a big-city slicker know his way around.

"That's how I come along, Mistuh Sanders. Me. He doesn't like that much, Washington Dancer King, but why give up a good thing just because there's another pickaninny bastard to feed? Doesn't eat much anyway. Not that he isn't a pain in the ass crying and interrupting a good piece of ass or a good game of dice with the boys when he's hungry. That's the way it works at first but the kid begins to grow up and he's not kooky like his mother. He mean shrewd like his daddy-o. He asks questions. 'Are you my daddy?' 'Why don't you come visit me no more?' 'Where do you go to work?' 'Play with me, Daddy.' And that *is* a pain in the ass. He don need that, none of it.

"Besides, it's after the war now and though there's a lot more travelin between the coasts, a lot more of it's by airplane now, and the old kinda white folks ain't travelin any more, them big tippers is all gone, and all that wartime gravy's over too. Besides, kooky Ellen-Mae ain't the way she used to be. She kookier and she like a old lady now of twenny-fo. He like 'em juicier an younger. So they have a big one, a gasser, a bust-out, a ball, one last time, and he leaves her a coupla hundred bucks—a big-time operator, Dancer King, ain't he?—an he never comes back." As he walked and talked, King rubbed his palms, twisting his hands, as if he were washing them with sand over and over again, his face livid with hatred.

Sympathetically Sanders again touched King's sleeve but King tore his arm away.

"You're just like him, just like him. A walker-outer. A take-a-powderer. A twenty-three skidooer. You cop out and cut out. Especially when the heat is on, when someone needs you." King was almost sobbing.

"Peter, what is it you're asking of me? What do you want?" Sanders asked and then, with an intimation of understanding, said, "I can't do that. I'm just not built that way, I'm not that kind of man."

"No? What kind of man are you?"

The question was always the same. And the answer. "I don't know," he confessed, "but I'm finding out."

King stopped and so did Sanders. King's eyes were mad, his breathing loud and wheezing. "Washington Dancer King, the father of my cunt-try. Toe-dancer King, smart-money man, don handle the dirty end of the stick; he leave that for someone else, leave the kooky little gal and black bastid tyke to hold the bag." He grabbed Sanders' shoulders and shook him again and again, shouting, "Kee-rist, you're the man George died for! You're *it*." Then, tossing him away, King stood staring at him as if he were a leper covered all over with sores, and with a gargled shriek King turned and ran frantically away down the street.

* * *

His report and pictures were good and they made a powerful lead-story and first-page combination. Sanders saw it, admitted it to himself without flattery but also without much pleasure. The main picture they'd used in the makeup was the one he'd taken of Murray Fillmore being carried to the paddy wagon by four police-men, the photograph so sharp that the Leica had caught the plead-ing accusation of Fillmore's face turned back to him. Now it blurred in his vision and became George's face and Peter King's and Lovett Carpenter Sanders' in turn, then a string of spittle and an anguished

[326]

cry from a blank face with a skewed mouth, shrieking, "So you're the man George died for. You're *it!*" *It.* What could have been more filled with contempt than that neuter?

Yet Sanders refused to let that stop him from writing the story for Tessier in another way so that it would make more sense to a French reader, more a magazine piece than a newspaper report. He cabled it and radiophotoed a dozen of the best pictures, carefully chosen, to Paris, following up with a dozen glossies airmail special delivery. Tessier would love the piece, an eyewitness picture story from the before-dawn empty street through the demonstration to the victorious if subdued entrance of the inductees to the final emptiness of the street at high noon, the wooden-horse barriers, some overturned, still blocking off the ends of the street, a quartet of police and a single prowl car left there, guarding, waiting.

When it was all written it was evening, the fluorescent light of the desk lamp harsh in his eyes, his mouth dry and bad-tasting, his shirt pasted clammily to his skin. "*What are you doing in there, David? What are you doing out there, Waldo?*" They'd begun the day properly, their reunion traditional, but Fillmore was no more Thoreau than he was Emerson. Emerson, his father's god.

Needham knocked and when there was no answer came in. "How'd it go?" he asked. "Finished?"

Sanders nodded, too tired to talk.

"How about a swim?"

The idea was appealing but Sanders was too bushed.

The deskmen had written the photo captions but he had changed one: "Minister Murray Fillmore, the Berkeley clergyman who led the demonstrators, being carried off by police." After "the Berkeley clergyman," Sanders had added, "and former military chaplain in Vietnam." How we appease our guilts, the small act of courage for failing to perform the larger one, the minuscule evasions and retributions which salvage our integrities, or give us the illusion of our salvation.

"Like old times. Big time. Paris all over again," Needham was saying happily. "Made me feel young. We parlayed it all over the lot, wire services, picture syndicates, even picture-magazine rights. Those were marvelous photos you took. A good day's work."

[327]

Sanders was grateful but unable to muster the response Needham wanted. A good day's work. For whom?

"Why don't we celebrate tonight? Come on out and have dinner with me, Sheila and me. Bring your girl, a girl, any girl. I've got a couple of bottles of champagne in the cooler—French *brut,* not local —so we can do it up right. What do you say?" His enthusiasm was boyish, infectious.

"I'm really tired. Got up at three-thirty A.M. so I could get to Oakland early," Sanders explained.

"Before the fun started."

Sanders remembered the quiet street, the morning coffee, the counterman's face turning hostile. The lieutenant with the bullhorn and his weary appeal to reason and legality, his genuine desire for order, the others' fervent sense of moral right, their burning desire for peace, and most of all Fillmore's face reproaching him, upbraiding him: *J'accuse.*

"Go on home, shower and have a nap," Needham advised. "You've got a couple of hours yet. We'll have dinner about eight-thirty. Okay?"

Sanders agreed; fatigued, he didn't have the energy to resist.

"I knew you'd make it," Needham remarked as he went to the door, "the minute I hired you. Lov Sanders' boy. How could I miss?"

"Did anyone doubt you?" He tried to temper the sarcastic tone but didn't quite succeed. How could he miss?

"A couple of cooler heads than mine around here had some reservations, I admit. But they didn't know your old man. Or you. By God, those photos are better than any Lov ever took."

"The cameras are better nowadays."

"I don't think I'll hear much of that from any of my people now, not after today. In fact, there was a lot of talk the other way this afternoon."

"Well, well, well," Sanders said, feeling stupid.

"Couldn't you be a little, well, friendlier with some of them? You know, have lunch with them, shoot the breeze now and then. Take a swim with the gang. Wouldn't hurt that much, would it?" Needham was not at all embarrassed.

Sanders threw up his hands. "I suppose I could, couldn't I?" And why not? Lovett Carpenter Sanders had been one of the boys; in fact, Needham had been one of the boys he'd been one of the boys with.

"See you later," Needham said into the silence that ensued, "about eight-thirty." Then he closed the door behind him.

* * *

Jason Howe's silent apartment soothed him though he had to turn his gaze deliberately away from the Paris street signs Laura had so naïvely and generously put on his walls. Jason Howe's discreet taste in furnishings had created a refuge from life for which Sanders was grateful, quiet and peaceful colors and graceful lines, but the recollection that he had probably had to do so because he was Negro edged Sanders' solace with remorse and distaste. After he'd poured himself a drink and put his feet up, he slouched back on the couch looking out at the sun plunging toward the mountains like a world aflame meteoring out of the universe and was filled with a biting melancholy, a melancholy that embraced Fillmore and the day's demonstrators. I can't believe any of it, any of it. I've seen too many wars, up too close. I can't believe the reasons for them and I can't bear the conduct of them. Patriotism, Marxism, neo-colonialism, wars of liberation, the paternalist Western Prometheuses bringing the "light of civilization" to the "benighted barbarians" East and West that always seemed to be borne on the flaming sword. Or in modern times on napalm. Their partisans, always required *Mort aux*—somebody. Death to the foreign devils, to the capitalist running dogs and jackals, to the Communist subversives, death to the blacks, the yellows, the reds, the whites, the Catholics, the Buddhists, the Jews, the heretics, the conformers. Always death. Always *à bas* something or someone, and the *à bas* became *là-bas,* a George buried somewhere, everywhere.

"It's not *my* war," Sanders said aloud into the silent apartment, conscious that he was negatively echoing and contesting his father's attestation, "This is *my* war!" not sure which war it was he was disowning, or war altogether, sure only that his nausea from the whole idiocy of laying down human life today as compost to fertilize the fields and prospects of human life the day after tomorrow was profound and insupportable. His father had considered that cowardice. Yet, with all his hatred of war, he had stood aside, an observer, and not joined Fillmore and his cohorts either. "I don't like holy wars either, not even that kind," but he felt himself hedging and he knew that Fillmore and Peter King thought that cowardice. For Peter King he was the supreme copout. So, too, for George Christiansen. "What happened to the good men? Where are all the honorable men? Where did they go?" George had demanded. Where indeed? They went down to dusty death biting the earth and stones in their final agony, hanging from crosses, drinking hemlock, left in the desert to die parched and bereft, alone with their visions; they took a bullet or a bayonet, a spear or an arrow in the guts, their skin and hair aflame with boiling oil or jellied gasoline in a last lethal fiery passion. Voltaire had called for tilling one's garden, but where was there a garden you could still till and who would leave you in peace to till it?

Needham had informed him that Fillmore would be leading another if somewhat different kind of demonstration the next day, but though Needham had been tipped off about it, he had not been able to discover just what type it would be. Earlier Sanders had called and discovered that Fillmore had already been bailed out on his own recognizance, so even that small alleviation of his guilt, bailing Fillmore out, had been denied him.

In the shower he kept thinking of Laura, worrying about her and about Peter King, feeling responsible for them, but he didn't know what he could do to help them. He called and sent a night letter to Laura as soon as he was dressed again, asking her to telephone him, but still he felt uneasy about her. No sooner had he put the receiver down than the phone rang again. It was Beth. "I was just going to call you," he said.

"Great minds," she chuckled.

"ESP." He was happy to hear her sound so gay, and making his mind up on the instant, he invited her to have dinner with him at Needham's.

"Aren't you afraid of what they'll think? That I'm someone special?"

"You are someone special," he said, weary of the coy game before it began, yet knowing no other way to deal with it than to play it.

Beth changed the conversation. "Steven looked at the plates. Nothing. Absolutely nothing. We took the stomach too, nothing there either."

"Nothing but *boule hystérique*," Sanders replied, dismayed and relieved.

"It will go away. I've seen dozens of such cases."

"Scant consolation. It simply means I belong to a much larger group of nuts than I thought."

"Don't be so morbid," she chastised him. "Look at the brighter side. It could have been cancer."

"I promise to try. And thanks for the news and the trouble you— and Prescott—took."

"You'll have to thank Steven yourself."

"I might just do that."

"I'll bet you will." Her uproarious laughter made Sanders vow to write Prescott a thank-you note immediately.

"Now, how about dinner with the Needhams?"

She hesitated.

"Already spoken for?" he asked wryly. "Prescott on tap?"

"I've got to wash my hair," she said, ignoring him. "Come on over. By the time you get here, I'll have a couple of drinks ready and then we can go on to the Needhams'." She asked him how she ought to dress and he told her he had confidence in her judgment in such matters, and she then said she'd leave the latch off in case she was in the shower, that he was to come right on in.

There was no answer when he rang and knocked so he walked inside. When he called her name, she summoned him to the bedroom where he found her wrapped in a huge white beach towel imprinted with pairs of red dice, all showing either sevens or elevens: the winning combinations, Sanders thought, if you began with them for openers, but the crap-out numbers if they arrived on the scene subsequently. Signs and portents? Or just the superstition born of the vagaries of dry-goods distribution in America? Still wet, Beth stood before a full-length mirror set into the walnut door of an open closet, turning this way and that, palms on her stomach, then on her buttocks, surveying herself with the identical self-conscious narcissism Laura had used to examine herself in that dressing-table mirror except that what Laura rejected with disdain Beth approved and enjoyed. "You'll do," Sanders commented wryly, not without admiration.

"But for whom? And when?" she asked somberly, then laughing she turned and on bare feet moved mincingly toward him, the red dice shaking humorously obscene on her breasts and belly and outstretched arms. "How's my favorite *boule hystérique?*"

Sanders took her in his arms, damp, smelling of soap and toilet water and the faintest odor of gin and toothpaste as she nuzzled his cheek and neck. "And how's my favorite *boule de suif?*" was his rejoinder.

She leaped back and returned to the mirror. "Beast! I haven't gained a pound since I was fourteen. *Boule de suif* indeed!" She looked piqued.

"Don't get hysterical, Beth, I was only teasing. And I wanted to see if you remembered any French, if your Aunt Katharine's tutelage had all gone for naught." Striding past her to the glass wall that gave out on the garden, he drew the portières. "Ain't you got no shame?"

"Men! You're just like George. Forever pulling the drapes to or closing the windows, except"—she brought herself up short—"for one time." Her face, naked and full of pain, was turned in on itself but seconds later its smiling flirtatiousness had returned. "Nobody can see through the fence and all that greenery back there. Even with a telescope. That's one of the reasons I bought this house. Privacy. I often sunbathe nude in the backyard and sometimes I even sleep nude out there in the hammock when the weather's warm, or when I have trouble sleeping."

"Dangerous, isn't it?"

"You mean someone might leap over the wall and rape me? Come on, Elliott. Besides, I generally have company." Quickly, she joshed him. "Now, Elliott, mustn't pout. You must learn to share, you know. That's what civilization is all about, sharing. You can't have everything to yourself." Her hilarity echoed through the house.

You can't have everything to yourself? You can't have anything to yourself: that was the law. A curious, shuffling noise like someone bustling through the shrubbery came from the garden. "There's someone out there," he said, "right now."

"Not someone"—Beth was still laughing—"some*thing*. It's Jo-Jo, the turtle, my pet turtle. George gave him to me a long, long time ago. Way back when. Come on, I'll introduce you, but first we've got to get him something to eat. I haven't fed him today and that's why he's making a ruckus. Scratches at the window when he's hungry. Imperious. Demanding. Just like a man. And expensive tastes, like a woman, Boston lettuce and endive." In the kitchen she broke some lettuce and cabbage leaves from the heads in the vegetable bin of the refrigerator, then went out into the garden. An outdoor switch turned on a battery of spotlights which illuminated the house and garden. "Come on"—she waved him along—"I know where Jo-Jo hides." And she did. Under clumps of fuchsia and fern and tangles of unstaked red and pink chrysanthemums, a mottled-gray-brown turtle shell huddled. Beth knelt and said, "It's only me, Jo-Jo, don't be afraid. You're not afraid of Elliott, are you? He's a friend." She poked some of the lettuce leaves under the shell but the turtle wouldn't stick his head out. "If you're going to be bad, you're going to be punished," she threatened, "and I might not feed you at all." She went to where a garden hose was wound around a metal reel bolted to the concrete pillar of the house. Pulling the nozzle at the end she spun off ten or twelve feet of it as she walked back to where she stood directly over the turtle. "Step back" she ordered and before Sanders had moved, she'd squeezed the chrome nozzle and sent a jet of water at the turtle's shell. The turtle's legs came out from under the shell, it turned, its rear braced against the stream of water, trying to dig in with its ugly rubbery legs, but Beth continued to play the water on it until the force of the water skidded the turtle along the muddy earth that now afforded him no purchase. "You going to behave, Jo-Jo?" Beth asked severely, relaxing the nozzle.

With the water off the turtle's head came out, tentatively, its elastic neck turning this way and that, its beady eyes surveying the landscape. Beth crouched, hiking the tightly wrapped bath towel up around her thighs. With her left hand she put down the vegetable leaves in front of the turtle, with the other hand she held the

[333]

hose nozzle. Clumsily, slowly, the turtle lumbered forward to the lettuce and cabbage, his mouth triangular and open, like a bird of prey's, the crunching on the cabbage leaf distinct and grinding. As the turtle began to chew through the edge of the greens, Beth, with a flashing chrome cast of the nozzle, flicked the turtle over on his shell and played an abrupt intense stream of water on its corrugated soft gray belly. The turtle's legs ran helplessly in the air and panic-stricken, his sinuous neck twisted in search of aid. Beth laughed and turned the stream off.

"Don't!" Sanders said sharply just an instant before she did, and reaching past her, flipped the turtle back on its legs, its clammy shell unpleasant to his touch.

"Sentimental, Elliott?"

"I hate to see living things abused and tormented uselessly."

"Even people?"

"Especially people."

"You're going to have to change the whole world, then, aren't you?" she asked and, giving the nozzle a jerk, let the rubber hose, like some living serpent, roll back across the ground, slithering onto the reel. Then she took a limp fragment of lettuce leaf and placed it on the turtle's shell just far enough back so that he could see but not reach the leaf with his beak. Immediately the turtle began to stretch its creased gray neck in an unwieldy but painstaking effort to get the lettuce off his back, tiny black eyes wild and staring, his whole posture tortured, unable even to concentrate on the food before him. After watching its convulsive efforts with a sleek Buddha-like grin, Beth said, "Come on, let's go back inside."

"You're not going to leave it like that?"

"Why not? It gives me pleasure. That's what Jo-Jo's for, to give me pleasure. That's what George gave him to me for."

"To abuse, to torment? It's only a dumb animal."

"*Only* a dumb animal," she snarled. "And what do you think people are, seraphim? It does nothing but eat and crap and lie in the sun. Is that such a bad life?"

"Do you envy it, a turtle?"

"Yes, I envy Jo-Jo. Often. Even now. Nothing to rankle the heart, no thorns in the flesh, nothing but a couple of lettuce and cabbage

[334]

leaves and a little warm morning sunshine to worry about. Look how ugly he is. His face and neck, that short snaky neck with that head on it, just like a—well, you know what it looks like." It did.

"Even less reason to abuse it, then."

"For you."

Sanders remembered the turtle's voracious diamond-shaped mouth, the rending beak. Should I consent to this torment because of my own experiences with the "snapping turtle," he asked himself rhetorically, but the cruelty offended him.

They were silent, the soft wind fluttering in the trees, the sounds of small insects a ground swell, the noises magnified in the early evening quiet.

"All right" Beth said at last, impatiently, "all right." She nudged the turtle over with her bare foot, the lettuce leaf dropped off and with her big toe she righted the turtle once again. Then she wheeled and went back into the house. With only a brief backward glance that confirmed that the turtle was already moving on that lettuce and cabbage, Sanders followed.

Before the bedroom mirror she gazed into her face as if it were something foreign, a stranger's face she did not recognize or control, a penalty life had exacted of her, which she had done nothing to deserve. "You think I'm cruel," she remarked to her own image but speaking to him, "don't you?"

"I don't think, I know."

Beth's fingers brushed her dark hair back from her pale temples, drew her eyelids up into an Oriental cast so that her eyes disappeared beneath the fringe of her lashes, massaged the lines of her mouth with fingers that tried but could not erase them. In a single fluent gesture she dropped the towel as if it were a pennant trailing in the dust, the dice proclaiming with her face the inexorable risks and certainties, victories and defeats. "Have we got time?" she asked, her voice an evasion and avowal together. Doubled in the mirror, her body was twice white and sharply sculptured by the overhead light which cruelly revealed that they were two bodies in one but not the same. Innocent and depraved, passionate and frigid, free and bound, the haughty breasts, the proud legs and lordly buttocks admitted only great victories; the betrayal and loss, grief and

[335]

bereavement, ruin and defeat spoke only from the fluted chalice of her belly, from her grass-green flecked eyes and uncertain voluble fingers. Snared in his desire, pity pledged him, but the memory of George's name, uttered in the rapture of their last lovemaking, was sand in his teeth; the recollection of the limp lettuce leaf he had just witnessed placed on the turtle carapace withheld his indulgence. Dead sons and dead lovers out of her womb, living lovers on her belly, jasmine and gardenias, all the meshes and toils she cast. By refusing to acknowledge his impassiveness, she blunted its force; lightly moving across the rug, guileless and resolute, she switched out all the lights except a single green-shaded bed lamp, and then, all guile and shadow, lay back on the velvet greensward bed, snare to be snared. Once more she had made him cry quits, provoking and extracting his surrender, however equivocally, on her own terms.

"We still have time," he heard himself say in spite of his willing not to, knowing he had considered more in his answer and in her question than she had intended, but trying hard to refuse to acquiesce to her need, though the unappeasable hungers stirred shakily, then with growing rigor in his loins. We have time for that, he thought, but neither world enough nor time enough for more: the much more he wanted and needed for what still remained to be done. As he lay down next to her on the bed, he knew she had not quite made him cry quits, only cry havoc.

* * *

The house on the Avenue Mozart was the product of architecture of another age, a solid robust tribute to the age of Haussmann and the classical revival. The apartment Sanders had rented for Monique was on the fifth floor, a walkup which he promised himself was good exercise but by which he hoped to limit her other "clients" and if not that at least to diminish their strength and ardor. Monique had left him no other viable choice, because she had set the conditions. When he first asked her if he could set her up in an apartment, he'd been amused, then irritated and finally furious not only with how she continued to postpone considering his proposition but also with how she simultaneously deferred to his needs, approaching the problem as their mutual concern with a candor and practicality that embarrassed him. And his realization that she was behaving more sensibly and less romantically than he was made him ashamed of his embarrassment. "There is no need to hurry, *chéri*," Monique cautioned. "Such things must be thought over carefully, chewed over many times. We both need time to think over the practical arrangements. And I am here and you are here, so it is not too bad, now, is it?" When, after four months of bringing the subject up, cajoling and threatening, earnest and humorous, she did agree to talk it over with him, she did it with a joke—"What is it, *chéri*, is the trip home from Rue Daunou too far and too inconvenient?"—that left him chagrined and dejected because there was enough pointed truth in it to puncture his pretenses. Yet since she spoke without rancor it did not leave him feeling diminished but quietly desired.

It was a *cinq à sept,* the evening graying in the unlit room, and lying there naked in the big brass bed, languorous and half asleep, Sanders was momentarily at peace. Monique got up and he almost reached out for her to keep the warmth of her flesh there next to him, but he was dreaming that he was bathing under a warm waterfall in the Connecticut hills where he used to camp out and fish in the sun-warmed green stream, so he let her go. When she switched on the lamp he waked. For the first time Monique was wearing the negligee he had bought for her the previous Christmas at Aux Printemps, a luxurious and expensive blue, pleated peignoir that was not quite diaphanous. He had searched for it for a long time, wanting to give her something she would not normally buy for herself both because it was too costly and because it offended her sense of what was "practical." But when she had opened the package in her slow, refusal-to-expect-anything way, he knew he'd made a mistake. She shook her head twice, too abrupt angry motions, and said, "You shouldn't have bought this for me. It is *her* style, not mine. Too rich and grand for my ass." It was a deliberate vulgarity, for she rarely used the words common to her trade; and she had never mentioned Elaine's name or worn the peignoir thereafter until now.

Sanders lay watching her slow, heavy grace as she brought slices of pear and Port de Salut and glasses of red wine from the kitchen and set them on the table next to the bed. It was the first time she offered him more than a drink in her flat and he knew that they

[337]

were either to celebrate or to mourn something. Her body, rosy and rounded, gleamed and moved beneath the blue nylon, and her face, newly scrubbed, its eyes blue and candid as ever, looked like a schoolgirl's—except for the plucked eyebrows. "You look beautiful, Mlle. Bardieu," Sanders said, sitting up in bed and admiring her.

"Thank you very much, M. Sanders"—she pronounced his name French style—"it is a beautiful negligee." She spoke without coquetry, mouth smiling, eyebrows arched and skeptical.

Monique handed him a slice of fruit and cheese together and a glass of wine, then took the same for herself. "*Salut!*" she toasted.

"*À votre,*" he responded, raising his glass to her. They ate and drank.

"I have thought about your offer," she began without further preamble, "and I have decided to accept."

Silently he raised his glass to her again. "But," she added, "there are conditions."

"What kind of conditions?"

"It is important, necessary, that we both understand what this arrangement means, what it doesn't mean, and how it is to be conducted."

"Why must we talk about such things now? I'm happy you've consented. And conditions? We are grown-up, sensible people. We can work things out."

"Though you are older," she said, "I have more experience in these matters. You are American and I am French. Our ways in these affairs are different."

Sanders bowed his head not only because he recognized the truth of what she said but because he hated it with a jealous rage.

The terms Monique set were simple but inflexible. She would permit, yes, that was the word, she would permit him to pay for the apartment and to pay for furnishing it, but she would not accept money for food and drink. He might pay for her clothes, but she would prefer to buy them herself though she would be happy to have him accompany her. In addition, he would have to give her a weekly stipend of 500 new francs and she would have to have a month in the summer, in August of course, to vacation in Normandy with her family. Three nights and two days a week, whichever days

[338]

and nights he chose, she wanted for herself, to see friends, to shop, to be alone; and to take other "clients."

That last was what he balked at, the other "clients," and where Monique was adamant. "I don't want you with anyone else," Sanders said, his wine glass tilting so that the bedsheets were stained red.

"I know *you* don't, but *I* do," she replied.

"Why do you have to have it your way, that way?"

"Because, Elliott"—it was also the first time she had used his Christian name to his face and she pronounced it French-style so that it sounded more like *idiot* than Elliott—"I cannot afford the risk of being your woman alone."

"You mean there's not enough money in it for you?" he sneered.

For a fraction of a second he thought Monique might fling either the pear and cheese, or the wine, into his face, but when she replied it was in the same composed voice as before. "Why must you always behave like a Tatar when your pride is hurt? *Orgeuil. Amour propre.* That's what men are, three-fifths pride and two-fifths lust."

"And women three-fifths greed and two-fifths mother love?"

Monique sat back in the chair, finished eating her cheese and fruit, drinking her wine. "You are a swine," she said when she was done, smiling disarmingly. "Do you love your wife?" she asked brusquely.

"What has that got to do with it?" Sanders was defensive.

"Everything. I cannot afford to love you, Elliott."

"Why not?"

"Is that what you want?"

He hesitated only a hair before replying, "Yes, that's what I want," but she had caught even that pause.

"What would I do when you go?"

"How do you know I'll go?" he countered.

"You'll go. Tomorrow, or in a year, you'll go," Monique said unconditionally.

"You are certain?"

"Absolutely."

"You're wrong."

Monique shrugged.

"You won't change your mind?"

"Not *will* not, Elliott, *can* not."

Sanders jumped out of bed and began to throw his clothes on. "No," he muttered, "no, I can't stand that. I won't stand that." Monique sat watching him, not moving, not speaking, until he began to knot his tie.

"Then we are to remain here," she asked, "in the Rue Daunou?" It was a question phrased without an iota of threat or ultimatum.

"No," he raged, "not here, not anywhere."

"You're leaving, then?" she asked.

"Yes, what did you expect?"

Monique began to laugh, a deep curdled humor bubbling up from her chest, her head thrown back, her blond hair even more golden in the lamplight, her scrubbed face naked and sad and good-natured.

"What's so funny?" he inquired.

Monique repeated their dialogue as if it were recorded, changing her voice to his and back to her own. *"What would I do when you go? How do you know I'll go? You'll go. Tomorrow, or in a year, you'll go."* By the time she'd finished repeating their words, he was laughing with her.

"All right," he said. "I surrender. You win."

"In these things, *chéri*," Monique said, the smile wiped off her face, "no one wins. Everybody loses."

Sanders pulled her out of the chair then and embraced her, felt her fingers at his back as he berated himself for being solemn, then her nails as he berated himself for his own blindness. When they were back in bed and he imbedded in her, rooted in the wet clutching of her earth, he knew something had passed between them that had not before, for in her rapture she wept and left the marks of her nails in the grooves of his ribs as she cried out, *"Baise-moi bien! Donne-moi ta foutre."* However uncertain he'd been before, he knew that in this there had been no feigning, no professional artifice; neither her body nor her grammar lied.

* * *

From the beginning it was clear that inviting Beth to the Needhams' was a mistake. The instant they met and subjected one another to that minute and uniquely female scrutiny that passed for an introduction but was much more, Beth and Sheila Needham struck sparks and though masked but not hidden by the veneer of good manners, sparks all the more easily fanned into fire because it was equally plain that Needham found Beth attractive and preened himself in a fashion that gave Sanders a glimpse of the younger newspaperman his father must have known in Paris, a cocky, masculine, suntanned Needham who made Sanders feel middle-aged.

Needham met them at the door, apologizing for Sheila's not being there to greet them and saying that she was not yet ready in such a way that Sanders realized that Sheila had already been at the bottle and needed time to compose herself. While Needham helped Beth off with her coat and gallantly admired the simple but beautifully fitted Spanish-style black dress she wore, Beth returned the compliment by admiring his house, its design, how cleverly placed it was, taking advantage of the high ground of the ridge and the surrounding trees, but when the three of them walked into the living room and Beth saw the panorama spread out below them through that expanse of glass wall, her sharp and audible intake of breath was more flattering than any words could have been.

They were sitting on the enormous couch that faced the glass wall, admiring the view, and Needham was at the bar mixing drinks, when Sheila made her entrance. It was melodramatic, so deliberately engineered that Sanders was instantly and sympathetically aware of the kind of shyness that must have inspired it. Sheila stood on the top of the three steps that led down into the living room dressed in a simple white togalike dinner gown with a high, beaded Chinese collar that not only hid her thickening body but the lines of her throat yet was in positively striking contrast to her carefully made-up face and flamboyant, once-blond hair. Sanders stood and Sheila, one silver-nailed hand on the wrought-iron rail, the other nervously clenched at her side, descended the three steps like a moving-picture starlet making her debut. "Elliott," she called in her whisky-hoarse voice, "I'm so glad to see you." Sanders met her halfway, kissed her cheeks French-style and felt her trembling as she embraced him. She hooked her arm in his for support and walked him back to the couch where Beth, spine erect, head arrogant, waited. "You're Elliott's girl," Sheila began, and Sanders felt the spark leap from her to Beth and back, like a short shock of static electricity people sometimes communicate when they touch on especially thick carpet.

Beth stood up then, the contrast of her short black cocktail dress and Sheila's long white dinner gown emphasizing the difference of age and taste and class. "Well, not exactly his girl," Beth said, a smirk turning the corners of her lips and then gone so swiftly that Sanders himself was not sure he'd seen it.

"Oh?" Sheila said, a little too wide-eyed, looking from one to the other. "I am sorry. I thought you—"

"No apologies are necessary." Beth was suave and relentless. "*Girl* is perhaps both too much and too little."

It continued that way through dinner, Sheila offering and drinking her special "martis" alone while they drank wine through superbly prepared shrimp bisque, turbot, leg of baby lamb and salad, imperturbably served by an unsmiling slender gray-haired Negro. In the living room the champagne waited in an ice bucket and Needham popped the cork with suitable ceremony and expertise, explaining that they were celebrating an important occasion, one of the best pieces of reporting he'd seen in a long time. He then raised his glass in a toast, "To Elliott Sanders, son of a great reporter and great friend, and a great reporter and friend himself."

"Hear! Hear!" Sheila chorused thickly.

Puzzled, Beth asked what it was about and Needham told her about the demonstration, and while he did she kept nodding her dark head, discreetly murmuring that she had read the story and seen the pictures. "First-class reporting, first-class pictures," Needham concluded, but Beth had already turned away.

"By the way, Elliott," Needham remarked, "that touch of jail seems to have discouraged Chaplain Fillmore. He called off that demonstration tomorrow, so you won't have to cover it."

"You don't know Murray Fillmore," Sanders said.

"Fillmore, Elliott?" Beth was alert. "Is that the same Chaplain Fillmore? The one who wrote to me?"

Needham looked discomfited. "Do you know him?"

"Well, not exactly," Beth replied.

"You're a 'well, not exactly'-type girl, aren't you?" Sheila said.

[342]

"Not exactly," Sanders said, trying for and getting the laughter he hoped would break the tension. "Beth heard from Fillmore when he was a chaplain in Vietnam. Beth's husband—"

"Oh, you're married," Sheila said, a note of equivocal triumph in her voice.

"—was killed," Sanders went on too quickly to stop, too slowly to stop her, "there."

"I'm so sorry," Sheila said, getting up and reeling a little. "That was nasty."

"That's quite all right, Mrs. Needham," Beth replied without leniency, "we all make mistakes."

Sheila caught the tone immediately. "Yes, don't we?" she said, but her chagrin remained.

"What were you doing with Chaplain Fillmore?" Beth asked. "Why didn't you tell me he was back in the States? Didn't he want to see me? What's this about his being jailed?" The barrage of questions was sharp.

"One question at a time, Beth," Sanders replied. "I just found out Fillmore was back. I saw him at the demonstration I covered for the paper and I talked to him. Then he was jailed by the police and almost immediately bailed out."

"Is he still in uniform?"

"No, he's resigned from the chaplains' corps, but I don't know the story. We didn't have time to talk."

"Did you know this guy before, Elliott?" Needham, suddenly vigilant, inquired.

"Yes, Jim, I knew him in Vietnam."

"Well, why didn't you say so in your piece?"

"I'm not ready yet. There's more to the story that I don't know and besides that wasn't today's assignment."

"No, that's true, it wasn't," Needham said reluctantly. "But you're going to, aren't you?"

"Oh, don't badger him, Jim," Sheila reprimanded him. "He's a good reporter, he'll do the job that has to be done—and well. Look at what he did today."

"I am, I am," Needham said, "but why didn't he say he knew Fillmore?"

"In a way, I did," Elliott explained about changing the caption.

Needham bounded up the three steps in a single leap and in moments was back with the day's issue, spread out. "You did. Front-page caption too."

"See, I told you, Jim," Sheila echoed loyally.

"Elliott," Beth said in a low voice, "I want to see Chaplain Fillmore."

"Why not?" Needham said. "Might make a good story too."

"No story," Beth said decisively.

"Don't you believe in freedom of the press?" Needham was half joking but only half.

"I believe only in the individual's right to privacy," she retorted, smiling to take the sting out of her reply.

The three of them turned expectantly to him but Sanders added no comment.

"Well?" Beth insisted.

"I don't see much point. Fillmore didn't know George, never saw him until—after—"

"That doesn't matter," Beth said, cutting him off impatiently. "I want to see him. If that letter meant anything, he'll want to see me too."

Sanders doubted it. He didn't point out to her that Fillmore had written to her before, had her address, and had he wanted to talk to her it would have been simple for him to get in touch with her by mail again. "If he does," Sanders promised, "I'll arrange it."

"How do I know you'll ask him?" she inquired suspiciously.

"You don't." He was unyielding. "You'll just have to take my word."

Needham broke the tense silence with an invitation to go see his gymnasium, and he and Beth, arm in arm, led the way while Sanders followed with Sheila. Sheila held his arm to stabilize her wavering walk and also as if she simply wanted, needed, the human warmth and contact. "Jim just wants to show off in front of your girl," she whispered in his ear, her breath laden with gin.

"She's really not my girl. She's the widow of a man who saved my life in Vietnam," Sanders protested softly. "That's all."

"That's all?" Her eyebrows were querulous. "Isn't that enough?"

[344]

He smiled. "In some ways too much."

"I can see that, but why are you sleeping with her?" It was not really a question so much as an expression of puzzled concern and disappointed recognition.

"What makes you think that?" he asked stiffly.

"Don't give me any of your stiff-necked hoity-toity, Elliott. I may be drunk but I'm not dumb. I can still see things and sense them." She squeezed his arm. "I like you, Elliott. She's not for you, this girl. Drop her."

"Sheila!"

"I know, I know, I'm butting in. I should be minding my own business. And what does an old drunken bitch know anyway? But about people and especially about women, I do know, I have a nose. Even Jim gives me that." She stumbled and he held her up, feeling her too soft flesh against his arm with distaste. "I could easily have been your mother," she continued. "I liked your parents. Not your father alone. I liked your mother too, a fine woman. They didn't belong together, but they were both wonderful human beings. I felt that I was speaking in their behalf before. Forgive me. Now I'll just shut up." She glanced earnestly at him just once, probing for some response she didn't get, and then turned her face away and walked silently next to him, controlling her movements very carefully, so carefully that she didn't stumble again until they arrived at the gymnasium.

The gymnasium itself was large, with two glass walls, ceiling spotlights and the entire array of athletic equipment one would normally find in such places: parallel bars, ropes, high bar, horse, rowing machine, all the devices Sanders had not seen or touched since college. Obviously proud, Needham was asking how they liked it and he made appropriate noises until like a circus impresario Needham waved them back against the wall and slipped his shirt off. Without it, his powerfully muscled tanned torso made him seem thirty years younger. And then, even more impressive, Needham went through a whirlwind demonstration of gymnastics, on the bars, the horse, the mats, the ropes, doing tumbles, headstands, handstands, kips, his muscles standing out sharply with effort, the sweat on his skin glittering in the hard light, his body graceful and strong.

[345]

As he watched entranced, Sanders recognized in a remote part of himself a shard of envy at this uninhibited display of disciplined skill and realized that had his father lived it was just the kind of thing Lovett Carpenter Sanders might have cultivated as his body began to age, just the kind of demonstration his father might have put on. Vanity in remaining youthful-looking and "trim," pride in physical strength and stamina, delight in display. Needham and Lovett Carpenter Sanders had more in common than he'd first discerned. Unexpectedly, fantastically, he saw Needham and by implication his father as a latter-day *jongleur de Notre Dame,* but what was it he was tumbling for and who was his lady? Only when that occurred to him did he notice that with every leap and maneuver successfully executed, Needham threw a triumphant glance at Sheila, a gloating look that seemed to proclaim his youth and masculinity. "The jackass," Sanders heard Sheila exclaim softly next to him. "Look, Ma, no hands! See me, way up there, graceful and easy, the Daring Young Man on the Flying Trapeze? Pan's Peter! The everlasting, everloving boy. As if he was fooling the fates. We don't get old, we don't get fat, we don't get tired. We don't drink too much and we can still screw as often and as long as we used to—from the chandeliers."

"What was that, Mrs. Needham?" Beth asked, not having heard, her eyes glued to Needham's gyrations.

"Nothing. Nothing," Sheila said and Sanders was constrained to put his arm around her shoulders.

When at last Needham swung off the high bar after a final two-and-a-half spin and kip, he came down lightly, on his toes, skipped over toward them, breathing hard but not heavily, looking as if he had just finished singing them a song. And he had. "Want to try, Elliott?" he panted.

"No, thanks, Jim," Sanders refused.

"Good for you, keeps you in trim."

"Marvelous!" Beth applauded and Needham bowed to her hand-clapping. "Come on, Elliott, let's see what you can do."

"Your friend," Sheila said under her breath.

"Why don't you try?" Needham coaxed.

"Let him alone if he doesn't feel like it," Sheila began, but the glares of the other two silenced her.

"All right," Sanders agreed unwillingly, "if that's what you want." He stripped to his waist and though he was much bigger and more heavily muscled than Needham he saw how poor a contrast his pale flesh and flabbiness made. Only Sheila's sharp intake of breath reminded him of the still-livid scars across his chest and belly. "Wound scars," he explained laconically, dramatically, as he stretched and walked gingerly toward the high bar, enjoying Needham's wince.

Uncomfortable now, Needham tried to back off, suggesting that perhaps he ought to wait until he'd come out and worked out first for a couple of times, but Sanders ignored him. They had wanted to see him make a fool of himself and now he wanted to make fools of them in return, though he knew his cooperation was almost certain to produce the result they, not he, hoped for. With a quick running start he leaped, caught the high bar and swung himself up, feeling the strain in his back, shoulder and stomach muscles. He did a series of slow swings, then another of rapid jackknife rolls and then a kip, but his timing was off and as he came down the highly polished wooden floor was too slippery for his leather soles and he went sprawling. In a moment Needham was at his side, helping him up, his face ashamed and gloating. "Pretty good," Needham commented, "for a man out of shape," but it was so clearly a placebo that no one was required to swallow it.

Sanders said nothing. He got to his feet, his chest red and slightly scraped from the slide along the floor, and stood unsteadily where he was. Sheila brought his shirt, helped him into it and fumbled badly with his buttons until he took the chore over from her himself, but Beth, eyes and smile fixed, neither spoke nor moved, showed neither solace nor sympathy.

They were finishing the champagne in the living room when, as if she'd been thinking of it all evening, Sheila Needham remarked, "How much like him you really are, Elliott. Truly *tel père, tel fils.*"

"Did you know Elliott's father, Mrs. Needham?" Beth's curiosity was kindled.

Sheila nodded. "Jim and I knew both his parents. Lovett Sanders and the two of us were all working press in Paris before the last big war."

"That long ago?" Beth asked, so innocently and nastily that Sanders wanted to slap her.

"That long ago," Sheila conceded.

"It's not all *that* long ago," Needham said, more jovial than was called for, almost flexing his muscles and displaying his tan.

"What sort of man was he?" Beth asked. The question was not asked casually.

"Good newspaperman," Needham interjected, "and a great ladies' man."

"Like Elliott," Beth gibed.

"Well, you'd know more about that than I," Sheila said levelly. She stood up, steadying herself with an effort, poured still another glass in spite of Needham's disapproving look, then went very carefully to the glass wall, put her forehead against the glass and peered into the night. Silently she stood there squinting for a long time, then drank her glass off in a single draught and stepped back. "Lovett Sanders was more than just a good newspaperman," she began, "he was a very *good* man. Not in the Rotary Club or Babbitt way—Lord knows he was no Babbitt and he wouldn't have gone over big with the little lady in Dubuque—but in a deeper, more important way. He loved his profession though he wasn't awed by it; in fact, I don't think he much liked most people who worked on papers.

"Lov Sanders had more damn charm than an impoverished Italian count on the make and he liked people. He got more stories that way just because people liked him. He even liked women, if they're people, and he especially liked to make love to them, if that's what a ladies' man is. But he was no Don Juan who had to keep score and make conquests"—she shot a glance at Sanders—"and he wasn't a perpetual boy who had to be mothered. You could do the town with him and have a stimulating, gay and delightful companion, full of laughs, who drank and could hold his liquor, who danced like a dream and loved to dance, who could walk with you in the rain and hold your hand. He was a man you could go to with a problem, a man on whose shoulder you could cry, who gave you solace and comfort, and didn't use the opportunity to score.

"No one went away from Lov Sanders poorer—in money, if you needed a fiver, or in fun, or in feeling, or even in information. More goddam Paris correspondents lived off the journalistic crumbs from his table than I can name, and a couple of them got famous off it too. I'm not ashamed to say that Jim and I did more than once too.

We both got better lessons in politics, history and economics, and sometimes just in writing a good English sentence, than either of us got in college. Eventually it all came in handy.

"He was fierce about facts and honesty: 'Say you don't know if you don't.' 'You're writing today's history for tomorrow, so make sure you know what you're putting down.' I think that stupid naïve bastard really believed that the truth shall make you free—"

"A dedicated man," Beth commented, the taunt clear.

Sheila spun on her heel. "Yes, miss, he was just that. He really took his duties to heart. Duties. Responsibilities. They weren't just words to him. He was what the fourth estate is really supposed to be; he really believed not only in exposing fraud and injustice and tyranny, but in fighting it. And he hated cant and humbug."

"He wanted to do good," Beth said, so poisonously sweet that even a jeer would have been better.

"Yes, and he died for it. He wanted to do good. Is that a vice nowadays? Or shameful?"

"Do-gooders do more harm than most people." Beth's tone was tough. "The road to hell is paved with bleeding hearts' intentions."

Bleeding hearts. George. The echo of Prescott shook him.

Sheila shrugged. "Maybe so. But Lovett Sanders was a very special man. Tough, hard, and persistent. Not a man to be led around by the nose or to lead others around that way. I once heard him say that your mother"—she turned to Sanders—"had given him the motto he'd have put on his escutcheon—if he had an escutcheon. It was the three words she'd learned from her grandfather, who was a doctor."

"Her father's father," Sanders said. "She was always proud of him because he'd studied with and remained friends with Oliver Wendell Holmes. He used to tell her that Holmes knew about childbirth fever and its causes long before Semmelweis and that he'd learned it from Holmes and had, therefore, never lost a patient to puerperal fever." He was surprised that he remembered that at all, but it had come tumbling out without even an effort at recall.

"What great motto was his guiding star?" Beth asked Sheila.

"A Latin saying, a warning to and advice for physicians. Marian's grandfather had passed it on to her father—who was a lawyer?"

Sanders nodded.

"Don't keep us in suspense any longer," Beth scoffed. "Give us this drink from the fount."

Slowly Sheila walked back to the champagne bottle, drew it from the ice bucket and poured herself the remains, watching patiently as the last golden drops fell sparkling into her glass. She raised the glass to her mouth as if it were a toast and said; "*Primum non nocere*. That was the motto: First do no harm."

Beth had understood the Latin even before Sheila had translated it for her and she flushed as if she'd been slapped.

"And now, you must excuse me," Sheila said. "It's late and I'm very drunk. No, Jim, you don't have to explain or apologize for me. I'm quite drunk, an old woman in her cups, talking too much; but I've spoken my piece. Good night to both of you." With shaky stateliness she walked to Sanders, kissed him on both cheeks and embraced him, then shook hands formally with Beth, brushed Needham's lips and, without touching the wrought-iron railing, walked up the stairs and unsteadily out of the room.

Needham got their coats and ushered them to the door, his murmured apologies and explanations too much. "Tired. Worn out. Rough half year. Not feeling well. Bit too much to drink. Sometimes like that. Lovett Sanders was an old friend. Good to her. Taught her, and me too, lots about our trade. Sheila a first-class newspaperwoman, one of the best. Seeing Lov's son a shock. You know, no children of her, of our own . . ." until the door closed behind them and they found themselves alone in the dark, their heels loud on the paved driveway as they walked toward the parked car.

They were down from the hills and not far from her house before Beth spoke. "Was that the way he was?"

"I don't know," Sanders replied. "I never knew him that way."

"But he was your father," she protested.

"Maybe that's why."

Beth shrugged that off impatiently. "It doesn't make sense."

"A lot doesn't—especially about parents. I never knew the same Lovett Carpenter Sanders Sheila and Jim Needham did." Or that his mother had, or John C. Ballinger, or Nathalie Blanchot, or Guitton. Or a host of others. "My father was a parent, a different species altogether, sometimes a devil, sometimes a demigod. I was not quite

[350]

fifteen when he died, not old enough to have a mature, informed view."

"Sometimes a child's-eye view is better."

"Maybe. I can remember how good-looking he was—dashing was the word my mother sometimes used, and other women used too. We'd go into a restaurant, or walk in the street, and people, men *and* women, would turn to look at him."

"Or at your mother?"

Sanders nodded. "Her too. They were a handsome couple. He was dark and dangerous-looking, smoldering as if he were about to burst into flame. Which he was. She was very beautiful, fair-haired and with the high Scottish coloring and fine features of her family and that baffling look of hauteur and serenity. They didn't seem to belong together at all, which was what, I suppose, made them so eye-catching. They looked as if they'd eloped before the age of consent which was, of course, in my mother's case, the way it happened."

"Romeo and Juliet."

"Well, mother was nineteen and not fourteen and my father twenty-four, but there were similarities. Certainly my mother's family didn't have much use for my father."

"Why?"

"I don't know."

"Weren't you curious? After my parents died, I tried to find out everything I could about them. I read letters Aunt Katharine had kept. I read ones that went back to their courtship. I talked to their old college chums, their horsey and bridge-playing cronies; in fact, I got involved with Bill Daulton, I think, because he knew them, had been their friend, and could talk about them as though they were alive."

"One time, after my father died," Sanders said, "I read everything he'd written, listened to the recordings of every broadcast he'd made, to see if I could find the man behind them. But I think that was more confusing than helpful. I never really understood Lovett Carpenter Sanders. I have a better insight now, but I don't think I understand him yet."

"Why not?"

"The parts of the man I knew could easily have fitted the parts I unearthed, or the parts the Needhams told about tonight. But so could a lot of other and different parts."

"Were you satisfied, are you satisfied, to let it go at that?"

"There isn't much choice." The man is dead, he added silently to himself, and besides that was in another country.

"I couldn't let go until I'd worked out a clear picture of my parents in my mind," Beth said. "When I did, I found they weren't much, flighty, superficial, useless rich people. If they'd lived I'm sure I wouldn't have liked them especially and I'm certain I wouldn't have had any respect for them at all."

"You're hard to please—and it's hard to know." The dead, he thought, have no one, really, to speak in their behalf. Who, what, speaks for the dead?

"But with Aunt Katharine it was harder, it still is." Her voice, filled with thwarted longing, hesitated and then broke.

" '*Je veux m'anéantir dans ta gorge profonde,*' " Sanders recited, " 'and find the freshness of the tomb on your breast.' "

"How in God's name do you make sense of that and the prim maiden aunt I knew?"

" '*Resigne-toi, mon coeur,*' " Sanders advised, not gently, " '*dors ton sommeil de brute.*' "

" 'Resign yourself, my heart; sleep your brutish sleep,' " Beth repeated pathetically after him. "I wish I hadn't been such an ass, such a complete ass, while she was alive. I loved her and I don't think she ever knew. How could she?" She shook herself impatiently. "When I didn't know myself until after she was gone."

At her door Beth asked him in for a nightcap but the evening had been too bruising, the day altogether overwhelming, and he felt drained and exhausted. Though he refused, she didn't leave the car; instead she slumped down in the seat next to him and in a small voice said, "This business of parents, genes, nature, nurture, I wish I knew what they all meant."

Sanders switched off the engine and headlights, put the emergency brake on and leaned back, resting his tense neck on the seat, peering up at the shadowy smooth upholstered ceiling of the car. "Your child?" he asked, instinctively feeling that was what she was referring to.

Beth glanced at him out of the corner of her eye. "You're very perceptive, Mr. Sanders, almost intuitive. The good reporter once more. *Tel père, tel fils?* Yes, *tel père, tel fils* is the question. My child. My Son. Steven Prescott's and mine."

"Not George's?"

"That was something different."

"Why?"

"Because the child didn't live long enough, because George didn't let it." She gestured in the shadows as if her hands were releasing a long-captive pigeon into the air. "He killed it."

"Because it was Prescott's?"

Beth shifted uncomfortably in her seat. "Maybe because it wasn't his. I don't know. And it finished things between us. Otherwise, no matter what you think, it might have worked out between us."

"The child?"

"Don't be so stupid, Elliott. Not the child, the marriage." Her anger burst through, then receded. "I didn't understand that either. Until later. Maybe. I'm still not sure. Always too little, too late."

Lovett Carpenter Sanders had always joked about O'Hara's laws and when finally Sanders asked him who O'Hara was, his father had laughed; but he had given him the laws: Nothing will go as you plan it; everything will take longer than you expect; and all of it will cost more than you anticipate. Sanders had found that if his father's O'Hara was apocryphal, his laws were nonetheless truly canonical. Sanders repeated the laws to Beth and tried to give them some of his father's O'Hara brogue in the delivery but Beth didn't smile, didn't acknowledge their rightness. "The child," she said, then irritably, "why do I go on calling it the child? Or worse, it? He had a name, we baptized him, though I didn't give a damn, didn't want to, but George insisted. John Marshall Christiansen, after George's great-grandfather, the one who brought the family to California from New England."

"With your family name in it," Sanders said, "it sounds as if the boy was named after the Chief Justice." And then Sanders remembered King had told him that Christiansen had baptized the child differently, named it after him, John King Christiansen. Which was it?

"Chief Justice," she snorted, "chief injustice! Phocomelia. That's what they called it. 'A not uncommon genetic defect,' the doctors said." She mocked the callous detachment of medical diagnosis. "A basket case. Chief justice, indeed."

In his throat, the lump seemed painfully swollen and beating like a separate heart. Sanders had the illusion that if someone simply jarred him slightly, or if he even hiccuped, he might spit out the lump and his heart, and his whole life, on the ground. His head was so heavy he was certain he could not lift it off the seat, and as he listened to her, felt her keening and wailing passion as something vibrating inside him, as something of his own, his hands began to tremble and he had to steady them by clutching the steering wheel.

"I loved it. I nursed it. I could feel it at my breast suckling as if it were connected to my heart, as if my blood were tied into its arteries, as if it were still attached to my placenta. How can you explain that to a man? You won't understand. You can't. George didn't understand—though he said he did, made believe he did. I stayed awake nights just looking at it. *It!* Why do I keep saying it? Jamie. A lovely baby, happy, blue-eyed, sparkling with life and intelligence.

"But when I saw the other mothers and their babies, and they were doing things with their hands and arms, and crawling with their legs, standing up in their carriages and cradles and playpens, I stayed awake crying all night. I couldn't stop myself, no matter what I did.

"My milk went bad. I was full of rage and hatred and the sense of being picked on, singled out, and that went right through my breast to Jamie. The pediatrician advised me to put him on formula but I wouldn't, I couldn't. And he began to get sick, to throw up, to be sleepless, and I slept even less and was more anxious than ever.

"After Jamie was born, after I came home from the hospital, George was very quiet. At first I thought it was because of the way Jamie'd been born, the phocomelia. He was very good with the baby, he could handle Jamie even better than I could, and he didn't seem to mind taking care of him, or getting up during the night if he cried, but he didn't say anything about that. And then I thought maybe it was because of the work at Berkeley. He was studying for the doctor's orals and he was working very hard, harder than I'd ever seen him work before. And I thought too that maybe it was

[354]

because of us, because everything was going wrong between us. I didn't have time for George because of Jamie. Even when we went to bed together, my body and mind were somewhere else and George knew it. I guess I didn't take too many pains to hide it either. I wasn't at my very best.

"When things got really bad and I couldn't sleep and the milk went sour and Jamie was unhappy, I could see George suffering. He lost weight, his eyes looked as if they were made of glass, his lips were pale all the time and he kept wetting them as if he was in a desert. And that tic was there all the time now, leaping across his face like little electric jolts trapped in his bones, and trying to break out of his flesh. But I couldn't talk to him about it, about Jamie, about anything. George tried to talk to me a couple of times, but I'd just start to cry and he'd stop.

"And then he killed Jamie. Don't look startled like that, again. Yes, George murdered him."

Insistently, wearily, but unable to raise his head to look at her, Sanders said, "George Christiansen was not a murderer."

Shrilly, like metal scratching glass, her voice cut through him. "He murdered the baby, I tell you! The doctors told us we'd have to be especially careful of pneumonia because the baby couldn't move around enough the way other babies did. George must have remembered that. Oh, yes, it must have stuck in his brain. Because one night, one of the few bitter-cold nights we had all that year, he left Jamie's windows wide open all night."

"An accident," Sanders said, the voice of reason so weak now he could barely hear it himself.

"It could have been but it wasn't. I hadn't been sleeping and I was half out of my mind by then so George gave me a couple of Nembutals that night and I went out like a light."

"Coincidence," Sanders croaked.

Beth ridiculed him. "Coincidence! When I woke up the next morning, bleary-eyed, and went into Jamie's room, the windows were wide-open, Jamie was uncovered, naked, his hair matted with frost. He was already coughing and his eyes were pasted together with that yellow rheum. George was gone. He'd left for Berkeley. He usually did that day because he had an early morning class, so

[355]

at first it didn't mean anything to me. But then I saw that the baby's bed had been moved across the room, from the wall to the windows, right under the open windows, and the blankets were on the floor. Coincidence?" She sat up stiffly. "When I called, the pediatrician came right over, took one look and sent us to the hospital, took us, in his car. They did everything they could—antibiotics, sucked out the mucus, put him in the oxygen tent—but in forty-eight hours Jamie was dead."

When her sobbing abated, Sanders asked softly, "Wasn't it better that way? What kind of life could Jamie look forward to without arms and legs?"

Violently she pounded her clenched fists against the seat upholstery. "No! No! Nothing is better than life. Nothing. Look at what they can do now with prosthesis. Look at—oh, what's the use of that? He's dead."

"Even if George left those windows open deliberately—"

"If! He always looked in on the baby during the night and before he left for school. And the bed was moved, across the room, from one wall to the other."

"—he might have been right. He knew the child would never be able to care for itself. He might have done it for both of your sakes."

"For my sake!" She laughed crazily. "He really helped me all right—right into a nervous breakdown. Postpartum psychosis, they called it. George-induced psychosis, that was what it was. He drove me right out of my mind."

"So it was all George's fault, huh?"

Unwillingly she admitted that George had been marvelous to her after that. He'd given up studying for the doctor's orals, stayed with her through the crying jags, the melancholia, the hallucinations, the terrible dreams, the desire to kill herself—and the attempts. The psychiatrists recommended that he put her in a mental hospital, at least a nursing home, but she was terrified and he refused. He had taken her for treatment, driven her for trips to Monterey, to Palm Springs, to Vegas, to the high country in the Sierras, had fed, bathed, dressed her, put her to sleep. "He took better care of me than he did of Jamie," she concluded.

[356]

"Maybe he had hope for you and none for the child," Sanders suggested.

"Hope. There's always hope. While there's life."

"Some people hang on to it longer than others."

"I see cancer patients every day, terminal ones too, and some of them have hope to the end."

"There are all kinds of ways to fool yourself. Hope is a whore. And when you traffic with whores," he began, but he thought of Monique and knew that it didn't apply, that whores were sometimes a hope too. "I still don't think George killed the boy."

"No. You wouldn't, you couldn't. Because you're so crazy tied up with him, what he was, how he died, with what you think he was. Good George, dear George, heroic George, do-gooder George."

Slowly the anger simmering in his chest and guts boiled up into his throat. "George loved you. He married you when your paramour wouldn't. Your good doctor. He gave the child his name. He saved your life and your sanity—"

"And he killed Jamie."

"Yes, he's dead, and so is George."

"Good, he deserved it."

Sanders exploded. "You bitch! You miserable ungrateful self-centered bitch! Get the hell out of this car! Do you hear me!" He reached across her, opened the car door and half shoved her out onto the sidewalk. She stood there for a moment, then put her face back inside through the car window and said, "And I don't like your goddam *nouveaux-riches* friends either!"

It was a long time after her door had slammed before Sanders could control his breathing, and then a powerful nausea swept over him until he was afraid he would throw up.

In the apartment, finally, spots exploding in front of his eyes, his body shaking with fever and chills, he collapsed over the washbasin and was sick. When the heaving and spasms were over, he managed to wash, brush his teeth and get into his pajamas before he fell prostrate into bed. The last thing that flashed through his mind like an illuminated news report was *Primum non nocere*, PRIMUM NON NOCERE, the type varying from the tiniest almost unreadable six-point to skyscraper-proportioned bold letters that thrust up into the clouds and were lost there, and then he dropped into coma. In the morning he knew he was sick: He had a fever, his nose and eyes ran, a cough racked his chest, but he could swallow—his phlegm—easily: the *boule hystérique* had gone.

* * *

It was a week of feverish restless sleep from which he came up as from unplumbed seas, rising up into the light for moments at first, then later for longer periods of time before plunging back down into the abyss. Where he swam he did not see clearly but he felt immersed in the sea of his past, not recollected in tranquility but revisited in terror. Between storms of recollection which shook him like agues, he knew he should call a doctor and didn't, he knew he could call Beth and wouldn't, wanted to call Laura but knew he couldn't, was conscious that he had to telephone Needham and did, twice dialing the wrong number, reporting sick and requesting that someone else cover the demonstrations while he was out and to keep the pictures and the original reports on file for him. Needham agreed, asked if he wanted any help and seemed immensely relieved when Sanders said he thought he'd get along. The third day, just after Sanders had managed to persuade the house superintendent with a five-dollar tip to shop for and deliver a mammoth order of groceries and whisky for him, Sheila Needham knocked at the door and, without waiting for his reply, entered like a ray of golden light in a yellow linen suit, smartly groomed, radiantly smiling, carrying a large wicker picnic hamper out of which came thick, hot onion soup with croutons and cheese, cold breast of chicken, still-warm *baguette*, and a bottle of dry white California wine. She kissed him on both cheeks, felt his forehead with a cool hand and then worldlessly and efficiently set about taking care of him. With almost professional ease that reminded him of Cathy Sullivan, she changed sheets without turning him out of bed, put the groceries the superintendent had left on the kitchen table and counters into the cupboards and refrigerator, and took all the refuse to the incinerator. She discovered a bed tray Jason Howe had and brought him his lunch on it with a single red rose in a small glass vase that had,

[358]

with the onion soup, chicken and French bread, come out of the capacious wicker basket. She didn't argue with him when he refused her offer to feed him but she waited until he found he couldn't hold the spoon steady or raise it easily to his mouth, and then, over his faint objections, Sheila propped him up on the pillows she had plumped and fed him.

For days thereafter he could not really distinguish which meals she fed him and which he somehow managed to take himself, stumbling from refrigerator to stove, living on heated tinned soups or whatever else Sheila Needham had left him neatly prepared, carefully wrapped, cooked, baked or roasted, or ingredients assembled for him to heat and eat. And even on the one day a week when the cleaning woman came and did for him, she seemed to be Sheila.

* * *

The flat in the Avenue Mozart was cheerful as the one in the Rue Daunou had not been. High ceilings and big windows that flooded it with light and sunshine for a good part of the day gave the apartment a feeling of airiness and spaciousness that Sanders found invigorating. Except for the brass bed which Monique insisted on bringing along from the Rue Daunou, all the other furnishings at the Avenue Mozart were newly acquired though not new because Monique both disliked modern furniture and could not bring her frugal Norman soul to buy anything except secondhand even with his money, so Sanders found himself finally ensconced in a second apartment almost the complete antithesis of his legal residence with Elaine. Unlike the cool modern Scandinavian straight lines, the comfortable overstuffed old-fashioned chairs and sofas, beautiful wooden tables and armoires, the patina of years having given the woods a dark glow and sheen that only long care and polishing could produce, were restful and had the dents and marks of having been lived with and enjoyed. Though it took several months to find and to buy the various pieces—Monique went everywhere for her sales and bargains, from the Flea Market to auctions and to the private homes of those recently bereaved by death or divorce, with a hard-driving skill and perseverance that reminded him of someone just stepped out of the pages of Balzac—she soon had the place more comfortable than his Quai de Passy flat. And only after Monique had finished buying what she thought she needed, down to some heavy heirloom silver she had found at a small-town Normandy auction, did she tell him that she'd been so successful in part because a lawyer friend of hers, a former "client"—she stressed the *former*—had given her tips on the auctions and on the deaths and divorces.

Sanders knew that Monique continued to have her "clients"— some of them he presumed were "regulars"—but she was discreet and he kept their prearranged agreement about time and her availability so that there were no embarrassing encounters or *flagrante delictos*. Monique never discussed her "friends" with him, or even her family and her past, and when he tried to pry she would turn his questions aside with either a joke or a secret smile which baffled and enraged him, or with a caress. She extended him the same privileges: She never asked about Elaine or his family, his past or his work. If he told her he had to leave Paris on an assignment, or couldn't see her on one of his usual days or evenings, she neither questioned him nor made any comment. Sometimes he thought of that as exquisite tact, other times as not giving a damn; but if he berated her she quickly stopped him. "You are a free man. You come and go as you please. You owe me nothing."

"And you owe me?"

"My time, my concern, my affection, my body."

"No more?"

She didn't answer.

"You owe me those things, but don't I owe you anything?"

"You take care of me."

"Money," he said, the disgust plain in his voice.

"Money, yes," Monique replied, unembarrassed, "but not only money. You are kind to me, you are good to me, you treat me like a person. And money is not nothing either. When, how much, how a man gives money tells a great deal."

Sanders wanted to press her further but just how far and for exactly what he wasn't sure, and something in her mien warned him not to trespass, not to cross rivers that could become, would become, Rubicons, and so he was constrained and—sometimes—held

[360]

his peace. In bed Monique fulfilled him as no other woman ever had, taking him into her with a gladness and generosity that had neither hypocrisy nor guile in it, though it knew bounds, bounds he felt but could not define, for no matter how deep and vigorous his thrust, how passionate her embrace and response, there were in her locked doors to which he had no keys. From her he drew calm and courage to return to the Quai de Passy and to Elaine and the mad circling of his marriage. There, in the bedroom that now seemed always to be darkly lit green even in daylight, Elaine waited, usually reclining on the bed and apparently reading poetry or the green paper-covered pornography which had now filled one bedstand bookcase and overflowed to another. At first she wouldn't reply to his greeting, feigning that she had not heard him or that she was immersed in her reading, and somehow, when he bent to kiss her, she always managed to turn her cheek just that fraction of an inch which made affection awkward and her lips impossible. "Working late again?" she asked, her face so close to his that he could almost feel the heat of pain and hatred darting from her eyes. He grunted to avoid the outright lie but the geyser would not be capped, the ugly scene spewed like oil from some underground spout under intolerable pressure and covered the landscape. "You're back? Finished? Have a good one?" When, as usual, he didn't answer, her tone grew more strident and accusing, cursing his ancestors, particularly his "fancy-dan, studhorse father, Cocksman Carpenter Sanders," then went on to berate his sluts, whores and prostitutes, and—when she was especially beyond his control—his cunts, a word she normally hated and avoided with a grim prudish fastidiousness. She painted pictures of his sexual proclivities and depravities that would have done justice to a Persian pasha, a Kashmiri prince or a Javanese voluptuary, reciting accounts of his extravagances that made the Kama Sutra an amateur's handbook and Krafft-Ebing a boy-scout manual until he was undressed and lay next to her in the great bed. There, enveloped in the cloud of *muguet* that was as much her scent as the smell of her flesh and hair, she began. *Lily of the valley. As the lily among thorns, so is my love among the maidens.* His mother's religious training put to his father's vices. A thorn among lilies, a valley among mountains, a desert with the ever-receding promise of oases green with date palms and water, she began, her touch nasty and nettled, harsh and hurtful, and at last a burning scourge until her icy lips, scarlet as blood, devoured him, her fingers kneaded him, drew him, her mouth bit his seed, a score of feminine wiles that denied him access left him limp and longing. *Give us this day our daily bed.*

Deliver us. . . . In the dark, neither mind nor body at peace, Sanders asked her for still another time how long, how long could he wait in the antechamber of her desire, how long kneel before her lunacy like a suppliant, her shudder his rebuke, her tightly joined thighs his reply. How much he needed to couple with her, to sink himself inside her, melding his flesh with hers, plowing her earth and planting his posterity there, only he knew. But no matter how he rehearsed it in his brain, coated the feeling in words that shaped but did not convey his desire, Elaine rebuffed them, engulfed in the fear that offered nothing in the darkness except the green night-light in the distance, wait and hope, begged him for time, raged that neither psychiatry nor argument nor understanding would help her.

From the moment that morning that he awoke and saw Elaine's funereal face scrutinizing his as if for some assurance in his features she could not find in their life together, Sanders knew in his bones it was going to be a bad day. The *flics* had captured a former French Army and now OAS Colonel, an Indochina and Algerian paratroop hero, trussed up in a truck, and had taken him into custody. On a tip, Sanders had arrived in the small street not far from Notre Dame only moments after the police. The only reporter there, he had been deliberately unobtrusive, taken pictures with both cameras, both equipped as usual with telescopic lenses, showing how the capture had been organized and how badly and unnecessarily the Colonel had been roughed up. The *flics* hadn't noticed him but two plainclothesmen had and they'd confiscated the Leica, though he managed to hide the Nikon just before they reached him. Two other tips from "contacts" had cost him more than 2,500 francs but had elicited the information that the Colonel had been drugged and kidnaped in Switzerland by the SDECE, flown out of the country and planted in Paris for the police to find. Though Sanders had written the story as another OAS *attentat* to murder the General thwarted by French security and counterintelligence forces, publication of the story and pictures he'd managed to save in the Nikon, hung by its strap behind the door in front of which he'd been standing when he saw the plainclothesmen, was sure to ruin whatever "cover story" the SDECE had invented for their coup. Tessier had behaved like a lunatic, ranting about proof and documentation as if he were a press attaché at the Ministry of Information instead of a magazine editor; he wouldn't even protest the confiscation of the Leica, howled that the magazine refused to pay the costs of replacing it, and displayed an irrational testiness Sanders could only attribute to resentment that an American had run down the story even though the American was in his employ. After quarreling about the lead, captions, about sentences describing the deliberate beating of the Colonel, about cropping pictures and using ones that showed the Colonel's battered face, Tessier sullenly initialed his copy and photos for press and shooed him out of the office.

Coming up the stairs at the Avenue Mozart, carrying a handful of azure irises with golden hearts that he had bought from an old-lady flower vendor in the street, Sanders was momentarily cheered, but when he heard the music from Monique's record player echoing down from above, the same sense of doom enveloped him. He'd insisted on giving her a record player shortly after they rented the flat because he knew how much she liked the French *chansons* of the streets and the cafés. The only modern and American furnishing in the flat, the phonograph looked remarkably out of place on the marble-topped antique sideboard where Monique had set it. Though the recording echoing down the stairwell was not one he'd bought for her, Sanders recognized it instantly, Patachou singing *J'Attendrai:*

> *J'attendrai*
> *Le jour et la nuit*
> *J'attendrai toujours ton retour.*

Was it *his* return Monique awaited always, day and night, or some one else's, some other man of whom he'd never heard? Had Mo-

[363]

nique bought the record for herself or had some "friend" or "client" given it to her for services remembered or rendered? His feet grew heavier, he slowed his steps, and the irises, so bright and lively, dimmed while the sophisticated longing of the song hung in the gloom like crepe.

> *J'attendrai*
> *Car l'oiseau qui s'enfuit*
> *Vient chercher l'oubli*
> *Dans le nid.*

Certainly he was the one bird who daily flew away and came back to seek his oblivion in her nest, but was he the only one?

At the door he could hear Monique pacing inside and singing softly along with the clear voice of Patachou:

> *Le temps passe et court*
> *En battant tristement*
> *Dans mon coeur plus lourd*
> *Et pourtant*
> *J'attendrai ton retour.*

Sanders knocked, Monique opened the door, expecting him, her eyes shining, and smilingly embraced him, then put her finger to his lips to keep silent and listen. Arm in arm, they leaned against the door and each other, the bouquet of irises dangling from his fist as the voice mourned:

> *Les fleurs palissent,*
> *L'ombre se glisse dans le jardin,*
> *L'horloge tisse,*
> *Je crois entendre ton pas.*
> *Le vent m'apporte des bruits lointains.*
> *Guettant ma porte j'écoute en vain.*
>
> *Hélas, plus rien, plus rien, plus rien ne vient.*
> *J'attendrai.*

When the record was over, Monique danced him into the bed-room in an uncommon burst of gaiety, plopped him on the bed and made swift and passionate love to him, not allowing him to take his clothes off, joking as she swayed astride that she was *dans une bonne position* (well-off), that such things often led to being *dans une position intéressante* (to being pregnant), and Sanders, the melancholy still draping his heart, tried to match her exhilaration by rejoining that he found himself in a *position fatigante,* even *embarrassante,* chiefly because he was *dans une position peu elevée* (in an inferior position) and if she kept doing what she was doing so skillfully, delightfully, he was not even sure he would *être en position de* (be able to) keep his *feux de position* (parking lights) on.

Earlier in the day he had phoned to tell Monique that he would have to leave early because Elaine had opera tickets for that evening and now, as they greedily ate the pâté out of the small crock she had put on the bed table and washed it down with red wine, Monique took a long slim packet out of the night-table drawer and handed him the first formal gift she'd ever made him. Wrapped in the paper and ribbon of one of the expensive Boulevard des Capucines men's shops, the box contained a white silk dress scarf with his monogram.

"You like it?" Monique asked.

"Beautiful," Sanders said, and it was, but how could he explain a third dress scarf to Elaine?

"You must wear it to the opera tonight, in my honor," Monique said, jubilantly winding it around his neck in the casual way his boyhood pilot heroes, Fonck and Guynemer, had worn theirs.

Sanders was touched, moved, but mistrustful of the felicity.

"You promise?" Monique insisted, mischievously tightening the scarf around his throat in a mock threat of strangulation.

"I promise."

Not until he was at the door, about to leave, did Monique tell him that she was going to Cannes for ten days with "an old friend," leaving the very next morning.

"Why didn't you tell me before?" he asked angrily.

"I didn't know for sure until yesterday," she said, "and I didn't want to spoil today." She covered his mouth with fingers that smelled of pâté, red wine and lovemaking. "Please, Elliott, no scenes, no quarrels. *Je ne te reproche rien.* I like this man but he is not important. Between us, between you and me now, things, feelings, are too intense, too intimate. I must go away for a time or I will lose my hold on myself. I cannot afford that and it will be bitter for both of us if I should. It is only ten days. I'll be back and it will be all right."

"Only ten days," he repeated, the days stretching interminable before him as he stood stubbornly in the doorway, reproaching her, until she pushed him out and shut the door behind him. As he went down the stairs, he heard the music begin once again and Patachou's cool weary *J'Attendrai* reverberated down the stairs again, parting and farewell.

"And how is your whore?" Elaine greeted him as soon as he walked in the door. It was the first time she'd used the singular that way and the entire day's foreboding told him that the worst was yet to come. Someone had seen him with Monique at Fouquet's; one of Elaine's old Avenue Foch crowd had reported it to her with evident relish—and doubtless to all of the de Besancourt crowd—and lavish details that included Monique's appearance, coiffure, dress and demeanor. No denials had worked when he was innocent; none now worked when he was guilty though he continued to assert, to explain, that in the course of his work he had to lunch or dine or drink with many women and he couldn't even remember which one this was that she referred to. The air was filled with Elaine's expletives, *putain, prostituée, bâtard, vagin, libertine,* as they dressed and then, worse, with an icy silence as they slouched on opposite sides of the cab that took them to the Opéra.

The opera was *Carmen* and they shared a box with a young Japanese couple, clearly on their honeymoon, who sat next to them wideeyed, bucktoothed and grinning, speaking no other language but their own, and listened enraptured to the thin, uncertain voices of the French, taking occasional and startling flash-bulb photographs of the stage—until the first intermission, when they bowed their way out of the box and never returned. But through the performance the only music Sanders heard was Patachou; and not even the frigid way in which Elaine held herself aloof from him, not deigning to touch even his sleeve, shook the quivering *J'Attendrai* from his ears until two words resounded from the stage like shots and, in aria and recitative, hung over him like fate. He heard the words together—*l'amour, la mort*—and didn't know whether it was mispronunciation, his imagination, or Bizet's intention. Love and death. *L'amour. La mort.*

Afterwards Elaine insisted on having supper at Fouquet's, as if by some compulsion she was forced to visit and make him revisit what she considered to be the scene of his crime. The weather was still warm, the sky bright with moonlight and soiled with stars, and the tables on the terrace were almost full, but Elaine wanted to sit indoors in the almost empty and luxurious melancholy of the restaurant, where she took as proof of his infidelity the *"Bon soir, M'sieu Sanders"* of the maître and their waiter though Sanders reminded her, had told her many times before, that because Fouquet's was close to his office it was one of the places where he often ate and drank. While Elaine slowly and sullenly ate *escargots de bourgogne, poule en chemise* and *mousse au café,* Sanders, unable to eat, drank brandy after brandy until by the time they rose to leave he was quite drunk. Outside, as he was about to hail a taxi, Elaine walked off and left him standing there, one arm foolishly raised like the Statue of Liberty. He followed her up the Champs-Élysées, strolling at her side, not touching her, Elaine breaking the silence only to remark on the prowling pairs of whores on foot, or those soliciting more obviously from automobiles which cruised slowly along the street close to the curbstones, asking him which of the *putains* he knew and what their specialties were, insisting he enumerate the virtues of their vices, as if he really knew them all and could explain them as simply as Fouquet's *carte.*

Only after they had walked half across the Étoile, through the Arch which memorialized in stone all those battles where French blood had been shed—Wagram, Austerlitz, Iéna—past the Unknown Soldier's flame sputtering in its brass cup buried in the concrete—*l'amour, la mort*—and after he'd taken her arm and, drunkenly loud, insisted that he wanted to go home, was he able to persuade her to get into a cab with him. And only after they'd crossed the rest of the Étoile and gone all the way round the perimeter to the Avenue Foch were they able to find a taxi. The driver took them down the Rue Paul-Valéry through Belloy and past the Place des États-Unis, which loomed up a surprise, the doughboy and poilu unmoving in their friendship, shadows hulking in the night—*l'amour, la mort*—before they turned into Iéna and headed for home.

Undressing, Elaine sat on the far side of the bed with her back to him, her long unblemished back, every vertebra beautifully articulated from coccyx to skull, a long xylophone of bones he wanted to caress, percuss, break. In bed she shrank from his touch, moving as far away from him as the confines of the double bed would permit, and his anger and passion, his melancholy and frustration, all inflamed by alcohol, flared. "You holier-than-thou bitch," he erupted, and grew angrier when her back went rigid, "what do you want to do, destroy me altogether?"

Elaine turned her body and cold eyes toward him, her warm breasts red-eyed beneath and peering through her sheer nightdress, another glance, a contradictory and ambivalent invitation, before she reached for him, eyes ardent now, all scratching nails and nipping teeth until, aroused, he tried and tried again to breach the barrier of her thighs, only to be put off, pushed off, until in despair, like a dog put out of doors for the night, he howled, "Let me—let me in," and she, heaving beneath him, terror-stricken, threw him off, put him off. In one ungovernable burst of rage then he pinned her beneath him and savagely slapped her face and buttocks and legs while she, thrashing beneath, struggled to throw him off again. But the harder she fought the more stingingly he slapped her and though she continued to resist he saw and felt her stirred, quickened, until a final slap at last unlocked her legs, her thighs parted and brutally he entered her as if he were bulling through a door, with a direct primitive thrust to the very bottom of her, knowing there had been others before but not caring, warlike and charging, drenched and turbulent in his own storms, seized and swept away by hers, until at her moment, if it was her moment, Elaine cried out in tormented ecstasy, "You—you—and your filthy prick!" and he came finally weeping to rest, crucified and crowned in a consummation that had brought him nothing he wanted. When at last he

[368]

could see her face, Sanders kissed her twisted, bitten and bleeding lips, her tear-soaked lashes and tear-stained cheeks, ashamed of the fingermarks he had splayed on her fair skin, conscience-stricken by what he knew was as much rape as anything else, and heard at the back of his head the quaking soprano of the diva in *Carmen* earlier that evening croaking her fatal *l'amour, la mort.*

* * *

By the end of the week Sanders was able to get his own meals, walk around the flat uncertainly and even sit, well wrapped in robe and blankets, on the balcony, numbly watching the sun go down behind the mountains into the sea, trying to put out of his mind every thought of Paris, every recollection of Elaine and Monique that came to him because they threatened to inundate him, sweep him away from himself, drag him under. Sitting there he felt like one of the tuberculars, removed from life, wrapped in a cocoon to bear the Alpine colds, like a character out of *The Magic Mountain* waiting to be told that he would never leave Davos to go down to the plains again, to do battle and to die in war. Everything he did remember, everything he turned to in the past, wounded and pained him: the hurtful things because he had endured them, the pleasant ones because they were gone. Memories become symptoms as wounds become scars, he thought: tics, *boules hystériques,* grippe, vaginismus, perhaps even cancer and· basket-case babies, not to speak of white slices across black palms, suicide and murder.

The sun was altogether gone, blotches of stars emerged on the feverish skin of sky soon to be deprived of all light when Sheila Needham came out and sat next to him. "Lovely view," she said kindly.

"Better than yours?" he asked.

"Depends on where you sit."

Having Sheila visit—she had missed only two days since he'd been sick and each time brought him marvelously prepared French food, tidying up the flat, changing linens, making beds, doing a host of other chores to make him more comfortable—left him deeply in her debt and uncomfortable. Yet she was discreet, sat with him as she was doing, silent when he did not feel like talking, talking when

[369]

he did, making no explicit demands on him except occasionally holding his hand without pressure as if merely wanting to be reassured that he was still there and alive.

"Why don't you go back to Paris?" Sheila asked. "America isn't for you, this place isn't for you. You've outgrown it."

"Maybe it's outgrown me."

"That too."

"Does it make so much difference where you are? You take yourself along all the time."

"It makes some difference," Sheila maintained. "How much depends—"

"Not much."

"You're staying on because of the girl, because of Beth?"

"You don't like her much, do you?"

"Not much," Sheila echoed. "She's not much good in bed and she can't cook."

"Is that all women are good for?"

Sheila eyed him askance. "That's quite a bit, wouldn't you say?"

"She has money. She's rich," Sanders said.

Sheila stared him down.

"Sheila," he began, with effort, "I'm so grateful, I can't tell you—"

"Then don't."

"I hate collecting interest on my father's principal."

"Principle?"

"Maybe that too."

"Most sons are delighted."

"I'm not most sons."

"Why are you jealous of him, Elliott? Why do you hate him so much? Your father was a good man, he really was, warm and considerate, and a hell of a fine reporter."

"I'm not sure I do hate him. I think I love him, only there's no way now to tell him, to show him, to find out. And I'd like to."

"Of course there is," she said, leaning toward him, brushing his hair out of his eyes—he needed a haircut badly—then pillowing his face on her bosom. Deep in a cloud of lavender perfume, he heard her add, "Your life tells him, the way you live shows him."

Sanders knew that was the only answer but not satisfactory. Lovett Carpenter Sanders was dead; if he couldn't see, couldn't know, if they couldn't come to some agreement or even argue about it, it was really no answer at all.

Sheila held his head, slowly stroking his hair, longingly, a low crooning of doves in her throat. "You could have been *my* son instead of hers," she said, speaking to herself so that there was no need for him to comment.

Gently extricating himself from her embrace, Sanders said, "You could have had children of your own—why didn't you?"

"We tried," Sheila answered, "but—"

"They do miracles now."

Sheila laughed discordantly. "Not that kind of miracle. Once I could have had children. A litter. But once, just one time, long ago, in Paris, I had a small abortion, just a tiny little curettage, that finished all that."

"Not my father?" Sanders asked, surprised by the horror he felt and heard in his voice.

"No, not Lov. Jim."

Sheila sat there, her head listless, eyes shut tight. "Jim wouldn't adopt. Not his sort of thing. Blood, you know. Blood will out. Now it's too late. All over. Jim has the paper, I have Jim, he has me, we both have the house and the cars and the money, and that's the whole ring-a-round-a-rosy. Loving a newspaperman's not front-page." Her voice cracked, only just skirting tears. "It's late-edition. We missed even that and now there's only the blue final left."

* * *

The first morning Sanders was back Needham called him into his office, shook his hand a bit cautiously—half apologetically, half viciously, Sheila had explained that Jim disliked sick people, never visited them, even in the hospital, and was afraid of germs, might, she added hastily, even wear those surgical face masks the Japanese were addicted to except that he felt conspicuous—asked briefly how he was feeling and then, without waiting for an answer, told him that Fillmore had scheduled another Oakland demonstration that morning. The demonstration was at eleven, and driving through the eerie morning ground fog, Sanders thought of Murray Fillmore and Fillmore's father, of Beth and Laura and Peter and George, and of their parents. Were the sins of the fathers always visited on the children? Was that the burden of personal, genetic history that was fate, the chain that could not be broken? Only cycles? What Levi Migdal, quoting his Viennese mentor and pessimistic Jew, had always maintained: the repetition compulsion in personal and human and national history. In the ten days of his illness Sanders had not called any of them, nor had any of them called him. About all except Beth he felt remiss, but Beth, he felt, should have called him. And Laura he should have called.

The counterman in the coffee shop across from the induction center was the same one who'd been there the last time and without waiting brought him a cup of hot coffee. "More trouble?" he asked, grimacing.

"What makes you think that?"

He gestured at Sanders' cameras. "Whenever I see any of you newspaper guys, there's trouble."

"Newspapermen don't make trouble, they only report it."

"Bullshit," the counterman said irascibly. "You guys need headlines. Make news if you got none. Get some fool kid to whong a cop, or some fool cop to whong a kid. Brave as hell, you guys are, with some other guy's ass."

"Had a lot of that the last couple of weeks?"

"Some. Stupid kids trying to close down that induction center, and of course they can't. Can't fight the government. Or the Army. Not that I blame the kids for trying. My nephew's over there and says he couldn't care less for the real estate. Who needs it? We don't go much for rice in this country anyway." Having said his piece, he walked back down the counter.

Once more hordes of foot and mounted police marched in orderly files into the garage across from the induction center and once again Sanders got fine sharp pictures of them. As he stood close up to the restaurant window taking them, the door opened, and in the doorway, almost filling it, stood Peter King. "I thought I'd find you here," Peter said, "taking your little pictures and making your little notes." King sat next to him at the counter, the counterman brought up another cup of coffee and King thanked him.

"Need a cuppa mornings like this. Gets the chill out of your bones," the counterman said. "You another one?" He nodded at Sanders.

"A newspaperman? God forbid!" King's horror was genuine, intense, and comic. "I'm one of those," he added, jerking his head toward the demonstrators in the street.

"Cop?" The counterman's distaste for the police was plain.

"Naw, demonstrator."

"Good for you," the counterman applauded, then went back down the counter.

"Were you looking for me?" Sanders asked.

Head bent over the cup he was holding in both hands, King blew on his coffee to cool it, then sipped noisily. "You ain't been around, man, how come?"

"Sick."

"Something serious, I hope?" King said, unsmiling. Then, switching voices, diction and erudition, he boomed oratorically, *"To live means to be sick a long time: I owe a cock to the god Aesculapius."* And again, "Yassuh, boss, us niggers live sick an die sick; we owes our cocks 'n' balls to tha great white fatha, the Man, Mistuh Charley."

"Why don't you come off it, Peter?"

"Why don't you come on it, Elliott? Scared? This thing too big for you? You've seen that rotten war, you saw what happened to George, and to a lot of others."

"The world's more complicated than you make it. Besides, I thought you were the boy who wanted to do a little kindly killing of your own."

"I am. I do," King said, "but that's in another war, one back here."

"How can you see the world so black and white?" Sanders asked, and the moment he'd said it he knew he'd phrased the question in the worst way possible.

"Man, that's where you miss. Sure is black *and* white, black *against* white."

"You're wrong about that too."

"You ain't seen many niggers at these get-outs, have you?"

"You're here."

[373]

"For my own reasons, but not many other black boys. We savin ourself for biggah things, not real nice, well-mannered stuff like this. We don't believe these preacher types, you know, don't buy this 'black and white together, we will not be moved' shit. We gonna have to do it ouhselves, without Mistuh Charley. For years we take an take. Now we tired of takin. We finished takin. You can tell your readers, Mistuh White Reporter, tell 'em all, we ain't takin no more. We gonna be dishin. I don't give a shit about dyin. I'm hardly livin. All us niggers is like that, hardly livin nohow and not givin a damn about dyin neither. Just as soon die heah as in Vietnam. An if'n ah die ah won't know nuthin bout it. He who dies today is quits tomorrow."

King slurped a little more coffee before he spoke again. "Demonstrations, marches, protests. Shit, man, honkies don care none bout them potatoes. Mistuh Charley, he don give a good crap you march, you carry signs, you lay down in fronta tha fuzz. Whitey, he git the cops to stomp you, beat up on you, an throw you in the paddy wagon. An he look the other way, cause he don like tha sight of blood. Dirty up the sidewalks. Not nuff law 'n' order. Besides, black man's blood runs red too, just like his, an mebbe that remind him. Remind him plenny. You git too uppity, the fuzz shoot you in tha belly and leave you an old jackknife or mebbe a letter opener, so they kin say you try ta cut 'em up first before they plug ya. Well, White Boy"—King poked his finger into Sanders' chest—"you tell 'em we gonna be shootin back. We gonna have rifles an pistols an shotguns an we gonna be shootin back."

"What does that get you, Peter, except a pine box?"

"Man, you a chickenshit honky, Sanders. You spend your whole life being scared, you die all the time, you die every day. You spen yo whole lahf dyin 'n' not livin. Everybody gits his pine box sooner or later. I git mine, you git yours, George, he git his—that's the way them snake eyes roll."

"But when and how you get yours and maybe even what for is what counts. Getting it in a riot is useless. What the hell do you expect to accomplish by killing some white men and probably the wrong ones at that?"

"This war, man. Only another kind of war. You don't understand,

[374]

Sanders, do you? Because you got a Mister Charley mentality. It's like being Samson"—he flexed his biceps and raised his powerful arms above his head as if he was going to tear down the cheap overhead chrome-and-glass lighting fixture with his bare hands— "strong, powerful, determined. You will the temple down on the Philistines' heads, and you pull down what you can yourself, and the Philistines is you, Sanders, and all the Mister Charleys."

"A marvelous gesture, Peter, full of sound and fury and great for a play, but that isn't the way political power is taken. That isn't life, that's one of those dramas you played for the sisters back in school. All Samson got was himself killed. The temple of Dagon was slightly damaged, a couple of thousand were killed among the Philistines, but the rest of them remained in power as before." Sanders remembered that Samson always came to grief because of women, Philistine prostitutes, Gaza harlots, who enticed him. Well, at least that was one temptation Peter King would be immune to.

"If'n ah can kill one of you cats, jus one, ah make mahself all white inside, ah cleanse mah soul," King whispered lovingly. "Just one of"—his eyes were full of love and longing, and his fists clenched and unclenched—"you." His fist clamped around Sanders' biceps and squeezed until Sanders broke the grip and stood up.

"You're crazy," Sanders said softly. *Eyeless in Gaza at the mill with slaves.* What was left but mania, mania to reach the pillars of the temple and pull them down?

"Crazy or not, that's what I want. Now you're mad and you want to fight. Good, good." King got up and slouched into a flatfooted boxer's stance, jabbing the air, then dancing away on his toes.

"I've taken as much guff from you as I'm going to," Sanders said angrily, slapping a dollar bill on the counter. "You want to fight? Okay. Come on outside and we'll try it." In the street the anger catching in his throat made him remember his recent *bolus hystericus* before he saw again the yearning in Peter King's voice and eyes, the craving for death and destruction, for love and fulfillment, the *Liebestod*. Pull down the temple, tear down the walls, kill your friends and allies with your enemies: *We shall overcome.*

In a moment King was at his side, subdued, and gently he put his hand on Sanders' arm. "I'm sorry," King apologized, "I don't

[375]

know what got into me." Then he heard what he'd said and laughed. "Ah, but I do, I do. A priestly prat boy, what can you expect? One of those Catholic schools I was in betweentimes—between the times my old lady was in the booby hatch, which means between times that she had some new man living in the house who I knew was not my daddy—had an Irish priest in it. Father"—he hesitated and Sanders sensed that he had changed the priest's real name in mid-passage—"Lindley, a young, very tormented man who should never have been a priest, certainly never put in charge of children, especially boys."

"He was homosexual?" Sanders asked, more uncomfortable with the word than with the question, uneasy because he knew that his question was a statement.

King nodded. "Queer as a three-dollar bill. And a passionate religious. He was the first white man who cared a damn about me and he gave me a priceless gift: he really taught me to read. He also taught me to pray, but always on our knees, always on the cold floor or the cold stones. I suppose in order to mortify his flesh he had to mortify ours. At night he came to the dormitory I slept in for lights-out to see that all was in order before we slept and he would harangue us about the horrors of sex and the flesh and the burning torments of hell that awaited any of us who indulged. He'd march down the aisle between our cots to see if anyone was 'building tents' and woe to anyone he caught who was. It was not only the harangue and the public embarrassment that terrified us—he'd strip the bedclothes back so that the boy's pathetic hard-on was there for everyone to see for the few seconds it stood in the fright and cold—but the public reminders and the penances and the painful strokes of the wooden classroom pointer he always carried. And he wasn't above reaching his hands under the sheets to see if you had your pajama bottoms on because if you didn't that was *prima facie* evidence that you were whacking off, or had, or would be soon.

"I heard the other kids talking about him, saying he was a fag, a queer, a homo, always fiddling their diddles, always around when the boys were taking showers, but I didn't believe any of it. Orphanages are like that, full of gossip, mean, vicious talk, and it was

[376]

some time before, in my innocence, I learned most of the talk was true. Then, one day, I was late in finishing an exam in Father . . . Lindley's Latin class. He was talking to two boys and had taken his wallet out to give them a dollar bill, for some collection they were making, for foreign missions, I think, and something fell to the floor. I had to finish the exam so I went back to writing, but when I looked up they were all gone and the little square of paper was still there next to the desk leg. I was supposed to leave my exam paper on the desk for him but before I did I picked up that other paper—by the feel of it I could tell it was a small snapshot—and put it into my pocket without even looking at it.

"Later that night, after lights-out, I remembered it and got it out of my trousers to look at it. It was a very sharp picture of a naked boy from the waist to the mid-thighs, showing his prick and balls and pubic hair. No face, no identifying marks, nothing except those genitals in clear close-up. I lay awake that night, all night, in a shaking sweat, my heart pounding, wondering what to do but I couldn't make up my mind. All next day I was taking that snapshot out of my pocket when I could, when no one was looking, and staring at it, excited and afraid, terrified I'd be caught with it. It was so worrisome I guess I never heard O'Ma—Lindley until someone hissed that he was watching and then he was bearing down on me with that wooden pointer. I had the snapshot in my fingers and I knew I couldn't hide it so I tore it up and put the pieces in my mouth and tried to swallow them. It was like trying to chew glass, hard-edged photographic paper doesn't chew well, and though I got one or two pieces down before he was on me, whacking my shoulder blades with the pointer, I couldn't swallow them all. He was roaring, 'Spit it out, spit it out,' and holding his cupped palm under my chin, his fingers trying to pry my jaws apart.

"I did. I spat into his hand and he took one look and knew immediately what I'd been chewing, and his fingers closed over the fragments into a clenched fist. He beat me till I was sore, and then, that night, for the first time but by no means the last, he came to me in the dormitory—"

A spray of hooting and catcalling interrupted him. It came from hecklers at the fringes of a small group of demonstrators at the head

[377]

of the street led by two ministers, one of them Murray Fillmore, three priests, two nuns and a rabbi. The protesters numbered no more than a few dozen, surrounded by a far greater horde of reporters, cameramen, police and hecklers. Three signs undulated over them: AN IMMORAL WAR; PEACE—NOW! and REFUSE TO GO! Only the signs spoke; otherwise they were a silent protest surrounded by noise.

"They're here," King said.

And we are here once again, Sanders thought, and then was taking photographs as quickly as he could. King had trotted down the street to the approaching demonstrators, was momentarily stopped, then passed through the police cordon to add another spot of color, the rare Negro face in the group, his great bulk now positioned between the group of protesters and the hecklers. Ensconced on the steps, Sanders took pictures of the protesters from that vantage point as they formed ragged ranks in front of the building entrance. All the clergy stood in the first row wearing black except for Murray Fillmore who was in his suntan military chaplain's uniform, the gold cross on his collar reflecting the noonday sun twice as intensely as the twin silver bars he wore on his shoulders. Next to him stood the thin colored minister who had been with him at the other demonstration and now behind both of them towered Peter King. The group stood there quietly for perhaps five minutes until at some imperceptible signal they all began to sing, their voices with that *a capella* nakedness and uncoordinated, like a sincere and ill-prepared church choir:

> *I'm gonna lay down that na-palm*
> *Down by the riverside . . .*
> *I'm gonna lay down that atomic bomb*
> *Down by the riverside . . .*
> *Ain't gonna study war no more, no more. . . . .*

When they'd finished they stood silently, expectantly, like children who, having chorused their Christmas carols, wait for coins and applause. In that interim Sanders' eye caught and engaged Fillmore's and received just the barest nod of recognition before Fillmore looked through him and then into the building entranceway. Though he was now surrounded by a clutch of other newsmen and TV cameramen and beyond them the police, Sanders felt uneasy, felt himself once more on the wrong side though he knew surely that if he were with Fillmore and the others he would be feeling the same disquietude, the same sense that all right did not inhere in his cause alone.

Fillmore raised his right hand and from the second rank of the column things were passed up to the clergy in the first rank, and the clergymen, not the nuns, moved out briskly toward the stairs. Not until they'd reached the first step and Sanders had them in focus in the viewfinder of his camera did he see that they were carrying flasks of blood. At almost the same moment the ministers, priests and rabbi unstopped the flasks and began to pour blood all over the steps, streams and puddles, and as they did Peter King came from behind them, leaped over the bloodied lower steps and on the top step unrolled a long streamer on which was daubed in scarlet the legend: LET THE BLOODSHED END HERE!

Let the bloodshed end here! Would that that were so. Recalling Peter King's paean of hate and his scowling face of half an hour before, Sanders felt it doubly ironic for King to have been the one to spread that streamer on the steps: King was not only waiting for the bloodshed to begin but knew that the bleeding had not yet even begun. A TV cameraman next to him, leaning his shoulder into the camera harness to get low shots of the blood dripping down the stairs, said, "What did you say?" and Sanders realized that he'd been mumbling to himself. A sudden deep-seated pang of suffering for his country convulsed him. My lucky country, he thought, not to have endured a war on its own soil for more than a hundred years. My unlucky country, so often called on to send its sons abroad to bleed and die in other countries, in other causes, and now once more its sons, black and white, were going to fight another civil war, the same civil war postponed to a later date, an uncivil bitter brother-against-brother battle. The TV cameraman next to him shouted and swiveled his camera and Sanders saw a Vietcong flag, green and red and with its single yellow star, raised at the rear of the demonstrators' ranks. Even as he took the picture of it, Sanders' gorge rose, his vision blurring so that he saw not what he was photographing but another picture he'd taken at another time in another country, one of the very best photographs he'd ever taken and one of the worst he'd had to endure: seven lines of empty jump boots lined up in uneven rows, dirty, walked in and worn, worn down at the heels and torn, mute personal remains of a hundred and thirty Americans killed in a hill-country skirmish with the VC. The boots were being given a farewell honor salute before the regimental colors and Old Glory, and nearby a shredded VC flag, dirtied and bloodstained, lay on the ground. VC. Victor Charley.

> *Victor Charley at Plei Me*
> *Threw a hand grenade at me.*
> *So I caught it in my palm,*
> *Threw it back and he was gone.*
> *Victor Charley, at Plei Me,*
> *Thanks a lot, you s.o.b.*

Sung to the tune of *Rock of Ages*, it had sounded almost sacrilegious when the troops had bawled it out. Charley. Charley was what Americans called the Cong; Mister Charley was what Negroes were calling whites at home. The jump boots, ridges and toe marks graven in the leather, stood laced and lonely, other men's shoes, everywhere other men's shoes.

As he moved toward the Cong banner Sanders saw the scuffle start and got half a dozen brilliant shots of it. Some of the hecklers, Oakland longshoremen and stevedores, had broken through the police lines and lunged at the boys carrying the VC flag. The fighting was short but bloody; the stevedores captured the flag and were setting fire to it, holding it up for the crowd of spectators and bystanders to see as it charred, crisped and burst into flame. There were cheers and some few began to sing "God Bless America." Two or three of the protesters, boys with noses bleeding, mouths cut, eyes already puffy, were being pulled to their feet by some of the other marchers as the police intervened, broke up the still-brawling men and shoved the dockwallopers back.

Behind him there were the sounds of another altercation and as he wheeled, refocused and kept clicking the shutter, Sanders saw that the police had come out of the building and begun to arrest the clergymen, leaving only the nuns, and trying to drag them inside the building. Peter King was fighting three policemen and going down under their clubs, carrying two of them to the steps with him. Confusion reigned briefly and then the demonstration was broken up, small groups of marchers being hustled down the street and two nuns led away in a stately walk by a personal escort of two uniformed police. Sanders tried to get into the induction center but police barred the entrance and would let no one pass, and so, after photographing the bloodstained stairs, Sanders once more took up his vigil outside of the building. He didn't have long to wait. The paddy wagon arrived and in short order about fourteen people were escorted out between columns of police and put into the van. Only Peter King came out struggling until a plainclothesman tapped him behind the ear with a blackjack and then two of them, one pulling his hair and hauling his shoulder, the other carrying his legs, dragged him along the ground, bouncing him liberally, then threw him into the back of the police van. Sanders shot that entire journey, frame after frame, twice on each camera, to make sure he had it, concentrating on the camera to keep himself from leaping at the detectives and trying to free King, but still ashamed, guilty, about his inaction. Was this what George Christiansen would have done? And had George done that in Saigon, where would he have been? Dead. Was this what Lovett Carpenter Sanders would have done? In this cul-de-sac or the one in Paris? If he had, where would he have been? Alive.

Sanders phoned the story in, drove back to the office to read and correct sheets, and pick the pictures. On the front page he featured three of the best photographs: one of the clergymen pouring blood over the steps (a libation? a transubstantiation?), the scuffle between protesters and dock wallopers over the VC flag, and the two cops dragging Peter King to the paddy wagon. And afterwards when the paper had finally been put to bed, he avoided Jim Needham and the others who wanted to celebrate, and went back by himself to Los Pueblos.

There he parked the car and on impulse, feeling a need for

something other than brick and glass and chrome and redwood and concrete, he walked past the braided redwood fence that guarded the swimming pool and its occupants from prying eyes into the adjacent apricot grove on which he had so often looked down from his balcony. The late afternoon shadows were long but not cool, the air under the trees, as if trapped there, was stifling, almost syrupy with the smell of fruit which hung ponderous and orange on the branches. Yet in spite of the heat Sanders was relieved to walk on the naked earth. He took off his shoes and socks so he could sink his feet into the warm loam and, feeling lighter, happier, walked down the lanes between the trees. Short-trunked, almost dwarfed apricot trees, heavy with green leaves and golden fruit, in orderly straight rows, carefully pruned and planted, they seemed paradisiacal, an Elysium of peace and fruitfulness and beauty so far removed from concrete human viciousness as he'd seen it that day. Not nature, he knew, but nature controlled and cultivated by men; but he felt the difference. He took off his jacket, shirt and tie, rolled them into a bolster, and then lay down under one of the trees, feeling the warm earth against his naked back, the leafy shade on his bare chest, putting the bolster comfortably under his neck so he could look up at the clear empty evening heavens with no sun, no moon, no stars, and no clouds. He reached up to take down an apricot, rubbed it clean on his forearm and then ate the slightly green still-tart fruit and was content.

Lying there in the hot silence, comfortable for the first time in many weeks, Sanders closed his eyes and felt himself being knit up and restored, his heart eased, as if his spirit for so long in thrall was slowly being unburdened and salved. Antaeus, and mother earth, he thought, almost drifting off to sleep, but what a small-sized Antaeus he was. On the edge of slumber he first heard the harsh grinding of gears, the growl of a motor, the powerful hiss of fluid under great pressure. Sleepily he opened his eyes, turned his head and saw a great dull-green metal beetle on immense wheels jouncing down the aisle once removed from the one in which he lay. Encased in an all-green plastic coverall, face mask, goggles and helmet, the man who drove it resembled a creature from another planet and so did the sprayer, a rumbling hissing mechanical monster spitting a smoking gray spray of insecticide that doused the fruit and the leaves of the apricot trees and filled the air of the only-a-moment-ago sylvan orchard with nauseating noise and reek.

Laboriously, Sanders rose and went up to his apartment, his limbs and mood heavy again with a weary oppression that neither a shower nor a change of clothing dissipated. He made himself a sandwich and a drink and as he sat out on the balcony eating and drinking he decided to postpone the French version of the article on the demonstration until the next day; instead, he was going back into town to bail Fillmore and King out of jail. Once the decision was made and he'd finished eating, he felt better, the oppression lifted somewhat, but at the police station it returned renewed. The desk sergeant told him that both Fillmore and King—in fact all the protesters who had been arrested for public nuisance and defacing a Federal building—had already been bailed out and released, though only a short while ago. Even that small responsibility was forfeit; even that minuscule attempt to be of some help had been thwarted.

Then, with shame and alarm, he remembered Laura and headed across the Bay bridge for San Francisco, the waters below already reflecting the first night stars splashed around a white-enamel washbasin of moon.

*　*　*

Laura Martin's door was firmly shut, apparently double-locked and bolted, and it was a long time after Sanders had knocked and announced who he was, in answer to the strange male voice who asked, before the door was opened. The man, or perhaps the boy, who stood there belligerently in the open doorway was a little hard to believe, and it took Sanders more than a few moments to get over his surprise. The boy looked like the pictures of Robert Louis Stevenson Sanders remembered from his childhood, with long hair down to his shoulders, lank and unwashed brunette locks, a drooping silky handlebar mustache, also brunette but shot through with red lights, a red velvet vest liberally stained with food, egg, cigarette ash and flecked by scorch marks, and a tubercular cough that bubbled through pale almost purple lips. Except for an ankh which hung from a single strand of chain down on his bony chest, it might have been the young Scottish student just returned from a night on the town in an Edinburgh howf.

"Good evening," Sanders said. "I'm Elliott Sanders, a friend of Laura's. Is she at home?"

The boy—he couldn't have been more than twenty-three or -four —looked him over suspiciously, still blocking the doorway, and Sanders, impressed by his belligerent bravery and amused by it, because he looked as if a strong wind might blow him out of the way, waited patiently, trying to see if Laura was somewhere behind him in the apartment. The boy took a long clay pipe out of the sagging pocket of the Norfolk tweed jacket he wore, put it in his mouth, struck a match across the lapel of the jacket and lit up. He blew a stream of smoke directly into Sanders' face and, bleary pale eyes peering, examined him closely. "Babe," he called back over his shoulder, talking out of the side of his mouth that was free of the pipe bit, "do you know a cat named Sanders?"

A faint kittenish cry came from behind him. "Elliott! Let him in, Clay, he's okay," but the boy seemed still reluctant, and so Sanders shouldered past his arm and into the room. Laura lay on the unmade divan in her soiled terry-cloth robe safety-pinned up to the throat, her feet covered by heavy maroon woolen socks, and a bright scarlet ribbon tying back her long tangled hair. Propped on four or five pillows in begrimed pillowcases, she held her arms away from her body as if she were trying to fly, her hands completely swathed in bandages already the worse for wear. Her face was like a porcelain doll's, eyes filmed, lips glossy, expression slack; it was clear she was high on marijuana. "H'lo," Laura said, raising her smudged-bandaged hands in what was like a benison. "It's been a long time."

Sanders took it for the rebuke it was. "I've been sick," he explained.

"So have I," she said, but her eyes, heavily caked with an eggshell-colored eyeshadow and starkly outlined with black pencil, seemed to recognize neither that anyone might be ill but her, nor the extent of her own illness.

"What happened to you," Sanders asked, "playing with matches?"

"Something like that," the boy replied, his voice a deep booming baritone altogether too large for his tubercular frame. He had shut and bolted the door and was standing with his back to it.

"Clay Bowen," Laura said, "Elliott Sanders."

They nodded, exchanging suspicious, assertive glances. "What happened?" Sanders repeated, this time to Bowen.

"Not matches, firecrackers the bird was playing with. Bike boys. They play rough, for keeps."

"Remember those motorcycle nuts who came here that last time you were here?" Laura asked, her pale eyes paler for the contrast of the makeup.

Sanders nodded, remembering with a chill the black leather maniacs on the freeway.

"They came back."

"The same night?"

"No, the next night, but they told me they'd been there the night before and that you'd thrown them out."

"And?"

"They crucified her," Bowen said, drawing on his pipe and spitting smoke out.

Sanders looked uncomprehendingly from Laura to Bowen and back again.

"They crucified her," Bowen repeated calmly.

"You're joking."

Laura shook her head and mutely raised her two gauze-encased hands in witness.

"Meth freaks," Bowen explained. "Blown their minds. And she" —he pointed at Laura with his pipestem—"had, as usual, left the door unlatched. They knew she put out and they wanted some but the bird wasn't having any. So they made her, first one, then the other, a little slapping around in the bargain, but the doll here wouldn't lie back and enjoy. She scratched and bit and fought so they got mad, meth-mad, and that's mighty mad, man, and nailed her to the door. The bathroom door, over there."

"I had a hammer and nails because I was fixing myself a new shelf, there." Laura pointed one clump of gauze at a raw-wood shelf on which a milk bottle rested with one single blood-red rose.

"Insane," Sanders muttered. "Absolutely crazy. Didn't the police find them?"

Bowen looked at Laura but neither spoke.

"Couldn't they find them? I can identify them easily. I even noted

[385]

down their license numbers—they tried to kill me on the freeway with their motorcycles."

"I didn't go to the police," Laura said.

"But why not?"

"The fuzz wouldn't do anything," Bowen said harshly. "And if they did, those bike boys would come back some night and tear her and this place apart. Besides, the fuzz would be snooping around and they'd get to us for the gauge."

"We went to the clinic. Clay found me. He has a doctor buddy there. He fixed me up."

"Sure, they fixed her up fine. Nothing vital hit. Lucky Laura. A couple of scars later, maybe on the palms and on the backs of the hands. Nothing more."

Peter King's white corrugations flashed before his eyes. The scarred palms. "Nothing more," Sanders raged. "You mean they didn't kill her?"

"Yeh, man, that's what I do mean," Bowen replied belligerently, "exactly what I mean."

"Why didn't you call me, Laura?" Sanders asked her directly, ignoring Bowen.

Shamefacedly, her eyes downcast, she raised her bandaged paws, and said, "I couldn't dial, and . . ."

"And?"

"She thought you'd got yours and run," Bowen explained, "that you were just another square in for a quick boff, that you didn't give a shit."

"I wasn't talking to you," Sanders flared.

"You wanted to know, so I'm telling you, man," Bowen replied, not giving ground. "Lucky I came by a couple hours later and took her down, otherwise—"

"Otherwise I might have died," Laura said, beginning to cry, soundlessly, the tears running out of the corners of her eyes tracking mascara and eye pencil down her cheeks like flecks of soot on her fair skin.

Stunned, Sanders stood staring at her, remembering her naked torso reflected again and again in the three-paneled dressing-table mirror and her agonized "Look at me, who wants this—this thing?" the naked breasts weeping red-eyed mourners. Well, the motorcycle boys had wanted her all right—and taken her. They'd spoken their I do's and—done her. He had been lucky, he supposed, to have put them off once; but to do more than that one had to be there, present, as Clay Bowen was there now, to lock and bolt the doors, to call for help and to fight if the leather jackets and Indian headbands broke the door down and invaded.

"Three-inch galvanized nails, right through the palms," Bowen remarked, a sadistic edge to his voice.

"I'm a doormat," Laura said in a small voice.

"Yes, you sure are," Bowen replied. He went to her and began to stroke her tangled hair. "But with 'Welcome' written all over it."

"In this world the password is love," Sanders commented bitterly.

"Yes," Bowen said rebelliously, "with us the password *is* love—in spite of the bike boys and the fuzz and the squares like . . ." He left unfinished the sentence which could only end "you."

On the shoji screen the scroll still defined the good life. *Neither be cynical about love; for in the face of all aridity & disenchantment it is perennial as the grass.* Undamaged and pristine, the scroll proclaimed its desire but Sanders didn't believe it for a moment. Perennial as grass, yes, but to be mowed down, to wither, to be made hay of by life and men, to be driven out by the weeds of hatred, the crabgrass of violence.

Bowen had walked to the door, slid the bolts and was holding the door open for him. "Goodbye, Sanders," he said.

Laura refused to meet his eyes.

"Will you be all right?" Sanders asked her.

"Maybe we'll make out," Laura said so softly that Sanders strained to hear her, but he thought she spoke without hope.

"We'll be fine," Bowen said, more confidently, louder, waving his pipe. "Don't you worry, we'll make out all right. Happy Mecca, that's us."

Sanders picked Laura's bandaged hand up in his and kissed it. A hot tear fell on his wrist and she flicked it away, then pulled his face down to hers and kissed him on the mouth once, hard, determined, irrevocable.

Going down the stairs, Sanders heard Bowen shoot the bolts and turn the lock and he knew that was over, done. Just before he found his car again he passed a graffito scrawled on a gray stucco wall in green crayon, GOD ISN'T DEAD—HE JUST DOESN'T WANT TO GET INVOLVED, and burst into tremulous laughter that almost became tears.

※　※　※

The two months that followed were nightmarish, full of horrors so real they seemed to him imaginary yet unimaginable. In a swift rush summer turned to autumn, the skies shot through with gray, the air sharper, the wind a presence. Like a volcano long dormant, there was a sudden surprising eruption of protest, a constant Vesuvius of hatred for the war and uncertainty about its outcome, an overflowing lava of protest and demonstration. Sanders was so busy covering the stories, taking the pictures, writing the pieces for Needham and Tessier, that he had neither time nor energy to do anything else. At the end of each day's work when he dropped exhausted into bed he knew how weakened he had been by the flu, and for a few clairvoyant instants before sleep came he thought about Beth and Laura, about Fillmore and King, both of whom he saw at various demonstrations and exchanged curt nods with in passing. A young boy who bought a can of gasoline at a nearby gas station drenched himself with it and turned himself into a torch on the induction-center steps to protest the war. Two passersby tried to save him, dousing the flames with a blanket and rushing the boy to a nearby hospital, but the boy with third-degree burns over most of his body—Sanders interviewed him, his parents, his girl friend, some of his schoolmates and teachers—died three days later. All who knew him said he'd been disturbed by the war, that he was a very religious boy who thought that killing was not what a godly Christian could endure. His girl friend confessed that he'd been on LSD and thought that maybe he'd had a bad trip. Six young college students fasted in front of the administration buildings of the university, drinking only weak tea and water for ten days in protest against the unjustified, immoral and illegal war Americans were fighting in Vietnam. Sanders talked to all six—they were eager to communicate so the press could make their protest widely known—before two passed out and all six were taken to the university hospital for exposure and malnutrition. All six could not reconcile themselves to Americans killing innocent people, defoliating and destroying peasants' crops, to American soldiers being used to prop up and bear the brunt of a war in defense of a government they thought corrupt and dictatorial, and allied troops they considered venal and cowardly, cruel and parasitic. More than two hundred physicians marched solemnly together in a public parade through the streets of the downtown portion of the city, wearing their white medical uniforms, their green surgical gowns, some with stethoscopes and face masks, all of them calling on the country to declare peace, not to destroy the people that America had set out to save. One of those turned out to be Steven Prescott, to Sanders' immense surprise, and after the ceremonial speeches were over, they talked.

"Have you seen Beth?" Sanders asked.

Prescott shook his head. "No. I've been busy and so has she. I've passed her a couple of times in the corridors, but we haven't had much time."

"Something wrong?"

"I don't think so. Daulton is up going over her financial position with her. She's wanted to be alone for a couple of weeks so I haven't seen much of her," Prescott explained. "I take it you haven't seen her?"

"Not for more than two months."

"That long!" Prescott's eyebrows rose. "Something wrong?"

"Lots of things."

They were near Fisherman's Wharf and they walked down to a restaurant and went in for drinks, sitting silently looking out at the fishing fleet's masts, the colorful maritime panorama of signal flags. "What are you doing with these?" Sanders asked finally.

"I'm for getting the hell out of there," Prescott said brusquely. "To hell with those yellow bastards. I'm not for Americans getting knocked off for people who don't want to fight for themselves."

"Is that the whole of it?"

"For me it is. I'm not a great political pundit—like you newspaper types are supposed to be. But the big ones are China and Russia and they're sitting there laughing, not losing a soldier, while we bleed ourselves white, men and money, in that godforsaken country. That's

[389]

stupid," Prescott said angrily. "If we want to be anti-Communist we've got to hit those two with the whole business, the big ones, A-bombs, H-bombs, rockets. The hell with it. None of this will do any good anyway, these marches and protests. Besides, I hate those inquiring-reporter questions about matters of public interest. Tell me how your throat is instead."

"I hate those doctors' questions too," Sanders said, but grinning, and admitted his throat was better. "You were right. It was hysterical."

In an unaccustomed gesture Prescott touched his sleeve. "I'm always right—in medicine. Well, not really even there. It's people I don't get. I know what happens to their bodies when the going gets rough—*boule hystérique,* ulcers, arthritis, high blood pressure, you name it, I've seen it—but I don't know what the hell to do about it."

"Nobody does, do they?" Sanders said.

"The shrinks think they do but most of them are up dry gulch. 'Medical bias,' my psychiatrist colleagues tell me, implying by that that physicians are altogether ignorant of what makes people tick." He finished his drink, morose now and beetle-browed. "Maybe they're right. Tell me, Sanders, you still married?"

"Divorced."

"You want to marry Beth?" Prescott, staring into his face, was evidently trying to gauge his sincerity.

"I don't know. Do you?"

Prescott nodded, vigorously, violently. "I don't know if I can live with her, but I can't seem to live without her."

"She's a very complicated creature," Sanders said noncommittally.

"That she is," Prescott assented. "And doubly strange this last six weeks or so, withdrawn, quiet, very much unlike her usual self—if she has a usual self. I thought it might be because you two were making it together."

"I told you"—Sanders' voice rose—"that I haven't seen her in almost two months."

"But you were making it together?" He peered at him shrewdly, then raised his hand. "I know you were because she told me."

"Don't believe everything Beth tells you, Prescott."

[390]

"Beth Marshall's lots of kooky things but not a liar. A layer, yes. Maybe it's Daulton again."

"Him too?" The two words rang false.

"She told me she wanted a few weeks to think things through carefully. And if she's got Daulton up here, bedding down or not, it's to go over her money and her property. Beth's always serious when she does that. You can tell she's a rich girl; she's always more serious about money than about sex. This going over her money affairs doesn't happen often. I've seen her do that only twice before, once after she married Christiansen, another time after the baby died and it looked like she might end up in the booby hatch for a spell."

"Emergencies," Sanders said, "crises."

"Exactly. I thought you might know what this one was."

"I don't, but the signs and portents"—he fumbled for words—"are there."

"I think she's trying to make up her mind about which of us to marry," Prescott said irresolutely, "and that's why neither of us has seen her . . ." The unfinished sentence left hanging in the air an unspoken phrase: "and neither of us has gone to bed with her."

It had an air of complicity Sanders wouldn't accept. "I haven't asked her," Sanders said.

"But you will."

"No, I don't think I will."

"If she wants you, if she wants you to, you will, Sanders, believe me, you will." His tone was fervid, grudging, admiring. He stood up and stuck out his hand.

Still sitting, Sanders took it and asked, "And now should we say, 'And may the best man win?' "

Prescott's face was a puzzle. "No, I don't think she deserves either of us," and before Sanders could get clear whether that meant that they were too good for her, or she was too good for them, Prescott was gone.

Students, logically, remained in the forefront of the protest activities, or disturbances, depending on the point of view, with sit-ins, happenings, rallies, marches, protests, demonstrations, all directed against the war, against personnel recruitment by the military and

[391]

intelligence services, and the manufacturers who supplied the armed forces with various kinds of weapons and material. At one of these, in front of the Federal building in San Francisco, Sanders met Fillmore and Peter King again, this time leading a group of students almost equally composed of blacks and whites, all protesting the draft. They were, instead of burning their draft cards, turning them in so that the government could prosecute them for nonpossession. Fillmore and King were carrying a large wicker basket together, the kind in which picnic lunches were usually carried, and they tried to present it to the Federal district attorney who was then on his way into the building where he worked and who graciously but firmly refused to accept it.

After waiting for a few moments, while some students talked to Fillmore and then departed with the wicker basket, Sanders caught Fillmore. The two of them, arm in arm but not speaking, walked past the library and sat in the Civic Center park in the pale midmorning sunshine watching the derelicts and winos stagger by, their wide-brimmed fedoras, sweatbands stained, from another era, their faces starched white or flushed with alcohol or fever, and Sanders remembered seeing those same men, in Paris in the winters, those same faces, looking for warm places on the sidewalks over the gratings where the heat came up from the Métro. One he remembered particularly near Saint-Sulpice where a free-for-all, kicking, biting, pummeling had broken out among such men fighting for the warmest spots on that cold, frost-stained night. As he sat there, facing the City Hall, San Francisco could almost have been Paris and again the cities' resemblances struck him—and not only in its bums and *clochards* that no one gave a damn about.

"You'd think," Fillmore said looking at those men, his eyes so naked with compassion that Sanders was immediately ashamed, "that this was a civilized country—if you didn't open your eyes."

Sanders remembered with a start his mother's quoting Anatole France to his father about the rich and poor having the same freedom to sleep under the Paris bridges—and without humor. "I tried to bail you out a couple of times," Sanders began, but he couldn't finish because Fillmore cut him off.

"I know," Fillmore said, "I heard."

"You sound somehow disappointed, as if you wanted something more of me." Sanders felt uneasy.

"I did. I do." Fillmore's face was unrelenting, his mouth pursed, as if he were considering defining just what he did want. "A lot more."

Sanders diverted him. "George Christiansen's wife would like to see you."

Fillmore stiffened. "What for?"

"I don't know," Sanders replied. "She didn't say."

Fillmore seemed to be turning that over in his mind.

"Will you see her?"

Fillmore nodded. "Bring her to services and I'll save some time for both of you afterwards." They arranged the time, Fillmore gave him the address and driving directions—the church was in Berkeley —and before there was time to say anything else, he got up, looked down piteously, and said, "God bless you, Sanders, and lift the burdens from your spirit," and then he turned and walked away.

*   *   *

Late that night Sanders called Beth from his apartment, trying to suppress his tremulous excitement as he waited for her to pick up the phone, angry with the lift of his heart when her guarded hello changed to a happy "Elliott! I was meaning to call you!" as she recognized his voice. "I really was. Steven told me he'd seen you at the doctors' demonstration."

"Yes, we talked and had a drink. Prescott said that *even he* hadn't seen you for a long time." Sanders bore down heavily on the *even he* in spite of himself.

"Steven exaggerates, but I have been busy." Her voice turned grave. "Lots of new c.a. cases so I've been working overtime. And one of the other senior technicians is out with, of all things, mumps, and one of the radiologists with an infarc— a heart attack. You know," she laughed ruefully, "the usual thing."

The usual thing. Cancer, mumps, heart attacks.

"What little time I have had," Beth continued, "has been devoted to trying to set my life in order. A kind of premenstrual cleaning obsession"—her laughter did not ring altogether true—"a desire to get things straightened out. Some business things, mostly, but a few things in my mind too. I've been moderately successful with the first, chiefly because Bill Daulton came up two or three times this past month to help put my business affairs in good order and to make out a new will for me."

"Intimations of mortality?" he asked, the echoing intimations of immorality loud and clear but unspoken in his throat.

"I'm not a boy scout, not even a girl scout, but 'Be prepared' is my motto." She tried to say it lightly.

"I believe that's your motto with Daulton and Prescott."

"Please, Elliott," Beth said wearily, "not again. Yes, I slept with both of them, Bill because he's been so kind and helpful to me this past couple of weeks, and because he was so eager, needed, wanted . . . for God's sake, Elliott, why do we have to go through this still another time?"

Sanders wanted to say it; his mouth shaped the words, but his teeth bit them back. He couldn't speak words like "I love you" or "I want to marry you," and he certainly couldn't use them as his *because,* for if he did, then what followed ceased to have meaning. It had to be given freely, without stint or threat, or else it turned sour for him; you could not say to someone you wanted to live with, "Do this, *because";* if you did, you had failed and it was the end.

The silence on the phone was broken only by the sounds of their breathing until Sanders, in another, impersonal voice, said that Chaplain Fillmore had agreed to see her at the end of the week, that he, Sanders, would drive her up there if she wished, but that if she preferred she was free to go herself.

"Will you come over tonight, now, and have a nightcap with me?" she asked, without coquetry.

"No," Sanders said, "I still have work to finish up tonight."

The silence was restored until Beth broke it with her own businesslike response, making the arrangements for their meeting to go to Fillmore's church.

*　*　*

When Sanders went into Needham's office the next morning, Needham was standing on his head. "Come on in, Elliott," he called, "just my morning yoga."

"Does that give you the publishers' viewpoint?" Sanders asked.

"No, this is to recapture the reporter's viewpoint," Needham replied. "You ought to try it."

"The yoga or the reporter's viewpoint?"

"The yoga, you idiot, your reporting is fine. So far. How are your French friends enjoying the stuff?"

"Tessier's too much of a curmudgeon to admit he likes anything, but he sent me a bonus check and for a French editor that is the equivalent of the Nobel Prize, it speaks a lot louder than words. But I think he wants me to come back to Paris. He's been dropping broad hints that I really ought to get back by the end of the year."

Needham did a neat somersault and landed springily on his feet. "Are you going back?"

Sanders shrugged. "Don't know yet."

"If you want to stay, permanently, I mean, we could work something out. I'm getting older and I'd like to take more time off, maybe take a trip or two with Sheila, do some reporting from Asia or Africa, even go back to Europe for a bit, just to get the old hand in. Do me good, Sheila too. Might even do you some good to sit in the editor's chair for a while."

"That's very kind of you, Jim, but—"

"No need to make your mind up now, Elliott. Just something to chew over. Wouldn't want Tessier and the French to have the only bid in." He patted Sanders' shoulder, then walked over behind his desk, picked up a slip of paper and handed it across. "This may look like a routine police reporter's assignment, but I don't think it is. A National Guard armory was broken into and a batch of guns and ammunition was stolen. I'd like you to cover it."

"Looks routine," Sanders said.

Needham slapped his palm against the nape of his neck. "Call it intuition, a hunch. There's something more here."

After Sanders showed his press pass, the policeman guarding the armory window where the thieves had broken in took him around to the front entrance, temporarily closed, and, for a fiver, let him in to wander around the inside of the dank, melancholy armory. At police headquarters Sanders was shunted to the press-relations man who told him that no accurate count had yet been established but the present estimate was that the burglars had taken forty rifles, seventeen carbines, four shotguns, three submachine guns, a dozen pistols and automatics, and perhaps three thousand rounds of various kinds of ammunition. Something too casual and flip about the press-relations man's account—especially his answers to questions about why nothing but arms and ammunition had been taken—disturbed him, so Sanders began to dig. It took him all morning but when he was finished he had found that more than a dozen recent robberies in the area involved stealing arms and ammunition, burglaries of the armory, two gunsmiths, a sports store, some private houses where men were known to be hunters, a department store. There had also been the theft and sale of weapons—guns, grenades, ammunition, bayonets—by soldiers at the Presidio and sailors in Alameda and at the Naval Supply Center. After reviewing the details of each case time and time again the only connecting link Sanders could find was that every case seemed to involve a Negro. It was then that Peter King's threats about the black day of reckoning with the white man came back to him and he called Needham at the paper. Needham was home for lunch, so Sanders called him there and Sheila answered the phone. "Elliott," she asked, sounding unguarded, tender and tentative, "how are you?" He explained that he wanted to talk to Jim, and Sheila, sounding as if he had interrupted their lovemaking, asked if it was urgent because Jim was taking his siesta and she didn't want to wake him. Sanders said that it was urgent and in about ten seconds, the time he estimated it took to make a brief explanation and hand the phone across the double bed, Needham was on the line. Sanders summarized what he'd learned and Needham listened without comment until he was finished. "You think it's what, a Negro plot?"

"I'm afraid it's preparation for a race riot," Sanders answered somberly.

Needham was silent. "Give me your number and sit tight," he said finally. "I'll call you back within ten minutes." Sanders gave him the booth phone number and waited. Eight minutes later the phone rang and Needham was at the other end. "Elliott? Go to police headquarters and see Dick Kenney. Be inconspicuous. Don't let any of the police-beat reporters spot you. Kenney would like to talk to you.

[396]

He's planning something. Persuade him to let you go along. If you do, you should get an interesting exclusive."

"Weren't you able to persuade them?" Sanders asked.

"Well, it's not like that. Let me put it this way: I think I've opened the door. If you put your face in and they like it, things will work out."

"Thanks. Sorry to have disturbed your siesta, Jim."

"No thanks necessary. It's my job and in my interest. And you couldn't have interrupted a siesta for a better reason. Keep me posted," he said and rang off.

The small gilt letters on the blank wooden door read RICHARD KENNEY, DEPUTY CHIEF OF DETECTIVES. A tall, broad-shouldered man in his middle forties, Kenney stood up to greet him. Kenney asked him to sit, offered him a pack of cigarettes, then took out a small brown cigar himself, lit up and sat back in a leather chair. "You're Elliott Sanders?" he asked, his pepper-and-salt hair and equine face offset by green eyes of extraordinary sparkle and shrewdness, his speculative cynical expression much like Albert Guitton's. Cops, Sanders thought, cops and soldiers and whores are alike all over the world; but he knew that was hogwash, a cliché that was useful only insofar as one wanted not really to confront the individual.

"I'm Elliott Sanders," he admitted. What more depressing confession could he make, he thought, and smiled.

Kenney smiled back. "Jim Needham called a while back and said you had some ideas about that armory business."

Sanders repeated what he had done, what he'd learned, and what he thought it meant, but he didn't mention Peter King.

Kenney's smile disappeared and his tobacco-stained uneven teeth were bared as they chomped the end of the cigar. "A riot, eh? They've got enough for an insurrection. What's more, I don't think that's what they're driving at." Kenney got up and walked around to the front of the desk, propped himself against it. "We've got some ideas about it here too and some tips from people—in the field."

"What do you think it is?" Sanders asked.

"We're hoping to find out a lot more in"—he looked at his wrist-watch—"about forty minutes."

"I'd like to go with you."

Kenney drew in on the cigar, contemplative, looking at a spot three feet over his head. "No story if I say no story?"

"You have my word."

"I'll have your head."

"My word is worth more."

Kenney laughed without mirth. "Your head will be more useful. You're Lovett Carpenter Sanders' son, aren't you?"

Sanders nodded.

"I remember his reporting during the war. My war. The big one. I met him once, a long time ago, in Devon, in England, when we were preparing for the invasion of France. Quite a guy. What happened to him?"

"He was killed in the war, in 1944."

"In France?"

"Yes."

"Funny, I never read about it in the newspapers." Kenney seemed genuinely chagrined, disappointed.

"Reporters aren't that important. A couple of small obits, that's about all."

"The same as for cops, sometimes not even that. Just a slab in the morgue and a widow's pension for the family. But we do our jobs," Kenney said.

"He did his job too," Sanders said, surprised that he meant it.

"I figured that was the way he bought it. Colorful type. Gutsy. Not too many of those around any more," Kenney remarked. He looked at his watch again, checked a pistol in his waistband, then buttoned his jacket over it. "We're off."

Three other plainclothesmen nodded when they got into the back of the unmarked black sedan but no one spoke. Sanders felt the tension, the fear; it was exactly the same as when he'd waited to go out on patrol with a squad in the jungle: You could almost smell and taste it. The house, a shabby brick tenement not far from where Peter King lived, had already been staked out. Four other unmarked cars with a dozen plainclothesmen surrounded the block. The apartment they were looking for was on the fifth floor, and as Sanders followed Kenney and three detectives up the stairs through the stench of bacon grease, urine and peeling plaster, the colored faces he saw were all frightened, suspicious, hostile. The news of their arrival had evidently preceded them and as they passed from flight to flight the half-opened doors closed quietly behind them, the faces looking out relieved but unfriendly. A detective kicked the door open but no one was inside and soon they all put their revolvers away except one man who stood guard outside the door. Inside there was almost no furniture. Unadorned bulbs hung from the ceilings, old green paint had been peeled away from the walls in great sheets showing a layer of pink paint and sometimes white plaster beneath. On the wall were graffiti—BLACK IS BEST; PEACE IS A COOL SCENE; INTEGRATE? NO! FORNICATE! FUZZ FUCKS CHICKENS!—and obscene drawings to match; and in red paint that had run like blood, KILL WHITEY! MURDER THE MAN! TAKE MISTER CHARLEY!

"They don't like us much, do they?" Kenney drawled, but there was little talk and everyone was edgy. A few stained and mildewed stinking mattresses were on the floor. Sanders noticed an old chipped enamel-topped kitchen table and wooden crates that had obviously served for chairs. In the bedroom were three rolls of clothesline, six five-gallon jerry cans of gasoline, three strips of rubber hose thin enough to be used to siphon gasoline out of an automobile gas tank and a dozen cardboard cartons of bottles neatly lined up against one wall. Along the other, guns and ammunition were just as carefully laid out on the floor. The detectives had also found reefers, some glassine envelopes of heroin and cocaine, bottles of pep pills and goof balls, and the various other tools of drug addiction: hypodermics, needles and the rest. On the bedroom walls were crudely drawn a black ram butting a naked and pathetic-looking white man's tail as he tried to run away; a black panther leaped on the back of another white man, hairy and Neanderthal-looking, his back already badly clawed, a cartoon balloon coming out of his mouth with GIT OFFA MAH BACK! in it. Rummaging around among the discolored fetid mattresses, which here too were strewn over the floor, Sanders saw the white back of the snapshot between two of the mattresses which had been pushed together. He bent, picked it up, and saw instantly that it was a picture of a white man or boy's genitals, a picture close up from waist to thighs only, a picture that had obviously been handled many times because the edges had been worn

[399]

round and frayed and the emulsion partly alligatored off. "You find anything, Sanders?" Kenney asked, calling from the doorway to the kitchen, and Sanders, palming the snapshot, stood up and shook his head. He pocketed the snapshot and followed Kenney back into the kitchen.

The detectives were agreed that the apartment was being used as a cache for a black nationalist group's weapons. Its members had apparently been forewarned of their arrival. Smoking cigarette butts were still in the ashtrays, and water in a blackened pot on the encrusted range burner was still warm. At the bottom of it were two hypodermic needles being boiled as if someone had been preparing a "fix." The weapons were only a small part of what had been stolen from the armory and from some of the other heists, but the serial numbers were going to have to be checked to be sure. Either the black nationalists had other arms caches, logical and likely, or, being forewarned, they had managed to spirit away a good part of what they had stored there and left the rest behind only because of lack of time or as a decoy. What alarmed Kenney most were the makings for the Molotov cocktails and he arranged for laboratory men to work the place over for fingerprints, for uniformed police to take all the contents of the flat down to headquarters subsequently and for the apartment to be sealed and guarded.

Warm noontime sunshine coated the streets and buildings when they got down to the street, and on the sidewalks and in the gutters they found more than two hundred Negroes, men, women and children, crowded around the apartment house entrance and the police sedan. The faces were laughing and sullen, glum and angry, many apathetic, but Sanders saw not a single friendly face. A bunch of colored teen-agers were rocking the police sedan, the springs and tires creaking loudly, while inside the detective, a small microphone in his fist, was calling for help. Kenney began to push his way toward the sedan, shouldering people aside to make headway. Even walking in Kenney's wake, Sanders found black men shoving, tripping, pummeling him until he began to push forward, thrusting his way among them. Hands clutched and tore at the cameras around his neck, but he fought them off. Silence surrounded them, as oppressive as the bodies crowding in on them, a heavy crushing quiet as tangible as flesh. Gradually it gave way to a hissing, growling, snarling "Fuzz! Mistuh Charley the boss man! Stickin their noses up people's business! Heah, man, stick yo nose up mah smelly asshole! Nevah you mind us, how 'bout them white-ass crooks takin the slice down to City Hall?" A yowl, first one voice, then others taking it up, "Whitey, yah! Let's burn them motherfuckers!"

The two detectives behind him put their hands under their coats but Kenney in an unbelievably loud voice shouted, "Let us through, let us pass! Goddam it, ain't you jokers never seen a lousy black Chevvy before? You'd think it was a solid gold Cadillac." Someone giggled, someone else laughed and the laughter rippled through the crowd like a chain of small firecrackers exploding. By the time it had faded away Kenney had the teen-agers off the car, had knocked on the window so the detective opened the door locks, and had them all secured inside and the doors locked once more. But no sooner were they there than the crowd closed in again, refusing to let the car move, and the teen-agers took to rocking it again until it seemed they would turn the sedan over. His face grim, Kenney said to the driver, "Okay, start moving!" The detective raced the engine and put the car in gear, and it began to inch forward but the crowd braced itself and held it back. "Give it gas!" Kenney commanded, and then from both ends of the street came the scream of sirens. Two prowl cars and two of the other unmarked police cars came roaring down from both ends of the street, and the crowd, like a black sea, parted and let them pass.

In Kenney's office, with his permission, Sanders telephoned the story in to the paper, reporting that he'd got pictures and would have them there in time for the morning edition. When he put the phone down, Kenney was pouring two paper cups of bourbon from a desk-drawer bottle. The detective, face pained, sat back in his leather chair and sipped the bourbon.

"They really hate us, don't they?" Sanders said quietly. "You live outside of the States for a while, the way I have, and you forget what it's like. Especially if you live in Paris and if you're a damn Connecticut Yankee to begin with. You read the papers there, but it doesn't come across. And because you're a newspaperman you believe only a fraction of what you read. You don't feel the hatred the way I felt it back there. Things have gotten a hell of a lot worse since I was in the States last."

"The blowoff comes when the lid's off, not when it's on. Doesn't make much sense, I suppose, but that's the way it is. I'm surprised hell didn't break loose a long time ago. During the war, in France, I was in the MPs and what I saw convinced me way back then that a war was brewing, another civil war between blacks and whites. They were already fighting then, about whores, whisky, about black-market graft and stealing on the red-ball express. It's been a long time coming. World War II's been over more than twenty years, but I could feel it inching up every day." Kenney's face was gloomy.

"I can't say I blame them, living like that," Sanders remarked. "Having to live like that."

"They don't have to," Kenney rejoined curtly. "They don't have to live like that at all if they don't want to. They don't give a damn."

"You believe that?"

"I really do. I've been a cop for more than twenty years now and I've spent a lot of time in that black ghetto. I know those people the way most white men never get to know them. You think the white man does them in, keeps them where they are—"

"Doesn't he?"

"You ought to see what they do to each other. Mugging, robbing, stomping, killing each other. Like animals. Sanders, you should see their own people, the middle-class ones, exploiting the hell out of them, slum lords, undertakers, preachers, con men, taking them for a ride."

"But the rest of us permit it, don't we? And the white man gets his share of the take too, doesn't he? Cheap labor. Docile votes. The whole business."

"We're no angels. Don't misunderstand me, we haven't been very decent either. But it's going to take a hundred and fifty years for those people to begin to live the way we do, no matter what the bleeding hearts say."

"We haven't got a hundred years to spare. And white people don't set them much of an example in the crime department."

Kenney shook his head in disgust. "I know that. Believe me, I have nightmares about it. We're sitting on a powder keg and not just

[402]

here. Every city with a large Negro slum's got the same problem. If it doesn't blow up in Oakland, it's Detroit or Baltimore or Newark or Kansas City or Memphis or Birmingham or New York."

"And you just sit and wait for it?"

"You do what you can to postpone it."

"No more."

"Life is postponing the inevitable. You got any suggestions? I'm a cop, not a big-shot politician or a fancy-dan college professor of sociology. I'm the guy they send out when the stores get looted and the merchants complain, when they burn the buildings and the land-lords beef, when someone gets mugged or his throat cut by some junkie who needs a fix. I protect life and property."

"You can't do that just with clubs and guns and jails—or even the gas chamber."

"You can't even do it with better jobs and houses and schools either. You've got to build a Negro life and respect, you've got to take these people and teach them everything from how to read to table manners and how to buy their groceries. Now, how the hell do you do that? They come from all over Africa, from a hundred different tribes and languages that had nothing in common except they had a black skin and got kidnaped and brought over here. They've been slaves and serfs for so long, I don't think they know— oh, what the hell!" He tossed off the rest of the bourbon, crumpled the paper cup and flipped it accurately into his wastebasket. "The only way to build themselves up is through power, and power means money or guns. Either will do, but both are better. Negroes with money haven't been free with it for their people—when did you last hear of a Negro endowing a college or a hospital for his own peo-ple?—and there aren't that many and they don't have that much long green either. So the rest of them are beginning to get the guns."

"You mean there's been a lot of the burglary I turned up, like that National Guard armory? More than I dug up?"

Glumly Kenney nodded.

"What happens when it blows up?"

"We'll crush them. Because we have the power and they don't. Black power is really the aim of black impotence. They'll make it so expensive that we may eventually have to give them power they

[403]

can't handle, don't know how to handle yet. Equality? Balls! What they want and need is special treatment, coddling, until you can build some kind of society *for* and *with* them, because they can't do it themselves. It's either that or sending them back to Africa, or putting them in special areas the way the South Africans have done. It may come to that yet."

"They learned something from the Irish and the British, the Jews and the British, the Mau Mau and the British," Sanders said.

"Except," Kenney pointed out, "that in those cases it was a white army, a white occupier that moved into their country. Here, it's them that were brought here into a white country. We're not a foreign occupying power."

"The Sioux and the Comanches and a few others might think so," Sanders offered.

"They got a right," Kenney conceded, grinning. "But not the Negroes. What do you do here, with only twenty million of them and one hundred eighty million of us?"

"A tenth of the population can make one hell of a mess of this country; they could fight a real guerrilla war."

"I suppose. But you know, Sanders, the Germans and the Russians pioneered the two most efficient, and most hideous, ways to handle the problem: The Nazis exterminated peoples; the Soviets picked them up, shoved 'em into cattle cars and sent them three thousand miles into Siberia. Thank God, this country doesn't do that kind of thing, yet."

"Yet?"

"Everything's possible. Or is that just a cynical cop's view of life? You burn down enough buildings, loot enough stores, kill enough people, and the reaction will come, sure as you're alive, and it won't be pretty. This is a goddam violent country once its dander is up—and even without its dander up."

"Can I quote you on all of this?"

Kenney's mouth turned sardonic. "Sanders, you do and I'll have your scalp. You have been away a long time. Of course, you can't quote me."

* * *

[404]

To Sanders' surprise he found Peter King leaning against the mottled wall of his tenement, a toothpick stuck jauntily between his marvelous white teeth. "You gittin mighty chummy with the fuzz these days, aintchu, Mr. Reporter?" Stationed in a rectangle of mellow late-afternoon sun warming the bricks, King looked like a combat-jacketed Othello framed for an open-air museum, warriorlike, huge, powerful.

"I go where the news is. That's my job."

"Cant. Someday you gonna take a trip with the fuzz and you don't come back, man, you know that?"

Mimicking his field-hand accent, Sanders replied, aware of the ironic echo of his father's old saw, "You pays your money, you takes your choice. That's what they used to say at headquarters when I went on S-and-D missions."

"What are they?"

"Search and destroy."

"Like that. Like that. We darkies gotta do more of that. Search and destroy."

Sanders looked around up and down the street, saw Negroes lolling at the entrances to buildings, others leaning out of windows, arms folded on windowsills, children playing in the street, women talking around their wire carts filled with laundry and groceries, and asked King to follow him into the hall for a minute. King looked him up and down appraisingly, the toothpick flicking back and forth between his teeth. "You changed your mind, Elliott?" King asked, his mouth lewd.

Sanders grimaced, not deigning to answer him, and preceded King into the semiobscurity of the hallway. A quick survey revealed that no one was in the corridor or on the stairs. In the privacy of that gloomy place Sanders took the snapshot out of his pocket, palmed it and extended his hand. Assuming that he wanted to shake hands, King put his own hand out but when he felt the snapshot against his palm instantly knew what it was and his fist convulsed painfully around Sanders' fingers. "Where did you get it?" he gritted. "You show it to the fuzz?"

"Let go of my hand," Sanders said.

King bore down more heavily still, crushing his fingers until he wanted to cry out. Instead, with a swift smash, Sanders brought his heel down on King's foot and King staggered back with an exclamation of pain, leaving the snapshot still in Sanders' palm, hopping around ludicrously on one foot, clutching the other shoe in his hands. "I said let go," Sanders repeated, "and I meant it."

"Brave boy, aren't you?" King mocked, hopping on one leg. "You're in *my* country now and you better watch your lily-white ass."

"This may be your country but it's mine too, and I can take care of my own ass, don't you worry about that," Sanders retorted. "You always think you can get things with force you couldn't get by other means. Well, let me tell you I came here to give that picture to you, because I didn't want to give it to the police. I wanted to warn you that you were a jackass to get involved in that kind of thing and that you were a sloppy fool to have left such a picture behind—"

"We had to leave there fast."

"Doubtless, but you shouldn't be carrying that kind of snapshot around. Bad enough you need it for your own kinky kicks, you sure as hell shouldn't be showing it to anyone else. How long do you think it would take the cops to run down the shop where it was developed and printed? And how many of your fag friends have you shown that thing to, to spice up the sex? You know how fast they're going to pin that picture on you, like the tail on a donkey, the first time a cop shows up and asks them? And how many people have you told that story about you and that priest to, so they'd feel sorry for you?" Sanders flayed him with each sentence as if it were a whip.

"No one, alive now, except you," King answered, almost shyly, and Sanders stopped short.

"George?"

King nodded.

Sanders felt guilt and remorse together. King had felt able to confide only in George Christiansen, his best friend, and in Elliott Sanders, both white. How goddam mixed up the man's feelings were, about himself, about others, about white men. "Listen, Peter," Sanders said, changing his tone, "you can't possibly win this kind of war," hearing Kenney's words echo in his.

"What will?" King, still on one foot but not hopping now, asked sullenly. "What do you want me, us, to be? More Booker T's and Uncle Toms?"

"I honestly don't know, but I do know this kind of war can bring only death and desolation to your own people."

"And to yours." King set his other foot down on the floor, gingerly, but gradually put his weight on it. "Some of us will die, that's true. A lot of us have died already. A lot more are likely to die still, but we'll take you down with us. We'll fight a guerrilla war, we'll assassinate your leaders—and ours. This country's already killed a couple of Presidents, don't you think we can knock off some Governors and Senators and Congressmen for good measure? And we'll burn down your cities and our ghettos at the same time, the way you're burning out those poor yellow bastards in Vietnam. Maybe we haven't got napalm, but we have got gasoline."

"I saw some of your Molotov cocktail preparations."

"There's more where that came from too."

"Sure there is, Peter, and then what? Okay, you've killed some leaders and you've burned out a couple of cities, or parts of them, what then?"

"Maybe the Man will see that we mean business this time, that we're serious, that we're not going to be bought off with another promise, with tokenism, with another couple of white man's niggers in the legislatures, another couple of Howards or Hamptons or Tuskegees where Mister Charley can educate himself some Sugar Hill niggers to live off the rest of us, to lord it over us and to help you keep us down."

"Is that the way it looks to you?"

"That's the way. We want to sit at the table, Elliott, not work in the kitchen, not wait on table, not eat the crumbs from it. We want a piece of that golden American apple pie, maybe even *à la mode,* with a big scoop of chocolate ice cream."

"I've seen a few revolutions, Peter, and mostly they leave things worse than before, not better."

[407]

"We've tried everything else. We got nowhere to go, man, but up."

"You know that's not true."

"We are at the end of our rope—"

"You'll be at the end of a rope."

" 'Southern trees bear a strange fruit'?" King gave the last word its homosexual meaning. "Nothing can stop us now, Elliott. That stuff you saw is only a little bit of what we got. There's plenty more stashed away and distributed to the soul brothers. Judgment Day's a-comin'. 'Ezekiel saw the wheel way up in the middle of the air.' King's face burned with a sexual hatred and ecstasy that made Sanders flinch and recoil. They stood there, frozen into their stances, until Sanders, feeling cold horror and impotence, handed him the snapshot again. This time King took it without a glance and with a vicious pleasure tore it into shreds and let them flutter out of his hands like snow. "Thanks," King said, "you are a friend." The words, wrenched from some dark place of his spirit, were spoken choked and hoarse, but they were intended as a benison.

"Even if I am white?"

"*Especially because* you're white."

* * *

Monique announced her return from the Côte d' Azur in a manner that pleased and flattered him far more than Sanders thought possible. She almost never called him at the office and absolutely never at home; it was he who invariably had to get in touch with her. That evening, he came out of the office and walked up the Champs-Élysées, head down, mind stirred with the recollection of the previous night with Elaine, and another night in which his father, drunkenly, had taunted his mother at the dinner table just before, cavalierly, telling her he was going out on the town. The memory of Elaine was still so intense in his mind that he could smell her flesh and hair and perfume on the night breeze that swept down from the Arc. The evening air was soft and wet, the smell of spring on it, although spring was more than one swallow away. An evening like that other night, a truly spring night, with the chestnut leaves and candles stiff with desire, opulent with sap, when his father, in response to his mother's softly spoken plea that he stay home that night, that they try once again to bring back some of the joy of their earlier years, had derisively told her that the bloom was off the peach and what could she expect. They were married, no longer lovers but people who shared each other's lives, had a child together, were united by fortune and misfortune. Sanders knew even then what his mother wanted because he had already discerned that special soft somnolent look her face took on, that special far-eyed stare, when she spoke of their coutrship and honeymoon that even a nine-year-old could see, if not understand, that halcyon time when all between them had been gay and meaningful, before, Sanders understood even then, he had been born. If his father had slapped his mother's face, he could no more clearly have left an imprint than his remark that at least she had memories and that Sacha Guitry had promised that "Memory is one paradise out of which we cannot be driven." His mother's bleak rejoinder, delivered with starched face and pressed lips, had thanked him for his generous reassurances, had been grateful to him for at least permitting her her memories. But Guitry was wrong, Sanders knew, an actor's reminiscent nostalgia for footlights and applause and first nights; memory was one hell from which we were never freed—except by death. And marriage was that curious relationship in which a woman might be your best and most intimate friend or your worst and coldest enemy, sometimes alternating between the two, sometimes being the two together.

A woman's high heels clacked behind him, then were at his side, and an arm slipped under his and a hoarse rough voice, its accent from Artois or Picardie, inquired, *"On fait l'amour?"*

"Pas ce soir, mademoiselle," Sanders replied curtly, without even a glance at the woman, preoccupied, trying to shrug her loose but she wouldn't free his arm.

"Tu veux que je te suce? Une partouze? Alors, donne-moi ton queue," she whispered hoarsely. As her hand reached for him Sanders intercepted it and moved away and then saw that it was Monique. "Ah, *mon homme,* I see you are, after all, and in your own way, faithful." The usual linen sheen of her skin was dark with sun, a healthy burnt-umber color that was a rebuke to winter and made her smile snowy. Sanders swept her into his arms, lifted her into the

air and whirled her around in unabashed delight until he saw people staring. Then he put her down, embraced her more formally, kissed both of her cheeks and breathed into her hair, "You're back, Monique, you're back."

"I told you it would only be ten days," she protested.

"I know. I know. But you didn't even send me a postcard."

"I didn't know where to send it." It was a subtle rebuke: She was telling him that she was unable to write openly to him either at home or at his office.

Monique took his arm again and they walked together up the avenue, Sanders warmed by her presence and by the insistent caress of her breast, her hip and thigh against him as they strolled. "I only returned at noon and I came here to 'pick you up' and surprise you."

Sanders knew how much it must have cost her to make such an overt gesture, such a demonstration of need and affection. "You surprised me all right. My God, Monique, it's good to see you again!"

"And you," she replied shyly, "but I've been waiting for a long time because I didn't want to miss you and I'm cold. You must buy me a drink."

"Of course, come on." They sat in the café at a small table way in the back, sipping coffee and brandy and looking at each other, speechless with pleasure, their legs locked, their hands glued together, her breast at his elbow. "Tell me about Cannes," Sanders began at long last, but she refused.

"You don't want to hear and I don't want to tell you."

"You look wonderful."

"Sun and sea and rest."

"And you've gained weight."

"I ate like a pig."

"It's becoming."

Monique drank the rest of her brandy before she spoke again. "Let's go home," she murmured, moving against him, her eyes and mouth wet; she had said *chez nous* not *chez moi*, and even if he couldn't forget the man or men she had gone with to Cannes, he knew she loved him, not perhaps as he wanted, not perhaps even as she might want, and the question that shaped in his teeth, though he did not utter it but drank it down with his brandy, was the same

[410]

one he had asked himself so many times before: Was that the only way that love came, the way you *didn't* want it?

Yet it was like coming home. The next three weeks were what he had always imagined his honeymoon with Elaine would be like and he spent every minute he could with Monique, going home late at night to find Elaine always waiting there for him, no matter how late, always in bed, always reading a book in the cone of yellow light from the bed lamp, her whole demeanor expectant but subdued. What she expected Sanders couldn't fathom, but there was no word of rebuke from her lips, not once the tidal wave of *cons, trottineuses, chats, radeuses, greffiers,* and other argot for whores he never knew how she'd learned; not once, moreover, did she make a move to touch him in the old luring way. Stymied by all of it, exhausted, Sanders let it go altogether and did not attempt to make love to her. Though politely attentive, he was remote; if they were not strangers, they were estranged, tied to each other with silken threads so fine he only knew they were steel when he tried to pull away from them. He bought Elaine flowers and candy, pâté and smoked oysters, and other delicacies she enjoyed; and on the nights when Monique still refused to see him—he had almost forgiven her for Cannes, almost forgotten that she had gone; as the sun faded out of her skin, as in wintry Paris she turned from burnt umber to tan to beige and then back to her native fairness, forgiving her for Cannes was easier; but he could not forgive her for insisting still on her "free nights"— he took Elaine to the movies, to the pelota games nearby, to the automobile show, for long silent walks in the park, or sat and watched her play double solitaire at a café near the frozen fountains of St. Cloud.

He saw that Elaine was suffering, that she wanted to speak and couldn't, but he wouldn't help her because he too couldn't; the next move had to be hers. They'd been married for more than a year and he didn't know what else to do; he'd done everything he knew how to, tried everything, even, he reminded himself with pain and chagrin, rape, but all of it had come to nothing. They walked together, they ate together, they slept together, but they were like the old French couples they saw in the parks, in Vincennes or Boulogne or the Champs de Mars, who sat on the benches next to each other like stone monoliths, not talking, not touching, clearly belonging to each other, more clearly having once truly belonged to one another.

With Monique it was the reverse, easy, intimate, passionate, though they did almost the same things together that he did with Elaine: They ate at bistros; they went to old movies; they listened to Monique's *chanteuses* and danced to her records—and each time he heard Patachou singing *J'Attendrai* it was with a chill at the base of his spine—they walked in the gray drizzle of the winter streets. But they touched; they could not keep their hands off each other and their lovemaking was like none Sanders had ever known before, an open joy in the flesh and its touch and taste and fragrance he had never before encountered. Though she did not speak the words, Monique told him in a myriad ways that she loved him, and though he strove to meet her intensity, though he felt deeply for her, though he enjoyed her sex as no other, he knew that he was tied to Elaine more profoundly and though he fought to free himself of those ties, he couldn't. And Monique sensed his struggle though he couldn't tell how, so that there was a faint desperation in her ardor, an immoderate overflow of passion that sometimes made him timorous, if only for moments, before he was carried away by his own wild luxurious feelings. One midnight, as he dressed to go back to the Quai de Passy, Monique drew him back down to the bed again, impatient with his clothes, overriding his protests that it was late, taking him into her with a thrust that was like a collision. They strove and heaved together until at the critical moment she stopped him, held him immobile, poised on the brink, her breast heaving, her mouth agape with pleasure, drank in air and passionately commanded; "Elliott, make me a child! Make me a son!" For a moment, glued together at their center, their writhing a torment, they hung there stopped in time until the last interminable lunge of his loins took him helplessly over the brink and he came into her, casting his spurt at her inmost flesh like a flower, sounding her depths like a bell whose peal he heard and felt like quivering flesh. But she had caught him naked, known him soft, seen his instant hesitation; he had fulfilled her mounted desire but balked her seeking love. She slid out from under him and went to the bidet.

Early next morning Sanders was interrupted at an editorial meeting with Tessier by Monique's call informing him that she was leaving Paris for a week or two of skiing at Bad Gastein, and with Tessier's sardonic eye on him Sanders sputteringly tried to persuade her to wait, not to leave until at least they could have lunch and talk it over, but she refused. She was leaving from Orly for Austria in two hours—she took care to convey to him that it was "Nous *venons de partir*" so he would know she wasn't going alone—and she was sorry but she wouldn't be able to wait for lunch.

Except for a single plaintive and angry postcard on whose face was the cloudless cobalt sky high over gray-and-white Radhausberg (2,651 meters), the snow-blue firs and pines which like legionnaires in phalanxes climbed from the red-roofed, brick-walled village in the cleft below up the steep sides of the mountains, Sanders did not hear from her for ten days. On the card Monique had scribbled the message that she was enjoying the high delights of the *idealer Wintersportplatz*, but that she was by no means missing the pleasures down below. He got the point, more painful and piercing than he thought it could be. Monique mailed the card to the office and it was lying there on his desk, text up, when Tessier came by to discuss some photographs of the de Gaulle press conference that they were going to use in the magazine but which needed cropping and saw it. "Ah, so that is why you are such a bear, your *petite amie* is off skiing in Austria."

"*Rognons!*" Sanders exploded.

"Why certainly, Sanders," Tessier rejoined, deceptively mild, "that's the menu for the whole world, *rognons* or *oignons*, those who eat and those who are eaten. In a manner of speaking we are all screwed and all screwing everyone else. That's people. That's politics. That's life." Pleased with his bons mots Tessier walked jauntily off but not without leaving the photographic prints for Sanders' cropping.

The fortnight Monique spent in Austria was even more tormenting than the ten days she'd spent on the Riviera because Sanders knew that they had passed a watershed that night, that he had failed her, been unable to meet the heights and depths of her passionate commitment, and he could not imagine what peaks and valleys lay beyond the divide. As if sensing that he was suffering through a

[413]

crisis, perhaps even understanding what it was, Elaine was quieter and more attentive to him than she had ever been before, showing an affectionate concern that had none of the old irate lewdness or provocative passion. She cooked for him every night things she knew he was especially fond of—she was a superb cook, the kitchen one of the few places she seemed almost completely serene—she left him by himself when he wanted to be alone, to stand in the dark on the balcony, sometimes in the middle of the night, wrapped in blankets, watching the dark oily Seine and the barges bringing fuel up from the coast. Until, at last, the night after he received Monique's post-card from Bad Gastein, Elaine found him on the balcony, shivering under the blankets, his teeth chattering, his bare feet blue with cold, and led him into the kitchen where she made him hot coffee, poured him brandy and then bundled him into bed. As he lay there still trembling, the warmth of coffee and brandy in his stomach only slowly beginning to radiate their fever through his limbs, Elaine be-gan to make love to him, arousing him gradually, tantalizing as before, but with a sadness so delicate, so utterly without hope or joy, that he was moved to tears. Yet he was unprepared and startled when at the moment he turned to her, as he had done on so many nights before, she opened herself wide to him and led him into her —but only a little way for she was dry and unreceptive and he could go no further. Lying there, her teeth sunk into her lower lip, her legs stiffly outstretched and welcoming only by an act of determination, her face, come to grief, was turned away from him into the pillow. Gently as he could, he moved patiently into her, felt and heard the parched tearing of her dry inner flesh, the warm ooze of her blood and its trickle against his thighs, and was transported by the knowl-edge that whatever, whoever, had gone before, this was his first night with her, her true defloration that was simultaneously her flowering, a rape that she had willed herself in love. Implanted in her dryness, her legs dangling askew around him like the broken hands of an old clock, he leaned to kiss her and with his fingers turned her face up from the pillow to him, saw the bloody third lip she had bitten into her chin. Painfully he kissed her teeth and lips free of that bite, tasted the salt of her blood, swallowed the unnerv-ing sob of her mouth, the echo of her aching cry, and found the

searching freedom of her tongue. Martyred but willing her martyrdom with bravery, she was at last his wife. She had violated the innermost clefts of her spirit; for him she had like Persephone taken
the first steps out of the darkness, up from the Hades of hatred
where her gnarled roots lay mired in panic, where her disheveled
spirit ran riot in terror. But if she was Persephone, Sanders understood that he was an unfit Orpheus to play her out of her hell. To
grow a sunny tree out of such nightmare roots required a miracle of
new birth, rebirth, an unfolding of such proportions that whatever
music his lyre was capable of would be inadequate. Willingly, eag-
erly, he assumed the burden of being her helpmeet; but it was she
who was heavy-laden and only her will to live and love could wring
freedom from the rotten-root skein of melancholy, mania and memory; only her courage and persistence could bring her to true flower
and unblemished fruit. She would have to learn the lonely lesson to
remember and forget not only her wounds but her very scars; to
convert and transform her most searing recollections to a serene forgetfulness.

For three successive nights it was the same, Elaine willing herself
accessible with so much palpable effort that it was another and
separate presence in their bed; so determined was she not to give in
to herself but to give in to him, that Sanders continued what was
physically unsatisfying if psychologically deeply moving, what was
pitiful and painful to him.

At his desk the following morning, not quite awake and stirred
by Elaine's courage and resolution, yet finding her sacrifice of the
maiden almost as difficult to bear and as lamentable as her earlier
closure, Sanders was drinking his coffee laced with brandy and eating a soggy brioche when Monique called. The instant he heard
her voice he was certain something was wrong. He blurted that Bad
Gastein must have been fun indeed since it was now more than two
weeks since she'd left, but she did not address herself to his rebuke.
"I want to talk to you right away, Elliott," she said. "I'm waiting for
you." *J'attendrai.*

"Can't you talk over the phone?"

"No. This must be face-to-face between us and right away." *Le
temps passe et court. . . .*

"Is something wrong?"

"Very wrong, Elliott. Come quickly." *En battant tristement, dans mon coeur plus lourd . . . j'attendrai.*

"I'll be there as soon as I can."

Because he had to go to the Quai d'Orsay that morning anyway no explanations were necessary for Tessier when he left almost immediately. In the taxi he tried to hold down the panic that filled him but he couldn't. As he walked up the stairs Patachou's *J'attendrai* rang in his ears though he knew no music was playing. He knocked, heard Monique's *"Entrez!"* and went in. Usually she came to the door to let him in, to greet and embrace him, but now sunk into a chair, her arms hanging limp over its sides, she had a cigarette between her fingers burned down almost to the filter so that it sent up a tiny corkscrewed funeral pyre of smoke. Her skin was burned dark by the Alpine winter sun, her blond hair was bleached by it; and wearing the blue pleated peignoir he'd given her, she looked beautiful, full of life—and completely dejected. She didn't rise to meet him but waved him leadenly to a chair facing her, never taking her eyes off him. When he was seated she began to speak in a soft uncertain voice that broke, as he had never heard it break before, full of unshed tears. "What I have to tell you is bad news, very bad news, and there is no way to make it easier. I am guilty and not guilty and even that doesn't matter because there is no way to make amends."

"We are alive," Sanders said, knowing it was a lie, "nothing can be that terrible." Controlling himself, he took the cigarette from her inert fingers, stubbed it out in an ashtray and then lit another one for her and gave it to her. "Now, tell me what it is."

Monique hunched her shoulders, spread her arms, dropped them dispiritedly in her lap. "I don't know where to begin, how to tell it . . ."

"Begin at the beginning, tell it naturally," Sanders advised, though he knew it was impossible advice. Then he said no more.

"You remember when I went to Cannes?" Monique asked shyly, and when he nodded, went on, "I went with an old friend, a man I've known for more than five years. He comes down from Lille and he's been very good to me, kind, decent, better to me than anyone

[416]

has been—except you. He visits Paris perhaps ten or twelve times a year, and sometimes he takes me with him on trips. Amsterdam, Dieppe, Brussels, the Schwarzwald, Copenhagen, Chamonix, Mallorca. Sometimes on business, sometimes just—to be with me. This year when he asked me to go to Cannes, I couldn't say no. And, as I told you, I wanted to get away from you for a time, put some distance between us." Monique stubbed her cigarette out without smoking it, rose and began impatiently to pace.

"Albert is a decent man. Lonely. A man who was always kind to me. When I came back from Bad Gastein—no, I didn't go to Austria with him, that was with some other people—he called to tell me . . . to tell me . . . that he was contaminated"—the expression she used was *il est plombé*—"that he had venereal disease. Syphilis." Her eyes, downcast, were fixed on the design in the old Oriental carpet, as if she were genuinely concerned with the figures in the pattern. Waiting for him to speak, she stood stock-still, unable to look at him.

"And you," Sanders asked, clearing his throat, "are infected also?"

Monique nodded. "Albert has several other women in Lille. One of them was infected and gave it to him."

"And he gave it to you?"

Again she nodded. "I couldn't believe it when he called. I went to two doctors, they both did the tests, and both are positive, though it seems—I have never been so fortunate as to know before—that it is difficult to be absolutely certain with women. Without the tests, that is."

"A woman in Lille to Albert to Monique to me," he said aloud, philosophically, and to himself, "and from me to Elaine." The chain was determined, the appointment in Samara, or Bad Gastein, or Cannes or Lille, a network of irreversible cause and effect.

"Perhaps you will be lucky," Monique said, but there was no hope in her voice.

"Me? Lucky?" Sanders said, heard the self-pity start into his voice and crushed it. "No, I don't think so."

"The doctors have already given me penicillin. It is nothing to be alarmed about, they say," she announced encouragingly. "They tell me that my fear and my revulsion are medieval. In a week or ten days it will all be over, forgotten like a bad dream." But he could see that the medical advice and cheer had not really convinced her.

Over, Sanders thought, but not forgotten. Not in ten days or ten years. Nothing is more tenacious, more pernicious, than recollection; the more you want to forget, the more vividly and frequently you remember.

Monique walked to his chair and in a movement so like collapse that he swiftly put out his hands to catch her, she knelt before him, head down, pleading, "Forgive me, Elliott, I did not mean—"

"There's nothing to forgive, Monique. Absolutely nothing. No one is at fault—and we're all at fault. This is the way life is."

Fiercely she shook her head. "No, no." She gulped. "She"—Monique couldn't speak Elaine's name—"must have it too and you will have to tell her, your wife, I mean, won't you?"

"There is no alternative; I will tell her."

"I'm so sorry and it's no good being sorry. Please say you forgive me."

"I forgive you, Monique," Sanders said, and to himself, "but I don't forgive me. Not for you, not for Elaine."

Monique raised her tear-stained face to him, eyes closed, lashes wet, murmuring, "Elliott, my love, take me here, take me now. Make love to me, love me." After an instant of recoil, Sanders bent through his revulsion and kissed her but he couldn't, he knew he couldn't, and though he held her close, kissed away her tears, his flesh would not rise to the occasion. Once again he knew he had failed her. Once again, and just as grievously, he'd failed her. Monique tried to move him as she had tried in the past and always succeeded, but his flesh shrank away from her, helplessly, obdurately.

At the corner bistro he called Michel Fejnstejn, one of his father's old friends and before the war their family physician. He had not seen or talked to Fejnstejn for a long time and Michel sounded surprised and pleased to hear from him, paid him compliments about the stories he'd read in the magazine, the pictures he'd seen, giving him the highest praise Fejnstejn could—he was the true son of his father—until, abruptly, Sanders cut in to explain why he was calling. "Oh, I see," Fejnstejn said sadly and then his voice changed, an old and smoothly oiled reflex, and grew professionally cheerful. "You know, Elliott, I have retired from practice, but I still see a few old patients and friends. Come along."

Fejnstejn's office was still in the same old and now genteel shabby building on the Boulevard Jourdan not far from the Porte d'Orléans, and six floors below his windows lay the gray frozen earth and grass of the Parc Montsouris. Fejnstejn greeted him himself, affectionate, embracing him, kissing him on both cheeks, his clear blue eyes appraising and candid. "It has been many years now, Elliott, altogether too many. But I have followed your career from a distance with pleasure." There was no rebuke, no recrimination, though Sanders had not called him in a decade, had done no more than send him an occasional Christmas card and the announcement of his wedding.

"How is Elaine?" Fejnstejn asked. Though he'd never met her, he'd remembered her name.

"I don't know," Sanders replied.

"You haven't told her what you think?"

"No, I didn't see any point to alarming her until I was certain."

Fejnstejn shook his white head sagely. "Sensible, sensible. Come" —he took Sanders' arm—"let's go into the office." There, donning a short green coat and his pince-nez, he briskly ordered Sanders to undress, then gave him a thorough physical examination. After an hour he spoke his first though preliminary verdict: There was no sign of venereal or any other disease. Had he, Sanders, noted any physical signs? Sanders confessed that he'd seen none. "The tests will tell," Fejnstejn said and, swiftly bringing up the blue vein in the crook of his left arm with a rubber tie, deftly inserted the needle, struck the vein the very first time and drew the blood, dark red, slowly out into the glass tube. "Call me tomorrow," Fejnstejn said, and Sanders heard the fatigue plainly in his voice. "I'll ask the laboratory to rush it through."

At the door of the flat Sanders turned to thank him but Fejnstejn waved his thanks aside. "Nothing, it's nothing, Elliott. I hope that the tests are negative."

"So do I," Sanders avowed fervently. Only then did he remember to ask about Babette, Fejnstejn's daughter and only child, and the one living remembrance of his wife Ilona, the beloved Tula of his own childhood, the one friend of his father's, the one woman friend, that is, who had also been a friend of his mother's, the Tula who had been his godmother, the Tula who had been taken by the Nazis to perish in the crematorium.

For an instant Fejnstejn's face was like a mirror smashed suddenly into slivers but still contained in its frame. "She died two years ago, a pulmonary embolism," Fejnstejn blurted.

His hand on the doorknob, Sanders stood there stunned, the door and his face ajar. "I didn't know," he finally managed. Babette, he knew, would have been twenty-four years old, because she'd been born in 1939, the same year that he and his mother had left France for America and left his father behind. And his parents had returned the compliment for Michel and Tula; they had served as Babette's godparents. The following year Lovett Carpenter Sanders, who had been counseling the Fejnstejns to leave France since 1937, had helped them escape over the Pyrenees into Spain but somehow Tula had been taken at the border, betrayed by one of the men paid to make their "contact," while Michel, after waiting for her—they went separately and had a rendezvous—with the infant Babette drugged and strapped to his back, had made it over the mountains with the two Basques who had taken almost his last franc but had saved their lives. Babette had gotten pneumonia then and had been a long time mending, but had, so far as Sanders knew, been fine thereafter.

"How? Why didn't you let me know?" he stammered.

"In childbirth. A pulmonary embolism. I sent you a notice of the funeral but when you didn't come I assumed you were out of the country."

"When was it, Michel?"

Fejnstejn told him and Sanders, remembering, explained that he'd been in the hospital in Algiers with malaria then and a lot of his mail had gone astray in transit.

"You had malaria?" Fejnstejn asked, removing his pince-nez and wearily rubbing the bridge of his nose with his fingers. "Why didn't you tell me?"

"You didn't ask me. Is it important?"

"I'll have to do another test. That will take two, perhaps three days, to confirm the Wassermann. Call me then."

Babette, Sanders thought, with the clear blue eyes and the blond hair of Fejnstejn's beloved Ilona, dead at twenty-four. How unimportant the syphilis seemed, how minor an anguish even hearing it from Monique, even telling it to Elaine, was compared to what he had seen as the naked despair on Michel Fejnstejn's face. "Her husband?" Sanders asked. "What happened to him?"

"He remarried a few months ago."

"Do you see him?"

Fejnstejn shook his head, briefly but decisively. "No, for both of us it is better not to."

"Why didn't you call me, get in touch with me?" Sanders asked, unreasonably angry, he knew, because he was ashamed to have let the relationship languish, ashamed because he had not made the effort to keep in closer, more personal touch with the old man, guilty because now, in his own emergency, he had without an instant's hesitation called on Fejnstejn for help.

"I thought you were busy, you know, an important job and a lot of traveling, and newly married," Fejnstejn replied apologetically.

You mean, Sanders said to himself, that you thought I was a stinking snob who forgot his old friends, and particularly his parents' old friends, so you spared me the embarrassment of calling me. Don't call us, we'll call you.

For the first time then Sanders saw Michel Fejnstejn with his reporter's eye, freed for the moment of his own fright and self-absorption, and saw a painfully emaciated old man, the lines so deep in his face that they seemed furrowed into the bone, the hair altogether white, even the thick clumps of eyebrow that had so delighted him as a child now snowy. An old man, though Fejnstejn couldn't have been more than sixty, was in fact younger than his father would have been had Lovett Carpenter Sanders lived. "Are you well, Michel?" Sanders asked.

"As well as you can expect an old man to be," Fejnstejn replied, the tone full of the false joviality of the professional physician. "After Babette passed away I had a coronary, which was why I stopped practicing—for a time. But I'm fine now. Collateral circulation is better than what I had before and I'm my old self again. And I've taken up a bit of practice again too." The explanation was brisk but not at all personally revealing and Fejnstejn's gaunt frame and haunted eyes belied it. Spontaneously, Sanders reached out and with both hands took Fejnstejn's in his.

"Michel," Sanders said, "I'm so sorry."

"It is the way life is," Fejnstejn said. "Life makes very few exceptions." The measured resignation of those sentences echoed his words to Monique earlier in the day. But neither Fejnstejn the man nor Fejnstejn the physician was content to say farewell on that somber note. "You'll see, Elliott, things will improve. You will be healthy, if you really are sick, and I am truly much stronger now than I was before. And when you and Elaine have a child, a son, or even"—his smile was close to tears—"a daughter—you know, we are obsessed with being fruitful and multiplying—you must promise to invite me. I shall bring the champagne and we shall celebrate."

"We'll make you godfather, Michel, to two generations," Sanders promised, not certain that he would ever have the child he wanted so much, son or daughter, with Elaine, but certain that he would not now forget Michel Fejnstejn for godfather.

The three days Sanders had to wait for the results of the blood tests were a torment. Because he could no longer contain himself after a day and a half he called Fejnstejn on the second day only to find that the Wassermann had been positive, which might mean nothing because of his bout of malaria, but which made waiting to have the confirmation of the dark field test absolutely necessary. When, at last, on the evening of the third day, he called Fejnstejn again, he was numb with certainty. "Michel," he said, his voice rising in spite of himself, "I've been sitting here for half an hour trying to get up the courage to call you, so please tell me swiftly and straight. Do I have *It?*"

"Yes," Fejnstejn said, after only the slightest pause, "the tests were conclusive. You have syphilis."

"Thank you," Sanders said, feeling only a surge of horrified relief that the waiting and uncertainty were over. "What do we do now?"

Fejnstejn asked if he had slept with anyone besides Elaine and the woman who had infected him, because if so he had to inform them and when Sanders said there was no one else, he said, "Good!" Then Fejnstejn described the treatment, asked him to come to the

[422]

office at two the next afternoon to begin it and to bring Elaine with him. Once more he was the poised professional physician.

"What for?" Sanders asked.

"For treatment, Elliott. You will almost surely have infected her but we must take tests to be sure. Have you told her yet?"

"I will tonight," Sanders promised, "and I'll bring her with me tomorrow."

Three times on the way home he stopped for drinks but the brandy didn't warm him or even get him tipsy; instead, it gave him an icy clarity of vision of a future that stretched interminably before him without either Elaine or Monique, linear-sharp and macadam-paved as a Chirico painting but without any hope of human warmth or connection. At home the elevator wasn't working and he had to climb the seven floors to their flat. He let himself in, hoping that Elaine would be out shopping, or somewhere else, praying that he might take a shower, have another drink, attempt to compose himself, perhaps be able to work out some way of telling her that would not be altogether horrifying for her and humiliating for him, but she was there, waiting for him, dressed in a dark-red plaid pleated Scottish kilt and deep-green turtlenecked sweater with a silver pin of two profiles kissing, melding into one another, one smiling, the other grimacing, so that you could not tell where weeping ended and laughing began. The pin seemed almost too appropriate not to have been planned: What was the French proverb his father had always scored off his mother with? "In every love affair the tragedy is that one kisses and the other permits himself to be kissed." And in every marriage.

Elaine came to kiss him, her face a torment of shyness and uncertainty that made him cringe when she touched him and that left her crestfallen when he barely brushed her cheek. They had dinner in silence and he drank more wine than he wanted, hoping to loosen his tongue, and instead felt deadened. Afterward she brought coffee and cognac to the chair at the window where he sat, a book in his lap, looking out at a black-and-silver sky flecked with gray stars, and sat at his feet, her head against his thigh. When he soothingly stroked her hair and said, haltingly, "Elaine, however bad it has been between us, however rotten it may seem to you tomorrow,

[423]

I love you," she turned her face into his leg and kissed his trouser, and while he continued to talk kept her face pressed there and did not take it away so that her expression was hidden from him. "I married you because no one had moved me, no one had touched me as you did, since my parents. I was glad to be alive when you came into a room. It was like sunlight on the darkest day of winter when spring and hope seem buried forever. And then afterwards I couldn't believe what was happening, I couldn't believe that it was going to go on like that. A couple of weeks, sure. The shyness and inexperience of a young girl, I told myself, but it wasn't that. Scarcely. After a while I thought it was not too little experience but too much." Her shudder ran into and through him like a shiver of his own. "And I wanted a family, a child, children, which I knew we couldn't have the way we were. I couldn't stand what you did to me, what I let you do to me, what I did to myself, and the more skillful, the more tantalizing, the more exciting it was, the worse it was, yet I couldn't stop because I thought that, in time, it would change, grow, become something else. That, in my all-too-American mind, it would turn out all right.

"Until after a while I couldn't bear it any more and I found . . . another woman. A prostitute"—he could barely bring himself to say that word, to describe Monique, insult her that way, for he knew that the world he had built with Monique could scarcely be described in those terms any more than she could be described as a *poule*—"but a good woman. She gave me something you couldn't or wouldn't give me and she made it possible, somehow, for me to go on trying with you.

"I know that sounds like a lie, an apology, a rationalization, but it isn't. At first, it was just for the simple natural physical relief she offered, the sense of my own masculinity made whole and normal again—"

"Thrust home, d'Artagnan!" Elaine mumbled into his thigh.

"What was that?"

Elaine repeated what she'd said, still not removing her face from the haven of his leg.

"Yes, thrust home. Just that, the homely sense of my normality made flesh. And it left me courage enough, patience enough, free

[424]

enough to go on trying to change our—to make our marriage over in another way." Even as he said that, he knew he loved Monique, not perhaps as he loved Elaine but in a quite separate but by no means less valuable way. He had the clear sense that Monique had never cheated him; she had given him syphilis but had played fair with him all the way right down the line, while Elaine had never played fair with him, was not even now playing fair with him, and yet why should she? Why was he obsessed with that childish hangover of his mother's character and religious insistence on fair play? Monique surely had not known about the syphilis before she'd given it to him and he was certain that if she had she would not have gone to bed with him, would have warned him off. But Elaine had known what her own past had been like, had known what those frozen thighs betokened, probably even how they had come to pass, and had not told him the truth. With wanton cruelty they had done each other in, for one thing had led to another and now, surely a poetic ironical justice for the sickness and frustration she had bestowed on him, he had given her syphilis just when with the wrenching of her spirit she had cloven herself apart for him, to him, made possible the home and family that he coveted.

"You loved her?" Elaine asked his leg.

"Yes," he admitted, newly aware, intent on the truth. "I think I did. Not as I did you, nor as I do you now, but I loved her. She was good to me, she restored my confidence, my manhood, my conviction, my hope that there was still hope for me, for us. She slept with other men, several of them"—Elaine's teeth bit sharply into his leg through his trouser—"and today I found out, she told me, I had the results of the tests, today . . . I have . . . she gave me syphilis." Elaine's teeth closed on his flesh so painfully he barely refrained from shouting, and then suddenly his flesh was freed and she sprawled away from him on the floor, beating her head against the carpet, shrieking hysterically.

"She gave you . . . syphilis . . . and I . . . opened myself . . . to . . . finally . . . opened myself wide . . . I let you . . . inside of . . . you gave it . . . to me!" Her shrieking laughter was transformed into a yowl, an animal at bay. "I tore myself open. I broke myself apart. I let you and your dirty, filthy, fucking prick inside

[425]

of me." She banged her head again and again, resoundingly, against the carpet until he pulled her to her feet and tried to hold her against him, to still her screaming and her shaking, but she tore herself out of his grasp.

"You dirtied me up inside. You filled me full of your vile germs, your obscene sperm. I hope I'm pregnant. I hope you have a child, I hope I have your child, syphilitic, blind, scabrous, moronic. It would serve you right. You and your whores and your whoring around! *Elaine,*" she mocked and mimicked him, "*however bad it has been between us, however rotten it may seem to you tomorrow, I love you.* What the hell do you know about love? Love, for you that's sticking that piece of diseased meat into someone. Rotten, rotten, rotten, that's what you are. Foul. I hate you. I hate your dirty, filthy, fucking prick!" Her gales and storms of laughter and weeping rose like a keening wail into a sirenlike hysterical screech that didn't stop until he slapped her face sharply with his open palm, once, twice, and then she tried to kick him, knee him, but he held her until she fell again to the floor, holding her belly, growling and moaning, chewing the carpet, slavering like a wounded and maddened animal. After a long time she lay there limp, her body curled up into a ball, whimpering, and he was able to carry her into the bedroom, but when he tried to undress her to put her to bed, she began once more to shriek in a cracked voice, trembling terribly, so that he was able only to lay her down on the bed, cover her with blankets and put out all the lights except that ironic green night-light of hers. Then he went out with his own blankets to sit and stare at the twisting Seine, to see if he could think his way out of the labyrinth in which he found himself.

In the morning while he was brewing coffee she came into the kitchen, wordlessly accepted a cup from him and, refusing to sit down, drank it standing at the table. She was perfectly groomed, her hair tied back with a narrow black velvet ribbon with tiny black sequins on it that glistened like raindrops in the pale-pink morning light, her black suit and ruffled white blouse impeccable. She looked so scrubbed and healthy, so lovely, that the nightmare vision of the illness he had sent crawling through her blood, seeping through her tissues, made him feel nauseated. Briefly he told her about Michel

Fejnstejn, that they were expected at his office that afternoon, but she would have none of it. In a cold, flat voice she said she wasn't going.

"You must have the tests," Sanders said desperately. "You might not have it."

"I have it," Elaine replied, "it couldn't happen any other way. It's right. It's justice. I deserve it and so I have it. I'm certain of that. But I don't want to go with *you*, I don't want *your* doctor, I don't want to have anything to do with *your* treatment. I'll do it in my own way."

"How?"

"What's the matter, Elliott, are you afraid I'll reinfect you?" Her sneering lips, like pale worms, writhed across her face. "Don't fret. You won't get another chance to infect me. I promise you that."

"That wasn't what concerned me, Elaine. I was worried about you—"

Elaine snorted.

"We've got to talk this out. We've got to make some effort not just to cure this—syphilis—but to cure what's ailing us. Come with me to Fejnstejn. He's a fine man. An old friend. A good doctor. He'll look after you."

"I'm going to the American Hospital."

"Isn't that a little public?"

"Does that bother you, Elliott? Afraid one of your newshound friends will get the story and make it pubic—I mean public? What does that matter now? Besides, it'll only raise your stock with the boys at the Crillon bar. I want to have an American doctor to talk to and to look after me," she said. She would brook no argument.

"All right, the American Hospital. What then?" he finally asked.

"I don't know—yet." Eyes wide with fright, she seemed uncertain for the first time that morning.

"Do you want me to leave, to stay at a hotel?"

"You want to run to your whore?" she flared. "Go! Go on!" Then she relented and shook her head. "No, not yet. I want to think for a while. But I want you in the guest room, not with me."

"If you want it that way—"

"I do want it that way."

[427]

"That's the way it started—"

"Well, fine. Maybe that's the way it will end."

"Eventually, Elaine, we have to talk. Why not now?"

"I can't. You can be rational and logical about this kind of thing, I know, but I can't. In the deepest, most intimate parts of me, I feel violated, sickened, betrayed in ways I have never been able to bear all my life. Your whore"—her face burned with bitterness, her voice flamed with it—"gave you this terrible disease that you've given me and that I feel I should be passing on to someone else, as if I were only a single link in a chain letter, and not a French letter either, which might have prevented the whole thing, and that if I don't pass it on it will kill me. I know it's not sensible but I can't be sensible about any of this."

"I know how you feel—"

"No you don't. You can't. You feel unlucky, Elliott, that's all, picked on by fate. It's all an accident, just one of those things, and you got caught. That's not the way I feel. This is my logical punishment, the reward for my inner rottenness that all my life has called for, that my character requires."

"You're making more of it than it is, Elaine. It is *not* the visitation of the gods, the scourge of the Lord for the unclean spirit—"

"For who would 'scape whipping? You're right and you're wrong, Elliott. This is my scourge, brought down on myself because I violated myself and so you violated me. Tit for tat. One good turn deserves another."

"That's sick."

"Yes, Elliott, I *am* sick and not just sick the way you made me sick. I was sick when we married, I didn't know how sick until then, and I can't talk to you now because my spirit is still sick. You helped me, at first. I could feel myself being pried apart, like the clams I used to try to rip open on the beach at Easthampton when I was a child, and I know how mulish clams are. And I tried, Elliott, believe me, I tried to cleave to you, to cleave myself open for you, to bring you inside of me like a healing spirit in my blood, like the penicillin I'm now going to have injected into me, to remake me into something I could feel more at home with, and I shouldn't have tried."

[428]

"You need a doctor, Elaine."

"A shrink? Elliott, I've seen three headshrinkers already, one American psychiatrist, one ex-Viennese psychoanalyst and one English behavioral psychologist, and none of them helped me a bit—though they got richer in the process. No, it wasn't a talking cure I needed, a medical cure; it was a living cure, a loving cure, someone who could take me by the hand and lead me out of my own wildernesses. For a while I thought I had that man in you."

"But you didn't?"

"No." She shook her head again, sadly, as if the weight of it and the ponderous awareness in it were too great for her slender neck to bear. "It was too much to ask, of you, of me. Too much to ask you to go beyond, even against, your natural instincts and marital rights, your lusts and your love, too much patience to ask of any person, too much passion to ask me to turn from this grimy caterpillar I am into a beautiful butterfly."

"If you could tell me, if you'd told me—"

"That wouldn't have helped. You know that. It would have made things worse. I've had experiences in those matters before, Elliott. This telling, it simply complicates things, adds another burden. Forgetfulness, forgetting, was the only medicine that could, might, cure me. Telling you would have made that impossible and made your nights sleepless, your days even more tormenting than I'm sure they were. To talk about it is to remember it, to burn in hell again and again; to tell someone else is to impress it on his brain, to bring him into your hell, willy-nilly."

"And what does *not* talking accomplish?"

"That, at least, left me, leaves you, in the cool winds and empty spaces of limbo."

"Where I burn."

"Yes, where we burn."

"But not together."

"No, Elliott, not together."

❋ ❋ ❋

Fillmore's church was a small, weathered and dignified gray granite building, a dour-faced turn-of-the-century hangover whose solemnity and steeple, even more than its small iron fenced-in close, set it apart from its frame and stucco neighbors. Walking toward it from across the street where he had parked the car, he saw that the only real color in the building was a semicircle of stained-glass panels set over the massive wooden doors with the crucifix of golden panes at its center. Sanders barely felt Beth's white-gloved hand on his arm, so lightly did her fingers rest on it, but he was insistently aware of her presence. Not far away the university campanile rose high and lonely over the city, its gilt top dulled by dusk, its clock's black hands curiously sharp at ten minutes before six o'clock. Thick and wet, the evening air tasted of sea salt and marsh flats and was hard to breathe. Inside the church yellow lanterns suspended from linked metal chains cast debilitated saffron light that darkened the ranks of mahogany pews that swept in orderly ranks down to the cleared space where a simple floor-level table served as an altar. Behind it the old raised pulpit was both beseiged and masked by a scarlet screen like an iconostasis which was decorated with a cross woven of evergreen branches, thorns and rusting barbed wire. From it pennants of paper headlines from the local newspapers streamered out, all with great black bold type telling of the war.

The first dozen rows of pews were packed but beyond those only a scattering of people sat singly or in twos around the benches. Sanders led Beth into one of the rear, empty rows and was surprised to note her automatic genuflection. Fillmore was conducting the service, a service such as Sanders had never before seen, to a congregation he found hard to believe: bearded, long-haired, booted and beaded, in Navajo and buckskin shirts, in dark sunglasses and great yellow granny glasses, many in the dyed castoffs of what had once been Army, Navy, Marine, police, fire and postal uniforms. But there were others there too, sober, serious, dressed conventionally, though not in the majority. The cymbals clashed, a sitar throbbed, and the congregation sang, the voices curiously harmonious and clear, "Praise God from whom all blessings flow . . ." and the varied worshipers all drank from a large smoky glass cup that served as a common chalice. When Fillmore began his sermon his voice was small and floundering in the church, echoing thinly like *a capella* song, as if he had not yet found his true voice, hit the proper pitch;

[430]

but soon after only the slightest tilt of his head indicated that he'd seen them, his voice rose to a powerful and persuasive emotional chant that rang in the old beamed rafters like an organ.

Christianity, Fillmore preached, was not merely a Sunday creed, a flat comfortable hypocrisy to mask hatred, greed, racism and violence; it was, instead, a daily delight and determination to love one's fellow man, to live in justice and in peace. American Christianity, like American life, was suffering severe illness, sickened by war, by racial hatred, violence in the streets, and unprecedented affluence. Small wonder the best of the younger generation were fed up and wanted either to overthrow or drop out of the society, wanted to get off the meaningless materialist merry-go-round their parents rode and recommended: house, car, TV, hi-fi, refrigerator, boat, air conditioner, credit card and bank mortgage. Jesus had also been a dropout in his own day, an Essene hippie of his time who had flaunted the Establishment; but he had not dropped out permanently, or turned away finally to drugs or to private concerns: He had ranged himself against society and its injustice and oppression and fought it, immersed himself in a struggle for peace and social justice, driven the moneychangers from the temple, accepted the downtrodden, succored the poor and broken in spirit, tried to change the quality of the life of his time and place and his people and in so doing had changed the quality of life for all time. *Thou shalt love thy neighbor as thyself* was then and remained now a revolutionary slogan, one which twentieth-century Americans had forgotten so that they could conveniently accumulate their possessions, luxuriate in their comforts, and forget about the poor, the Negroes, the Mexicans, the Indians, the Jews, the Vietnamese peasants perishing in flaming napalm, the Bolivian peasants in abysmal poverty, the Indian untouchables starving in the parched provinces of the subcontinent. . . .

The clammy air of the unheated church, the citrine light, the palpable steady thrumming of sitar and drone of tambours in the background, the sonorous rise and fall of Fillmore's oratorical delivery lulled and infuriated Sanders. He had heard it all so many times before, the same exhortation to reason and Christian good will and love, to charity, grace and unselfishness. Useless. Absurd. Man's history showed that men scarcely relied on their reason and even

[431]

less expressed their love and good will. His own experience of life, however jaundiced it might be by his profession, had convinced him that men reacted very little to exhortation, and when they did respond their responses were almost always short-lived—especially if the exhortation was to their "better natures."

Men acted out of other springs, driving selfishness and self-assertiveness, lust and obsession, the desire to master, deprive and manipulate others; out of the deeper clefts and recesses of their natures they were driven by subterranean rivers whose existence they could not often discern and control, rivers which carried them along in their swift currents like chips, and lofty words were only puffs of sound that neither stayed nor drove a single sail. Yet, he reminded himself, yet George Christiansen had died for him on a sidewalk in Saigon, yet Lovett Carpenter Sanders had gone to a Gestapo-tortured death silently to save his comrades, yet his mother had forsaken his father, whom she loved, and gone back to America to save his, her son's, life in another way. And he himself, Lord help him, had striven for others, however cautiously, however cowardly, had committed his heart, if not his mind; and, as Beth stirred next to him, he knew that he was still trying. No, the shoji iconostasis in Laura Martin's apartment had spoken a more modest truth, more modest truths, in a tone not of exhortation but of quiet advice: *Go placidly among the noise & haste, & remember what peace there may be in silence . . . everywhere life is full of heroism. . . . Neither be cynical about love; for in the face of all aridity & disenchantment it is perennial as the grass. . . .*

Beth, suddenly rigid beside him, recalled his strayed attention to Fillmore's words: "It was during the first assaults on that hill that Peter Agnielli was killed. I knew him for a long time, a middle-aged man a little thick in the waist and thin in the hair, plain-faced with steel-rimmed glasses, from a poor slum family in one of our large but not great Eastern cities. A priest from his earliest youth and for seventeen years a priest in the slums of the city where he grew up, a man dedicated to working with the young, he had volunteered to go where he thought the priesthood was needed most, to the battlefield, though by now he was a major and a battalion chaplain and could easily have refrained from the front lines.

"Some of you will imagine that Pete Agnielli was not afraid, that men of God do not tremble when the 'incoming mail' arrives, when a fire fight begins, when bayonet charges begin, but you are wrong. We all tremble, even the earth trembles, for this is Armageddon, where every man trembles for life and limb.

"From their higher ground on the hill the enemy attacked our lines near the base of the hill, a mortar and infantry assault that drove our men back and downhill. Half a dozen of our people were wounded and lay out on the perimeter crying in pain, for medics, for morphine, for help, but the medic had been killed by a mortar burst.

"Peter Agnielli was a chaplain, a man of God, and he carried no weapons. It wasn't his job, you might say, and you might also say that he had no other job. He ran out and one by one he dragged those 'grunts' to safety, and miraculously he wasn't hit. A gray-haired bespectacled middle-aged chaplain doesn't sprint, doesn't run the hundred, the way he did when he was twenty, but Agnielli managed.

"It was a six-day fight for that hill, a seesaw struggle that in the sight of man and God seemed to make no sense and was an abomination. The next day Agnielli took a flesh wound in the hip by our own Thunderchiefs. The enemy was pressing hard and the F-105s were called in for close air-ground support. They miscalculated, bombed our own lines, and Agnielli was wounded and a dozen other men were killed.

"The third day was the worst. Our battalion was retreating from the parched hills, working its way carefully through rice paddies bordered by jungle, when an enemy battalion struck with mortars and automatic weapons. In the ambush men everywhere were screaming and dying, the air was filled with fire, but Pete scrambled out of his hole and began to pray with the wounded, began to give the dying the last rites. A mortar burst blew three fingers off his left hand, and through the hail of machine-gun fire he continued to crawl from wounded to wounded, from dead to dead, until he was hit. The last time anyone saw him alive, Father Agnielli was crouching over a dying boy giving him Extreme Unction.

" 'Greater love hath no man than this, that a man lay down his life for his friends,' for his fellow man.

"There was another such man who was able to transcend the

brutality and ugliness, the hatred and killing, a man who went to school here, who heard the carillons in the university campaniles at Stanford and Berkeley, who loved the high arches of the Bay bridges, the chaparral and the madrona, the buckeye and the laurel, the streams and the inlets of the Bay region, a man who had lived here all of his very young life before he was killed. His name was"— Fillmore began; then, looking straight at them, so that a number of heads turned to see where his eyes were fixed, Fillmore changed his mind—"well, what his name was doesn't really matter, he was a true son of Christ—"

"A true son of Christ," Beth said under her breath, "a Christian-son."

"—though himself not officially religious, neither a minister nor a priest, only a young man appalled by what he saw. That man saw a VC throw a grenade in front of a café in Saigon where innocent people were sitting and walking, where he was sitting with his friend, and that young man threw himself on that grenade and was killed by the explosion. That man fell on a hand grenade on a Saigon sidewalk to save his friend and an old Vietnamese woman and a young Vietnamese girl. 'Greater love. . . .' "

Sanders heard his own sharp intake of breath and knew Beth had heard too, and now, keeping his face directly forward, looking at Fillmore but not hearing a word he spoke, he saw out of the corner of his eye Beth's angry stare before he felt her sharp elbow at his ribs. "Is that what happened? Is that the way George died?" she whispered. "Tell me!"

Sanders nodded. "That's the way it was," he replied out of the side of his mouth.

"So he had to sacrifice himself. Somehow he had to make himself a martyr once more. And that was why you came back here to pick up the threads of his life instead of your own. Because he died for you!" Her voice was full of awe and disgust. "And died because of me!"

Again Sanders nodded.

"Nations, civilizations, worlds are as mortal as men, as the men who people them and make them. Like men nations go down into the pit, never to be heard of again. The graveyard of history can hold cultures as well as individuals, the shards of civilizations as well as the bones and hair of men and women. And we are now at the brink of the abyss and no brinksmanship can continue to keep us out of the abyss unless we turn our backs on it and walk away from its edge; unless men are aware that this pit, this fused-glass, cobalt-poisoned menace, will destroy not only a single civilization but all civilization on this earth, all men on this earth, men cannot survive. Man either transcends his nature, transcends his hatreds, prejudices, aggressions, or this earth will be slag and cinders and lava. . . ."

With all its sham, drudgery & broken dreams, Sanders thought bitterly, *it is still a beautiful world. Be careful. Strive to be happy. . . . And whether or not it is clear to you, no doubt the universe is unfolding as it should.*

Beth said no more but slumped down in the pew next to him, her fingers nervously tying knots in a tiny elegant lace-edged white handkerchief, her pale face growing increasingly pale. The service was at last over, the congregation filtered slowly down the aisles, ankle bells chiming, metal talismans sounding, the sitar and tambour musicians continuing their rhythms out of the doors.

When the church was empty, they rose and followed in Fillmore's wake into the rectory, a small room which also apparently served as study, library and perhaps even bedroom. A single tarnished brass lamp was lit but its green shade cut off almost all the light it cast except two cones of brightness which shone down on an old paper-littered secretary-desk and up onto the ceiling, but left most of the rest of the room in semidarkness.

Fillmore motioned them to two slatted folding chairs while he removed his vestments and carefully stored them in a dark wooden closet. From the secretary he produced a carafe and three slender-stemmed wineglasses. "Sherry?" he asked, having already poured three glasses. He passed them around and raised his glass: "To George Christiansen, may he rest in peace."

"Amen," Beth echoed fervently and sipped her wine.

Sanders drank his sherry silently. The specter of George's broken body on the pavement, having once been roused in the church, now refused to be laid to rest. Leaning back in a worn red leather chair next to the secretary, Fillmore scrutinized Beth closely from over his wineglass, and while he did so Sanders saw how deeply chiseled the lines in his face were now, how much tighter his expression, how much he had aged since Vietnam. Beth was looking uncomfortably down at the black grosgrain bows of her patent-leather shoes and Sanders remembered that Elaine had had shoes like that, only the bows on hers were black velvet. They were called Mary Jane shoes, Elaine had once told him sarcastically, the shoes well-bred proper little rich girls wore.

"Am I different from what you were expecting?" Beth asked self-consciously.

Fillmore nodded. "Very."

"How?"

Fillmore was awkward. "More beautiful, more—"

"Arrogant, richer, shrewder," Sanders filled in for him.

Fillmore was gallant. "That wasn't exactly what I meant. Mr. Sanders is quite a bit more fluent than I am, but sometimes he says things he doesn't really mean. He says them to shock, for the sake of effect. A journalist's training and temperament."

"And a preacher's."

The exchange and the collar had put Beth off. "I'm very grateful for the letter you sent me about Elliott," she said shyly, then realized she'd made a gaffe.

"Saved you from a fate worse than death, didn't it, Beth?" Sanders asked straight-faced.

Beth flushed and Fillmore, embarrassed, by that and by the public recognition of a letter he had clearly not wanted Sanders to see, rushed in with the question: "Did Sanders give you your husband's effects?"

"Beth showed your letter to me, Fillmore, and I object to being described as unhinged."

"You were unhinged, Sanders, and you still are."

"You and those kooks back in there are sane?"

"The world is insane, of which you are part." Fillmore turned on his most engaging pastoral smile. "A most curious congregation, that, wouldn't you say?"

"Most curious." Beth echoed his words and his smile.

"Bells on their fingers and rings in their noses," Sanders charged. "Their greatest vice, though, isn't their ridiculous costumes; it's that they don't know any history."

"And their virtue," Fillmore said. "Their idealism wouldn't work for them if they did know too much history, if they knew what men in the past have tried to do and failed to accomplish. They'd only be burdened down by history, discouraged by the prospects before them. Maybe you just can't be old and young at the same time. The young have their own wisdom, different from ours. It would be inappropriate, impossible, for us to have theirs, just as they, deprived of our experience, can't have ours."

"But they have you, Fillmore, their pastor, for a leader."

"I don't want them to be altogether deprived of historical perspective"—Fillmore smiled again—"so I try to do what little I can to fill the gap. But not too much."

"Will they believe you? After all, you're over thirty."

"They do trust some few of us who are that ancient."

"The childish ones."

"Perhaps. Perhaps only the child*like* ones, the ones who can in a complex age seek out and act on basic simplicities."

"Which basic oversimplifications are you recommending?"

"Thou shalt not kill! Thou shalt love thy neighbor as thyself!"

Lord, Sanders thought, he really means it. "And what if thy neighbor chooses to kill thee?"

"Ultimately," Fillmore replied slowly, "even if thy neighbor tries to kill thee."

"And you think *I'm* insane!"

"Unless somewhere, some of us dig in our heels and say no more killing, unless we can persuade the world, we shall all go down the drain, all mankind and the whole fair green earth with us."

"Remember what you wrote in that charming letter to Mrs. Christiansen here? 'Nothing is to be gained by shouldering unbearable burdens or undertaking unpayable debts.' That line has remained in my head. Perhaps you should seriously consider your own advice."

"I have, and it was why I had to leave the Army. Because shouldering unbearable burdens and undertaking unpayable debts is a minister's job."

[437]

"No, Fillmore, that's Christ's role, a superhuman role, not a human one."

"We are Christ's surrogates on earth, here to minister to men's needs, duly authorized by the church to preach the gospel, to administer the sacraments, to conduct Christian worship—"

"Was that Christian worship back there?"

"Yes, the content is what counts."

"What do those kids know about form or content, Filly? They're so shaken with lusts and fears and uncertainties, they're so young and have such small experience of life, that they want either to overthrow everything or give way to everything; either they're on the barricades, nostrils distended, the veins in their necks showing, their arms raised with flags or grenades or Molotov cocktails, or they're lying back in a haze of drugs, their eyes closed, clutching themselves for comfort and solace, or clutching whoever else is within arm's reach."

"Are they much different from us?" Beth asked.

"No, not very much," Sanders admitted readily, "though they think so."

" 'Time is the rider that breaks youth,' " Fillmore declared.

His mother's favorite poet, that poet of reluctant religious ecstasy, that commonsense lucid intelligence and knotty feeling heart that had flowered in the Bemerton parsonage, George Herbert had been Marian Stuart Sanders' kind of man, the raging passions and intellectual contradictions held in balance with a tightly controlled wisdom of ordinary life and a profound belief in God. "Herbert said two other things my mother was especially fond of quoting, Fillmore, 'Life is half spent before we know what it is'; and 'Love your neighbour, yet pull not down your hedge.' "

"Or your pants," Beth said, deliberately vulgar, shocking both of them.

Fillmore, uncomfortable, said, "You see how wrong that man could be. He also insisted that 'Words are women, deeds are men.' "

"Words sometimes are deeds and women men," Sanders said, deliberately insulting, but Beth seemed serene.

"Did you know George, personally?" Beth asked Fillmore.

"I'm sorry. I saw him only after he was dead, in the hospital."

Beth winced but pressed him further. "Why did George do it? Why did he commit suicide that way?"

"Suicide? I couldn't call it that. He saw his duty and he did it. Deeds are, indeed, men, Beth"—it was the first time he had called her by name and Fillmore spoke the Christian name softly, sensuously, caressing it with his mouth—"and men are the sum of their deeds."

"And of their intentions too?" Sanders asked.

"That too," Fillmore granted.

"Are you married, Mr. Fillmore?" Beth asked, her voice sweet and innocent, crossing her legs so that their silken whisper was loud in the small room and drew both their eyes.

Fillmore shook his head sadly. "I was a late developer, or at least that's what my mother said, and then, at the seminary, when I began to see the kind of minister I wanted to be, I knew that to marry would not only give hostages to fortune but make those hostages liable to the most excruciating anguish."

"And so you gave up the idea of marriage and children?" Beth was intrigued, skeptical.

"Inflicting pain on those I loved did not seem to be what I was after."

"No, martyrdom was what you were after, Fillmore," Sanders said brusquely. "And you were right not to involve any others in your lust for it. Martyrs leave only mourning widows and orphaned children."

"You speak in the bitterness of your soul," Fillmore said calmly, compassionately. "But I suppose you're right. Idealists often have to pay their way with the comfort, the peace of mind, even the lives, of their families. I didn't want to be one of those idealists."

"Martyrs," Sanders corrected, realizing as he did so that he was abusing Lovett Carpenter Sanders, berating his father for what he had had to pay, for what his mother had had to pay, for his father's ideals and ambitions. Take what you want and pay for it, indeed!

"No, Sanders, I didn't set out to be a martyr. I was never that—"

"Catholic? Poverty, obedience, chastity?"

[439]

"—arrogant or falsely humble. I wanted to be useful and not be used badly, or exploited. That was why I went into the Army and why I left it."

"Which was why you went into this peace movement and why you'll be leaving it."

"Are you really so cynical about what can be done, Sanders? You saw that war, you've seen many of them. You saw how hopeless, cruel, brutalizing to us and to them—"

"And occasionally ennobling too. Rarely, I admit, but sometimes. George. That Catholic priest you mentioned in your sermon today. Others."

"Are you for this war?" Fillmore asked, his face dismayed.

"No."

"Are you against it?"

"Yes."

"Then you want to stop it."

"I do."

"How?"

"I don't know how."

"Why not just stop fighting?"

"And leave behind the innocent to slaughter?"

"That government?"

"No, the local doctor, headman, farmer, teacher who wouldn't play ball."

"They can be saved too."

"How?"

Fillmore was irritated. "So you do nothing?"

"I report. I'm a newspaperman. I try to tell people what is really happening. What I see. What I know. I do what I can in my own way."

"But others don't have your option."

"You're a minister. Can you tear the roots of violence and evil and greed out of men's hearts, even yours or mine? That's your job."

"Trying to arouse people's hearts, move their minds, picketing draft-induction centers, demonstrating, marching, protesting against an evil immoral cancerous war accomplishes nothing?"

[440]

"*Primum non nocere*. What you do does express dissatisfaction but it offers no solution and it's a perpetual incitement to riot, to its own violence."

"Letting the government know how the people feel is democracy. It changes the course of policy."

"I doubt that. I'm not even sure the expression of your dissatisfaction that way helps the causes you espouse. You have the ballot, you have referendum and recall, you have the mails to carry petitions and letters to your representatives. All that would do far more than one more turbulent protest."

"Was George a martyr?" Beth suddenly asked, as if she hadn't even heard what they were arguing about. It was a question Sanders longed to hear answered and he waited for Fillmore's reply.

Fillmore looked at his hands for some time before he said, "I have never been quite sure I knew what the word *martyr* meant."

"A martyr," Sanders said angrily, "is someone who deliberately lays down his life for a cause, for his religion, for a principle, for a friend, for his wife and children."

"Who suffers death gladly," Beth added.

"No," Sanders said louder than he intended. "Those words *suffer* and *gladly* don't go together; at least," he added lamely, "they shouldn't."

"Death is sometimes a release and a relief," Fillmore said to Beth.

"Is that what George was searching for, release? And why should he want release from life?" Beth asked.

"Perhaps because he found life insupportable," Fillmore ventured.

Insupportable. Inconsolable. Unbearable. Men always used hyperbole. Difficult to support and insupportable were very different things; most men found life difficult to bear, to endure; most human relations lacked consolation; but insupportable, unbearable and inconsolable were something else again. Only a few men, relatively, found life so dire, only a few were sensitive enough to be rubbed so raw by it, and George had been one of those.

"Why else?" Fillmore inquired gently.

"Because of me," Beth replied.

They were talking to each other now and he was excluded, his presence not only superfluous but an intrusion, yet though he sensed the restraint his being there imposed on them, Sanders could not bring himself to leave them alone. Together, their talk had the quality of catechism and confessional combined.

"Are you certain?" Fillmore asked.

"I am responsible for his death," Beth answered.

"Why? How?"

"Because I was not what he needed—"

"But what he wanted?"

"Yes, that, but I betrayed him even there, and at every turn."

"Was he responsible for the betrayals or were you?"

"I, at least in part, but not altogether."

"Did you want him to go to war?"

"Yes."

"Did you encourage him?"

"No."

"Did you try to prevent him?"

"Yes, but only halfheartedly."

"Did you want him to die?"

Beth's voice was a croak. "I wanted him to die. I wanted to kill him."

"And so you think you did kill him and feel responsible for his actual death."

"I could have saved him. A few gestures of affection, of concern, a hand held out—and he wouldn't have gone."

"But you couldn't make those gestures?"

"I hated him. I couldn't reach across the bed and touch him. I couldn't look at his face. I hated having him in the same room with me, in the same house."

"In the same bed," Fillmore said, completing her thought with a current of his own passion. "Why did you hate him so much?"

"He killed my son."

Shocked, visibly shaken, Fillmore slumped farther down in the red chair. "His own son?"

"Not *our* son, *my* son."

"Did he know it wasn't his son?"

"He knew. That's how he came to marry me, because the real father refused."

[442]

"And you were grateful," Fillmore said sadly, "and so you had no choice but to hate him."

She had no choice. Sanders knew that wasn't true. She had had a choice. And so had George. And so had he himself. Listening to them, he heard himself thinking and arguing and feeling about, for, against Elaine, Monique, his father and mother.

Her head bowed, her eyes fixed miserably on the worn gray carpet, Beth slipped off the chair onto her knees and dragged herself across the short distance to Fillmore's chair that way, the silken scraping of her hose a rasp in the silent room. She put her head on his knees and groaned, "I want to be forgiven, I need to be pardoned, so I can go on living, go on with my life, so I won't die, shrivel up, kill myself."

Slowly Fillmore raised her head and they looked into each other's faces like lovers; and Sanders, conscience-stricken and abashed, filled with loathing for the recollection of the Avenue Foch, feeling as if they had made him, permitted him, to make himself a voyeur and a participant, rose as silently and swiftly as he could; and, in the presence of a scene he had once endured and found truly unendurable, a scene he no longer had to endure, he tiptoed out of the room, tiptoed but almost ran. Whether what he'd witnessed was hallowed or impious, devout or profane, he didn't know, but it stifled him with grief. "Nothing is to be gained," Fillmore had written to Beth in that letter, "by shouldering unbearable burdens or undertaking unpayable debts." Yet who didn't do both? And who did not carry the burdens of unbearable recollections and unpayable forgivenesses? Perhaps Fillmore could persuade Beth of the sense of what he'd written to her and so perhaps relieve her of both debts and burdens, but Sanders doubted it. For himself, he knew he could be relieved of neither, either on the Quai de Passy, the Avenue Mozart or the Avenue Foch, in Paris, or Connecticut, or California. The longer he lived, the more he understood anything about himself and his life, however imperfectly he understood it still, the more he was convinced that human beings were probably no more important than the unpayable debts they'd undertaken, of no more value than the unbearable burdens they'd shouldered, and perhaps even of the inconsolable memories they carried all their lives and to the grave.

The telephone call wakened him early in the morning. A man's voice he neither knew nor liked, the voice querulous and full of petty authority, asked if he was Elliott Sanders, and when Sanders had thickly agreed that it was truly he, the voice went on to say that Joseph Christiansen wanted to see him, today, as early in the day as possible.

"Is it an emergency?" Sanders inquired.

"Christiansen's dying," the voice said flatly, without regret or apology or equivocation, with no attempt to soften the impact of what he'd said, only the irascibility of having to convey it spiky in tone.

"How long has he got?" Sanders, fully awake, asked.

"Hours, maybe, maybe a couple of days. A week at most."

"Sure?"

"We're sure." All the tyranny and majesty and unanswerable arrogance of the royal *we*.

When Sanders arrived at the hospital a light greasy drizzle fell steadily out of an overcast sky, and in the time it took him to run from the parking lot to the hospital he got soaked. While he tried to shake and stamp himself dry in the lobby, Sanders' eyes, almost on their own, sought the yellow hillside beyond the highway where he had seen the horses and colts romping, but nothing moved there now under the drenched live oaks and on the sodden rutted brown earth. No one was in Christiansen's room; the beds were perfectly made and turned down for occupants who weren't there, everything was neat and in place, but without a sign of life. For an instant he was sure that the old man had been buried, that the phone call was a dream and his hurried trip a wild goose chase, until by an act of discipline he made himself realize that less than an hour had elapsed since he'd received that phone call. No one, he assured himself, could have imagined that snide stinking authority of tone he'd been treated to over the telephone; that could not be a dream, not even a nightmare: it had to be real. He searched the corridor until he found a nurse who told him that Christiansen had been transferred to another room. There a skeleton Christiansen lay in bed shriveled as if a searing sirocco had passed over him soaking his flesh and his life from his bones in a great sweat to leave him a weary and emaciated carcass pale as the sheets he lay on: There was no question now, this was a dying man. The once-piercing blue eyes, now cloudy and remote, searched the ceiling above as if for reasons, the thin lips bared over the teeth that were now too large for the face already half set in the sardonic laugh of death.

"Mr. Christiansen," Sanders said, softly at first, then louder when there was no response, "it's Elliott Sanders."

"Sanders," Christiansen sighed, his eyes focusing, the broomstick forearms jutting exposed from the blue pajama sleeves reaching for, searching for and finally finding the rimless glasses on the bed stand next to him. It took those shaking hands a long time to don and position those gold earpieces, and when they were in place the whole face seemed more alive and determined, more in control than those palsied hands and pallid arms indicated. "I'm glad you could come," he said and he made the terse sentence seem like an admission of weakness, a failure he couldn't easily endure.

"How are you feeling?" Sanders asked, trying to sound cheerful and cheering. "You're looking much better than when I saw you last."

Christiansen's eyes sparked. "Don't talk nonsense, Sanders. In the Corps we'd say you talked like a man with a paper asshole. I'm dying, so don't talk nonsense. That isn't why I asked you to come here."

Sanders had to bite back his "Then why did you?" but he waited. However, if there was a point Christiansen wanted to make, he seemed in no hurry to make it.

"I was lying there, my mind singing songs by itself," Christiansen said, "and I was listening to them at the same time. I realized that they were all killing songs, war songs." In a flawed, faltering baritone, unexpectedly lyrical and moving, Christiansen sang:

> I'll eat when I'm hungry,
>   I'll drink when I'm dry.
> If the Yankees don't kill me,
>   I'll live till I die.

[445]

He laughed. "My daddy used to sing that and I think he heard it from his daddy, the one who was killed in the Civil War." Again he sang:

> *Keep your head down, Fritzie Boy!*
> *Keep your head down, Fritzie Boy!*
> *If you wanna see your "Vater" in your Vaterland,*
> *Keep your head down, Fritzie Boy.*

"I learned that one myself. At Belleau Wood. I liked it too. I liked war and soldiering. I liked the killing too. I liked the life. Not like George, not like George at all. He was like her. It was exciting and boring, frightening, your feelings going up and down so you was dizzy and you knew the next drop might be into the grave, one foot on a banana peel; that made it real, for keeps, none of this foolishness of fighting for a lousy couple of greenbacks so you could have a new icebox or a fancy car with a rumble seat or more little numbers in a bankbook. I couldn't stand that.

"Christiansens were all alike. Like a bulldog I once had I taught to fetch. A great retriever, that dog, but once he fetched he couldn't let go what he had his teeth into. All of us was like that, even George, only he got his teeth into books—and into Beth Marshall. Bad diet. Makes your teeth rotten and your soul like Swiss cheese. Like his mother's soul.

"My skill is obsolete. An infantryman's skill, a rifleman's skill, a hunter's skill. The other thing that counts is heart. I call that passion. We Christiansens all had heart, all of us, even her, even the women we married. Even Beth Marshall. Soldiers shouldn't marry, shouldn't have kids. Only whores. Only girls in different ports. Not homes. Not kids. Not wives.

"Did you know that Alameda is Spanish for 'the place where the poplars grow'? I was there when I met her. Beautiful, she was, straight and clean and green like a poplar, but like a poplar couldn't bend. But neither could I. The boy like both of us. Christiansens not benders nor bowers; stand straight, even against each other.

"Now it's all over. It was a good life. I got what I wanted. Almost. Except for George—and her, always making me feel guilty, trying to

[446]

make me feel sorry for being away, for being in the Corps, for not sending enough cash home, always something, as if I wasn't doing my job, wasn't doing things right.

"Only this is dumb." His hands gestured at the body that lay in the bed, the room, the hospital. "Dying's dying. Everybody's gotta go one time or another, but at least if you go useful, taking one of them with you, whichever them it is, a greaser or a Fritzie or a slopehead, it's okay. Gooks, all of em. Do em a favor doing em in. But stretched out here on a bed with clean sheets your blood and guts turning white, turning to water, inside you, that's a waste, dumb, a favor to nobody."

"At least they're not turning yellow," Sanders tried to comfort him.

"Goddam right they're not!" Christiansen lay there exhausted as if the talking had been too much for him, but in a few moments a surge of strength seemed to go through him. "I called to tell you I arranged for my funeral." He raised his palm, traffic-cop style. "Don't say anything, just listen. I don't want no one there, no one. I was never one of them grinning slobs, sucking up to people, and I don't want anyone sucking up to me at my funeral just because they're glad I'm dead. Especially her, that bitch Beth Marshall, especially not her, which is why I'm telling you, so you can tell her."

"Do you want me to—?" Sanders began, knowing that this was what George Christiansen would have wanted, knowing that this was something he could truly do in living out George's life, but reluctant because Christiansen was Christiansen.

"Nobody!" Christiansen tried to bellow but what came out of his mouth was hollow-sounding. "Don't want nobody there. Fuck em all except six—and save them for pallbearers. The Corps'll take care of them. Up at Presidio. Six gyrenes in dress blues. Wanted to be buried next to George but there's no room there already, no place next to him. Those places fill up fast. Maybe that's the way it should be, me and George was never close in life, guess it's justice we not be close in death. There'll be the Corps honor guard. That's enough for any man. You tell that bitch, you tell her for me."

"I'll tell her," Sanders agreed, relieved and guilty because Christiansen had taken him off the hook. He didn't have to go, though he felt he should, felt obscurely that it would make up for never having gone to Lovett Carpenter Sanders' funeral, never having found his burial place.

"Tell her too that she doesn't get a dime, not a dime. Whatever I got goes to the Corps fund, every dime, my bank account, my service life insurance, even my share of George's insurance. Miss Richbitch Marshall gets nothing, d'you hear?"

"I hear," Sanders answered. "But the Marine Corps doesn't need your money. Why don't you leave some of it, at least George's insurance money, to Peter King?"

"That nigger nance!"

"He can use it."

"You can use it too. Who can't use money?"

"Mr. Christiansen, Beth is rich. She doesn't need your money. Neither do I. I've got more than enough to do me. But Peter's black and dirt-poor. He's got two strikes on him already and to him the money would be a leg up, a blessing."

Weakly Christiansen's hands balled into loose fists, the ropy blue veins standing out of the pale skin. "I don't want to give him a leg up, I don't want to bless him. The answer is no."

There was no point in pleading. The old man had made up his mind and he was implacable.

Sanders saw how much effort of will it took for Christiansen to speak, to maintain his resolve, even to keep his eyes open. His skin, bloodless-white, his body paper-thin, he looked as if he was gradually being resolved into the bed linens and would in moments disappear, leaving only a creased white sheet and a rumpled blanket. "The chess set," he said, "the one George sent."

"Yes?"

"I want you to have it."

"You want to leave *me* something?"

"Naw. I know you. I know George didn't send that to me, or to Beth either. I knew him better than that. It was your idea, and I want you to have it back. It's under the bed." He pointed weakly toward the foot of the bed and Sanders slowly retrieved the box.

"That's all there is, I guess," Christiansen said. "That's the whole kit and kaboodle. George is dead. His boy is dead. I'm dying. The

[448]

Christiansens are finished, washed up, through. The last of 'em dies here."

"I'm sorry," Sanders blurted.

"You're sorry." Christiansen laughed. "You're sorry. As if that ever made a difference to anyone, anywhere. Six generations in this country come to nothing. No," he said, correcting himself very carefully, trying and failing to pull himself erect, "not nothing. We helped build it, make it, and we'll be buried up there on that bluff looking out to sea and smelling those eucalyptus trees and the Pacific salt."

Sanders only just managed to hold back his tears and his fury.

"So long, Sanders, and thanks for telling me about George, how he died and all that." He reached out his hand and Sanders took it. It was the failing grip of a dying man.

"Goodbye, Mr. Christiansen," Sanders said, gently putting the hand back on the sheets and the bony chest beneath.

"You better get on now, I need a little shut-eye," Christiansen said, his eyes already closing, "just a little sleep."

At the door Sanders turned back, the chess set a burden under his arm, and Christiansen waved a weak hand at him, once. "See you in hell," he called faintly, one eye open, and then he turned his face away.

* * *

Torn between his desire to tell Beth about Joseph Christiansen's imminent death and his promise not to tell, Sanders tried for a few days to make himself call her but he could never dial more than three digits of her telephone number before he put the receiver down, nor could he drive his car closer than a dozen blocks from her house. And the more he tried to telephone or visit, the harder it became for him. The chess set, a mute reminder and rebuke, sat on Jason Howe's sideboard and each morning Sanders gave it a furtive sidelong glance and a Japanese bow as if paying respects he was unable to fulfill, his mind always beginning with the mocking "Honorable ancestors . . ." and then never going any further because he realized that it wasn't funny. He recognized that part of the reluctance was an intuition that something had come to a head between him and Beth there in Fillmore's rectory, that some decisive change in their relationship was brewing like coffee that had been too long on the boil, had overflowed onto the burner and sent a rank brown burned stench into the recesses of his spirit; but he knew it for a postponement, not for a decision, and he was certain he would have to see Beth, talk to her, hear her out, before the directions their lives were to take could be mapped.

Because Jim Needham had taken Sheila down to Mexicali for a fortnight—confidentially, Jim reported that he wanted to dry Sheila out, that she'd been drinking even more heavily than before, just why he couldn't tell, "martis" before breakfast even, but maybe if he could keep her swimming and riding and sightseeing, and away from the mescal and tequila, she'd come back home refreshed, sober and healthier—Sanders was left to his own devices in the office and spoke to almost no one except in the most routine, businesslike way. But he worked. He drove all around the Bay area, down the Peninsula as far south as Point Lobos, as far north as Eureka, and inland to Sacramento, searching for answers to the questions which came unbidden, witless sometimes, but which did not let him rest. Again he was obsessed, and his obsession with the country, he knew, was inextricably connected with his obsession about George Christiansen, though he could not ascertain how they were connected. More and more Sanders felt he did understand what was happening in America and less and less did he like it, less and less did he want to be part of it; yet a part of it he was, willy-nilly. The physical beauty of the land itself, sometimes even its barrenness, stirred him as had few of the other countries in which he'd lived, worked or traveled; it was a magnificent country with a grandeur that only a few other places he'd seen had: the Alps, the Côte d'Azur, the Dalmatian coast, the mountain and lake country around Fuji and around Como and Garda. But it wasn't simply that the natural setting was superb and only man vile: As he looked, poked in government publications, talked to local and state officials, university teachers and students, businessmen, doctors, lawyers, Mexican bean pickers, Negro laborers, Italian winegrowers, Anglo bankers and shipping-interest people, all that rich racial mixture the American melting pot had never melted down enough to fuse into a new metal, a picture of a deeply troubled and torn society emerged, a society afflicted with provincialism and a new urbanity, old idealism and older cynicism,

[450]

violence and individualism and pacificism and collectivism, all in a troublesome mixture unleavened by clarity of purpose or overriding ethic. The pieces of it began to fit together, the war and peace impulses, the Negroes and civil-rights movements, the hippies and the squares, and the sense of overriding disillusion in the goals and possibilities of American life: The American dream had become the American nightmare, in glass, chrome and ferroconcrete. How much industry around San Francisco and in California at large was involved with the war, with military and naval effort—electronics, shipping, aircraft, railroads, research, lumbering, farming—surprised and alarmed him. In essence, if slightly exaggerated in form, the area seemed to be a microcosm of the major problems of the nation at large.

At bottom Sanders was gradually made aware that one problem was most pernicious: America's slogan of "Business is business" had become bone and gristle of the land. Competition had been enshrined and institutionalized as God. Private profit meant public good and where the two diverged almost inevitably the public good suffered. A commercialism so crass had swept the face of the nation that it had left a festering sore of materialism, a suppurating wound on the body politic that would not heal. Poisoned air and polluted water, spoiled food and tasteless crops, plundered natural resources, were the most dramatic and visible evidence, but what had filtered into the minds and hearts of men was even more lethal. The "Gimme" and "What's in it for me?" vied with "You goddam well better do it" and "If you don't you'll be taken care of": Violence and corruption were yoked and all men feared the furrow they plowed including those who drove the oxen and chose the field. Take what you want, his father had said, and then pay for it; well, the nation had taken what it wanted and it was paying for it, and would continue to pay for it for a long time.

The notions his French friends might bring to bear, mostly Marxist, were outlandish and unsophisticated, but the economics were pertinent, crucial, if older Christian notions seemed more penetrating and appropriate. It was all subsumed by one human difficulty, that of transcending personal, material and immediate gratification. How did one learn, or teach others, to give up anything now—sov-

[451]

ereignty, political power, economic wealth, life itself if need be—for the public good now or later? In history peoples had often been coerced into self-sacrifice, self-transcendence, but the means were always awful and bloody and consequently so were the ends. The Nazis and the Communists, among others, had gone down that blind alley to the very end, the entire route slippery with blood, for the *Volk* and the *State;* and every other cause—God, Justice, Equality, Freedom—had had its day and its slogans, but how did one learn, and teach others, to transcend pride and greed, lust and anger, gluttony and envy, and sloth—sloth and indifference? Could you ask any man to love his neighbor as he did himself? And if you did, didn't you forget his self-hatred? His hatred for his own as well as his hatred for others? Didn't you ask the impossible? Could you ask a man to lay down his life for a friend? In spite of George, in spite of Peter Agnielli, he didn't believe you could ask and expect men to do so; only a God could do so, and perhaps even not a God. Yet if men didn't learn to think, feel, work, for other men, then it was only a matter of years before the cobalt snow shone blue in the sun and the silent deserted planet lay absolved and ravished beneath the unfeeling sky. What profit it a man if he conquer the city and lose his own soul? the religious had asked; but they might also have said, should have said, that if a man loses his soul he loses the city too: He doesn't conquer it unless he conquers himself.

The questions Sanders asked of himself and of those he spoke to left him daily more uneasy, not alone because he could unearth no satisfactory answer but because he saw how intricately his own personal life was tied to both questions and answers, how he was trying to diagnose not only the crisis of nerve of his society, perhaps even of his time, but also his own personal crisis. The macrocosm, for all the power and impersonality of the state, was not yet entirely removed from the microcosm; in fact, though once they might have met asymptotic to infinity, like parallel lines, he knew they were now diverging lines, moving with increasing speed in different directions, expanding universes in antithesis. If he could arrive at any answers, in either sphere, they could be applied to the other and bring some relief, some improvement, perhaps even some kind of salvation. And questions and answers alike stuck in his throat as discordantly as all too recently his *boule hystérique* had. That he owed George Christiansen his life was clear, but had the effort to take up George's life been only the neurotic obsession Fillmore saw, or was it a genuine and deep-seated effort to live out another man's life truly, to walk however imperfectly in another man's shoes?

If only he could arrive at some insight about transcendence, some understanding of what made men act against what seemed like their explicit personal interests, then he was convinced that all the important relationships of his life would be suddenly and brilliantly illuminated; from the dark labyrinth of lurking motive and ambiguous intent he would come to see a clear thread to lead him out of the depths and the fear of the Minotaur. His father and mother, Elaine, Monique, Beth, Laura, George, all of them and all of the others would take on new dimensions. Rationality and irrationality, unity and diversity, good and evil, love and hatred, war and peace, would suddenly, like the colored chips in a kaleidoscope after shaking, assume a new and more meaningful configuration. Something Laura had said to him in bed one night after she had turned on and he had refused came back to him, and with it the painful thought of Laura: "You're the last of another generation," she'd muttered through the smoke, "and we are the first of a new. The drugs are the way out. I know, I know, you think I'm just high and dopey but I'm not. I'm not putting you on either. What we do means something. Maybe we're an experiment that mankind is trying, to learn how to deal with the bomb and the machine. Isn't that what we've got to do?"

Sanders had nodded, not taking her quite seriously, sure it was the marijuana talking, but intrigued by her earnestness.

"The machines're gonna be working the machines pretty soon and no one will have anything to do. Maybe we're the guinea pigs of how to live in a world that has no work. A world in which you have got to have people who don't want to kill. Who don't even want anything special, a special girl, a special job, only a special kick. A psychedelic world. A world in which cats have to work at playing. And maybe the drugs are the way to turn off the work-fight-kill world and turn on the play-love-flowers world. We're the flower children, remember? The love-in generation? Turned on and tuned out."

"How about the bomb?" he's asked her.

"Man's the bomb," she'd said, inhaling deeply and holding the smoke in her lungs. "You got to defuse the bomb. Maybe jive won't do it. Maybe acid won't either. Maybe none of the stuff we have now'll do it, but some stuff will. It's got to take the killer out of cats. Once you do that, the bomb doesn't matter."

The killer and the worker: didn't the two go together? Once you needed them both and now you didn't, Laura thought, and maybe she was right. Maybe she was really exploring the opening to a new world, a not-so-brave but not-so-rash world, one he wouldn't like, one his father and mother would have hated, but one in which mankind in some form could persist on the planet, brave-new-worldly, smack into 1984. That was transcendence of a kind, self-transcendence indeed, if drug-induced. In time men might even learn to manage in other ways that the novelists if not the politicians had predicted and foreseen, manipulating the genetic inheritance and makeup, using organ transplants and hormonic surgery, with hypnopedia and subliminal education and Pavlovian conditioning, with God knew what other as yet unheard-of means. That world was one he could not live in comfortably but then he wasn't living that comfortably in the world as it was, and neither were most of the globe's people. Drugs and chemicals and surgery to deal with modern man's malaises, to keep mankind from overpeopling the globe, to restrain him from the atomic violence that would depopulate it permanently, to make him serene if not happy, to prolong the length of his life by reducing the breadth of it: Perhaps *homo sapiens* had gone as far as he could go; now at last it was time for *homo felix*.

Ten days after the first call, on a sunny morning not yet in full flush, the telephone woke him and the same officious voice without a trace of concern or compassion told him that Joseph Farnum Christiansen had been buried up at the Presidio the day before. The voice said that the old man had left specific instructions that Sanders was to be called and, it added with a kind of macabre glee, given the grave and plot number, but *only after the burial*. Sanders was, confusedly, able to elicit the further information that Christiansen had lingered on a few days more after he'd seen him, semicomatose, and then had "passed on" without being in great pain during the night. A blessing. "Sure," Sanders thought, "but whose blessing? and who blesses?" But he didn't ask that cold metallic voice those questions. It was over. When he hung up the phone, Sanders knew he would call Beth and tell her; the time for delay was over. He didn't wait: Early as it was, he dialed her number, not without that little lurch of effort after the first three digits, and he had no sooner spoken her name into the mouthpiece than she exclaimed, "Elliott, I wondered when you'd get around to calling me." She sounded delighted to be talking to him but that had happened so many times before and turned sour that Sanders did not feel his spirits lift. "Dinner tonight?" she invited, and with a premonition that it would be their last supper he accepted, angry at his alacrity, wondering why he didn't simply and straightforwardly—and finally? —tell her then the news of old man Christiansen's death and leave it at that. He knew that wouldn't be enough, he knew he wanted more than that; he wanted to see her, make love to her, relieve himself of a desolation that he felt and couldn't fathom. He wanted to tell her, at last, finally, that he knew he did not want her, would not and could not marry her.

It was dusk when he arrived at her house, the bouquet of red roses in hand. At the florist he'd ruled out gardenias and jasmine for obvious reasons and there seemed no other choice but red roses. The door was ajar but he rang and heard Beth calling for him to come in, she was in the kitchen. For a fraction of a second Sanders saw her before she saw him, intent over the stove, a lock of her hair spilled on her forehead, a neatly starched white apron partly covering her pearl-gray tailored shirt and black velvet toreador trousers. "Elliott," she said, making his spoken name an endearment. Pushing back the lock of hair with her forearm, still clutching the whisk she'd been using, she met him, embraced him and kissed him on the mouth, before she noticed the roses he was carrying. She took them from him, eyes wide, and buried her face in the petals before she silently found a white porcelain vase with slender branched tan bamboos designed on it and set the flowers on the living-room cocktail table. "Anyone who brings me red roses can have what he wants of me," Beth said softly. "Just ask, Elliott."

[455]

"Anyone?" Sanders inquired. "And anything?"

"Well," Beth amended, catching his tone and hardening her own, "almost anyone and not quite but almost anything." She promised she'd be ready in a little while and, handing him a wedge of lettuce and another of cabbage, directed him outdoors to feed Jo-Jo the turtle. Sanders found the turtle easily, hearing its clumsy noises first in the shrubbery, then its hard-nailed scraping on the patio flags. No sooner did he drop the vegetables within its reach than the turtle's head, legs and tail disappeared under its shell and remained there, armored, hidden. Sanders sat in the hammock and watched as the ugly black-and-yellow head and neck gradually reemerged, the beady eyes wary, the birdlike beak biting sharply, tearing at the lettuce and cabbage with a crunching sound. The single-mindedness of the turtle's attack on the food was both horrifying and fascinating.

In a little while Beth came out of the house, drinks in hand, her apron discarded, a black sweater studded with pearls thrown over her shoulders, a single red rose pinned to the lapel of her shirt. She handed him a glass, sat down and asked what he'd been doing since she'd seen him. He told her he'd been working, mostly, and hadn't done much else, and then she wanted to know why he hadn't called. There was no coyness in the question, only a forceful directness, but he chose to bypass it and instead told her about the morning call that had informed him that old man Christiansen was dead and buried. She didn't seem to hear him but sat there toying with the rose, tilting her head to it as if it were a child she was nursing, raising the shirt lapel and the flower to her nose, eyes closed, her face a distant ecstasy.

"Did you hear me, Beth?" Sanders asked, swinging slowly in the hammock, his heels dragging against the flagstones. "Joseph Farnum Christiansen's dead. They buried him up near George at the Presidio."

"Not too near," Beth murmured, not opening her eyes. "Not too near, I hope, because George hated his guts."

"The old man was the last of his line. Now the Christiansens are cut off, root and branch."

"Good! I'm glad! It's what they deserved!" Her eyes were now pressed tightly shut. "It's what they asked for. If Jamie—if Jamie had

[456]

lived, they'd have been carried on, both of them, and their name too."

"If George had lived," Sanders said, "maybe you could have had another child, other children, with him, really his own flesh and blood, Christiansens, perhaps healthier, but—"

"George is dead! Jamie's dead!" she said too loudly, her eyes now open and blazing. "Dead, dead, dead! That's all over and done with. Forever. I'm glad he's dead. He was a miserly mean old man."

"Mean and miserly he was," Sanders agreed. "I saw him a little while before—"

"He died?"

"Yes. He asked me to come to the hospital for the last time so he could warn me that he was leaving his money to the Marine Corps, to tell me he wanted no one to come to his funeral—"

"I know, fuck 'em all except six and save those for pallbearers!" Beth laughed discordantly. "How did I know? He was always saying that, even to George, even when there was no prospect of his dying. Oh, yes, that leopard never changed his spots."

"I felt sorry for him there, at the end."

"Joseph Farnum Christiansen was a sonofabitch. He didn't deserve your sympathy or anyone else's."

"He was George's father."

Beth shrugged her shoulders impatiently, the rose falling away from her face. "That little spurt of sperm, that biological act of paternity, counts a great deal more with you than it does with me."

Sanders only just avoided saying "I'd never have known," and instead remarked lightly, "They still don't make children without it, do they?"

"They will, don't worry, Elliott, they will."

"I'll be sorry when they do—even if it makes an improvement in the breed."

"The breed can use it."

"Yes," he agreed, "I'm sure it can." He drank and watched the turtle snapping at the heels of the lettuce and cabbage. "Even at the end there was something magnificent about the old bastard, unregenerate, tough, miserable, aggressive, mean as he was—"

[457]

"Yes, I know, the kind of man who made the West—yesterday—and is destroying it today."

In the gathering dusk they sat until she said very carefully, angrily, picking each word and enunciating the separate syllables as if precision were absolutely essential to her, as if she wanted no ambiguity about her intentions, "I'm going to marry Steven Prescott, Elliott. I've been thinking about it a great deal these past weeks and I've made up my mind. It hasn't been easy, making up my mind, and it isn't easy to tell you."

"Well, it must have been easier telling him," Sanders said, his palm frozen to the icy glass.

"I haven't told him yet. I wanted to tell *you* first."

"Why?"

"Because I love you, Elliott."

"That makes sense, Beth. You love me and therefore you marry Steven Prescott. I thought you tried that once before, with George, and it didn't work out quite as you hoped."

She ignored the heavy-handed irony. "I'm going to marry him and quit my job, move up to Atherton and join the country club. I'm going to live the life of a socialite matron who's a proper doctor's wife. I'm going to play tennis and golf, ride horses, give parties, and go on vacations to Maui and Mexico. . . . And I'm going to have children, three or four of them."

His venom would not be stayed. "Isn't that going to be something of a problem considering how the last one with Steven Prescott turned out?"

Beth flinched. "That was a freak"—she stopped herself, aware of the other meaning of what she'd said—"an accident. Phocomelia, like lightning, doesn't strike twice in the same spot."

The look on her face made him reverse his field. "For your sake, and for the child's, I hope not."

"Not for Steven's?"

"He's not very different from old man Christiansen, you know."

"I love him."

"Him too?"

"In another way." When she spoke again, she was not changing the subject but was concerned: "What will *you* do?"

[458]

"I don't know, yet," he said. "The news comes as a bit of a shock, yet I'm not surprised. I had the feeling in my bones that it was going to work out this way."

"Why?"

"Fate. I don't know exactly. The only thing that stood in the way between you and Steven was the money; you could never be sure that wasn't what he was after, and—"

"Bill Daulton was up and arranged the whole property thing for me. He was a big help. He understood the problems and he's arranged to help me preserve the estate. After all, California has a community property law. That's the way Aunt Katharine would have wanted it done. Steven will understand it and it won't make any difference. He's got enough money now so that it won't matter a bit."

"What did Daulton say about that? Is his penchant for you done with, the fever in the blood turned cold? Or is the saving of the estate enough for him?"

"I went to bed with him," Beth announced again.

"Oh, was that the price? That's either a very high or a very low fee, depending, for a good lawyer."

"I went to bed with him, Elliott, because he pleaded and cried and carried on, and because he wanted it so much. And I was grateful to him. And giving him something made me feel strong and compassionate and generous. He was doing so much for me."

"No, Beth, darling"—the term of endearment had an edge—"it was much more than that."

"More?"

"You went to bed with him so you could tell me and tell Prescott, so you can let us know—and poor Daulton too—that you belong to no one, that nobody owns Beth Marshall Christiansen."

"I'm free, my own woman, if that's what you're driving at."

"Maybe that just means you're not anybody's wife, or not capable of being anybody's wife."

"Nonsense!"

"I don't think so. If you don't belong to anyone else, you don't belong to yourself either. George found that out. I've found it. You still have a way to go before you find it out."

"I belong to no one, not to Steven, not to you, not to George, not even to Aunt Katharine or my parents, not to the living or to the dead. No one, do you understand?"

"Yes," Sanders replied, "I do understand."

"I'm going to tell Steven too so that he'll know, so he'll see clearly that I'm not a thing, not a property, not chattel, not to be owned by anyone."

Beth sniffed the air and ran for the house. When he found her in the kitchen she was leaning over a kettle on the stove, vigorously stirring it and plaintively announcing that she'd burned the *boeuf bourguignon*. It did not seem to him that it was the most important thing she'd burned that evening, nor was the smell of the scorched meat the only odor of charring flesh in his nostrils.

The food was fine, a cold gazpacho, the beef in burgundy, delicious though overdone, a lemon meringue she had whisked into unbelievable airiness, but Sanders did not enjoy the dinner. Beth was a good cook and obviously relished serving him so that he ate and tried to be hearty and cheerful, and properly appreciative, but the effort told on him and he knew he was not altogether successful. They sat in the living room, lingering over brandy and coffee for a long time, not talking much and avoiding each other's eyes until Beth asked him, boldly not shyly, to make love to her and it was his turn to quail. "I don't think I could manage that now," he replied, "under the circumstances."

"Let me try," she challenged. Her demeanor was arrogant, her voice assured. She was so like Elaine in her proud skill, her confident address, that his flesh did not at first rise to the occasion but when it finally did, in tribute to her persistent craft, he hated her so that he thrust into her like a sword, wanting to cut her in two, wanting to tear up her insides as his were torn up. There on the living-room floor, he fell away from her at last, his hand bleeding where the thorn of the rose or the pin that held it to her sweater had stabbed his palm; if he hated her, Sanders despised himself because he wished he could not perform out of hatred, wished he could not make love when there was no longer love; but he could. Next to him Beth's face was set in lines of mourning, the face of a widow, the skin stretched tight across the bones so that for a moment he could see how she would look when she was old, emptied of passion, and he saw what her Aunt Katharine must have looked like, been like. "I'll miss you, Elliott," Beth moaned, an elegy for something coveted and lost, for something enjoyed and relinquished, bereavement once more. "I'll miss you a long time." It was a promise she meant but fortunately wouldn't, couldn't, keep.

"If you ever see Murray Fillmore again," Beth whispered after a time, "please thank him for me."

"I will, Beth," Sanders promised, "but what shall I thank him for?" He didn't, couldn't, bring himself to ask if that too was for services rendered: Had she also slept with Fillmore as she had with Bill Daulton, or was it a seduction, a mutual seduction, of another kind?

"The chaplain released me. He forgave me so I could forgive myself."

"So you could marry Prescott?"

Her head made a soft thud against the carpet as, nodding, she brought her head up and back twice.

"I'm glad for you."

"Are you, Elliott?"

"Nothing is to be gained"—he made himself smile—"by shouldering unbearable burdens or undertaking unpayable debts. I'm glad for you that you can go on, have the strength and the purpose to go on into the future."

"Do you think I'll be a good wife and mother?" With her head turned to him, eyes wide and searching, she was asking not only for his forgiveness but for absolution, an acquiescence that would wipe the slate clean and permit her to begin afresh—or as afresh as would be possible to one so scarred and wounded. But as he had made love in hatred, so he preserved his hatred in his love, undissolved by charity or forgiveness, and he couldn't give her any more forbearance and remission than the cold comfort of "You'll be a good mother, Beth—if you try."

"And a happy wife. Say it, Elliott, please."

"Happy? No one's happy, Beth, and especially not wives and husbands."

In his own apartment Sanders sat drinking and looking out at the huddled black mountains that barred his access to the sea, re-

membering through the night pieces of his life until the first faint
scars of dawn were cut burning across the sky. Elaine's note was
burning in his mind by then, as he had once set it aflame and
watched it burn to ashes in his hand before grinding it to powered
ash beneath his heel, but it was harder, impossible in fact, to grind
it out of his memory: His fingers could still feel that parchment-stiff
linen paper, the faint blue border boxing the eggshell, the embossed
three-initial monogram a deeper blue and in angular modern type,
just as the words were seared into his brain:

DEAR ELLIOTT:

Look—I've got to tell you what a wonderful, terrible happi-
ness I feel now. They are all wrong who talk of dignity and
its attainment. Malraux and the other half of the world—and
we can find meaning and dignity through a union with another
person or a cause. Hurray for causes, because in them—as well
as in another person—we can lose ourselves and find "dignity."

In the other corner of the ring, dear sir, are those who have
already given up. Flat on their backs. No such thing for them
as hoping for a realization of these words in terms of them-
selves. Dignity and meaning? No such thing. Don't exist. But
they keep on trying—on their backs, of course—to confirm their
own existence in terms of futility. That's not right, Elliott, is it?
No. Goddammit! In isolation, in anguish itself, is the nearest we
can come to dignity. Impossible to seek it out of context! Man
can come just so close to his escapes in space but never near at
all in time.

And when you stand unarmed, and make a dignity of an-
guish, create a meaning of isolation, you get pretty close—
maybe closest—to reality. You can't give of yourself and re-
tain the you that is dignity—it isn't at all logical. In this sense
love as such is only that same self-confirmation, not dignity
but degradation. And do I have to sit on a pile of dung with
Giono or moan in a garbage pail with Beckett or mumble my
scorn with Genêt? I don't think so.

What was that Air Force Colonel but a last attempt to en-

ter into such a disgraceful compromise—narcissism, perhaps
(spelled right?)?

And having had nearly all of the choices, I have yet to try
myself. Oh, hope with me, Elliott, hope with me that I've got
guts enough.

I have loved you.

ELAINE

The letter had arrived too late and he had not understood all of
it the day Tessier had handed it to him. He'd just returned from a
long assignment in Japan, writing and photographing a series on the
revival of Japanese nationalism—the industrialists, the militarists,
the Zengakuren and other recalcitrant students, the intellectuals,
the resurrection of a disciplined, skilled and energetic people from
defeat and disaster to the rank of the fifth most powerful nation on
earth—and he was still suffering from "culture shock," the return
from East to West, from Orient to Occident, from Nippon to France,
remembering like a samisen refrain over and over the story one
Buddhist had told him about how the Gautama's final life had been
a triumph over sickness, old age and death and how that triumph
had begun under the sacred fig tree with the defeat of temptation.
Every man under his own fig tree—even the Buddha. He'd stood
there not quite hearing Tessier's congratulations on the quality of
the text and pictures, nodding automatically at the right breath
pauses, but concentrating on the feeling in his fingertips as they ran
over the paper of the envelope as if it were Elaine's flesh, as if they
were once more brushing her cheek or her breast or her buttock or
that soft inner helplessness of thigh, telling himself with his own
perverse self-punishing irony that it was laid-stock linen paper.

His mother's words to his father, her farewell words before they'd
left his father in Europe to his fate, to France's, echoed in his head,
phrases he knew his mother had never intended her son to overhear,
their Biblical ring an echo of her own uprightness and puritan up-
bringing, of her sturdiness and stubbornness. "Lovett," she had said
to his father then, "from all those who have taught me have I become wise; from all those who have opposed me have I become

[463]

strong; from all those who have tried to demean me have I bolstered
my pride; from all those who have hated me, or have tried to turn me
to hatred in turn, have I learned how to love."

"You mean me?" his father had asked, blanching as he rarely did.

"I mean you, more than anyone else."

"But not to love me enough to stay?"

"To love you, yes, Lovett, but Elliott more—and myself, of necessity, if I would survive, for him—and if and when you change your
mind, for you." Because his mother knew her own mind and was
strong and determined—his father would have said self-righteous—
and his father no less was convinced of his own needs and rightness,
his mother had taken him home to America in spite of his father
from a Europe already aflame with war and stinking with burning
corpses.

* * *

How the weeks passed or how many Sanders didn't know, but at
the edge of his consciousness he was aware that the Paris fall was
chilling imperceptibly into winter, the days grayer and thicker, the
rain a daily recurrence. Dutifully he visited Fejnstejn and Elaine
went to the American Hospital for their respective treatments. At
home they rarely spoke and when they did Elaine's clinical fascina-
tion with the treatment, the twenty-million-unit doses of penicillin,
the repeated blood tests to make sure that their veins were no longer
hosts to the pallid visitors from other bodies repelled him because
it seemed only to stand between them and to be a parallel sickness,
because it couldn't cure the syphilis of the soul with which they
were afflicted, the illness that coursed through their minds raging
and rampant, immune to any antibiotics of the spirit. There was a
delight with filth, with corruption, with infection of the flesh and
the womb, an identification of the burrowing spirochete with the
mounting sperm that sickened him to his marrow. It was as if Elaine
was plainly striving to tell him, "You wanted to spill your seed into
me like a disease, an illness that I was to harbor in my bowels and
grow into a child for you, and you did; but now, with the help of
medicine, I am rooting it out of me, spewing forth your semen so
that it will not contaminate my womb and infect my tissues: I will
not commit myself to you, to myself, to life, to the future, because

[464]

they are all diseased." What man had joined, however imperfectly, man had torn asunder.

Deranged as it was, Sanders tried to hold on to some comprehension of what it was Elaine was enduring—and yet could not because it was mad. One night, not long after the fortnight of treatment was over and Fejnstejn had told him he was cured and could resume his sexual life—and, though insisting he spoke as a physician, not as a friend or godfather, smiling not altogether happily and saying that perhaps he spoke only as an old Jewish patriarch—Fejnstejn had in avuncular fashion advised him to have a child. Fejnstejn had been the only one he'd been able to talk to about what was happening with Elaine and the old man had nodded sympathetically. "Not uncommon, Elliott," he'd commented, "it happens this way to many women and not just with venereal disease. Where the man doesn't want a child, where there is an abortion, a miscarriage, a stillbirth; sometimes only where the man has had another affair and his wife suspects it or has actually discovered it. Trust." He spread his hands and shrugged his shoulders. "What is it? The cement and lubrication between people. But what it's made of, how it's established, no one knows, and therefore when it's fractured or broken, no one knows how to splint it up, how to repair matters."

"Then what do I do?"

"You go on being affectionate and considerate, tender and decent, if you can manage it, in the face of any and all rebuffs, and you go on hoping."

"I don't know how long I can manage."

"You manage as long as you must, as long as you care for Elaine."

"Or she cares for me."

"Yes, that too, though that matters less."

"How long can I go on, can she go on, living in yesterdays?" he'd cried out, hating himself for that appeal, recognizing by the narrowed eyes how it hit Fejnstejn where he himself lived in lonely anguish.

"There are more yesterdays to come," Fejnstejn said sadly, putting his hand on Elliott's shoulder in a move spontaneous and paternal and very like a Biblical blessing.

That evening he'd come back to the flat with the taste of desolation in his mouth like mildewed mushrooms. The day had been long and trying and he'd quarreled with Tessier who'd wanted him to fly to Vienna to cover the Austrian elections. Austria's role in European politics had not, in Sanders' judgment, been really important since the Russians had accepted its independence and neutrality. The country, the leadership and the people had interpreted both of those to mean that they were to keep their noses clean to maintain their freedom, and so they had made no effort to serve as a bridge between East and West, to encourage and facilitate rapprochement between the divided worlds; they'd simply sighed with relief at their good fortune to have slipped out from under the barbed wire and the truncheon and had settled back to enjoy their newfound prosperity, their old *Schlag* and *Schlamperei*. Tessier had balked at sending one of the younger French staff reporters and a photographer Sanders recommended, maintaining that because Sanders was an American and because of his contacts among the Austrian socialists, he would have entree to people and places that a Frenchman and a relatively inexperienced journalist would not; besides, he'd have to send two men, a photographer too, while with Sanders, only one staff man need go. Sanders knew Tessier was right but he obstinately refused to acknowledge it. He hated trading on his nationality or his father's old friends and contacts though after more than a decade and a half he knew those people in Vienna better than Lovett Carpenter Sanders ever had and they were, in fact, now his own friends and acquaintances. But what was at the bottom of his refusal to go to Vienna on that assignment was his personal reluctance to leave Elaine even for a week. If he told that to Tessier, Tessier would accuse him of uxoriousness, sneer at him, and talk about American men being doormats. Yet he wanted to stay as close to Elaine as he could, do his best to try to rebuild a new life for them out of the bombed-out rubble they were living in that was no longer a marriage but the ruins of one: If he did not succeed now, he would never succeed.

Elaine was, as usual, in bed reading when he came into the bedroom and didn't look up. Eyes still on the book, she asked in an offhand voice if he had had his dinner—she had not cooked a single

[466]

meal for him since he'd told her about the syphilis—and he acknowledged that he hadn't eaten. He went into the guestroom, what was now his bedroom, to which one morning while he was at work Elaine had transferred all his clothing, his suits neatly pressed and hung on hangers in the closet, his other clothes carefully and symmetrically laid away in the armoire, his shoes shined and treed in a shoe rack on the back of a closet door. He undressed, put on a robe and went to the bathroom to shower. When he came out, feeling very little refreshed, he found the kitchen table set, flowers on it for the first time in weeks, tightly closed yellow tulips on grass-green stalks, and a diced ham omelet, a tomato salad, a glass of red wine and a bakery-fresh half a *baguette* waiting for him.

Sanders went to the bedroom where Elaine, odalisque on the bed, was concentrating too deliberately on her book to be reading. "Thanks," he said, hoping that she had made the first gesture of reconciliation, her first gesture.

Mock innocently, eyes wide, Elaine looked up and asked, "What for?"

"For dinner, the flowers. Want to join me?"

"I've already eaten." In the past she had always wanted to take her meals with him no matter what time he ate, even morning breakfasts though Sanders knew she hated to get up early in the day and had for years before they were married never gotten out of bed before midday if she could help it and certainly not to make anyone, or even herself, breakfast. Elaine rose from the bed so reluctantly that he was instantly sorry he'd asked her, and as if further to show her disinclination she took her book with her, finger held in her place between the leaves of the book as she preceded him into the kitchen. He held her chair for her, she sat gravely, not glancing at or touching him, before he went around the table to his own place, the whole strained formality as chilling and difficult as always. The omelet was piping hot and so was the plate, so he knew she'd timed it to his entrance and her exit, but he didn't know what to make of that either. Though all the food was tasty he had no appetite, and after a few desultory mouthfuls of food, he pushed the plates back and devoted himself to the wine, rinsing his mouth with it, letting it trickle down his tightened throat, hoping the alcohol would scour the mushroom taste of desolation from his tongue and palate but it didn't.

"You ought to eat," Elaine admonished him quietly. "You're looking positively gaunt."

"I have no appetite," he said.

"That's okay," she said insinuatingly, "losing your appetite sometimes helps you to survive."

"Unless you starve to death or you lose your appetite to live altogether."

"Is life only a bundle of appetites, Elliott?"

He bobbed his head, watching the wine seesaw crazily in his glass, unable to gaze into her beautiful face, now the face of a familiar stranger, the long eyelashes masking the eyes and grazing the cheek, the vulnerable mouth held stern. "Man is an *I want* animal," he replied.

"And woman?"

Though her face remained serious, solemn, Sanders couldn't help smiling. "Woman is an *I want more* animal, maybe even more animal too."

"That's the way it has to be?"

"That's the way it is."

"For everyone?"

"I don't think there are many exceptions," he said slowly, reflectively, his mother, John C. Ballinger, Michel Fejnstejn flashing through his mind, "but everyone learns to curb the *I want* and the animal and to make do."

"You couldn't do that, could you?" Her voice, tremulous, rose, and Sanders saw her effort to control it, to bring it down, to talk at all.

He shook his head. "I don't think so. Not in this."

"You wouldn't try?"

"I *have* tried, Elaine, very hard. You know that. For more than a year. It's been a long and not very happy time." He sighed and poured himself some more wine. "Besides, I want children, don't you?"

"We could adopt them."

"Yes, we could. Under other circumstances, if we had to, it

[468]

wouldn't matter; well, it would matter, but I could live with it, but not this way. Don't you even want to give birth to your own, if you can, hand down whatever part of you that you can?" What other immortality is there? he thought. What other eternal link with the past and with the future?

Her shudder quivered through the table to his elbows, propped on it, a distinct quaver like a small earth tremor. "God, no," she said, mortified, fervent. "Isn't one like me more than enough?"

"One like you is enough for me," Sanders said, knowing that he might easily say that one of her was too much for him, knowing too that he was promising something he might not be able to fulfill and suddenly hearing his own voice like the echo of his father's explaining to his mother, being obscurely gallant and chivalrous. He put down his wineglass and reached across the table to take Elaine's hand in his but she recoiled, her hands now clutching her book, the book pressed to her breasts. "Come to bed with me," he said.

"I can't," she said, shaking as if with fever.

"Is it because of the syphilis?"

Dumbly Elaine looked at the tablecloth.

"It's over," he insisted. "We're cured, at least of that. But if we don't go ahead, work our way back to some more . . . normal, sensible life, we'll have it forever. Look at me," he commanded, but she wouldn't. "Am I so loathsome to you?"

Elaine shook her head, wildly, eyes panicky looking left and right, searching for some way out, like an animal trapped and searching for escape, about to bolt. "It's not you," she whispered.

"Then who? what?"

"It's me." Sanders could barely hear her. "It . . . I'm so loathsome to myself." She leaped up, the book fell out of her hands and slammed on the floor and she fled. He followed her into the bedroom where she was lying face down on the bed, shoulders heaving, hands over her ears as if trying to shut out, or in, the sound of her sobbing, her face burrowing into the pillow. Sitting on the bed next to her, stroking her back, feeling her muscles go rigid beneath his hands until his patient fingers fondled them limp, Sanders wanted to plead, exhort, command, rage, even pray, but he had no confidence in any of those means to help them. How long, O Lord, he thought, how

[469]

long? When at last she was still he turned her over on her back, wiped her tears away, brushed her hair back from her face, lay down next to her and held her in his arms. She clung to him like a child, her face buried in his shoulder, and softly, as if it were a lullaby, Sanders sang to her a song he remembered from his childhood. The song seemed to soothe her and soon she dozed. While she was half asleep, her free hand, without artifice, sought and found him, fell between his legs and held him, gripped him, clasped him tight. *Thy rod and Thy staff, they comfort me*—sometimes—he thought, wondering if that was blasphemy or true religion; and in wondering he saw the cleavage between his parents clear. But he knew he walked in the valley of the shadow of death, and he feared evil, he was terrified of what was happening to them, of what would happen to them. Eyes closed, hands clenched, Elaine accepted his kisses, his caresses, her response slow and shivering until, her nipple urgent against his palm, between his fingers, announced her readiness that was no readiness, her willingness that was not yet able to be willed into reality, and when he was poised over her, his legs and his trunk trying to separate her branches so that he could find her living pulp, she reared and bucked, the cry in her throat torn out of it a gargling wound, her fingernails slashing at his face, her whole body holding, pushing him off while he pleaded, groveled, heard his supplications with self-hatred and contempt and despair, until her knee rose and sent the rejection flaming painfully through his vitals, throwing him off her, off the bed and onto the floor where he lay in a heap holding himself together, hearing his own voice, a stranger's in his ears, still clamoring for her to open, to open to him, begging her, please.

The next afternoon Sanders flew out of Orly for Vienna, having brought his bag and cameras to the office, made banking and travel arrangements, wired three or four key people in Austria that he was arriving and giving them a list of people he wanted to see and lunching with Tessier before he left for the airport. In the morning Elaine's bedroom door had been closed and though he made enough noise getting dressed and packing his bags to wake her the door remained shut. When he nudged it open a crack and peered in, her body was twisted in her nightdress, turned away from him so that he couldn't see her face, but coiled like a great cat's about to spring out of sleep, bed and nightdress; yet he couldn't tell if she was truly asleep. He left her a brief note in the kitchen, giving her the address of his hotel in Vienna, telling her he'd be gone for perhaps a week or ten days in Austria, perhaps slightly more. It was, on rereading, a curt note, cold and withdrawn, and he couldn't bring himself to soften it with terms of endearment he didn't feel. He wasn't even able to sign it "Love" or "Fondly," however ambiguous he knew those terms to be; the best he could manage was "Yrs.," abbreviated, and he wondered "Yrs." what?

Sanders had telephoned Monique almost every day for weeks since he'd begun the treatment with Fejnstejn, but he had had no answer and the silence stirred the coals of his shame to fire; he couldn't make himself go to the flat without speaking to her on the telephone first, but he couldn't leave France to go to Austria without seeing her, talking to her. Leaving Paris, leaving the country, had another kind of finality whose demands couldn't be brooked. So, with the pretext of leaving the country in hand, he had the taxi wait at the Avenue Mozart flat on his way to the office, went up the stairs half hoping to hear Patachou's longing resounding in the stairwell:

J'attendrai
Car l'oiseau qui s'enfuit
Vient chercher l'oubli
Dans son nid.

but her door was locked, there was no response to the bell or to his knock. Then he noticed the small embossed card below the bell had been removed. Downstairs the concierge informed him that Mme. Bardieu had moved almost two weeks before and had left no forwarding address. If he was M. Sanders, which the concierge knew he was, having seen him visiting her often enough, then Mme. Bardieu had left him a message. A five-franc note produced the envelope which Sanders tore open only after he was back in the cab being driven to the office. Monique's handwriting was a schoolgirl scrawl, that of someone schooled neither long enough nor well enough, and who was unused to writing; but the letter nonetheless jarred him to his roots.

[471]

MY DEAREST:

> *I never got a letter. I never received a call. Not a word. The days went on. I could not sleep or do anything because I was waiting. I knew it was finished, but I could not make my heart believe.*
>
> *Today the damp chill has gone. The morning is fresh. I have been awake since daybreak. Today I am certain. Done. Finished. No need to wait any more.*
>
> *I knew I had permitted us to go too far, too deep, We needed more space between us, or less. Much less. The space between me and other people is a shock now after our brief but imaginary closeness. I am not even a companion to myself.*
>
> *Like a tidy housewife I must now clean up my desolation, stuff my disorder and unhappiness out of sight, prepare myself again for the horror and the humor of being until the will to life flows back.*
>
> *Complaints are useless. Regrets foolish. We choose our life, or it chooses us.*

It was signed with her initial only, nothing more, not even the date.

Sanders had not been in Vienna since the autumn of 1956 but the city was not much changed. The weather and the Danube were still gray and depressing, but they were offset at least in part by the music, the theater, the food, the lights, the shops, and the girls—or boys, if you were inclined that way—handsome and agreeable, and the gray weathered architectural reminders of the once-imposing Austro-Hungarian Empire's power and grandeur. His interviews went smoothly, he filled his notebooks with facts and insights, he took hundreds of photographs, and he even managed—it turned out, correctly—to predict the way the elections would go; but he didn't enjoy any of it, either the professional probing, usually a keen satisfaction, or the personal encounters with his old acquaintances, or the music and theater, though both were excellent. Again and again at the most inappropriate times—drinking the autumn wine in the Heuriger cafés up at Grinzing, listening to music at the State Opera, or the violinists, accordionists, guitarists and zither players in the cafés; even on the one night on the town he took with an old trade-union friend, who brought him to a restaurant and bar where he saw the best striptease he'd ever seen, the most beautiful, sinuous and desirable girls, all of whom when he talked to them turned out to be English or French, he couldn't take any of them to the rooms up-stairs—he found himself without desire for anything but writing letters in his head, making up conversations, arguments, explana-tions for Elaine—and for Monique—silent, unanswered and unan-swerable, but perpetual as *La Ronde*.

The old pernicious uneasiness about living in a German-speaking country was with him again as much as the interminable talks he had in the privacy of his skull with Elaine and Monique. They had killed his father, the Germans, but how many other fathers and children had they murdered? And could anyone who knew, much less who had felt their heavy hand personally, be at ease with them, always wondering which face, which hands, belonged to a murderer? Sanders wished he were one of those whose memories were less acute, one who could let bygones be bygones, the dead bury their dead, but he wasn't. He couldn't tell if the old symptoms he saw— the resurfacing of a neo-Nazi political life, the revival of the student societies, the continuation and virulence of anti-Semitism, the schiz-oid division between conservative and socialist, worker and farmer, town and country—were the same old malignant disease once more, or about to be, or whether he saw them askew, was looking for them, exaggerating them, and hence seeing things, symptoms, writ larger than they actually were.

The two together—his personal internal dialogue and his profes-sional external dialogue, his psychological and political unhappi-nesses—combined, and three days earlier than he had planned, hav-ing gotten everything he could use except the final voting tallies and some photos of the actual polling, both of which he arranged for with a local stringer, Sanders sent Elaine a wire—he had in all those bitter, humorous, carefully thought-out epistolary reflections not managed to confide a single word to paper or to mail a single letter —saying that he'd be home the next day and in the morning took a plane back for Paris. Drowsing, plying himself with whisky, which did not shut out his awareness that he knew no better now what to do than when he had left Paris, Sanders tried once more to see if

[473]

there was any way he could rebuild a life, his life, their lives, and fell asleep without either conclusion or consolation.

It was midafternoon before he was back in the Quai de Passy flat and no one was there. His wire was in the mail slot, still uncalled for, and the apartment was in perfect order, as if no one had slept or lived there since his departure. After an hour of unpacking, showering, changing his clothes, and calling Tessier to report that he was back and would bring in the films and the other materials, Sanders grew increasingly uneasy about Elaine's absence and was abruptly certain that, like Monique, she had simply left him, moved out of the apartment preparatory to a divorce. Or worse. He went into her bedroom and opened the closets, to be flayed by the whip of perfume that lingered on her clothes there, all neatly arrayed— coats, dresses, suits, shoes in order—so he thought that if she had gone she had left only temporarily. Unless? The river. He remembered the lady suicide he'd once seen washed up next to the quai, her flesh trailing like streamers in the filthy Seine, her face eaten away until bone jutted from bruised black-and-green flesh, naked except for a trench coat which hung from around her neck by one button, like a cape. He'd gotten a prize for the pictures he took of her, but he had never caught the rot of it, the stench, that awful color of putrefaction.

After another hour of waiting, having gone through the various explanations that seemed logical—she'd gone shopping, or to a movie, or for a walk in the Bois—he knew where she was, with a certainty that was beyond argument: back in the de Besancourts' Avenue Foch apartment. Elaine had a spare key and she always knew when they were out of town—even he knew that they were now in Tangiers—but as he went downstairs to look for a cab he didn't know why he was positive she was there. He loved her, though, he knew that, and he wanted to make a life with her that would permit them to build a family, a future, together—even without Monique—but still he didn't know how, because he always wanted it without those closed thighs and what they stood for and would not stand for.

The house was an old gray stone mansion not far from the Porte Dauphine, huge, elegant, its bellied windows tall and barred to the afternoon sunlight by high green shutters. Set back in a splendid garden amid masses of shrubbery and towering chestnut and acacia trees, even in November it still looked green, even now, a hundred and fifty years after it had been built, converted as it was now to a series of flats for more than seventy-five years, it bespoke luxury, hauteur, and the unmistakable odor of wealth. Seeing it again for the first time in a very long while, Sanders realized how much he had always hated that place, how assiduously he had avoided that part of the Avenue Foch because of it, and when the cab pulled up in front of the S-shaped walk that led to the black grilled iron-and-glass doorway, he almost gave the driver the order to continue to his office, but driven as he was, he could not.

The self-service elevator rose noiselessly—it was a modern one, American, and had only recently been installed—and when he stood at the door of the flat and hesitantly knocked and no one came to the door, he almost turned and fled again. But the door was ajar, there was a crack of light like a thin uneven pallid splash of paint on the corridor rug, and he opened the door and went inside. He forced himself through the foyer and down the long hall toward where he heard sounds he couldn't quite identify, didn't quite want to recognize, until at last he came into the high-ceilinged, crystal-chandeliered parlor. Over the years in Paris Sanders had heard about *partouzes*, the parties that began with a chain of cars skirting the edge of the Bois picking up a daisy chain of different and exotic people to combine in a general and venereal orgy, but he had never been to one or witnessed one; and faced with it now, he found it altogether unreal, a painting by Ingres or David, an adolescent's dream of a Byzantine seraglio, a moving-picture version of a Victorian brothel all rolled into one. The parlor was filled with Directoire furniture and decorated with opulence; heavy gold-framed Impressionist paintings on the walls glowed colorfully under the buttery light of their tiny brass overhead lamps, tapestries on the walls that might have been Aubusson or Gobelin showed stags and harts, hunts, classical nymphs and satyrs, intricate bronzes and weighty marble statuary were here a Cupid there a Bacchus, and beyond a porcelain group of ladies and gallants from Marie Antoinette's court made sport. In his first startled glance around the room, in the dim light of the late autumn afternoon filtering through the drawn portières, the shuttered windows, Sanders glimpsed a Moroccan captain in French Army uniform, an Arab in galibiyah, a Sikh in green turban and oxford-gray flannels, a Eurasian girl in scarlet cheongsam, a German in Italian-style clothes but wearing a monocle, an effete Englishman in Harris tweeds and a great-breasted epicene woman also in tweeds, English or German or perhaps Scandinavian, a tiny Annamese girl in *ao dai*, an Indian girl replete with brilliant orange-and-gold sari, Brahmin caste mark on her forehead and tiny diamond glittering in her nostril, a burning-eyed dark Indian or Pakistani in a dhoti, and an African in native regalia whose origins Sanders couldn't identify. Men and women, though various and variously dressed, were all of a similar class, well-groomed and gowned and barbered, and in various states of undress they were draped over chairs and couches and hassocks, stretched out on Oriental carpets, in every posture of sexual abandon, in every kind of *bizarrerie* and languor he had ever seen. He felt that some liveried footman in powdered wig and ruff, in silk stockings and undone codpiece, should announce him, bawl in high-pitched flawless French that the Marquis de Sanders was on the scene; but failing that, that he should at the very least introduce himself, speak his own name, be recognized. No one, however, paid him much attention; no one came forward as host or hostess to ask him who he was; only a few languid heads turned, only a few sets of glazed eyes glided indifferently over his presence.

Turning on his heel, about to leave, he saw Elaine near one of the windows, seated on her haunches on the rug, her dark head pressed between the hairy legs of an American Air Force Colonel who wore only his khaki shirt, command pilot's wings and silver eagles adorning it, and who was leaning over her solicitously and slowly beating, stroking, her bare back with his quirt. Her eyes were closed, her face weary and ecstatic together, heavy with passion, her whole face like an overripe cluster of grapes about to burst into red wine; he had never seen her like that and he could not believe he saw her still. He heard the Colonel saying, breathing heavily, speaking in soft, drawling Southern English, "Eat, my dear. Taste its pride, you cunt. Now, don't bite!" and then he slapped his quirt smartly across her back, her thighs, her shoulders, raising new welts on her pale

[476]

flesh where others splashed like jagged wine stains. Elaine quivered, writhed, coiled and uncoiled, her mouth and throat working, moving away, crying out in French, "Beat me! Hurt me! Punish me! I love—" before the Colonel's other hand brought her back, while the one with the crop slashed across her breasts.

The cry must have escaped him unawares, perhaps he had even spoken her name as one speaks it in a nightmare, impelled. Elaine heard, her eyes opened, and she looked straight at him. Their visions engaged, hers heavy-lidded, drugged, with only the faintest spark of recognition at first; then completely cognizant, heeding, she paused, stopped, and the inexorable quirt cruel across her bosom like the leathery slap of an open palm against a soft cheek brought her renewed spasmodic efforts. Deliberately she averted her eyes, turned her head away and burrowed into the refuge and punishment of those limbs that bestrode her world, wincing joyously, passionately under the blows of her fate.

By the time Sanders was back down on the street, looking maniacally for a taxi, the whole phantasm had frozen into a stone hallucination, a graffito on an ancient tomb, Herculaneum or Angkor Wat, he was never going to able to erase from his memory. Deliberately he recalled the days of his childhood in the Bois nearby, his mother taking him through the delights of the Jardin d'Acclimatation, the *plein-air* summer camps and picnics on the slopes of St. Cloud, Bellevue and Mendon just beyond, hoping to set those halcyon recollections of his youth between himself and what he had just witnessed, the crucifix between himself and the evil eye, but it didn't help. Though he knew he would in time be able to put some distance, some space, between himself and that apparition, it would only be by converting it into the Ingres or David painting it might have been, the suggestive Italian moving picture of modern depravity, the pornographic fantasy of an aging roué, but even that could not deprive the scene of the violation, the convulsion, that shook him each and every time it sprang into his head full-grown. Racing up and down the street waving at any automobile that looked like a taxi, he heard with some surprise his own shriek, the "EEe-ee!" bursting out of him like a wind under great pressure, a hurricane in the making, and he only just managed to stop it when a taxi pulled up to the curb. He jumped in, gave the magazine's address and, flashing past a street sign that read AVENUE FOCH, remembered that once, in the not-too-distant past, the boulevard had been called the Avenue de l'Impératrice. That seemed woundingly funny to him and though he laughed he tried to stifle his laughter until it became sobs so wracking that the taxi driver, who thought he had hiccups, suggested that he swallow air. But swallow as he did, Sanders could not swallow it, nor stop himself, until he stopped the taxi, paid the driver, and began blindly to walk. And walk, until he found himself once more facing the statue of the doughboy and the poilu, suddenly looming up in the early fall deciduous nakedness of the Place des États-Unis. He sat there in the park for a very long time, oblivious to everyone, oblivious of everything, until it was dark and the street lights yellowed, and then he started slowly making his way back toward the Quai de Passy.

No one was there and nothing had changed since he left that afternoon—but everything had changed. " 'Paris changes, but nothing in my melancholy has changed,' " he thought; "once more Baudelaire comes back to haunt, taunt me." Wrapped in a blanket, drinking brandy from the bottle, Sanders sat and looked out at the river until dawn came up over its oil slicks pink and green, the Seine empty, and Elaine had not come home. She did not come back that night, or any of the other nights he waited for her thereafter; she never came back and he never saw her again, not even from a distance as he'd seen Monique across the white islands of tables at the Grand Véfour. Finally, he asked one of the secretaries at the magazines to pack all Elaine's things and he had them sent to the de Besancourts' at the Avenue Foch and when he came back that same day and last evening to pack his own belongings before moving into one of the smaller hotels near the Gare Montparnasse, the only reminders of her were the lingering scent of lily of the valley and the green nightlight which with one blow he smashed beneath his heel, splintering the brown bakelite and green glass, and twisting permanently out of shape the brass metal prongs.

* * *

Needham's return from Mexico—he was browner, rested-looking, and even more energetic than always—posed a new problem. Needham cornered him one evening in the office, just after he had returned from covering another Fillmore demonstration, this time one the chaplain had not been able to get off from scot-free. Fillmore and half a dozen youths, Peter King among them, had been arrested for a nighttime tour through Berkeley and Oakland spraying antiwar and black-power slogans on the walls of buildings with paint cans. NO MORE WAR and BLACK POWER had been plastered on two dozen buildings before an energetic milk-wagon driver, curious and impelled to do his civic duty, had reported them to the police and the police had picked the group up. Sanders had managed to get to the Oakland police station before they were all free on bond and Fillmore would make no statement, would not even acknowledge his greeting, and Peter King stared through him as if he were the invisible man. Needham came straight to the point. "Look, Elliott," he began, brusque because he was feeling awkward, "I want you to stay here on the paper with me. The climate's good, you can swim or ski most of the year, Mexico and Hawaii and Canada aren't too far off—"

"You sound like the Chamber of Commerce," Sanders kidded him, leaning back from the typewriter, trying to massage the crick out his neck from having been hunched over for so long. "You trying to sell me a bill of goods?"

Needham nodded assertively. "I sure am. You've kicked around the world long enough—"

"More than fifteen years!" Sanders expostulated, and even as he said it felt proud and wasteful.

"So you've had enough of that. You can settle down here, buy a house in the hills, make a home for yourself. You can marry that girl, Beth, even if Sheila doesn't think she's good enough for you. Have a family."

It was the kind of offer, Sanders recognized, that he'd hoped for for years but now it made no sense at all, so he said nothing.

"I'll make it worth your while," Needham continued. "You can step in as executive editor and I'll throw in a piece of the action too. You'll be ownership and second man on the paper. What do you say?"

"That's a generous offer, Jim, more than I deserve—"

"Modesty will get you nowhere. You're a helluva good man, a good reporter—better, I think, than even your old man, in a way. The stuff you've written's been good for the paper. More people are reading it, talking about it and so the advertising's going up. I think I'm going to raise the space rates after the first of the year. We've even picked up a batch of subsidiary income from your stuff, the pictures too. You're good for us and we'll be good for and good to you." He stopped pacing and slid into a chair across the desk. "And it would be a big favor to me. You know, I'd like to take it a little easier, take a little more time off, spend it with Sheila. I owe that to her. You know, Elliott, while we were down Mejico way she was off the sauce altogether. Well, almost altogether. You should see her. She looks great, ten years younger. And we had a good time together, one of the best times in years."

"I'd like to do it for *you*, Jim, but—"

"You ought to do it for yourself," Needham said softly. "When are you going to stop running? When are you gonna quit fooling yourself and settle down and have a family? Don't make the mistake we did. Without kids most of it doesn't make sense."

"I'd like to, Jim. My God, how I'd like to."

"But?" Needham's eyes narrowed, his lips pursed. "She said no. She's going to marry that doctor." He wasn't asking; he was telling.

Sanders nodded.

"I *am* sorry," Needham said, and spontaneously reached across the desk and patted his sleeve. "That's tough."

"Here," Sanders said, ripping the sheet out of the typewriter, slipping the carbon and the yellow out, then collating the rest of the article, "have a look at this."

While Needham read, he tried to recover himself, but unbidden the memory of her face telling him about Daulton, about becoming an Atherton matron, stabbed his recollection as the rose thorn that night had pricked his palm. Beth, he almost said aloud, Beth, but it was a cry so deep out of the depths that he knew no one would ever hear it, and if they did, Beth or Elaine, Monique or Laura, no one would answer.

The last time he'd seen Monique was at the Grand Véfour. Tessier and he were dining with a couple of Swiss newspapermen and when he looked up there she was, a half-dozen tables away, her head proudly held, her hair swept up in a new way that made her at once more haughty and defenseless. She was sitting with a middle-aged, mustached, very attentive Frenchman, quietly dressed, a bourgeois surely and just as surely not a Parisian. They looked well together, Sanders thought, as if they belonged to one another, and that hurt him even more. He was half out of his chair to go to her when he realized that she'd seen him, and her gesture, incomplete but unmistakable, subtle but brooking no questions, told him that she didn't want him to recognize her, didn't want him to come to her table, or show in any way that they had ever known each other. After that he couldn't remember a single word the two Swiss or Tessier had said, though Tessier called him to attention quite sharply on several occasions. He drank brandy after brandy, and discreetly as he could watched Monique, aware again of how lovely she was, how warm and easy, so that when she and the Frenchman finally rose to go, his eyes felt strained and torn from having glanced sidelong at her for all that while. The Frenchman helped Monique on with her wrap and Sanders was pleased that the man was just a shade too short for her and had to reach. Monique walked past without a word, so close that for an instant he thought—or had he only imagined?—that he felt her nails graze the material of his sleeve, but her whole body was turned to the man she was with, her arm hooked in his, and the man had eyes for no one, for nothing, else.

Needham tossed the sheets back onto the desk, nodding. "It's good, very good. You've caught this peace-movement thing in a way no one else I've read has. Their moral outrage, their outrageous morality, their disregard for the law, their notion of politics as demonstration, their disregard of the simplest notions of political organization. Their whole 'Fight for Peace' posture. Same as with our colored brethren."

Sanders thought he had been able to put down only a small part of what he'd seen and felt, and had the same old frustrating sense of what he'd left out, of how much was lost, warped in the communicating. "Fillmore sprayed only one sign himself, you know," he said. "At least that's what the milkman witness testified. It was FOR GOD'S SAKE, STOP IT NOW! When I asked him what IT was, Fillmore wouldn't answer but one of the boys with him did. 'Everything,' he said. 'The killing, the napalm, the bombing, the shelling, the destruction. *No more war!* And no more war at home against the black man. No more segregation and slums, no more racial bias in getting jobs, no more social hatred for the kids in schools. That's IT. Those are the ITS!' " It had been Peter King who spoke out for Fillmore and not, on the face of it, with Fillmore's permission to be his spokesman. King had spoken right into the TV and radio reporters' microphones too, not to him alone, simply looking through him as if he weren't there, as if he hadn't asked the question at all.

"You know the word's out to get Fillmore, to treat him like a crank," Needham said, "a crackpot."

"You get up-to-date fast, don't you, Jim?"

"My job. I'm supposed to know. But I thought you ought to know too."

"I did. Some of the TV boys dropped the word to me. I would have known anyway from the way the photographers were shooting him, so he'd look like a kook—one of them even mussed his hair and pulled his collar crooked—and the questions they were feeding him. No wonder he clammed up."

"Is he a kook?"

Sanders shook his head. "Sane. Decent. Intelligent. He saw it and he's had a bellyful. He doesn't care about anything now except saving mankind."

"Isn't that what a kook is?"

Sanders thought about that. "Maybe. If that's what you mean by a kook, then he is."

"That kind asks for it. He wants someone to make him a martyr."

"He's a Christian minister."

"I know. He really believes the Gospel and not only on Sundays, but his parishioners, all the rest of us, aren't up to it for the whole week. They can barely make it on Sunday morning—especially after Saturday night."

[482]

"Fillmore wants to buy time, to give them a chance and to do what he's got to to keep anyone from pressing the button for the 'big bang.'"

"You think he's right?"

"I think he's right about that. I think it's either no more wars or no more world. There's no middle ground left."

"Better red than dead?"

"Better alive and free, if it can be managed, but better for mankind to survive. Tyrannies pass. The Attilas, the Neros and Caligulas, even the Hitlers and Stalins, pass. They die and the systems they build change and—"

"Usually get worse," Needham growled.

"Sometimes they do, Jim, sometimes they do, but not usually. Mostly things ease up, give people more elbow room, get better. Very slowly, it's true, but better."

"I think you're wrong, Elliott."

"I could be. I have been, often. But without a world government, without an end to nuclear and popular explosions, we're a doomed planet and a doomed species," Sanders said.

"And with a world government, are we much better off? That kind of government with its instruments of violence and prying—computer bank dossiers, nuclear weapons, the whole business of political police and repressive instruments and controlled propaganda—could make life not worth living. They'll reshape your genes, bring up your kids conditioned the way they want them, they'll tell you where to live and how, and finally they'll make people just the way they preprint radio circuits, all tuned to one frequency, one broadcast."

"Men are too complicated, too cunning, too raunchy, too goddam mean to be preprinted, Jim," Sanders said, "or to stay preprinted. Life will find a way. Men will."

"Even with the drugs and the hypnosis, with the fooling around with the DNA and the RNA? Elliott, in another fifty years they'll even make people love it; and if you don't, they'll tranquilize you, hypnotize you, lobotomize you and psychoanalyze you until you do."

"What do you recommend, Jim?"

"I don't have any recommendations, Elliott. I'd like to go back maybe thirty years, maybe a little more, back to the twenties maybe,

[483]

and hold the line, but I know that's out of the question. And maybe it's only because I was young then and that's what I'm after. But I'm glad at least for that one reason, that I don't have any kids to pass this heap on to."

"You don't think it can be stopped, do you?"

"No, Elliott. None of it. The big bang least of all. Everyone I've talked to, the big boys and the man in the street, thinks it's coming. Nuclear war. Race war. Biological warfare. Mushroom peril, yellow peril, black peril. Just peril, and probably all of them will come together."

"That's the end, the very bitter end."

"Maybe not. Some of the deep-think types say there'll only be a small one—you know, India and Pakistan, Egypt and Israel, a race war in South Africa or Angola or Rhodesia; and if that one's bloody enough and not too bloody, maybe the rest of the world will wise up."

"You have any confidence in that?"

Quietly, almost serenely, Needham shook his head. Somberly, they stared at each other across the desk until Sanders repeated, "Murray Fillmore's no crackpot. He's saner than either of us."

"That makes it even tougher for him," Needham said sympathetically. "The kooks manage, somehow. The others end up drinking hemlock or getting themselves crucified."

"By the press?" Sanders forced a laugh, but he was thinking of George spreadeagled on the sidewalk.

"It's no laughing matter. Even a journalistic crucifixion is painful, Elliott, and you have to go on living with it." Needham stood up, rearranged the creases of his trousers and straightened his tie.

"We see things so differently, yet you're willing to make me your heir apparent."

It was Needham's turn to laugh. "Why not? *I* believe in peace and freedom, racial equality and economic opportunity, even if the rest of the world doesn't. I'm for giving people an even break—even the suckers." More solemnly, after a moment, he added, "Besides, I don't think we're that far apart in our thinking and feeling. And I have no other heir, apparent or transparent, so think it over, will you?"

[484]

"I will, Jim. Seriously. And, however it turns out, I'm really grateful for the offer."

At the door Needham turned, grinning, and said, "Tessier'll be furious if you stay, won't he?"

"He's written that he wants me back in Paris after the first of the year." Tessier had told him that the magazine had absorbed just about as much material on what he'd been covering as it could. Either he moved east, doing a series across the United States, and ending up at "the center of things"—Washington and New York— or he returned to Paris at the end of the year. Tessier really preferred his return to France for there were other assignments that now seemed more important to the magazine. Sanders quickly explained what was happening.

"You want to go back?"

"No. Not yet, anyway. I want to follow through on those peace and civil-rights stories. Then, whichever way I decide, stay or go, I'll want to go back to tell Tessier personally. He's been very decent to me. And I have some affairs to settle up in Paris if I come here."

"Sure. I wouldn't have it any other way. Just give yourself plenty of time to think it over."

Sanders was having breakfast at a local diner before going to work, not yet wakened from the frightful dreams which now regularly pursued him through the nights until morning brought him fatigued relief, when over his coffee cup he saw Peter King's photograph in someone else's newspaper. The man obligingly rose shortly thereafter and left his paper and Sanders slid over into his seat and read the article. A group of some two dozen armed Negroes had burst into the state legislature as a protest against a bill being considered to limit carrying loaded weapons within the city confines; all of the protestors were carrying loaded arms in the chamber themselves: rifles, shotguns, pistols. The two dozen led by Peter King had walked past gaping police and groups of schoolchildren on an outing who were scheduled to have a fried-chicken lunch with the Governor on the capitol's west lawn. Surrounded by television reporters and cameramen, the intruders had stormed silently into the chamber brandishing their weapons until state police, alerted by the Assembly sergeant-at-arms, had come to their senses and after a brief scuffle disarmed all the Negroes and escorted them out of the chamber. The Negroes had told the reporters that they were protesting Oakland's racist police force and its methods, but with the microphones stuck into their faces and a storm of questions, Peter King was put forward to make their statement for them. He protested that they had every constitutional right to bear arms and that "the state legislature, poisoned by racial bias and hatred, was intent on passing laws which would, by denying black men arms, keep them powerless and make them unable to resist the growing forces of racism in the country, forces which increasingly resorted to cruelty, repression, terror and murder of black citizens." If the words didn't sound like King, even filtered through reporters and deskmen, the lilt of anger, the surge of violence beneath them, did.

Sanders sat there in the diner, his coffee growing cold, staring at the picture of those young black men; even in the blurred newsprint their faces were fierce and warlike; their hands clutched the stocks of their weapons tightly, more as if they were spears to be thrown than rifles to be fired; their heads—in outlandish turbans, silly caps, fezzes, bristling and bare—were held high and aggressively, thrust forward on their necks; and their leather jackets and cast-off Army battle jackets gave them the appearance of a group of irregular militia or guerrillas. There was no mistaking the meaning of those flared nostrils, those jutting lips, those angry eyes; these were men full of hatred, eager for revenge, intent on violence for evils, real and fancied, committed against them. Sanders had seen those faces before, closed-in, determined, explosive, beyond reasoning with and hardened against compassion: in Algerian FLN assassins, among Hungarian Freedom Fighters, in Japanese students in the Zengakuren, in Chinese Communist terrorists in Hong Kong, in German *Suddeutsche* revanchists, in black-pajamaed Vietcong. They had a cause, and whatever their cause, however just or meritorious, he had never learned to like them; fanatic, committed to bloodshed and lusting for mayhem, they were bringers of chaos in whatever place they lived, in whatever cause they were enlisted.

The year was dying in a gray shroud, chill, bleak, funereal, the mountains bare and stony, the Bay black and white-capped, and

[486]

he felt a wintry solstice of the spirit, a melancholy so bitter that as he drove through the raw December streets of Oakland toward the induction center it made him want to turn back. He was not, he thought, excessively sentimental about Christmas but it was one of the holidays that had really been merry for him as a child, one he had deliberately cherished as an adult and, no matter where he'd been, how far from home and hearth, he had tried to make the season memorable. This year he knew that if the holiday were memorable it would be so only in a negative sense. Jim and Sheila Needham were giving a Christmas Day party for all the paper's staff and their families, and he had of course been asked. The mail a few days before had brought a small thick linen envelope which contained an embossed card from Elizabeth Marshall Christiansen and Dr. Steven Prescott announcing their engagement and inviting him to a Christmas Eve party at which it would be celebrated. Sanders didn't think he'd attend either party, but he had not yet made up his mind to fly back to Paris either though he knew there would be a great party on Christmas Day, Tessier's only staff gathering of the year and usually a festive occasion. Though there were only days left in which he could make up his mind, he felt no haste, no urgency; if anything, it was as if he were snow-shoeing through fields of gruel in a sticky lethargy.

It was a small demonstration, no more than two hundred young people, probably most of them college students whom Murray Fillmore, ensconced on the building steps, had brought down from Berkeley. They were braced, arm in arm, in front of the main entrance to the building like fresh-faced kids, their faces white in the gray morning, their signs—WE REFUSE TO GO! AN IMMORAL WAR! PUT CHRIST IN CHRISTMAS; TAKE OUT WAR!—bobbing over their heads like sails. Off to one side Peter King was at the head of a contingent of black faces—the Magi, bearing what gifts?—clustered together, a single placard over it, a large cloth mainsail tacked between two poles and bellying in the air. It was simply inscribed: IT'S A WAR OF COLOR. In the camera's telescopic sight King's face looked sadder and more frantic, wilder but more cast down, and as Sanders focused on it and snapped photos of it, King's mouth opened, the mouths around him opened, the expressions on their faces filled with bellowing anger, anguished pleading, as smoking from their mouths their songs rose above the crowd like mist into the frosty morning. The voices were deeply moving as they sang carol after carol and when, in *"O Holy Night,"* they chanted:

Fall on your knees! O hear the angel voices!
O night divine! O night when Christ was born!

Fillmore fell on his knees first and then, as if he were a stone thrown into a pond that sent ripples out to its farthest edge, those around him knelt, then others, eddy after eddy, out to the last rim of the crowd. In silence they continued to kneel, their heads bent, their hands together in prayer, until they lifted their heads to sing once more:

Hark! the herald angels sing
Glory to the newborn king,
Peace on earth and mercy mild,
God and sinners reconciled!

Remembering his mother's thin soprano singing that same carol to him, Sanders found tears in his eyes. When the students got to their feet again they were suddenly transformed into a field of flowers. Everywhere in their hands white and yellow daisies sprouted and they held the flowers high, chanting in unison, "No more war!" and "Peace on earth, good will to men!"

Five busloads of inductees arrived just as the overcast skies began to drizzle. Policemen in yellow rain suits moved in and began to clear the young protesters from the steps and entrance to the building. Those who, however passively, resisted were carried or dragged to the waiting paddy wagons while others, in pairs, one protectively holding an umbrella over the other, passed out leaflets to police, to bystanders, to reporters and photographers, that said that those arrested would refuse bail and would instead, in protest, spend Christmas and New Year's behind bars. As the inductees were trotted out of the buses and into the induction center the drizzle became a downpour but the remaining protesters, held back by a thin yellow line of police, refused to leave; instead, they stood fast and sang over and over again:

> Silent night, Holy night!
> Shepherds quake at the sight!
> Glories stream from heaven afar,
> Heavenly hosts sing Hallelujah;
> Christ the Saviour is born!
> Christ the Saviour is born.

until all the draftees had entered the building and the doors were closed behind them.

As he drove away Sanders saw that neither Fillmore nor Peter King was among those arrested. Fillmore, a raincoat tented over his head and shoulders, walked with a group of students but was not of them. Bedraggled, hunched over, exhausted-looking, he greeted Sanders' hailed invitation from the car with a tired smile and after a brief word with some of the students got into the front seat of the car with a sigh. "Can you take a few more?" he asked.

"Sure," Sanders agreed. "Just leave one place for King. He's up the street there, a little way ahead." Fillmore called to the students and two girls and a boy hopped into the back seat of the car. "Be careful of the cameras back there, please," Sanders requested, and in the rear mirror saw the questioning, then the smirking exchange of glances.

Slowly Sanders pulled abreast of the Negro group—their banner was now limp but not furled, yet all of its sign that was visible was WAR and COLOR—and called out to King, but King kept walking, his face obstinately averted. Though he had obviously heard, several of his companions turned to stare, first at the car and then at King, but King paid no attention until Fillmore summoned him. "Want a lift?" Sanders asked when King's black, rain-speckled face presented itself at the car window.

"Us field-hand darkies don know nuff to come in outta tha rain, boss. Wanna live, gotta pick cotton."

"Come on, Peter, I'll drive the chaplain up to Berkeley and then take you back down to Oakland," Sanders coaxed.

King looked at the five white faces in the car, then slowly shook his head. "I'll stay with my own."

Fillmore's clucking was loud. "Peter," he said, the gentlest of rebukes.

"We've got another demonstration of our own, in Oakland, Reverend. I'd better not." The explanation was courteous but cool, and Sanders sensed that Fillmore felt and had been rebuffed.

"Fine, if you think so," Fillmore said, and subsided.

"I'd like to talk to you this afternoon, Peter," Sanders said, "after the demonstration. I'll come by your place, say about four, okay?"

"Okay," King agreed, neutrally, and then walked off without another word.

"What's biting him?" one of the girls in the back of the car asked.

"Not what, who?" the boy said, and the three of them giggled.

They drove through the rain in silence, the windshield wipers loud and slapping, until they dropped the three young people off at a coffee house on Telegraph Avenue, and then as they drove on toward the church, Fillmore told Sanders he thought that what was biting King was the increasingly tense race relations between blacks and whites in the East Bay. Fillmore told how King had led the group of arms-bearing Negroes into the state legislature, how white and black alike were so fearful and suspicious that there'd been a run all over the East Bay and in San Francisco too on sporting-goods stores and pawnshops with whites and blacks alike buying pistols, rifles, shotguns. The spiraling fear, hatred and suspicion was bound to lead to an outbreak, and last week it had almost gotten out of hand and he'd been lucky enough to help stop it—for the moment at least. A bunch of leather-jacketed motorcycle boys from Richmond had decided to run down to Oakland to "kill them some niggers." Fortunately, one of the boys in the gang had come to the church to warn Fillmore of the impending raid but he wouldn't or couldn't give any more information. Fillmore had called the police immediately and luckily they'd been interrogating five young girls they knew were dolls of the motorcycle gang. The girls were in custody in an investigation for beating and robbing

[490]

two Negro girls earlier in the week, and when the police questioned them further, one of the arrested girls had broken down and given them the information they needed: that their boyfriends were right at that moment on their way to "get some spades." Descriptions of the boyfriends' cars were radioed to the Berkeley police and the two cars were spotted, boxed in by four prowl cars, and stopped. Police had found four rifles, a sawed-off shotgun, and three revolvers, all loaded, in the two cars. The seven young men in the cars were all part of a single motorcycle gang and admitted that they were going to East Oakland to avenge a slight that several of them had endured, or thought they'd endured, or invented, a few nights previous, and were all booked on charges of carrying concealed weapons and conspiracy to commit murder. Fillmore had seen them arraigned, because he had hoped to talk to them, persuade them, plead for clemency in their behalf, but all of them, long-haired, wearing earrings, in heavy stomping boots, their denim jackets emblazoned with Luftwaffe wings, *Hakenkreuzen* hanging on chains around their necks, had so offended him, had so filled him with loathing, that he could think of only one thing: "They were Nazis, really and truly Nazis, only their intended victims were Negroes instead of Jews. You should have heard them talk, Sanders, they sounded like a bunch of storm-trooper hoodlums."

"And you thought you'd come home from the wars, eh?" Sanders asked, as he drew up and parked in front of the church.

"I've come home from one war to others," Fillmore said moodily, "and I hate it."

In the gray daylight Fillmore's rectory seemed even shabbier and the brass lamp he lit didn't drive away the mote-filled gloom or the wet damp. Fillmore brought a bottle from the secretary drawer, poured them quarter glasses of bourbon and then, with a silent toast, drank his off shuddering.

"Caught a chill?" Sanders asked.

Fillmore's face was seraphic. "I feel cold inside all the time now. Not even whisky thaws me out."

"Too much living alone. Too many causes, protests, demon-

[491]

strations, marches. No home, no hearth, no wife and children."
Sanders spelled it out, altogether too conscious that he was also
describing his own predicament.

Fillmore leaned back in the red leather chair, his legs outstretched,
his eyes closed, the empty bourbon glass precariously balanced on
his chest. "Birds of a feather?" he asked softly.

"Birds of a father," Sanders said. He heard the mistake and
amended, "I mean feather."

" 'No man can serve two masters; for either he will hate the one,
and love the other; or else he will hold to the one, and despise the
other. Ye cannot serve God and Mammon.' " Fillmore chanted. "That
goes for Peter King too. Another bird of the same feather, but
unfortunately not of the same color."

"Blackbird? Crow? Raven?"

"Blackbird, crowing and ravening all together," Fillmore said.
"King's had to decide between home and hearth, children and
wife, and doing something for his people."

"Like you?"

"Well, like me," Fillmore admitted grudgingly, "and not like me."
He looked again at the bourbon bottle he'd left uncorked on the
secretary, then at the glass on his chest, and apparently decided
no. "A wife and children are less tempting to him than to me.
For me they might be a burden but they would be a solace. A
great solace." He paused. "But King sees how miserable it is in
the ghetto for black men who carry the burden of family on their
backs, feed and house and care for wives and children. It makes
him so scared and so angry he can't see that it's building up inside
him like a volcano ready to erupt—"

"And when it does, watch out!"

"Unless we change things quickly, make a normal life for black
men possible."

"Too late now. The volcano's going to blow anyway." Sanders
hadn't intended it but the *double-entendre* hung in the air between them.

"He's a homosexual, isn't he?" Fillmore finally asked.

Sanders nodded.

"I thought as much. How much worse and grinding the desire in him for home and hearth. Fear and anger and hatred always cripple. In more than one way."

"Are you sure that's the way it happened?"

Fillmore eyed the bottle and this time he changed his mind. Unfolding, he reached over, poured himself half a glass, and then, motioning for Sanders to help himself, lay back in the chair again, sipping his whisky slowly, intermittently, with evident relish. "No," he said, "I'm *not* sure." He shuddered again, the spasm visibly running the length of his frame, and then closed his eyes. "His mother just died. Makes him more overwrought than ever. Somewhere in a mental institution, Mendocino, I think, but he didn't say exactly."

"My God!" Sanders exclaimed.

"I wish you wouldn't use that expression," Fillmore said plaintively.

"You mean I'm taking the Lord's name in vain, or that he's not *my* God at all?"

"Neither. Only every time someone says that in circumstances of deprivation or misfortune, pain or tragedy, it seems to me to be a cry signaling the Lord's absence, His blindness, His ineffable indifference. *De profundis clamavi*—and no one listens."

"Maybe He's got His eye on the sparrow and can't see man. You know, old age and senile nearsightedness."

"God sees in His own way." Fillmore tried to smile but couldn't quite. "It's impossible for men to understand, almost impossible for men to bear."

"Faith wavering, Murray? That why you're so cold inside? The Lord's fire gone out and you're no longer able to warm your hands over the questioning doubting coals?" Sanders asked, and seeing how exhausted Fillmore was, barely able to stay awake, felt guilty for baiting him.

" 'And there shall be signs in the sun, and in the moon, and in the stars; and upon the earth distress of nations, with perplexity; the sea and the waves roaring;

" 'Men's hearts failing them for fear, and for looking after those things which are coming on earth: for the powers of heaven shall be shaken.

" 'And then shall they see the Son of man coming in a cloud with power and great glory.

" 'And when these things begin to come to pass, then look up, and lift up your heads; for your redemption draweth nigh.' "

Fillmore spoke the Biblical lines with power, his head raised, his eyes flashing, his voice suddenly restored, but now again his head nodded, his eyes were hooded, his whole demeanor faded. Then he roused himself and asked, "She's not going to marry you, is she?"

"Thanks to you, she can't."

"No thanks to me, thanks to you. Herself. Christiansen. She can't turn over her old life, can't make herself new."

"Not even with God's grace? And you're glad, Murray, aren't you?"

"Glad?" The pale eyes looked at him, bleared and blinking, before he nodded. "Yes. Glad. Beth not for you. You not for Beth. All sick, mad, neurotic, wrong relations, wrong reasons."

"Meddler!"

"Friend."

"Same thing, isn't it?" Sanders smiled.

Fillmore's smile was sleepy. "Minister," he said.

"You're just jealous, Murray, not high-minded. You wanted her for yourself. Christiansen's wife, Christiansen's life."

"No, you, not me."

"You don't believe that."

" 'Who shall change our vile body, that it may be fashioned like unto his glorious body, according to the working whereby He is able even to subdue all things unto Himself,' " Fillmore declaimed, but the words lacked ring and resonance; they breathed fatigue.

"Fraud!"

Fillmore's head fell, his eyes sightless. "Maybe. I wanted. Beautiful. Beth. Temptation. Wife. Children. But wrong, wrong. Destroy with love. My work. My ministry. My hopes. No!"

"When was the last time you had a good night's sleep, Murray?" Sanders asked.

"Sleep?" Fillmore smiled stupidly. "What's that? Pills and whisky. So much, too much, to do. No time. Can't sleep anyway. Keep thinking. War. Killing. Blood." His eyes closed and his breathing,

[494]

labored, was audible. With great effort he tried to shake himself awake, his eyes flickering, his dry lips parted, whispering, "Why don't you go home?"

"Where's home?"

"Home. Place you can make beginning. New life. Put roots. Connecticut."

"Too many tombstones there."

"Where?"

"Connecticut."

"Tombstones everywhere. World a graveyard. Got to build on graveyards, plant in cemeteries. Make new world. Yesterday's tombstones today's lesson, tomorrow's hope. With God's help—"

"God is dead, Murray! Dead as a doornail."

"God is *not* dead," Fillmore muttered, eyes still shut. "He can't be dead. D'you hear, Sanders? He can't be . . ." and then his chin fell on his chest.

Sanders sat there listening to Fillmore's asthmatic breathing, watching his gray, lined tormented face, then reached over and took the empty glass from his hand. When he stood up, Fillmore stirred. "Didn't work out," he murmured, "did it? Couldn't." But his eyes remained closed and he sank back into the chair, asleep, so that Sanders didn't know whether Fillmore was aware of what he was saying or what it meant.

As he removed his coat from the old-fashioned, antlered clothes tree, Sanders saw a silver chain on the peg beneath; from it, swinging slightly, was a silver-and-black *Hakenkreuz*. Was it the memento the boy had left behind who had come to tell Fillmore about the gang going to Oakland to get itself a couple of "spades"? The swastika. The crooked cross. The true cross. Was the first only the true cross with its arms bent at right angles, or were they more intimately connected than that, the cross itself crucified?

On the drive down toward Oakland the windshield wipers' to-and-fro rhythm became that swastika pendant on that silver chain, swinging up and back like a hypnotic medallion glinting in the half-light of his recollection, mesmerizing him.

* * *

Sanders could not have been more than nine years old. It was in the apartment near La Motte-Picquet late in the fall of the year, cold because he could remember how his urine smoked in the outdoor pissoir at l'école. It was evening and he had finished doing his *devoir* and was playing the usual game of cribbage with his mother before going up to bed when, as always when his father was away, his mother had stood up and gone to turn on the radio to catch his father's broadcast. He heard the familiar voice, choked and excited and full of anger from the very first: "This is Lovett Carpenter Sanders in Berlin. All over the Third Reich last night there was the sound of shattered glass and in the light of the cold moon the shards shone steely as bayonets, for last night the Nazis organized the largest pogrom against Jews in the history of modern Europe. Because a miserable Jewish refugee from Germany, Herschel Grynszpan, a seventeen-year-old boy whose family had been expelled from Hanover, shot third secretary Ernst vom Rath, a minor official in the Reich Embassy in Paris, what the Nazis here are calling the *Kristallnacht*, which might be translated both as the 'crystal night' or the 'night of broken glass,' was organized by the government. Before the night of wrecking, looting, burning and killing was over, more than twenty thousand Jews were arrested and sent to concentration camps at Buchenwald, Dachau and Sachsenhausen. Everywhere Jewish shops and property were smashed and plundered, hundreds were burned to the ground and thousands were robbed of everything of value that was portable. All over the Reich synagogues were put to the torch, almost two hundred of them set aflame. . . ."

His mother sat at the table, rigid, her hands prayerfully frozen together over the cribbage board, listening to his father's voice as if she were hypnotized as his father described the beatings and the killings, the arson and looting, the crowds passively watching thousands of Jews being herded into trucks and vans and taken to the concentration camps, doing nothing. "This is Europe's last chance to declare and defend its humanity, its traditions, not only to help these helpless Jews, but to prevent the blood tide of brutality

[496]

from engulfing the world. If we do not act now, Europe will go down into the pit; and over it, over all of the once-civilized world will glower the *Hakenkreuz,* will wave the steel helmet, the mailed fist and the jackboot. Barbarism will have become the order of the day: *the new order.*"

His father had finished and his mother snapped the radio receiver off, then came round to his side of the table and stood behind his chair, her hands on his shoulders. "That was your father," she said, "broadcasting from Berlin."

"I know, Mama, I heard him and recognized his voice. He was very angry."

"Yes, Elliott, he was angry because of the terrible things the Germans are doing and he was brave to broadcast it."

"Will he come home now?"

"The Germans will expel him, I think."

"What's expel?"

"They won't let him broadcast from Germany any longer."

He clapped his hands. "Then he'll be coming home?"

"Yes," she replied, "he'll be coming back to Paris."

When he was in bed she came to kiss him good night and sat on his bed, singing him lullabies until he grew sleepy. "You should be very proud of your father tonight, Elliott," she said.

"Are you proud of him, Mama?" he asked.

"Very proud. Your father's a good man who believes in fighting for justice."

"What's justice, Mama?"

"What's right and fair."

"Then why must Daddy fight for what's right and fair?"

"Because life is full of unfairness and injustice."

"Then why doesn't God make things right?"

"I don't know, Elliott. Maybe God does make it right by making people like your father who will fight for what they think is right."

"Won't Daddy get hurt if he has to fight?" He remembered how his own scuffles with Philippe and Antoine at school were painful.

"Maybe. Sometimes it's necessary to be hurt and to hurt if you know you are right. But let's hope nothing will happen to Daddy. We'll pray for him, won't we?" And then, when she learned that

[497]

he'd not yet said his prayers, she made him get out of bed to kneel on the cold floor and say them and when he'd spoken the last words and gotten back into bed, she repeated them over him: "Bless Daddy and bring him home safe from Germany." She'd kissed him, on both cheeks, French style, and then put out the night-light.

* * *

In Oakland Sanders had to park blocks away from Peter King's flat because everywhere the streets were filled with people and cars were parked bumper to bumper in all the free spaces closer by. The demonstration begun that morning at the induction center seemed to have grown and swelled; but it was now all black and more a civil-rights protest than a peace protest, although the two were almost indistinguishable in the signs and placards that appeared everywhere and the songs the demonstrators sang as Sanders tried to work his way back through the crowds to King's tenement. TV trucks and portable cameras and reporters were already circulating through the crowds and Sanders saw one TV cameraman urging a teen-age black boy to heave a brick through a store window so he could get a good photo of it. A group of grim young men were walking, then snake-dancing down the center of the street, shouting, "What do you want?" and the crowds in the street and on the sidewalks responded, "Peace *now!*"

"What do you want?"

"Bring the troops home, *now!*"

Abruptly the snake-dancing men began to roar, "Black power!"

"All the way!" the crowd roared back.

"Black power!"

"Gotta have it!"

"Black power!"

"Good for you!"

"Black power!"

"Every day!"

"Black power!"

"All the time!"

"Black power!"

"We need it!"

[498]

It was a growling antiphonal chorus, surging, threatening; it was a religious chant, hoping, praying, incandescent.

Everywhere signs with only place names carried a heavy freight of meaning: SELMA. OXFORD. NEWARK. DETROIT. One read, HARLEM IS MISSISSIPPI IN CONCRETE. Here and there policemen stood uncertainly and watched, or walked warily on the sidewalks, while in the new dark shopkeepers were already putting up the metal shutters and grates which guarded their windows. White faces gleamed among the black, infrequent and frightened. In the black faces, antagonistic, fierce eyes engaged his but looked through him when he took pictures; the Negroes pretended that they saw neither him nor his cameras, refusing him the courtesy of a direct confrontation, making him feel invisible, making him feel that he had intruded on their privacy and provoked their rage. Not until he was in the hallway of Peter King's building did he realize that he'd been afraid, that his hands were clammy and his shirt stuck to his shoulders with sweat.

King was sitting on the paillasse, head in his hands, when Sanders walked through the open door. Despondently, he lifted his head and lamented, "Leave your door open, can't tell what'll roll in, can you?"

"Hello, Peter," Sanders greeted him.

"We been seeing so much of each other lately at those demonstrations, I almost thought you were one of us. Getting much? I mean big-time news scoops."

"I'm sorry about your mother, Peter. Fillmore told me."

"Well, ain't that nice, Mistuh Charley. You're sorry about my little old dark-faced kooky Mama. My fat old, skinny, crazy Aunt Jemima. That's mighty nice, mighty kind of yuh. She like livin in this heah U-oo-nited States, so fine she inside de walls most time, up there in Mendocino, an livin mighty good, pretty high on de hawg. No worries bout rent 'n' feedin tha kids. He-ll, no. The state take care of all dat. Ain't even able to see her lil ole pickaninny son no mo, rub his Brillo haid fer comfort, 'cause she don have no visitors, she ain with it nuff to be with her colored chile an put some of them fine cuts on his palms. Mebbe hard to believe, white man, but listen anyway. You realize, that po little ole coon lady only forty years ole. Forty! An she caint bear it no longer. She have trouble breathin the white man's air, an walkin the white man's streets, an eatin the white man's shit. She fed up. She so fed up she feed herself a little more, not much, just enough. She drink some lye and it go down mighty easy, burning, searing her guts out, but no worse, no more heat, no more killin than all that shit-eatin she had to do all her life because she was black. Because she black, man! Black! No other reason.

"She don do no one no harm. She like to drink a lil and she like to fuck a lil—yeh, white boy, we come by that motherfucker epithet naturally, we see em all fuckin our mothers, black an white, transient gennumen who come by and stay one night, or many, an pay fo it. And lots who don pay, who git it for what they call luv. Man, you evah heah such sh-i-t? Sometimes they even give a kid a buck, a whole dollah, to git lost for a while, buy him some ice cream so he go to sleep early in the next room, and the next room usually the kitchen floor, sometimes the toilet with a blanket in the tub, fightin the roaches and the silverfish and the rats, an the best place to see his mother come in with the douche bag, if she smart enough and not too drunk, or every now and then to see the big-man john come in to peel off his fishskin and drop it in the bowl. . . ."

Peter King's speech had been so incoherent, so assaulting, that Sanders actually stumbled two or three steps back as if he'd been pushed, before he was able to realize that King's mother had committed suicide.

"Yeh, Mistuh Sanders, old Mammy drank lye up in Mendocino State Hospital for the Medically Insane. Some lard-ass cleaning woman left some lye around and Mama made herself her last drink. Seven n seven her favorite cause she don like the taste of whisky, only the feelin it give her, and the Seven-up make it sweet, lak candy. She died. She committed suicide. She kill herself. She tossed off those three fingers of white lye lightning like it was some moonshine she bought up at a white man's still that make you blind. They do try to save her up there, the good doctors, good people, good white men, cause they don understand nuthin. They think she sufferin from what they call paranoia—paranoid schizophrenia was the fancy term they had for it, that they put on her records, that they

[500]

told me she died from—and she thinks everybody after her, everybody tryin to kill her, poison her, but she poison herself. And they can't cure what really ailin her: she black, black. She maybe paranoid, but that don kill her; she black, an that do. They pump her stomach an they cut her throat open so she can breathe an they try to sew the tubes together where they burned through an fulla holes so maybe she kin live, but she don wanna live no more, and the lye kill her anyway. They got no medicine to change her skin to white, to make her life over white, so she give them all the lye, she give life the lye, she take the lye and her life; they hers to take an give, the only things the white man leave her, an they got nuthin for her there so she take her leave of all of 'em."

In Christ's name, Fillmore, Sanders cried out inside himself, how do we build on such graveyards? How do we make these cemeteries into gardens and playgrounds, Pastor? How do we make these tombstones talk, Minister, so that tomorrow's speech won't have the word *nigger* in it? Standing there, head bowed, as Peter King beat him unrelentingly over the head with those burning, tumultuous words, Sanders felt as if he'd been worked over with a blackjack. He slumped into a chair across the room from King, a beat-up canvas camp chair.

"Mebbe I ought to go out on the street and sing real loud, real sad. 'I gotta right to sing the blues, I gotta right to say I'm sad.' . . . 'Sometimes ah feel like a motherless chile.' . . . An mebbe some of yo good white folks they throw pennies an nickels in mah cap. You could get real good pictures of that, Elliott." King pointed to the two cameras hung around his neck. "Front-page stuff for your papers. 'Negro Militant's Mother Dies in Asylum. Black Power Leader's Mother Suicide.' Yah, boy, serves them spades right. Kooks, every motherfucking one! Mebbe I even git me some dark glasses an a white cane, mebbe even a seein-eye dog, an I peddle me some pencils. Put Mistuh Charley on. You make more beggin anyway if tha fuzz don git to yuh. That make good copy too, eh?"

Sanders put his head in his hands, hid his face from those glowing-coal eyes, that burning-brand accusation.

"What the hell *you* lookin so sad for? You been writin good stories

[501]

around the Bay area, Elliott. Clear. Careful. Objective. But like you're a neutral, man. Ain't no neutrals in this here war, Elliott, none at all. Everybody's got to be a belligerent."

"Thanks, but no thanks," Sanders spoke through the prison bars of his fingers.

"Ain't no other way."

"This is no way either; taking sides is one thing, being a belligerent another." He sat up and looked straight at King. "And you're smart enough to know it."

"All that due process and with all due deliberate speed, huh? Be good. Don't break any of Whitey's crockery. Don't hurry. Too late for all that bullshit. . . . They gonna promote you for those stories? They gonna give you a prize? a medal? or just some more money for such *responsible* journalism?" He threw back his head and chortled.

Wearily Sanders shook his head. "I'm through. I'm going back to Paris after the new year," he added slowly. He hadn't realized until then that he'd made the decision, but as he said it, he knew it for what he wanted to do, had to do. Neither France nor America, he knew, exempted him from remembrance: In Paris the recollections of Elaine and Monique did not enhance the city any more than Beth and Laura enhanced San Francisco; and in both countries the remembrances of his parents were so painful as to be just short of insupportable. Unlike his father, he was at home in neither country; unlike his mother, he could not be at home in the United States. As his father's passionate commitment had made him the man and reporter that Lovett Carpenter Sanders was, so too had his own dispassionate neutrality and objectivity made him the man and reporter he was. That people should identify him casually with his father's viewpoint was one of those ironies he had learned to live with, if not enjoy; he had nonetheless walked in his father's footsteps and since coming home had tried to walk in George's, but never had he truly walked in his own. What he had set out to do was beyond him, impossible. He would, could, walk only in his own shoes, however confining, even crippling, they were, on his own feet, however inadequate, however fallen the arches and calloused the soles, however afflicted with chilblains and trench foot that the

[502]

fixed and mobile warfares of his life had engendered. Was that what Elaine had meant in her final note?

"What's the matter," King sneered, "you running? Too much heat in the kitchen, you gotta git out? Or maybe you're just washed up with Beth the Bitch Marshall."

"She's going to marry Prescott."

"Well, I'll be goddamned. Finally, after all these years."

"Just by being here I guess I helped make up her mind—in Prescott's favor," Sanders commented ruefully.

King laughed again. "She did *you* a favor, man. That woman's bad news, real bad news." Somberly, he added, "She killed George, she'd get you too."

"All she had to do was ask."

"What's the matter, you accident-prone? She'd ask all right. You better believe that."

"When do I put on my dunce cap?"

"Any head'll do," King said. "I told you, you should have tried my way."

"I guess I can't try your way, in this or other things either," Sanders replied, with no resentment. "You know that the old man, George's father, died?"

"No. Old man Christiansen, the Great Pioneer?"

"The same."

"Sanders, you're a bringer of glad tidings. You almost cheer me. The old sonofabitch finally bought it. Well, it couldn't happen to a meaner man. I'm delighted." King leaped to his feet, bounded across the room, his face now wreathed in smiles, and pounded his back. From the kitchen he brought a half-empty, half-gallon jug of red wine and a couple of empty glass jars. He poured the jars full and passed one over. "Let's drink to that man's departure."

"*De mortuis nil nisi bonum—*"

"Balls! I'm glad he's dead. He was half stone-cold-dead fish while he was alive. But, man, George was right to send you home in his place. You're his avenger: the old man dead and Beth going to marry Prescott."

"George didn't send me, I came," Sanders admitted reluctantly, holding up his wine jar to the naked bulb—the jar looked as if it

[503]

had only a short time before held peanut butter—"and I didn't come as an avenger."

"Old Joe gone and beautiful Beth married to the good doctor," King exulted. "Everybody gets his or hers." The planes in his face shifted. "Well, almost everybody. Tell on, Sanders, I'm gonna enjoy hearing it, the whole thing." So Sanders told him, told him as much of the story with as many details as he could bear to repeat. When he was done and they'd several times filled and emptied the jars, King, tongue clucking, remarked, "He never did change, that ornery bastard! Mean to the last breath. Did he really turn over all that green to the Marines?"

"That's what he said and I believe him. I tried to persuade him to leave at least his share of George's insurance to you, but he wouldn't. You were only incidental; what he really wanted to make sure of was that Beth didn't get a dime."

King roared with laughter. "Mean, misanthropic, nigger-hating honky. He always had the red-ass for her. Said she took his boy away from him. Shit, he drove George away. He was just as big a shit as my old man, bigger, because he was white and didn't have to be. My poor old lye-drinkin mama, she only cut my hands." He bared those scarred palms. "But those two, they killed George, sure as shootin."

They killed George. Had *they* murdered him? Had *he* killed himself? Or had he *chosen* to sacrifice his life for someone else? Now, after all of this, did he know any better than he had on that sidewalk in Saigon? He doubted it.

With a sigh Sanders unburdened himself of the cameras, laying them carefully on the table, then sat back with his wine. For a long time they sat silently drinking, slowly, savoring the wine, and Sanders felt that at last, in the silence, they had reached and sealed their friendship, a loyal affectionate acceptance of their differences, black and white, homo- and heterosexual, militant and progressive; the tension between them was for the first time removed, not abated as in the past, but absent; and he felt serene.

The pounding feet up the stairs broke the spell. They stopped at the door, pounded quickly, and King was at the door in a flash, holding it ajar, blocking the opening with his body so that Sanders could see only an indistinct black face or two, but Sanders could hear the "It's begun. It's started. They rampagin all over tha lot, breakin windows, an settin fires to cars."

"How'd it start?" King asked.

"Some kid heaved a brick through a window and the soul folk started haulin the stuff out. A cop burned the kid, in the back, an then it took time to git a hospital ambulance to come."

"Good!" King said. "That's the beginning. You know what to do. You know where the stuff is."

"How bout what we got here?"

King looked uncomfortably over his shoulder and whispered, "I got me a visitor. Later."

"Ain got much time."

The door shut, the footfalls separated, pounded upstairs, clattered down, doors opening and slamming. King turned and said, "Elliott, you better get out of here. Get into your car and get out of Oakland. All hell's gonna break loose."

Sanders stood up, slipped the camera straps over his head.

"And don't make like a newspaperman. No photos, no interviews, no reporting. Just get out."

"Reporting's my job."

"You might get yourself hurt."

Sanders shrugged. "I've been shot at before."

Hands on hips, King eyed him as if he were insane and ready for commitment, then on the run brought a crowbar from the other room, shifted the paillasse from the wall and carefully pried a piece of the baseboard away. On his knees he pulled a bundle out that looked like an emaciated corpse in a dirty winding sheet. When he had quickly and efficiently stripped the oil-stained rags off, it turned out to be a rifle with a telescopic sight. He donned his khaki battle jacket and grabbed Sanders' arm. "Come on," he ordered, "I'm gonna see that you get to your car safe. After that, if you're crazy enough to stay, you're on your own. Okay?"

Sanders said nothing.

"And no pictures here and no mention of me or what you saw here. Okay?"

Sanders agreed, but very reluctantly.

[505]

"It's dark outside now"—King grinned, without humor or cheer—
"so maybe if you follow me and stick in the shadows, they'll think
you're one of us, one of the soul folk, and you'll get by."

In the hallway there were others waiting, at least a dozen, and
no sooner had they run the gauntlet of their vengeful eyes and begun to thump down the stairs than he heard the group of them
rushing into King's rooms for what else lay behind the baseboards.
As Sanders turned at the landing, he could see the first man already
coming out of King's flat with a pistol in his hand and starting down
the stairs in their wake.

Outside the rain had stopped, the air was still heavy with mois-
ture, and a half-moon, the face in it eroded as if from cancer of the
cheek and jawbone, shone fitfully behind bulky gray clouds. The
street before them was littered with garbage and broken glass, and
a little way down two cars, one overturned, the other like a beached
whale with its hood open, burned. People were everywhere, in ones
and twos, in groups, all running, and there was a festive air as of
Mardi Gras or carnival with something still more hectic and intense
like the low and then rising scream of a distant siren, a great cat in
pain and anger in the concrete jungle. "They've really gone and done
it," King said between his teeth, and Sanders couldn't tell whether
that spoke of hope or fear, or how much of both. King sped down
the street and Sanders trotted after him, his coat collar up to hide
his white face, his cameras hidden as best he could in the folds of
his coat. They went by a furniture store with a line of people like a
bucket brigade passing out television sets, radios, small tables, chairs,
and even a couch through the smashed windows and broken-down
doors. A little farther on a liquor store, windows and door smashed
too, was also being looted, men and boys handing bottles out of
the windows, one old lady staggering off with a carton of whisky
on her bent back, and an immensely fat black man weaving across
the street with bottles in both hands was drinking whisky first from
one then from the other, the whisky running down his chin and
over his shirtfront. "Soul brothers," he called out to them, holding
his prizes high, "have a lil drink with me. On the house." His laughter was a high feminine yawp. King ran past him and Sanders followed. They finally found his car, still unmolested, and King said

to him. "Listen to me, Elliott, get out of here. Out of Oakland. As far away as you can. This is no night for any white man to be here."

"But I am here, and I'm a newspaperman."

"You're white."

"And there are no white friends, no white allies, no white sympathizers? Not even any sympathetic if objective reporters?"

"None."

"Why don't you let me go with you, or give me one of your people to take me around?"

"There are no safe-conduct passes here, no official guides either," King replied tartly.

"I don't expect either. I'll take my chances."

"If you stay, you'll have to. You're the enemy."

"You're still wrong, Peter. I am *not* the enemy."

"Goodbye, Elliott," King said hurriedly. He seized his hand and shook it so roughly, so strongly, that again, shuddering, Sanders felt those ridged palms like rasps. "Good luck. We could have been friends once," King said gently. "Now it's too late, too late for friendships, too late for lots of things. No more amenities. Even George and I couldn't be friends any more." Before Sanders could say a word or make a gesture, King was gone, running down the darkened street toward where flames were already bloodying the night sky. Watching him go until he disappeared around a corner, Sanders knew that at last he was home from the wars, for good or for ill, to new wars; and feeling so old in years, so unborn still, he unlocked the car and got in behind the wheel.

About the Author

Abraham Rothberg is a native New Yorker who has traveled widely in Europe, Latin America, the Far East and the United States, sometimes under U.S. Army auspices. Educated at Brooklyn College, the University of Iowa, and Columbia University, where he took his Ph.D., he has had a wide variety of jobs, among them professional singer and table waiter, production manager in an electronics firm, and Ford Fellow, university teacher, editor, journalist, political analyst and writer. He was a roving European correspondent for *The National Observer* and special correspondent for *The (Manchester) Guardian,* and now devotes his full time to writing.